The Bluest Eye
Sula
Song of Solomon

by Toni Morrison

The Bluest Eye (1970)

Sula (1974)

Song of Solomon (1977)

Tar Baby (1981)

Beloved (1987)

Jazz (1992)

Playing in the Dark (1992)

Race-ing Justice, En-Gendering Power (1992; editor)

The Nobel Lecture in Literature (1994)

Birth of a Nation'hood (1996; coeditor
with Claudia Brodsky Lacour)

The Dancing Mind (1996)

Paradise (1998)

The Big Box (1999; with Slade Morrison)

The Book of Mean People (2002; with Slade Morrison)

Who's Got Game? (2003; with Slade Morrison)

The Bluest Eye
Sula
Song of Solomon

TONI MORRISON

QUALITY PAPERBACK BOOK CLUB
NEW YORK

The Bluest Eye

To the two who gave me life
and the one who made me free

Here is the house. It is green and white. It has a red door. It is very pretty. Here is the family. Mother, Father, Dick, and Jane live in the green-and-white house. They are very happy. See Jane. She has a red dress. She wants to play. Who will play with Jane? See the cat. It goes meow-meow. Come and play. Come play with Jane. The kitten will not play. See Mother. Mother is very nice. Mother, will you play with Jane? Mother laughs. Laugh, Mother, laugh. See Father. He is big and strong. Father, will you play with Jane? Father is smiling. Smile, Father, smile. See the dog. Bowwow goes the dog. Do you want to play with Jane? See the dog run. Run, dog, run. Look, look. Here comes a friend. The friend will play with Jane. They will play a good game. Play, Jane, play.

Here is the house it is green and white it has a red door it is very pretty here is the family mother father dick and jane live in the green-and-white house they are very happy see jane she has a red dress she wants to play who will play with jane see the cat it goes meow-meow come and play come play with jane the kitten will not play see mother mother is very nice mother will you play with jane mother laughs laugh mother laugh see father he is big and strong father will you play with jane father is smiling smile father smile see the dog bowwow goes the dog do you want to play do you want to play with jane see the dog run run dog run look look here comes a friend the friend will play with jane they will play a good game play jane play

Hereisthehouseitisgreenandwhiteithasareddooritisveryprettyhereisthefa
milymotherfatherdickandjaneliveinthegreenandwhitehousetheyareveryh
appyseejaneshehasareddressshewantstoplaywhowillplaywithjaneseetheca
titgoesmeowmeowcomeandplaycomeplaywithjanethekittenwillnotplays
eemothermotherisverynicemotherwillyouplaywithjanemotherlaughslau
ghmotherlaughseefatherheisbigandstrongfatherwillyouplaywithjanefath
erissmilingsmilefathersmileseethedogbowwowgoesthedogdoyouwantto
playdoyouwanttoplaywithjaneseethedogrunrundogrunlooklookherecom
esafriendthefriendwillplaywithjanetheywillplayagoodgameplayjaneplay

Quiet as it's kept, there were no marigolds in the fall of 1941. We thought, at the time, that it was because Pecola was having her father's baby that the marigolds did not grow. A little examination and much less melancholy would have proved to us that our seeds were not the only ones that did not sprout; nobody's did. Not even the gardens fronting the lake showed marigolds that year. But so deeply concerned were we with the health and safe delivery of Pecola's baby we could think of nothing but our own magic: if we planted the seeds, and said the right words over them, they would blossom, and everything would be all right.

It was a long time before my sister and I admitted to ourselves that no green was going to spring from our seeds. Once we knew, our guilt was relieved only by fights and mutual accusations about who was to blame. For years I thought my sister was right: it was my fault. I had planted them too far down in the earth. It never occurred to either of us that the earth itself might have been un-yielding. We had dropped our seeds in our own little plot of black dirt just as Pecola's father had dropped his seeds in his own plot of black dirt. Our inno-cence and faith were no more productive than his lust or despair. What is clear now is that of all of that hope, fear, lust, love, and grief, nothing remains but Pecola and the unyielding earth. Cholly Breedlove is dead; our innocence too. The seeds shriveled and died; her baby too.

There is really nothing more to say—except why. But since why *is difficult to handle, one must take refuge in* how.

Autumn

Nuns go by as quiet as lust, and drunken men with sober eyes sing in the lobby of the Greek hotel. Rosemary Villanucci, our next-door friend who lives above her father's café, sits in a 1939 Buick eating bread and butter. She rolls down the window to tell my sister Frieda and me that we can't come in. We stare at her, wanting her bread, but more than that wanting to poke the arrogance out of her eyes and smash the pride of ownership that curls her chewing mouth. When she comes out of the car we will beat her up, make red marks on her white skin, and she will cry and ask us do we want her to pull her pants down. We will say no. We don't know what we should feel or do if she does, but whenever she asks us, we know she is offering us something precious and that our own pride must be asserted by refusing to accept.

School has started, and Frieda and I get new brown stockings and cod-liver oil. Grown-ups talk in tired, edgy voices about Zick's Coal Company and take us along in the evening to the railroad tracks where we fill burlap sacks with the tiny pieces of coal lying about. Later we walk home, glancing back to see the great carloads of slag being dumped, red hot and smoking, into the ravine that skirts the steel mill. The dying fire lights the sky with a dull orange glow. Frieda and I lag behind, staring at the patch of color surrounded by black. It is impossible not to feel a shiver when our feet leave the gravel path and sink into the dead grass in the field.

Our house is old, cold, and green. At night a kerosene lamp lights one large room. The others are braced in darkness, peopled by roaches and mice. Adults do not talk to us—they give us directions. They issue orders without providing information. When we trip and fall down they glance at us; if we cut or bruise ourselves, they ask us are we crazy. When we catch colds, they shake their heads in disgust at our lack of consideration. How, they ask us, do you expect anybody to get anything done if you all are sick? We cannot answer them. Our illness is treated with contempt, foul Black Draught, and castor oil that blunts our minds.

When, on a day after a trip to collect coal, I cough once, loudly, through bronchial tubes already packed tight with phlegm, my mother frowns. "Great Jesus. Get on in that bed. How many times do I have to tell you to wear something on your head? You must be the biggest fool in this town. Frieda? Get some rags and stuff that window."

Frieda restuffs the window. I trudge off to bed, full of guilt and self-pity. I lie down in my underwear, the metal in my black garters hurts my legs, but I do not take them off, for it is too cold to lie stockingless. It takes a long time for my body to heat its place in the bed. Once I have generated a silhouette of warmth, I dare not move, for there is a cold place one-half inch in any direction. No one speaks to me or asks how I feel. In an hour or two my mother comes. Her hands are large and rough, and when she rubs the Vicks salve on my chest, I am rigid with pain. She takes two fingers' full of it at a time, and massages my chest until I am faint. Just when I think I will tip over into a scream, she scoops out a little of the salve on her forefinger and puts it in my mouth, telling me to swallow. A hot flannel is wrapped about my neck and chest. I am covered up with heavy quilts and ordered to sweat, which I do—promptly.

Later I throw up, and my mother says, "What did you puke on the bed clothes for? Don't you have sense enough to hold your head out the bed? Now, look what you did. You think I got time for nothing but washing up your puke?"

The puke swaddles down the pillow onto the sheet—green-gray, with flecks of orange. It moves like the insides of an uncooked egg. Stubbornly clinging to its own mass, refusing to break up and be removed. How, I wonder, can it be so neat and nasty at the same time?

My mother's voice drones on. She is not talking to me. She is talking to the puke, but she is calling it my name: Claudia. She wipes it up as best she can and puts a scratchy towel over the large wet place. I lie down again. The rags have fallen from the window crack, and the air is cold. I dare not call her back and am reluctant to leave my warmth. My mother's anger humiliates me; her words chafe my cheeks, and I am crying. I do not know that she is not angry at me, but at my sickness. I believe she despises my weakness for letting the sickness "take holt." By and by I will not get sick; I will refuse to. But for now I am crying. I know I am making more snot, but I can't stop.

My sister comes in. Her eyes are full of sorrow. She sings to me: "When the deep purple falls over sleepy garden walls, someone thinks of me. . . ." I doze, thinking of plums, walls, and "someone."

But was it really like that? As painful as I remember? Only mildly. Or rather, it was a productive and fructifying pain. Love, thick and dark as Alaga syrup, eased up into that cracked window. I could smell it—taste it—sweet, musty, with an edge of wintergreen in its base—everywhere in that house. It stuck, along with my tongue, to the frosted windowpanes. It coated my chest, along with the salve, and when the flannel came undone in my sleep, the clear, sharp curves of air outlined its presence on my throat. And in the night, when my coughing was dry and tough, feet padded into the room, hands repinned the flannel, readjusted the quilt, and rested a moment on my forehead. So when I think of autumn, I think of somebody with hands who does not want me to die.

It was autumn too when Mr. Henry came. Our roomer. Our roomer. The words ballooned from the lips and hovered about our heads—silent, separate, and pleasantly mysterious. My mother was all ease and satisfaction in discussing his coming.

"You know him," she said to her friends. "Henry Washington. He's been living over there with Miss Della Jones on Thirteenth Street. But she's too addled now to keep up. So he's looking for another place."

"Oh, yes." Her friends do not hide their curiosity. "I been wondering how long he was going to stay up there with her. They say she's real bad off. Don't know who he is half the time, and nobody else."

"Well, that old crazy nigger she married up with didn't help her head none."

"Did you hear what he told folks when he left her?"

"Uh-uh. What?"

"Well, he run off with that trifling Peggy—from Elyria. You know."

"One of Old Slack Bessie's girls?"

"That's the one. Well, somebody asked him why he left a nice good church woman like Della for that heifer. You know Della always did keep a good house. And he said the honest-to-God real reason was he couldn't take no more of that violet water Della Jones used. Said he wanted a woman to smell like a woman. Said Della was just too clean for him."

"Old dog. Ain't that nasty!"

"You telling me. What kind of reasoning is that?"

"No kind. Some men just dogs."

"Is that what give her them strokes?"

"Must have helped. But you know, none of them girls wasn't too bright. Remember that grinning Hattie? She wasn't never right. And their Auntie Julia is still trotting up and down Sixteenth Street talking to herself."

"Didn't she get put away?"

"Naw. County wouldn't take her. Said she wasn't harming anybody."

"Well, she's harming me. You want something to scare the living shit out of you, you get up at five-thirty in the morning like I do and see that old hag floating by in that bonnet. Have mercy!"

They laugh.

Frieda and I are washing Mason jars. We do not hear their words, but with grown-ups we listen to and watch out for their voices.

"Well, I hope don't nobody let me roam around like that when I get senile. It's a shame."

"What they going to do about Della? Don't she have no people?"

"A sister's coming up from North Carolina to look after her. I expect she wants to get aholt of Della's house."

"Oh, come on. That's a evil thought, if ever I heard one."

"What you want to bet? Henry Washington said that sister ain't seen Della in fifteen years."

"I kind of thought Henry would marry her one of these days."

"That old woman?"

"Well, Henry ain't no chicken."

"No, but he ain't no buzzard, either."

"He ever been married to anybody?"

"No."

"How come? Somebody cut it off?"

"He's just picky."

"He ain't picky. You see anything around here you'd marry?"

"Well . . . no."

"He's just sensible. A steady worker with quiet ways. I hope it works out all right."

"It will. How much you charging?"

"Five dollars every two weeks."

"That'll be a big help to you."

"I'll say."

Their conversation is like a gently wicked dance: sound meets sound, curtsies, shimmies, and retires. Another sound enters but is upstaged by still another: the two circle each other and stop. Sometimes their words move in lofty spirals; other times they take strident leaps, and all of it is punctuated with warm-pulsed laughter—like the throb of a heart made of jelly. The edge, the curl, the thrust of their emotions is always clear to Frieda and me. We do not, cannot, know the meanings of all their words, for we are nine and ten years old. So we watch their faces, their hands, their feet, and listen for truth in timbre.

So when Mr. Henry arrived on a Saturday night, we smelled him. He smelled wonderful. Like trees and lemon vanishing cream, and Nu Nile Hair Oil and flecks of Sen-Sen.

He smiled a lot, showing small even teeth with a friendly gap in the middle. Frieda and I were not introduced to him—merely pointed out. Like, here is the bathroom; the clothes closet is here; and these are my kids, Frieda and Claudia; watch out for this window; it don't open all the way.

We looked sideways at him, saying nothing and expecting him to say nothing. Just to nod, as he had done at the clothes closet, acknowledging our existence. To our surprise, he spoke to us.

"Hello there. You must be Greta Garbo, and you must be Ginger Rogers."

We giggled. Even my father was startled into a smile.

"Want a penny?" He held out a shiny coin to us. Frieda lowered her head, too pleased to answer. I reached for it. He snapped his thumb and forefinger, and the penny disappeared. Our shock was laced with delight. We searched all over him, poking our fingers into his socks, looking up the inside back of his coat. If happiness is anticipation with certainty, we were happy. And while we waited for the coin to reappear, we knew we were amusing Mama and Daddy. Daddy was smiling, and Mama's eyes went soft as they followed our hands wandering over Mr. Henry's body.

We loved him. Even after what came later, there was no bitterness in our memory of him.

She slept in the bed with us. Frieda on the outside because she is brave—it never occurs to her that if in her sleep her hand hangs over the edge of the bed "something" will crawl out from under it and bite her fingers off. I sleep near the wall because that thought *has* occurred to me. Pecola, therefore, had to sleep in the middle.

Mama had told us two days earlier that a "case" was coming—a girl who had no place to go. The county had placed her in our house for a few days until they could decide what to do, or, more precisely, until the family was reunited. We were to be nice to her and not fight. Mama didn't know "what got into people," but that old Dog Breedlove had burned up his house, gone upside his wife's head, and everybody, as a result, was outdoors.

Outdoors, we knew, was the real terror of life. The threat of being outdoors surfaced frequently in those days. Every possibility of excess was curtailed with it. If somebody ate too much, he could end up outdoors. If somebody used too much coal, he could end up outdoors. People could gamble themselves outdoors, drink themselves outdoors. Sometimes mothers put their sons outdoors, and when that happened, regardless of what the son had done, all sympathy was with him. He was outdoors, and his own flesh had done it. To be put outdoors by a landlord was one thing—unfortunate, but an aspect of life over which you had no control, since you could not control your income. But to be slack enough to put oneself outdoors, or heartless enough to put one's own kin outdoors—that was criminal.

There is a difference between being put *out* and being put out*doors*. If you are put out, you go somewhere else; if you are outdoors, there is no place to go. The distinction was subtle but final. Outdoors was the end of something, an irrevocable, physical fact, defining and complementing our metaphysical condition. Being a minority in both caste and class, we moved about anyway on the hem of life, struggling to consolidate our weaknesses and hang on, or to creep singly up into the major folds of the garment. Our peripheral existence, however, was something we had learned to deal with—probably because it was abstract. But the concreteness of being outdoors was another matter—like the difference between the concept of death and being, in fact, dead. Dead doesn't change, and outdoors is here to stay.

Knowing that there was such a thing as outdoors bred in us a
hunger for property, for ownership. The firm possession of a yard, a
porch, a grape arbor. Propertied black people spent all their energies,
all their love, on their nests. Like frenzied, desperate birds, they
overdecorated everything; fussed and fidgeted over their hard-won
homes; canned, jellied, and preserved all summer to fill the cupboards
and shelves; they painted, picked, and poked at every corner of their
houses. And these houses loomed like hothouse sunflowers among the
rows of weeds that were the rented houses. Renting blacks cast furtive
glances at these owned yards and porches, and made firmer
commitments to buy themselves "some nice little old place." In the
meantime, they saved, and scratched, and piled away what they could
in the rented hovels, looking forward to the day of property.

Cholly Breedlove, then, a renting black, having put his family
outdoors, had catapulted himself beyond the reaches of human
consideration. He had joined the animals; was, indeed, an old dog, a
snake, a ratty nigger. Mrs. Breedlove was staying with the woman she
worked for; the boy, Sammy, was with some other family; and Pecola
was to stay with us. Cholly was in jail.

She came with nothing. No little paper bag with the other dress, or
a nightgown, or two pair of whitish cotton bloomers. She just appeared
with a white woman and sat down.

We had fun in those few days Pecola was with us. Frieda and I
stopped fighting each other and concentrated on our guest, trying hard
to keep her from feeling outdoors.

When we discovered that she clearly did not want to dominate us,
we liked her. She laughed when I clowned for her, and smiled and
accepted gracefully the food gifts my sister gave her.

"Would you like some graham crackers?"

"I don't care."

Frieda brought her four graham crackers on a saucer and some milk
in a blue-and-white Shirley Temple cup. She was a long time with the
milk, and gazed fondly at the silhouette of Shirley Temple's dimpled

face. Frieda and she had a loving conversation about how cu-ute Shirley Temple was. I couldn't join them in their adoration because I hated Shirley. Not because she was cute, but because she danced with Bojangles, who was *my* friend, *my* uncle, *my* daddy, and who ought to have been soft-shoeing it and chuckling with me. Instead he was enjoying, sharing, giving a lovely dance thing with one of those little white girls whose socks never slid down under their heels. So I said, "I like Jane Withers."

They gave me a puzzled look, decided I was incomprehensible, and continued their reminiscing about old squint-eyed Shirley.

Younger than both Frieda and Pecola, I had not yet arrived at the turning point in the development of my psyche which would allow me to love her. What I felt at that time was unsullied hatred. But before that I had felt a stranger, more frightening thing than hatred for all the Shirley Temples of the world.

It had begun with Christmas and the gift of dolls. The big, the special, the loving gift was always a big, blue-eyed Baby Doll. From the clucking sounds of adults I knew that the doll represented what they thought was my fondest wish. I was bemused with the thing itself, and the way it looked. What was I supposed to do with it? Pretend I was its mother? I had no interest in babies or the concept of motherhood. I was interested only in humans my own age and size, and could not generate any enthusiasm at the prospect of being a mother. Motherhood was old age, and other remote possibilities. I learned quickly, however, what I was expected to do with the doll: rock it, fabricate storied situations around it, even sleep with it. Picture books were full of little girls sleeping with their dolls. Raggedy Ann dolls usually, but they were out of the question. I was physically revolted by and secretly frightened of those round moronic eyes, the pancake face, and orangeworms hair.

The other dolls, which were supposed to bring me great pleasure, succeeded in doing quite the opposite. When I took it to bed, its hard unyielding limbs resisted my flesh—the tapered fingertips on those

dimpled hands scratched. If, in sleep, I turned, the bone-cold head
collided with my own. It was a most uncomfortable, patently
aggressive sleeping companion. To hold it was no more rewarding.
The starched gauze or lace on the cotton dress irritated any embrace. I
had only one desire: to dismember it. To see of what it was made, to
discover the dearness, to find the beauty, the desirability that had
escaped me, but apparently only me. Adults, older girls, shops,
magazines, newspapers, window signs—all the world had agreed that
a blue-eyed, yellow-haired, pink-skinned doll was what every girl child
treasured. "Here," they said, "this is beautiful, and if you are on this
day 'worthy' you may have it." I fingered the face, wondering at the
single-stroke eyebrows; picked at the pearly teeth stuck like two piano
keys between red bowline lips. Traced the turned-up nose, poked the
glassy blue eyeballs, twisted the yellow hair. I could not love it. But I
could examine it to see what it was that all the world said was lovable.
Break off the tiny fingers, bend the flat feet, loosen the hair, twist the
head around, and the thing made one sound—a sound they said was
the sweet and plaintive cry "Mama," but which sounded to me like the
bleat of a dying lamb, or, more precisely, our icebox door opening on
rusty hinges in July. Remove the cold and stupid eyeball, it would
bleat still, "Ahhhhhh," take off the head, shake out the sawdust, crack
the back against the brass bed rail, it would bleat still. The gauze back
would split, and I could see the disk with six holes, the secret of the
sound. A mere metal roundness.

Grown people frowned and fussed: "You-don't-know-how-to-take-
care-of-nothing. I-never-had-a-baby-doll-in-my-whole-life-and-used-to-
cry-my-eyes-out-for-them. Now-you-got-one-a-beautiful-one-and-you-
tear-it-up-what's-the-matter-with-you?"

How strong was their outrage. Tears threatened to erase the
aloofness of their authority. The emotion of years of unfulfilled
longing preened in their voices. I did not know why I destroyed those
dolls. But I did know that nobody ever asked me what I wanted for
Christmas. Had any adult with the power to fulfill my desires taken me

seriously and asked me what I wanted, they would have known that I did not want to have anything to own, or to possess any object. I wanted rather to feel something on Christmas day. The real question would have been, "Dear Claudia, what experience would you like on Christmas?" I could have spoken up, "I want to sit on the low stool in Big Mama's kitchen with my lap full of lilacs and listen to Big Papa play his violin for me alone." The lowness of the stool made for my body, the security and warmth of Big Mama's kitchen, the smell of the lilacs, the sound of the music, and, since it would be good to have all of my senses engaged, the taste of a peach, perhaps, afterward.

Instead I tasted and smelled the acridness of tin plates and cups designed for tea parties that bored me. Instead I looked with loathing on new dresses that required a hateful bath in a galvanized zinc tub before wearing. Slipping around on the zinc, no time to play or soak, for the water chilled too fast, no time to enjoy one's nakedness, only time to make curtains of soapy water careen down between the legs. Then the scratchy towels and the dreadful and humiliating absence of dirt. The irritable, unimaginative cleanliness. Gone the ink marks from legs and face, all my creations and accumulations of the day gone, and replaced by goose pimples.

I destroyed white baby dolls.

But the dismembering of dolls was not the true horror. The truly horrifying thing was the transference of the same impulses to little white girls. The indifference with which I could have axed them was shaken only by my desire to do so. To discover what eluded me: the secret of the magic they weaved on others. What made people look at them and say, "Awwwww," but not for me? The eye slide of black women as they approached them on the street, and the possessive gentleness of their touch as they handled them.

If I pinched them, their eyes—unlike the crazed glint of the baby doll's eyes—would fold in pain, and their cry would not be the sound of an icebox door, but a fascinating cry of pain. When I learned how repulsive this disinterested violence was, that it was repulsive because

it was disinterested, my shame floundered about for refuge. The best
hiding place was love. Thus the conversion from pristine sadism to
fabricated hatred, to fraudulent love. It was a small step to Shirley
Temple. I learned much later to worship her, just as I learned to
delight in cleanliness, knowing, even as I learned, that the change was
adjustment without improvement.

"Three quarts of milk. That's what was *in* that icebox yesterday.
Three whole quarts. Now they ain't none. Not a drop. I don't mind
folks coming in and getting what they want, but three quarts of milk!
What the devil does *any*body need with *three* quarts of milk?"
The "folks" my mother was referring to was Pecola. The three of
us, Pecola, Frieda, and I, listened to her downstairs in the kitchen
fussing about the amount of milk Pecola had drunk. We knew she was
fond of the Shirley Temple cup and took every opportunity to drink
milk out of it just to handle and see sweet Shirley's face. My mother
knew that Frieda and I hated milk and assumed Pecola drank it out of
greediness. It was certainly not for us to "dispute" her. We didn't
initiate talk with grown-ups; we answered their questions.
Ashamed of the insults that were being heaped on our friend, we
just sat there: I picked toe jam, Frieda cleaned her fingernails with her
teeth, and Pecola finger-traced some scars on her knee—her head
cocked to one side. My mother's fussing soliloquies always irritated
and depressed us. They were interminable, insulting, and although
indirect (Mama never named anybody—just talked about folks and
some people), extremely painful in their thrust. She would go on like
that for hours, connecting one offense to another until all of the things
that chagrined her were spewed out. Then, having told everybody and
everything off, she would burst into song and sing the rest of the day.
But it was such a long time before the singing part came. In the
meantime, our stomachs jellying and our necks burning, we listened,
avoided each other's eyes, and picked toe jam or whatever.
". . . I don't know what I'm supposed to be running here, a

charity ward, I guess. Time for me to get out of the *giving* line and get in the *getting* line. I guess I ain't sup*posed* to have nothing. I'm sup*posed* to end up in the poorhouse. Look like nothing I do is going to keep me out of there. Folks just spend all their time trying to figure out ways to send *me* to the poorhouse. I got about as much business with another mouth to feed as a cat has with side pockets. As if I don't have trouble enough trying to feed my own and keep out the poorhouse, now I got something else in here that's just going to *drink* me on in there. Well, naw, she ain't. Not long as I got strength in my body and a tongue in my head. There's a limit to everything. I ain't got nothing to just throw *away*. Don't *no*body need *three* quarts of milk. Henry *Ford* don't need three quarts of milk. That's just downright *sin*ful. I'm willing to do what I can for folks. Can't nobody say I ain't. But this has got to stop, and I'm just the one to stop it. Bible say watch as *well* as pray. Folks just dump they children off on you and go on 'bout they business. Ain't nobody even *peeped* in here to see whether that child has a loaf of bread. Look like they would just *peep* in to see whether I had a loaf of bread to give her. But naw. That thought don't cross they mind. That old trifling Cholly been out of jail *two* whole days and ain't been here *yet* to see if his own child was 'live or dead. She could be *dead* for all he know. And that *mama* neither. What kind of something is that?"

When Mama got around to Henry Ford and all those people who didn't care whether she had a loaf of bread, it was time to go. We wanted to miss the part about Roosevelt and the CCC camps.

Frieda got up and started down the stairs. Pecola and I followed, making a wide arc to avoid the kitchen doorway. We sat on the steps of the porch, where my mother's words could reach us only in spurts.

It was a lonesome Saturday. The house smelled of Fels Naphtha and the sharp odor of mustard greens cooking. Saturdays were lonesome, fussy, soapy days. Second in misery only to those tight, starchy, cough-drop Sundays, so full of "don'ts" and "set'cha self downs."

If my mother was in a singing mood, it wasn't so bad. She would sing about hard times, bad times, and somebody-done-gone-and-left-me times. But her voice was so sweet and her singing-eyes so melty I found myself longing for those hard times, yearning to be grown without "a thin di-i-ime to my name." I looked forward to the delicious time when "my man" would leave me, when I would "hate to see that evening sun go down . . ." 'cause then I would know "my man has left this town." Misery colored by the greens and blues in my mother's voice took all of the grief out of the words and left me with a conviction that pain was not only endurable, it was sweet.

But without song, those Saturdays sat on my head like a coal scuttle, and if Mama was fussing, as she was now, it was like somebody throwing stones at it.

". . . and here I am poor as a bowl of yak-me. What do they think I am? Some kind of Sandy Claus? Well, they can just take they stocking down 'cause it *ain't* Christmas. . . ."

We fidgeted.

"Let's do something," Frieda said.

"What do you want to do?" I asked.

"I don't know. Nothing." Frieda stared at the tops of the trees. Pecola looked at her feet.

"You want to go up to Mr. Henry's room and look at his girlie magazines?"

Frieda made an ugly face. She didn't like to look at dirty pictures. "Well," I continued, "we could look at his Bible. *That's* pretty." Frieda sucked her teeth and made a *phtt* sound with her lips. "O.K., then. We could go thread needles for the half-blind lady. She'll give us a penny."

Frieda snorted. "Her eyes look like snot. I don't feel like looking at them. What *you* want to do Pecola?"

"I don't care," she said. "Anything you want."

I had another idea. "We could go up the alley and see what's in the trash cans."

"Too cold," said Frieda. She was bored and irritable.

"I know. We could make some fudge."

"You kidding? With Mama in there fussing? When she starts fussing at the walls, you know she's gonna be at it all day. She wouldn't even let us."

"Well, let's go over to the Greek hotel and listen to them cuss."

"Oh, who wants to do *that?* Besides, they say the same old words all the time."

My supply of ideas exhausted, I began to concentrate on the white spots on my fingernails. The total signified the number of boyfriends I would have. Seven.

Mama's soliloquy slid into the silence ". . . Bible say feed the hungry. That's fine. That's all right. But I ain't feeding no elephants. . . . Anybody need three quarts of milk to *live* need to get out of here. They in the wrong place. What is this? Some kind of *dairy* farm?"

Suddenly Pecola bolted straight up, her eyes wide with terror. A whinnying sound came from her mouth.

"What's the matter with *you?*" Frieda stood up too.

Then we both looked where Pecola was staring. Blood was running down her legs. Some drops were on the steps. I leaped up. "Hey. You cut yourself? Look. It's all over your dress."

A brownish-red stain discolored the back of her dress. She kept whinnying, standing with her legs far apart.

Frieda said, "Oh. Lordy! I know. I know what that is!"

"What?" Pecola's fingers went to her mouth.

"That's ministratin'."

"What's that?"

"You know."

"Am I going to die?" she asked.

"Noooo. You won't die. It just means you can have a baby!"

"What?"

"How do *you* know?" I was sick and tired of Frieda knowing everything.

"Mildred told me, and Mama too."

"I don't believe it."

"You don't have to, dummy. Look. Wait here. Sit down, Pecola. Right here." Frieda was all authority and zest. "And you," she said to me, "you go get some water."

"Water?"

"Yes, stupid. Water. And be quiet, or Mama will hear you."

Pecola sat down again, a little less fear in her eyes. I went into the kitchen.

"What you want, girl?" Mama was rinsing curtains in the sink.

"Some water, ma'am."

"Right where I'm working, naturally. Well, get a glass. Not no clean one neither. Use that jar."

I got a Mason jar and filled it with water from the faucet. It seemed a long time filling.

"Don't nobody never want nothing till they see me at the sink. Then everybody got to drink water. . . ."

When the jar was full, I moved to leave the room.

"Where you going?"

"Outside."

"Drink that water right here!"

"I ain't gonna break nothing."

"You don't know what you gonna do."

"Yes, ma'am. I do. Lemme take it out. I won't spill none."

"You bed' not."

I got to the porch and stood there with the Mason jar of water. Pecola was crying.

"What you crying for? Does it hurt?"

She shook her head.

"Then stop slinging snot."

Frieda opened the back door. She had something tucked in her blouse. She looked at me in amazement and pointed to the jar. "What's that supposed to do?"

"You told me. You *said* get some water."

"Not a little old jar full. Lots of water. To scrub the steps with, dumbbell!"

"How was I supposed to know?"

"Yeah. How was you. Come on." She pulled Pecola up by the arm. "Let's go back here." They headed for the side of the house where the bushes were thick.

"Hey. What about me? I want to go."

"Shut uuuup," Frieda stage-whispered. "Mama will hear you. You wash the steps."

They disappeared around the corner of the house.

I was going to miss something. Again. Here was something important, and I had to stay behind and not see any of it. I poured the water on the steps, sloshed it with my shoe, and ran to join them.

Frieda was on her knees; a white rectangle of cotton was near her on the ground. She was pulling Pecola's pants off. "Come on. Step out of them." She managed to get the soiled pants down and flung them at me. "Here."

"What am I supposed to do with these?"

"Bury them, moron."

Frieda told Pecola to hold the cotton thing between her legs.

"How she gonna walk like that?" I asked.

Frieda didn't answer. Instead she took two safety pins from the hem of her skirt and began to pin the ends of the napkin to Pecola's dress.

I picked up the pants with two fingers and looked about for something to dig a hole with. A rustling noise in the bushes startled me, and turning toward it, I saw a pair of fascinated eyes in a dough-white face. Rosemary was watching us. I grabbed for her face and succeeded in scratching her nose. She screamed and jumped back.

"Mrs. MacTeer! Mrs. MacTeer!" Rosemary hollered. "Frieda and Claudia are out here playing nasty! Mrs. MacTeer!"

Mama opened the window and looked down at us.

"What?"

"They're playing nasty, Mrs. MacTeer. Look. And Claudia hit me 'cause I seen them!"

Mama slammed the window shut and came running out the back door.

"What you all doing? Oh. Uh-huh. Uh-huh. Playing nasty, huh?" She reached into the bushes and pulled off a switch. "I'd rather raise pigs than some nasty girls. Least I can slaughter *them!*"

We began to shriek. "No, Mama. No, ma'am. We wasn't! She's a liar! No, ma'am, Mama! No, ma'am, Mama!"

Mama grabbed Frieda by the shoulder, turned her around, and gave her three or four stinging cuts on her legs. "Gonna be nasty, huh? Naw you ain't!"

Frieda was destroyed. Whippings wounded and insulted her.

Mama looked at Pecola. "You too!" she said. "Child of mine or not!" She grabbed Pecola and spun her around. The safety pin snapped open on one end of the napkin, and Mama saw it fall from under her dress. The switch hovered in the air while Mama blinked. "What the devil is going on here?"

Frieda was sobbing. I, next in line, began to explain. "She was bleeding. We was just trying to stop the blood!"

Mama looked at Frieda for verification. Frieda nodded. "She's ministratin'. We was just helping."

Mama released Pecola and stood looking at her. Then she pulled both of them toward her, their heads against her stomach. Her eyes were sorry. "All right, all right. Now, stop crying. I didn't know. Come on, now. Get on in the house. Go on home, Rosemary. The show is over."

We trooped in, Frieda sobbing quietly, Pecola carrying a white tail, me carrying the little-girl-gone-to-woman pants.

Mama led us to the bathroom. She prodded Pecola inside, and taking the underwear from me, told us to stay out.

We could hear water running into the bathtub.

"You think she's going to drown her?"

"Oh, Claudia. You so dumb. She's just going to wash her clothes and all."

"Should we beat up Rosemary?"

"No. Leave her alone."

The water gushed, and over its gushing we could hear the music of my mother's laughter.

That night, in bed, the three of us lay still. We were full of awe and respect for Pecola. Lying next to a real person who was really ministratin' was somehow sacred. She was different from us now—grown-up-like. She, herself, felt the distance, but refused to lord it over us.

After a long while she spoke very softly. "Is it true that I can have a baby now?"

"Sure," said Frieda drowsily. "Sure you can."

"But . . . how?" Her voice was hollow with wonder.

"Oh," said Frieda, "somebody has to love you."

"Oh."

There was a long pause in which Pecola and I thought this over. It would involve, I supposed, "my man," who, before leaving me, would love me. But there weren't any babies in the songs my mother sang. Maybe that's why the women were sad: the men left before they could make a baby.

Then Pecola asked a question that had never entered my mind. "How do you do that? I mean, how do you get somebody to love you?" But Frieda was asleep. And I didn't know.

HEREISTHEHOUSEITISGREENANDWHITEITHASAREDDO
ORITISVERYPRETTYITISVERYPRETTYPRETTYPRETTYP

There is an abandoned store on the southeast corner of Broadway and
Thirty-fifth Street in Lorain, Ohio. It does not recede into its
background of leaden sky, nor harmonize with the gray frame houses
and black telephone poles around it. Rather, it foists itself on the eye
of the passerby in a manner that is both irritating and melancholy.
Visitors who drive to this tiny town wonder why it has not been torn
down, while pedestrians, who are residents of the neighborhood,
simply look away when they pass it.

At one time, when the building housed a pizza parlor, people saw
only slow-footed teen-aged boys huddled about the corner. These
young boys met there to feel their groins, smoke cigarettes, and plan
mild outrages. The smoke from their cigarettes they inhaled deeply,
forcing it to fill their lungs, their hearts, their thighs, and keep at bay
the shiveriness, the energy of their youth. They moved slowly, laughed
slowly, but flicked the ashes from their cigarettes too quickly, too
often, and exposed themselves, to those who were interested, as
novices to the habit. But long before the sound of their lowing and the
sight of their preening, the building was leased to a Hungarian baker,
modestly famous for his brioche and poppy-seed rolls. Earlier than
that, there was a real-estate office there, and even before that, some
gypsies used it as a base of operations. The gypsy family gave the large
plate-glass window as much distinction and character as it ever had.
The girls of the family took turns sitting between yards of velvet
draperies and Oriental rugs hanging at the windows. They looked out
and occasionally smiled, or winked, or beckoned—only occasionally.
Mostly they looked, their elaborate dresses, long-sleeved and
long-skirted, hiding the nakedness that stood in their eyes.

So fluid has the population in that area been, that probably no one remembers longer, longer ago, before the time of the gypsies and the time of the teen-agers when the Breedloves lived there, nestled together in the storefront. Festering together in the debris of a realtor's whim. They slipped in and out of the box of peeling gray, making no stir in the neighborhood, no sound in the labor force, and no wave in the mayor's office. Each member of the family in his own cell of consciousness, each making his own patchwork quilt of reality—collecting fragments of experience here, pieces of information there. From the tiny impressions gleaned from one another, they created a sense of belonging and tried to make do with the way they found each other.

The plan of the living quarters was as unimaginative as a first-generation Greek landlord could contrive it to be. The large "store" area was partitioned into two rooms by beaverboard planks that did not reach to the ceiling. There was a living room, which the family called the front room, and the bedroom, where all the living was done. In the front room were two sofas, an upright piano, and a tiny artificial Christmas tree which had been there, decorated and dust-laden, for two years. The bedroom had three beds: a narrow iron bed for Sammy, fourteen years old, another for Pecola, eleven years old, and a double bed for Cholly and Mrs. Breedlove. In the center of the bedroom, for the even distribution of heat, stood a coal stove. Trunks, chairs, a small end table, and a cardboard "wardrobe" closet were placed around the walls. The kitchen was in the back of this apartment, a separate room. There were no bath facilities. Only a toilet bowl, inaccessible to the eye, if not the ear, of the tenants.

There is nothing more to say about the furnishings. They were anything but describable, having been conceived, manufactured, shipped, and sold in various states of thoughtlessness, greed, and indifference. The furniture had aged without ever having become familiar. People had owned it, but never known it. No one had lost a penny or a brooch under the cushions of either sofa and remembered the place and time of the loss or the finding. No one had clucked and said, "But I *had* it just a minute ago. I was sitting right there talking to . . ." or "Here it is. It must have slipped down while I was feeding the baby!" No one had given birth in one of the beds—or remembered with fondness the peeled paint places, because that's what the baby, when he learned to pull himself up, used to pick loose. No thrifty child had tucked a wad of gum under the table. No happy drunk—a friend of the family, with a fat neck, unmarried, you know, but God how he eats!— had sat at the piano and played "You Are My Sunshine." No young girl had stared at the tiny Christmas tree and remembered when she had decorated it, or wondered if that blue ball was going to hold, or if HE would ever come back to see it.

There were no memories among those pieces. Certainly no memories to be cherished. Occasionally an item provoked a physical reaction: an increase of acid irritation in the upper intestinal tract, a light flush of perspiration at the back of the neck as circumstances surrounding the piece of furniture were recalled. The sofa, for example. It had been purchased new, but the fabric had split straight across the back by the time it was delivered. The store would not take the responsibility. . . .

"Looka here, buddy. It was O.K. when I put it on the truck. The store can't do anything about it once it's on the truck. . . ." Listerine and Lucky Strike breath.

"But I don't want no tore couch if'n it's bought new." Pleading eyes and tightened testicles.

"Tough shit, buddy. *Your* tough shit. . . ."

You could hate a sofa, of course—that is, if you could hate a sofa. But it didn't matter. You still had to get together $4.80 a month. If you had to pay $4.80 a month for a sofa that started off split, no good, and humiliating—you couldn't take any joy in owning it. And the joylessness stank, pervading everything. The stink of it kept you from painting the beaverboard walls; from getting a matching piece of material for the chair; even from sewing up the split, which became a gash, which became a gaping chasm that exposed the cheap frame and cheaper upholstery. It withheld the refreshment in a sleep slept on it. It imposed a furtiveness on the loving done on it. Like a sore tooth that is not content to throb in isolation, but must diffuse its own pain to other parts of the body—making breathing difficult, vision limited, nerves unsettled, so a hated piece of furniture produces a fretful malaise that asserts itself throughout the house and limits the delight of things not related to it.

The only living thing in the Breedloves' house was the coal stove, which lived independently of everything and everyone, its fire being "out," "banked," or "up" at its own discretion, in spite of the fact that the family fed it and knew all the details of its regimen: sprinkle, do not dump, not too much. . . . The fire seemed to live, go down, or die according to its own schemata. In the morning, however, it always saw fit to die.

The Breedloves did not live in a storefront because they were having temporary difficulty adjusting to the cutbacks at the plant. They lived there because they were poor and black, and they stayed there because they believed they were ugly. Although their poverty was traditional and stultifying, it was not unique. But their ugliness was unique. No one could have convinced them that they were not relentlessly and aggressively ugly. Except for the father, Cholly, whose ugliness (the result of despair, dissipation, and violence directed toward petty things and weak people) was behavior, the rest of the family—Mrs. Breedlove, Sammy Breedlove, and Pecola Breedlove—wore their ugliness, put it on, so to speak, although it did not belong to them. The eyes, the small eyes set closely together under narrow foreheads. The low, irregular hairlines, which seemed even more irregular in contrast to the straight, heavy eyebrows which nearly met. Keen but crooked noses, with insolent nostrils. They had high cheekbones, and their ears turned forward. Shapely lips which called attention not to themselves but to the rest of the face. You looked at them and wondered why they were so ugly; you looked closely and could not find the source. Then you realized that it came from conviction, their conviction. It was as though some mysterious all-knowing master had given each one a cloak of ugliness to wear, and they had each accepted it without question. The master had said, "You are ugly people." They had looked about themselves and saw nothing to contradict the statement; saw, in fact, support for it leaning at them from every billboard, every movie, every glance. "Yes," they had said. "You are right." And they took the ugliness in their hands, threw it as a mantle over them, and went about the world with it. Dealing with it each according to his way. Mrs.

Breedlove handled hers as an actor does a prop: for the articulation of character, for support of a role she frequently imagined was hers—martyrdom. Sammy used his as a weapon to cause others pain. He adjusted his behavior to it, chose his companions on the basis of it: people who could be fascinated, even intimidated by it. And Pecola. She hid behind hers. Concealed, veiled, eclipsed—peeping out from behind the shroud very seldom, and then only to yearn for the return of her mask.

This family, on a Saturday morning in October, began, one by one, to stir out of their dreams of affluence and vengeance into the anonymous misery of their storefront.

Mrs. Breedlove slipped noiselessly out of bed, put a sweater on over her nightgown (which was an old day dress), and walked toward the kitchen. Her one good foot made hard, bony sounds; the twisted one whispered on the linoleum. In the kitchen she made noises with doors, faucets, and pans. The noises were hollow, but the threats they implied were not. Pecola opened her eyes and lay staring at the dead coal stove. Cholly mumbled, thrashed about in the bed for a minute, and then was quiet.

Even from where Pecola lay, she could smell Cholly's whiskey. The noises in the kitchen became louder and less hollow. There was direction and purpose in Mrs. Breedlove's movements that had nothing to do with the preparation of breakfast. This awareness, supported by ample evidence from the past, made Pecola tighten her stomach muscles and ration her breath.

Cholly had come home drunk. Unfortunately he had been too drunk to quarrel, so the whole business would have to erupt this morning. Because it had not taken place immediately, the oncoming fight would lack spontaneity; it would be calculated, uninspired, and deadly.

Mrs. Breedlove came swiftly into the room and stood at the foot of the bed where Cholly lay.

"I need some coal in this house."

Cholly did not move.

"Hear me?" Mrs. Breedlove jabbed Cholly's foot.

Cholly opened his eyes slowly. They were red and menacing. With no exception, Cholly had the meanest eyes in town.

"Awwwwww, woman!"

"I said I need some coal. It's as cold as a witch's tit in this house. Your whiskey ass wouldn't feel hellfire, but I'm cold. I got to do a lot of things, but I ain't got to freeze."

"Leave me lone."

"Not until you get me some coal. If working like a mule don't give me the right to be warm, what am I doing it for? You sure ain't bringing in nothing. If it was left up to you, we'd all be dead. . . ." Her voice was like an earache in the brain. ". . . If you think I'm going to wade out in the cold and get it myself, you'd better think again."

"I don't give a shit how you get it." A bubble of violence burst in his throat.

"You going to get your drunk self out of that bed and get me some coal or not?"

Silence.

"Cholly!"

Silence.

"Don't try me this morning, man. You say one more word, and I'll split you open!"

Silence.

"All right. All right. But if I sneeze once, just once, God help your butt!"

Sammy was awake now too, but pretending to be asleep. Pecola still held her stomach muscles taut and conserved her breath. They all knew that Mrs. Breedlove could have, would have, and had, gotten coal from the shed, or that Sammy or Pecola could be directed to get it. But the unquarreled evening hung like the first note of a dirge in sullenly expectant air. An escapade of drunkenness, no matter how routine, had its own ceremonial close. The tiny, undistinguished days that

Mrs. Breedlove lived were identified, grouped, and classed by these quarrels. They gave substance to the minutes and hours otherwise dim and unrecalled. They relieved the tiresomeness of poverty, gave grandeur to the dead rooms. In these violent breaks in routine that were themselves routine, she could display the style and imagination of what she believed to be her own true self. To deprive her of these fights was to deprive her of all the zest and reasonableness of life. Cholly, by his habitual drunkenness and orneriness, provided them both with the material they needed to make their lives tolerable. Mrs. Breedlove considered herself an upright and Christian woman, burdened with a no-count man, whom God wanted her to punish. (Cholly was beyond redemption, of course, and redemption was hardly the point—Mrs. Breedlove was not interested in Christ the Redeemer, but rather Christ the Judge.) Often she could be heard discoursing with Jesus about Cholly, pleading with Him to help her "strike the bastard down from his pea-knuckle of pride." And once when a drunken gesture catapulted Cholly into the red-hot stove, she screamed, "Get him, Jesus! Get him!" If Cholly had stopped drinking, she would never have forgiven Jesus. She needed Cholly's sins desperately. The lower he sank, the wilder and more irresponsible he became, the more splendid she and her task became. In the name of Jesus.

No less did Cholly need her. She was one of the few things abhorrent to him that he could touch and therefore hurt. He poured out on her the sum of all his inarticulate fury and aborted desires. Hating her, he could leave himself intact. When he was still very young, Cholly had been surprised in some bushes by two white men while he was newly but earnestly engaged in eliciting sexual pleasure from a little country girl. The men had shone a flashlight right on his behind. He had stopped, terrified. They chuckled. The beam of the flashlight did not move. "Go on," they said. "Go on and finish. And, nigger, make it good." The flashlight did not move. For some reason Cholly had not hated the white men; he hated, despised, the girl. Even a half-remembrance of this episode, along with myriad other humiliations, defeats, and emasculations, could stir him into flights of depravity that surprised himself—but only himself. Somehow he could not astound. He could only be astounded. So he gave that up, too.

Cholly and Mrs. Breedlove fought each other with a darkly brutal formalism that was paralleled only by their lovemaking. Tacitly they had agreed not to kill each other. He fought her the way a coward fights a man—with feet, the palms of his hands, and teeth. She, in turn, fought back in a purely feminine way—with frying pans and pokers, and occasionally a flat iron would sail toward his head. They did not talk, groan, or curse during these beatings. There was only the muted sound of falling things, and flesh on unsurprised flesh.

There was a difference in the reaction of the children to these battles. Sammy cursed for a while, or left the house, or threw himself into the fray. He was known, by the time he was fourteen, to have run away from home no less than twenty-seven times. Once he got to Buffalo and stayed three months. His returns, whether by force or circumstance, were sullen. Pecola, on the other hand, restricted by youth and sex, experimented with methods of endurance. Though the methods varied, the pain was as consistent as it was deep. She struggled between an overwhelming desire that one would kill the other, and a profound wish that she herself could die. Now she was whispering, "Don't, Mrs. Breedlove. Don't." Pecola, like Sammy and Cholly, always called her mother Mrs. Breedlove.

"Don't, Mrs. Breedlove. Don't."

But Mrs. Breedlove did.

By the grace, no doubt, of God, Mrs. Breedlove sneezed. Just once.

She ran into the bedroom with a dishpan full of cold water and threw it in Cholly's face. He sat up, choking and spitting. Naked and ashen, he leaped from the bed, and with a flying tackle, grabbed his wife around the waist, and they hit the floor. Cholly picked her up and knocked her down with the back of his hand. She fell in a sitting position, her back supported by Sammy's bed frame. She had not let go of the dishpan, and began to hit at Cholly's thighs and groin with it. He put his foot in her chest, and she dropped the pan. Dropping to his knee, he struck her several times in the face, and she might have succumbed early had he not hit his hand against the metal bed frame when his wife ducked. Mrs. Breedlove took advantage of this momentary suspension of blows and slipped out of his reach. Sammy, who had watched in silence their struggling at his bedside, suddenly began to hit his father about the head with both fists, shouting "You naked fuck!" over and over and over. Mrs. Breedlove, having snatched up the round, flat stove lid, ran tippy-toe to Cholly as he was pulling himself up from his knees, and struck him two blows, knocking him right back into the senselessness out of which she had provoked him. Panting, she threw a quilt over him and let him lie.

Sammy screamed, "Kill him! Kill him!"

Mrs. Breedlove looked at Sammy with surprise. "Cut out that noise, boy." She put the stove lid back in place, and walked toward the kitchen. At the doorway she paused long enough to say to her son, "Get up from there anyhow. I need some coal."

Letting herself breathe easy now, Pecola covered her head with the quilt. The sick feeling, which she had tried to prevent by holding in her stomach, came quickly in spite of her precaution. There surged in her the desire to heave, but as always, she knew she would not.

"Please, God," she whispered into the palm of her hand. "Please make me disappear." She squeezed her eyes shut. Little parts of her body faded away. Now slowly, now with a rush. Slowly again. Her fingers went, one by one; then her arms disappeared all the way to the elbow. Her feet now. Yes, that was good. The legs all at once. It was hardest above the thighs. She had to be real still and pull. Her stomach would not go. But finally it, too, went away. Then her chest, her neck. The face was hard, too. Almost done, almost. Only her tight, tight eyes were left. They were always left.

Try as she might, she could never get her eyes to disappear. So what was the point? They were everything. Everything was there, in them. All of those pictures, all of those faces. She had long ago given up the idea of running away to see new pictures, new faces, as Sammy had so often done. He never took her, and he never thought about his going ahead of time, so it was never planned. It wouldn't have worked anyway. As long as she looked the way she did, as long as she was ugly, she would have to stay with these people. Somehow she belonged to them. Long hours she sat looking in the mirror, trying to discover the secret of the ugliness, the ugliness that made her ignored or despised at school, by teachers and classmates alike. She was the only member of her class who sat alone at a double desk. The first letter of her last name forced her to sit in the front of the room always. But what about Marie Appolonaire? Marie was in front of her, but she shared a desk with Luke Angelino. Her teachers had always treated her this way. They tried never to glance at her, and called on her only when everyone was required to respond. She also knew that when one of the girls at school wanted to be particularly insulting to a boy, or wanted to get an immediate response from him, she could say, "Bobby loves Pecola Breedlove! Bobby loves Pecola Breedlove!" and never fail to get peals of laughter from those in earshot, and mock anger from the accused.

It had occurred to Pecola some time ago that if her eyes, those eyes that held the pictures, and knew the sights—if those eyes of hers were different, that is to say, beautiful, she herself would be different. Her teeth were good, and at least her nose was not big and flat like some of those who were thought so cute. If she looked different, beautiful, maybe Cholly would be different, and Mrs. Breedlove too. Maybe they'd say, "Why, look at pretty-eyed Pecola. We mustn't do bad things in front of those pretty eyes."

Pretty eyes. Pretty blue eyes. Big blue pretty eyes. Run, Jip, run. Jip runs, Alice runs. Alice has blue eyes. Jerry has blue eyes. Jerry runs. Alice runs. They run with their blue eyes. Four blue eyes. Four pretty blue eyes. Blue-sky eyes.

Blue-like Mrs. Forrest's blue blouse eyes. Morning-glory-blue-eyes. Alice-and-Jerry-blue-storybook-eyes.

Each night, without fail, she prayed for blue eyes. Fervently, for a year she had prayed. Although somewhat discouraged, she was not without hope. To have something as wonderful as that happen would take a long, long time.

Thrown, in this way, into the binding conviction that only a miracle could relieve her, she would never know her beauty. She would see only what there was to see: the eyes of other people.

She walks down Garden Avenue to a small grocery store which sells penny candy. Three pennies are in her shoe—slipping back and forth between the sock and the inner sole. With each step she feels the painful press of the coins against her foot. A sweet, endurable, even cherished irritation, full of promise and delicate security. There is plenty of time to consider what to buy. Now, however, she moves down an avenue gently buffeted by the familiar and therefore loved images. The dandelions at the base of the telephone pole. Why, she wonders, do people call them weeds? She thought they were pretty. But grown-ups say, "Miss Dunion keeps her yard so nice. Not a dandelion anywhere." Hunkie women in black babushkas go into the fields with baskets to pull them up. But they do not want the yellow heads—only the jagged leaves. They make dandelion soup. Dandelion wine. Nobody loves the head of a dandelion. Maybe because they are so many, strong, and soon.

There was the sidewalk crack shaped like a Y, and the other one that lifted the concrete up from the dirt floor. Frequently her sloughing step had made her trip over that one. Skates would go well over this sidewalk—old it was, and smooth; it made the wheels glide evenly, with a mild whirr. The newly paved walks were bumpy and uncomfortable, and the sound of skate wheels on new walks was grating.

These and other inanimate things she saw and experienced. They were real to her. She knew them. They were the codes and touchstones of the world, capable of translation and possession. She owned the crack that made her stumble; she owned the clumps of dandelions whose white heads, last fall, she had blown away; whose yellow heads, this fall, she peered into. And owning them made her part of the world, and the world a part of her.

She climbs four wooden steps to the door of Yacobowski's Fresh Veg. Meat and Sundries Store. A bell tinkles as she opens it. Standing before the counter, she looks at the array of candies. All Mary Janes, she decides. Three for a penny. The resistant sweetness that breaks open at last to deliver peanut butter—the oil and salt which complement the sweet pull of caramel. A peal of anticipation unsettles her stomach.

She pulls off her shoe and takes out the three pennies. The gray head of Mr. Yacobowski looms up over the counter. He urges his eyes out of his thoughts to encounter her. Blue eyes. Blear-dropped. Slowly, like Indian summer moving imperceptibly toward fall, he looks toward her. Somewhere between retina and object, between vision and view, his eyes draw back, hesitate, and hover. At some fixed point in time and space he senses that he need not waste the effort of a glance. He does not see her, because for him there is nothing to see. How can a fifty-two-year-old white immigrant storekeeper with the taste of potatoes and beer in his mouth, his mind honed on the doe-eyed Virgin Mary, his sensibilities blunted by a permanent awareness of loss, *see* a little black girl? Nothing in his life even suggested that the feat was possible, not to say desirable or necessary.

"Yeah?"

She looks up at him and sees the vacuum where curiosity ought to lodge. And something more. The total absence of human recognition —the glazed separateness. She does not know what keeps his glance suspended. Perhaps because he is grown, or a man, and she a little girl. But she has seen interest, disgust, even anger in grown male eyes. Yet this vacuum is not new to her. It has an edge; somewhere in the bottom lid is the distaste. She has seen it lurking in the eyes of all white people. So. The distaste must be for her, her blackness. All things in her are flux and anticipation. But her blackness is static and dread. And it is the blackness that accounts for, that creates, the vacuum edged with distaste in white eyes.

She points her finger at the Mary Janes—a little black shaft of finger, its tip pressed on the display window. The quietly inoffensive assertion of a black child's attempt to communicate with a white adult.

"Them." The word is more sigh than sense.

"What? These? These?" Phlegm and impatience mingle in his voice.

She shakes her head, her fingertip fixed on the spot which, in her view, at any rate, identifies the Mary Janes. He cannot see her view— the angle of his vision, the slant of her finger, makes it incomprehensible to him. His lumpy red hand plops around in the glass casing like the agitated head of a chicken outraged by the loss of its body.

"Christ. Kantcha talk?"

His fingers brush the Mary Janes.

She nods.

"Well, why'nt you say so? One? How many?"

Pecola unfolds her fist, showing the three pennies. He scoots three Mary Janes toward her—three yellow rectangles in each packet. She holds the money toward him. He hesitates, not wanting to touch her hand. She does not know how to move the finger of her right hand from the display counter or how to get the coins out of her left hand. Finally he reaches over and takes the pennies from her hand. His nails graze her damp palm.

Outside, Pecola feels the inexplicable shame ebb.

Dandelions. A dart of affection leaps out from her to them. But they do not look at her and do not send love back. She thinks, "They *are* ugly. They *are* weeds." Preoccupied with that revelation, she trips on the sidewalk crack. Anger stirs and wakes in her; it opens its mouth, and like a hot-mouthed puppy, laps up the dredges of her shame.

Anger is better. There is a sense of being in anger. A reality and

presence. An awareness of worth. It is a lovely surging. Her thoughts
fall back to Mr. Yacobowski's eyes, his phlegmy voice. The anger will
not hold; the puppy is too easily surfeited. Its thirst too quickly
quenched, it sleeps. The shame wells up again, its muddy rivulets seep-
ing into her eyes. What to do before the tears come. She remembers
the Mary Janes.

Each pale yellow wrapper has a picture on it. A picture of little
Mary Jane, for whom the candy is named. Smiling white face. Blond
hair in gentle disarray, blue eyes looking at her out of a world of clean
comfort. The eyes are petulant, mischievous. To Pecola they are simply
pretty. She eats the candy, and its sweetness is good. To eat the candy
is somehow to eat the eyes, eat Mary Jane. Love Mary Jane. Be Mary
Jane.

Three pennies had bought her nine lovely orgasms with Mary Jane.
Lovely Mary Jane, for whom a candy is named.

Three whores lived in the apartment above the Breedloves' storefront. China, Poland, and Miss Marie. Pecola loved them, visited them,
and ran their errands. They, in turn, did not despise her.

On an October morning, the morning of the stove-lid triumph, Pecola climbed the stairs to their apartment.

Even before the door was opened to her tapping, she could hear
Poland singing—her voice sweet and hard, like new strawberries:

> I got blues in my mealbarrel
> Blues up on the shelf
> I got blues in my mealbarrel
> Blues up on the shelf
> Blues in my bedroom
> Cause I'm sleepin' by myself

"Hi, dumplin'. Where your socks?" Marie seldom called Pecola the
same thing twice, but invariably her epithets were fond ones chosen
from menus and dishes that were forever uppermost in her mind.

"Hello, Miss Marie. Hello, Miss China. Hello, Miss Poland."

"You heard me. Where your socks? You as bare-legged as a yard dog."

"I couldn't find any."

"Couldn't find any? Must be somethin' in your house that loves socks."

China chuckled. Whenever something was missing, Marie attributed its disappearance to "something in the house that loved it." "There is somethin' in this house that loves brassieres," she would say with alarm.

Poland and China were getting ready for the evening. Poland, forever ironing, forever singing. China, sitting on a pale-green kitchen chair, forever and forever curling her hair. Marie never got ready.

The women were friendly, but slow to begin talk. Pecola always took the initiative with Marie, who, once inspired, was difficult to stop.

"How come you got so many boyfriends, Miss Marie?"

"*Boy*friends? *Boy*friends? Chittlin', I ain't seen a *boy* since nineteen and twenty-seven."

"You didn't see none then." China stuck the hot curlers into a tin of Nu Nile hair dressing. The oil hissed at the touch of the hot metal.

"How come, Miss Marie?" Pecola insisted.

"How come what? How come I ain't seen a boy since nineteen and twenty-seven? Because they ain't *been* no boys since then. That's when they stopped. Folks started gettin' born old."

"You mean that's when *you* got old," China said.

"I ain't never got old. Just fat."

"Same thing."

"You think 'cause you skinny, folks think you young? You'd make a haint buy a girdle."

"And you look like the north side of a southbound mule."

"All I know is, them bandy little legs of yours is every bit as old as mine."

"Don't worry 'bout my bandy legs. That's the first thing they push aside."

All three of the women laughed. Marie threw back her head. From deep inside, her laughter came like the sound of many rivers, freely, deeply, muddily, heading for the room of an open sea. China giggled spastically. Each gasp seemed to be yanked out of her by an unseen hand jerking an unseen string. Poland, who seldom spoke unless she was drunk, laughed without sound. When she was sober she hummed mostly or chanted blues songs, of which she knew many.

Pecola fingered the fringe of a scarf that lay on the back of a sofa. "I never seen nobody with as many boyfriends as you got, Miss Marie. How come they all love you?"

Marie opened a bottle of root beer. "What else they gone do? They know I'm rich and good-lookin'. They wants to put their toes in my curly hair, and get at my money."

"You rich, Miss Marie?"

"Puddin', I got money's mammy."

"Where you get it from? You don't do no work."

"Yeah," said China, "where you get it from?"

"Hoover give it me. I did him a favor once, for the F. B. and I."

"What'd you do?"

"I did him a favor. They wanted to catch this crook, you see. Name of Johnny. He was as low-down as they come. . . ."

"We *know* that." China arranged a curl.

". . . the F. B. and I. wanted him bad. He killed more people than TB. And if you *crossed* him? Whoa, Jesus! He'd run you as long as there was ground. Well, I was little and cute then. No more than ninety pounds, soaking wet."

"You ain't never been soaking wet," China said.

"Well, you ain't never been dry. Shut up. Let me tell you, sweetnin'. To tell it true, I was the only one could handle him. He'd go out and rob a bank or kill some people, and I'd say to him, soft-like, 'Johnny, you shouldn't do that.' And he'd say he just had to bring me pretty things. Lacy drawers and all. And every Saturday we'd get a case of beer and fry up some fish. We'd fry it in meal and egg batter, you know, and when it was all brown and crisp—not hard, though—we'd break open that cold beer. . . ." Marie's eyes went soft as the memory of just such a meal sometime, somewhere transfixed her. All her stories were subject to breaking down at descriptions of food. Pecola saw Marie's teeth settling down into the back of crisp sea bass; saw the fat fingers putting back into her mouth tiny flakes of white, hot meat that had escaped from her lips; she heard the "pop" of the beer-bottle cap; smelled the acridness of the first stream of vapor; felt the cold beeriness hit the tongue. She ended the daydream long before Marie.

"But what about the money?" she asked.

China hooted. "She's makin' like she's the Lady in Red that told on Dillinger. Dillinger wouldn't have come near you lessen he was going hunting in Africa and shoot you for a hippo."

"Well, this hippo had a ball back in Chicago. Whoa Jesus, ninety-nine!"

"How come you always say 'Whoa Jesus' and a number?" Pecola had long wanted to know.

"Because my mama taught me never to cuss."

"Did she teach you not to drop your drawers?" China asked.

"Didn't have none," said Marie. "Never saw a pair of drawers till I was fifteen, when I left Jackson and was doing day work in Cincinnati. My white lady gave me some old ones of hers. I thought they was some kind of stocking cap. I put it on my head when I dusted. When she saw me, she liked to fell out."

"You must have been one dumb somebody." China lit a cigarette and cooled her irons.

"How'd I know?" Marie paused. "And what's the use of putting on something you got to keep taking off all the time? Dewey never let me keep them on long enough to get used to them."

"Dewey who?" This was a somebody new to Pecola.

"Dewey who? Chicken! You never heard me tell of *Dewey?* " Marie was shocked by her negligence.

"No, ma'am."

"Oh, honey, you've missed half your life. Whoa Jesus, one-nine-five. You talkin' 'bout smooth! I met him when I was fourteen. We ran away and lived together like married for three years. You know all those klinker-tops you see runnin' up here? Fifty of 'em in a bowl wouldn't make a Dewey Prince ankle bone. Oh, Lord. How that man loved me!"

China arranged a fingerful of hair into a bang effect. "Then why he left you to sell tail?"

"Girl, when I found out I could sell it—that somebody would pay cold cash for it, you could have knocked me over with a feather."

Poland began to laugh. Soundlessly. "Me too. My auntie whipped me good that first time when I told her I didn't get no money. I said 'Money? For what? He didn't owe me nothin'.' She said, 'The hell he didn't!' "

They all dissolved in laughter.

Three merry gargoyles. Three merry harridans. Amused by a long-ago time of ignorance. They did not belong to those generations of prostitutes created in novels, with great and generous hearts, dedicated, because of the horror of circumstance, to ameliorating, the luckless, barren life of men, taking money incidentally and humbly for their "understanding." Nor were they from that sensitive breed of young girl, gone wrong at the hands of fate, forced to cultivate an outward brittleness in order to protect her springtime from further shock, but knowing full well she was cut out for better things, and could make the right man happy. Neither were they the sloppy, inadequate whores who, unable to make a living at it alone, turn to drug consumption and traffic or pimps to help complete their scheme of self-destruction, avoiding suicide only to punish the memory of some absent father or to sustain the misery of some silent mother. Except for Marie's fabled love for Dewey Prince, these women hated men, all men, without shame, apology, or discrimination. They abused their visitors with a scorn grown mechanical from use. Black men, white men, Puerto Ricans, Mexicans, Jews, Poles, whatever—all were inadequate and weak, all came under their jaundiced eyes and were the recipients of their disinterested wrath. They took delight in cheating them. On one occasion the town well knew, they lured a Jew up the stairs, pounced on him, all three, held him up by the heels, shook everything out of his pants pockets, and threw him out of the window.

Neither did they have respect for women, who, although not their colleagues, so to speak, nevertheless deceived their husbands—regularly or irregularly, it made no difference. "Sugar-coated whores," they called them, and did not yearn to be in their shoes. Their only respect was for what they would have described as "good Christian colored women." The woman whose reputation was spotless, and who tended to her family, who didn't drink or smoke or run around. These women had their undying, if covert, affection. They would sleep with their husbands, and take their money, but always with a vengeance.

Nor were they protective and solicitous of youthful innocence. They looked back on their own youth as a period of ignorance, and regretted that they had not made more of it. They were not young girls in whores' clothing, or whores regretting their loss of innocence. They were whores in whores' clothing, whores who had never been young and had no word for innocence. With Pecola they were as free as they were with each other. Marie concocted stories for her because she was a child, but the stories were breezy and rough. If Pecola had announced her intention to live the life they did, they would not have tried to dissuade her or voiced any alarm.

"You and Dewey Prince have any children, Miss Marie?"

"Yeah. Yeah. We had some." Marie fidgeted. She pulled a bobby pin from her hair and began to pick her teeth. That meant she didn't want to talk anymore.

Pecola went to the window and looked down at the empty street. A tuft of grass had forced its way up through a crack in the sidewalk,

only to meet a raw October wind. She thought of Dewey Prince and
how he loved Miss Marie. What did love feel like? she wondered.
How do grown-ups act when they love each other? Eat fish together?
Into her eyes came the picture of Cholly and Mrs. Breedlove in bed.
He making sounds as though he were in pain, as though something
had him by the throat and wouldn't let go. Terrible as his noises were,
they were not nearly as bad as the no noise at all from her mother. It
was as though she was not even there. Maybe that was love. Choking
sounds and silence.

Turning her eyes from the window, Pecola looked at the women.

China had changed her mind about the bangs and was arranging a
small but sturdy pompadour. She was adept in creating any number of
hair styles, but each one left her with a pinched and harassed look.
Then she applied makeup heavily. Now she gave herself surprised eyebrows and a cupid-bow mouth. Later she would make Oriental eyebrows and an evilly slashed mouth.

Poland, in her sweet strawberry voice, began another song:

> I know a boy who is sky-soft brown
> I know a boy who is sky-soft brown
> The dirt leaps for joy when his feet touch the ground.
>> His strut is a peacock
>> His eye is burning brass
>> His smile is sorghum syrup drippin' slow-sweet to the last
> I know a boy who is sky-soft brown

Marie sat shelling peanuts and popping them into her mouth. Pecola looked and looked at the women. Were they real? Marie belched,
softly, purringly, lovingly.

Winter

❄

My daddy's face is a study. Winter moves into it and presides there. His eyes become a cliff of snow threatening to avalanche; his eyebrows bend like black limbs of leafless trees. His skin takes on the pale, cheerless yellow of winter sun; for a jaw he has the edges of a snowbound field dotted with stubble; his high forehead is the frozen sweep of the Erie, hiding currents of gelid thoughts that eddy in darkness. Wolf killer turned hawk fighter, he worked night and day to keep one from the door and the other from under the windowsills. A Vulcan guarding the flames, he gives us instructions about which doors to keep closed or opened for proper distribution of heat, lays kindling by, discusses qualities of coal, and teaches us how to rake, feed, and bank the fire. And he will not unrazor his lips until spring.

Winter tightened our heads with a band of cold and melted our eyes. We put pepper in the feet of our stockings, Vaseline on our faces, and stared through dark icebox mornings at four stewed prunes, slippery lumps of oatmeal, and cocoa with a roof of skin.

But mostly we waited for spring, when there could be gardens.

By the time this winter had stiffened itself into a hateful knot that nothing could loosen, something did loosen it, or rather someone. A someone who splintered the knot into silver threads that tangled us, netted us, made us long for the dull chafe of the previous boredom.

This disrupter of seasons was a new girl in school named Maureen Peal. A high-yellow dream child with long brown hair braided into two lynch ropes that hung down her back. She was rich, at least by our standards, as rich as the richest of the white girls, swaddled in comfort and care. The quality of her clothes threatened to derange Frieda and me. Patent-leather shoes with buckles, a cheaper version of which we got only at Easter and which had disintegrated by the end of May.

Fluffy sweaters the color of lemon drops tucked into skirts with pleats so orderly they astounded us. Brightly colored knee socks with white borders, a brown velvet coat trimmed in white rabbit fur, and a matching muff. There was a hint of spring in her sloe green eyes, something summery in her complexion, and a rich autumn ripeness in her walk.

She enchanted the entire school. When teachers called on her, they smiled encouragingly. Black boys didn't trip her in the halls; white boys didn't stone her, white girls didn't suck their teeth when she was assigned to be their work partners; black girls stepped aside when she wanted to use the sink in the girls' toilet, and their eyes genuflected under sliding lids. She never had to search for anybody to eat with in the cafeteria—they flocked to the table of her choice, where she opened fastidious lunches, shaming our jelly-stained bread with egg-salad sandwiches cut into four dainty squares, pink-frosted cupcakes, sticks of celery and carrots, proud, dark apples. She even bought and liked white milk.

Frieda and I were bemused, irritated, and fascinated by her. We looked hard for flaws to restore our equilibrium, but had to be content at first with uglying up her name, changing Maureen Peal to Meringue Pie. Later a minor epiphany was ours when we discovered that she had a dog tooth—a charming one to be sure—but a dog tooth nonetheless. And when we found out that she had been born with six fingers on each hand and that there was a little bump where each extra one had been removed, we smiled. They were small triumphs, but we took what we could get—snickering behind her back and calling her Six-finger-dog-tooth-meringue-pie. But we had to do it alone, for none of the other girls would cooperate with our hostility. They adored her.

When she was assigned a locker next to mine, I could indulge my jealousy four times a day. My sister and I both suspected that we were secretly prepared to be her friend, if she would let us, but I knew it would be a dangerous friendship, for when my eye traced the white border patterns of those Kelly-green knee socks, and felt the pull and slack of my brown stockings, I wanted to kick her. And when I thought of the unearned haughtiness in her eyes, I plotted accidental slammings of locker doors on her hand.

As locker friends, however, we got to know each other a little, and I was even able to hold a sensible conversation with her without visualizing her fall off a cliff, or giggling my way into what I thought was a clever insult.

One day, while I waited at the locker for Frieda, she joined me.

"Hi."

"Hi."

"Waiting for your sister?"

"Uh-huh."

"Which way do you go home?"

"Down Twenty-first Street to Broadway."

"Why don't you go down Twenty-second Street?"

" 'Cause I live on Twenty-first Street."

"Oh. I can walk that way, I guess. Partly, anyway."

"Free country."

Frieda came toward us, her brown stockings straining at the knees because she had tucked the toe under to hide a hole in the foot.

"Maureen's gonna walk part way with us."

Frieda and I exchanged glances, her eyes begging my restraint, mine promising nothing.

It was a false spring day, which, like Maureen, had pierced the shell of a deadening winter. There were puddles, mud, and an inviting warmth that deluded us. The kind of day on which we draped our coats over our heads, left our galoshes in school, and came down with croup the following day. We always responded to the slightest change in weather, the most minute shifts in time of day. Long before seeds were stirring, Frieda and I were scruffing and poking at the earth, swallowing air, drinking rain. . . .

As we emerged from the school with Maureen, we began to moult immediately. We put our head scarves in our coat pockets, and our coats on our heads. I was wondering how to maneuver Maureen's fur muff into a gutter when a commotion in the playground distracted us. A group of boys was circling and holding at bay a victim, Pecola Breedlove.

Bay Boy, Woodrow Cain, Buddy Wilson, Junie Bug—like a necklace of semiprecious stones they surrounded her. Heady with the smell of their own musk, thrilled by the easy power of a majority, they gaily harassed her.

"Black e mo. Black e mo. Yadaddsleepsnekked. Black e mo black e mo ya dadd sleeps nekked. Black e mo . . ."

They had extemporized a verse made up of two insults about matters over which the victim had no control; the color of her skin and speculations on the sleeping habits of an adult, wildly fitting in its incoherence. That they themselves were black, or that their own father had similarly relaxed habits was irrelevant. It was their contempt for their own blackness that gave the first insult its teeth. They seemed to have taken all of their smoothly cultivated ignorance, their exquisitely learned self-hatred, their elaborately designed hopelessness and sucked it all up into a fiery cone of scorn that had burned for ages in the hollows of their minds—cooled—and spilled over lips of outrage, consuming whatever was in its path. They danced a macabre ballet around the victim, whom, for their own sake, they were prepared to sacrifice to the flaming pit.

> Black e mo Black e mo Ya daddy sleeps nekked.
> Stch ta ta stch ta ta
> stach ta ta ta ta ta

Pecola edged around the circle crying. She had dropped her notebook, and covered her eyes with her hands.

We watched, afraid they might notice us and turn their energies our way. Then Frieda, with set lips and Mama's eyes, snatched her coat from her head and threw it on the ground. She ran toward them and brought her books down on Woodrow Cain's head. The circle broke. Woodrow Cain grabbed his head.

"Hey, girl!"

"You cut that out, you hear?" I had never heard Frieda's voice so loud and clear.

Maybe because Frieda was taller than he was, maybe because he saw her eyes, maybe because he had lost interest in the game, or maybe because he had a crush on Frieda, in any case Woodrow looked frightened just long enough to give her more courage.

"Leave her 'lone, or I'm gone tell everybody what you did!"

Woodrow did not answer; he just walled his eyes.

Bay Boy piped up, "Go on, gal. Ain't nobody bothering you."

"You shut up, Bullet Head." I had found my tongue.

"Who you calling Bullet Head?"

"I'm calling you Bullet Head, Bullet Head."

Frieda took Pecola's hand. "Come on."

"You want a fat lip?" Bay Boy drew back his fist at me.

"Yeah. Gimme one of yours."

"You gone get one."

Maureen appeared at my elbow, and the boys seemed reluctant to continue under her springtime eyes so wide with interest. They buckled in confusion, not willing to beat up three girls under her watchful gaze. So they listened to a budding male instinct that told them to pretend we were unworthy of their attention.

"Come on, man."

"Yeah. Come on. We ain't got time to fool with them."

Grumbling a few disinterested epithets, they moved away.

I picked up Pecola's notebook and Frieda's coat, and the four of us left the playground.

"Old Bullet Head, he's always picking on girls."

Frieda agreed with me. "Miss Forrester said he was incorrigival."

"Really?" I didn't know what that meant, but it had enough of a doom sound in it to be true of Bay Boy.

While Frieda and I clucked on about the near fight, Maureen, suddenly animated, put her velvet-sleeved arm through Pecola's and began to behave as though they were the closest of friends.

"I just moved here. My name is Maureen Peal. What's yours?"

"Pecola."

"Pecola? Wasn't that the name of the girl in *Imitation of Life?*"

"I don't know. What is that?"

"The picture show, you know. Where this mulatto girl hates her mother 'cause she is black and ugly but then cries at the funeral. It was real sad. Everybody cries in it. Claudette Colbert too."

"Oh." Pecola's voice was no more than a sigh.

"Anyway, her name was Pecola too. She was so pretty. When it comes back, I'm going to see it again. My mother has seen it four times."

Frieda and I walked behind them, surprised at Maureen's friendliness to Pecola, but pleased. Maybe she wasn't so bad, after all. Frieda had put her coat back on her head, and the two of us, so draped, trotted along enjoying the warm breeze and Frieda's heroics.

"You're in my gym class, aren't you?" Maureen asked Pecola.

"Yes."

"Miss Erkmeister's legs sure are bow. I bet she thinks they're cute. How come she gets to wear real shorts, and we have to wear those old bloomers? I want to die every time I put them on."

Pecola smiled but did not look at Maureen.

"Hey." Maureen stopped short. "There's an Isaley's. Want some ice cream? I have money."

She unzipped a hidden pocket in her muff and pulled out a multifolded dollar bill. I forgave her those knee socks.

"My uncle sued Isaley's." Maureen said to the three of us. "He sued the Isaley's in Akron. They said he was disorderly and that that was why they wouldn't serve him, but a friend of his, a policemen, came in and beared the witness, so the suit went through."

"What's a suit?"

"It's when you can beat them up if you want to and won't anybody do nothing. Our family does it all the time. We believe in suits."

At the entrance to Isaley's Maureen turned to Frieda and me, asking, "You all going to buy some ice cream?"

We looked at each other. "No," Frieda said.

Maureen disappeared into the store with Pecola.

Frieda looked placidly down the street; I opened my mouth, but quickly closed it. It was extremely important that the world not know that I fully expected Maureen to buy us some ice cream, that for the past 120 seconds I had been selecting the flavor, that I had begun to like Maureen, and that neither of us had a penny.

We supposed Maureen was being nice to Pecola because of the boys, and were embarrassed to be caught—even by each other—thinking that she would treat us, or that we deserved it as much as Pecola did.

The girls came out. Pecola with two dips of orange-pineapple, Maureen with black raspberry.

"You should have got some," she said. "They had all kinds. Don't eat down to the tip of the cone," she advised Pecola.

"Why?"

"Because there's a fly in there."

"How you know?"

"Oh, not really. A girl told me she found one in the bottom of hers once, and ever since then she throws that part away."

"Oh."

We passed the Dreamland Theater, and Betty Grable smiled down at us.

"Don't you just love her?" Maureen asked.

"Uh-huh," said Pecola.

I differed. "Hedy Lamarr is better."

Maureen agreed. "Ooooo yes. My mother told me that a girl named Audrey, she went to the beauty parlor where we lived before, and asked the lady to fix her hair like Hedy Lamarr's, and the lady said, 'Yeah, when you grow some hair like Hedy Lamarr's.' " She laughed long and sweet.

"Sounds crazy," said Frieda.

"She sure is. Do you know she doesn't even menstrate yet, and she's sixteen. Do you, yet?"

"Yes." Pecola glanced at us.

"So do I." Maureen made no attempt to disguise her pride. "Two months ago I started. My girl friend in Toledo, where we lived before, said when she started she was scared to death. Thought she had killed herself."

"Do you know what it's for?" Pecola asked the question as though hoping to provide the answer herself.

"For babies." Maureen raised two pencil-stroke eyebrows at the obviousness of the question. "Babies need blood when they are inside you, and if you are having a baby, then you don't menstrate. But when you're not having a baby, then you don't have to save the blood, so it comes out."

"How do babies get the blood?" asked Pecola.

"Through the like-line. You know. Where your belly button is. That is where the like-line grows from and pumps the blood to the baby."

"Well, if the belly buttons are to grow like-lines to give the baby blood, and only girls have babies, how come boys have belly buttons?"

Maureen hesitated. "I don't know," she admitted. "But boys have all sorts of things they don't need." Her tinkling laughter was somehow stronger than our nervous ones. She curled her tongue around the edge of the cone, scooping up a dollop of purple that made my eyes water. We were waiting for a stop light to change. Maureen kept scooping the ice cream from around the cone's edge with her tongue; she didn't bite the edge as I would have done. Her tongue circled the cone. Pecola had finished hers; Maureen evidently liked her things to last. While I was thinking about her ice cream, she must have been thinking about her last remark, for she said to Pecola, "Did you ever see a naked man?"

Pecola blinked, then looked away. "No. Where would I see a naked man?"

"I don't know. I just asked."

"I wouldn't even look at him, even if I did see him. That's dirty. Who wants to see a naked man?" Pecola was agitated. "Nobody's father would be naked in front of his own daughter. Not unless he was dirty too."

"I didn't say 'father.' I just said 'a naked man.' "

"Well . . ."

"How come you said 'father'?" Maureen wanted to know.

"Who else would she see, dog tooth?" I was glad to have a chance to show anger. Not only because of the ice cream, but because we had seen our own father naked and didn't care to be reminded of it and feel the shame brought on by the absence of shame. He had been walking down the hall from the bathroom into his bedroom and passed the open door of our room. We had lain there wide-eyed. He stopped and looked in, trying to see in the dark room whether we were really asleep—or was it his imagination that opened eyes were looking at him? Apparently he convinced himself that we were sleeping. He moved away, confident that his little girls would not lie open-eyed like that, staring, staring. When he had moved on, the dark took only him away, not his nakedness. That stayed in the room with us. Friendly-like.

"I'm not talking to you," said Maureen. "Besides, I don't care if she sees her father naked. She can look at him all day if she wants to. Who cares?"

"You do," said Frieda. "That's all you talk about."

"It is not."

"It is so. Boys, babies, and somebody's naked daddy. You must be boy-crazy."

"You better be quiet."

"Who's gonna make me?" Frieda put her hand on her hip and jutted her face toward Maureen.

"You all ready made. Mammy made."

"You stop talking about my mama."

"Well, you stop talking about my daddy."

"Who said anything about your old daddy?"

"You did."

"Well, you started it."

"I wasn't even talking to you. I was talking to Pecola."

"Yeah. About seeing her naked daddy."

"So what if she did see him?"

Pecola shouted, "I never saw my daddy naked. Never."

"You did too," Maureen snapped. "Bay Boy said so."

"I did not."

"You did."

"I did not."

"Did. Your own daddy, too!"

Pecola tucked her head in—a funny, sad, helpless movement. A kind of hunching of the shoulders, pulling in of the neck, as though she wanted to cover her ears.

"You stop talking about her daddy," I said.

"What do I care about her old black daddy?" asked Maureen.

"Black? Who you calling black?"

"You!"

"You think you so cute!" I swung at her and missed, hitting Pecola in the face. Furious at my clumsiness, I threw my notebook at her, but it caught her in the small of her velvet back, for she had turned and was flying across the street against traffic.

Safe on the other side, she screamed at us, "I *am* cute! And you ugly! Black and ugly black e mos. I *am* cute!"

She ran down the street, the green knee socks making her legs look like wild dandelion stems that had somehow lost their heads. The

weight of her remark stunned us, and it was a second or two before
Frieda and I collected ourselves enough to shout,
"Six-finger-dog-tooth-meringue-pie!" We chanted this most powerful
of our arsenal of insults as long as we could see the green stems and
rabbit fur.

Grown people frowned at the three girls on the curbside, two with
their coats draped over their heads, the collars framing the eyebrows
like nuns' habits, black garters showing where they bit the tops of
brown stockings that barely covered the knees, angry faces knotted like
dark cauliflowers.

Pecola stood a little apart from us, her eyes hinged in the direction
in which Maureen had fled. She seemed to fold into herself, like a
pleated wing. Her pain antagonized me. I wanted to open her up, crisp
her edges, ram a stick down that hunched and curving spine, force her
to stand erect and spit the misery out on the streets. But she held it in
where it could lap up into her eyes.

Frieda snatched her coat from her head. "Come on, Claudia. 'Bye,
Pecola."

We walked quickly at first, and then slower, pausing every now and
then to fasten garters, tie shoelaces, scratch, or examine old scars. We
were sinking under the wisdom, accuracy, and relevance of Maureen's
last words. If she was cute—and if anything could be believed, she
was—then we were not. And what did that mean? We were lesser.
Nicer, brighter, but still lesser. Dolls we could destroy, but we could
not destroy the honey voices of parents and aunts, the obedience in the
eyes of our peers, the slippery light in the eyes of our teachers when
they encountered the Maureen Peals of the world. What was the
secret? What did we lack? Why was it important? And so what?
Guileless and without vanity, we were still in love with ourselves then.
We felt comfortable in our skins, enjoyed the news that our senses
released to us, admired our dirt, cultivated our scars, and could not
comprehend this unworthiness. Jealousy we understood and thought
natural—a desire to have what somebody else had; but envy was a

strange, new feeling for us. And all the time we knew that Maureen Peal was not the Enemy and not worthy of such intense hatred. The *Thing* to fear was the *Thing* that made *her* beautiful, and not us.

The house was quiet when we opened the door. The acrid smell of simmering turnips filled our cheeks with sour saliva.

"Mama!"

There was no answer, but a sound of feet. Mr. Henry shuffled part of the way down the stairs. One thick, hairless leg leaned out of his bathrobe.

"Hello there, Greta Garbo; hello, Ginger Rogers."

We gave him the giggle he was accustomed to. "Hello, Mr. Henry. Where's Mama?"

"She went to your grandmaw's. Left word for you to cut off the turnips and eat some graham crackers till she got back. They in the kitchen."

We sat in silence at the kitchen table, crumbling the crackers into anthills. In a little while Mr. Henry came back down the stairs. Now he had his trousers on under his robe.

"Say. Wouldn't you all like some cream?"

"Oh, yes, sir."

"Here. Here's a quarter. Gone over to Isaley's and get yourself some cream. You been good girls, ain't you?"

His light-green words restored color to the day. "Yes, sir. Thank you, Mr. Henry. Will you tell Mama for us if she comes?"

"Sure. But she ain't due back for a spell."

Coatless, we left the house and had gotten all the way to the corner when Frieda said, "I don't want to go to Isaley's."

"What?"

"I don't want ice cream. I want potato chips."

"They got potato chips at Isaley's."

"I know, but why go all that long way? Miss Bertha got potato chips."

"But I want ice cream."

"No you don't, Claudia."

"I do too."

"Well, you go on to Isaley's. I'm going to Miss Bertha's."

"But you got the quarter, and I don't want to go all the way up there by myself."

"Then let's go to Miss Bertha's. You like her candy, don't you?"

"It's always stale, and she always runs out of stuff."

"Today is Friday. She orders fresh on Friday."

"And then that crazy old Soaphead Church lives there."

"So what? We're together. We'll run if he does anything at us."

"He scares me."

"Well, I don't want to go up by Isaley's. Suppose Meringue Pie is hanging around. You want to run into her, Claudia?"

"Come on, Frieda. I'll get candy."

Miss Bertha had a small candy, snuff, and tobacco store. One brick room sitting in her front yard. You had to peep in the door, and if she wasn't there, you knocked on the door of her house in back. This day she was sitting behind the counter reading a Bible in a tube of sunlight.

Frieda bought potato chips, and we got three Powerhouse bars for ten cents, and had a dime left. We hurried back home to sit under the lilac bushes on the side of the house. We always did our Candy Dance there so Rosemary could see us and get jealous. The Candy Dance was a humming, skipping, foot-tapping, eating, smacking combination that overtook us when we had sweets. Creeping between the bushes and the side of the house, we heard voices and laughter. We looked into the living-room window, expecting to see Mama. Instead we saw Mr. Henry and two women. In a playful manner, the way grandmothers do with babies, he was sucking the fingers of one of the women, whose laughter filled a tiny place over his head. The other woman was buttoning her coat. We knew immediately who they were, and our flesh crawled. One was China, and the other was called the Maginot Line. The back of my neck itched. These were the fancy women of the maroon nail polish that Mama and Big Mama hated. And in our house.

China was not too terrible, at least not in our imaginations. She was thin, aging, absentminded, and unaggressive. But the Maginot Line. That was the one my mother said she "wouldn't let eat out of one of her plates." That was the one church women never allowed their eyes to rest on. That was the one who had killed people, set them on fire, poisoned them, cooked them in lye. Although I thought the Maginot Line's face, hidden under all that fat, was really sweet, I had heard too many black and red words about her, seen too many mouths go triangle at the mention of her name, to dwell on any redeeming features she might have.

Showing brown teeth, China seemed to be genuinely enjoying Mr. Henry. The sight of him licking her fingers brought to mind the girlie magazines in his room. A cold wind blew somewhere in me, lifting little leaves of terror and obscure longing. I thought I saw a mild lonesomeness cross the face of the Maginot Line. But it may have been my own image that I saw in the slow flaring of her nostrils, in her eyes that reminded me of waterfalls in movies about Hawaii.

The Maginot Line yawned and said, "Come on, China. We can't hang in here all day. Them people be home soon." She moved toward the door.

Frieda and I dropped down to the ground, looking wildly into each other's eyes. When the women were some distance away, we went inside. Mr. Henry was in the kitchen opening a bottle of pop.

"Back already?"

"Yes, sir."

"Cream all gone?" His little teeth looked so kindly and helpless. Was that really our Mr. Henry with China's fingers?

"We got candy instead."

"You did huh? Ole sugar-tooth Greta Garbo."

He wiped the bottle sweat and turned it up to his lips—a gesture that made me uncomfortable.

"Who were those women, Mr. Henry?"

He choked on the pop and looked at Frieda. "What you say?"

"Those women," she repeated, "who just left. Who were they?"

"Oh." He laughed the grown-up getting-ready-to-lie laugh. A heh-heh we knew well.

"Those were some members of my Bible class. We read the scriptures together, and so they came today to read with me."

"Oh," said Frieda. I was looking at his house slippers to keep from seeing those kindly teeth frame a lie. He walked toward the stairs and then turned back to us.

"Bed' not mention it to your mother. She don't take to so much Bible study and don't like me having visitors, even if they good Christians."

"No, sir, Mr. Henry. We won't."

He rapidly mounted the stairs.

"Should we?" I asked. "Tell Mama?"

Frieda sighed. She had not even opened her Powerhouse bar or her potato chips, and now she traced the letters on the candy wrappers with her fingers. Suddenly she lifted her head and began to look all around the kitchen.

"No. I guess not. No plates are out."

"Plates? What you talking about now?"

"No plates are out. The Maginot Line didn't eat out of one of Mama's plates. Besides, Mama would just fuss all day if we told her."

We sat down and looked at the graham-cracker anthills we had made.

"We better cut off the turnips. They'll burn, and Mama will whip us," she said.

"I know."

"But if we let them burn, we won't have to eat them."

"Heyyy, what a lovely idea," I thought.

"Which you want? A whipping and no turnips, or turnips and no whippings?"

"I don't know. Maybe we could burn them just a little so Mama and Daddy can eat them, but we can say we can't."

"O.K."

I made a volcano out of my anthill.

"Frieda?"

"What?"

"What did Woodward do that you was gonna tell?"

"Wet the bed. Mrs. Cain told Mama he won't quit."

"Old nasty."

The sky was getting dark; I looked out of the window and saw snow falling. I poked my finger down into the mouth of my volcano, and it toppled, dispersing the golden grains into little swirls. The turnip pot crackled.

SEETHECATITGOESMEOWMEOWCOMEANDPLAYCOMEPL
AYWITHJANETHEKITTENWILLNOTPLAYPLAYPLAYPLA

They come from Mobile. Aiken. From Newport News. From Marietta. From Meridian. And the sounds of these places in their mouths make you think of love. When you ask them where they are from, they tilt their heads and say "Mobile" and you think you've been kissed. They say "Aiken" and you see a white butterfly glance off a fence with a torn wing. They say "Nagadoches" and you want to say "Yes, I will." You don't know what these towns are like, but you love what happens to the air when they open their lips and let the names ease out.

Meridian. The sound of it opens the windows of a room like the first four notes of a hymn. Few people can say the names of their home towns with such sly affection. Perhaps because they don't have home towns, just places where they were born. But these girls soak up the juice of their home towns, and it never leaves them. They are thin brown girls who have looked long at hollyhocks in the backyards of Meridian, Mobile, Aiken, and Baton Rouge. And like hollyhocks they are narrow, tall, and still. Their roots are deep, their stalks are firm, and only the top blossom nods in the wind. They have the eyes of people who can tell what time it is by the color of the sky. Such girls live in quiet black neighborhoods where everybody is gainfully employed. Where there are porch swings hanging from chains. Where the grass is cut with a scythe, where rooster combs and sunflowers grow in the yards, and pots of bleeding heart, ivy, and mother-in-law tongue line the steps and windowsills. Such girls have bought watermelon and snapbeans from the fruit man's wagon. They have put in the window the cardboard sign that has a pound measure printed on each of three edges—10 lbs., 25 lbs., 50 lbs.—and NO ICE on the fourth. These particular brown girls from Mobile and Aiken are not like some of their sisters. They are not fretful, nervous, or shrill; they do not have lovely black necks that stretch as though against an invisible collar; their eyes do not bite. These sugar-brown Mobile girls move through the streets without a stir. They are as sweet and plain as buttercake. Slim ankles; long, narrow feet. They wash themselves with orange-colored Lifebuoy soap, dust themselves with Cashmere Bouquet talc, clean their teeth with salt on a piece of rag, soften their skin with Jergens Lotion. They smell like wood, newspapers, and vanilla. They straighten their hair with Dixie Peach, and part it on the side. At night they curl it in paper from brown bags, tie a print scarf around their heads, and sleep with hands folded across their stomachs. They do not drink, smoke, or swear, and they still call sex "nookey." They sing second soprano in the choir, and although their voices are clear and steady, they are never picked to solo. They are in the second row, white blouses starched, blue skirts almost purple from ironing.

They go to land-grant colleges, normal schools, and learn how to do the white man's work with refinement: home economics to prepare his food; teacher education to instruct black children in obedience; music to soothe the weary master and entertain his blunted soul. Here they learn the rest of the lesson begun in those soft houses with porch swings and pots of bleeding heart: how to behave. The careful development of thrift, patience, high morals, and good manners. In short, how to get rid of the funkiness. The dreadful funkiness of passion, the funkiness of nature, the funkiness of the wide range of human emotions.

Wherever it erupts, this Funk, they wipe it away; where it crusts, they dissolve it; wherever it drips, flowers, or clings, they find it and fight it until it dies. They fight this battle all the way to the grave. The laugh that is a little too loud; the enunciation a little too round; the gesture a little too generous. They hold their behind in for fear of a sway too free; when they wear lipstick, they never cover the entire mouth for fear of lips too thick, and they worry, worry, worry about the edges of their hair.

They never seem to have boyfriends, but they always marry. Certain men watch them, without seeming to, and know that if such a girl is in his house, he will sleep on sheets boiled white, hung out to dry on juniper bushes, and pressed flat with a heavy iron. There will be pretty paper flowers decorating the picture of his mother, a large Bible in the front room. They feel secure. They know their work clothes will be mended, washed, and ironed on Monday, that their Sunday shirts will billow on hangers from the door jamb, stiffly starched and white. They look at her hands and know what she will do with biscuit dough; they smell the coffee and the fried ham; see the white, smoky grits with a dollop of butter on top. Her hips assure them that she will bear children easily and painlessly. And they are right.

What they do not know is that this plain brown girl will build her nest stick by stick, make it her own inviolable world, and stand guard over its every plant, weed, and doily, even against him. In silence will she return the lamp to where she put it in the first place; remove the dishes from the table as soon as the last bite is taken; wipe the doorknob after a greasy hand has touched it. A sidelong look will be enough to tell him to smoke on the back porch. Children will sense instantly that they cannot come into her yard to retrieve a ball. But the men do not know these things. Nor do they know that she will give him her body sparingly and partially. He must enter her surreptitiously, lifting the hem of her nightgown only to her navel. He must rest his weight on his elbows when they make love, ostensibly to avoid hurting her breasts but actually to keep her from having to touch or feel too much of him.

While he moves inside her, she will wonder why they didn't put the necessary but private parts of the body in some more convenient place —like the armpit, for example, or the palm of the hand. Someplace one could get to easily, and quickly, without undressing. She stiffens when she feels one of her paper curlers coming undone from the activity of love; imprints in her mind which one it is that is coming loose so she can quickly secure it once he is through. She hopes he will not sweat—

the damp may get into her hair; and that she will remain dry between her legs—she hates the glucking sound they make when she is moist. When she senses some spasm about to grip him, she will make rapid movements with her hips, press her fingernails into his back, suck in her breath, and pretend she is having an orgasm. She might wonder again, for the six hundredth time, what it would be like to have *that* feeling while her husband's penis is inside her. The closest thing to it was the time she was walking down the street and her napkin slipped free of her sanitary belt. It moved gently between her legs as she walked. Gently, ever so gently. And then a slight and distinctly delicious sensation collected in her crotch. As the delight grew, she had to stop in the street, hold her thighs together to contain it. That must be what it is like, she thinks, but it never happens while he is inside her. When he withdraws, she pulls her nightgown down, slips out of the bed and into the bathroom with relief.

Occasionally some living thing will engage her affections. A cat, perhaps, who will love her order, precision, and constancy; who will be as clean and quiet as she is. The cat will settle quietly on the windowsill and caress her with his eyes. She can hold him in her arms, letting his back paws struggle for footing on her breast and his forepaws cling to her shoulder. She can rub the smooth fur and feel the unresisting flesh underneath. At her gentlest touch he will preen, stretch, and open his mouth. And she will accept the strangely pleasant sensation that comes when he writhes beneath her hand and flattens his eyes with a surfeit of sensual delight. When she stands cooking at the table, he will circle about her shanks, and the trill of his fur spirals up her legs to her thighs, to make her fingers tremble a little in the pie dough.

Or, as she sits reading the "Uplifting Thoughts" in *The Liberty Magazine,* the cat will jump into her lap. She will fondle that soft hill of hair and let the warmth of the animal's body seep over and into the deeply private areas of her lap. Sometimes the magazine drops, and she opens her legs just a little, and the two of them will be still together, perhaps shifting a little together, sleeping a little together, until four o'clock, when the intruder comes home from work vaguely anxious about what's for dinner.

The cat will always know that he is first in her affections. Even after she bears a child. For she does bear a child—easily, and painlessly. But only one. A son. Named Junior.

One such girl from Mobile, or Meridian, or Aiken who did not sweat in her armpits nor between her thighs, who smelled of wood and vanilla, who had made soufflés in the Home Economics Department, moved with her husband, Louis, to Lorain, Ohio. Her name was Geraldine. There she built her nest, ironed shirts, potted bleeding hearts, played with her cat, and birthed Louis Junior.

Geraldine did not allow her baby, Junior, to cry. As long as his needs were physical, she could meet them—comfort and satiety. He was always brushed, bathed, oiled, and shod. Geraldine did not talk to him, coo to him, or indulge him in kissing bouts, but she saw that every other desire was fulfilled. It was not long before the child discovered the difference in his mother's behavior to himself and the cat. As he grew older, he learned how to direct his hatred of his mother to the cat, and spent some happy moments watching it suffer. The cat survived, because Geraldine was seldom away from home, and could effectively soothe the animal when Junior abused him.

Geraldine, Louis, Junior, and the cat lived next to the playground of Washington Irving School. Junior considered the playground his own, and the schoolchildren coveted his freedom to sleep late, go home for lunch, and dominate the playground after school. He hated to see the swings, slides, monkey bars, and seesaws empty and tried to get kids to stick around as long as possible. White kids; his mother did not like him to play with niggers. She had explained to him the difference between colored people and niggers. They were easily identifiable. Colored people were neat and quiet; niggers were dirty and loud. He belonged to the former group: he wore white shirts and blue trousers; his hair was cut as close to his scalp as possible to avoid any suggestion of wool, the part was etched into his hair by the barber. In winter his mother put Jergens Lotion on his face to keep the skin from becoming ashen. Even though he was light-skinned, it was possible to ash. The line between colored and nigger was not always clear; subtle and telltale signs threatened to erode it, and the watch had to be constant.

Junior used to long to play with the black boys. More than anything in the world he wanted to play King of the Mountain and have them push him down the mound of dirt and roll over him. He wanted to feel their hardness pressing on him, smell their wild blackness, and say "Fuck you" with that lovely casualness. He wanted to sit with them on curbstones and compare the sharpness of jackknives, the distance and arcs of spitting. In the toilet he wanted to share with them the laurels of being able to pee far and long. Bay Boy and P. L. had at one time been his idols. Gradually he came to agree with his mother that neither Bay Boy nor P. L. was good enough for him. He played only with Ralph Nisensky, who was two years younger, wore glasses, and didn't want to *do* anything. More and more Junior enjoyed bullying girls. It was easy making them scream and run. How he laughed when they fell down and their bloomers showed. When they got up, their faces red and crinkled, it made him feel good. The nigger girls he did not pick on very much. They usually traveled in packs, and once when he threw a stone at some of them, they chased, caught, and beat him witless. He lied to his mother, saying Bay Boy did it. His mother was very upset. His father just kept on reading the Lorain *Journal*.

When the mood struck him, he would call a child passing by to come play on the swings or the seesaw. If the child wouldn't, or did and left too soon, Junior threw gravel at him. He became a very good shot.

Alternately bored and frightened at home, the playground was his joy. On a day when he had been especially idle, he saw a very black girl taking a shortcut through the playground. She kept her head down as she walked. He had seen her many times before, standing alone, always alone, at recess. Nobody ever played with her. Probably, he thought, because she was ugly.

Now Junior called to her. "Hey! What are you doing walking through my yard?"

The girl stopped.

"Nobody can come through this yard 'less I say so."

"This ain't your yard. It's the school's."

"But I'm in charge of it."

The girl started to walk away.

"Wait." Junior walked toward her. "You can play in it if you want to. What's your name?"

"Pecola. I don't want to play."

"Come on. I'm not going to bother you."

"I got to go home."

"Say, you want to see something? I got something to show you."

"No. What is it?"

"Come on in my house. See, I live right there. Come on. I'll show you."

"Show me what?"

"Some kittens. We got some kittens. You can have one if you want."

"Real kittens?"

"Yeah. Come on."

He pulled gently at her dress. Pecola began to move toward his house. When he knew she had agreed, Junior ran ahead excitedly, stopping only to yell back at her to come on. He held the door open for her, smiling his encouragement. Pecola climbed the porch stairs and hesitated there, afraid to follow him. The house looked dark. Junior said, "There's nobody here. My ma's gone out, and my father's at work. Don't you want to see the kittens?"

Junior turned on the lights. Pecola stepped inside the door.

How beautiful, she thought. What a beautiful house. There was a big red-and-gold Bible on the dining-room table. Little lace doilies were everywhere—on arms and backs of chairs, in the center of a large dining table, on little tables. Potted plants were on all the windowsills. A color picture of Jesus Christ hung on a wall with the prettiest paper flowers fastened on the frame. She wanted to see everything slowly, slowly. But Junior kept saying, "Hey, you. Come on. Come on." He pulled her into another room, even more beautiful than the first. More doilies, a big lamp with green-and-gold base and white shade. There was even a rug on the floor, with enormous dark-red flowers. She was deep in admiration of the flowers when Junior said, "Here!" Pecola turned. "Here is your kitten!" he screeched. And he threw a big black cat right in her face. She sucked in her breath in fear and surprise and felt fur in her mouth. The cat clawed her face and chest in an effort to right itself, then leaped nimbly to the floor.

Junior was laughing and running around the room clutching his stomach delightedly. Pecola touched the scratched place on her face and felt tears coming. When she started toward the doorway, Junior leaped in front of her.

"You can't get out. You're my prisoner," he said. His eyes were merry but hard.

"You let me go."

"No!" He pushed her down, ran out the door that separated the rooms, and held it shut with his hands. Pecola's banging on the door increased his gasping, high-pitched laughter.

The tears came fast, and she held her face in her hands. When something soft and furry moved around her ankles, she jumped, and saw it was the cat. He wound himself in and about her legs. Momentarily distracted from her fear, she squatted down to touch him, her hands wet from the tears. The cat rubbed up against her knee. He was black all over, deep silky black, and his eyes, pointing down toward his nose, were bluish green. The light made them shine like blue ice. Pecola rubbed the cat's head; he whined, his tongue flicking with pleasure. The blue eyes in the black face held her.

Junior, curious at not hearing her sobs, opened the door, and saw her squatting down rubbing the cat's back. He saw the cat stretching its head and flattening its eyes. He had seen that expression many times as the animal responded to his mother's touch.

"Gimme my cat!" His voice broke. With a movement both awkward and sure he snatched the cat by one of its hind legs and began to swing it around his head in a circle.

"Stop that!" Pecola was screaming. The cat's free paws were stiffened, ready to grab anything to restore balance, its mouth wide, its eyes blue streaks of horror.

Still screaming, Pecola reached for Junior's hand. She heard her dress rip under her arm. Junior tried to push her away, but she grabbed the arm which was swinging the cat. They both fell, and in falling, Junior let go the cat, which, having been released in mid-motion, was thrown full force against the window. It slithered down and fell on the radiator behind the sofa. Except for a few shudders, it was still. There was only the slightest smell of singed fur.

Geraldine opened the door.

"What is this?" Her voice was mild, as though asking a perfectly reasonable question. "Who is this girl?"

"She killed our cat," said Junior. "Look." He pointed to the radiator, where the cat lay, its blue eyes closed, leaving only an empty, black, and helpless face.

Geraldine went to the radiator and picked up the cat. He was limp in her arms, but she rubbed her face in his fur. She looked at Pecola. Saw the dirty torn dress, the plaits sticking out on her head, hair matted where the plaits had come undone, the muddy shoes with the wad of gum peeping out from between the cheap soles, the soiled socks, one of which had been walked down into the heel of the shoe. She saw the safety pin holding the hem of the dress up. Up over the hump of the cat's back she looked at her. She had seen this little girl all of her life. Hanging out of windows over saloons in Mobile, crawling over the porches of shotgun houses on the edge of town, sitting in bus stations holding paper bags and crying to mothers who kept saying

"Shet up!" Hair uncombed, dresses falling apart, shoes untied and caked with dirt. They had stared at her with great uncomprehending eyes. Eyes that questioned nothing and asked everything. Unblinking and unabashed, they stared up at her. The end of the world lay in their eyes, and the beginning, and all the waste in between.

They were everywhere. They slept six in a bed, all their pee mixing together in the night as they wet their beds each in his own candy-and-potato-chip dream. In the long, hot days, they idled away, picking plaster from the walls and digging into the earth with sticks. They sat in little rows on street curbs, crowded into pews at church, taking space from the nice, neat, colored children; they clowned on the playgrounds, broke things in dime stores, ran in front of you on the street, made ice slides on the sloped sidewalks in winter. The girls grew up knowing nothing of girdles, and the boys announced their manhood by turning the bills of their caps backward. Grass wouldn't grow where they lived. Flowers died. Shades fell down. Tin cans and tires blossomed where they lived. They lived on cold black-eyed peas and orange pop. Like flies they hovered; like flies they settled. And this one had settled in her house. Up over the hump of the cat's back she looked.

"Get out," she said, her voice quiet. "You nasty little black bitch. Get out of my house."

The cat shuddered and flicked his tail.

Pecola backed out of the room, staring at the pretty milk-brown lady in the pretty gold-and-green house who was talking to her through the cat's fur. The pretty lady's words made the cat fur move; the breath of each word parted the fur. Pecola turned to find the front door and saw Jesus looking down at her with sad and unsurprised eyes, his long brown hair parted in the middle, the gay paper flowers twisted around his face.

Outside, the March wind blew into the rip in her dress. She held her head down against the cold. But she could not hold it low enough to avoid seeing the snowflakes falling and dying on the pavement.

Spring

The first twigs are thin, green, and supple. They bend into a complete circle, but will not break. Their delicate, showy hopefulness shooting from forsythia and lilac bushes meant only a change in whipping style. They beat us differently in the spring. Instead of the dull pain of a winter strap, there were these new green switches that lost their sting long after the whipping was over. There was a nervous meanness in these long twigs that made us long for the steady stroke of a strap or the firm but honest slap of a hairbrush. Even now spring for me is shot through with the remembered ache of switchings, and forsythia holds no cheer.

Sunk in the grass of an empty lot on a spring Saturday, I split the stems of milkweed and thought about ants and peach pits and death and where the world went when I closed my eyes. I must have lain long in the grass, for the shadow that was in front of me when I left the house had disappeared when I went back. I entered the house, as the house was bursting with an uneasy quiet. Then I heard my mother singing something about trains and Arkansas. She came in the back door with some folded yellow curtains which she piled on the kitchen table. I sat down on the floor to listen to the song's story, and noticed how strangely she was behaving. She still had her hat on, and her shoes were dusty, as though she had been walking in deep dirt. She put on some water to boil and then swept the porch; then she hauled out the curtain stretcher, but instead of putting the damp curtains on it, she swept the porch again. All the time singing about trains and Arkansas.

When she finished, I went to look for Frieda. I found her upstairs lying on our bed, crying the tired, whimpering cry that follows the first wailings—mostly gasps and shudderings. I lay on the bed and looked at the tiny bunches of wild roses sprinkled over her dress. Many washings had faded their color and dimmed their outlines.

"What happened, Frieda?"

She lifted a swollen face from the crook of her arm. Shuddering still, she sat up, letting her thin legs dangle over the bedside. I knelt on the bed and picked up the hem of my dress to wipe her running nose. She never liked wiping noses on clothes, but this time she let me. It was the way Mama did with her apron.

"Did you get a whipping?"

She shook her head no.

"Then why you crying?"

"Because."

"Because what?"

"Mr. Henry."

"What'd he do?"

"Daddy beat him up."

"What for? The Maginot Line? Did he find out about the Maginot Line?"

"No."

"Well, what, then? Come on, Frieda. How come I can't know?"

"He . . . *picked* at me."

"Picked at you? You mean like Soaphead Church?"

"Sort of."

"He showed his privates at you?"

"Noooo. He touched me."

"Where?"

"Here and here." She pointed to the tiny breasts that, like two fallen acorns, scattered a few faded rose leaves on her dress.

"Really? How did it feel?"

"Oh, Claudia." She sounded put-out. I wasn't asking the right questions.

"It didn't feel like anything."

"But wasn't it supposed to? Feel good, I mean?" Frieda sucked her teeth. "What'd he do? Just walk up and pinch them?"

She sighed. "First he said how pretty I was. Then he grabbed my arm and touched me."

"Where was Mama and Daddy?"

"Over at the garden weeding."

"What'd you say when he did it?"

"Nothing. I just ran out the kitchen and went to the garden."

"Mama said we was never to cross the tracks by ourselves."

"Well, what would you do? Set there and let him pinch you?"

I looked at my chest. "I don't have nothing to pinch. I'm never going to have nothing."

"Oh, Claudia, you're jealous of everything. You *want* him to?"

"No, I just get tired of having everything last."

"You do not. What about scarlet fever? You had that first."

"Yes, but it didn't last. Anyway, what happened at the garden?"

"I told Mama, and she told Daddy, and we all come home, and he was gone, so we waited for him, and when Daddy saw him come up on the porch, he threw our old tricycle at his head and knocked him off the porch."

"Did he die?"

"Naw. He got up and started singing 'Nearer My God to Thee.' Then Mama hit him with a broom and told him to keep the Lord's name out of his mouth, but he wouldn't stop, and Daddy was cussing, and everybody was screaming."

"Oh, shoot, I always miss stuff."

"And Mr. Buford came running out with his gun, and Mama told him to go somewhere and sit down, and Daddy said no, give him the gun, and Mr. Buford did, and Mama screamed, and Mr. Henry shut up and started running, and Daddy shot at him and Mr. Henry jumped out of his shoes and kept on running in his socks. Then Rosemary came out and said that Daddy was going to jail, and I hit her."

"Real hard?"

"Real hard."

"Is that when Mama whipped you?"

"She didn't whip me, I told you."

"Then why you crying?"

"Miss Dunion came in after everybody was quiet, and Mama and Daddy was fussing about who let Mr. Henry in anyway, and she said that Mama should take me to the doctor, because I might be ruined, and Mama started screaming all over again."

"At you?"

"No. At Miss Dunion."

"But why were you crying?"

"I don't want to be *ruined!*"

"What's ruined?"

"You know. Like the Maginot Line. She's ruined. Mama said so." The tears came back.

An image of Frieda, big and fat, came to mind. Her thin legs swollen, her face surrounded by layers of rouged skin. I too begin to feel tears.

"But, Frieda, you could exercise and not eat."

She shrugged.

"Besides, what about China and Poland? They're ruined too, aren't they? And they ain't fat."

"That's because they drink whiskey. Mama says whiskey ate them up."

"You could drink whiskey."

"Where would I get whiskey?"

We thought about this. Nobody would sell it to us; we had no money, anyway. There was never any in our house. Who would have some?

"Pecola," I said. "Her father's always drunk. She can get us some."

"You think so?"

"Sure. Cholly's always drunk. Let's go ask her. We don't have to tell her what for."

"Now?"

"Sure, now."

"What'll we tell Mama?"

"Nothing. Let's just go out the back. One at a time. So she won't notice."

"O.K. You go first, Claudia."

We opened the fence gate at the bottom of the backyard and ran down the alley.

Pecola lived on the other side of Broadway. We had never been in her house, but we knew where it was. A two-story gray building that had been a store downstairs and had an apartment upstairs.

Nobody answered our knock on the front door, so we walked around to the side door. As we approached, we heard radio music and looked to see where it came from. Above us was the second-story porch, lined with slanting, rotting rails, and sitting on the porch was the Maginot Line herself. We stared up and automatically reached for the other's hand. A mountain of flesh, she lay rather than sat in a rocking chair. She had no shoes on, and each foot was poked between a railing: tiny baby toes at the tip of puffy feet; swollen ankles smoothed and tightened the skin; massive legs like tree stumps parted wide at the knees, over which spread two roads of soft flabby inner thigh that kissed each other deep in the shade of her dress and closed. A dark-brown root-beer bottle, like a burned limb, grew out of her dimpled hand. She looked at us down through the porch railings and emitted a low, long belch. Her eyes were as clean as rain, and again I remembered the waterfall. Neither of us could speak. Both of us imagined we were seeing what was to become of Frieda. The Maginot Line smiled at us.

"You all looking for somebody?"

I had to pull my tongue from the roof of my mouth to say, "Pecola—she live here?"

"Uh-huh, but she ain't here now. She gone to her mama's work place to git the wash."

"Yes, ma'am. She coming back?"

"Uh-huh. She got to hang up the clothes before the sun goes down."

"Oh."

"You can wait for her. Wanna come up here and wait?"

We exchanged glances. I looked back up at the broad cinnamon roads that met in the shadow of her dress.

Frieda said, "No, ma'am."

"Well," the Maginot Line seemed interested in our problem. "You can go to her mama's work place, but it's way over by the lake."

"Where by the lake?"

"That big white house with the wheelbarrow full of flowers."

It was a house that we knew, having admired the large white wheelbarrow tilted down on spoked wheels and planted with seasonal flowers.

"Ain't that too far for you all to go walking?"

Frieda scratched her knee.

"Why don't you wait for her? You can come up here. Want some pop?" Those rain-soaked eyes lit up, and her smile was full, not like the pinched and holding-back smile of other grown-ups.

I moved to go up the stairs, but Frieda said, "No, ma'am, we ain't allowed."

I was amazed at her courage, and frightened of her sassiness. The smile of the Maginot Line slipped. "Ain't 'llowed?"

"No'm."

"Ain't 'llowed to what?"

"Go in your house."

"Is that right?" The waterfalls were still. "How come?"

"My mama said so. My mama said you ruined."

The waterfalls began to run again. She put the root-beer bottle to her lips and drank it empty. With a graceful movement of the wrist, a gesture so quick and small we never really saw it, only remembered it afterward, she tossed the bottle over the rail at us. It split at our feet, and shards of brown glass dappled our legs before we could jump back. The Maginot Line put a fat hand on one of the folds of her stomach and laughed. At first just a deep humming with her mouth closed, then a larger, warmer sound. Laughter at once beautiful and frightening. She let her head tilt sideways, closed her eyes, and shook her massive trunk, letting the laughter fall like a wash of red leaves all around us. Scraps and curls of the laughter followed us as we ran. Our breath gave out at the same time our legs did. After we rested against a tree, our heads on crossed forearms, I said, "Let's go home."

Frieda was still angry—fighting, she believed, for her life. "No, we got to get it now."

"We can't go all the way to the lake."

"Yes we can. Come on."

"Mama gone get us."

"No she ain't. Besides, she can't do nothing but whip us."

That was true. She wouldn't kill us, or laugh a terrible laugh at us, or throw a bottle at us.

We walked down tree-lined streets of soft gray houses leaning like tired ladies. . . . The streets changed; houses looked more sturdy, their paint was newer, porch posts straighter, yards deeper. Then came brick houses set well back from the street, fronted by yards edged in shrubbery clipped into smooth cones and balls of velvet green.

The lakefront houses were the loveliest. Garden furniture, ornaments, windows like shiny eyeglasses, and no sign of life. The backyards of these houses fell away in green slopes down to a strip of sand, and then the blue Lake Erie, lapping all the way to Canada. The orange-patched sky of the steel-mill section never reached this part of town. This sky was always blue.

We reached Lake Shore Park, a city park laid out with rosebuds, fountains, bowling greens, picnic tables. It was empty now, but sweetly expectant of clean, white, well-behaved children and parents who would play there above the lake in summer before half-running, half-stumbling down the slope to the welcoming water. Black people were not allowed in the park, and so it filled our dreams.

Right before the entrance to the park was the large white house with the wheelbarrow full of flowers. Short crocus blades sheathed the purple-and-white hearts that so wished to be first they endured the chill and rain of early spring. The walkway was flagged in calculated disorder, hiding the cunning symmetry. Only fear of discovery and the knowledge that we did not belong kept us from loitering. We circled the proud house and went to the back.

There on the tiny railed stoop sat Pecola in a light red sweater and blue cotton dress. A little wagon was parked near her. She seemed glad to see us.

"Hi."

"Hi."

"What you all doing here?" She was smiling, and since it was a rare thing to see on her, I was surprised at the pleasure it gave me.

"We're looking for you."

"Who told you I was here?"

"The Maginot Line."

"Who is that?"

"That big fat lady. She lives over you."

"Oh, you mean Miss Marie. Her name is Miss Marie."

"Well, everybody calls her Miss Maginot Line. Ain't you scared?"

"Scared of what?"

"The Maginot Line."

Pecola looked genuinely puzzled. "What for?"

"Your mama let you go in her house? And eat out of her plates?"

"She don't know I go. Miss Marie is nice. They all nice."

"Oh, yeah," I said, "she tried to kill us."

"Who? Miss Marie? She don't bother nobody."

"Then how come your mama don't let you go in her house if she so nice?"

"I don't know. She say she's bad, but they ain't bad. They give me stuff all the time."

"What stuff?"

"Oh, lots of stuff, pretty dresses, and shoes. I got more shoes than I ever wear. And jewelry and candy and money. They take me to the movies, and once we went to the carnival. China gone take me to Cleveland to see the square, and Poland gone take me to Chicago to see the Loop. We going everywhere together."

"You lying. You don't have no pretty dresses."

"I do, too."

"Oh, come on, Pecola, what you telling us all that junk for?" Frieda asked.

"It ain't junk." Pecola stood up ready to defend her words, when the door opened.

Mrs. Breedlove stuck her head out the door and said, "What's going on out here? Pecola, who are these children?"

"That's Frieda and Claudia, Mrs. Breedlove."

"Whose girls are you?" She came all the way out on the stoop. She looked nicer than I had ever seen her, in her white uniform and her hair in a small pompadour.

"Mrs. MacTeer's girls, ma'am."

"Oh, yes. Live over on Twenty-first Street?"

"Yes, ma'am."

"What are you doing 'way over here?"

"Just walking. We came to see Pecola."

"Well, you better get on back. You can walk with Pecola. Come on in while I get the wash."

We stepped into the kitchen, a large spacious room. Mrs. Breedlove's skin glowed like taffeta in the reflection of white porcelain, white woodwork, polished cabinets, and brilliant copperware. Odors of meat, vegetables, and something freshly baked mixed with a scent of Fels Naphtha.

"I'm gone get the wash. You all stand stock still right there and don't mess up nothing." She disappeared behind a white swinging door, and we could hear the uneven flap of her footsteps as she descended into the basement.

Another door opened, and in walked a little girl, smaller and younger than all of us. She wore a pink sunback dress and pink fluffy bedroom slippers with two bunny ears pointed up from the tips. Her hair was corn yellow and bound in a thick ribbon. When she saw us, fear danced across her face for a second. She looked anxiously around the kitchen.

"Where's Polly?" she asked.

The familiar violence rose in me. Her calling Mrs. Breedlove Polly, when even Pecola called her mother Mrs. Breedlove seemed reason enough to scratch her.

"She's downstairs," I said.

"Polly!" she called.

"Look," Frieda whispered, "look at that." On the counter near the stove in a silvery pan was a deep-dish berry cobbler. The purple juice bursting here and there through crust. We moved closer.

"It's still hot," Frieda said.

Pecola stretched her hand to touch the pan, lightly, to see if it was hot.

"Polly, come here," the little girl called again.

It may have been nervousness, awkwardness, but the pan tilted under Pecola's fingers and fell to the floor, splattering blackish blueberries everywhere. Most of the juice splashed on Pecola's legs, and the burn must have been painful, for she cried out and began hopping about just as Mrs. Breedlove entered with a tightly packed laundry bag. In one gallop she was on Pecola, and with the back of her hand knocked her to the floor. Pecola slid in the pie juice, one leg folding under her. Mrs. Breedlove yanked her up by the arm, slapped her again, and in a voice thin with anger, abused Pecola directly and Frieda and me by implication.

"Crazy fool . . . my floor, mess . . . look what you . . .

work . . . get on out . . . now that . . . crazy . . . my
floor, my floor . . . my floor." Her words were hotter and darker than
the smoking berries, and we backed away in dread.

The little girl in pink started to cry. Mrs. Breedlove turned to her.
"Hush, baby, hush. Come here. Oh, Lord, look at your dress. Don't cry
no more. Polly will change it." She went to the sink and turned tap
water on a fresh towel. Over her shoulder she spit out words to us like
rotten pieces of apple. "Pick up that wash and get on out of here, so I
can get this mess cleaned up."

Pecola picked up the laundry bag, heavy with wet clothes, and we
stepped hurriedly out the door. As Pecola put the laundry bag in the
wagon, we could hear Mrs. Breedlove hushing and soothing the tears
of the little pink-and-yellow girl.

"Who were they, Polly?"

"Don't worry none, baby."

"You gonna make another pie?"

" 'Course I will."

"Who were they, Polly?"

"Hush. Don't worry none," she whispered, and the honey in her
words complemented the sundown spilling on the lake.

SEEMOTHERMOTHERISVERYNICEMOTHERWILLYOUPLA
YWITHJANEMOTHERLAUGHSLAUGHMOTHERLAUGHLA

The easiest thing to do would be to build a case out of her foot. That
is what she herself did. But to find out the truth about how dreams die,
one should never take the word of the dreamer. The end of her lovely
beginning was probably the cavity in one of her front teeth. She preferred, however, to think always of her foot. Although she was the
ninth of eleven children and lived on a ridge of red Alabama clay seven
miles from the nearest road, the complete indifference with which a
rusty nail was met when it punched clear through her foot during her
second year of life saved Pauline Williams from total anonymity. The
wound left her with a crooked, archless foot that flopped when she
walked—not a limp that would have eventually twisted her spine, but
a way of lifting the bad foot as though she were extracting it from little whirlpools that threatened to pull it under. Slight as it was, this deformity explained for her many things that would have been otherwise
incomprehensible: why she alone of all the children had no nickname;
why there were no funny jokes and anecdotes about funny things she
had done; why no one ever remarked on her food preferences—no sav-
ing of the wing or neck for her—no cooking of the peas in a separate
pot without rice because she did not like rice; why nobody teased her;
why she never felt at home anywhere, or that she belonged anyplace.
Her general feeling of separateness and unworthiness she blamed on
her foot. Restricted, as a child, to this cocoon of her family's spinning,
she cultivated quiet and private pleasures. She liked, most of all, to arrange things. To line things up in rows—jars on shelves at canning,
peach pits on the step, sticks, stones, leaves—and the members of her
family let these arrangements be. When by some accident somebody
scattered her rows, they always stopped to retrieve them for her, and

she was never angry, for it gave her a chance to rearrange them again. Whatever portable plurality she found, she organized into neat lines, according to their size, shape, or gradations of color. Just as she would never align a pine needle with the leaf of a cottonwood tree, she would never put the jars of tomatoes next to the green beans. During all of her four years of going to school, she was enchanted by numbers and depressed by words. She missed—without knowing what she missed— paints and crayons.

Near the beginning of World War I, the Williamses discovered, from returning neighbors and kin, the possibility of living better in another place. In shifts, lots, batches, mixed in with other families, they migrated, in six months and four journeys, to Kentucky, where there were mines and millwork.

"When all us left from down home and was waiting down by the depot for the truck, it was nighttime. June bugs was shooting everywhere. They lighted up a tree leaf, and I seen a streak of green every now and again. That was the last time I seen real june bugs. These things up here ain't june bugs. They's something else. Folks here call them fireflies. Down home they was different. But I recollect that streak of green. I recollect it well."

In Kentucky they lived in a real town, ten to fifteen houses on a single street, with water piped right into the kitchen. Ada and Fowler Williams found a five-room frame house for their family. The yard was bounded by a once-white fence against which Pauline's mother planted flowers and within which they kept a few chickens. Some of her brothers joined the Army, one sister died, and two got married, increasing the living space and giving the entire Kentucky venture a feel of luxury. The relocation was especially comfortable to Pauline, who was old enough to leave school. Mrs. Williams got a job cleaning and cooking for a white minister on the other side of town, and Pauline, now the oldest girl at home, took over the care of the house. She kept the fence in repair, pulling the pointed stakes erect, securing them with bits of

wire, collected eggs, swept, cooked, washed, and minded the two
younger children—a pair of twins called Chicken and Pie, who were
still in school. She was not only good at housekeeping, she enjoyed it.
After her parents left for work and the other children were at school or
in mines, the house was quiet. The stillness and isolation both calmed
and energized her. She could arrange and clean without interruption
until two o'clock, when Chicken and Pie came home.

When the war ended and the twins were ten years old, they too left
school to work. Pauline was fifteen, still keeping house, but with less
enthusiasm. Fantasies about men and love and touching were drawing
her mind and hands away from her work. Changes in weather began to
affect her, as did certain sights and sounds. These feelings translated
themselves to her in extreme melancholy. She thought of the death of
newborn things, lonely roads, and strangers who appear out of nowhere simply to hold one's hand, woods in which the sun was always
setting. In church especially did these dreams grow. The songs caressed
her, and while she tried to hold her mind on the wages of sin, her body
trembled for redemption, salvation, a mysterious rebirth that would
simply happen, with no effort on her part. In none of her fantasies was
she ever aggressive; she was usually idling by the river bank, or gathering berries in a field when a someone appeared, with gentle and pene-
trating eyes, who—with no exchange of words—understood; and before whose glance her foot straightened and her eyes dropped. The
someone had no face, no form, no voice, no odor. He was a simple
Presence, an all-embracing tenderness with strength and a promise of
rest. It did not matter that she had no idea of what to do or say to the
Presence—after the wordless knowing and the soundless touching, her
dreams disintegrated. But the Presence would know what to do. She
had only to lay her head on his chest and he would lead her away to
the sea, to the city, to the woods . . . forever.

There was a woman named Ivy who seemed to hold in her mouth
all of the sounds of Pauline's soul. Standing a little apart from the
choir, Ivy sang the dark sweetness that Pauline could not name; she

sang the death-defying death that Pauline yearned for; she sang of the
Stranger who *knew* . . .

> Precious Lord take my hand
> Lead me on, let me stand
> I am tired, I am weak, I am worn.
> Through the storms, through the night
> Lead me on to the light
> Take my hand, precious Lord, lead me on.
>
> When my way grows drear
> Precious Lord linger near,
> When my life is almost gone
> Hear my cry hear my call
> Hold my hand lest I fall
> Take my hand, precious Lord, lead me on.

Thus it was that when the Stranger, the someone, did appear out of
nowhere, Pauline was grateful but not surprised.

He came, strutting right out of a Kentucky sun on the hottest day
of the year. He came big, he came strong, he came with yellow eyes,
flaring nostrils, and he came with his own music.

Pauline was leaning idly on the fence, her arms resting on the cross-
rail between the pickets. She had just put down some biscuit dough
and was cleaning the flour from under her nails. Behind her at some
distance she heard whistling. One of these rapid, high-note riffs that
black boys make up as they go while sweeping, shoveling, or just
walking along. A kind of city-street music where laughter belies anxiety, and joy is as short and straight as the blade of a pocketknife. She
listened carefully to the music and let it pull her lips into a smile. The
whistling got louder, and still she did not turn around, for she wanted
it to last. While smiling to herself and holding fast to the break in
somber thoughts, she felt something tickling her foot. She laughed
aloud and turned to see. The whistler was bending down tickling her
broken foot and kissing her leg. She could not stop her laughter—not

until he looked up at her and she saw the Kentucky sun drenching the yellow, heavy-lidded eyes of Cholly Breedlove.

"When I first seed Cholly, I want you to know it was like all the bits of color from that time down home when all us chil'ren went berry picking after a funeral and I put some in the pocket of my Sunday dress, and they mashed up and stained my hips. My whole dress was messed with purple, and it never did wash out. Not the dress nor me. I could feel that purple deep inside me. And that lemonade Mama used to make when Pap came in out the fields. It be cool and yellowish, with seeds floating near the bottom. And that streak of green them june bugs made on the trees the night we left from down home. All of them colors was in me. Just sitting there. So when Cholly come up and tickled my foot, it was like them berries, that lemonade, them streaks of green the june bugs made, all come together. Cholly was thin then, with real light eyes. He used to whistle, and when I heerd him, shivers come on my skin."

Pauline and Cholly loved each other. He seemed to relish her company and even to enjoy her country ways and lack of knowledge about city things. He talked with her about her foot and asked, when they walked through the town or in the fields, if she were tired. Instead of ignoring her infirmity, pretending it was not there, he made it seem like something special and endearing. For the first time Pauline felt that her bad foot was an asset.

And he did touch her, firmly but gently, just as she had dreamed. But minus the gloom of setting suns and lonely river banks. She was secure and grateful; he was kind and lively. She had not known there was so much laughter in the world.

They agreed to marry and go 'way up north, where Cholly said steel mills were begging for workers. Young, loving, and full of energy, they came to Lorain, Ohio. Cholly found work in the steel mills right away, and Pauline started keeping house.

And then she lost her front tooth. But there must have been a speck, a brown speck easily mistaken for food but which did not leave, which sat on the enamel for months, and grew, until it cut into the surface and then to the brown putty underneath, finally eating away to the root, but avoiding the nerves, so its presence was not noticeable or uncomfortable. Then the weakened roots, having grown accustomed to the poison, responded one day to severe pressure, and the tooth fell free, leaving a ragged stump behind. But even before the little brown speck, there must have been the conditions, the setting that would allow it to exist in the first place.

In that young and growing Ohio town whose side streets, even, were paved with concrete, which sat on the edge of a calm blue lake, which boasted an affinity with Oberlin, the underground railroad station, just thirteen miles away, this melting pot on the lip of America facing the cold but receptive Canada—What could go wrong?

"Me and Cholly was getting along good then. We come up north; supposed to be more jobs and all. We moved into two rooms up over a furniture store, and I set about housekeeping. Cholly was working at the steel plant, and everything was looking good. I don't know what all happened. Everything changed. It was hard to get to know folks up here, and I missed my people. I weren't used to so much white folks. The ones I seed before was something hateful, but they didn't come around too much. I mean, we didn't have too much truck with them. Just now and then in the fields, or at the commissary. But they want all over us. Up north they was everywhere—next door, downstairs, all over the streets—and colored folks few and far between. Northern colored folk was different too. Dicty-like. No better than whites for meanness. They could make you feel just as no-count, 'cept I didn't expect it from them. That was the lonesomest time of my life. I 'member looking out them front windows just waiting for Cholly to come home at three o'clock. I didn't even have a cat to talk to."

In her loneliness, she turned to her husband for reassurance, entertainment, for things to fill the vacant places. Housework was not enough; there were only two rooms, and no yard to keep or move about in. The women in the town wore high-heeled shoes, and when Pauline tried to wear them, they aggravated her shuffle into a pronounced limp. Cholly was kindness still, but began to resist her total dependence on him. They were beginning to have less and less to say to each other. He had no problem finding other people and other things to occupy him—men were always climbing the stairs asking for him, and he was happy to accompany them, leaving her alone.

Pauline felt uncomfortable with the few black women she met. They were amused by her because she did not straighten her hair. When she tried to make up her face as they did, it came off rather badly. Their goading glances and private snickers at her way of talking (saying "chil'ren") and dressing developed in her a desire for new clothes. When Cholly began to quarrel about the money she wanted, she decided to go to work. Taking jobs as a day worker helped with the clothes, and even a few things for the apartment, but it did not help with Cholly. He was not pleased with her purchases and began to tell her so. Their marriage was shredded with quarrels. She was still no more than a girl, and still waiting for that plateau of happiness, that hand of a precious Lord who, when her way grew drear, would always linger near. Only now she had a clearer idea of what drear meant. Money became the focus of all their discussions, hers for clothes, his for drink. The sad thing was that Pauline did not really care for clothes and makeup. She merely wanted other women to cast favorable glances her way.

After several months of doing day work, she took a steady job in the home of a family of slender means and nervous, pretentious ways.

"Cholly commenced to getting meaner and meaner and wanted to fight me all of the time. I give him as good as I got. Had to. Look like working for that woman and fighting Cholly was all I did. Tiresome. But I holt on to my jobs, even though working for that woman was more than a notion. It wasn't so much her meanness as just simpleminded. Her whole family was. Couldn't get along with one another worth nothing. You'd think with a pretty house

*like that and all the money they could holt on to, they would enjoy one
another. She haul off and cry over the leastest thing. If one of her friends cut
her short on the telephone, she'd go to crying. She should of been glad she had
a telephone. I ain't got one yet. I recollect oncet how her baby brother who she
put through dentistry school didn't invite them to some big party he throwed.
They was a big to-do about that. Everybody stayed on the telephone for days.
Fussing and carrying on. She asked me, 'Pauline, what would you do if your
own brother had a party and didn't invite you?' I said ifn I really wanted to
go to that party, I reckoned I'd go anyhow. Never mind what he want. She
just sucked her teeth a little and made out like what I said was dumb. All the
while I was thinking how dumb she was. Whoever told her that her brother
was her friend? Folks can't like folks just 'cause they has the same mama. I
tried to like that woman myself. She was good about giving me stuff, but I
just couldn't like her. Soon as I worked up a good feeling on her account, she'd
do something ignorant and start in to telling me how to clean and do. If I left
her on her own, she'd drown in dirt. I didn't have to pick up after Chicken
and Pie the way I had to pick up after them. None of them knew so much as
how to wipe their behinds. I know, 'cause I did the washing. And couldn't pee
proper to save their lives. Her husband ain't hit the bowl yet. Nasty white
folks is about the nastiest things they is. But I would have stayed on 'cepting
for Cholly come over by where I was working and cut up so. He come there
drunk wanting some money. When that white woman see him, she turned red.
She tried to act strong-like, but she was scared bad. Anyway, she told Cholly
to get out or she would call the police. He cussed her and started pulling on
me. I would of gone upside his head, but I don't want no dealings with the
police. So I taken my things and left. I tried to get back, but she didn't want
me no more if I was going to stay with Cholly. She said she would let me stay
if I left him. I thought about that. But later on it didn't seem none too bright
for a black woman to leave a black man for a white woman. She didn't never
give me the eleven dollars she owed me, neither. That hurt bad. The gas man
had cut the gas off, and I couldn't cook none. I really begged that woman for
my money. I went to see her. She was mad as a wet hen. Kept on telling me I
owed her for uniforms and some old broken-down bed she give me. I didn't*

know if I owed her or not, but I needed my money. She wouldn't let up none, neither, even when I give her my word that Cholly wouldn't come back there no more. Then I got so desperate I asked her if she would loan it to me. She was quiet for a spell, and then she told me I shouldn't let a man take advantage over me. That I should have more respect, and it was my husband's duty to pay the bills, and if he couldn't, I should leave and get alimony. All such simple stuff. What was he gone give me alimony on? I seen she didn't understand that all I needed from her was my eleven dollars to pay the gas man so I could cook. She couldn't get that one thing through her thick head. 'Are you going to leave him, Pauline?' she kept on saying. I thought she'd give me my money if I said I would, so I said 'Yes, ma'am.' 'All right,' she said. 'You leave him, and then come back to work, and we'll let bygones be bygones.' 'Can I have my money today?' I said. 'No' she said. 'Only when you leave him. I'm only thinking of you and your future. What good is he, Pauline, what good is he to you?' How you going to answer a woman like that, who don't know what good a man is, and say out of one side of her mouth she's thinking of your future but won't give you your own money so you can buy you something besides baloney to eat? So I said, 'No good, ma'am. He ain't no good to me. But just the same, I think I'd best stay on.' She got up, and I left. When I got outside, I felt pains in my crotch, I had held my legs together so tight trying to make that woman understand. But I reckon now she couldn't understand. She married a man with a slash in his face instead of a mouth. So how could she understand?"

One winter Pauline discovered she was pregnant. When she told Cholly, he surprised her by being pleased. He began to drink less and come home more often. They eased back into a relationship more like the early days of their marriage, when he asked if she were tired or wanted him to bring her something from the store. In this state of ease, Pauline stopped doing day work and returned to her own house-keeping. But the loneliness in those two rooms had not gone away. When the winter sun hit the peeling green paint of the kitchen chairs, when the smoked hocks were boiling in the pot, when all she could hear was the truck delivering furniture downstairs, she thought about back home, about how she had been all alone most of the time then too, but that this lonesomeness was different. Then she stopped staring at the green chairs, at the delivery truck; she went to the movies instead. There in the dark her memory was refreshed, and she succumbed to her earlier dreams. Along with the idea of romantic love, she was introduced to another—physical beauty. Probably the most destructive ideas in the history of human thought. Both originated in envy, thrived in insecurity, and ended in disillusion. In equating physical beauty with virtue, she stripped her mind, bound it, and collected self-contempt by the heap. She forgot lust and simple caring for. She regarded love as possessive mating, and romance as the goal of the spirit. It would be for her a well-spring from which she would draw the most destructive emotions, deceiving the lover and seeking to imprison the beloved, curtailing freedom in every way.

She was never able, after her education in the movies, to look at a face and not assign it some category in the scale of absolute beauty, and the scale was one she absorbed in full from the silver screen. There at last were the darkened woods, the lonely roads, the river banks, the gentle knowing eyes. There the flawed became whole, the blind sighted, and the lame and halt threw away their crutches. There death was dead, and people made every gesture in a cloud of music. There the black-and-white images came together, making a magnificent whole—all projected through the ray of light from above and behind.

It was really a simple pleasure, but she learned all there was to love and all there was to hate.

"The onliest time I be happy seem like was when I was in the picture show. Every time I got, I went. I'd go early, before the show started. They'd cut off the lights, and everything be black. Then the screen would light up, and I'd move right on in them pictures. White men taking such good care of they women, and they all dressed up in big clean houses with the bathtubs right in the same room with the toilet. Them pictures gave me a lot of pleasure, but it

*made coming home hard, and looking at Cholly hard. I don't know. I
'member one time I went to see Clark Gable and Jean Harlow. I fixed my hair
up like I'd seen hers on a magazine. A part on the side, with one little curl on
my forehead. It looked just like her. Well, almost just like. Anyway, I sat in
that show with my hair done up that way and had a good time. I thought I'd
see it through to the end again, and I got up to get me some candy. I was
sitting back in my seat, and I taken a big bite of that candy, and it pulled a
tooth right out of my mouth. I could of cried. I had good teeth, not a rotten
one in my head. I don't believe I ever did get over that. There I was, five
months pregnant, trying to look like Jean Harlow, and a front tooth gone.
Everything went then. Look like I just didn't care no more after that. I let my
hair go back, plaited it up, and settled down to just being ugly. I still went to
the pictures, though, but the meanness got worse. I wanted my tooth back.
Cholly poked fun at me, and we started fighting again. I tried to kill him. He
didn't hit me too hard, 'cause I were pregnant I guess, but the fights, once they
got started up again, kept up. He begin to make me madder than anything I
knowed, and I couldn't keep my hands off him. Well, I had that baby—a
boy—and after that got pregnant again with another one. But it weren't like
I thought it was gone be. I loved them and all, I guess, but maybe it was
having no money, or maybe it was Cholly, but they sure worried the life out of
me. Sometimes I'd catch myself hollering at them and beating them, and I'd
feel sorry for them, but I couldn't seem to stop. When I had the second one, a
girl, I 'member I said I'd love it no matter what it looked like. She looked like
a black ball of hair. I don't recollect trying to get pregnant that first time. But
that second time, I actually tried to get pregnant. Maybe 'cause I'd had one
already and wasn't scairt to do it. Anyway, I felt good, and wasn't thinking
on the carrying, just the baby itself. I used to talk to it whilst it be still in the
womb. Like good friends we was. You know. I be hanging wash and I
knowed lifting weren't good for it. I'd say to it holt on now I gone hang up
these few rags, don't get froggy; it be over soon. It wouldn't leap or nothing. Or
I be mixing something in a bowl for the other chile and I'd talk to it then too.
You know, just friendly talk. On up til the end I felted good about that baby.
I went to the hospital when my time come. So I could be easeful. I didn't want*

to have it at home like I done with the boy. They put me in a big room with a whole mess of women. The pains was coming, but not too bad. A little old doctor come to examine me. He had all sorts of stuff. He gloved his hand and put some kind of jelly on it and rammed it up between my legs. When he left off, some more doctors come. One old one and some young ones. The old one was learning the young ones about babies. Showing them how to do. When he got to me he said now these here women you don't have any trouble with. They deliver right away and with no pain. Just like horses. The young ones smiled a little. They looked at my stomach and between my legs. They never said nothing to me. Only one looked at me. Looked at my face, I mean. I looked right back at him. He dropped his eyes and turned red. He knowed, I reckon, that maybe I weren't no horse foaling. But them others. They didn't know. They went on. I seed them talking to them white women: 'How you feel? Gonna have twins?' Just shucking them, of course, but nice talk. Nice friendly talk. I got edgy, and when them pains got harder, I was glad. Glad to have something else to think about. I moaned something awful. The pains wasn't as bad as I let on, but I had to let them people know having a baby was more than a bowel movement. I hurt just like them white women. Just 'cause I wasn't hooping and hollering before didn't mean I wasn't feeling pain. What'd they think? That just 'cause I knowed how to have a baby with no fuss that my behind wasn't pulling and aching like theirs? Besides, that doctor don't know what he talking about. He must never seed no mare foal. Who say they don't have no pain? Just 'cause she don't cry? 'Cause she can't say it, they think it ain't there? If they looks in her eyes and see them eyeballs lolling back, see the sorrowful look, they'd know. Anyways, the baby come. Big old healthy thing. She looked different from what I thought. Reckon I talked to it so much before I conjured up a mind's eye view of it. So when I seed it, it was like looking at a picture of your mama when she was a girl. You knows who she is, but she don't look the same. They give her to me for a nursing, and she liked to pull my nipple off right away. She caught on fast. Not like Sammy, he was the hardest child to feed. But Pecola look like she knowed right off what to do. A right smart baby she was. I used to like to watch her. You know they makes them greedy sounds. Eyes all soft and wet. A cross between a puppy and

*a dying man. But I knowed she was ugly. Head full of pretty hair, but Lord
she was ugly."*

When Sammy and Pecola were still young Pauline had to go back
to work. She was older now, with no time for dreams and movies. It
was time to put all of the pieces together, make coherence where before there had been none. The children gave her this need; she herself
was no longer a child. So she became, and her process of becoming was
like most of ours: she developed a hatred for things that mystified or
obstructed her; acquired virtues that were easy to maintain; assigned
herself a role in the scheme of things; and harked back to simpler
times for gratification.

She took on the full responsibility and recognition of breadwinner
and returned to church. First, however, she moved out of the two
rooms into a spacious first floor of a building that had been built as a
store. She came into her own with the women who had despised her,
by being more moral than they; she avenged herself on Cholly by forcing him to indulge in the weaknesses she despised. She joined a church
where shouting was frowned upon, served on Stewardess Board No. 3,
and became a member of Ladies Circle No. 1. At prayer meeting she
moaned and sighed over Cholly's ways, and hoped God would help her
keep the children from the sins of the father. She stopped saying
"chil'ren" and said "childring" instead. She let another tooth fall, and
was outraged by painted ladies who thought only of clothes and men.
Holding Cholly as a model of sin and failure, she bore him like a
crown of thorns, and her children like a cross.

It was her good fortune to find a permanent job in the home of a
well-to-do family whose members were affectionate, appreciative, and
generous. She looked at their houses, smelled their linen, touched their
silk draperies, and loved all of it. The child's pink nightie, the stacks of
white pillow slips edged with embroidery, the sheets with top hems
picked out with blue cornflowers. She became what is known as an
ideal servant, for such a role filled practically all of her needs. When

she bathed the little Fisher girl, it was in a porcelain tub with silvery taps running infinite quantities of hot, clear water. She dried her in fluffy white towels and put her in cuddly night clothes. Then she brushed the yellow hair, enjoying the roll and slip of it between her fingers. No zinc tub, no buckets of stove-heated water, no flaky, stiff, grayish towels washed in a kitchen sink, dried in a dusty backyard, no tangled black puffs of rough wool to comb. Soon she stopped trying to keep her own house. The things she could afford to buy did not last, had no beauty or style, and were absorbed by the dingy storefront. More and more she neglected her house, her children, her man—they were like the afterthoughts one has just before sleep, the early-morning and late-evening edges of her day, the dark edges that made the daily life with the Fishers lighter, more delicate, more lovely. Here she could arrange things, clean things, line things up in neat rows. Here her foot flopped around on deep pile carpets, and there was no uneven sound. Here she found beauty, order, cleanliness, and praise. Mr. Fisher said, "I would rather sell her blueberry cobblers than real estate." She reigned over cupboards stacked high with food that would not be eaten for weeks, even months; she was queen of canned vegetables bought by the case, special fondants and ribbon candy curled up in tiny silver dishes. The creditors and service people who humiliated her when she went to them on her own behalf respected her, were even intimidated by her, when she spoke for the Fishers. She refused beef slightly dark or with edges not properly trimmed. The slightly reeking fish that she accepted for her own family she would all but throw in the fish man's face if he sent it to the Fisher house. Power, praise, and luxury were hers in this household. They even gave her what she had never had—a nickname—Polly. It was her pleasure to stand in her kitchen at the end of a day and survey her handiwork. Knowing there were soap bars by the dozen, bacon by the rasher, and reveling in her shiny pots and pans and polished floors. Hearing, "We'll never let her go. We could never find anybody like Polly. She will *not* leave the kitchen until everything is in order. Really, she is the ideal servant."

Pauline kept this order, this beauty, for herself, a private world, and never introduced it into her storefront, or to her children. Them she bent toward respectability, and in so doing taught them fear: fear of being clumsy, fear of being like their father, fear of not being loved by God, fear of madness like Cholly's mother's. Into her son she beat a loud desire to run away, and into her daughter she beat a fear of grow-ing up, fear of other people, fear of life.

All the meaningfulness of her life was in her work. For her virtues were intact. She was an active church woman, did not drink, smoke, or carouse, defended herself mightily against Cholly, rose above him in every way, and felt she was fulfilling a mother's role conscientiously when she pointed out their father's faults to keep them from having them, or punished them when they showed any slovenliness, no matter how slight, when she worked twelve to sixteen hours a day to support them. And the world itself agreed with her.

It was only sometimes, sometimes, and then rarely, that she thought about the old days, or what her life had turned to. They were musings, idle thoughts, full sometimes of the old dreaminess, but not the kind of thing she cared to dwell on.

"I started to leave him once, but something came up. Once, after he tried to set the house on fire, I was all set in my mind to go. I can't even 'member now what held me. He sure ain't give me much of a life. But it wasn't all bad. Sometimes things wasn't all bad. He used to come easing into bed sometimes, not too drunk. I make out like I'm asleep, 'cause it's late, and he taken three dollars out of my pocketbook that morning or something. I hear him breathing, but I don't look around. I can see in my mind's eye his black arms thrown back behind his head, the muscles like great big peach stones sanded down, with veins running like little swollen rivers down his arms. Without touching him I be feeling those ridges on the tips of my fingers. I sees the palms of his hands calloused to granite, and the long fingers curled up and still. I think about the thick, knotty hair on his chest, and the two big swells his breast muscles make. I want to rub my face hard in his chest and feel the hair

cut my skin. I know just where the hair growth slacks out—just above his navel—and how it picks up again and spreads out. Maybe he'll shift a little, and his leg will touch me, or I feel his flank just graze my behind. I don't move even yet. Then he lift his head, turn over, and put his hand on my waist. If I don't move, he'll move his hand over to pull and knead my stomach. Soft and slow-like. I still don't move, because I don't want him to stop. I want to pretend sleep and have him keep on rubbing my stomach. Then he will lean his head down and bite my tit. Then I don't want him to rub my stomach anymore. I want him to put his hand between my legs. I pretend to wake up, and turn to him, but not opening my legs. I want him to open them for me. He does, and I be soft and wet where his fingers are strong and hard. I be softer than I ever been before. All my strength in his hand. My brain curls up like wilted leaves. A funny, empty feeling is in my hands. I want to grab holt of something, so I hold his head. His mouth is under my chin. Then I don't want his hand between my legs no more, because I think I am softening away. I stretch my legs open, and he is on top of me. Too heavy to hold, and too light not to. He puts his thing in me. In me. In me. I wrap my feet around his back so he can't get away. His face is next to mine. The bed springs sounds like them crickets used to back home. He puts his fingers in mine, and we stretches our arms outwise like Jesus on the cross. I hold on tight. My fingers and my feet hold on tight, because everything else is going, going. I know he wants me to come first. But I can't. Not until he does. Not until I feel him loving me. Just me. Sinking into me. Not until I know that my flesh is all that be on his mind. That he couldn't stop if he had to. That he would die rather than take his thing out of me. Of me. Not until he has let go of all he has, and give it to me. To me. To me. When he does, I feel a power. I be strong, I be pretty, I be young. And then I wait. He shivers and tosses his head. Now I be strong enough, pretty enough, and young enough to let him make me come. I take my fingers out of his and put my hands on his behind. My legs drop back onto the bed. I don't make no noise, because the chil'ren might hear. I begin to feel those little bits of color floating up into me—deep in me. That streak of green from the june-bug light, the purple from the berries trickling along my thighs, Mama's lemonade yellow runs sweet in me. Then I feel like I'm laughing *between my legs, and the laughing gets all mixed up with the colors, and I'm afraid I'll come, and afraid I won't. But I know I will. And I do. And it be rainbow all inside. And it lasts and lasts and lasts. I want to thank him, but don't know how, so I pat him like you do a baby. He asks me if I'm all right. I say yes. He gets off me and lies down to sleep. I want to say something, but I don't. I don't want to take my mind offen the rainbow. I should get up and go to the toilet, but I don't. Besides, Cholly is asleep with his leg throwed over me. I can't move and don't want to.*

"But it ain't like that anymore. Most times he's thrashing away inside me before I'm woke, and through when I am. The rest of the time I can't even be next to his stinking drunk self. But I don't care 'bout it no more. My Maker will take care of me. I know He will. I know He will. Besides, it don't make no difference about this old earth. There is sure to be a glory. Only thing I miss sometimes is that rainbow. But like I say, I don't recollect it much anymore."

SEEFATHERHEISBIGANDSTRONGFATHERWILLYOUPLAY WITHJANEFATHERISSMILINGSMILEFATHERSMILESMILE

When Cholly was four days old, his mother wrapped him in two blankets and one newspaper and placed him on a junk heap by the railroad. His Great Aunt Jimmy, who had seen her niece carrying a bundle out of the back door, rescued him. She beat his mother with a razor strap and wouldn't let her near the baby after that. Aunt Jimmy raised Cholly herself, but took delight sometimes in telling him of how she had saved him. He gathered from her that his mother wasn't right in the head. But he never had a chance to find out, because she ran away shortly after the razor strap, and no one had heard of her since.

Cholly was grateful for having been saved. Except sometimes. Sometimes when he watched Aunt Jimmy eating collards with her fingers, sucking her four gold teeth, or smelled her when she wore the asafetida bag around her neck, or when she made him sleep with her for warmth in winter and he could see her old, wrinkled breasts sagging in her nightgown—then he wondered whether it would have been just as well to have died there. Down in the rim of a tire under a soft black Georgia sky.

He had four years of school before he got courage enough to ask his aunt who and where his father was.

"That Fuller boy, I believe it was," his aunt said. "He was hanging around then, but he taken off pretty quick before you was born. I think he gone to Macon. Him or his brother. Maybe both. I hear old man Fuller say something bout it once."

"What name he have?" asked Cholly.

"Fuller, Foolish."

"I mean what his given name?"

"Oh." She closed her eyes to think, and sighed. "Can't recollect nothing no more. Sam, was it? Yeh. Samuel. No. No, it wasn't. It was Samson. Samson Fuller."

"How come you all didn't name me Samson?" Cholly's voice was low.

"What for? He wasn't nowhere around when you was born. Your mama didn't name you nothing. The nine days wasn't up before she throwed you on the junk heap. When I got you I named you myself on the ninth day. You named after my dead brother. Charles Breedlove. A good man. Ain't no Samson never come to no good end."

Cholly didn't ask anything else.

Two years later he quit school to take a job at Tyson's Feed and Grain Store. He swept up, ran errands, weighed bags, and lifted them onto the drays. Sometimes they let him ride with the drayman. A nice old man called Blue Jack. Blue used to tell him old-timey stories about how it was when the Emancipation Proclamation came. How the black people hollered, cried, and sang. And ghost stories about how a white man cut off his wife's head and buried her in the swamp, and the headless body came out at night and went stumbling around the yard, knocking over stuff because it couldn't see, and crying all the time for a comb. They talked about the women Blue had had, and the fights he'd been in when he was younger, about how he talked his way out of getting lynched once, and how others hadn't.

Cholly loved Blue. Long after he was a man, he remembered the good times they had had. How on a July 4 at a church picnic a family was about to break open a watermelon. Several children were standing around watching. Blue was hovering about on the periphery of the circle—a faint smile of anticipation softening his face. The father of the family lifted the melon high over his head—his big arms looked taller than the trees to Cholly, and the melon blotted out the sun. Tall, head forward, eyes fastened on a rock, his arms higher than the pines, his hands holding a melon bigger than the sun, he paused an instant to get his bearing and secure his aim. Watching the figure etched against the bright blue sky, Cholly felt goose pimples popping along his arms and neck. He wondered if God looked like that. No. God was a nice old white man, with long white hair, flowing white beard, and little blue eyes that looked sad when people died and mean when they were bad It must be the devil who looks like that—holding the world in his hands, ready to dash it to the ground and spill the red guts so niggers could eat the sweet, warm insides. If the devil did look like that, Cholly preferred him. He never felt anything thinking about God, but just the idea of the devil excited him. And now the strong, black devil was blotting out the sun and getting ready to split open the world.

Far away somebody was playing a mouth organ; the music slithered over the cane fields and into the pine grove; it spiraled around the tree trunks and mixed itself with the pine scent, so Cholly couldn't tell the difference between the sound and the odor that hung about the heads of the people.

The man swung the melon down to the edge of a rock. A soft cry of disappointment accompanied the sound of smashed rind. The break was a bad one. The melon was jagged, and hunks of rind and red meat scattered on the grass.

Blue jumped. "Aw—awww," he moaned, "dere go da heart." His voice was both sad and pleased. Everybody looked to see the big red chunk from the very center of the melon, free of rind and sparse of seed which had rolled a little distance from Blue's feet. He stooped to pick it up. Blood red, its planes dull and blunted with sweetness, its edges rigid with juice. Too obvious, almost obscene, in the joy it promised.

"Go 'head, Blue," the father laughed. "You can have it."

Blue smiled and walked away. Little children scrambled for the pieces on the ground. Women picked out the seeds for the smallest ones and broke off little bits of the meat for themselves. Blue's eye caught Cholly's. He motioned to him. "Come on, boy. Les' you and me eat the heart."

Together the old man and the boy sat on the grass and shared the heart of the watermelon. The nasty-sweet guts of the earth.

It was in the spring, a very chilly spring, that Aunt Jimmy died of peach cobbler. She went to a camp meeting that took place after a rainstorm, and the damp wood of the benches was bad for her. For four or five days afterward, she felt poorly. Friends came to see about her. Some made camomile tea; others rubbed her with liniment. Miss Alice, her closest friend, read the Bible to her. Still she was declining. Advice was prolific, if contradictory.

"Don't eat no whites of eggs."

"Drink new milk."

"Chew on this root."

Aunt Jimmy ignored all but Miss Alice's Bible reading. She nodded in drowsy appreciation as the words from First Corinthians droned over her. Sweet amens fell from her lips as she was chastised for all her sins. But her body would not respond.

Finally it was decided to fetch M'Dear. M'Dear was a quiet woman who lived in a shack near the woods. She was a competent midwife and decisive diagnostician. Few could remember when M'Dear was not around. In any illness that could not be handled by ordinary means— known cures, intuition, or endurance—the word was always, "Fetch M'Dear."

When she arrived at Aunt Jimmy's house, Cholly was amazed at the sight of her. He had always pictured her as shriveled and hunched over, for he knew she was very, very old. But M'Dear loomed taller than the preacher who accompanied her. She must have been over six feet tall. Four big white knots of hair gave power and authority to her soft black face. Standing straight as a poker, she seemed to need her hickory stick not for support but for communication. She tapped it lightly on the floor as she looked down at Aunt Jimmy's wrinkled face. She stroked the knob with the thumb of her right hand while she ran her left one over Aunt Jimmy's body. The backs of her long fingers she placed on the patient's cheek, then placed her palm on the forehead. She ran her fingers through the sick woman's hair, lightly scratching the scalp, and then looking at what the fingernails revealed. She lifted

Aunt Jimmy's hand and looked closely at it—fingernails, back skin, the flesh of the palm she pressed with three fingertips. Later she put her ear on Aunt Jimmy's chest and stomach to listen. At M'Dear's request, the women pulled the slop jar from under the bed to show the stools. M'Dear tapped her stick while looking at them.

"Bury the slop jar and everything in it," she said to the women. To Aunt Jimmy she said, "You done caught cold in your womb. Drink pot liquor and nothing else."

"Will it pass?" asked Aunt Jimmy. "Is I'm gone be all right?"

"I reckon."

M'Dear turned and left the room. The preacher put her in his buggy to take her home.

That evening the women brought bowls of pot liquor from black-eyed peas, from mustards, from cabbage, from kale, from collards, from turnips, from beets, from green beans. Even the juice from a boiling hog jowl.

Two evenings later Aunt Jimmy had gained much strength. When Miss Alice and Mrs. Gaines stopped in to check on her, they remarked on her improvement. The three women sat talking about various miseries they had had, their cure or abatement, what had helped. Over and over again they returned to Aunt Jimmy's condition. Repeating its cause, what could have been done to prevent the misery from taking hold, and M'Dear's infallibility. Their voices blended into a threnody of nostalgia about pain. Rising and falling, complex in harmony, uncertain in pitch, but constant in the recitative of pain. They hugged the memories of illnesses to their bosoms. They licked their lips and clucked their tongues in fond remembrance of pains they had endured—childbirth, rheumatism, croup, sprains, backaches, piles. All of the bruises they had collected from moving about the earth—harvesting, cleaning, hoisting, pitching, stooping, kneeling, picking—always with young ones underfoot.

But they had been young once. The odor of their armpits and haunches had mingled into a lovely musk; their eyes had been furtive,

their lips relaxed, and the delicate turn of their heads on those slim
black necks had been like nothing other than a doe's. Their laughter
had been more touch than sound.

Then they had grown. Edging into life from the back door. Becoming. Everybody in the world was in a position to give them orders.
White women said, "Do this." White children said, "Give me that."
White men said, "Come here." Black men said, "Lay down." The only
people they need not take orders from were black children and each
other. But they took all of that and re-created it in their own image.
They ran the houses of white people, and knew it. When white men
beat their men, they cleaned up the blood and went home to receive
abuse from the victim. They beat their children with one hand and
stole for them with the other. The hands that felled trees also cut um-
bilical cords; the hands that wrung the necks of chickens and butch-
ered hogs also nudged African violets into bloom; the arms that loaded
sheaves, bales, and sacks rocked babies into sleep. They patted biscuits
into flaky ovals of innocence—and shrouded the dead. They plowed all
day and came home to nestle like plums under the limbs of their men.
The legs that straddled a mule's back were the same ones that straddled their men's hips. And the difference was all the difference there
was.

Then they were old. Their bodies honed, their odor sour. Squatting
in a cane field, stooping in a cotton field, kneeling by a river bank, they
had carried a world on their heads. They had given over the lives of
their own children and tendered their grandchildren. With relief they
wrapped their heads in rags, and their breasts in flannel; eased their
feet into felt. They were through with lust and lactation, beyond tears
and terror. They alone could walk the roads of Mississippi, the lanes of
Georgia, the fields of Alabama unmolested. They were old enough to
be irritable when and where they chose, tired enough to look forward
to death, disinterested enough to accept the idea of pain while ignoring
the presence of pain. They were, in fact and at last, free. And the lives

of these old black women were synthesized in their eyes—a purée of tragedy and humor, wickedness and serenity, truth and fantasy.

They chattered far into the night. Cholly listened and grew sleepy. The lullaby of grief enveloped him, rocked him, and at last numbed him. In his sleep the foul odor of an old woman's stools turned into the healthy smell of horse shit, and the voices of the three women were muted into the pleasant notes of a mouth organ. He was aware, in his sleep, of being curled up in a chair, his hands tucked between his thighs. In a dream his penis changed into a long hickory stick, and the hands caressing it were the hands of M'Dear.

On a wet Saturday night, before Aunt Jimmy felt strong enough to get out of the bed, Essie Foster brought her a peach cobbler. The old lady ate a piece, and the next morning when Cholly went to empty the slop jar, she was dead. Her mouth was a slackened O, and her hands, those long fingers with a man's hard nails, having done their laying by, could now be dainty on the sheet. One open eye looked at him as if to say, "Mind how you take holt of that jar, boy." Cholly stared back, unable to move, until a fly settled at the corner of her mouth. He fanned it away angrily, looked back at the eye, and did its bidding.

Aunt Jimmy's funeral was the first Cholly had ever attended. As a member of the family, one of the bereaved, he was the object of a great deal of attention. The ladies had cleaned the house, aired everything out, notified everybody, and stitched together what looked like a white wedding dress for Aunt Jimmy, a maiden lady, to wear when she met Jesus. They even produced a dark suit, white shirt, and tie for Cholly. The husband of one of them cut his hair. He was enclosed in fastidious tenderness. Nobody talked to him; that is, they treated him like the child he was, never engaging him in serious conversation; but they anticipated wishes he never had: meals appeared, hot water for the wooden tub, clothes laid out. At the wake he was allowed to fall asleep, and arms carried him to bed. Only on the third day after the death—the day of the funeral—did he have to share the spotlight. Aunt Jimmy's people came from nearby towns and farms. Her brother

O. V., his children and wife, and lots of cousins. But Cholly was still the major figure, because he was "Jimmy's boy, the last thing she loved," and "the one who found her." The solicitude of the women, the head pats of the men, pleased Cholly, and the creamy conversations fascinated him.

"What'd she die from?"

"Essie's pie."

"Don't say?"

"Uh-huh. She was doing fine, I saw her the very day before. Said she wanted me to bring her some black thread to patch some things for the boy. I should of known just from her wanting black thread that was a sign."

"Sure was."

"Just like Emma. 'Member? She kept asking for thread. Dropped dead that very evening."

"Yeah. Well, she was determined to have it. Kept on reminding me. I told her I had some to home, but naw, she wanted it new. So I sent Li'l June to get some that very morning when she was laying dead. I was just fixing to bring it over, 'long with a piece of sweet bread. You know how she craved my sweet bread."

"Sure did. Always bragged on it. She was a good friend to you."

"I believe it. Well, I had no more got my clothes on when Sally bust in the door hollering about how Cholly here had been over to Miss Alice saying she was dead. You could have knocked me over, I tell you."

"Guess Essie feels mighty bad."

"Oh, Lord, yes. But I told her the Lord giveth and the Lord taketh away. Wasn't her fault none. She makes good peach pies. But she bound to believe it was the pie did it, and I 'spect she right."

"Well, she shouldn't worry herself none 'bout that. She was just doing what we all would of done."

"Yeah. 'Cause I was sure wrapping up that sweet bread, and that could of done it too."

"I doubts that. Sweet bread is pure. But a pie is the worse thing to give anybody ailing. I'm surprised Jimmy didn't know better."

"If she did, she wouldn't let on. She would have tried to please. You know how she was. So good."

"I'll say. Did she leave anything?"

"Not even a pocket handkerchief. The house belongs to some white folks in Clarksville."

"Oh, yeah? I thought she owned it."

"May have at one time. But not no more. I hear the insurance folks been down talking to her brother."

"How much do it come to?"

"Eighty-five dollars, I hear."

"That all?"

"Can she get in the ground on that?"

"Don't see how. When my daddy died last year this April it costed one hundred and fifty dollars. 'Course, we had to have everything just so. Now Jimmy's people may all have to chip in. That undertaker that lays out black folks ain't none too cheap."

"Seems a shame. She been paying on that insurance all her life."

"Don't I know?"

"Well, what about the boy? What he gone do?"

"Well, caint nobody find that mama, so Jimmy's brother gone take him back to his place. They say he got a nice place. Inside toilet and everything."

"That's nice. He seems like a good Christian man. And the boy need a man's hand."

"What time's the funeral?"

"Two clock. She ought to be in the ground by four."

"Where's the banquet? I heard Essie wanted it at her house."

"Naw, it's at Jimmy's. Her brother wanted it so."

"Well, it will be a big one. Everybody liked old Jimmy. Sure will miss her in the pew."

The funeral banquet was a peal of joy after the thunderous beauty of the funeral. It was like a street tragedy with spontaneity tucked softly into the corners of a highly formal structure. The deceased was the tragic hero, the survivors the innocent victims; there was the omnipresence of the deity, strophe and antistrophe of the chorus of mourners led by the preacher. There was grief over the waste of life, the stunned wonder at the ways of God, and the restoration of order in nature at the graveyard.

Thus the banquet was the exultation, the harmony, the acceptance of physical frailty, joy in the termination of misery. Laughter, relief, a steep hunger for food.

Cholly had not yet fully realized his aunt was dead. Everything was so interesting. Even at the graveyard he felt nothing but curiosity, and when his turn had come to view the body at the church, he had put his hand out to touch the corpse to see if it were really ice cold like everybody said. But he drew his hand back quickly. Aunt Jimmy looked so private, and it seemed wrong somehow to disturb that privacy. He had trudged back to his pew dry-eyed amid tearful shrieks and shouts of others, wondering if he should try to cry.

Back in his house, he was free to join in the gaiety and enjoy what he really felt—a kind of carnival spirit. He ate greedily and felt good enough to try to get to know his cousins. There was some question, according to the adults, as to whether they were his real cousins or not, since Jimmy's brother O. V. was only a half-brother, and Cholly's mother had been the daughter of Jimmy's sister, but that sister was from the second marriage of Jimmy's father, and O. V. was from the first marriage.

One of these cousins interested Cholly in particular. He was about fifteen or sixteen years old. Cholly went outside and found the boy standing with some others near the tub where Aunt Jimmy used to boil her clothes.

He ventured a tentative "Hey." They responded with another. The fifteen-year-old named Jake offered Cholly a rolled-up cigarette. Cholly took it, but when he held the cigarette at arm's length and stuck the tip of it into the match flame, instead of putting it in his mouth and drawing on it, they laughed at him. Shamefaced, he threw the cigarette down. He felt it important to do something to reinstate himself with Jake. So when he asked Cholly if he knew any girls, Cholly said, "Sure."

All the girls Cholly knew were at the banquet, and he pointed to a cluster of them standing, hanging, draping on the back porch. Darlene too. Cholly hoped Jake wouldn't pick her.

"Let's get some and walk around," said Jake.

The two boys sauntered over to the porch. Cholly didn't know how to begin. Jake wrapped his legs around the rickety porch rail and just sat there staring off into space as though he had no interest in them at all. He was letting them look him over, and guardedly evaluating them in return.

The girls pretended they didn't see the boys and kept on chattering. Soon their talk got sharp; the gentle teasing they had been engaged in with each other changed to bitchiness, a serious kind of making fun. That was Jake's clue; the girls were reacting to him. They had gotten a whiff of his manhood and were shivering for a place in his attention.

Jake left the porch rail and walked right up to a girl named Suky, the one who had been most bitter in her making fun.

"Want to show me 'round?" He didn't even smile.

Cholly held his breath, waiting for Suky to shut Jake up. She was good at that, and well known for her sharp tongue. To his enormous surprise, she readily agreed, and even lowered her lashes. Taking courage, Cholly turned to Darlene and said, "Come on 'long. We just going down to the gully." He waited for her to screw up her face and say no, or what for, or some such thing. His feelings about her were mostly fear—fear that she would not like him, and fear that she would.

His second fear materialized. She smiled and jumped down the three leaning steps to join him. Her eyes were full of compassion, and Cholly remembered that he was the bereaved.

"If you want to," she said, "but not too far. Mama said we got to leave early, and its getting dark."

The four of them moved away. Some of the other boys had come to the porch and were about to begin that partly hostile, partly indifferent, partly desperate mating dance. Suky, Jake, Darlene, and Cholly walked through several backyards until they came to an open field. They ran across it and came to a dry riverbed lined with green. The object of the walk was a wild vineyard where the muscadine grew. Too new, too tight to have much sugar, they were eaten anyway. None of them wanted—not then—the grape's easy relinquishing of all its dark juice. The restraint, the holding off, the promise of sweetness that had yet to unfold, excited them more than full ripeness would have done. At last their teeth were on edge, and the boys diverted themselves by pelting the girls with the grapes. Their slim black boy wrists made G clefs in the air as they executed the tosses. The chase took Cholly and Darlene away from the lip of the gully, and when they paused for breath, Jake and Suky were nowhere in sight. Darlene's white cotton dress was stained with juice. Her big blue hair bow had come undone, and the sundown breeze was picking it up and fluttering it about her head. They were out of breath and sank down in the green-and-purple grass on the edge of the pine woods.

Cholly lay on his back panting. His mouth full of the taste of muscadine, listening to the pine needles rustling loudly in their anticipation of rain. The smell of promised rain, pine, and muscadine made him giddy. The sun had gone and pulled away its shreds of light. Turning his head to see where the moon was, Cholly caught sight of Darlene in moonlight behind him. She was huddled into a D—arms encircling drawn-up knees, on which she rested her head. Cholly could see her bloomers and the muscles of her young thighs.

"We bed' get on back," he said.

"Yeah." She stretched her legs flat on the ground and began to retie her hair ribbon. "Mama gone whup me."

"Naw she ain't."

"Uh-huh. She told me she would if I get dirty."

"You ain't dirty."

"I am too. Looka that." She dropped her hands from the ribbon and smoothed out a place on her dress where the grape stains were heaviest.

Cholly felt sorry for her; it was just as much his fault. Suddenly he realized that Aunt Jimmy was dead, for he missed the fear of being whipped. There was nobody to do it except Uncle O. V., and he was the bereaved too.

"Let me," he said. He rose to his knees facing her and tried to tie her ribbon. Darlene put her hands under his open shirt and rubbed the damp tight skin. When he looked at her in surprise, she stopped and laughed. He smiled and continued knotting the bow. She put her hands back under his shirt.

"Hold still," he said. "How I gone get this?"

She tickled his ribs with her fingertips. He giggled and grabbed his rib cage. They were on top of each other in a moment. She corkscrewing her hands into his clothes. He returning the play, digging into the neck of her dress, and then under her dress. When he got his hand in her bloomers, she suddenly stopped laughing and looked serious. Cholly, frightened, was about to take his hand away, but she held his wrist so he couldn't move it. He examined her then with his fingers, and she kissed his face and mouth. Cholly found her muscadine-lipped mouth distracting. Darlene released his head, shifted her body, and pulled down her pants. After some trouble with the buttons, Cholly dropped his pants down to his knees. Their bodies began to make sense to him, and it was not as difficult as he had thought it would be. She moaned a little, but the excitement collecting inside him made him close his eyes and regard her moans as no more than pine sighs over his head. Just as he felt an explosion threaten, Darlene froze and cried out. He thought he had hurt her, but when he looked at her face, she was staring wildly at something over his shoulder. He jerked around.

There stood two white men. One with a spirit lamp, the other with a flashlight. There was no mistake about their being white; he could smell it. Cholly jumped, trying to kneel, stand, and get his pants up all in one motion. The men had long guns.

"Hee hee hee heeeee." The snicker was a long asthmatic cough.

The other raced the flashlight all over Cholly and Darlene.

"Get on wid it, nigger," said the flashlight one.

"Sir?" said Cholly, trying to find a buttonhole.

"I said, get on wid it. An' make it good, nigger, make it good."

There was no place for Cholly's eyes to go. They slid about furtively searching for shelter, while his body remained paralyzed. The flashlight man lifted his gun down from his shoulder, and Cholly heard the clop of metal. He dropped back to his knees. Darlene had her head averted, her eyes staring out of the lamplight into the surrounding darkness and looking almost unconcerned, as though they had no part in the drama taking place around them. With a violence born of total helplessness, he pulled her dress up, lowered his trousers and underwear.

"Hee hee hee hee heeeeee."

Darlene put her hands over her face as Cholly began to simulate what had gone on before. He could do no more than make-believe. The flashlight made a moon on his behind.

"Hee hee hee hee heeee."

"Come on, coon. Faster. You ain't doing nothing for her."

"Hee hee hee hee heeee."

Cholly, moving faster, looked at Darlene. He hated her. He almost wished he could do it—hard, long, and painfully, he hated her so much. The flashlight wormed its way into his guts and turned the sweet taste of muscadine into rotten fetid bile. He stared at Darlene's hands covering her face in the moon and lamplight. They looked like baby claws.

"Hee hee hee hee heee."

Some dogs howled. "Thas them. Thas them. I know thas Old Honey."

"Yep," said the spirit lamp.

"Come on." The flashlight turned away, and one of them whistled to Honey.

"Wait," said the spirit lamp, "the coon ain't comed yet."

"Well, he have to come on his own time. Good luck, coon baby."

They crushed the pine needles underfoot. Cholly could hear them whistling for a long time, and then the dogs' answer no longer a howl, but warm excited yelps of recognition.

Cholly raised himself and in silence buttoned his trousers. Darlene did not move. Cholly wanted to strangle her, but instead he touched her leg with his foot. "We got to get, girl. Come on!"

She reached for her underwear with her eyes closed, and could not find them. The two of them patted about in the moonlight for the panties. When she found them, she put them on with the movements of an old woman. They walked away from the pine woods toward the road. He in front, she plopping along behind. It started to rain. "That's good," Cholly thought. "It will explain away our clothes."

When they got back to the house, some ten or twelve guests were still there. Jake was gone, Suky too. Some people had gone back for more helpings of food—potato pie, ribs. All were engrossed in early-night reminiscences about dreams, figures, premonitions. Their stuffed comfort was narcotic and had produced recollections and fabrications of hallucinations.

Cholly and Darlene's entrance produced only a mild stir.

"Ya'll soaked, ain't you?"

Darlene's mother was only vaguely fussy. She had eaten and drunk too much. Her shoes were under her chair, and the side snaps of her dress were opened. "Girl. Come on in here. Thought I told you . . ."

Some of the guests thought they would wait for the rain to slacken. Others, who had come in wagons, thought they'd best leave now. Cholly went into the little storeroom which had been made into a bedroom for him. Three infants were sleeping on his cot. He took off his rain- and pine-soaked clothes and put on his coveralls. He didn't know where to go. Aunt Jimmy's room was out of the question, and Uncle O. V. and his wife would be using it later anyway. He took a quilt from a trunk, spread it on the floor, and lay down. Somebody was brewing coffee, and he had a sharp craving for it, just before falling asleep.

The next day was cleaning-out day, settling accounts, distributing Aunt Jimmy's goods. Mouths were set in downward crescents, eyes veiled, feet tentative.

Cholly floated about aimlessly, doing chores as he was told. All the glamour and warmth the adults had given him on the previous day were replaced by a sharpness that agreed with his mood. He could think only of the flashlight, the muscadines, and Darlene's hands. And when he was not thinking of them, the vacancy in his head was like the space left by a newly pulled tooth still conscious of the rottenness that had once filled it. Afraid of running into Darlene, he would not go far from the house, but neither could he endure the atmosphere of his dead Aunt's house. The picking through her things, the comments on the "condition" of her goods. Sullen, irritable, he cultivated his hatred of Darlene. Never did he once consider directing his hatred toward the hunters. Such an emotion would have destroyed him. They were big, white, armed men. He was small, black, helpless. His subconscious knew what his conscious mind did not guess—that hating them would have consumed him, burned him up like a piece of soft coal, leaving only flakes of ash and a question mark of smoke. He was, in time, to discover that hatred of white men—but not now. Not in impotence but later, when the hatred could find sweet expression. For now, he hated the one who had created the situation, the one who bore witness to his failure, his impotence. The one whom he had not been able to protect, to spare, to cover from the round moon glow of the flashlight. The hee-hee-hee's. He recalled Darlene's dripping hair ribbon, flapping against her face as they walked back in silence in the rain. The loathing that galloped through him made him tremble. There was no one to talk to. Old Blue was too drunk too often these days to make sense. Besides, Cholly doubted if he could reveal his shame to Blue. He would have to lie a little to tell Blue, Blue the woman-killer. It seemed to him that lonely was much better than alone.

The day Cholly's uncle was ready to leave, when everything was packed, when the quarrels about who gets what had seethed down to a sticking gravy on everybody's tongue, Cholly sat on the back porch waiting. It had occurred to him that Darlene might be pregnant. It was a wildly irrational, completely uninformed idea, but the fear it produced was complete enough.

He had to get away. Never mind the fact that he was leaving that very day. A town or two away was not far enough, especially since he did not like or trust his uncle, and Darlene's mother could surely find him, and Uncle O. V. would turn him over to her. Cholly knew it was wrong to run out on a pregnant girl, and recalled, with sympathy, that his father had done just that. Now he understood. He knew then what he must do—find his father. His father would understand. Aunt Jimmy said he had gone to Macon.

With no more thought than a chick leaving its shell, he stepped off the porch. He had gotten a little way when he remembered the treasure; Aunt Jimmy had left something, and he had forgotten all about it. In a stove flue no longer used, she had hidden a little meal bag which she called her treasure. He slipped into the house and found the room empty. Digging into the flue, he encountered webs and soot, and then the soft bag. He sorted the money; fourteen one-dollar bills, two two-dollar bills, and lots of silver change . . . twenty-three dollars in all. Surely that would be enough to get to Macon. What a good, strong-sounding word, *Macon.*

Running away from home for a Georgia black boy was not a great problem. You just sneaked away and started walking. When night came you slept in a barn, if there were no dogs, a cane field, or an empty sawmill. You ate from the ground and bought root beer and licorice in little country stores. There was always an easy tale of woe to tell inquiring black adults, and whites didn't care, unless they were looking for sport.

When he was several days away, he could go to the back door of nice houses and tell the black cook or white mistress that he wanted a job weeding, plowing, picking, cleaning, and that he lived nearby. A week or more there, and he could take off. He lived this way through the turn of summer, and only the following October did he reach a town big enough to have a regular bus station. Dry-mouthed with excitement and apprehension, he went to the colored side of the counter to buy his ticket.

"How much to Macon, sir?"

"Eleven dollars. Five-fifty for children under twelve."

Cholly had twelve dollars and four cents.

"How old you be?"

"Just on twelve, sir, but my mama only give me ten dollars."

"You jest about the biggest twelve I ever seed."

"Please, sir, I got to get to Macon. My mama's sick."

"Thought you said you mama give you ten dollars."

"That's my play mama. My real mama is in Macon, sir."

"I reckon I knows a lying nigger when I sees one, but jest in case you ain't, jest in case one of them mammies is really dyin' and wants to see her little old smoke before she meets her maker, I gone do it."

Cholly heard nothing. The insults were part of the nuisances of life, like lice. He was happier than he had ever remembered being, except that time with Blue and the watermelon. The bus wasn't leaving for four hours, and the minutes of those hours struggled like gnats on fly paper—dying slow, exhausted with the fight to stay alive. Cholly was afraid to stir, even to relieve himself. The bus might leave while he was gone. Finally, rigid with constipation, he boarded the bus to Macon.

He found a window seat in the back all to himself, and all of Georgia slid before his eyes, until the sun shrugged out of sight. Even in the dark, he hungered to see, and only after the fiercest fight to keep his eyes open did he fall asleep. When he awoke it was very well into day, and a fat black lady was nudging him with a biscuit gashed with cold bacon. With the taste of bacon still in his teeth, they sidled into Macon.

At the end of the alley he could see men clustered like grapes. One large whooping voice spiraled over the heads of the bended forms. The kneeling forms, the leaning forms, all intent on one ground spot. As he came closer, he inhaled a rife and stimulating man smell. The men were gathered, just as the man in the pool hall had said, for and about dice and money. Each figure was decorated some way with the slight pieces of green. Some of them had separated their money, folded the bills around their fingers, clenched the fingers into fists, so the neat ends of the money stuck out in a blend of daintiness and violence. Others had stacked their bills, creased them down the middle, and held the wad as though they were about to deal cards. Still others had left their money in loosely crumpled balls. One man had money sticking out from under his cap. Another stroked his bills with a thumb and fore-finger. There was more money in those black hands than Cholly had ever seen before. He shared their excitement, and the dry-mouthed ap-prehension on meeting his father gave way to the saliva flow of excite-ment. He glanced at the faces, looking for the one who might be his father. How would he know him? Would he look like a larger version of himself? At that moment Cholly could not remember what his own self looked like. He only knew he was fourteen years old, black, and al-ready six feet tall. He searched the faces and saw only eyes, pleading eyes, cold eyes, eyes gone flat with malice, others laced with fear—all focused on the movement of a pair of dice that one man was throwing, snatching up, and throwing again. Chanting a kind of litany to which the others responded, rubbing the dice as though they were two hot coals, he whispered to them. Then with a whoop the cubes flew from his hand to a chorus of amazements and disappointments. Then the thrower scooped up money, and someone shouted, "Take it and crawl, you water dog, you, the best I know." There was some laughter, and a noticeable release of tension, during which some men exchanged money.

Cholly tapped an old white-haired man on the back.

"Can you tell me is Samson Fuller 'round here somewhere?"

"Fuller?" The name was familiar to the man's tongue. "I don't know, he here somewhere. They he is. In the brown jacket." The man pointed.

A man in a light-brown jacket stood at the far end of the group. He was gesturing in a quarrelsome, agitated manner with another man. Both of them had folded their faces in anger. Cholly edged around to where they stood, hardly believing he was at the end of his journey. There was his father, a man like any other man, but there indeed were his eyes, his mouth, his whole head. His shoulders lurked beneath that jacket, his voice, his hands—all real. They existed, really existed, some-where. Right here. Cholly had always thought of his father as a giant of a man, so when he was very close it was with a shock that he discov-ered that he was taller than his father. In fact, he was staring at a bald-ing spot on his father's head, which he suddenly wanted to stroke. While thus fascinated by the pitiable clean space hedged around by neglected tufts of wool, the man turned a hard, belligerent face to him.

"What you want, boy?"

"Uh. I mean . . . is you Samson Fuller?"

"Who sent you?"

"Huh?"

"You Melba's boy?"

"No, sir, I'm . . ." Cholly blinked. He could not remember his mother's name. Had he ever known it? What could he say? Whose boy was he? He couldn't say, "I'm your boy." That sounded disrespect-ful.

The man was impatient. "Something wrong with your head? Who told you to come after me?"

"Nobody." Cholly's hands were sweating. The man's eyes frightened him. "I just thought . . . I mean, I was just wandering around, and, uh, my name is Cholly. . . ."

But Fuller had turned back to the game that was about to begin anew. He bent down to toss a bill on the ground, and waited for a throw. When it was gone, he stood up and in a vexed and whiny voice shouted at Cholly, "Tell that bitch she get her money. Now, get the fuck outta my face!"

Cholly was a long time picking his foot up from the ground. He was trying to back up and walk away. Only with extreme effort could he get the first muscle to cooperate. When it did, he walked back up the alley, out of its shade, toward the blazing light of the street. As he emerged into the sun, he felt something in his legs give way. An orange crate with a picture of clasping hands pasted on its side was upended on the sidewalk. Cholly sat down on it. The sunshine dropped like honey on his head. A horse-drawn fruit wagon went by, its driver singing: "Fresh from the vine, sweet as sugar, red as wine."

Noises seemed to increase in volume. The clic-cloc of the women's heels, the laughter of idling men in doorways. There was a streetcar somewhere. Cholly sat. He knew if he was very still he would be all right. But then the trace of pain edged his eyes, and he had to use everything to send it away. If he was very still, he thought, and kept his eyes on one thing, the tears would not come. So he sat in the dripping honey sun, pulling every nerve and muscle into service to stop the fall of water from his eyes. While straining in this way, focusing every erg of energy on his eyes, his bowels suddenly opened up, and before he could realize what he knew, liquid stools were running down his legs. At the mouth of the alley where his father was, on an orange crate in the sun, on a street full of grown men and women, he had soiled himself like a baby.

In panic he wondered should he wait there, not moving until nighttime? No. His father would surely emerge and see him and laugh. Oh, Lord. He would laugh. Everybody would laugh. There was only one thing to do.

Cholly ran down the street, aware only of silence. People's mouths moved, their feet moved, a car jugged by—but with no sound. A door slammed in perfect soundlessness. His own feet made no sound. The air seemed to strangle him, hold him back. He was pushing through a world of invisible pine sap that threatened to smother him. Still he ran, seeing only silent moving things, until he came to the end of buildings, the beginning of open space, and saw the Ocmulgee River winding ahead. He scooted down a gravelly slope to a pier jutting out over the shallow water. Finding the deepest shadow under the pier, he crouched in it, behind one of the posts. He remained knotted there in fetal position, paralyzed, his fists covering his eyes, for a long time. No sound, no sight, only darkness and heat and the press of his knuckles on his eyelids. He even forgot his messed-up trousers.

Evening came. The dark, the warmth, the quiet, enclosed Cholly like the skin and flesh of an elderberry protecting its own seed.

Cholly stirred. The ache in his head was all he felt. Soon, like bright bits of glass, the events of that afternoon cut into him. At first he saw only money in black fingers, then he thought he was sitting on an uncomfortable chair, but when he looked, it turned out to be the head of a man, a head with a bald spot the size of an orange. When finally these bits merged into full memory, Cholly began to smell himself. He stood up and found himself weak, trembling, and dizzy. He leaned for a moment on the pier post, then took off his pants, underwear, socks, and shoes. He rubbed handfuls of dirt on his shoes; then he crawled to the river edge. He had to find the water's beginning with his hands, for he could not see it clearly. Slowly he swirled his clothes in the water and rubbed them until he thought they were clean. Back near his post, he took off his shirt and wrapped it around his waist, then spread his trousers and underwear on the ground. He squatted down and picked at the rotted wood of the pier. Suddenly he thought of his Aunt Jimmy, her asafetida bag, her four gold teeth, and the purple rag she wore around her head. With a longing that almost split him open, he thought of her handing him a bit of smoked hock out of her dish. He remembered just how she held it—clumsy-like, in three fingers, but with so much affection. No words, just picking up a bit of meat and holding it out to him. And then the tears rushed down his cheeks, to make a bouquet under his chin.

Three women are leaning out of two windows. They see the long clean neck of a new young boy and call to him. He goes to where they are. Inside, it is dark and warm. They give him lemonade in a Mason jar. As he drinks, their eyes float up to him through the bottom of the jar, through the slick sweet water. They give him back his manhood, which he takes aimlessly.

The pieces of Cholly's life could become coherent only in the head of a musician. Only those who talk their talk through the gold of curved metal, or in the touch of black-and-white rectangles and taut skins and strings echoing from wooden corridors, could give true form to his life. Only they would know how to connect the heart of a red watermelon to the asafetida bag to the muscadine to the flashlight on his behind to the fists of money to the lemonade in a Mason jar to a man called Blue and come up with what all of that meant in joy, in pain, in anger, in love, and give it its final and pervading ache of freedom. Only a musician would sense, know, without even knowing that he knew, that Cholly was free. Dangerously free. Free to feel whatever he felt—fear, guilt, shame, love, grief, pity. Free to be tender or violent, to whistle or weep. Free to sleep in doorways or between the white sheets of a singing woman. Free to take a job, free to leave it. He could go to jail and not feel imprisoned, for he had already seen the furtiveness in the eyes of his jailer, free to say, "No, suh," and smile, for he had already killed three white men. Free to take a woman's insults, for his body had already conquered hers. Free even to knock her in the head, for he had already cradled that head in his arms. Free to be gentle when she was sick, or mop her floor, for she knew what and

where his maleness was. He was free to drink himself into a silly helplessness, for he had already been a gandy dancer, done thirty days on a
chain gang, and picked a woman's bullet out of the calf of his leg. He
was free to live his fantasies, and free even to die, the how and the
when of which held no interest for him. In those days, Cholly was
truly free. Abandoned in a junk heap by his mother, rejected for a crap
game by his father, there was nothing more to lose. He was alone with
his own perceptions and appetites, and they alone interested him.

It was in this godlike state that he met Pauline Williams. And it
was Pauline, or rather marrying her, that did for him what the flashlight did not do. The constantness, varietylessness, the sheer weight of
sameness drove him to despair and froze his imagination. To be
required to sleep with the same woman forever was a curious and
unnatural idea to him; to be expected to dredge up enthusiasms for old
acts, and routine ploys; he wondered at the arrogance of the female.
When he had met Pauline in Kentucky, she was hanging over a fence
scratching herself with a broken foot. The neatness, the charm, the joy
he awakened in her made him want to nest with her. He had yet to
discover what destroyed that desire. But he did not dwell on it. He
thought rather of whatever had happened to the curiosity he used to
feel. Nothing, nothing, interested him now. Not himself, not other
people. Only in drink was there some break, some floodlight, and
when that closed, there was oblivion.

But the aspect of married life that dumbfounded him and rendered
him totally disfunctional was the appearance of children. Having no
idea of how to raise children, and having never watched any parent
raise himself, he could not even comprehend what such a relationship
should be. Had he been interested in the accumulation of things, he
could have thought of them as his material heirs; had he needed to
prove himself to some nameless "others," he could have wanted them
to excel in his own image and for his own sake. He had not been alone
in the world since he was thirteen, knowing only a dying old woman
who felt responsible for him, but whose age, sex, and interests were so

remote from his own, he might have felt a stable connection between himself and the children. As it was, he reacted to them, and his reactions were based on what he felt at the moment.

So it was on a Saturday afternoon, in the thin light of spring, he staggered home reeling drunk and saw his daughter in the kitchen. She was washing dishes. Her small back hunched over the sink. Cholly saw her dimly and could not tell what he saw or what he felt. Then he became aware that he was uncomfortable; next he felt the discomfort dissolve into pleasure. The sequence of his emotions was revulsion, guilt, pity, then love. His revulsion was a reaction to her young, helpless, hopeless presence. Her back hunched that way; her head to one side as though crouching from a permanent and unrelieved blow. Why did she have to look so whipped? She was a child—unburdened—why wasn't she happy? The clear statement of her misery was an accusation. He wanted to break her neck—but tenderly. Guilt and impotence rose in a bilious duet. What could he do for her—ever? What give her? What say to her? What could a burned-out black man say to the hunched back of his eleven-year-old daughter? If he looked into her face, he would see those haunted, loving eyes. The hauntedness would irritate him—the love would move him to fury. How dare she love him? Hadn't she any sense at all? What was he supposed to do about that? Return it? How? What could his calloused hands produce to make her smile? What of his knowledge of the world and of life could be useful to her? What could his heavy arms and befuddled brain accomplish that would earn him his own respect, that would in turn allow him to accept her love? His hatred of her slimed in his stomach and threatened to become vomit. But just before the puke moved from anticipation to sensation, she shifted her weight and stood on one foot scratching the back of her calf with her toe. It was a quiet and pitiful gesture. Her hands were going around and around a frying pan, scraping flecks of black into cold, greasy dishwater. The timid, tucked-in look of the scratching toe—that was what Pauline was doing the first time he saw her in Kentucky. Leaning over a fence staring at nothing in particular. The creamy toe of her bare foot scratching a velvet leg. It was such a small and simple gesture, but it filled him then with a wondering softness. Not the usual lust to part tight legs with his own, but a tenderness, a protectiveness. A desire to cover her foot with his hand and gently nibble away the itch from the calf with his teeth. He did it then, and startled Pauline into laughter. He did it now.

The tenderness welled up in him, and he sank to his knees, his eyes on the foot of his daughter. Crawling on all fours toward her, he raised his hand and caught the foot in an upward stroke. Pecola lost her balance and was about to careen to the floor. Cholly raised his other hand to her hips to save her from falling. He put his head down and nibbled at the back of her leg. His mouth trembled at the firm sweetness of the flesh. He closed his eyes, letting his fingers dig into her waist. The rigidness of her shocked body, the silence of her stunned throat, was better than Pauline's easy laughter had been. The confused mixture of his memories of Pauline and the doing of a wild and forbidden thing excited him, and a bolt of desire ran down his genitals, giving it length, and softening the lips of his anus. Surrounding all of this lust was a border of politeness. He wanted to fuck her—tenderly. But the tenderness would not hold. The tightness of her vagina was more than he could bear. His soul seemed to slip down to his guts and fly out into her, and the gigantic thrust he made into her then provoked the only sound she made—a hollow suck of air in the back of her throat. Like the rapid loss of air from a circus balloon.

Following the disintegration—the falling away—of sexual desire, he was conscious of her wet, soapy hands on his wrists, the fingers clenching, but whether her grip was from a hopeless but stubborn struggle to be free, or from some other emotion, he could not tell.

Removing himself from her was so painful to him he cut it short and snatched his genitals out of the dry harbor of her vagina. She appeared to have fainted. Cholly stood up and could see only her grayish panties, so sad and limp around her ankles. Again the hatred mixed with tenderness. The hatred would not let him pick her up; the tenderness forced him to cover her.

So when the child regained consciousness, she was lying on the kitchen floor under a heavy quilt, trying to connect the pain between her legs with the face of her mother looming over her.

SEETHEDOGBOWBOWGOESTHEDOGDOYOUWANTTOPL
AYDOYOUWANTTOPLAYWITHJANESEETHEDOGRUNR

Once there was an old man who loved things, for the slightest contact
with people produced in him a faint but persistent nausea. He could
not remember when this distaste began, nor could he remember ever
being free of it. As a young boy he had been greatly disturbed by this
revulsion which others did not seem to share, but having got a fine education, he learned, among other things, the word "misanthrope."
Knowing his label provided him with both comfort and courage, he
believed that to name an evil was to neutralize if not annihilate it.
Then, too, he had read several books and made the acquaintance of several great misanthropes of the ages, whose spiritual company soothed
him and provided him with yardsticks for measuring his whims, his
yearnings, and his antipathies. Moreover, he found misanthropy an excellent means of developing character: when he subdued his revulsion
and occasionally touched, helped, counseled, or befriended somebody,
he was able to think of his behavior as generous and his intentions as
noble. When he was enraged by some human effort or flaw, he was
able to regard himself as discriminating, fastidious, and full of nice
scruples.

As in the case of many misanthropes, his disdain for people led him
into a profession designed to serve them. He was engaged in a line of
work that was dependent solely on his ability to win the trust of others, and one in which the most intimate relationships were necessary.
Having dallied with the priesthood in the Anglican Church, he
abandoned it to become a caseworker. Time and misfortune, however,
conspired against him, and he settled finally on a profession that
brought him both freedom and satisfaction. He became a "Reader,

Adviser, and Interpreter of Dreams." It was a profession that suited him well. His hours were his own, the competition was slight, the clientele was already persuaded and therefore manageable, and he had numerous opportunities to witness human stupidity without sharing it or being compromised by it, and to nurture his fastidiousness by viewing physical decay. Although his income was small, he had no taste for luxury—his experience in the monastery had solidified his natural asceticism while it developed his preference for solitude. Celibacy was a haven, silence a shield.

All his life he had had a fondness for things—not the acquisition of wealth or beautiful objects, but a genuine love of worn objects: a coffee pot that had been his mother's, a welcome mat from the door of a rooming house he once lived in, a quilt from a Salvation Army store counter. It was as though his disdain of human contact had converted itself into a craving for things humans had touched. The residue of the human spirit smeared on inanimate objects was all he could withstand of humanity. To contemplate, for example, evidence of human footsteps on the mat—absorb the smell of the quilt and wallow in the sweet certainty that many bodies had sweated, slept, dreamed, made love, been ill, and even died under it. Wherever he went, he took along his things, and was always searching for others. This thirst for worn things led him to casual but habitual examinations of trash barrels in alleys and wastebaskets in public places. . . .

All in all, his personality was an arabesque: intricate, symmetrical, balanced, and tightly constructed—except for one flaw. The careful design was marred occasionally by rare but keen sexual cravings.

He could have been an active homosexual but lacked the courage. Bestiality did not occur to him, and sodomy was quite out of the question, for he did not experience sustained erections and could not endure the thought of somebody else's. And besides, the one thing that disgusted him more than entering and caressing a woman was caressing and being caressed by a man. In any case, his cravings, although intense, never relished physical contact. He abhorred flesh on flesh. Body odor, breath odor, overwhelmed him. The sight of dried matter in the corner of the eye, decayed or missing teeth, ear wax, blackheads, moles, blisters, skin crusts—all the natural excretions and protections the body was capable of—disquieted him. His attentions therefore gradually settled on those humans whose bodies were least offensive—children. And since he was too diffident to confront homosexuality, and since little boys were insulting, scary, and stubborn, he further limited his interests to little girls. They were usually manageable and frequently seductive. His sexuality was anything but lewd; his patronage of little girls smacked of innocence and was associated in his mind with cleanliness. He was what one might call a very clean old man.

A cinnamon-eyed West Indian with lightly browned skin.

Although his given name was printed on the sign in his kitchen window, and on the business cards he circulated, he was called by the townspeople Soaphead Church. No one knew where the "Church" part came from—perhaps somebody's recollection of his days as a guest preacher—those reverends who had been called but who had no flock or coop, and were constantly visiting other churches, sitting on the altar with the host preacher. But everybody knew what "Soaphead" meant—the tight, curly hair that took on and held a sheen and wave when pomaded with soap lather. A sort of primitive process.

He had been reared in a family proud of its academic accomplishments and its mixed blood—in fact, they believed the former was based on the latter. A Sir Whitcomb, some decaying British nobleman, who chose to disintegrate under a sun more easeful than England's, had introduced the white strain into the family in the early 1800's. Being a gentleman by order of the King, he had done the civilized thing for his mulatto bastard—provided it with three hundred pounds sterling, to the great satisfaction of the bastard's mother, who felt that fortune had smiled on her. The bastard too was grateful, and regarded as his life's goal the hoarding of this white strain. He bestowed his favors on a fifteen-year-old girl of similar parentage. She, like a good Victorian parody, learned from her husband all that was worth learning—to separate herself in body, mind, and spirit from all that suggested Africa; to cultivate the habits, tastes, preferences that her absent father-in-law and foolish mother-in-law would have approved.

They transferred this Anglophilia to their six children and sixteen grandchildren. Except for an occasional and unaccountable insurgent who chose a restive black, they married "up," lightening the family complexion and thinning out the family features.

With the confidence born of a conviction of superiority, they performed well at schools. They were industrious, orderly, and energetic, hoping to prove beyond a doubt De Gobineau's hypothesis that "all civilizations derive from the white race, that none can exist without its help, and that a society is great and brilliant only so far as it preserves the blood of the noble group that created it." Thus, they were seldom overlooked by schoolmasters who recommended promising students for study abroad. The men studied medicine, law, theology, and emerged repeatedly in the powerless government offices available to the native population. That they were corrupt in public and private practice, both lecherous and lascivious, was considered their noble right, and thoroughly enjoyed by most of the less gifted population.

As the years passed, due to the carelessness of some of the Whitcomb brothers, it became difficult to maintain their whiteness, and some distant and some not so distant relatives married each other. No obviously bad effects were noticed from these ill-advised unions, but one or two old maids or gardener boys marked a weakening of faculties and a disposition toward eccentricity in some of the children. Some flaw outside the usual alcoholism and lechery. They blamed the flaw on intermarriage with the family, however, not on the original genes of the decaying lord. In any case, there were flukes. No more than in any other family, to be sure, but more dangerous because more powerful. One of them was a religious fanatic who founded his own secret sect and fathered four sons, one of whom became a schoolmaster known for the precision of his justice and the control in his violence. This schoolmaster married a sweet, indolent half-Chinese girl for whom the fatigue of bearing a son was too much. She died soon after childbirth. Her son, named Elihue Micah Whitcomb, provided the schoolmaster with ample opportunity to work out his theories of education, discipline, and the good life. Little Elihue learned everything he needed to know well, particularly the fine art of self-deception. He read greedily but understood selectively, choosing the bits and pieces of other men's ideas that supported whatever predilection he had at the moment. Thus he chose to remember Hamlet's abuse of Ophelia, but not Christ's love of Mary Magdalene; Hamlet's frivolous politics, but not Christ's serious anarchy. He noticed Gibbon's acidity, but not his tolerance, Othello's love for the fair Desdemona, but not Iago's perverted love of Othello. The works he admired most were Dante's; those he despised most were Dostoyevsky's. For all his exposure to the best minds of the Western world, he allowed only the narrowest interpretation to touch him. He responded to his father's controlled violence by developing hard habits and a soft imagination. A hatred of, and fascination with, any hint of disorder or decay.

At seventeen, however, he met his Beatrice, who was three years his senior. A lovely, laughing big-legged girl who worked as a clerk in a Chinese department store. Velma. So strong was her affection and zest for life, she did not eliminate the frail, sickly Elihue from it. She found his fastidiousness and complete lack of humor touching, and longed to introduce him to the idea of delight. He resisted the introduction, but she married him anyway, only to discover that he was suffering from and enjoying an invincible melancholy. When she learned two months into the marriage how important his melancholy was to him, that he was very interested in altering her joy to a more academic gloom, that he equated lovemaking with communion and the Holy Grail, she simply left. She had not lived by the sea all those years, listened to the wharfman's songs all that time, to spend her life in the soundless cave of Elihue's mind.

He never got over her desertion. She was to have been the answer to his unstated, unacknowledged question—where was the life to counter the encroaching nonlife? Velma was to rescue him from the nonlife he had learned on the flat side of his father's belt. But he resisted her with such skill that she was finally driven out to escape the inevitable boredom produced by such a dainty life.

Young Elihue was saved from visible shattering by the steady hand of his father, who reminded him of the family's reputation and Velma's questionable one. He then pursued his studies with more vigor than before and decided at last to enter the ministry. When he was advised that he had no avocation, he left the island, came to America to study the then budding field of psychiatry. But the subject required too much truth, too many confrontations, and offered too little support to a failing ego. He drifted into sociology, then physical therapy. This diverse education continued for six years, when his father refused to support him any longer, until he "found" himself. Elihue, not knowing where to look, was thrown back on his own devices, and "found" himself quite unable to earn money. He began to sink into a rapidly fraying gentility, punctuated with a few of the white-collar occupations available to black people, regardless of their noble bloodlines, in America: desk clerk at a colored hotel in Chicago, insurance agent, traveling salesman for a cosmetics firm catering to blacks. He finally settled in Lorain, Ohio, in 1936, palming himself off as a minister, and inspiring awe with the way he spoke English. The women of the town early discovered his celibacy, and not being able to comprehend his rejection of them, decided that he was supernatural rather than unnatural.

Once he understood their decision, he quickly followed through, accepting the name (Soaphead Church) and the role they had given him. He rented a kind of back-room apartment from a deeply religious old lady named Bertha Reese. She was clean, quiet, and very close to total deafness. The lodgings were ideal in every way but one. Bertha Reese had an old dog, Bob, who, although as deaf and quiet as she, was not as clean. He slept most of his days away on the back porch, which was Elihue's entrance. The dog was too old to be of any use, and Bertha Reese had not the strength or presence of mind to care for him properly. She fed him, and watered him, left him alone. The dog was mangy; his exhausted eyes ran with a sea-green matter around which gnats and flies clustered. Soaphead was revolted by Bob and wished he would hurry up and die. He regarded this wish for the dog's death as humane, for he could not bear, he told himself, to see anything suffer. It did not occur to him that he was really concerned about his own suffering, since the dog had adjusted himself to frailty and old age. Soaphead finally determined to put an end to the animal's misery, and bought some poison with which to do it. Only the horror of having to go near him had prevented Soaphead from completing his mission. He waited for rage or blinding revulsion to spur him.

Living there among his worn things, rising early every morning from dreamless sleeps, he counseled those who sought his advice.

His business was dread. People came to him in dread, whispered in dread, wept and pleaded in dread. And dread was what he counseled.

Singly they found their way to his door, wrapped each in a shroud stitched with anger, yearning, pride, vengeance, loneliness, misery, defeat, and hunger. They asked for the simplest of things: love, health, and money. Make him love me. Tell me what this dream means. Help me get rid of this woman. Make my mother give me back my clothes. Stop my left hand from shaking. Keep my baby's ghost off the stove. Break so-and-so's fix. To all of these requests he addressed himself. His practice was to do what he was bid—not to suggest to a party that perhaps the request was unfair, mean, or hopeless.

With only occasional, and increasingly rare, encounters with the little girls he could persuade to be entertained by him, he lived rather peaceably among his things, admitting to no regrets. He was aware, of course, that something was awry in his life, and all lives, but put the problem where it belonged, at the foot of the Originator of Life. He believed that since decay, vice, filth, and disorder were pervasive, they must be in the Nature of Things. Evil existed because God had created it. He, God, had made a sloven and unforgivable error in judgment: designing an imperfect universe. Theologians justified the presence of corruption as a means by which men strove, were tested, and triumphed. A triumph of cosmic neatness. But this neatness, the neatness of Dante, was in the orderly sectioning and segregating of all levels of evil and decay. In the world it was not so. The most exquisite-looking ladies sat on toilets, and the most dreadful-looking had pure and holy yearnings. God had done a poor job, and Soaphead suspected that he himself could have done better. It was in fact a pity that the Maker had not sought his counsel.

Soaphead was reflecting once again on these thoughts one late hot afternoon when he heard a tap on his door. Opening it, he saw a little girl, quite unknown to him. She was about twelve or so, he thought, and seemed to him pitifully unattractive. When he asked her what she wanted, she did not answer, but held out to him one of his cards advertising his gifts and services: "If you are overcome with trouble and conditions that are not natural, I can remove them; Overcome Spells, Bad Luck, and Evil Influences. Remember, I am a true Spiritualist and Psychic Reader, born with power, and I will help you. Satisfaction in one visit. During many years of practice I have brought together many in marriage and reunited many who were separated. If you are unhappy, discouraged, or in distress, I can help you. Does bad luck seem to follow you? Has the one you love changed? I can tell you why. I will tell you who your enemies and friends are, and if the one you love is true or false. If you are sick, I can show you the way to health. I locate lost and stolen articles. Satisfaction guaranteed."

Soaphead Church told her to come in.

"What can I do for you, my child?"

She stood there, her hands folded across her stomach, a little protruding pot of tummy. "Maybe. Maybe you can do it for me."

"Do what for you?"

"I can't go to school no more. And I thought maybe you could help me."

"Help you how? Tell me. Don't be frightened."

"My eyes."

"What about your eyes?"

"I want them blue."

Soaphead pursed his lips, and let his tongue stroke a gold inlay. He thought it was at once the most fantastic and the most logical petition he had ever received. Here was an ugly little girl asking for beauty. A surge of love and understanding swept through him, but was quickly replaced by anger. Anger that he was powerless to help her. Of all the wishes people had brought him—money, love, revenge—this seemed to him the most poignant and the one most deserving of fulfillment. A little black girl who wanted to rise up out of the pit of her blackness and see the world with blue eyes. His outrage grew and felt like power. For the first time he honestly wished he could work miracles. Never before had he really wanted the true and holy power—only the power to make others believe he had it. It seemed so sad, so frivolous, that mere mortality, not judgment, kept him from it. Or did it?

With a trembling hand he made the sign of the cross over her. His flesh crawled; in that hot, dim little room of worn things, he was chilled.

"I can do nothing for you, my child. I am not a magician. I work only through the Lord. He sometimes uses me to help people. All I can do is offer myself to Him as the instrument through which he works. If He wants your wish granted, He will do it."

Soaphead walked to the window, his back to the girl. His mind raced, stumbled, and raced again. How to frame the next sentence? How to hang on to the feeling of power. His eye fell on old Bob sleeping on the porch.

"We must make, ah, some offering, that is, some contact with nature. Perhaps some simple creature might be the vehicle through which He will speak. Let us see."

He knelt down at the window, and moved his lips. After what seemed a suitable length of time, he rose and went to the icebox that stood near the other window. From it he removed a small packet wrapped in pinkish butcher paper. From a shelf he took a small brown bottle and sprinkled some of its contents on the substance inside the paper. He put the packet, partly opened, on the table.

"Take this food and give it to the creature sleeping on the porch. Make sure he eats it. And mark well how he behaves. If nothing happens, you will know that God has refused you. If the animal behaves strangely, your wish will be granted on the day following this one."

The girl picked up the packet; the odor of the dark, sticky meat made her want to vomit. She put a hand on her stomach.

"Courage. Courage, my child. These things are not granted to faint hearts."

She nodded and swallowed visibly, holding down the vomit. Soaphead opened the door, and she stepped over the threshold.

"Good-bye, God bless," he said and quickly shut the door. At the window he stood watching her, his eyebrows pulled together into waves of compassion, his tongue fondling the worn gold in his upper jaw. He saw the girl bending down to the sleeping dog, who, at her touch, opened one liquid eye, matted in the corners with what looked like green glue. She reached out and touched the dog's head, stroking him gently. She placed the meat on the floor of the porch, near his nose. The odor roused him; he lifted his head, and got up to smell it better. He ate it in three or four gulps. The girl stroked his head again, and the dog looked up at her with soft triangle eyes. Suddenly he coughed, the cough of a phlegmy old man—and got to his feet. The girl jumped. The dog gagged, his mouth chomping the air, and promptly fell down. He tried to raise himself, could not, tried again, and half-fell down the steps. Choking, stumbling, he moved like a broken toy around the yard. The girl's mouth was open, a little petal of

tongue showing. She made a wild, pointless gesture with one hand and
then covered her mouth with both hands. She was trying not to vomit.
The dog fell again, a spasm jerking his body. Then he was quiet. The
girl's hands covering her mouth, she backed away a few feet, then
turned, ran out of the yard and down the walk.

Soaphead Church went to the table. He sat down, with folded hands
balancing his forehead on the balls of his thumbs. Then he rose and
went to a tiny night table with a drawer, from which he took paper
and a fountain pen. A bottle of ink was on the same shelf that held the
poison. With these things he sat again at the table. Slowly, carefully,
relishing his penmanship, he wrote the following letter:

Att: TO HE WHO GREATLY ENNOBLED HUMAN NATURE
BY CREATING IT
Dear God:

The Purpose of this letter is to familiarize you with facts which either have escaped your notice, or which you have chosen to ignore.

Once upon a time I lived greenly and youngish on one of your
islands. An island of the archipelago in the South Atlantic between
North and South America, enclosing the Caribbean Sea and the Gulf
of Mexico: divided into the Greater Antilles, the Lesser Antilles, and
the Bahama Islands. Not the Windward or Leeward Island colonies,
mark you, but within, of course, the Greater of the two Antilles (while
the precision of my prose may be, at times, laborious, it is necessary
that I identify myself to you clearly).

Now.

We in this colony took as our own the most dramatic, and the most
obvious, of our white master's characteristics, which were, of course,
their worst. In retaining the identity of our race, we held fast to those
characteristics most gratifying to sustain and least troublesome to
maintain. Consequently we were not royal but snobbish, not aristo-
cratic but class-conscious; we believed authority was cruelty to our infe-
riors, and education was being at school. We mistook violence for pas-

sion, indolence for leisure, and thought recklessness was freedom. We raised our children and reared our crops; we let infants grow, and property develop. Our manhood was defined by acquisitions. Our womanhood by acquiescence. And the smell of your fruit and the labor of your days we abhorred.

This morning, before the little black girl came, I cried—for Velma. Oh, not aloud. There is no wind to carry, bear, or even refuse to bear, a sound so heavy with regret. But in my silent own lone way, I cried—for Velma. You need to know about Velma to understand what I did today.

She (Velma) left me the way people leave a hotel room. A hotel room is a place to be when you are doing something else. Of itself it is of no consequence to one's major scheme. A hotel room is convenient. But its convenience is limited to the time you need it while you are in that particular town on that particular business; you hope it is comfortable, but prefer, rather, that it be anonymous. It is not, after all, where you *live*.

When you no longer need it, you pay a little something for its use; say, "Thank you, sir," and when your business in that town is over, you go away from that room. Does anybody regret leaving a hotel room? Does anybody, who has a home, a real home somewhere, want to stay there? Does anybody look back with affection, or even disgust, at a hotel room when they leave it? You can only love or despise whatever *living* was done in that room. But the room itself? But you take a souvenir. Not, oh, not, to remember the room. To remember, rather, the time and the place of your business, your adventure. What can anyone feel for a hotel room? One doesn't any more feel for a hotel room than one expects a hotel room to feel for its occupant.

That, heavenly, heavenly Father, was how she left me; or rather, she never left me, because she was never ever there.

You remember, do you, how and of what we are made? Let me tell you now about the breasts of little girls. I apologize for the inappropriateness (is that it?), the imbalance of loving them at awkward times of day, and in awkward places, and the tastelessness of loving those which belonged to members of my family. Do I have to apologize for loving strangers?

But you too are amiss here, Lord. How, why, did you allow it to happen? How is it I could lift my eyes from the contemplation of Your Body and fall deeply into the contemplation of theirs? The buds. The buds on some of these saplings. They were mean, you know, mean and tender. Mean little buds resisting the touch, springing like rubber. But aggressive. Daring me to touch. Commanding me to touch. Not a bit shy, as you'd suppose. They stuck out at me, oh yes, at me. Slender-chested, finger-chested lassies. Have you ever seen them, Lord? I mean, really seen them? One could not see them and not love them. You who made them must have considered them lovely even as an idea— how much more lovely is the manifestation of that idea. I couldn't, as you must recall, keep my hands, my mouth, off them. Salt-sweet. Like not quite ripe strawberries covered with the light salt sweat of running days and hopping, skipping, jumping hours.

The love of them—the touch, taste, and feel of them—was not just an easy luxurious human vice; they were, for me, A Thing To Do Instead. Instead of papa, instead of the Cloth, instead of Velma, and I *chose* not to do without them. But I didn't go into the church. At least I didn't do that. As to what I did do? I told people I knew all about You. That I had received Your Powers. It was not a complete *lie;* but it was a *complete* lie. I should never have, I admit, I should never have taken their money in exchange for well-phrased, well-placed, well-faced lies. But, mark you, I hated it. Not for a moment did I love the lies or the money.

But consider: The woman who left the hotel room.

Consider: The greentime, the noontime of the archipelago.

Consider: Their hopeful eyes that were outdone only by their hoping breasts.

Consider: How I needed a comfortable evil to prevent my knowing what I could not bear to know.

Consider: How I hated and despised the money.

And now, consider: Not according to my just deserts, but according to *my* mercy, the little black girl that came a-looning at me today. Tell me, Lord, how could you leave a lass so long so lone that she could find her way to me? How could you? I weep for you, Lord. And it is because I weep for You that I had to do your work for You.

Do you know what she came for? Blue eyes. New, blue eyes, she said. Like she was buying shoes. "I'd like a pair of new blue eyes." She must have asked you for them for a very long time, and you hadn't replied. (A habit, I could have told her, a long-ago habit broken for Job —but no more.) She came to *me* for them. She had one of my cards. (Card enclosed.) By the way, I added the Micah—Micah Elihue Whitcomb. But I am called Soaphead Church. I cannot remember how or why I got the name. What makes one name more a person than another? Is the name the real thing, then? And the person only what his name says? Is that why to the simplest and friendliest of questions: "What is your name?" put to you by Moses, You would not say, and said instead "I am who I am." Like Popeye? I Yam What I Yam? Afraid you were, weren't you, to give out your name? Afraid they would know the name and then know you? Then they wouldn't fear you? It's quite all right. Don't be vexed. I mean no offense. I understand. I have been a bad man too, and an unhappy man too. But someday *I* will die. I was always so kind. Why do I have to die? The little girls. The little girls are the only things I'll miss. Do you know that when I touched their sturdy little tits and bit them—just a little—I felt I was being friendly? I didn't want to kiss their mouths or sleep in the bed with them or take a child bride for my own. Playful, I felt, and friendly. Not like the newspapers said. Not like the people whispered. And they didn't mind at all. Not at all. Remember how so many of them came back? No one would even try to understand that. If I'd been hurting them, would they have come back? Two of them, Doreen and Sugar Babe, they'd come together. I gave them mints, money, and they'd eat ice cream with their legs open while I played with them. It was like a party. And there wasn't nastiness, and there wasn't any filth, and there wasn't any odor, and there wasn't any groaning—just the light white laughter of little girls and me. And there wasn't any look— any long funny look—any long funny Velma look afterward. No look that makes you feel dirty afterward. That makes you want to die. With little girls it is all clean and good and friendly.

You have to understand that, Lord. You said, "Suffer little children to come unto me, and harm them not." Did you forget? Did you forget about the children? Yes. You forgot. You let them go wanting, sit on road shoulders, crying next to their dead mothers. I've seen them charred, lame, halt. You forgot, Lord. You forgot how and when to be God.

That's why I changed the little black girl's eyes for her, and I didn't touch her; not a finger did I lay on her. But I gave her those blue eyes she wanted. Not for pleasure, and not for money. I did what You did not, could not, would not do: I looked at that ugly little black girl, and I loved her. I played You. And it was a very good show!

I, I have caused a miracle. I gave her the eyes. I gave her the blue, blue, two blue eyes. Cobalt blue. A streak of it right out of your own blue heaven. No one else will see her blue eyes. But *she* will. And she will live happily ever after. I, I have found it meet and right so to do.

Now you are jealous. You are jealous of me.

You see? I, too, have created. Not aboriginally, like you, but creation is a heady wine, more for the taster than the brewer.

Having therefore imbibed, as it were, of the nectar, I am not afraid of You, of Death, not even of Life, and it's all right about Velma; and it's all right about Papa; and it's all right about the Greater and the Lesser Antilles. Quite all right. Quite.

With kindest regards, I remain,

Your,

Micah Elihue Whitcomb

Soaphead Church folded the sheets of paper into three equal parts and slipped them into an envelope. Although he had no seal, he longed for sealing wax. He removed a cigar box from under the bed and rummaged about in it. There were some of his most precious things: a sliver of jade that had dislodged from a cuff link at the Chicago hotel; a gold pendant shaped like a Y with a piece of coral attached to it that had belonged to the mother he never knew; four large hairpins that Velma had left on the rim of the bathroom sink; a powder blue grosgrain ribbon from the head of a little girl named Precious Jewel; a blackened faucet head from the sink in a jail cell in Cincinnati; two marbles he had found under a bench in Morningside Park on a very fine spring day; an old Lucky Hart catalog that smelled still of nut-brown and mocha face powder, and lemon vanishing cream. Distracted by his things, he forgot what he had been looking for. The effort to recall was too great; there was a buzzing in his head, and a wash of fatigue overcame him. He closed his box, eased himself out on the bed, and slipped into an ivory sleep from which he could not hear the tiny yelps of an old lady who had come out of her candy store and found the still carcass of an old dog named Bob.

Summer

I have only to break into the tightness of a strawberry, and I see summer—its dust and lowering skies. It remains for me a season of storms. The parched days and sticky nights are undistinguished in my mind, but the storms, the violent sudden storms, both frightened and quenched me. But my memory is uncertain; I recall a summer storm in the town where we lived and imagine a summer my mother knew in 1929. There was a tornado that year, she said, that blew away half of south Lorain. I mix up her summer with my own. Biting the strawberry, thinking of storms, I see her. A slim young girl in a pink crepe dress. One hand is on her hip; the other lolls about her thigh—waiting. The wind swoops her up, high above the houses, but she is still standing, hand on hip. Smiling. The anticipation and promise in her lolling hand are not altered by the holocaust. In the summer tornado of 1929, my mother's hand is unextinguished. She is strong, smiling, and relaxed while the world falls down about her. So much for memory. Public fact becomes private reality, and the seasons of a Midwestern town become the *Moirai* of our small lives.

The summer was already thick when Frieda and I received our seeds. We had waited since April for the magic package containing the packets and packets of seeds we were to sell for five cents each, which would entitle us to a new bicycle. We believed it, and spent a major part of every day trooping about the town selling them. Although Mama had restricted us to the homes of people she knew or the neighborhoods familiar to us, we knocked on all doors, and floated in and out of every house that opened to us: twelve-room houses that sheltered half as many families, smelling of grease and urine; tiny wooden four-room houses tucked into bushes near the railroad tracks; the up-over places—apartments up over fish markets, butcher shops, furniture stores, saloons, restaurants; tidy brick houses with flowered carpets and glass bowls with fluted edges.

During that summer of the seed selling we thought about the money, thought about the seeds, and listened with only half an ear to what people were saying. In the houses of people who knew us we were asked to come in and sit, given cold water or lemonade; and while we sat there being refreshed, the people continued their conversations or went about their chores. Little by little we began to piece a story together, a secret, terrible, awful story. And it was only after two or three such vaguely overheard conversations that we realized that the story was about Pecola. Properly placed, the fragments of talk ran like this:

"Did you hear about that girl?"

"What? Pregnant?"

"Yas. But guess who?"

"Who? I don't know all these little old boys."

"That's just it. Ain't no little old boy. They say it's Cholly."

"Cholly? Her daddy?"

"Uh-huh."

"Lord. Have mercy. That dirty nigger."

" 'Member that time he tried to burn them up? I knew he was crazy for sure then."

"What's she gone do? The mama?"

"Keep on like she been, I reckon. He taken off."

"County ain't gone let her keep that baby, is they?"

"Don't know."

"None of them Breedloves seem right anyhow. That boy is off somewhere every minute, and the girl was always foolish."

"Don't nobody know nothing about them anyway. Where they come from or nothing. Don't seem to have no people."

"What you reckon make him do a thing like that?"

"Beats me. Just nasty."

"Well, they ought to take her out of school."

"Ought to. She carry some of the blame."

"Oh, come on. She ain't but twelve or so."

"Yeah. But you never know. How come she didn't fight him?"

"Maybe she did."

"Yeah? You never know."

"Well, it probably won't live. They say the way her mama beat her she lucky to be alive herself."

"She be lucky if it don't live. Bound to be the ugliest thing walking."

"Can't help but be. Ought to be a law: two ugly people doubling up like that to make more ugly. Be better off in the ground."

"Well, I wouldn't worry none. It be a miracle if it live."

Our astonishment was short-lived, for it gave way to a curious kind of defensive shame; we were embarrassed for Pecola, hurt for her, and finally we just felt sorry for her. Our sorrow drove out all thoughts of the new bicycle. And I believe our sorrow was the more intense because nobody else seemed to share it. They were disgusted, amused, shocked, outraged, or even excited by the story. But we listened for the one who would say, "Poor little girl," or, "Poor baby," but there was only head-wagging where those words should have been. We looked for eyes creased with concern, but saw only veils.

I thought about the baby that everybody wanted dead, and saw it very clearly. It was in a dark, wet place, its head covered with great O's of wool, the black face holding, like nickels, two clean black eyes, the flared nose, kissing-thick lips, and the living, breathing silk of black skin. No synthetic yellow bangs suspended over marble-blue eyes, no pinched nose and bowline mouth. More strongly than my fondness for Pecola, I felt a need for someone to want the black baby to live—just to counteract the universal love of white baby dolls, Shirley Temples, and Maureen Peals. And Frieda must have felt the same thing. We did not think of the fact that Pecola was not married; lots of girls had babies who were not married. And we did not dwell on the fact that the baby's father was Pecola's father too; the process of having a baby

by any male was incomprehensible to us—at least she knew her father.
We thought only of this overwhelming hatred for the unborn baby.
We remembered Mrs. Breedlove knocking Pecola down and soothing
the pink tears of the frozen doll baby that sounded like the door of our
icebox. We remembered the knuckled eyes of schoolchildren under the
gaze of Meringue Pie and the eyes of these same children when they
looked at Pecola. Or maybe we didn't remember; we just knew. We
had defended ourselves since memory against everything and
everybody, considered all speech a code to be broken by us, and all
gestures subject to careful analysis; we had become headstrong,
devious, and arrogant. Nobody paid us any attention, so we paid very
good attention to ourselves. Our limitations were not known to
us—not then. Our only handicap was our size; people gave us orders
because they were bigger and stronger. So it was with confidence,
strengthened by pity and pride, that we decided to change the course of
events and alter a human life.

"What we gone do, Frieda?"

"What can we do? Miss Johnson said it would be a miracle if it
lived."

"So let's make it a miracle."

"Yeah, but how?"

"We could pray."

"That's not enough. Remember last time with the bird?"

"That was different; it was half-dead when we found it."

"I don't care, I still think we have to do something really strong this
time."

"Let's ask Him to let Pecola's baby live and promise to be good for
a whole month."

"O.K. But we better give up something so He'll know we really
mean it this time."

"Give up what? We ain't got nothing. Nothing but the seed
money, two dollars."

"We could give that. Or, you know what? We could give up the bicycle. Bury the money and . . . plant the seeds."

"All of the money?"

"Claudia, do you want to do it or not?"

"O.K. I just thought . . . O.K."

"We have to do it *right*, now. We'll bury the money over by her house so we can't go back and dig it up, and we'll plant the seeds out back of our house so we can watch over them. And when they come up, we'll know everything is all right. All right?"

"All right. Only let me sing this time. You say the magic words."

LOOKLOOKHERECOMESAFRIENDTHEFRIENDWILLPLAY
WITHJANETHEYWILLPLAYAGOODGAMEPLAYJANEPLA

How many times a minute are you going to look inside that old thing?
I didn't look in a long time.
You did too–
So what? I can look if I want to.
I didn't say you couldn't. I just don't know why you have to look every minute. They aren't going anywhere.
I know it. I just like to look.
You scared they might go away?
Of course not. How can they go away?
The others went away.
They didn't go away. They changed.
Go away. Change. What's the difference?
A lot. Mr. Soaphead said they would last forever.
Forever and ever Amen?
Yes, if you want to know.
You don't have to be so smarty when you talk to me.
I'm not being smarty. You started it.
I'd just like to do something else besides watch you stare in that mirror.
You're just jealous.
I am not.
You are. You wish you had them.
Ha. What would I look like with blue eyes?
Nothing much.
If you're going to keep this up, I may as well go on off by myself.
No. Don't go. What you want to do?
We could go outside and play, I guess.
But it's too hot.

You can take your old mirror. Put it in your coat pocket, and you can look at yourself up and down the street.

Boy! I never would have thought you'd be so jealous.

Oh, come on!

You are.

Are what?

Jealous.

O.K. So I'm jealous.

See. I told you.

No. I told you.

Are they really nice?

Yes. Very nice.

Just "very nice"?

Really, truly, very nice.

Really, truly, bluely nice?

Oh, God. You are crazy.

I am not!

I didn't meant it that way.

Well, what did you mean?

Come on. It's too hot in here.

Wait a minute. I can't find my shoes.

Here they are.

Oh. Thank you.

Got your mirror?

Yes dearie. . . .

Well, let's go then. . . . Ow!

What's the matter?

The sun is too bright. It hurts my eyes.

Not mine. I don't even blink. Look. I can look right at the sun.

Don't do that.

Why not? It doesn't hurt. I don't even have to blink.

Well, blink anyway. You make me feel funny, staring at the sun like that.

Feel funny how?

I don't know.

Yes, you do. Feel funny how?

I told you, I don't know.

Why don't you look at me when you say that? You're looking drop-eyed like Mrs. Breedlove.

Mrs. Breedlove look drop-eyed at you?

Yes. Now she does. Ever since I got my blue eyes, she look away from me all of the time. Do you suppose she's jealous too?

Could be. They are pretty, you know.

I know. He really did a good job. Everybody's jealous. Every time I look at somebody, they look off.

Is that why nobody has told you how pretty they are?

Sure it is. Can you imagine? Something like that happening to a person, and nobody but nobody saying anything about it? They all try to pretend they don't see them. Isn't that funny? . . . I said, isn't that funny?

Yes.

You are the only one who tells me how pretty they are.

Yes.

You are a real friend. I'm sorry about picking on you before. I mean, saying you were jealous and all.

That's all right.

No. Really. You are my very best friend. Why didn't I know you before?

You didn't need me before.

Didn't need you?

I mean . . . you were so unhappy before. I guess you didn't notice me before.

I guess you're right. And I was so lonely for friends. And you were right here. Right before my eyes.

No, honey. Right after your eyes.

What?

What does Maureen think about your eyes?

She doesn't say anything about them. Has she said anything to you about them?

No. Nothing.

Do you like Maureen?

Oh. She's all right. For a half-white girl, that is.

I know what you mean. But would you like to be her friend? I mean, would you like to go around with her or anything?

No.

Me neither. But she sure is popular.

Who wants to be popular?

Not me.

Me neither.

But you couldn't be popular anyway. You don't even go to school.

You don't either.

I know. But I used to.

What did you stop for?

They made me.

Who made you?

I don't know. After that first day at school when I had my blue eyes. Well, the next day they had Mrs. Breedlove come out. Now I don't go anymore. But I don't care.

You don't?

No, I don't. They're just prejudiced, that's all.

Yes, they sure are prejudiced.

Just because I got blue eyes, bluer than theirs, they're prejudiced.

That's right.

They are bluer, aren't they?

Oh, yes. Much bluer.

Bluer than Joanna's?

Much bluer than Joanna's.

And bluer than Michelena's?

Much bluer than Michelena's.

I thought so. Did Michelena say anything to you about my eyes?

No. Nothing.

Did you say anything to her?

No.

How come?

How come what?

How come you don't talk to anybody?

I talk to you.

Besides me.

I don't like anybody besides you.

Where do you live?

I told you once.

What is your mother's name?

Why are you so busy meddling me?

I just wondered. You don't talk to anybody. You don't go to school. And nobody talks to you.

How do you know nobody talks to me?

They don't. When you're in the house with me, even Mrs. Breedlove doesn't say anything to you. Ever. Sometimes I wonder if she even sees you.

Why wouldn't she see me?

I don't know. She almost walks right over you.

Maybe she doesn't feel too good since Cholly's gone.

Oh, yes. You must be right.

She probably misses him.

I don't know why she would. All he did was get drunk and beat her up.

Well, you know how grown-ups are.

Yes. No. How are they?

Well, she probably loved him anyway.

HIM?

Sure. Why not? Anyway, if she didn't love him, she sure let him do it to her a lot.

That's nothing.

How do you know?

I saw them all the time. She didn't like it.

Then why'd she let him do it to her?

Because he made her.

How could somebody make you do something like that?

Easy.

Oh, yeah? How easy?

They just make you, that's all.

I guess you're right. And Cholly could make anybody do anything.

He could not.

He made you, didn't he?

Shut up!

I was only teasing.

Shut up!

O.K. O.K.

He just tried, see? He didn't do anything. You hear me?

I'm shutting up.

You'd better. I don't like that kind of talk.

I said I'm shutting up.

You always talk so dirty. Who told you about that, anyway?

I forget.

Sammy?

No. You did.

I did not.

You did. You said he tried to do it to you when you were sleeping on the couch.

See there! You don't even know what you're talking about. It was when I was washing dishes.

Oh, yes. Dishes.

By myself. In the kitchen.

Well, I'm glad you didn't let him.

Yes.

Did you?

Did I what?
Let him.
Now who's crazy?
I am, I guess.
You sure are.
Still . . .
Well. Go ahead. Still what?
I wonder what it would be like.
Horrible.
Really?
Yes. Horrible.
Then why didn't you tell Mrs. Breedlove?
I did tell her!
I don't mean about the first time. I mean about the second time, when you were sleeping on the couch.
I wasn't sleeping! I was reading!
You don't have to shout.
You don't understand anything, do you? She didn't even believe me when I told her.
So that's why you didn't tell her about the second time?
She wouldn't have believed me then either.
You're right. No use telling her when she wouldn't believe you.
That's what I'm trying to get through your thick head.
O.K. I understand now. Just about.
What do you mean, just about?
You sure are mean today.
You keep on saying mean and sneaky things. I thought you were my friend.
I am. I am.
Then leave me alone about Cholly.
OK.
There's nothing more to say about him, anyway. He's gone, anyway.
Yes. Good riddance.

Yes. Good riddance.

And Sammy's gone too.

And Sammy's gone too.

So there's no use talking about it. I mean them.

No. No use at all.

It's all over now.

Yes.

And you don't have to be afraid of Cholly coming at you anymore.

No.

That was horrible, wasn't it?

Yes.

The second time too?

Yes.

Really? The second time too?

Leave me alone! You better leave me alone.

Can't you take a joke? I was only funning.

I don't like to talk about dirty things.

Me neither. Let's talk about something else.

What? What will we talk about?

Why, your eyes.

Oh, yes. My eyes. My blue eyes. Let me look again.

See how pretty they are.

Yes. They get prettier each time I look at them.

They are the prettiest I've ever seen.

Really?

Oh, yes.

Prettier than the sky?

Oh, yes. Much prettier than the sky.

Prettier than Alice-and-Jerry Storybook eyes?

Oh, yes. Much prettier than Alice-and-Jerry Storybook eyes.

And prettier than Joanna's?

Oh, yes. And bluer too.

Bluer than Michelena's?

Yes.

Are you sure?

Of course I'm sure.

You don't sound sure. . . .

Well, I am sure. Unless. . . .

Unless what?

Oh, nothing. I was just thinking about a lady I saw yesterday. Her eyes sure were blue. But no. Not bluer than yours.

Are you sure?

Yes. I remember them now. Yours are bluer.

I'm glad.

Me too. I'd hate to think that there was anybody around with bluer eyes than yours. I'm sure there isn't. Not around here, anyway.

But you don't know, do you? You haven't seen everybody, have you?

No. I haven't.

So there could be, couldn't there?

Not hardly.

But maybe. Maybe. You said "around here." Nobody "around here" probably has bluer eyes. What about someplace else? Even if my eyes are bluer than Joanna's and bluer than Michelena's and bluer than that lady's you saw, suppose there is somebody way off somewhere with bluer eyes than mine?

Don't be silly.

There could be. Couldn't there?

Not hardly.

But suppose. Suppose a long way off. In Cincinnati, say, there is somebody whose eyes are bluer than mine? Suppose there are *two* people with bluer eyes?

So what? You asked for blue eyes. You got blue eyes.

He should have made them bluer.

Who?

Mr. Soaphead.

Did you say what color blue you wanted them?
No. I forgot.
Oh. Well.
Look. Look over there. At that girl. Look at her eyes. Are they bluer than mine?
No, I don't think so.
Did you look real good?
Yes.
Here comes someone. Look at his. See if they're bluer.
You're being silly. I'm not going to look at everybody's eyes.
You have to.
No I don't.
Please. If there is somebody with bluer eyes than mine, then maybe there is somebody with the bluest eyes. The bluest eyes in the whole world.
That's just too bad, isn't it?
Please help me look.
No.
But suppose my eyes aren't blue enough?
Blue enough for what?
Blue enough for . . . I don't know. Blue enough for something. Blue enough . . . for you!
I'm not going to play with you anymore.
Oh. Don't leave me.
Yes. I am.
Why? Are you mad at me?
Yes.
Because my eyes aren't blue enough? Because I don't have the bluest eyes?
No. Because you're acting silly.
Don't go. Don't leave me. Will you come back if I get them?
Get what?
The bluest eyes. Will you come back then?

Of course I will. I'm just going away for a little while.
You promise?
Sure. I'll be back. Right before your very eyes.

So it was.

A little black girl yearns for the blue eyes of a little white girl, and the horror at the heart of her yearning is exceeded only by the evil of fulfillment.

We saw her sometimes, Frieda and I—after the baby came too soon and died. After the gossip and the slow wagging of heads. She was so sad to see. Grown people looked away; children, those who were not frightened by her, laughed outright.

The damage done was total. She spent her days, her tendril, sap-green days, walking up and down, up and down, her head jerking to the beat of a drummer so distant only she could hear. Elbows bent, hands on shoulders, she flailed her arms like a bird in an eternal, gro-tesquely futile effort to fly. Beating the air, a winged but grounded bird, intent on the blue void it could not reach—could not even see—but which filled the valleys of the mind.

We tried to see her without looking at her, and never, never went near. Not because she was absurd, or repulsive, or because we were frightened, but because we had failed her. Our flowers never grew. I was convinced that Frieda was right, that I had planted them too deeply. How could I have been so sloven? So we avoided Pecola Breed-love—forever.

And the years folded up like pocket handkerchiefs. Sammy left town long ago; Cholly died in the workhouse; Mrs. Breedlove still does housework. And Pecola is somewhere in that little brown house she and her mother moved to on the edge of town, where you can see her even now, once in a while. The birdlike gestures are worn away to a mere picking and plucking her way between the tire rims and the sun-flowers, between Coke bottles and milkweed, among all the waste and beauty of the world—which is what she herself was. All of our waste which we dumped on her and which she absorbed. And all of our beauty, which was hers first and which she gave to us. All of us—all who knew her—felt so wholesome after we cleaned ourselves on her. We were so beautiful when we stood astride her ugliness. Her simplicity decorated us, her guilt sanctified us, her pain made us glow with health, her awkwardness made us think we had a sense of humor. Her inarticulateness made us believe we were eloquent. Her poverty kept us generous. Even her waking dreams we used—to silence our own nightmares. And she let us, and thereby deserved our contempt. We honed our egos on her, padded our characters with her frailty, and yawned in the fantasy of our strength.

And fantasy it was, for we were not strong, only aggressive; we were not free, merely licensed; we were not compassionate, we were polite; not good, but well behaved. We courted death in order to call ourselves brave, and hid like thieves from life. We substituted good grammar for intellect; we switched habits to simulate maturity; we rearranged lies and called it truth, seeing in the new pattern of an old idea the Revelation and the Word.

She, however, stepped over into madness, a madness which protected her from us simply because it bored us in the end.

Oh, some of us "loved" her. The Maginot Line. And Cholly loved her. I'm sure he did. He, at any rate, was the one who loved her enough to touch her, envelop her, give something of himself to her. But his touch was fatal, and the something he gave her filled the matrix of her agony with death. Love is never any better than the lover. Wicked people love wickedly, violent people love violently, weak people love weakly, stupid people love stupidly, but the love of a free man is never safe. There is no gift for the beloved. The lover alone possesses his gift of love. The loved one is shorn, neutralized, frozen in the glare of the lover's inward eye.

And now when I see her searching the garbage—for what? The thing we assassinated? I talk about how I did *not* plant the seeds too deeply, how it was the fault of the earth, the land, of our town. I even think now that the land of the entire country was hostile to marigolds that year. This soil is bad for certain kinds of flowers. Certain seeds it will not nurture, certain fruit it will not bear, and when the land kills of its own volition, we acquiesce and say the victim had no right to live. We are wrong, of course, but it doesn't matter. It's too late. At least on the edge of my town, among the garbage and the sunflowers of my town, it's much, much, much too late.

Afterword

We had just started elementary school. She said she wanted blue eyes. I looked around to picture her with them and was violently repelled by what I imagined she would look like if she had her wish. The sorrow in her voice seemed to call for sympathy, and I faked it for her, but, astonished by the desecration she proposed, I "got mad" at her instead.

Until that moment I had seen the pretty, the lovely, the nice, the ugly, and although I had certainly used the word "beautiful," I had never experienced its shock—the force of which was equaled by the knowledge that no one else recognized it, not even, or especially, the one who possessed it.

It must have been more than the face I was examining: the silence of the street in the early afternoon, the light, the atmosphere of confession. In any case it was the first time I knew beautiful. Had imagined it for myself. Beauty was not simply something to behold; it was something one could *do*.

The Bluest Eye was my effort to say something about that; to say something about why she had not, or possibly ever would have, the experience of what she possessed and also why she prayed for so radical an alteration. Implicit in her desire was racial self-loathing. And twenty years later I was still wondering about how one learns that. Who told her? Who made her feel that it was better to be a freak than what she was? Who had looked at her and found her so wanting, so small a weight on the beauty scale? The novel pecks away at the gaze that condemned her.

The reclamation of racial beauty in the sixties stirred these thoughts, made me think about the necessity for the claim. Why, although reviled by others, could this beauty not be taken for granted within the community? Why did it need wide public articulation to exist? These are not clever questions. But in 1962 when I began this story, and in 1965 when it began to be a book, the answers were not as obvious to me as they quickly became and are now. The assertion of racial beauty was not a reaction to the self-mocking, humorous critique of cultural/racial foibles common in all groups, but against the damaging internalization of assumptions of immutable inferiority originating in an outside gaze. I focused, therefore, on how something as grotesque as the demonization of an entire race could take root inside the most delicate member of society: a child; the most vulnerable member: a female. In trying to dramatize the devastation that even casual racial contempt can cause, I chose a unique situation, not a representative one. The extremity of Pecola's case stemmed largely from a crippled and crippling family—unlike the average black family and unlike the narrator's. But singular as Pecola's life was, I believed some aspects of her woundability were lodged in all young girls. In exploring the social and domestic aggression that could cause a child to literally fall apart, I mounted a series of rejections, some routine, some exceptional, some monstrous, all the while trying hard to avoid complicity in the demonization process Pecola was subjected to. That is, I did not want to dehumanize the characters who trashed Pecola and contributed to her collapse.

One problem was centering: the weight of the novel's inquiry on so delicate and vulnerable a character could smash her and lead readers into the comfort of pitying her rather than into an interrogation of themselves for the smashing. My solution—break the narrative into parts that had to be reassembled by the reader—seemed to me a good idea, the execution of which does not satisfy me now. Besides, it didn't work: many readers remain touched but not moved.

The other problem, of course, was language. Holding the despising glance while sabotaging it was difficult. The novel tried to hit the raw nerve of racial self-contempt, expose it, then soothe it not with narcotics but with language that replicated the agency I discovered in my first experience of beauty. Because that moment was so racially infused (my revulsion at what my school friend wanted: very blue eyes in a very black skin; the harm she was doing to *my* concept of the beautiful), the struggle was for writing that was indisputably black. I don't yet know quite what that is, but neither that nor the attempts to disqualify an effort to find out keeps me from trying to pursue it.

Some time ago I did the best job I could of describing strategies for grounding my work in race-specific yet race-free prose. Prose free of racial hierarchy and triumphalism. Parts of that description are as follows.

The opening phrase of the first sentence, "Quiet as it's kept," had several attractions for me. First, it was a familiar phrase, familiar to me as a child listening to adults; to black women conversing with one another, telling a story, an anecdote, gossip about some one or event within the circle, the family, the neighborhood. The words are conspiratorial. "Shh, don't tell anyone else," and "No one is allowed to know this." It is a secret between us and a secret that is being kept from us. The conspiracy is both held and withheld, exposed and sustained. In some sense it was precisely what the act of writing the book was: the public exposure of a private confidence. In order to comprehend fully the duality of that position, one needs to be reminded of the political climate in which the writing took place, 1965–69, a time of great social upheaval in the lives of black people. The publication (as opposed to the writing) involved the exposure; the writing was the disclosure of secrets, secrets "we" shared and those withheld from us by ourselves and by the world outside the community.

"Quiet as it's kept" is also a figure of speech that is written, in this instance, but clearly chosen for how speakerly it is, how it speaks and bespeaks a particular world and its ambience. Further, in addition to its "back fence" connotation, its suggestion of illicit gossip, of thrilling revelation, there is also, in the "whisper," the assumption (on the part of the reader) that the teller is on the inside, knows something others do not, and is going to be generous with this privileged information. The intimacy I was aiming for, the intimacy between the reader and the page, could start up immediately because the secret is being shared, at best, and eavesdropped upon, at the least. Sudden familiarity or instant intimacy seemed crucial to me. I did not want the reader to have time to wonder, "What do I have to do, to give up, in order to read this? What defense do I need, what distance maintain?" Because I know (and the reader does not—he or she has to wait for the second sentence) that this is a terrible story about things one would rather not know anything about.

What, then, is the Big Secret about to be shared? The thing we (reader and I) are "in" on? A botanical aberration. Pollution, perhaps. A skip, perhaps, in the natural order of things: a September, an autumn, a fall without marigolds. Bright, common, strong and sturdy marigolds. When? In 1941, and since that is a momentous year (the beginning of World War II for the United States), the "fall" of 1941, just before the declaration of war, has a "closet" innuendo. In the temperate zone where there is a season known as "fall" during which one expects marigolds to be at their peak, in the months before the beginning of U.S. participation in World War II, something grim is about to be divulged. The next sentence will make it clear that the sayer, the one who knows, is a child speaking, mimicking the adult black women on the porch or in the backyard. The opening phrase is an effort to be grown-up about this shocking information. The point of view of a child alters the priority an adult would assign the information. "We thought . . . it was because Pecola was having her father's baby that the mari-golds did not grow" foregrounds the flowers, backgrounds illicit, traumatic, incomprehensible sex coming to its dreaded fruition. This forgrounding of "trivial" informa-tion and backgrounding of shocking knowledge secures the point of view but gives the reader pause about whether the voice of children can be trusted at all or is more trustworthy than an adult's. The reader is thereby protected from a confrontation too soon with the painful details, while simul-taneously provoked into a desire to know them. The novelty, I thought, would be in having this story of female violation revealed from the vantage point of the victims or could-be victims of rape—the persons no one inquired of (certainly not in 1965): the girls themselves. And since the victim does not have the vocabulary to understand the violence or its context, gullible, vulnerable girlfriends, looking back as the knowing adults they pretended to be in the beginning, would have to do that for her, and would have to fill those silences with their own reflective lives. Thus, the opening provides the stroke that announces something more than a secret shared, but a silence broken, a void filled, an unspeakable thing spoken at last. And it draws the connection between a minor destabilization in seasonal flora and the insignificant destruction of a black girl. Of course "minor" and "insignificant" represent the outside world's view—for the girls, both phenomena are earthshaking depositories of information they spend that whole year of childhood (and afterward) trying to fathom, and cannot. If they have any success, it will be in transferring the problem of fathoming to the presumably adult reader, to the inner circle of listeners. At the least they have distributed the weight of these problematical questions to a larger constituency, and justified the public exposure of a privacy. If the conspiracy that the opening words announce is entered into by the reader, then the book can be seen to open with its close: a speculation on the disruption of "nature" as being a social disruption with tragic individual consequences in which the reader, as part of the population of the text, is implicated.

However, a problem lies in the central chamber of the novel. The shattered world I built (to complement what is happening to Pecola), its pieces held together by seasons in childtime and commenting at every turn on the incompatible and barren white-family primer, does not in its present form handle effectively the silence at its center: the void that is Pecola's "unbeing." It should have had a shape—like the emptiness left by a boom or a cry. It required a sophistication unavailable to me, and some deft manipulation of the voices around her. She is not *seen* by herself until she hallucinates a self. And the fact of her hallucination becomes a kind of outside-the-book conversation.

Also, although I was pressing for a female expressiveness, it eluded me for the most part, and I had to content myself with female personae because I was not able to secure throughout the work the feminine subtext that is present in the opening sentence (the women gossiping, eager and aghast in "Quiet as it's kept"). The shambles this struggle became is most evident in the section on Pauline Breedlove, where I resorted to two voices, hers and the urging narrator's, both of which are extremely unsatisfactory to me. It is interesting to me now that where I thought I would have the most difficulty subverting the language to a feminine mode, I had the least: connecting Cholly's "rape" by the whitemen to his own of his daughter. This most masculine act of aggression becomes feminized in my language, "passive," and, I think, more accurately repellent when deprived of the male "glamour of shame" rape is (or once was) routinely given.

My choices of language (speakerly, aural, colloquial), my reliance for full comprehension on codes embedded in black culture, my effort to effect immediate co-conspiracy and intimacy (without any distancing, explanatory fabric), as well as my attempt to shape a silence while breaking it are attempts to transfigure the complexity and wealth of Black-American culture into a language worthy of the culture.

Thinking back now on the problems expressive language presented to me, I am amazed by their currency, their tenacity. Hearing "civilized" languages debase humans, watching cultural exorcisms debase literature, seeing oneself preserved in the amber of disqualifying metaphors—I can say that my narrative project is as difficult today as it was thirty years ago.

With very few exceptions, the initial publication of *The Bluest Eye* was like Pecola's life: dismissed, trivialized, misread. And it has taken twenty-five years to gain for her the respectful publication this edition is.

Princeton, New Jersey
November, 1993

Sula

*It is sheer good fortune to miss
somebody long before they leave you.
This book is for Ford and Slade, whom
I miss although they have not left me.*

*"Nobody knew my rose of the world
but me. . . . I had too much glory.
They don't want glory like that
in nobody's heart."*

—The Rose Tattoo

PART ONE

In that place, where they tore the nightshade and black-berry patches from their roots to make room for the Medallion City Golf Course, there was once a neighbor-hood. It stood in the hills above the valley town of Medal-lion and spread all the way to the river. It is called the suburbs now, but when black people lived there it was called the Bottom. One road, shaded by beeches, oaks, maples and chestnuts, connected it to the valley. The beeches are gone now, and so are the pear trees where children sat and yelled down through the blossoms to passersby. Generous funds have been allotted to level the stripped and faded buildings that clutter the road from Medallion up to the golf course. They are going to raze the Time and a Half Pool Hall, where feet in long tan shoes once pointed down from chair rungs. A steel ball will knock to dust Irene's Palace of Cosmetology, where women used to lean their heads back on sink trays and doze while Irene lathered Nu Nile into their hair. Men in khaki work clothes will pry loose the slats of Reba's Grill, where the owner cooked in her hat because she couldn't remember the ingredients without it.

There will be nothing left of the Bottom (the foot-bridge that crossed the river is already gone), but perhaps it is just as well, since it wasn't a town anyway: just a neighborhood where on quiet days people in valley houses could hear singing sometimes, banjos sometimes, and, if a valley man happened to have business up in those hills—collecting rent or insurance payments—he might see a dark woman in a flowered dress doing a bit of cakewalk, a bit of black bottom, a bit of "messing around" to the lively notes of a mouth organ. Her bare feet would raise the saffron dust that floated down on the coveralls and bunion-split shoes of the man breathing music in and out of his harmonica. The black people watching her would laugh and rub their knees, and it would be easy for the valley man to hear the laughter and not notice the adult pain that rested somewhere under the eyelids, somewhere under their head rags and soft felt hats, somewhere in the palm of the hand, somewhere behind the frayed lapels, some-where in the sinew's curve. He'd have to stand in the back of Greater Saint Matthew's and let the tenor's voice dress him in silk, or touch the hands of the spoon carvers (who had not worked in eight years) and let the fingers that danced on wood kiss his skin. Otherwise the pain would escape him even though the laughter was part of the pain.

A shucking, knee-slapping, wet-eyed laughter that could even describe and explain how they came to be where they were.

A joke. A nigger joke. That was the way it got started. Not the town, of course, but that part of town where the Negroes lived, the part they called the Bottom in spite of the fact that it was up in the hills. Just a nigger joke. The kind white folks tell when the mill closes down and they're looking for a little comfort somewhere. The kind colored folks tell on themselves when the rain doesn't come, or comes for weeks, and they're looking for a little comfort somehow.

A good white farmer promised freedom and a piece of bottom land to his slave if he would perform some very difficult chores. When the slave completed the work, he asked the farmer to keep his end of the bargain. Freedom was easy—the farmer had no objection to that. But he didn't want to give up any land. So he told the slave that he was very sorry that he had to give him valley land. He had hoped to give him a piece of the Bottom. The slave blinked and said he thought valley land was bottom land. The master said, "Oh, no! See those hills? That's bottom land, rich and fertile."

"But it's high up in the hills," said the slave.

"High up from us," said the master, "but when God looks down, it's the bottom. That's why we call it so. It's the bottom of heaven—best land there is."

So the slave pressed his master to try to get him some. He preferred it to the valley. And it was done. The nigger got the hilly land, where planting was backbreaking, where the soil slid down and washed away the seeds, and where the wind lingered all through the winter.

Which accounted for the fact that white people lived on the rich valley floor in that little river town in Ohio, and the blacks populated the hills above it, taking small consolation in the fact that every day they could literally look down on the white folks.

Still, it was lovely up in the Bottom. After the town grew and the farm land turned into a village and the village into a town and the streets of Medallion were hot and dusty with progress, those heavy trees that sheltered the shacks up in the Bottom were wonderful to see. And the hunters who went there sometimes wondered in private if maybe the white farmer was right after all. Maybe it was the bottom of heaven.

The black people would have disagreed, but they had no time to think about it. They were mightily preoccupied with earthly things—and each other, wondering even as early as 1920 what Shadrack was all about, what that little girl Sula who grew into a woman in their town was all about, and what they themselves were all about, tucked up there in the Bottom.

1919

Except for World War II, nothing ever interfered with the celebration of National Suicide Day. It had taken place every January third since 1920, although Shadrack, its founder, was for many years the only celebrant. Blasted and permanently astonished by the events of 1917, he had returned to Medallion handsome but ravaged, and even the most fastidious people in the town sometimes caught themselves dreaming of what he must have been like a few years back before he went off to war. A young man of hardly twenty, his head full of nothing and his mouth re-calling the taste of lipstick, Shadrack had found himself in December, 1917, running with his comrades across a field in France. It was his first encounter with the enemy and he didn't know whether his company was running toward them or away. For several days they had been marching, keeping close to a stream that was frozen at its edges. At one point they crossed it, and no sooner had he stepped foot on the other side than the day was adangle with shouts and explosions. Shellfire was all around him, and though he knew that this was something called *it*, he could not muster up the proper feeling—the feeling that would accommodate *it*. He expected to be terrified or exhilarated—to feel *something* very strong. In fact, he felt

only the bite of a nail in his boot, which pierced the ball
of his foot whenever he came down on it. The day was
cold enough to make his breath visible, and he wondered
for a moment at the purity and whiteness of his own
breath among the dirty, gray explosions surrounding him.
He ran, bayonet fixed, deep in the great sweep of men
flying across this field. Wincing at the pain in his foot, he
turned his head a little to the right and saw the face of a
soldier near him fly off. Before he could register shock, the
rest of the soldier's head disappeared under the inverted
soup bowl of his helmet. But stubbornly, taking no direction from the brain, the body of the headless soldier ran
on, with energy and grace, ignoring altogether the drip
and slide of brain tissue down its back.

When Shadrack opened his eyes he was propped up in a
small bed. Before him on a tray was a large tin plate
divided into three triangles. In one triangle was rice, in
another meat, and in the third stewed tomatoes. A small
round depression held a cup of whitish liquid. Shadrack
stared at the soft colors that filled these triangles: the
lumpy whiteness of rice, the quivering blood tomatoes, the
grayish-brown meat. All their repugnance was contained
in the neat balance of the triangles—a balance that soothed
him, transferred some of its equilibrium to him. Thus re-
assured that the white, the red and the brown would stay
where they were—would not explode or burst forth from
their restricted zones—he suddenly felt hungry and looked
around for his hands. His glance was cautious at first, for he
had to be very careful—anything could be anywhere. Then

he noticed two lumps beneath the beige blanket on either side of his hips. With extreme care he lifted one arm and was relieved to find his hand attached to his wrist. He tried the other and found it also. Slowly he directed one hand toward the cup and, just as he was about to spread his fingers, they began to grow in higgledy-piggledy fashion like Jack's beanstalk all over the tray and the bed. With a shriek he closed his eyes and thrust his huge growing hands under the covers. Once out of sight they seemed to shrink back to their normal size. But the yell had brought a male nurse.

"Private? We're not going to have any trouble today, are we? Are we, Private?"

Shadrack looked up at a balding man dressed in a green-cotton jacket and trousers. His hair was parted low on the right side so that some twenty or thirty yellow hairs could discreetly cover the nakedness of his head.

"Come on. Pick up that spoon. Pick it up, Private. Nobody is going to feed you forever."

Sweat slid from Shadrack's armpits down his sides. He could not bear to see his hands grow again and he was frightened of the voice in the apple-green suit.

"Pick it up, I said. There's no point to this . . ." The nurse reached under the cover for Shadrack's wrist to pull out the monstrous hand. Shadrack jerked it back and overturned the tray. In panic he raised himself to his knees and tried to fling off and away his terrible fingers, but succeeded only in knocking the nurse into the next bed.

When they bound Shadrack into a straitjacket, he was both relieved and grateful, for his hands were at last hidden and confined to whatever size they had attained.

Laced and silent in his small bed, he tried to tie the loose cords in his mind. He wanted desperately to see his own face and connect it with the word "private"—the word the nurse (and the others who helped bind him) had called him. "Private" he thought was something secret, and he wondered why they looked at him and called him a secret. Still, if his hands behaved as they had done, what might he expect from his face? The fear and longing were too much for him, so he began to think of other things. That is, he let his mind slip into whatever cave mouths of memory it chose.

He saw a window that looked out on a river which he knew was full of fish. Someone was speaking softly just outside the door . . .

Shadrack's earlier violence had coincided with a memorandum from the hospital executive staff in reference to the distribution of patients in high-risk areas. There was clearly a demand for space. The priority or the violence earned Shadrack his release, $217 in cash, a full suit of clothes and copies of very official-looking papers.

When he stepped out of the hospital door the grounds overwhelmed him: the cropped shrubbery, the edged lawns, the undeviating walks. Shadrack looked at the cement stretches: each one leading clearheadedly to some presumably desirable destination. There were no fences, no warnings, no obstacles at all between concrete and green grass, so one could easily ignore the tidy sweep of stone and cut out in another direction—a direction of one's own. Shadrack stood at the foot of the hospital steps watching the heads of trees tossing ruefully but harmlessly, since their trunks were rooted too deeply in the earth to threaten him. Only the walks made him uneasy. He shifted his weight, wondering how he could get to the gate without stepping on the concrete. While plotting his course—where he would have to leap, where to skirt a clump of bushes—a loud guffaw startled him. Two men were going up the steps. Then he noticed that there were many people about, and that he was just now seeing them, or else they had just materialized. They were thin slips, like paper dolls floating down the walks. Some were seated in chairs with wheels, propelled by other paper figures from behind. All seemed to be smoking, and their arms and legs curved in the breeze. A good high wind would pull them up and away and they would land perhaps among the tops of the trees.

Shadrack took the plunge. Four steps and he was on the grass heading for the gate. He kept his head down to avoid seeing the paper people swerving and bending here and there, and he lost his way. When he looked up, he was standing by a low red building separated from the main building by a covered walkway. From somewhere came a sweetish smell which reminded him of something painful. He looked around for the gate and saw that he had gone directly away from it in his complicated journey over the grass. Just to the left of the low building was a graveled driveway that appeared to lead outside the grounds. He trotted quickly to it and left, at last, a haven of more than a year, only eight days of which he fully recollected.

Once on the road, he headed west. The long stay in the

hospital had left him weak—too weak to walk steadily on the gravel shoulders of the road. He shuffled, grew dizzy, stopped for breath, started again, stumbling and sweating but refusing to wipe his temples, still afraid to look at his hands. Passengers in dark, square cars shuttered their eyes at what they took to be a drunken man.

The sun was already directly over his head when he came to a town. A few blocks of shaded streets and he was already at its heart—a pretty, quietly regulated downtown.

Exhausted, his feet clotted with pain, he sat down at the curbside to take off his shoes. He closed his eyes to avoid seeing his hands and fumbled with the laces of the heavy high-topped shoes. The nurse had tied them into a double knot, the way one does for children, and Shadrack, long unaccustomed to the manipulation of intricate things, could not get them loose. Uncoordinated, his fingernails tore away at the knots. He fought a rising hysteria that was not merely anxiety to free his aching feet; his very life depended on the release of the knots. Suddenly without raising his eyelids, he began to cry. Twenty-two years old, weak, hot, frightened, not daring to acknowledge the fact that he didn't even know who or what he was . . . with no past, no language, no tribe, no source, no address book, no comb, no pencil, no clock, no pocket handkerchief, no rug, no bed, no can opener, no faded postcard, no soap, no key, no tobacco pouch, no soiled underwear and nothing nothing nothing to do . . . he was sure of one thing only: the unchecked monstrosity of his hands. He cried soundlessly at the curbside of a small Midwestern town wondering where the window was, and the river, and the soft voices just outside the door . . .

Through his tears he saw the fingers joining the laces, tentatively at first, then rapidly. The four fingers of each hand fused into the fabric, knotted themselves and zigzagged in and out of the tiny eyeholes.

By the time the police drove up, Shadrack was suffering from a blinding headache, which was not abated by the comfort he felt when the policemen pulled his hands away from what he thought was a permanent entanglement with his shoelaces. They took him to jail, booked him for vagrancy and intoxication, and locked him in a cell. Lying on a cot, Shadrack could only stare helplessly at the wall, so paralyzing was the pain in his head. He lay in this agony for a long while and then realized he was staring at the painted-over letters of a command to fuck himself. He studied the phrase as the pain in his head subsided.

Like moonlight stealing under a window shade an idea insinuated itself: his earlier desire to see his own face. He looked for a mirror; there was none. Finally, keeping his hands carefully behind his back he made his way to the toilet bowl and peeped in. The water was unevenly lit by the sun so he could make nothing out. Returning to his cot he took the blanket and covered his head, rendering the water dark enough to see his reflection. There in the toilet water he saw a grave black face. A black so definite, so unequivocal, it astonished him. He had been harboring a skittish apprehension that he was not real—that he didn't exist at all. But when the blackness greeted him with its indisputable presence, he wanted nothing more. In his joy he took the risk of letting one edge of the blanket drop and glanced at his hands. They were still. Courteously still.

Shadrack rose and returned to the cot, where he fell into

the first sleep of his new life. A sleep deeper than the hospital drugs; deeper than the pits of plums, steadier than the condor's wing; more tranquil than the curve of eggs.

The sheriff looked through the bars at the young man with the matted hair. He had read through his prisoner's papers and hailed a farmer. When Shadrack awoke, the sheriff handed him back his papers and escorted him to the back of a wagon. Shadrack got in and in less than three hours he was back in Medallion, for he had been only twenty-two miles from his window, his river, and his soft voices just outside the door.

In the back of the wagon, supported by sacks of squash and hills of pumpkins, Shadrack began a struggle that was to last for twelve days, a struggle to order and focus experience. It had to do with making a place for fear as a way of controlling it. He knew the smell of death and was terrified of it, for he could not anticipate it. It was not death or dying that frightened him, but the unexpectedness of both. In sorting it all out, he hit on the notion that if one day a year were devoted to it, everybody could get it out of the way and the rest of the year would be safe and free. In this manner he instituted National Suicide Day.

On the third day of the new year, he walked through the Bottom down Carpenter's Road with a cowbell and a hangman's rope calling the people together. Telling them that this was their only chance to kill themselves or each other.

At first the people in the town were frightened; they

knew Shadrack was crazy but that did not mean that he didn't have any sense or, even more important, that he had no power. His eyes were so wild, his hair so long and matted, his voice was so full of authority and thunder that he caused panic on the first, or Charter, National Suicide Day in 1920. The next one, in 1921, was less frightening but still worrisome. The people had seen him a year now in between. He lived in a shack on the riverbank that had once belonged to his grandfather long time dead. On Tuesday and Friday he sold the fish he had caught that morning, the rest of the week he was drunk, loud, obscene, funny and outrageous. But he never touched anybody, never fought, never caressed. Once the people understood the boundaries and nature of his madness, they could fit him, so to speak, into the scheme of things.

Then, on subsequent National Suicide Days, the grown people looked out from behind curtains as he rang his bell; a few stragglers increased their speed, and little children screamed and ran. The tetter heads tried goading him (although he was only four or five years older then they) but not for long, for his curses were stingingly personal.

As time went along, the people took less notice of these January thirds, or rather they thought they did, thought they had no attitudes or feelings one way or another about Shadrack's annual solitary parade. In fact they had simply stopped remarking on the holiday because they had absorbed it into their thoughts, into their language, into their lives.

Someone said to a friend, "You sure was a long time delivering that baby. How long was you in labor?"

And the friend answered, "'Bout three days. The pains

started on Suicide Day and kept up till the following Sunday. Was borned on Sunday. All my boys is Sunday boys."

Some lover said to his bride-to-be, "Let's do it after New Years, 'stead of before. I get paid New Year's Eve."

And his sweetheart answered, "OK, but make sure it ain't on Suicide Day. I ain't 'bout to be listening to no cowbells whilst the weddin's going on."

Somebody's grandmother said her hens always started a laying of double yolks right after Suicide Day.

Then Reverend Deal took it up, saying the same folks who had sense enough to avoid Shadrack's call were the ones who insisted on drinking themselves to death or womanizing themselves to death. "May's well go on with Shad and save the Lamb the trouble of redemption."

Easily, quietly, Suicide Day became a part of the fabric of life up in the Bottom of Medallion, Ohio.

1920

It had to be as far away from the Sundown House as possible. And her grandmother's middle-aged nephew who lived in a Northern town called Medallion was the one chance she had to make sure it would be. The red shutters had haunted both Helene Sabat and her grandmother for sixteen years. Helene was born behind those shutters, daughter of a Creole whore who worked there. The grandmother took Helene away from the soft lights and flowered carpets of the Sundown House and raised her under the dolesome eyes of a multicolored Virgin Mary, counseling her to be constantly on guard for any sign of her mother's wild blood.

So when Wiley Wright came to visit his Great Aunt Cecile in New Orleans, his enchantment with the pretty Helene became a marriage proposal—under the pressure of both women. He was a seaman (or rather a lakeman, for he was a ship's cook on one of the Great Lakes lines), in port only three days out of every sixteen.

He took his bride to his home in Medallion and put her in a lovely house with a brick porch and real lace curtains at the window. His long absences were quite bearable for Helene Wright, especially when, after some nine years of marriage, her daughter was born.

Her daughter was more comfort and purpose than she had ever hoped to find in this life. She rose grandly to the occasion of motherhood—grateful, deep down in her heart, that the child had not inherited the great beauty that was hers: that her skin had dusk in it, that her lashes were substantial but not undignified in their length, that she had taken the broad flat nose of Wiley (although Helene expected to improve it somewhat) and his generous lips.

Under Helene's hand the girl became obedient and polite. Any enthusiasms that little Nel showed were calmed by the mother until she drove her daughter's imagination underground.

Helene Wright was an impressive woman, at least in Medallion she was. Heavy hair in a bun, dark eyes arched in a perpetual query about other people's manners. A woman who won all social battles with presence and a conviction of the legitimacy of her authority. Since there was no Catholic church in Medallion then, she joined the most conservative black church. And held sway. It was Helene who never turned her head in church when latecomers arrived; Helene who established the practice of seasonal altar flowers; Helene who introduced the giving of banquets of welcome to returning Negro veterans. She lost only one battle—the pronunciation of her name. The people in the Bottom refused to say Helene. They called her Helen Wright and left it at that.

All in all her life was a satisfactory one. She loved her house and enjoyed manipulating her daughter and her husband. She would sigh sometimes just before falling asleep, thinking that she had indeed come far enough away from the Sundown House.

So it was with extremely mixed emotions that she read a letter from Mr. Henri Martin describing the illness of her grandmother, and suggesting she come down right away. She didn't want to go, but could not bring herself to ignore the silent plea of the woman who had rescued her.

It was November. November, 1920. Even in Medallion there was a victorious swagger in the legs of white men and a dull-eyed excitement in the eyes of colored veterans.

Helene thought about the trip South with heavy misgiving but decided that she had the best protection: her manner and her bearing, to which she would add a beautiful dress. She bought some deep-brown wool and three-fourths of a yard of matching velvet. Out of this she made herself a heavy but elegant dress with velvet collar and pockets.

Nel watched her mother cutting the pattern from newspapers and moving her eyes rapidly from a magazine model to her own hands. She watched her turn up the kerosene lamp at sunset to sew far into the night.

The day they were ready, Helene cooked a smoked ham, left a note for her lake-bound husband, in case he docked early, and walked head high and arms stiff with luggage ahead of her daughter to the train depot.

It was a longer walk than she remembered, and they saw the train steaming up just as they turned the corner. They ran along the track looking for the coach pointed out to them by the colored porter. Even at that they made a mistake. Helene and her daughter entered a coach peopled by some twenty white men and women. Rather than go back and down the three wooden steps again, Helene decided to spare herself some embarrassment and walk on through to the colored car. She carried two pieces of luggage and a string purse; her daughter carried a covered basket of food.

As they opened the door marked COLORED ONLY, they saw a white conductor coming toward them. It was a chilly day but a light skim of sweat glistened on the woman's face as she and the little girl struggled to hold the door open, hang on to their luggage and enter all at once. The conductor let his eyes travel over the pale yellow woman and then stuck his little finger into his ear, jiggling it free of wax. "What you think you doin', gal?"

Helene looked up at him.

So soon. So soon. She hadn't even begun the trip back. Back to her grandmother's house in the city where the red shutters glowed, and already she had been called "gal." All the old vulnerabilities, all the old fears of being somehow flawed gathered in her stomach and made her hands tremble. She had heard only that one word; it dangled above her wide-brimmed hat, which had slipped, in her exertion, from its carefully leveled placement and was now tilted in a bit of a jaunt over her eye.

Thinking he wanted her tickets, she quickly dropped both the cowhide suitcase and the straw one in order to search for them in her purse. An eagerness to please and an apology for living met in her voice. "I have them. Right here somewhere, sir..."

The conductor looked at the bit of wax his fingernail

had retrieved. "What was you doin' back in there? What was you doin' in that coach yonder?"

Helene licked her lips. "Oh . . . I . . ." Her glance moved beyond the white man's face to the passengers seated behind him. Four or five black faces were watching, two belonging to soldiers still in their shit-colored uniforms and peaked caps. She saw their closed faces, their locked eyes, and turned for compassion to the gray eyes of the conductor.

"We made a mistake, sir. You see, there wasn't no sign. We just got in the wrong car, that's all. Sir."

"We don't 'low no mistakes on this train. Now git your butt on in there."

He stood there staring at her until she realized that he wanted her to move aside. Pulling Nel by the arm, she pressed herself and her daughter into the foot space in front of a wooden seat. Then, for no earthly reason, at least no reason that anybody could understand, certainly no reason that Nel understood then or later, she smiled. Like a street pup that wags its tail at the very doorjamb of the butcher shop he has been kicked away from only moments before, Helene smiled. Smiled dazzlingly and coquettishly at the salmon-colored face of the conductor.

Nel looked away from the flash of pretty teeth to the other passengers. The two black soldiers, who had been watching the scene with what appeared to be indifference, now looked stricken. Behind Nel was the bright and blazing light of her mother's smile; before her the midnight eyes of the soldiers. She saw the muscles of their faces tighten, a movement under the skin from blood to marble. No change in the expression of the eyes, but a hard wetness that veiled them as they looked at the stretch of her mother's foolish smile.

As the door slammed on the conductor's exit, Helene walked down the aisle to a seat. She looked about for a second to see whether any of the men would help her put the suitcases in the overhead rack. Not a man moved. Helene sat down, fussily, her back toward the men. Nel sat opposite, facing both her mother and the soldiers, neither of whom she could look at. She felt both pleased and ashamed to sense that these men, unlike her father, who worshiped his graceful, beautiful wife, were bubbling with a hatred for her mother that had not been there in the beginning but had been born with the dazzling smile. In the silence that preceded the train's heave, she looked deeply at the folds of her mother's dress. There in the fall of the heavy brown wool she held her eyes. She could not risk letting them travel upward for fear of seeing that the hooks and eyes in the placket of the dress had come undone and exposed the custard-colored skin underneath. She stared at the hem, wanting to believe in its weight but knowing that custard was all that it hid. If this tall, proud woman, this woman who was very particular about her friends, who slipped into church with unequaled elegance, who could quell a roustabout with a look, if *she* were really custard, then there was a chance that Nel was too.

It was on that train, shuffling toward Cincinnati, that she resolved to be on guard—always. She wanted to make certain that no man ever looked at her that way. That no midnight eyes or marbled flesh would ever accost her and turn her into jelly.

For two days they rode; two days of watching sleet turn to rain, turn to purple sunsets, and one night knotted on the wooden seats (their heads on folded coats), trying not to hear the snoring soldiers. When they changed trains in Birmingham for the last leg of the trip, they discovered what luxury they had been in through Kentucky and Tennessee, where the rest stops had all had colored toilets. After Birmingham there were none. Helene's face was drawn with the need to relieve herself, and so intense was her distress she finally brought herself to speak about her problem to a black woman with four children who had got on in Tuscaloosa.

"Is there somewhere we can go to use the restroom?"

The woman looked up at her and seemed not to understand. "Ma'am?" Her eyes fastened on the thick velvet collar, the fair skin, the high-tone voice.

"The restroom," Helene repeated. Then, in a whisper, "The toilet."

The woman pointed out the window and said, "Yes, ma'am. Yonder."

Helene looked out of the window halfway expecting to see a comfort station in the distance; instead she saw gray-green trees leaning over tangled grass. "Where?"

"Yonder," the woman said. "Meridian. We be pullin' in direc'lin." Then she smiled sympathetically and asked, "Kin you make it?"

Helene nodded and went back to her seat trying to think of other things—for the surest way to have an accident would be to remember her full bladder.

At Meridian the women got out with their children. While Helene looked about the tiny stationhouse for a door that said COLORED WOMEN, the other woman stalked off to a field of high grass on the far side of the track. Some white men were leaning on the railing in front of the stationhouse. It was not only their tongues curling around toothpicks that kept Helene from asking information of them. She looked around for the other woman and, seeing just the top of her head rag in the grass, slowly realized where "yonder" was. All of them, the fat woman and her four children, three boys and a girl, Helene and her daughter, squatted there in the four o'clock Meridian sun. They did it again in Ellisville, again in Hattiesburg, and by the time they reached Slidell, not too far from Lake Pontchartrain, Helene could not only fold leaves as well as the fat woman, she never felt a stir as she passed the muddy eyes of the men who stood like wrecked Dorics under the station roofs of those towns.

The lift in spirit that such an accomplishment produced in her quickly disappeared when the train finally pulled into New Orleans.

Cecile Sabat's house leaned between two others just like it on Elysian Fields. A Frenchified shotgun house, it sported a magnificent garden in the back and a tiny wrought-iron fence in the front. On the door hung a black crepe wreath with purple ribbon. They were too late. Helene reached up to touch the ribbon, hesitated, and knocked. A man in a collarless shirt opened the door. Helene identified herself and he said he was Henri Martin and that he was there for the settin'-up. They stepped into the house. The

Virgin Mary clasped her hands in front of her neck three times in the front room and once in the bedroom where Cecile's body lay. The old woman had died without seeing or blessing her granddaughter.

No one other than Mr. Martin seemed to be in the house, but a sweet odor as of gardenias told them that someone else had been. Blotting her lashes with a white handkerchief, Helene walked through the kitchen to the back bedroom where she had slept for sixteen years. Nel trotted along behind, enchanted with the smell, the candles and the strangeness. When Helene bent to loosen the ribbons of Nel's hat, a woman in a yellow dress came out of the garden and onto the back porch that opened into the bedroom. The two women looked at each other. There was no recognition in the eyes of either. Then Helene said, "This is your . . . grandmother, Nel." Nel looked at her mother and then quickly back at the door they had just come out of.

"No. That was your great-grandmother. This is your grandmother. My . . . mother."

Before the child could think, her words were hanging in the gardenia air. "But she looks so young."

The woman in the canary-yellow dress laughed and said she was forty-eight, "an old forty-eight."

Then it was she who carried the gardenia smell. This tiny woman with the softness and glare of a canary. In that somber house that held four Virgin Marys, where death sighed in every corner and candles sputtered, the gardenia smell and canary-yellow dress emphasized the funeral atmosphere surrounding them.

The woman smiled, glanced in the mirror and said, throwing her voice toward Helene, "That your only one?"

"Yes," said Helene.

"Pretty. A lot like you."

"Yes. Well. She's ten now."

"Ten? Vrai? Small for her age, no?"

Helene shrugged and looked at her daughter's questioning eyes. The woman in the yellow dress leaned forward. "Come. Come, chere."

Helene interrupted. "We have to get cleaned up. We been three days on the train with no chance to wash or . . ."

"Comment t'appelle?"

"She doesn't talk Creole."

"Then you ask her."

"She wants to know your name, honey."

With her head pressed into her mother's heavy brown dress, Nel told her and then asked, "What's yours?"

"Mine's Rochelle. Well. I must be going on." She moved closer to the mirror and stood there sweeping hair up from her neck back into its halo-like roll, and wetting with spit the ringlets that fell over her ears. "I been here, you know, most of the day. She pass on yesterday. The funeral tomorrow. Henri takin' care." She struck a match, blew it out and darkened her eyebrows with the burnt head. All the while Helene and Nel watched her. The one in a rage at the folded leaves she had endured, the wooden benches she had slept on, all to miss seeing her grandmother and seeing instead that painted canary who never said a word of greeting or affection or . . .

Rochelle continued. "I don't know what happen to de

house. Long time paid for. You be thinkin' on it? Oui?"
Her newly darkened eyebrows queried Helene.

"Oui." Helene's voice was chilly. "I be thinkin' on it."

"Oh, well. Not for me to say . . ."

Suddenly she swept around and hugged Nel—a quick
embrace tighter and harder than one would have imagined
her thin soft arms capable of.

"'Voir! 'Voir!" and she was gone.

In the kitchen, being soaped head to toe by her mother,
Nel ventured an observation. "She smelled so nice. And her
skin was so soft."

Helene rinsed the cloth. "Much handled things are always soft."

"What does 'vwah' mean?"

"I don't know," her mother said. "I don't talk Creole."
She gazed at her daughter's wet buttocks. "And neither do
you."

When they got back to Medallion and into the quiet
house they saw the note exactly where they had left it
and the ham dried out in the icebox.

"Lord, I've never been so glad to see this place. But
look at the dust. Get the rags, Nel. Oh, never mind. Let's
breathe awhile first. Lord, I never thought I'd get back
here safe and sound. Whoo. Well, it's over. Good and
over. Praise His name. Look at that. I told that old fool
not to deliver any milk and there's the can curdled to beat
all. What gets into people? I told him not to. Well, I got
other things to worry 'bout. Got to get a fire started. I left
it ready so I wouldn't have to do nothin' but light it. Lord,

it's cold. Don't just sit there, honey. You could be pulling your nose . . ."

Nel sat on the red-velvet sofa listening to her mother but remembering the smell and the tight, tight hug of the woman in yellow who rubbed burned matches over her eyes.

Late that night after the fire was made, the cold supper eaten, the surface dust removed, Nel lay in bed thinking of her trip. She remembered clearly the urine running down and into her stockings until she learned how to squat properly; the disgust on the face of the dead woman and the sound of the funeral drums. It had been an exhilarating trip but a fearful one. She had been frightened of the soldiers' eyes on the train, the black wreath on the door, the custard pudding she believed lurked under her mother's heavy dress, the feel of unknown streets and unknown people. But she had gone on a real trip, and now she was different. She got out of bed and lit the lamp to look in the mirror. There was her face, plain brown eyes, three braids and the nose her mother hated. She looked for a long time and suddenly a shiver ran through her.

"I'm me," she whispered. "Me."

Nel didn't know quite what she meant, but on the other hand she knew exactly what she meant.

"I'm me. I'm not their daughter. I'm not Nel. I'm me. Me."

Each time she said the word *me* there was a gathering in her like power, like joy, like fear. Back in bed with her discovery, she stared out the window at the dark leaves of the horse chestnut.

"Me," she murmured. And then, sinking deeper into the

quilts, "I want . . . I want to be . . . wonderful. Oh, Jesus, make me wonderful."

The many experiences of her trip crowded in on her. She slept. It was the last as well as the first time she was ever to leave Medallion.

For days afterward she imagined other trips she would take, alone though, to faraway places. Contemplating them was delicious. Leaving Medallion would be her goal. But that was before she met Sula, the girl she had seen for five years at Garfield Primary but never played with, never knew, because her mother said that Sula's mother was sooty. The trip, perhaps, or her new found me-ness, gave her the strength to cultivate a friend in spite of her mother.

When Sula first visited the Wright house, Helene's curdled scorn turned to butter. Her daughter's friend seemed to have none of the mother's slackness. Nel, who regarded the oppressive neatness of her home with dread, felt comfortable in it with Sula, who loved it and would sit on the red-velvet sofa for ten to twenty minutes at a time—still as dawn. As for Nel, she preferred Sula's woolly house, where a pot of something was always cooking on the stove; where the mother, Hannah, never scolded or gave directions; where all sorts of people dropped in; where newspapers were stacked in the hallway, and dirty dishes left for hours at a time in the sink, and where a one-legged grandmother named Eva handed you goobers from deep inside her pockets or read you a dream.

1921

Sula Peace lived in a house of many rooms that had been built over a period of five years to the specifications of its owner, who kept on adding things: more stairways—there were three sets to the second floor—more rooms, doors and stoops. There were rooms that had three doors, others that opened out on the porch only and were inaccessible from any other part of the house; others that you could get to only by going through somebody's bedroom. The creator and sovereign of this enormous house with the four sickle-pear trees in the front yard and the single elm in the back yard was Eva Peace, who sat in a wagon on the third floor directing the lives of her children, friends, strays, and a constant stream of boarders. Fewer than nine people in the town remembered when Eva had two legs, and her oldest child, Hannah, was not one of them. Unless Eva herself introduced the subject, no one ever spoke of her disability; they pretended to ignore it, unless, in some mood of fancy, she began some fearful story about it—generally to entertain children. How the leg got up by itself one day and walked on off. How she hobbled after it but it ran too fast. Or how she had a corn on her toe and it just grew and grew and grew until her whole foot was a corn and then it traveled on up her leg and wouldn't stop growing until she put a red rag at the top but by that time it was already at her knee.

Somebody said Eva stuck it under a train and made them pay off. Another said she sold it to a hospital for $10,000—at which Mr. Reed opened his eyes and asked, "Nigger gal legs goin' for $10,000 a *piece?*" as though he could understand $10,000 a *pair*—but for *one?*

Whatever the fate of her lost leg, the remaining one was magnificent. It was stockinged and shod at all times and in all weather. Once in a while she got a felt slipper for Christmas or her birthday, but they soon disappeared, for Eva always wore a black laced-up shoe that came well above her ankle. Nor did she wear overlong dresses to disguise the empty place on her left side. Her dresses were mid-calf so that her one glamorous leg was always in view as well as the long fall of space below her left thigh. One of her men friends had fashioned a kind of wheelchair for her: a rocking-chair top fitted into a large child's wagon. In this contraption she wheeled around the room, from bedside to dresser to the balcony that opened out the north side of her room or to the window that looked out on the back yard. The wagon was so low that children who spoke to her standing up were eye level with her, and adults, standing or sitting, had to look down at her. But they didn't know it. They all had the impression that they were looking up at her, up into the open distances of her eyes, up into the soft black of her nostrils and up at the crest of her chin.

Eva had married a man named BoyBoy and had three

children: Hannah, the eldest, and Eva, whom she named after herself but called Pearl, and a son named Ralph, whom she called Plum.

After five years of a sad and disgruntled marriage Boy-Boy took off. During the time they were together he was very much preoccupied with other women and not home much. He did whatever he could that he liked, and he liked womanizing best, drinking second, and abusing Eva third. When he left in November, Eva had $1.65, five eggs, three beets and no idea of what or how to feel. The children needed her; she needed money, and needed to get on with her life. But the demands of feeding her three children were so acute she had to postpone her anger for two years until she had both the time and the energy for it. She was confused and desperately hungry. There were very few black families in those low hills then. The Suggs, who lived two hundred yards down the road, brought her a warm bowl of peas, as soon as they found out, and a plate of cold bread. She thanked them and asked if they had a little milk for the older ones. They said no, but Mrs. Jackson, they knew, had a cow still giving. Eva took a bucket over and Mrs. Jackson told her to come back and fill it up in the morning, because the evening milking had already been done. In this way, things went on until near December. People were very willing to help, but Eva felt she would soon run her welcome out; winters were hard and her neighbors were not that much better off. She would lie in bed with the baby boy, the two girls wrapped in quilts on the floor, thinking. The oldest child,

Hannah, was five and too young to take care of the baby alone, and any housework Eva could find would keep her away from them from five thirty or earlier in the morning until dark—way past eight. The white people in the valley weren't rich enough then to want maids; they were small farmers and tradesmen and wanted hard-labor help if anything. She thought also of returning to some of her people in Virginia, but to come home dragging three young ones would have to be a step one rung before death for Eva. She would have to scrounge around and beg through the winter, until her baby was at least nine months old, then she could plant and maybe hire herself out to valley farms to weed or sow or feed stock until something steadier came along at harvest time. She thought she had probably been a fool to let BoyBoy haul her away from her people, but it had seemed so right at the time. He worked for a white carpenter and toolsmith who insisted on BoyBoy's accompanying him when he went West and set up in a squinchy little town called Medallion. BoyBoy brought his new wife and built them a one-room cabin sixty feet back from the road that wound up out of the valley, on up into the hills and was named for the man he worked for. They lived there a year before they had an outhouse.

Sometime before the middle of December, the baby, Plum, stopped having bowel movements. Eva massaged his stomach and gave him warm water. Something must be wrong with my milk, she thought. Mrs. Suggs gave her castor oil, but even that didn't work. He cried and fought so they couldn't get much down his throat anyway. He seemed in great pain and his shrieks were pitched high in outrage and suffering. At one point, maddened by his own crying, he gagged, choked and looked as though he was strangling to death. Eva rushed to him and kicked over the earthen slop jar, washing a small area of the floor with the child's urine. She managed to soothe him, but when he took up the cry again late that night, she resolved to end his misery once and for all. She wrapped him in blankets, ran her finger around the crevices and sides of the lard can and stumbled to the outhouse with him. Deep in its darkness and freezing stench she squatted down, turned the baby over on her knees, exposed his buttocks and shoved the last bit of food she had in the world (besides three beets) up his ass. Softening the insertion with the dab of lard, she probed with her middle finger to loosen his bowels. Her fingernail snagged what felt like a pebble; she pulled it out and others followed. Plum stopped crying as the black hard stools ricocheted onto the frozen ground. And now that it was over, Eva squatted there wondering why she had come all the way out there to free his stools, and what was she doing down on her haunches with her beloved baby boy warmed by her body in the almost total darkness, her shins and teeth freezing, her nostrils assailed. She shook her head as though to juggle her brains around, then said aloud, "Uh uh. Nooo." Thereupon she returned to the house and her bed. As the grateful Plum slept, the silence allowed her to think.

Two days later she left all of her children with Mrs. Suggs, saying she would be back the next day.

Eighteen months later she swept down from a wagon with two crutches, a new black pocketbook, and one leg. First she reclaimed her children, next she gave the surprised Mrs. Suggs a ten-dollar bill, later she started building a house on Carpenter's Road, sixty feet from BoyBoy's one-room cabin, which she rented out.

When Plum was three years old, BoyBoy came back to town and paid her a visit. When Eva got the word that he was on his way, she made some lemonade. She had no idea what she would do or feel during that encounter. Would she cry, cut his throat, beg him to make love to her? She couldn't imagine. So she just waited to see. She stirred lemonade in a green pitcher and waited.

BoyBoy danced up the steps and knocked on the door.

"Come on in," she hollered.

He opened the door and stood smiling, a picture of prosperity and good will. His shoes were a shiny orange, and he had on a citified straw hat, a light-blue suit, and a cat's-head stickpin in his tie. Eva smiled and told him to sit himself down. He smiled too.

"How you been, girl?"

"Pretty fair. What you know good?" When she heard those words come out of her own mouth she knew that their conversation would start off polite. Although it remained to be seen whether she would still run the ice pick through the cat's-head pin.

"Have some lemonade."

"Don't mind if I do." He swept his hat off with a satisfied gesture. His nails were long and shiny. "Sho is hot, and I been runnin' around all day."

Eva looked out of the screen door and saw a woman in a pea-green dress leaning on the smallest pear tree.

Glancing back at him, she was reminded of Plum's face when he managed to get the meat out of a walnut all by himself. Eva smiled again, and poured the lemonade.

Their conversation was easy: she catching him up on all the gossip, he asking about this one and that one, and like everybody else avoiding any reference to her leg. It was like talking to somebody's cousin who just stopped by to say howdy before getting on back to wherever he came from. BoyBoy didn't ask to see the children, and Eva didn't bring them into the conversation.

After a while he rose to go. Talking about his appointments and exuding an odor of new money and idleness, he danced down the steps and strutted toward the pea-green dress. Eva watched. She looked at the back of his neck and the set of his shoulders. Underneath all of that shine she saw defeat in the stalk of his neck and the curious tight way he held his shoulders. But still she was not sure what she felt. Then he leaned forward and whispered into the ear of the woman in the green dress. She was still for a moment and then threw back her head and laughed. A high-pitched big-city laugh that reminded Eva of Chicago. It hit her like a sledge hammer, and it was then that she knew what to feel. A liquid trail of hate flooded her chest.

Knowing that she would hate him long and well filled her with pleasant anticipation, like when you know you are going to fall in love with someone and you wait for the happy signs. Hating BoyBoy, she could get on with it, and have the safety, the thrill, the consistency of that hatred as long as she wanted or needed it to define and strengthen her or protect her from routine vulnerabilities.

(Once when Hannah accused her of hating colored people, Eva said she only hated one, Hannah's father BoyBoy, and it was hating him that kept her alive and happy.)

Happy or not, after BoyBoy's visit she began her retreat to her bedroom, leaving the bottom of the house more and more to those who lived there: cousins who were passing through, stray folks, and the many, many newly married couples she let rooms to with housekeeping privileges, and after 1910 she didn't willingly set foot on the stairs but once and that was to light a fire, the smoke of which was in her hair for years.

Among the tenants in that big old house were the children Eva took in. Operating on a private scheme of preference and prejudice, she sent off for children she had seen from the balcony of her bedroom or whose circumstances she had heard about from the gossipy old men who came to play checkers or read the *Courier*, or write her number. In 1921, when her granddaughter Sula was eleven, Eva had three such children. They came with woolen caps and names given to them by their mothers, or grandmothers, or somebody's best friend. Eva snatched the caps off their heads and ignored their names. She looked at the first child closely, his wrists, the shape of his head and the temperament that showed in his eyes and said, "Well. Look at Dewey. My my mymymy." When later that same year she sent for a child who kept falling down off the porch across the street, she said the same thing. Somebody said, "But, Miss Eva, you calls the other one Dewey."

"So? This here's another one."

When the third one was brought and Eva said
"Dewey" again, everybody thought she had simply run
out of names or that her faculties had finally softened.

"How is anybody going to tell them apart?" Hannah
asked her.

"What you need to tell them apart for? They's all
deweys."

When Hannah asked the question it didn't sound very
bright, because each dewey was markedly different from
the other two. Dewey one was a deeply black boy with a
beautiful head and the golden eyes of chronic jaundice.
Dewey two was light-skinned with freckles everywhere
and a head of tight red hair. Dewey three was half Mexi-
can with chocolate skin and black bangs. Besides, they
were one and two years apart in age. It was Eva saying
things like, "Send one of them deweys out to get me some
Garret, if they don't have Garret, get Buttercup," or,
"Tell them deweys to cut out that noise," or, "Come here,
you dewey you," and, "Send me a dewey," that gave
Hannah's question its weight.

Slowly each boy came out of whatever cocoon he was
in at the time his mother or somebody gave him away, and
accepted Eva's view, becoming in fact as well as in name
a dewey—joining with the other two to become a trinity
with a plural name . . . inseparable, loving nothing and no
one but themselves. When the handle from the icebox fell
off, all the deweys got whipped, and in dry-eyed silence
watched their own feet as they turned their behinds high
up into the air for the stroke. When the golden-eyed
dewey was ready for school he would not go without the
others. He was seven, freckled dewey was five, and Mexi-

can dewey was only four. Eva solved the problem by having them all sent off together. Mr. Buckland Reed said, "But one of them's only four."

"How you know? They all come here the same year," Eva said.

"But that one there was one year old when he came, and that was three years ago."

"You don't know how old he was when he come here and neither do the teacher. Send 'em."

The teacher was startled but not unbelieving, for she had long ago given up trying to fathom the ways of the colored people in town. So when Mrs. Reed said that their names were Dewey King, that they were cousins, and all were six years old, the teacher gave only a tiny sigh and wrote them in the record book for the first grade. She too thought she would have no problem distinguishing among them, because they looked nothing alike, but like everyone else before her, she gradually found that she could not tell one from the other. The deweys would not allow it. They got all mixed up in her head, and finally she could not literally believe her eyes. They spoke with one voice, thought with one mind, and maintained an annoying privacy. Stouthearted, surly, and wholly unpredictable, the deweys remained a mystery not only during all of their lives in Medallion but after as well.

The deweys came in 1921, but the year before Eva had given a small room off the kitchen to Tar Baby, a beautiful, slight, quiet man who never spoke above a whisper. Most people said he was half white, but Eva said he was all white. That she knew blood when she saw it, and he didn't have none. When he first came to Medallion, the people called him Pretty Johnnie, but Eva looked at his milky skin and cornsilk hair and out of a mixture of fun and meanness called him Tar Baby. He was a mountain boy who stayed to himself, bothering no one, intent solely on drinking himself to death. At first he worked in a poultry market, and after wringing the necks of chickens all day, he came home and drank until he slept. Later he began to miss days at work and frequently did not have his rent money. When he lost his job altogether, he would go out in the morning, scrounge around for money doing odd jobs, bumming or whatever, and come home to drink. Because he was no bother, ate little, required nothing, and was a lover of cheap wine, no one found him a nuisance. Besides, he frequently went to Wednesday-night prayer meetings and sang with the sweetest hill voice imaginable "In the Sweet By-and-By." He sent the deweys out for his liquor and spent most of his time in a heap on the floor or sitting in a chair staring at the wall.

Hannah worried about him a little, but only a very little. For it soon became clear that he simply wanted a place to die privately but not quite alone. No one thought of suggesting to him that he pull himself together or see a doctor or anything. Even the women at prayer meeting who cried when he sang "In the Sweet By-and-By" never tried to get him to participate in the church activities. They just listened to him sing, wept and thought very graphically of their own imminent deaths. The people either accepted his own evaluation of his life, or were indifferent to it. There was, however, a measure of contempt in their indifference, for they had little patience with people who took themselves that seriously. Seriously enough to try to die. And it was natural that he, after all, became the first one to join Shadrack—Tar Baby and the deweys—on National Suicide Day.

Under Eva's distant eye, and prey to her idiosyncrasies, her own children grew up stealthily: Pearl married at fourteen and moved to Flint, Michigan, from where she posted frail letters to her mother with two dollars folded into the writing paper. Sad little nonsense letters about minor troubles, her husband's job and who the children favored. Hannah married a laughing man named Rekus who died when their daughter Sula was about three years old, at which time Hannah moved back into her mother's big house prepared to take care of it and her mother forever.

With the exception of BoyBoy, those Peace women loved all men. It was manlove that Eva bequeathed to her daughters. Probably, people said, because there were no men in the house, no men to run it. But actually that was not true. The Peace women simply loved maleness, for its own sake. Eva, old as she was, and with one leg, had a regular flock of gentleman callers, and although she did not participate in the act of love, there was a good deal of teasing and pecking and laughter. The men wanted to see her lovely calf, that neat shoe, and watch the focusing that sometimes swept down out of the distances in her eyes. They wanted to see the joy in her face as they settled down to play checkers, knowing that even when she beat them, as she almost always did, somehow, in her presence, it was they who had won something. They would read the newspaper aloud to her and make observations on its content, and Eva would listen feeling no obligation to agree and, in fact, would take them to task about their interpretation of events. But she argued with them with such an absence of bile, such a concentration of manlove, that they felt their convictions solidified by her disagreement.

With other people's affairs Eva was equally prejudiced about men. She fussed interminably with the brides of the newly wed couples for not getting their men's supper ready on time; about how to launder shirts, press them, etc. "Yo' man be here direc'lin. Ain't it 'bout time you got busy?"

"Aw, Miss Eva. It'll be ready. We just having spaghetti."

"Again?" Eva's eyebrows fluted up and the newlywed pressed her lips together in shame.

Hannah simply refused to live without the attentions of a man, and after Rekus' death had a steady sequence of lovers, mostly the husbands of her friends and neighbors. Her flirting was sweet, low and guileless. Without ever a pat of the hair, a rush to change clothes or a quick application of paint, with no gesture whatsoever, she rippled with sex. In her same old print wraparound, barefoot in the summer, in the winter her feet in a man's leather slippers with the backs flattened under her heels, she made men aware of her behind, her slim ankles, the dew-smooth skin and the incredible length of neck. Then the smile-eyes, the turn of the head—all so welcoming, light and playful. Her voice trailed, dipped and bowed; she gave a chord to the simplest words. Nobody, but nobody, could say "hey sugar" like Hannah. When he heard it, the man tipped his hat down a little over his eyes, hoisted his trousers and thought about the hollow place at the base of her neck. And all this without the slightest confusion about work and responsibilities. While Eva tested and argued with her men, leaving them feeling as though they had been in combat with a worthy, if amiable, foe, Hannah rubbed no edges, made no demands, made the man feel as though he were complete and wonderful just as he was—he didn't need fixing—and so he relaxed and swooned in the Hannah-light that shone on him simply because he was. If the man entered and Hannah was carrying a coal scuttle up from the basement, she handled it in such a way that it became a gesture of love. He made no move to help her with it simply because he wanted to see how her thighs looked when she bent to put it down, knowing that she wanted him to see them too.

But since in that crowded house there were no places for private and spontaneous lovemaking, Hannah would take the man down into the cellar in the summer where it was cool back behind the coal bin and the newspapers, or in the winter they would step into the pantry and stand up against the shelves she had filled with canned goods, or lie on the flour sack just under the rows of tiny green peppers. When those places were not available, she would slip into the seldom-used parlor, or even up to her bedroom. She liked the last place least, not because Sula slept in the room with her but because her love mate's tendency was always to fall asleep afterward and Hannah was fastidious about whom she slept with. She would fuck practically anything, but sleeping with someone implied for her a measure of trust and a definite commitment. So she ended up a daylight lover, and it was only once actually that Sula came home from school and found her mother in the bed, curled spoon in the arms of a man.

Seeing her step so easily into the pantry and emerge looking precisely as she did when she entered, only happier, taught Sula that sex was pleasant and frequent, but otherwise unremarkable. Outside the house, where children giggled about underwear, the message was different. So she watched her mother's face and the face of the men when they opened the pantry door and made up her own mind.

Hannah exasperated the women in the town—the "good" women, who said, "One thing I can't stand is a nasty woman"; the whores, who were hard put to find trade among black men anyway and who resented Hannah's generosity; the middling women, who had both husbands and affairs, because Hannah seemed too unlike them, having no passion attached to her relationships and being wholly incapable of jealousy. Hannah's friendships with women were, of course, seldom and short-lived, and the newly married couples whom her mother took in soon learned what a hazard she was. She could break up a marriage before it had even become one—she would make love to the new groom and wash his wife's dishes all in an afternoon. What she wanted, after Rekus died, and what she succeeded in having more often than not, was some touching every day.

The men, surprisingly, never gossiped about her. She was unquestionably a kind and generous woman and that, coupled with her extraordinary beauty and funky elegance of manner, made them defend her and protect her from any vitriol that newcomers or their wives might spill.

Eva's last child, Plum, to whom she hoped to bequeath everything, floated in a constant swaddle of love and affection, until 1917 when he went to war. He returned to the States in 1919 but did not get back to Medallion until 1920. He wrote letters from New York, Washington, D.C., and Chicago full of promises of homecomings, but there was obviously something wrong. Finally some two or three days after Christmas, he arrived with just the shadow of his old dip-down walk. His hair had been neither cut nor combed in months, his clothes were pointless and he had no socks. But he did have a black bag, a paper sack, and a sweet, sweet smile. Everybody welcomed him and gave him a warm room next to Tar Baby's and waited for him to tell them whatever it was he wanted them to know. They waited in vain for his telling but not long for the knowing. His habits were much like Tar Baby's but there were no bottles, and Plum was sometimes cheerful and animated. Hannah watched and Eva waited. Then he began to steal from them, take trips to Cincinnati and sleep for days in his room with the record player going. He got even thinner, since he ate only snatches of things at beginnings or endings of meals. It was Hannah who found the bent spoon black from steady cooking.

So late one night in 1921, Eva got up from her bed and put on her clothes. Hoisting herself up on her crutches, she was amazed to find that she could still manage them, although the pain in her armpits was severe. She practiced a few steps around the room, and then opened the door. Slowly, she manipulated herself down the long flights of stairs, two crutches under her left arm, the right hand grasping the banister. The sound of her foot booming in comparison to the delicate pat of the crutch tip. On each landing she stopped for breath. Annoyed at her physical condition, she closed her eyes and removed the crutches from under her arms to relieve the unaccustomed pressure. At the foot of the stairs she redistributed her weight between the crutches and swooped on through the front room, to the dining room, to the kitchen, swinging and swooping like a giant heron, so graceful sailing about in its own habitat but awkward and comical when it folded its wings and tried to walk. With a swing and a swoop she arrived at Plum's door and pushed it open with the tip of one crutch. He was lying in bed barely visible in the light coming from a single bulb. Eva swung over to the bed and propped her crutches at its foot. She sat down and gathered Plum into her arms. He woke, but only slightly.

"Hey, man. Hey. You holdin' me, Mamma?" His voice was drowsy and amused. He chuckled as though he had heard some private joke. Eva held him closer and began to rock. Back and forth she rocked him, her eyes wandering around his room. There in the corner was a half-eaten store-bought cherry pie. Balled-up candy wrappers and empty pop bottles peeped from under the dresser. On the floor by her foot was a glass of strawberry crush and a *Liberty* magazine. Rocking, rocking, listening to Plum's occasional chuckles, Eva let her memory spin, loop and fall. Plum in the tub that time as she leaned over him. He reached up and dripped water into her bosom and laughed. She was angry, but not too, and laughed with him.

"Mamma, you so purty. You so purty, Mamma."

Eva lifted her tongue to the edge of her lip to stop the tears from running into her mouth. Rocking, rocking. Later she laid him down and looked at him a long time. Suddenly she was thirsty and reached for the glass of strawberry crush. She put it to her lips and discovered it was blood-tainted water and threw it to the floor. Plum woke up and said, "Hey, Mamma, whyn't you go on back to bed? I'm all right. Didn't I tell you? I'm all right. Go on, now."

"I'm going, Plum," she said. She shifted her weight and pulled her crutches toward her. Swinging and swooping, she left his room. She dragged herself to the kitchen and made grating noises.

Plum on the rim of a warm light sleep was still chuckling. Mamma. She sure was somethin'. He felt twilight. Now there seemed to be some kind of wet light traveling over his legs and stomach with a deeply attractive smell. It wound itself—this wet light—all about him, splashing and running into his skin. He opened his eyes and saw what he imagined was the great wing of an eagle pouring a wet lightness over him. Some kind of baptism, some kind of blessing, he thought. Everything is going to be all right, it said. Knowing that it was so he closed his eyes and sank back into the bright hole of sleep.

Eva stepped back from the bed and let the crutches rest under her arms. She rolled a bit of newspaper into a tight stick about six inches long, lit it and threw it onto the bed where the kerosene-soaked Plum lay in snug delight.

Quickly, as the *whoosh* of flames engulfed him, she shut the door and made her slow and painful journey back to the top of the house.

Just as she got to the third landing she could hear Hannah and some child's voice. She swung along, not even listening to the voices of alarm and the cries of the deweys. By the time she got to her bed someone was bounding up the stairs after her. Hannah opened the door. "Plum! Plum! He's burning, Mamma! We can't even open the door! Mamma!"

Eva looked into Hannah's eyes. "Is? My baby? Burning?" The two women did not speak, for the eyes of each were enough for the other. Then Hannah closed hers and ran toward the voices of neighbors calling for water.

1922

It was too cool for ice cream. A hill wind was blowing dust and empty Camels wrappers about their ankles. It pushed their dresses into the creases of their behinds, then lifted the hems to peek at their cotton underwear. They were on their way to Edna Finch's Mellow House, an ice-cream parlor catering to nice folks—where even children would feel comfortable, you know, even though it was right next to Reba's Grill and just one block down from the Time and a Half Pool Hall. It sat in the curve of Carpenter's Road, which, in four blocks, made up all the sporting life available in the Bottom. Old men and young ones draped themselves in front of the Elmira Theater, Irene's Palace of Cosmetology, the pool hall, the grill and the other sagging business enterprises that lined the street. On sills, on stoops, on crates and broken chairs they sat tasting their teeth and waiting for something to distract them. Every passerby, every motorcar, every alteration in stance caught their attention and was commented on. Particularly they watched women. When a woman approached, the older men tipped their hats; the younger ones opened and closed their thighs. But all of them, whatever their age, watched her retreating view with interest.

Nel and Sula walked through this valley of eyes chilled by the wind and heated by the embarrassment of appraising stares. The old men looked at their stalklike legs, dwelled on the cords in the backs of their knees and remembered old dance steps they had not done in twenty years. In their lust, which age had turned to kindness, they moved their lips as though to stir up the taste of young sweat on tight skin.

Pig meat. The words were in all their minds. And one of them, one of the young ones, said it aloud. Softly but definitively and there was no mistaking the compliment. His name was Ajax, a twenty-one-year-old pool haunt of sinister beauty. Graceful and economical in every movement, he held a place of envy with men of all ages for his magnificently foul mouth. In fact he seldom cursed, and the epithets he chose were dull, even harmless. His reputation was derived from the way he handled the words. When he said "hell" he hit the *h* with his lungs and the impact was greater than the achievement of the most imaginative foul mouth in the town. He could say "shit" with a nastiness impossible to imitate. So, when he said "pig meat" as Nel and Sula passed, they guarded their eyes lest someone see their delight.

It was not really Edna Finch's ice cream that made them brave the stretch of those panther eyes. Years later their own eyes would glaze as they cupped their chins in remembrance of the inchworm smiles, the squatting haunches, the track-rail legs straddling broken chairs. The cream-colored trousers marking with a mere seam the place where the mystery curled. Those smooth vanilla crotches invited them; those lemon-yellow gabardines beckoned to them.

They moved toward the ice-cream parlor like tightrope walkers, as thrilled by the possibility of a slip as by the maintenance of tension and balance. The least sideways glance, the merest toe stub, could pitch them into those creamy haunches spread wide with welcome. Somewhere beneath all of that daintiness, chambered in all that neatness, lay the thing that clotted their dreams.

Which was only fitting, for it was in dreams that the two girls had first met. Long before Edna Finch's Mellow House opened, even before they marched through the chocolate halls of Garfield Primary School out onto the playground and stood facing each other through the ropes of the one vacant swing ("Go on." "No. You go."), they had already made each other's acquaintance in the delirium of their noon dreams. They were solitary little girls whose loneliness was so profound it intoxicated them and sent them stumbling into Technicolored visions that always included a presence, a someone, who, quite like the dreamer, shared the delight of the dream. When Nel, an only child, sat on the steps of her back porch surrounded by the high silence of her mother's incredibly orderly house, feeling the neatness pointing at her back, she studied the poplars and fell easily into a picture of herself lying on a flowered bed, tangled in her own hair, waiting for some fiery prince. He approached but never quite arrived. But always, watching the dream along with her, were some smiling sympathetic eyes. Someone as interested as she herself in the flow of her imagined hair, the thickness of the mattress of flowers, the voile sleeves that closed below her elbows in gold-threaded cuffs.

Similarly, Sula, also an only child, but wedged into a

household of throbbing disorder constantly awry with things, people, voices and the slamming of doors, spent hours in the attic behind a roll of linoleum galloping through her own mind on a gray-and-white horse tasting sugar and smelling roses in full view of a someone who shared both the taste and the speed.

So when they met, first in those chocolate halls and next through the ropes of the swing, they felt the ease and comfort of old friends. Because each had discovered years before that they were neither white nor male, and that all freedom and triumph was forbidden to them, they had set about creating something else to be. Their meeting was fortunate, for it let them use each other to grow on. Daughters of distant mothers and incomprehensible fathers (Sula's because he was dead; Nel's because he wasn't), they found in each other's eyes the intimacy they were looking for.

Nel Wright and Sula Peace were both twelve in 1922, wishbone thin and easy-assed. Nel was the color of wet sandpaper—just dark enough to escape the blows of the pitch-black truebloods and the contempt of old women who worried about such things as bad blood mixtures and knew that the origins of a mule and a mulatto were one and the same. Had she been any lighter-skinned she would have needed either her mother's protection on the way to school or a streak of mean to defend herself. Sula was a heavy brown with large quiet eyes, one of which featured a birthmark that spread from the middle of the lid toward the eyebrow, shaped something like a stemmed rose. It gave her otherwise plain face a broken excitement and blue-blade threat like the keloid scar of the razored man who sometimes played checkers with her grandmother. The birthmark was to grow darker as the years passed, but now it was the same shade as her gold-flecked eyes, which, to the end, were as steady and clean as rain.

Their friendship was as intense as it was sudden. They found relief in each other's personality. Although both were unshaped, formless things, Nel seemed stronger and more consistent than Sula, who could hardly be counted on to sustain any emotion for more than three minutes. Yet there was one time when that was not true, when she held on to a mood for weeks, but even that was in defense of Nel.

Four white boys in their early teens, sons of some newly arrived Irish people, occasionally entertained themselves in the afternoon by harassing black schoolchildren. With shoes that pinched and woolen knickers that made red rings on their calves, they had come to this valley with their parents believing as they did that it was a promised land—green and shimmering with welcome. What they found was a strange accent, a pervasive fear of their religion and firm resistance to their attempts to find work. With one exception the older residents of Medallion scorned them. The one exception was the black community. Although some of the Negroes had been in Medallion before the Civil War (the town didn't even have a name then), if they had any hatred for these newcomers it didn't matter because it didn't show. As a matter of fact, baiting them was the one activity that the white Protestant residents concurred in. In part their place in this world was secured only when they echoed the old residents' attitude toward blacks.

These particular boys caught Nel once, and pushed her from hand to hand until they grew tired of the frightened helpless face. Because of that incident, Nel's route home from school became elaborate. She, and then Sula, managed to duck them for weeks until a chilly day in November when Sula said, "Let's us go on home the shortest way."

Nel blinked, but acquiesced. They walked up the street until they got to the bend of Carpenter's Road where the boys lounged on a disused well. Spotting their prey, the boys sauntered forward as though there were nothing in the world on their minds but the gray sky. Hardly able to control their grins, they stood like a gate blocking the path. When the girls were three feet in front of the boys, Sula reached into her coat pocket and pulled out Eva's paring knife. The boys stopped short, exchanged looks and dropped all pretense of innocence. This was going to be better than they thought. They were going to try and fight back, and with a knife. Maybe they could get an arm around one of their waists, or tear . . .

Sula squatted down in the dirt road and put everything down on the ground: her lunchpail, her reader, her mittens, her slate. Holding the knife in her right hand, she pulled the slate toward her and pressed her left forefinger down hard on its edge. Her aim was determined but inaccurate. She slashed off only the tip of her finger. The four boys stared open-mouthed at the wound and the scrap of flesh, like a button mushroom, curling in the cherry blood that ran into the corners of the slate.

Sula raised her eyes to them. Her voice was quiet. "If I

can do that to myself, what you suppose I'll do to you?"

The shifting dirt was the only way Nel knew that they were moving away; she was looking at Sula's face, which seemed miles and miles away.

But toughness was not their quality—adventuresomeness was—and a mean determination to explore everything that interested them, from one-eyed chickens highstepping in their penned yards to Mr. Buckland Reed's gold teeth, from the sound of sheets flapping in the wind to the labels on Tar Baby's wine bottles. And they had no priorities. They could be distracted from watching a fight with mean razors by the glorious smell of hot tar being poured by roadmen two hundred yards away.

In the safe harbor of each other's company they could afford to abandon the ways of other people and concentrate on their own perceptions of things. When Mrs. Wright reminded Nel to pull her nose, she would do it enthusiastically but without the least hope in the world.

"While you sittin' there, honey, go 'head and pull your nose."

"It hurts, Mamma."

"Don't you want a nice nose when you grow up?"

After she met Sula, Nel slid the clothespin under the blanket as soon as she got in the bed. And although there was still the hateful hot comb to suffer through each Saturday evening, its consequences—smooth hair—no longer interested her.

Joined in mutual admiration they watched each day as though it were a movie arranged for their amusement. The new theme they were now discovering was men. So they met regularly, without even planning it, to walk down the road to Edna Finch's Mellow House, even though it was too cool for ice cream.

Then summer came. A summer limp with the weight of blossomed things. Heavy sunflowers weeping over fences; iris curling and browning at the edges far away from their purple hearts; ears of corn letting their auburn hair wind down to their stalks. And the boys. The beautiful, beautiful boys who dotted the landscape like jewels, split the air with their shouts in the field, and thickened the river with their shining wet backs. Even their footsteps left a smell of smoke behind.

It was in that summer, the summer of their twelfth year, the summer of the beautiful black boys, that they became skittish, frightened and bold—all at the same time.

In that mercury mood in July, Sula and Nel wandered about the Bottom barefoot looking for mischief. They decided to go down by the river where the boys sometimes swam. Nel waited on the porch of 7 Carpenter's Road while Sula ran into the house to go to the toilet. On the way up the stairs, she passed the kitchen where Hannah sat with two friends, Patsy and Valentine. The two women were fanning themselves and watching Hannah put down some dough, all talking casually about one thing and another, and had gotten around, when Sula passed by, to the problems of child rearing.

"They a pain."

"Yeh. Wish I'd listened to mamma. She told me not to have 'em too soon."

"Any time atall is too soon for me."

"Oh, I don't know. My Rudy minds his daddy. He just wild with me. Be glad when he growed and gone."

Hannah smiled and said, "Shut your mouth. You love the ground he pee on."

"Sure I do. But he still a pain. Can't help loving your own child. No matter what they do."

"Well, Hester grown now and I can't say love is exactly what I feel."

"Sure you do. You love her, like I love Sula. I just don't like her. That's the difference."

"Guess so. Likin' them is another thing."

"Sure. They different people, you know..."

She only heard Hannah's words, and the pronounce-ment sent her flying up the stairs. In bewilderment, she stood at the window fingering the curtain edge, aware of a sting in her eye. Nel's call floated up and into the win-dow, pulling her away from dark thoughts back into the bright, hot daylight.

They ran most of the way.

Heading toward the wide part of the river where trees grouped themselves in families darkening the earth below. They passed some boys swimming and clowning in the water, shrouding their words in laughter.

They ran in the sunlight, creating their own breeze, which pressed their dresses into their damp skin. Reaching a kind of square of four leaf-locked trees which promised cooling, they flung themselves into the four-cornered shade to taste their lip sweat and contemplate the wildness that had come upon them so suddenly. They lay in the grass, their foreheads almost touching, their bodies stretched away from each other at a 180-degree angle. Sula's head rested on her arm, an undone braid coiled around her wrist. Nel leaned on her elbows and worried long blades of grass with her fingers. Underneath their dresses flesh tightened and shivered in the high coolness, their small breasts just now beginning to create some pleasant discomfort when they were lying on their stomachs.

Sula lifted her head and joined Nel in the grass play. In concert, without ever meeting each other's eyes, they stroked the blades up and down, up and down. Nel found a thick twig and, with her thumbnail, pulled away its bark until it was stripped to a smooth, creamy innocence. Sula looked about and found one too. When both twigs were undressed Nel moved easily to the next stage and began tearing up rooted grass to make a bare spot of earth. When a generous clearing was made, Sula traced intricate patterns in it with her twig. At first Nel was content to do the same. But soon she grew impatient and poked her twig rhythmically and intensely into the earth, making a small neat hole that grew deeper and wider with the least manipulation of her twig. Sula copied her, and soon each had a hole the size of a cup. Nel began a more strenuous digging and, rising to her knee, was careful to scoop out the dirt as she made her hole deeper. Together they worked until the two holes were one and the same. When the depression was the size of a small dishpan, Nel's twig broke. With a gesture of disgust she threw the pieces into the hole they had made. Sula threw hers in too. Nel saw a bottle cap and tossed it in as well. Each then looked around for more debris to throw into the hole: paper, bits of glass, butts of cigarettes, until all of the small defiling things they could find were collected there. Carefully they replaced the soil and covered the entire grave with uprooted grass.

Neither one had spoken a word.

They stood up, stretched, then gazed out over the swift dull water as an unspeakable restlessness and agitation held them. At the same instant each girl heard footsteps in the grass. A little boy in too big knickers was coming up from the lower bank of the river. He stopped when he saw them and picked his nose.

"Your mamma tole you to stop eatin' snot, Chicken," Nel hollered at him through cupped hands.

"Shut up," he said, still picking.

"Come up here and say that."

"Leave him 'lone, Nel. Come here, Chicken. Lemme show you something."

"Naw."

"You scared we gone take your bugger away?"

"Leave him 'lone, I said. Come on, Chicken. Look. I'll help you climb a tree."

Chicken looked at the tree Sula was pointing to—a big double beech with low branches and lots of bends for sitting.

He moved slowly toward her.

"Come on, Chicken, I'll help you up."

Still picking his nose, his eyes wide, he came to where they were standing. Sula took him by the hand and coaxed him along. When they reached the base of the beech, she lifted him to the first branch, saying, "Go on. Go on. I got you." She followed the boy, steadying him, when he needed it, with her hand and her reassuring voice. When they were as high as they could go, Sula pointed to the far side of the river.

"See? Bet you never saw that far before, did you?"

"Uh uh."

"Now look down there." They both leaned a little and peered through the leaves at Nel standing below, squinting up at them. From their height she looked small and fore-shortened.

Chicken Little laughed.

"Y'all better come on down before you break your neck," Nel hollered.

"I ain't never coming down," the boy hollered back.

"Yeah. We better. Come on, Chicken."

"Naw. Lemme go."

"Yeah, Chicken. Come on, now."

Sula pulled his leg gently.

"Lemme go."

"OK, I'm leavin' you." She started on.

"Wait!" he screamed.

Sula stopped and together they slowly worked their way down.

Chicken was still elated. "I was way up there, wasn't I? Wasn't I? I'm a tell my brovver."

Sula and Nel began to mimic him: "I'm a tell my brov-ver; I'm a tell my brovver."

Sula picked him up by his hands and swung him out-ward then around and around. His knickers ballooned and his shrieks of frightened joy startled the birds and the fat grasshoppers. When he slipped from her hands and sailed away out over the water they could still hear his bubbly laughter.

The water darkened and closed quickly over the place where Chicken Little sank. The pressure of his hard and tight little fingers was still in Sula's palms as she stood looking at the closed place in the water. They expected him to come back up, laughing. Both girls stared at the water.

Nel spoke first. "Somebody saw." A figure appeared briefly on the opposite shore.

The only house over there was Shadrack's. Sula glanced at Nel. Terror widened her nostrils. Had he seen?

The water was so peaceful now. There was nothing but the baking sun and something newly missing. Sula cupped her face for an instant, then turned and ran up to the little plank bridge that crossed the river to Shadrack's house. There was no path. It was as though neither Shadrack nor anyone else ever came this way.

Her running was swift and determined, but when she was close to the three little steps that led to his porch, fear crawled into her stomach and only the something newly missing back there in the river made it possible for her to walk up the three steps and knock at the door.

No one answered. She started back, but thought again of the peace of the river. Shadrack would be inside, just behind the door ready to pounce on her. Still she could not go back. Ever so gently she pushed the door with the tips of her fingers and heard only the hinges weep. More. And then she was inside. Alone. The neatness, the order startled her, but more surprising was the restfulness. Everything was so tiny, so common, so unthreatening. Perhaps this was not the house of the Shad. The terrible Shad who

walked about with his penis out, who peed in front of
ladies and girl-children, the only black who could curse
white people and get away with it, who drank in the road
from the mouth of the bottle, who shouted and shook in
the streets. This cottage? This sweet old cottage? With its
made-up bed? With its rag rug and wooden table? Sula
stood in the middle of the little room and in her wonder
forgot what she had come for until a sound at the door
made her jump. He was there in the doorway looking at
her. She had not heard his coming and now he was looking at her.

More in embarrassment than terror she averted her
glance. When she called up enough courage to look back
at him, she saw his hand resting upon the door frame. His
fingers, barely touching the wood, were arranged in a
graceful arc. Relieved and encouraged (no one with hands
like that, no one with fingers that curved around wood so
tenderly could kill her), she walked past him out of the
door, feeling his gaze turning, turning with her.

At the edge of the porch, gathering the wisps of courage
that were fast leaving her, she turned once more to look
at him, to ask him . . . had he . . . ?

He was smiling, a great smile, heavy with lust and time
to come. He nodded his head as though answering a question, and said, in a pleasant conversational tone, a tone of
cooled butter, "Always."

Sula fled down the steps, and shot through the greenness
and the baking sun back to Nel and the dark closed place
in the water. There she collapsed in tears.

Nel quieted her. "Sh, sh. Don't, don't. You didn't mean

it. It ain't your fault. Sh. Sh. Come on, le's go, Sula. Come on, now. Was he there? Did he see? Where's the belt to your dress?"

Sula shook her head while she searched her waist for the belt.

Finally she stood up and allowed Nel to lead her away. "He said, 'Always. Always.' "

"What?"

Sula covered her mouth as they walked down the hill. Always. He had answered a question she had not asked, and its promise licked at her feet.

A bargeman, poling away from the shore, found Chicken late that afternoon stuck in some rocks and weeds, his knickers ballooning about his legs. He would have left him there but noticed that it was a child, not an old black man, as it first appeared, and he prodded the body loose, netted it and hauled it aboard. He shook his head in disgust at the kind of parents who would drown their own children. When, he wondered, will those people ever be anything but animals, fit for nothing but substitutes for mules, only mules didn't kill each other the way niggers did. He dumped Chicken Little into a burlap sack and tossed him next to some egg crates and boxes of wool cloth. Later, sitting down to smoke on an empty lard tin, still bemused by God's curse and the terrible burden his own kind had of elevating Ham's sons, he suddenly became alarmed by the thought that the corpse in this heat would have a terrible odor, which might get into the fabric of his woolen cloth. He dragged the sack away and hooked it over the side, so that the Chicken's body was half in and half out of the water.

Wiping the sweat from his neck, he reported his find to the sheriff at Porter's Landing, who said they didn't have no niggers in their county, but that some lived in those hills 'cross the river, up above Medallion. The bargeman said he couldn't go all the way back there, it was every bit of two miles. The sheriff said whyn't he throw it on back into the water. The bargeman said he never shoulda taken it out in the first place. Finally they got the man who ran the ferry twice a day to agree to take it over in the morning.

That was why Chicken Little was missing for three days and didn't get to the embalmer's until the fourth day, by which time he was unrecognizable to almost everybody who once knew him, and even his mother wasn't deep down sure, except that it just had to be him since nobody could find him. When she saw his clothes lying on the table in the basement of the mortuary, her mouth snapped shut, and when she saw his body her mouth flew wide open again and it was seven hours before she was able to close it and make the first sound.

So the coffin was closed.

The Junior Choir, dressed in white, sang "Nearer My God to Thee" and "Precious Memories," their eyes fastened on the songbooks they did not need, for this was the first time their voices had presided at a real-life event.

Nel and Sula did not touch hands or look at each other during the funeral. There was a space, a separateness, between them. Nel's legs had turned to granite and she ex-

pected the sheriff or Reverend Deal's pointing finger at
any moment. Although she knew she had "done nothing,"
she felt convicted and hanged right there in the pew—
two rows down from her parents in the children's section.

Sula simply cried. Soundlessly and with no heaving and
gasping for breath, she let the tears roll into her mouth and
slide down her chin to dot the front of her dress.

As Reverend Deal moved into his sermon, the hands of
the women unfolded like pairs of raven's wings and flew
high above their hats in the air. They did not hear all of
what he said; they heard the one word, or phrase, or inflection that was for them the connection between the
event and themselves. For some it was the term "Sweet
Jesus." And they saw the Lamb's eye and the truly innocent victim: themselves. They acknowledged the innocent
child hiding in the corner of their hearts, holding a sugar-
and-butter sandwich. That one. The one who lodged deep
in their fat, thin, old, young skin, and was the one the
world had hurt. Or they thought of their son newly
killed and remembered his legs in short pants and wondered where the bullet went in. Or they remembered how
dirty the room looked when their father left home and
wondered if that is the way the slim, young Jew felt, he
who for them was both son and lover and in whose downy
face they could see the sugar-and-butter sandwiches and
feel the oldest and most devastating pain there is: not the
pain of childhood, but the remembrance of it.

Then they left their pews. For with some emotions one
has to stand. They spoke, for they were full and needed to
say. They swayed, for the rivulets of grief or of ecstasy
must be rocked. And when they thought of all that life

and death locked into that little closed coffin they danced and screamed, not to protest God's will but to acknowledge it and confirm once more their conviction that the only way to avoid the Hand of God is to get in it.

In the colored part of the cemetery, they sank Chicken Little in between his grandfather and an aunt. Butterflies flew in and out of the bunches of field flowers now loosened from the top of the bier and lying in a small heap at the edge of the grave. The heat had gone, but there was still no breeze to lift the hair of the willows.

Nel and Sula stood some distance away from the grave, the space that had sat between them in the pews had dissolved. They held hands and knew that only the coffin would lie in the earth; the bubbly laughter and the press of fingers in the palm would stay aboveground forever. At first, as they stood there, their hands were clenched together. They relaxed slowly until during the walk back home their fingers were laced in as gentle a clasp as that of any two young girlfriends trotting up the road on a summer day wondering what happened to butterflies in the winter.

1923

The second strange thing was Hannah's coming into her mother's room with an empty bowl and a peck of Kentucky Wonders and saying, "Mamma, did you ever love us?" She sang the words like a small child saying a piece at Easter, then knelt to spread a newspaper on the floor and set the basket on it; the bowl she tucked in the space between her legs. Eva, who was just sitting there fanning herself with the cardboard fan from Mr. Hodges' funeral parlor, listened to the silence that followed Hannah's words, then said, "Scat!" to the deweys who were playing chain gang near the window. With the shoelaces of each of them tied to the laces of the others, they stumbled and tumbled out of Eva's room.

"Now," Eva looked up across from her wagon at her daughter. "Give me that again. Flat out to fit my head."

"I mean, did you? You know. When we was little."

Eva's hand moved snail-like down her thigh toward her stump, but stopped short of it to realign a pleat. "No. I don't reckon I did. Not the way you thinkin'."

"Oh, well. I was just wonderin'." Hannah appeared to be through with the subject.

"An evil wonderin' if I ever heard one." Eva was not through.

"I didn't mean nothing by it, Mamma."

"What you mean you didn't *mean* nothing by it? How you gone not mean something by it?"

Hannah pinched the tips off the Kentucky Wonders and snapped their long pods. What with the sound of the cracking and snapping and her swift-fingered movements, she seemed to be playing a complicated instrument. Eva watched her a moment and then said, "You gone can them?"

"No. They for tonight."

"Thought you was gone can some."

"Uncle Paul ain't brought me none yet. A peck ain't enough to can. He say he got two bushels for me."

"Triflin'."

"Oh, he all right."

"Sho he all right. Everybody all right. 'Cept Mamma. Mamma the only one ain't all right. Cause she didn't *love* us."

"Awww, Mamma."

"Awww, Mamma? Awww, Mamma? You settin' here with your healthy-ass self and ax me did I love you? Them big old eyes in your head would a been two holes full of maggots if I hadn't."

"I didn't mean that, Mamma. I know you fed us and all. I was talkin' 'bout something else. Like. Like. Playin' with us. Did you ever, you know, play with us?"

"Play? Wasn't nobody playin' in 1895. Just 'cause you got it good now you think it was always this good? 1895 was a killer, girl. Things was bad. Niggers was dying like flies. Stepping tall, ain't you? Uncle Paul gone bring me *two* bushels. Yeh. And they's a melon downstairs, ain't they? And I bake every Saturday, and Shad brings fish on Friday, and they's a pork barrel full of meal, and we float eggs in a crock of vinegar . . ."

"Mamma, what you talkin' 'bout?"

"I'm talkin' 'bout 18 and 95 when I set in that house five days with you and Pearl and Plum and three beets, you snake-eyed ungrateful hussy. What would I look like leapin' 'round that little old room playin' with youngins with three beets to my name?"

"I know 'bout them beets, Mamma. You told us that a million times."

"Yeah? Well? Don't that count? Ain't that love? You want me to tinkle you under the jaw and forget 'bout them sores in your mouth? Pearl was shittin' worms and I was supposed to play rang-around-the-rosie?"

"But Mamma, they had to be some time when you wasn't thinkin' 'bout . . ."

"No time. They wasn't no time. Not none. Soon as I got one day done here come a night. With you all coughin' and me watchin' so TB wouldn't take you off and if you was sleepin' quiet I thought, O Lord, they dead and put my hand over your mouth to feel if the breath was comin' what you talkin' 'bout did I love you girl I stayed alive for you can't you get that through your thick head or what is that between your ears, heifer?"

Hannah had enough beans now. With some tomatoes and hot bread, she thought, that would be enough for everybody, especially since the deweys didn't eat vegetables no how and Eva never made them and Tar Baby was living off air and music these days. She picked up the basket and stood with it and the bowl of beans over her mother. Eva's face was still asking her last question. Hannah looked into her mother's eyes.

"But what about Plum? What'd you kill Plum for, Mamma?"

It was a Wednesday in August and the ice wagon was coming and coming. You could hear bits of the driver's song. Now Mrs. Jackson would be tipping down her porch steps. "Jes a piece. You got a lil ole piece layin' 'round in there you could spare?" And as he had since the time of the pigeons, the iceman would hand her a lump of ice saying, "Watch it now, Mrs. Jackson. That straw'll tickle your pretty neck to death."

Eva listened to the wagon coming and thought about what it must be like in the icehouse. She leaned back a little and closed her eyes trying to see the insides of the icehouse. It was a dark, lovely picture in this heat, until it reminded her of that winter night in the outhouse holding her baby in the dark, her fingers searching for his asshole and the last bit of lard scooped from the sides of the can, held deliberately on the tip of her middle finger, the last bit of lard to keep from hurting him when she slid her finger in and all because she had broken the slop jar and the rags had frozen. The last food staple in the house she had rammed up her baby's behind to keep from hurting him too much when she opened up his bowels to pull the stools out. He had been screaming fit to kill, but when she found his hole at last and stuck her finger up in it, the shock was so great he was suddenly quiet. Even now on the hottest day anyone in Medallion could remember—a day so hot flies slept and cats were splaying their fur like quills, a day so hot pregnant wives leaned up against trees and cried, and women remembering some three-month-old hurt put ground glass in their lovers' food and the men looked at the food and wondered if there was glass in it and ate it anyway because it was too hot to resist eating it —even on this hottest of days in the hot spell, Eva shivered from the biting cold and stench of that outhouse.

Hannah was waiting. Watching her mother's eyelids. When Eva spoke at last it was with two voices. Like two people were talking at the same time, saying the same thing, one a fraction of a second behind the other.

"He give me such a time. Such a time. Look like he didn't even want to be born. But he come on out. Boys is hard to bear. You wouldn't know that but they is. It was such a carryin' on to get him born and to keep him alive. Just to keep his little heart beating and his little old lungs cleared and look like when he came back from that war he wanted to git back in. After all that carryin' on, just gettin' him out and keepin' him alive, he wanted to crawl back in my womb and well . . . I ain't got the room no more even if he could do it. There wasn't space for him in my womb. And he was crawlin' back. Being helpless and thinking baby thoughts and dreaming baby dreams and messing up his pants again and smiling all the time. I had room enough in my heart, but not in my womb, not no more. I birthed him once. I couldn't do it again. He was growed, a big old thing. Godhavemercy, I couldn't birth him twice. I'd be laying here at night and he be downstairs in that room, but when I closed my eyes I'd see him . . . six feet tall smilin' and crawlin' up the stairs quietlike so I wouldn't hear and opening the door soft so I wouldn't hear and he'd be creepin' to the bed trying to spread my legs trying to get back up in my womb. He was a man, girl, a big old growed-up man. I didn't have that much room. I kept on dreaming it. Dreaming it and I knowed it was true. One night it wouldn't be no dream. It'd be true and I would have done it, would have let him if I'd've had the room but a big man can't be a baby all wrapped up inside his mamma no more; he suffocate. I done everything I could to make him leave me and go on and live and be a man but he wouldn't and I had to keep him out so I just thought of a way he could die like a man not all scrunched up inside my womb, but like a man."

Eva couldn't see Hannah clearly for the tears, but she looked up at her anyway and said, by way of apology or explanation or perhaps just by way of neatness, "But I held him close first. Real close. Sweet Plum. My baby boy."

Long after Hannah turned and walked out of the room, Eva continued to call his name while her fingers lined up the pleats in her dress.

Hannah went off to the kitchen, her old man's slippers plopping down the stairs and over the hardwood floors. She turned the spigot on, letting water break up the tight knots of Kentucky Wonders and float them to the top of the bowl. She swirled them about with her fingers, poured the water off and repeated the process. Each time the green tubes rose to the surface she felt elated and collected whole handfuls at a time to drop in twos and threes back into the water.

Through the window over the sink she could see the deweys still playing chain gang; their ankles bound one to the other, they tumbled, struggled back to their feet and tried to walk single file. Hens strutted by with one suspicious eye on the deweys, another on the brick fireplace where sheets and mason jars were boiled. Only the deweys could play in this heat. Hannah put the Kentucky Wonders over the fire and, struck by a sudden sleepiness, she went off to lie down in the front room. It was even hotter there, for the windows were shut to keep out the sunlight. Hannah straightened the shawl that draped the couch and lay down. She dreamed of a wedding in a red bridal gown until Sula came in and woke her.

But before the second strange thing, there had been the wind, which was the first. The very night before the day Hannah had asked Eva if she had ever loved them, the wind tore over the hills rattling roofs and loosening doors. Everything shook, and although the people were frightened they thought it meant rain and welcomed it. Windows fell out and trees lost arms. People waited up half the night for the first crack of lightning. Some had even uncovered barrels to catch the rain water, which they loved to drink and cook in. They waited in vain, for no lightning no thunder no rain came. The wind just swept through, took what dampness there was out of the air, messed up the yards, and went on. The hills of the Bottom, as always, protected the valley part of town where the white people lived, and the next morning all the people were grateful because there was a dryer heat. So they set about their work early, for it was canning time, and who knew but what the wind would come back this time with a cooling rain. The men who worked in the valley got up at four thirty in the morning and looked at the sky where the sun was already rising like a hot white bitch. They beat the brims of their hats against their legs before putting them on and trudged down the road like old promises nobody wanted kept.

On Thursday, when Hannah brought Eva her fried tomatoes and soft scrambled eggs with the white left out for good luck, she mentioned her dream of the wedding in the red dress. Neither one bothered to look it up for they both knew the number was 522. Eva said she'd play it when Mr. Buckland Reed came by. Later she would remember it as the third strange thing. She had thought it odd even then, but the red in the dream confused her. But she wasn't certain that it was third or not because Sula was acting up, fretting the deweys and meddling the newly married couple. Because she was thirteen, everybody supposed her nature was coming down, but it was hard to put up with her sulking and irritation. The birthmark over her eye was getting darker and looked more and more like a stem and rose. She was dropping things and eating food that belonged to the newly married couple and started in to worrying everybody that the deweys needed a bath and she was going to give it to them. The deweys, who went wild at the thought of water, were crying and thundering all over the house like colts.

"We ain't got to, do we? Do we got to do what she says? It ain't Saturday." They even woke up Tar Baby, who came out of his room to look at them and then left the house in search of music.

Hannah ignored them and kept on bringing mason jars out of the cellar and washing them. Eva banged on the floor with her stick but nobody came. By noon it was quiet. The deweys had escaped, Sula was either in her room or gone off somewhere. The newly married couple, energized by their morning lovemaking, had gone to look for a day's work happily certain that they would find none.

The air all over the Bottom got heavy with peeled fruit and boiling vegetables. Fresh corn, tomatoes, string beans, melon rinds. The women, the children and the old men who had no jobs were putting up for a winter they understood so well. Peaches were stuffed into jars and black cherries (later, when it got cooler, they would put up jellies and preserves). The greedy canned as many as forty-two a day even though some of them, like Mrs. Jackson, who ate ice, had jars from 1920.

Before she trundled her wagon over to the dresser to get her comb, Eva looked out the window and saw Hannah bending to light the yard fire. And that was the fifth (or fourth, if you didn't count Sula's craziness) strange thing. She couldn't find her comb. Nobody moved stuff in Eva's room except to clean and then they put everything right back. But Eva couldn't find it anywhere. One hand pulling her braids loose, the other searching the dresser drawers, she had just begun to get irritated when she felt it in her blouse drawer. Then she trundled back to the window to catch a breeze, if one took a mind to come by, while she combed her hair. She rolled up to the window and it was then she saw Hannah burning. The flames from the yard fire were licking the blue cotton dress, making her dance. Eva knew there was time for nothing in this world other than the time it took to get there and cover her daughter's body with her own. She lifted her heavy frame up on her good leg, and with fists and arms smashed the windowpane. Using her stump as a support on the window sill, her good leg as a lever, she threw herself out of the window. Cut and bleeding she clawed the air trying to aim her body toward the flaming, dancing figure. She missed and came crashing down some twelve feet from Hannah's smoke. Stunned but still conscious, Eva dragged herself toward her firstborn, but Hannah, her senses lost, went flying out of the yard gesturing and bobbing like a sprung jack-in-the-box.

Mr. and Mrs. Suggs, who had set up their canning apparatus in their front yard, saw her running, dancing toward them. They whispered, "Jesus, Jesus," and together hoisted up their tub of water in which tight red tomatoes floated and threw it on the smoke-and-flame-bound woman. The water did put out the flames, but it also made steam, which seared to sealing all that was left of the beautiful Hannah Peace. She lay there on the wooden sidewalk planks, twitching lightly among the smashed tomatoes, her face a mask of agony so intense that for years the people who gathered 'round would shake their heads at the recollection of it.

Somebody covered her legs with a shirt. A woman unwrapped her head rag and placed it on Hannah's shoulder. Somebody else ran to Dick's Fresh Food and Sundries to call the ambulance. The rest stood there as helpless as sunflowers leaning on a fence. The deweys came and stepped in the tomatoes, their eyes raked with wonder. Two cats sidled through the legs of the crowd, sniffing the burned flesh. The vomiting of a young girl finally broke the profound silence and caused the women to talk to each other and to God. In the midst of calling Jesus they heard the hollow clang of the ambulance bell struggling up the hill, but not the "Help me, ya'll" that the dying woman whispered. Then somebody remembered to go and see about Eva. They found her on her stomach by the forsythia bushes calling Hannah's name and dragging her body through the sweet peas and clover that grew under the forsythia by the side of the house. Mother and daughter were placed on stretchers and carried to the ambulance. Eva was wide awake. The blood from her face cuts filled her eyes so she could not see, could only smell the familiar odor of cooked flesh.

Hannah died on the way to the hospital. Or so they said. In any case, she had already begun to bubble and blister so badly that the coffin had to be kept closed at the funeral and the women who washed the body and dressed it for death wept for her burned hair and wrinkled breasts as though they themselves had been her lovers.

When Eva got to the hospital they put her stretcher on the floor, so preoccupied with the hot and bubbling flesh of the other (some of them had never seen so extreme a burn case before) they forgot Eva, who would have bled to death except Old Willy Fields, the orderly, saw blood staining his just-mopped floors and went to find out where it was coming from. Recognizing Eva at once he shouted to a nurse, who came to see if the bloody one-legged black woman was alive or dead. From then on Willy boasted that he had saved Eva's life—an indisputable fact which she herself admitted and for which she cursed him every day for thirty-seven years thereafter and would have cursed him for the rest of her life except by then she was already ninety years old and forgot things.

Lying in the colored ward of the hospital, which was a

screened corner of a larger ward, Eva mused over the perfection of the judgment against her. She remembered the wedding dream and recalled that weddings always meant death. And the red gown, well that was the fire, as she should have known. She remembered something else too, and try as she might to deny it, she knew that as she lay on the ground trying to drag herself through the sweet peas and clover to get to Hannah, she had seen Sula standing on the back porch just looking. When Eva, who was never one to hide the faults of her children, mentioned what she thought she'd seen to a few friends, they said it was natural. Sula was probably struck dumb, as anybody would be who saw her own mamma burn up. Eva said yes, but inside she disagreed and remained convinced that Sula had watched Hannah burn not because she was paralyzed, but because she was interested.

1927

Old people were dancing with little children. Young boys with their sisters, and the church women who frowned on any bodily expression of joy (except when the hand of God commanded it) tapped their feet. Somebody (the groom's father, everybody said) had poured a whole pint jar of cane liquor into the punch, so even the men who did not sneak out the back door to have a shot, as well as the women who let nothing stronger than Black Draught enter their blood, were tipsy. A small boy stood at the Victrola turning its handle and smiling at the sound of Bert Williams' "Save a Little Dram for Me."

Even Helene Wright had mellowed with the cane, waving away apologies for drinks spilled on her rug and paying no attention whatever to the chocolate cake lying on the arm of her red-velvet sofa. The tea roses above her left breast had slipped from the brooch that fastened them and were hanging heads down. When her husband called her attention to the children wrapping themselves into her curtains, she merely smiled and said, "Oh, let them be." She was not only a little drunk, she was weary and had been for weeks. Her only child's wedding—the culmination of all she had been, thought or done in this world— had dragged from her energy and stamina even she did not know she possessed. Her house had to be thoroughly cleaned, chickens had to be plucked, cakes and pies made, and for weeks she, her friends and her daughter had been sewing. Now it was all happening and it took only a little cane juice to snap the cords of fatigue and damn the white curtains that she had pinned on the stretcher only the morning before. Once this day was over she would have a lifetime to rattle around in that house and repair the damage.

A real wedding, in a church, with a real reception afterward, was rare among the people of the Bottom. Expensive for one thing, and most newlyweds just went to the courthouse if they were not particular, or had the preacher come in and say a few words if they were. The rest just "took up" with one another. No invitations were sent. There was no need for that formality. Folks just came, bringing a gift if they had one, none if they didn't. Except for those who worked in valley houses, most of them had never been to a big wedding; they simply assumed it was rather like a funeral except afterward you didn't have to walk all the way out to Beechnut Cemetery.

This wedding offered a special attraction, for the bridegroom was a handsome, well-liked man—the tenor of Mount Zion's Men's Quartet, who had an enviable reputation among the girls and a comfortable one among men. His name was Jude Greene, and with the pick of some eight or ten girls who came regularly to services to hear him sing, he had chosen Nel Wright.

He wasn't really aiming to get married. He was twenty then, and although his job as a waiter at the Hotel Medallion was a blessing to his parents and their seven other children, it wasn't nearly enough to support a wife. He had brought the subject up first on the day the word got out that the town was building a new road, tarmac, that would wind through Medallion on down to the river, where a great new bridge was to be built to connect Medallion to Porter's Landing, the town on the other side. The war over, a fake prosperity was still around. In a state of euphoria, with a hunger for more and more, the council of founders cast its eye toward a future that would certainly include trade from cross-river towns. Towns that needed more than a house raft to get to the merchants of Medallion. Work had already begun on the New River Road (the city had always meant to name it something else, something wonderful, but ten years later when the bridge idea was dropped for a tunnel it was still called the New River Road).

Along with a few other young black men, Jude had gone down to the shack where they were hiring. Three old colored men had already been hired, but not for the road work, just to do the picking up, food bringing and other small errands. These old men were close to feeble, not good for much else, and everybody was pleased they were taken on; still it was a shame to see those white men laughing with the grandfathers but shying away from the young black men who could tear that road up. The men like Jude who could do real work. Jude himself longed more than anybody else to be taken. Not just for the good money, more for the work itself. He wanted to swing the pick or kneel down with the string or shovel the gravel. His arms ached for something heavier than trays, for something dirtier than peelings; his feet wanted the heavy work shoes, not the thin-soled black shoes that the hotel required. More than anything he wanted the camaraderie of the road men: the lunch buckets, the hollering, the body movement that in the end produced something real, something he could point to. "I built that road," he could say. How much better sundown would be than the end of a day in the restaurant, where a good day's work was marked by the number of dirty plates and the weight of the garbage bin. "I built that road." People would walk over his sweat for years. Perhaps a sledge hammer would come crashing down on his foot, and when people asked him how come he limped, he could say, "Got that building the New Road."

It was while he was full of such dreams, his body already feeling the rough work clothes, his hands already curved to the pick handle, that he spoke to Nel about getting married. She seemed receptive but hardly anxious. It was after he stood in lines for six days running and saw the gang boss pick out thin-armed white boys from the Virginia hills and the bull-necked Greeks and Italians and heard over and over, "Nothing else today. Come back tomorrow," that he got the message. So it was rage, rage and a determination to take on a man's role anyhow that made him press Nel about settling down. He needed some of his appetites filled, some posture of adulthood recognized, but mostly he wanted someone to care about his hurt, to care very deeply. Deep enough to hold him, deep enough to rock him, deep enough to ask, "How you feel? You all right? Want some coffee?" And if he were to be a man, that someone could no longer be his mother. He chose the girl who had always been kind, who had never seemed hell-bent to marry, who made the whole venture seem like his idea, his conquest.

The more he thought about marriage, the more attractive it became. Whatever his fortune, whatever the cut of his garment, there would always be the hem—the tuck and fold that hid his raveling edges; a someone sweet, industrious and loyal to shore him up. And in return he would shelter her, love her, grow old with her. Without that someone he was a waiter hanging around a kitchen like a woman. With her he was head of a household pinned to an unsatisfactory job out of necessity. The two of them together would make one Jude.

His fears lest his burst dream of road building discourage her were never realized. Nel's indifference to his hints about marriage disappeared altogether when she discovered his pain. Jude could see himself taking shape in her eyes. She actually wanted to help, to soothe, and was it true what Ajax said in the Time and a Half Pool Hall? That "all they want, man, is they own misery. Ax em to die for you and they yours for life."

Whether he was accurate in general, Ajax was right about Nel. Except for an occasional leadership role with Sula, she had no aggression. Her parents had succeeded in rubbing down to a dull glow any sparkle or splutter she had. Only with Sula did that quality have free reign, but their friendship was so close, they themselves had difficulty distinguishing one's thoughts from the other's. During all of her girlhood the only respite Nel had had from her stern and undemonstrative parents was Sula. When Jude began to hover around, she was flattered—all the girls liked him—and Sula made the enjoyment of his attentions keener simply because she seemed always to want Nel to shine. They never quarreled, those two, the way some girlfriends did over boys, or competed against each other for them. In those days a compliment to one was a compliment to the other, and cruelty to one was a challenge to the other.

Nel's response to Jude's shame and anger selected her away from Sula. And greater than her friendship was this new feeling of being needed by someone who saw her singly. She didn't even know she had a neck until Jude remarked on it, or that her smile was anything but the spreading of her lips until he saw it as a small miracle.

Sula was no less excited about the wedding. She thought it was the perfect thing to do following their graduation from general school. She wanted to be the bridesmaid. No others. And she encouraged Mrs. Wright to go all out, even to borrowing Eva's punch bowl. In fact, she handled most of the details very efficiently, capitalizing on the fact that most people were anxious to please her since she had lost her mamma only a few years back and they still remembered the agony in Hannah's face and the blood on Eva's.

So they danced up in the Bottom on the second Saturday in June, danced at the wedding where everybody realized for the first time that except for their magnificent teeth, the deweys would never grow. They had been forty-eight inches tall for years now, and while their size was unusual it was not unheard of. The realization was based on the fact that they remained boys in mind. Mischievous, cunning, private and completely unhousebroken, their games and interests had not changed since Hannah had them all put into the first grade together.

Nel and Jude, who had been the stars all during the wedding, were forgotten finally as the reception melted into a dance, a feed, a gossip session, a playground and a love nest. For the first time that day they relaxed and looked at each other, and liked what they saw. They began to dance, pressed in among the others, and each one turned his thoughts to the night that was coming on fast. They had taken a housekeeping room with one of Jude's aunts (over the protest of Mrs. Wright, who had rooms to spare, but Nel didn't want to make love to her husband in her mother's house) and were getting restless to go there.

As if reading her thoughts, Jude leaned down and whispered, "Me too." Nel smiled and rested her cheek on his shoulder. The veil she wore was too heavy to allow her to feel the core of the kiss he pressed on her head. When she raised her eyes to him for one more look of reassurance, she saw through the open door a slim figure in blue, gliding, with just a hint of a strut, down the path toward the road. One hand was pressed to the head to hold down the large hat against the warm June breeze. Even from the rear Nel could tell that it was Sula and that she was smiling; that something deep down in that litheness was amused. It would be ten years before they saw each other again, and their meeting would be thick with birds.

PART
TWO

PART
TWO

1937

Accompanied by a plague of robins, Sula came back to Medallion. The little yam-breasted shuddering birds were everywhere, exciting very small children away from their usual welcome into a vicious stoning. Nobody knew why or from where they had come. What they did know was that you couldn't go anywhere without stepping in their pearly shit, and it was hard to hang up clothes, pull weeds or just sit on the front porch when robins were flying and dying all around you.

Although most of the people remembered the time when the sky was black for two hours with clouds and clouds of pigeons, and although they were accustomed to excesses in nature—too much heat, too much cold, too little rain, rain to flooding—they still dreaded the way a relatively trivial phenomenon could become sovereign in their lives and bend their minds to its will.

In spite of their fear, they reacted to an oppressive oddity, or what they called evil days, with an acceptance that bordered on welcome. Such evil must be avoided, they felt, and precautions must naturally be taken to protect themselves from it. But they let it run its course, fulfill itself, and never invented ways either to

SULA / 90

alter it, to annihilate it or to prevent its happening again. So also were they with people.

What was taken by outsiders to be slackness, slovenliness or even generosity was in fact a full recognition of the legitimacy of forces other than good ones. They did not believe doctors could heal—for them, none ever had done so. They did not believe death was accidental—life might be, but death was deliberate. They did not believe Nature was ever askew—only inconvenient. Plague and drought were as "natural" as springtime. If milk could curdle, God knows robins could fall. The purpose of evil was to survive it and they determined (without ever knowing they had made up their minds to do it) to survive floods, white people, tuberculosis, famine and ignorance. They knew anger well but not despair, and they didn't stone sinners for the same reason they didn't commit suicide—it was beneath them.

Sula stepped off the Cincinnati Flyer into the robin shit and began the long climb up into the Bottom. She was dressed in a manner that was as close to a movie star as anyone would ever see. A black crepe dress splashed with pink and yellow zinnias, foxtails, a black felt hat with the veil of net lowered over one eye. In her right hand was a black purse with a beaded clasp and in her left a red leather traveling case, so small, so charming—no one had seen anything like it ever before, including the mayor's wife and the music teacher, both of whom had been to Rome.

Walking up the hill toward Carpenter's Road, the heels and sides of her pumps edged with drying bird shit, she attracted the glances of old men sitting on stone benches in front of the courthouse, housewives throwing buckets of water on their sidewalks, and high school students on their way home for lunch. By the time she reached the Bottom, the news of her return had brought the black people out on their porches or to their windows. There were scattered hellos and nods but mostly stares. A little boy ran up to her saying, "Carry yo' bag, ma'am?" Before Sula could answer his mother had called him, "You, John. Get back in here."

At Eva's house there were four dead robins on the walk. Sula stopped and with her toe pushed them into the bordering grass.

Eva looked at Sula pretty much the same way she had looked at BoyBoy that time when he returned after he'd left her without a dime or a prospect of one. She was sitting in her wagon, her back to the window she had jumped out of (now all boarded up) setting fire to the hair she had combed out of her head. When Sula opened the door she raised her eyes and said, "I might have knowed them birds meant something. Where's your coat?"

Sula threw herself on Eva's bed. "The rest of my stuff will be on later."

"I should hope so. Them little old furry tails ain't going to do you no more good than they did the fox that was wearing them."

"Don't you say hello to nobody when you ain't seen them for ten years?"

"If folks let somebody know where they is and when they coming, then other folks can get ready for them. If they don't—if they just pop in all sudden like—then they got to take whatever mood they find."

"How you been doing, Big Mamma?"

"Gettin' by. Sweet of you to ask. You was quick enough when you wanted something. When you needed a little change or . . ."

"Don't talk to me about how much you gave me, Big Mamma, and how much I owe you or none of that."

"Oh? I ain't supposed to mention it?"

"OK. Mention it." Sula shrugged and turned over on her stomach, her buttocks toward Eva.

"You ain't been in this house ten seconds and already you starting something."

"Takes two, Big Mamma."

"Well, don't let your mouth start nothing that your ass can't stand. When you gone to get married? You need to have some babies. It'll settle you."

"I don't want to make somebody else. I want to make myself."

"Selfish. Ain't no woman got no business floatin' around without no man."

"You did."

"Not by choice."

"Mamma did."

"Not by choice, I said. It ain't right for you to want to stay off by yourself. You need . . . I'm a tell you what you need."

Sula sat up. "I need you to shut your mouth."

"Don't nobody talk to me like that. Don't nobody . . ."

"This body does. Just 'cause you was bad enough to cut

off your own leg you think you got a right to kick every-body with the stump."

"Who said I cut off my leg?"

"Well, you stuck it under a train to collect insurance."

"Hold on, you lyin' heifer!"

"I aim to."

"Bible say honor thy father and thy mother that thy days may be long upon the land thy God giveth thee."

"Mamma must have skipped that part. Her days wasn't too long."

"Pus mouth! God's going to strike you!"

"Which God? The one watched you burn Plum?"

"Don't talk to me about no burning. You watched your own mamma. You crazy roach! You the one should have been burnt!"

"But I ain't. Got that? I ain't. Any more fires in this house, I'm lighting them!"

"Hellfire don't need lighting and it's already burning in you..."

"Whatever's burning in me is mine!"

"Amen!"

"And I'll split this town in two and everything in it before I'll let you put it out!"

"Pride goeth before a fall."

"What the hell do I care about falling?"

"Amazing Grace."

"You sold your life for twenty-three dollars a month."

"You throwed yours away."

"It's mine to throw."

"One day you gone need it."

"But not you. I ain't never going to need you. And you know what? Maybe one night when you dozing in that wagon flicking flies and swallowing spit, maybe I'll just tip on up here with some kerosene and—who knows—you may make the brightest flame of them all."

So Eva locked her door from then on. But it did no good. In April two men came with a stretcher and she didn't even have time to comb her hair before they strapped her to a piece of canvas.

When Mr. Buckland Reed came by to pick up the number, his mouth sagged at the sight of Eva being carried out and Sula holding some papers against the wall, at the bottom of which, just above the word "guardian," she very carefully wrote Miss Sula Mae Peace.

⊚ ⊚ ⊚

Nel alone noticed the peculiar quality of the May that followed the leaving of the birds. It had a sheen, a glimmering as of green, rain-soaked Saturday nights (lit by the excitement of newly installed street lights); of lemon-yellow afternoons bright with iced drinks and splashes of daffodils. It showed in the damp faces of her children and the river-smoothness of their voices. Even her own body was not immune to the magic. She would sit on the floor to sew as she had done as a girl, fold her legs up under her or do a little dance that fitted some tune in her head. There were easy sun-washed days and purple dusks in which Tar Baby sang "Abide With Me" at prayer meetings, his lashes darkened by tears, his silhouette limp with regret against the whitewashed walls of Greater Saint Matthew's. Nel listened and was moved to smile. To smile at the sheer loveliness that pressed in from the windows and touched his grief, making it a pleasure to behold.

Although it was she alone who saw this magic, she did not wonder at it. She knew it was all due to Sula's return to the Bottom. It was like getting the use of an eye back, having a cataract removed. Her old friend had come home. Sula. Who made her laugh, who made her see old things with new eyes, in whose presence she felt clever, gentle and a little raunchy. Sula, whose past she had lived through and with whom the present was a constant sharing of perceptions. Talking to Sula had always been a conversation with herself. Was there anyone else before whom she could never be foolish? In whose view inadequacy was mere idiosyncrasy, a character trait rather than a deficiency? Anyone who left behind that aura of fun and complicity? Sula never competed; she simply helped others define themselves. Other people seemed to turn their volume on and up when Sula was in the room. More than any other thing, humor returned. She could listen to the crunch of sugar underfoot that the children had spilled without reaching for the switch; and she forgot the tear in the living-room window shade. Even Nel's love for Jude, which over the years had spun a steady gray web around her heart, became a bright and easy affection, a playfulness that was reflected in their lovemaking.

Sula would come by of an afternoon, walking along with her fluid stride, wearing a plain yellow dress the same way her mother, Hannah, had worn those too-big house dresses—with a distance, an absence of a relationship to clothes which emphasized everything the fabric covered. When she scratched the screen door, as in the old days, and stepped inside, the dishes piled in the sink looked as though they belonged there; the dust on the lamps sparkled; the hair brush lying on the "good" sofa in the living room did not have to be apologetically retrieved, and Nel's grimy intractable children looked like three wild things happily insouciant in the May shine.

"Hey, girl." The rose mark over Sula's eye gave her glance a suggestion of startled pleasure. It was darker than Nel remembered.

"Hey yourself. Come on in here."

"How you doin'?" Sula moved a pile of ironed diapers from a chair and sat down.

"Oh, I ain't strangled nobody yet so I guess I'm all right."

"Well, if you change your mind call me."

"Somebody need killin'?"

"Half this town need it."

"And the other half?"

"A drawn-out disease."

"Oh, come on. Is Medallion that bad?"

"Didn't nobody tell you?"

"You been gone too long, Sula."

"Not too long, but maybe too far."

"What's that supposed to mean?" Nel dipped her fingers into the bowl of water and sprinkled a diaper.

"Oh, I don't know."

"Want some cool tea?"

"Mmmm. Lots of ice, I'm burnin' up."

"Iceman don't come yet, but it's good and cold."

"That's fine."

"Hope I didn't speak too soon. Kids run in and out of here so much." Nel bent to open the icebox.

"You puttin' it on, Nel. Jude must be wore out."

"*Jude* must be wore out? You don't care nothin' 'bout my back, do you?"

"Is that where it's at, in your back?"

"Hah! Jude thinks it's everywhere."

"He's right, it is everywhere. Just be glad he found it, wherever it is. Remember John L.?"

"When Shirley said he got her down by the well and tried to stick it in her hip?" Nel giggled at the remembrance of that teen-time tale. "She should have been grateful. Have you seen her since you been back?"

"Mmm. Like a ox."

"That was one dumb nigger, John L."

"Maybe. Maybe he was just sanitary."

"Sanitary?"

"Well. Think about it. Suppose Shirley was all splayed out in front of you? Wouldn't you go for the hipbone instead?"

Nel lowered her head onto crossed arms while tears of laughter dripped into the warm diapers. Laughter that weakened her knees and pressed her bladder into action. Her rapid soprano and Sula's dark sleepy chuckle made a duet that frightened the cat and made the children run in from the back yard, puzzled at first by the wild free sounds, then delighted to see their mother stumbling merrily toward the bathroom, holding on to her stomach, fairly singing through the laughter: "Aw. Aw. Lord. Sula. Stop." And the other one, the one with the scary black thing over her eye, laughing softly and egging their mother on: "Neatness counts. You know what cleanliness is next to . . ."

"Hush." Nel's plea was clipped off by the slam of the bathroom door.

"What y'all laughing at?"

"Old time-y stuff. Long gone, old time-y stuff."

"Tell us."

"Tell *you?*" The black mark leaped.

"Uh huh. Tell us."

"What tickles us wouldn't tickle you."

"Uh huh, it would."

"Well, we was talking about some people we used to know when we was little."

"Was my mamma little?"

"Of course."

"What happened?"

"Well, some old boy we knew name John L. and a girl name . . ."

Damp-faced, Nel stepped back into the kitchen. She felt new, soft and new. It had been the longest time since she had had a rib-scraping laugh. She had forgotten how deep and down it could be. So different from the miscellaneous giggles and smiles she had learned to be content with these past few years.

"O Lord, Sula. You haven't changed none." She wiped her eyes. "What was all that about, anyway? All that scramblin' we did trying to do it and not do it at the same time?"

"Beats me. Such a simple thing."

"But we sure made a lot out of it, and the boys were dumber than we were."

"Couldn't nobody be dumber than I was."

"Stop lying. All of 'em liked you best."

"Yeah? Where are they?"

"They still here. You the one went off."

"Didn't I, though?"

"Tell me about it. The big city."

"Big is all it is. A big Medallion."

"No. I mean the life. The nightclubs, and parties . . ."

"I was in college, Nellie. No nightclubs on campus."

"Campus? That what they call it? Well. You wasn't in no college for—what—ten years now? And you didn't write to nobody. How come you never wrote?"

"You never did either."

"Where was I going to write to? All I knew was that you was in Nashville. I asked Miss Peace about you once or twice."

"What did *she* say?"

"I couldn't make much sense out of her. You know she been gettin' stranger and stranger after she come out the hospital. How is she anyway?"

"Same, I guess. Not so hot."

"No? Laura, I know, was doing her cooking and things. Is she still?"

"No. I put her out."

"Put her out? What for?"

"She made me nervous."

"But she was doing it for nothing, Sula."

"That's what you think. She was stealing right and left."

"Since when did you get froggy about folks' stealing?"
Sula smiled. "OK. I lied. You wanted a reason."

"Well, give me the real one."

"I don't know the real one. She just didn't belong in
that house. Digging around in the cupboards, picking up
pots and ice picks..."

"You sure have changed. That house was always full of
people digging in cupboards and carrying on."

"That's the reason, then."

"Sula. Come on, now."

"You've changed too. I didn't used to have to explain
everything to you."

Nel blushed. "Who's feeding the deweys and Tar
Baby? You?"

"Sure me. Anyway Tar Baby don't eat and the deweys
still crazy."

"I heard one of 'em's mamma came to take him back but
didn't know which was hern."

"Don't nobody know."

"And Eva? You doing the work for her too?"

"Well, since you haven't heard it, let me tell you. Eva's
real sick. I had her put where she could be watched and
taken care of."

"Where would that be?"

"Out by Beechnut."

"You mean that home the white church run? Sula! That
ain't no place for Eva. All them women is dirt poor with
no people at all. Mrs. Wilkens and them. They got dropsy
and can't hold their water—crazy as loons. Eva's odd, but
she got sense. I don't think that's right, Sula."

"I'm scared of her, Nellie. That's why..."

"Scared? Of Eva?"

"You don't know her. Did you know she burnt Plum?"

"Oh, I heard that years ago. But nobody put no stock in it."

"They should have. It's true. I saw it. And when I got back here she was planning to do it to me too."

"Eva? I can't hardly believe that. She almost died trying to get to your mother."

Sula leaned forward, her elbows on the table. "You ever known me to lie to you?"

"No. But you could be mistaken. Why would Eva . . ."

"All I know is I'm scared. And there's no place else for me to go. We all that's left, Eva and me. I guess I should have stayed gone. I didn't know what else to do. Maybe I should have talked to you about it first. You always had better sense than me. Whenever I was scared before, you knew just what to do."

The closed place in the water spread before them. Nel put the iron on the stove. The situation was clear to her now. Sula, like always, was incapable of making any but the most trivial decisions. When it came to matters of grave importance, she behaved emotionally and irresponsibly and left it to others to straighten out. And when fear struck her, she did unbelievable things. Like that time with her finger. Whatever those hunkies did, it wouldn't have been as bad as what she did to herself. But Sula was so scared she had mutilated herself, to protect herself.

"What should I do, Nellie? Take her back and sleep with my door locked again?"

"No. I guess it's too late anyway. But let's work out a plan for taking care of her. So she won't be messed over."

"Anything you say."

"What about money? She got any?"

Sula shrugged. "The checks come still. It's not much, like it used to be. Should I have them made over to me?"

"Can you? Do it, then. We can arrange for her to have special comforts. That place is a mess, you know. A doctor don't never set foot in there. I ain't figured out yet how they stay alive in there as long as they do."

"Why don't I have the checks made over to you, Nellie? You better at this than I am."

"Oh no. People will say I'm scheming. You the one to do it. Was there insurance from Hannah?"

"Yes. Plum too. He had all that army insurance."

"Any of it left?"

"Well I went to college on some. Eva banked the rest. I'll look into it, though."

". . . and explain it all to the bank people."

"Will you go down with me?"

"Sure. It's going to be all right."

"I'm glad I talked to you 'bout this. It's been bothering me."

"Well, tongues will wag, but so long as we know the truth, it don't matter."

Just at that moment the children ran in announcing the entrance of their father. Jude opened the back door and walked into the kitchen. He was still a very good-looking man, and the only difference Sula could see was the thin pencil mustache under his nose, and a part in his hair.

"Hey, Jude. What you know good?"

"White man running it—nothing good."

Sula laughed while Nel, high-tuned to his moods, ignored her husband's smile saying, "Bad day, honey?"

"Same old stuff," he replied and told them a brief tale of some personal insult done him by a customer and his boss—a whiney tale that peaked somewhere between anger and a lapping desire for comfort. He ended it with the observation that a Negro man had a hard row to hoe in this world. He expected his story to dovetail into milkwarm commiseration, but before Nel could excrete it, Sula said she didn't know about that—it looked like a pretty good life to her.

"Say what?" Jude's temper flared just a bit as he looked at this friend of his wife's, this slight woman, not exactly plain, but not fine either, with a copperhead over her eye. As far as he could tell, she looked like a woman roaming the country trying to find some man to burden down with a lot of lip and a lot of mouths.

Sula was smiling. "I mean, I don't know what the fuss is about. I mean, everything in the world loves you. White men love you. They spend so much time worrying about your penis they forget their own. The only thing they want to do is cut off a nigger's privates. And if that ain't love and respect I don't know what is. And white women? They chase you all to every corner of the earth, feel for you under every bed. I knew a white woman wouldn't leave the house after 6 o'clock for fear one of you would snatch her. Now ain't that love? They think rape soon's they see you, and if they don't get the rape they looking for, they scream it anyway just so the search won't be in vain. Colored women worry themselves into bad health

just trying to hang on to your cuffs. Even little children—
white and black, boys and girls—spend all their childhood
eating their hearts out 'cause they think you don't love
them. And if that ain't enough, you love yourselves.
Nothing in this world loves a black man more than another
black man. You hear of solitary white men, but niggers?
Can't stay away from one another a whole day. So. It looks
to me like you the envy of the world."

Jude and Nel were laughing, he saying, "Well, if that's
the only way they got to show it—cut off my balls and
throw me in jail—I'd just as soon they left me alone." But
thinking that Sula had an odd way of looking at things
and that her wide smile took some of the sting from that
rattlesnake over her eye. A funny woman, he thought, not
that bad-looking. But he could see why she wasn't married;
she stirred a man's mind maybe, but not his body.

⊚ ⊚ ⊚

He left his tie. The one with the scriggly yellow lines
running lopsided across the dark-blue field. It hung over
the top of the closet door pointing steadily downward
while it waited with every confidence for Jude to return.

Could he be gone if his tie is still here? He will remember it and come back and then she would . . . uh. Then she
could . . . tell him. Sit down quietly and tell him. "But
Jude," she would say, "you *knew* me. All those days and
years, Jude, you *knew* me. My ways and my hands and
how my stomach folded and how we tried to get Mickey
to nurse and how about that time when the landlord said
. . . but you said . . . and I cried, Jude. You knew me and
had listened to the things I said in the night, and heard me

in the bathroom and laughed at my raggedy girdle and I laughed too because I knew you too, Jude. So how could you leave me when you knew me?"

But they had been down on all fours naked, not touching except their lips right down there on the floor where the tie is pointing to, on all fours like (uh huh, go on, say it) like dogs. Nibbling at each other, not even touching, not even looking at each other, just their lips, and when I opened the door they didn't even look for a minute and I thought the reason they are not looking up is because they are not doing that. So it's all right. I am just standing here. They are not doing that. I am just standing here and seeing it, but they are not really doing it. But then they did look up. Or you did. You did, Jude. And if only you had not looked at me the way the soldiers did on the train, the way you look at the children when they come in while you are listening to Gabriel Heatter and break your train of thought —not focusing exactly but giving them an instant, a piece of time, to remember what they are doing, what they are interrupting, and to go on back to wherever they were and let you listen to Gabriel Heatter. And I did not know how to move my feet or fix my eyes or what. I just stood there seeing it and smiling, because maybe there was some explanation, something important that I did not know about that would have made it all right. I waited for Sula to look up at me any minute and say one of those lovely college words like *aesthetic* or *rapport,* which I never understood but which I loved because they sounded so comfortable and firm. And finally you just got up and started putting on your clothes and your privates were hanging down, so soft, and you buckled your pants belt but forgot to button the fly and she was sitting on the bed not even bothering to put on her clothes because actually she didn't need to because somehow she didn't look naked to me, only you did. Her chin was in her hand and she sat like a visitor from out of town waiting for the hosts to get some quarreling done and over with so the card game could continue and me wanting her to leave so I could tell you privately that you had forgotten to button your fly because I didn't want to say it in front of her, Jude. And even when you began to talk, I couldn't hear because I was worried about you not knowing that your fly was open and scared too because your eyes looked like the soldiers' that time on the train when my mother turned to custard.

Remember how big that bedroom was? Jude? How when we moved here we said, Well, at least we got us a real big bedroom, but it was small then, Jude, and so shambly, and maybe it was that way all along but it would have been better if I had gotten the dust out from under the bed because I was ashamed of it in that small room. And then you walked past me saying, "I'll be back for my things." And you did but you left your tie.

The clock was ticking. Nel looked at it and realized that it was two thirty, only forty-five minutes before the children would be home and she hadn't even felt anything right or sensible and now there was no time or wouldn't be until nighttime when they were asleep and she could get into bed and maybe she could do it then. Think. But who could think in that bed where *they* had been and where they *also* had been and where only she was now?

She looked around for a place to be. A small place. The closet? No. Too dark. The bathroom. It was both small and bright, and she wanted to be in a very small, very bright place. Small enough to contain her grief. Bright enough to throw into relief the dark things that cluttered her. Once inside, she sank to the tile floor next to the toilet. On her knees, her hand on the cold rim of the bathtub, she waited for something to happen . . . inside. There was stirring, a movement of mud and dead leaves. She thought of the women at Chicken Little's funeral. The women who shrieked over the bier and at the lip of the open grave. What she had regarded since as unbecoming behavior seemed fitting to her now; they were screaming at the neck of God, his giant nape, the vast back-of-the-head that he had turned on them in death. But it seemed to her now that it was not a fist-shaking grief they were keening but rather a simple obligation to say something, do something, feel something about the dead. They could not let that heart-smashing event pass unrecorded, unidentified. It was poisonous, unnatural to let the dead go with a mere whimpering, a slight murmur, a rose bouquet of good taste. Good taste was out of place in the company of death, death itself was the essence of bad taste. And there must be much rage and saliva in its presence. The body must move and throw itself about, the eyes must roll, the hands should have no peace, and the throat should release all the yearning, despair and outrage that accompany the stupidity of loss.

"The real hell of Hell is that it is forever." Sula said

that. She said doing anything forever and ever was hell. Nel didn't understand it then, but now in the bathroom, trying to feel, she thought, "If I could be sure that I could stay here in this small white room with the dirty tile and water gurgling in the pipes and my head on the cool rim of this bathtub and never have to go out the door, I would be happy. If I could be certain that I never had to get up and flush the toilet, go in the kitchen, watch my children grow up and die, see my food chewed on my plate . . . Sula was wrong. Hell ain't things lasting forever. Hell is change." Not only did men leave and children grow up and die, but even the misery didn't last. One day she wouldn't even have that. This very grief that had twisted her into a curve on the floor and flayed her would be gone. She would lose that too.

"Why, even in hate here I am thinking of what Sula said."

Hunched down in the small bright room Nel waited. Waited for the oldest cry. A scream not for others, not in sympathy for a burnt child, or a dead father, but a deeply personal cry for one's own pain. A loud, strident: "Why me?" She waited. The mud shifted, the leaves stirred, the smell of overripe green things enveloped her and announced the beginnings of her very own howl.

But it did not come.

The odor evaporated; the leaves were still, the mud settled. And finally there was nothing, just a flake of something dry and nasty in her throat. She stood up frightened. There was something just to the right of her, in the air, just out of view. She could not see it, but she knew exactly what it looked like. A gray ball hovering just there. Just there. To the right. Quiet, gray, dirty. A ball of muddy strings, but without weight, fluffy but terrible in its malevolence. She knew she could not look, so she closed her eyes and crept past it out of the bathroom, shutting the door behind her. Sweating with fear, she stepped to the kitchen door and onto the back porch. The lilac bushes preened at the railing, but there were no lilacs yet. Wasn't it time? Surely it was time. She looked over the fence to Mrs. Rayford's yard. Hers were not in bloom either. Was it too late? She fastened on this question with enthusiasm, all the time aware of something she was not thinking. It was the only way she could get her mind off the flake in her throat.

She spent a whole summer with the gray ball, the little ball of fur and string and hair always floating in the light near her but which she did not see because she never looked. But that was the terrible part, the effort it took not to look. But it was there anyhow, just to the right of her head and maybe further down by her shoulder, so when the children went to a monster movie at the Elmira Theater and came home and said, "Mamma, can you sleep with us tonight?" she said all right and got into bed with the two boys, who loved it, but the girl did not. For a long time she could not stop getting in the bed with her children and told herself each time that they might dream a dream about dragons and would need her to comfort them. It was so nice to think about their scary dreams and not about a ball of fur. She even hoped their dreams would rub off on her and give her the wonderful relief of a nightmare so she could stop going around scared to turn her head this way or that lest she see it. That was the scary part—seeing it. It was not coming at her; it never did that, or tried to pounce on her. It just floated there for the seeing, if she wanted to, and O my God for the touching if she wanted to. But she didn't want to see it, ever, for if she saw it, who could tell but what she might actually touch it, or want to, and then what would happen if she actually reached out her hand and touched it? Die probably, but no worse than that. Dying was OK because it was sleep and there wasn't no gray ball in death, was there? Was there? She would have to ask somebody about that, somebody she could confide in and who knew a lot of things, like Sula, for Sula would know or if she didn't she would say something funny that would make it all right. Ooo no, not Sula. Here she was in the midst of it, hating it, scared of it, and again she thought of Sula as though they were still friends and talked things over. That was too much. To lose Jude and not have Sula to talk to about it because it was Sula that he had left her for.

Now her thighs were really empty. And it was then that what those women said about never looking at another man made some sense to her, for the real point, the heart of what they said, was the word *looked*. Not to promise never to make love to another man, not to refuse to marry another man, but to promise and know that she could never afford to look again, to see and accept the way in which their heads cut the air or see moons and tree limbs framed by their necks and shoulders . . . never to look, for now she could not risk looking—and anyway, so what? For now her thighs were truly empty and dead too, and it was Sula who had taken the life from them and Jude who smashed her heart and the both of them who left her with no thighs and no heart just her brain raveling away.

And what am I supposed to do with these old thighs now, just walk up and down these rooms? What good are they, Jesus? They will never give me the peace I need to get from sunup to sundown, what good are they, are you trying to tell me that I am going to have to go all the way through these days all the way, O my god, to that box with four handles with never nobody settling down between my legs even if I sew up those old pillow cases and rinse down the porch and feed my children and beat the rugs and haul the coal up out of the bin even then nobody, O Jesus, I could be a mule or plow the furrows with my hands if need be or hold these rickety walls up with my back if need be if I knew that somewhere in this world in the pocket of some night I could open my legs to some cowboy lean hips but you are trying to tell me no and O my sweet Jesus what kind of cross is that?

1939

When the word got out about Eva being put in Sunnydale, the people in the Bottom shook their heads and said Sula was a roach. Later, when they saw how she took Jude, then ditched him for others, and heard how he bought a bus ticket to Detroit (where he bought but never mailed birthday cards to his sons), they forgot all about Hannah's easy ways (or their own) and said she was a bitch. Everybody remembered the plague of robins that announced her return, and the tale about her watching Hannah burn was stirred up again.

But it was the men who gave her the final label, who fingerprinted her for all time. They were the ones who said she was guilty of the unforgivable thing—the thing for which there was no understanding, no excuse, no compassion. The route from which there was no way back, the dirt that could not ever be washed away. They said that Sula slept with white men. It may not have been true, but it certainly could have been. She was obviously capable of it. In any case, all minds were closed to her when that word was passed around. It made the old women draw their lips together; made small children look away from her in shame; made young men fantasize elaborate torture for her—just to get the saliva back in their mouths when they saw her.

Every one of them imagined the scene, each according to his own predilections—Sula underneath some white man —and it filled them with choking disgust. There was nothing lower she could do, nothing filthier. The fact that their own skin color was proof that it had happened in their own families was no deterrent to their bile. Nor was the willingness of black men to lie in the beds of white women a consideration that might lead them toward tolerance. They insisted that all unions between white men and black women be rape; for a black woman to be willing was literally unthinkable. In that way, they regarded integration with precisely the same venom that white people did.

So they laid broomsticks across their doors at night and sprinkled salt on porch steps. But aside from one or two unsuccessful efforts to collect the dust from her footsteps, they did nothing to harm her. As always the black people looked at evil stony-eyed and let it run.

Sula acknowledged none of their attempts at counter-conjure or their gossip and seemed to need the services of nobody. So they watched her far more closely than they watched any other roach or bitch in the town, and their alertness was gratified. Things began to happen.

First off, Teapot knocked on her door to see if she had any bottles. He was the five-year-old son of an indifferent mother, all of whose interests sat around the door of the Time and a Half Pool Hall. Her name was Betty but she was called Teapot's Mamma because being his mamma was

precisely her major failure. When Sula said no, the boy
turned around and fell down the steps. He couldn't get up
right away and Sula went to help him. His mother, just
then tripping home, saw Sula bending over her son's pained
face. She flew into a fit of concerned, if drunken, motherhood, and dragged Teapot home. She told everybody that
Sula had pushed him, and talked so strongly about it she
was forced to abide by the advice of her friends and take
him to the county hospital. The two dollars she hated to
release turned out to be well spent, for Teapot did have a
fracture, although the doctor said poor diet had contributed substantially to the daintiness of his bones. Teapot's
Mamma got a lot of attention anyway and immersed herself in a role she had shown no inclination for: motherhood. The very idea of a grown woman hurting her boy
kept her teeth on edge. She became the most devoted
mother: sober, clean and industrious. No more nickels for
Teapot to go to Dick's for a breakfast of Mr. Goodbars
and soda pop: no more long hours of him alone or wandering the roads while she was otherwise engaged. Her
change was a distinct improvement, although little Teapot
did miss those quiet times at Dick's.

Other things happened. Mr. Finley sat on his porch
sucking chicken bones, as he had done for thirteen years,
looked up, saw Sula, choked on a bone and died on the
spot. That incident, and Teapot's Mamma, cleared up for
everybody the meaning of the birthmark over her eye; it
was not a stemmed rose, or a snake, it was Hannah's ashes
marking her from the very beginning.

She came to their church suppers without underwear,
bought their steaming platters of food and merely picked

at it—relishing nothing, exclaiming over no one's ribs or cobbler. They believed that she was laughing at their God.

And the fury she created in the women of the town was incredible—for she would lay their husbands once and then no more. Hannah had been a nuisance, but she was complimenting the women, in a way, by wanting their husbands. Sula was trying them out and discarding them without any excuse the men could swallow. So the women, to justify their own judgment, cherished their men more, soothed the pride and vanity Sula had bruised.

Among the weighty evidence piling up was the fact that Sula did not look her age. She was near thirty and, unlike them, had lost no teeth, suffered no bruises, developed no ring of fat at the waist or pocket at the back of her neck. It was rumored that she had had no childhood diseases, was never known to have chicken pox, croup or even a runny nose. She had played rough as a child—where were the scars? Except for a funny-shaped finger and that evil birthmark, she was free of any normal signs of vulnerability. Some of the men, who as boys had dated her, remembered that on picnics neither gnats nor mosquitoes would settle on her. Patsy, Hannah's one-time friend, agreed and said not only that, but she had witnessed the fact that when Sula drank beer she never belched.

The most damning evidence, however, came from Dessie, who was a big Daughter Elk and knew things. At one of the social meetings she revealed something to her friends.

"Yeh, well I noticed something long time ago. Ain't said nothing 'bout it 'cause I wasn't sure what it meant. Well . . . I did mention it to Ivy but not nobody else. I disremember how long ago. 'Bout a month or two I guess 'cause I hadn't put down my new linoleum yet. Did you see it, Cora? It's that kind we saw in the catalogue."

"Naw."

"Get on with it, Dessie."

"Well, Cora was with me when we looked in the catalogue..."

"We all know 'bout your linoleum. What we don't know is..."

"OK. Let me tell it, will you? Just before the linoleum come I was out front and seed Shadrack carryin' on as usual ... up by the well ... walkin' 'round it salutin' and carryin' on. You know how he does ... hollerin' commands and..."

"Will you get on with it?"

"Who's tellin' this? Me or you?"

"You."

"Well, let me tell it then. Like I say, he was just cuttin' up as usual when Miss Sula Mae walks by on the other side of the road. And quick as that"—she snapped her fingers—"he stopped and cut on over 'cross the road, steppin' over to her like a tall turkey in short corn. And guess what? He tips his hat."

"Shadrack don't wear no hat."

"I know that but he tipped it anyway. You know what I mean. He acted like he had a hat and reached up for it and tipped it at her. Now you know Shadrack ain't civil to nobody!"

"Sure ain't."

"Even when you buyin' his fish he's cussin'. If you ain't got the right change he cussin' you. If you act like a fish

ain't too fresh he snatch it out of your hand like he doin'
you the favor."

"Well, everybody know he a reprobate."

"Yeh, so how come he tip his hat to Sula? How come he
don't cuss her?"

"Two devils."

"Exactly!"

"What'd she do when he tipped it? Smile and give him
a curtsey?"

"No, and that was the other thing. It was the first time
I see her look anything but hateful. Like she smellin' you
with her eyes and don't like your soap. When he tipped his
hat she put her hand on her throat for a minute and *cut*
out. Went runnin' on up the road to home. And him still
standin' there tippin' away. And—this the point I was
comin' to—when I went back in the house a big sty come
on my eye. And I ain't never had no sty before. Never!"

"That's 'cause you saw it."

"Exactly."

"Devil all right."

"No two ways about it," Dessie said, and she popped the
rubber band off the deck of cards to settle them down for
a nice long game of bid whist.

Their conviction of Sula's evil changed them in account-
able yet mysterious ways. Once the source of their personal misfortune was identified, they had leave to protect
and love one another. They began to cherish their husbands and wives, protect their children, repair their homes
and in general band together against the devil in their

midst. In their world, aberrations were as much a part of nature as grace. It was not for them to expel or annihilate it. They would no more run Sula out of town than they would kill the robins that brought her back, for in their secret awareness of Him, He was not the God of three faces they sang about. They knew quite well that He had four, and that the fourth explained Sula. They had lived with various forms of evil all their days, and it wasn't that they believed God would take care of them. It was rather that they knew God had a brother and that brother hadn't spared God's son, so why should he spare them?

There was no creature so ungodly as to make them destroy it. They could kill easily if provoked to anger, but not by design, which explained why they could not "mob kill" anyone. To do so was not only unnatural, it was undignified. The presence of evil was something to be first recognized, then dealt with, survived, outwitted, triumphed over.

Their evidence against Sula was contrived, but their conclusions about her were not. Sula was distinctly different. Eva's arrogance and Hannah's self-indulgence merged in her and, with a twist that was all her own imagination, she lived out her days exploring her own thoughts and emotions, giving them full reign, feeling no obligation to please anybody unless their pleasure pleased her. As willing to feel pain as to give pain, to feel pleasure as to give pleasure, hers was an experimental life—ever since her mother's remarks sent her flying up those stairs, ever since her one major feeling of responsibility had been exorcised on the bank of a river with a closed place in the middle. The first experience taught her there was no other that you could count on; the second that there was no self to count on either. She had no center, no speck around which to grow. In the midst of a pleasant conversation with someone she might say, "Why do you chew with your mouth open?" not because the answer interested her but because she wanted to see the person's face change rapidly. She was completely free of ambition, with no affection for money, property or things, no greed, no desire to command attention or compliments—no ego. For that reason she felt no compulsion to verify herself—be consistent with herself.

She had clung to Nel as the closest thing to both an other and a self, only to discover that she and Nel were not one and the same thing. She had no thought at all of causing Nel pain when she bedded down with Jude. They had always shared the affection of other people: compared how a boy kissed, what line he used with one and then the other. Marriage, apparently, had changed all that, but having had no intimate knowledge of marriage, having lived in a house with women who thought all men available, and selected from among them with a care only for their tastes, she was ill prepared for the possessiveness of the one person she felt close to. She knew well enough what other women said and felt, or said they felt. But she and Nel had always seen through them. They both knew that those women were not jealous of other women; that they were only afraid of losing their jobs. Afraid their husbands would discover that no uniqueness lay between their legs.

Nel was the one person who had wanted nothing from her, who had accepted all aspects of her. Now she wanted everything, and all because of *that*. Nel was the first person who had been real to her, whose name she knew, who had seen as she had the slant of life that made it possible to stretch it to its limits. Now Nel was one of *them*. One of the spiders whose only thought was the next rung of the web, who dangled in dark dry places suspended by their own spittle, more terrified of the free fall than the snake's breath below. Their eyes so intent on the wayward stranger who trips into their net, they were blind to the cobalt on their own backs, the moonshine fighting to pierce their corners. If they were touched by the snake's breath, however fatal, they were merely victims and knew how to behave in that role (just as Nel knew how to behave as the wronged wife). But the free fall, oh no, that required— demanded—invention: a thing to do with the wings, a way of holding the legs and most of all a full surrender to the downward flight if they wished to taste their tongues or stay alive. But alive was what they, and now Nel, did not want to be. Too dangerous. Now Nel belonged to the town and all of its ways. She had given herself over to them, and the flick of their tongues would drive her back into her little dry corner where she would cling to her spittle high above the breath of the snake and the fall.

It had surprised her a little and saddened her a good deal when Nel behaved the way the others would have. Nel was one of the reasons she had drifted back to Medallion, that and the boredom she found in Nashville, Detroit, New Orleans, New York, Philadelphia, Macon and San Diego. All those cities held the same people, working the same mouths, sweating the same sweat. The men who took her to one or another of those places had merged into one large personality: the same language of love, the same

entertainments of love, the same cooling of love. Whenever she introduced her private thoughts into their rub-
bings or goings, they hooded their eyes. They taught her
nothing but love tricks, shared nothing but worry, gave
nothing but money. She had been looking all along for a
friend, and it took her a while to discover that a lover was
not a comrade and could never be—for a woman. And that
no one would ever be that version of herself which she
sought to reach out to and touch with an ungloved hand.
There was only her own mood and whim, and if that was
all there was, she decided to turn the naked hand toward it,
discover it and let others become as intimate with their
own selves as she was.

In a way, her strangeness, her naïveté, her craving for
the other half of her equation was the consequence of an
idle imagination. Had she paints, or clay, or knew the
discipline of the dance, or strings; had she anything to engage her tremendous curiosity and her gift for metaphor,
she might have exchanged the restlessness and preoccupation with whim for an activity that provided her with all
she yearned for. And like any artist with no art form, she
became dangerous.

She had lied only once in her life—to Nel about the
reason for putting Eva out, and she could lie to her only
because she cared about her. When she had come back
home, social conversation was impossible for her because
she could not lie. She could not say to those old acquaint-
ances, "Hey, girl, you looking good," when she saw how
the years had dusted their bronze with ash, the eyes that
had once opened wide to the moon bent into grimy sickles
of concern. The narrower their lives, the wider their hips.

Those with husbands had folded themselves into starched coffins, their sides bursting with other people's skinned dreams and bony regrets. Those without men were like sour-tipped needles featuring one constant empty eye. Those with men had had the sweetness sucked from their breath by ovens and steam kettles. Their children were like distant but exposed wounds whose aches were no less intimate because separate from their flesh. They had looked at the world and back at their children, back at the world and back again at their children, and Sula knew that one clear young eye was all that kept the knife away from the throat's curve.

She was pariah, then, and knew it. Knew that they despised her and believed that they framed their hatred as disgust for the easy way she lay with men. Which was true. She went to bed with men as frequently as she could. It was the only place where she could find what she was looking for: misery and the ability to feel deep sorrow. She had not always been aware that it was sadness that she yearned for. Lovemaking seemed to her, at first, the creation of a special kind of joy. She thought she liked the sootiness of sex and its comedy; she laughed a great deal during the raucous beginnings, and rejected those lovers who regarded sex as healthy or beautiful. Sexual aesthetics bored her. Although she did not regard sex as ugly (ugliness was boring also), she liked to think of it as wicked. But as her experiences multiplied she realized that not only was it not wicked, it was not necessary for her to conjure up the idea of wickedness in order to participate fully. During the lovemaking she found and needed to find the cutting edge. When she left off cooperating with her body and began to assert herself in the act, particles of strength gathered in her like steel shavings drawn to a spacious magnetic center, forming a tight cluster that nothing, it seemed, could break. And there was utmost irony and outrage in lying under someone, in a position of surrender, feeling her own abiding strength and limitless power. But the cluster did break, fall apart, and in her panic to hold it together she leaped from the edge into soundlessness and went down howling, howling in a stinging awareness of the endings of things: an eye of sorrow in the midst of all that hurricane rage of joy. There, in the center of that silence was not eternity but the death of time and a loneliness so profound the word itself had no meaning. For loneliness assumed the absence of other people, and the solitude she found in that desperate terrain had never admitted the possibility of other people. She wept then. Tears for the deaths of the littlest things: the castaway shoes of children; broken stems of marsh grass battered and drowned by the sea; prom photographs of dead women she never knew; wedding rings in pawnshop windows; the tidy bodies of Cornish hens in a nest of rice.

When her partner disengaged himself, she looked up at him in wonder trying to recall his name; and he looked down at her, smiling with tender understanding of the state of tearful gratitude to which he believed he had brought her. She waiting impatiently for him to turn away and settle into a wet skim of satisfaction and light disgust, leaving her to the postcoital privateness in which she met herself, welcomed herself, and joined herself in matchless harmony.

At twenty-nine she knew it would be no other way for

her, but she had not counted on the footsteps on the porch, and the beautiful black face that stared at her through the blue-glass window. Ajax.

Looking for all the world as he had seventeen years ago when he had called her pig meat. He was twenty-one then, she twelve. A universe of time between them. Now she was twenty-nine, he thirty-eight, and the lemon-yellow haunches seemed not so far away after all.

She opened the heavy door and saw him standing on the other side of the screen door with two quarts of milk tucked into his arms like marble statues. He smiled and said, "I been lookin' all over for you."

"Why?" she asked.

"To give you these," and he nodded toward one of the quarts of milk.

"I don't like milk," she said.

"But you like bottles don't you?" He held one up. "Ain't that pretty?"

And indeed it was. Hanging from his fingers, framed by a slick blue sky, it looked precious and clean and permanent. She had the distinct impression that he had done something dangerous to get them.

Sula ran her fingernails over the screen thoughtfully for a second and then, laughing, she opened the screen door.

Ajax came in and headed straight for the kitchen. Sula followed slowly. By the time she got to the door he had undone the complicated wire cap and was letting the cold milk run into his mouth.

Sula watched him—or rather the rhythm in his throat —with growing interest. When he had had enough, he poured the rest into the sink, rinsed the bottle out and presented it to her. She took the bottle with one hand and his wrist with the other and pulled him into the pantry. There was no need to go there, for not a soul was in the house, but the gesture came to Hannah's daughter naturally. There in the pantry, empty now of flour sacks, void of row upon row of canned goods, free forever of strings of tiny green peppers, holding the wet milk bottle tight in her arm she stood wide-legged against the wall and pulled from his track-lean hips all the pleasure her thighs could hold.

He came regularly then, bearing gifts: clusters of black berries still on their branches, four meal-fried porgies wrapped in a salmon-colored sheet of the Pittsburgh *Courier*, a handful of jacks, two boxes of lime Jell-Well, a hunk of ice-wagon ice, a can of Old Dutch Cleanser with the bonneted woman chasing dirt with her stick; a page of Tillie the Toiler comics, and more gleaming white bottles of milk.

Contrary to what anybody would have suspected from just seeing him lounging around the pool hall, or shooting at Mr. Finley for beating his own dog, or calling filthy compliments to passing women, Ajax was very nice to women. His women, of course, knew it, and it provoked them into murderous battles over him in the streets, brawling thick-thighed women with knives disturbed many a Friday night with their bloodletting and attracted whooping crowds. On such occasions Ajax stood, along with the crowd, and viewed the fighters with the same golden-eyed indifference with which he watched old men playing checkers. Other than his mother, who sat in her shack with six younger sons working roots, he had never met an interesting woman in his life.

His kindness to them in general was not due to a ritual of seduction (he had no need for it) but rather to the habit he acquired in dealing with his mother, who inspired thoughtfulness and generosity in all her sons.

She was an evil conjure woman, blessed with seven adoring children whose joy it was to bring her the plants, hair, underclothing, fingernail parings, white hens, blood, camphor, pictures, kerosene and footstep dust that she needed, as well as to order Van Van, High John the Conqueror, Little John to Chew, Devil's Shoe String, Chinese Wash, Mustard Seed and the Nine Herbs from Cincinnati. She knew about the weather, omens, the living, the dead, dreams and all illnesses and made a modest living with her skills. Had she any teeth or ever straightened her back, she would have been the most gorgeous thing alive, worthy of her sons' worship for her beauty alone, if not for the absolute freedom she allowed them (known in some quarters as neglect) and the weight of her hoary knowledge.

This woman Ajax loved, and after her—airplanes. There was nothing in between. And when he was not sitting enchanted listening to his mother's words, he thought of airplanes, and pilots, and the deep sky that held them both. People thought that those long trips he took to large cities in the state were for some sophisticated good times they could not imagine but only envy; actually he was leaning against the barbed wire of airports, or nosing around hangars just to hear the talk of the men who were fortunate enough to be in the trade. The rest of the time, the time he was not watching his mother's magic or thinking of airplanes, he spent in the idle pursuits of bachelors without work in small towns. He had heard all the stories about Sula, and they aroused his curiosity. Her elusiveness and indifference to established habits of behavior reminded him of his mother, who was as stubborn in her pursuits of the occult as the women of Greater Saint Matthew's were in the search for redeeming grace. So when his curiosity was high enough he picked two bottles of milk off the porch of some white family and went to see her, suspecting that this was perhaps the only other woman he knew whose life was her own, who could deal with life efficiently, and who was not interested in nailing him.

Sula, too, was curious. She knew nothing about him except the word he had called out to her years ago and the feeling he had excited in her then. She had grown quite accustomed to the clichés of other people's lives as well as her own increasing dissatisfaction with Medallion. If she could have thought of a place to go, she probably would have left, but that was before Ajax looked at her through the blue glass and held the milk aloft like a trophy.

But it was not the presents that made her wrap him up in her thighs. They were charming, of course (especially the jar of butterflies he let loose in the bedroom), but her real pleasure was the fact that he talked to her. They had genuine conversations. He did not speak down to her or at her, nor content himself with puerile questions about her life or monologues of his own activities. Thinking she was possibly brilliant, like his mother, he seemed to expect brilliance from her, and she delivered. And in all of it, he listened more than he spoke. His clear comfort at being in her presence, his lazy willingness to tell her all about fixes and the powers of plants, his refusal to baby or protect her, his assumption that she was both tough and wise—all of that coupled with a wide generosity of spirit only occasionally erupting into vengeance sustained Sula's interest and enthusiasm.

His idea of bliss (on earth as opposed to bliss in the sky) was a long bath in piping-hot water—his head on the cool white rim, his eyes closed in reverie.

"Soaking in hot water give you a bad back." Sula stood in the doorway looking at his knees glistening just at the surface of the soap-gray water.

"Soaking in Sula give me a bad back."

"Worth it?"

"Don't know yet. Go 'way."

"Airplanes?"

"Airplanes."

"Lindbergh know about you?"

"Go 'way."

She went and waited for him in Eva's high bed, her head turned to the boarded-up window. She was smiling, thinking how like Jude's was his craving to do the white man's work, when two deweys came in with their beautiful teeth and said, "We sick."

Sula turned her head slowly and murmured, "Get well."

"We need some medicine."

"Look in the bathroom."

"Ajax in there."

"Then wait."

"We sick now."

Sula leaned over the bed, picked up a shoe and threw it at them.

"Cocksucker!" they screamed, and she leaped out of the bed naked as a yard dog. She caught the redheaded dewey by his shirt and held him by the heels over the banister until he wet his pants. The other dewey was joined by the third, and they delved into their pockets for stones, which they threw at her. Sula, ducking and tottering with laughter, carried the wet dewey to the bed-room and when the other two followed her, deprived of all weapons except their teeth, Sula had dropped the first dewey on the bed and was fishing in her purse. She gave each of them a dollar bill which they snatched and then scooted off down the stairs to Dick's to buy the catarrh remedy they loved to drink.

Ajax came sopping wet into the room and lay down on the bed to let the air dry him. They were both still for a long time until he reached out and touched her arm.

He liked for her to mount him so he could see her towering above him and call soft obscenities up into her face. As she rocked there, swayed there, like a Georgia pine on its knees, high above the slipping, falling smile, high above the golden eyes and the velvet helmet of hair, rocking, swaying, she focused her thoughts to bar the creeping disorder that was flooding her hips. She looked down, down from what seemed an awful height at the head of the man whose lemon-yellow gabardines had been the first sexual excitement she'd known. Letting her thoughts dwell on his face in order to confine, for just a while longer, the drift of her flesh toward the high silence of orgasm.

If I take a chamois and rub real hard on the bone, right on the ledge of your cheek bone, some of the black will disappear. It will flake away into the chamois and underneath there will be gold leaf. I can see it shining through the black. I know it is there . . .

How high she was over his wand-lean body, how slippery was his sliding sliding smile.

And if I take a nail file or even Eva's old paring knife— that will do—and scrape away at the gold, it will fall away and there will be alabaster. The alabaster is what gives your face its planes, its curves. That is why your mouth smiling does not reach your eyes. Alabaster is giving it a gravity that resists a total smile.

The height and the swaying dizzied her, so she bent down and let her breasts graze his chest.

Then I can take a chisel and small tap hammer and tap away at the alabaster. It will crack then like ice under the pick, and through the breaks I will see the loam, fertile, free of pebbles and twigs. For it is the loam that is giving you that smell.

She slipped her hands under his armpits, for it seemed as though she would not be able to dam the spread of weakness she felt under her skin without holding on to something.

I will put my hand deep into your soil, lift it, sift it with my fingers, feel its warm surface and dewy chill below.

She put her head under his chin with no hope in the world of keeping anything at all at bay.

I will water your soil, keep it rich and moist. But how much? How much water to keep the loam moist? And how much loam will I need to keep my water still? And when do the two make mud?

He swallowed her mouth just as her thighs had swallowed his genitals, and the house was very, very quiet.

◉ ◉ ◉

Sula began to discover what possession was. Not love, perhaps, but possession or at least the desire for it. She was astounded by so new and alien a feeling. First there was the morning of the night before when she actually wondered if Ajax would come by that day. Then there was an afternoon when she stood before the mirror finger-tracing the laugh lines around her mouth and trying to decide whether she was good-looking or not. She ended this deep perusal by tying a green ribbon in her hair. The green silk made a rippling whisper as she slid it into her hair—a whisper that could easily have been Hannah's chuckle, a soft slow nasal hiss she used to emit when something amused her. Like women sitting for two hours under the marcelling irons only to wonder two days later how soon they would need another appointment. The ribbon-tying was followed by other activity, and when Ajax came that evening, bringing her a reed whistle he had carved that morning, not only was the green ribbon still in her hair, but the bathroom was gleaming, the bed was made, and the table was set for two.

He gave her the reed whistle, unlaced his shoes and sat in the rocking chair in the kitchen.

Sula walked toward him and kissed his mouth. He ran his fingers along the nape of her neck.

"I bet you ain't even missed Tar Baby, have you?" he asked.

"Missed? No. Where is he?"

Ajax smiled at her delicious indifference. "Jail."

"Since when?"

"Last Saturday."

"Picked up for drunk?"

"Little bit more than that," he answered and went ahead to tell her about his own involvement in another of Tar Baby's misfortunes.

On Saturday afternoon Tar Baby had stumbled drunk into traffic on the New River Road. A woman driver swerved to avoid him and hit another car. When the police came, they recognized the woman as the mayor's niece and arrested Tar Baby. Later, after the word got out, Ajax and two other men went to the station to see about him. At first they wouldn't let them in. But they relented after Ajax and the other two just stood around for one hour and a half and repeated their request at regular intervals. When they finally got permission to go in and looked in at him in the cell, he was twisted up in a corner badly beaten and dressed in nothing but extremely soiled underwear. Ajax and the other men asked the officer why Tar Baby couldn't have back his clothes. "It ain't right," they said, "to let a grown man lay around in his own shit."

The policeman, obviously in agreement with Eva, who had always maintained that Tar Baby was white, said that if the prisoner didn't like to live in shit, he should come down out of those hills, and live like a decent white man.

More words were exchanged, hot words and dark, and the whole thing ended with the arraignment of the three black men, and an appointment to appear in civil court Thursday next.

Ajax didn't seem too bothered by any of it. More annoyed and inconvenienced than anything else. He had had several messes with the police, mostly in gambling raids, and regarded them as the natural hazards of Negro life.

But Sula, the green ribbon shining in her hair, was flooded with an awareness of the impact of the outside world on Ajax. She stood up and arranged herself on the arm of the rocking chair. Putting her fingers deep into the velvet of his hair, she murmured, "Come on. Lean on me."

Ajax blinked. Then he looked swiftly into her face. In her words, in her voice, was a sound he knew well. For the first time he saw the green ribbon. He looked around and saw the gleaming kitchen and the table set for two and detected the scent of the nest. Every hackle on his body rose, and he knew that very soon she would, like all of her sisters before her, put to him the death-knell question "Where you been?" His eyes dimmed with a mild and momentary regret.

He stood and mounted the stairs with her and entered the spotless bathroom where the dust had been swept from underneath the claw-foot tub. He was trying to remember the date of the air show in Dayton. As he came into the bedroom, he saw Sula lying on fresh white sheets, wrapped in the deadly odor of freshly applied cologne.

He dragged her under him and made love to her with the steadiness and the intensity of a man about to leave for Dayton.

Every now and then she looked around for tangible evidence of his having ever been there. Where were the butterflies? the blueberries? the whistling reed? She could find nothing, for he had left nothing but his stunning absence. An absence so decorative, so ornate, it was diffi-cult for her to understand how she had ever endured, without falling dead or being consumed, his magnificent presence.

The mirror by the door was not a mirror by the door, it was an altar where he stood for only a moment to put on his cap before going out. The red rocking chair was a rocking of his own hips as he sat in the kitchen. Still, there was nothing of his—his own—that she could find. It was as if she were afraid she had hallucinated him and needed proof to the contrary. His absence was every-where, stinging everything, giving the furnishings primary colors, sharp outlines to the corners of rooms and gold light to the dust collecting on table tops. When he was there he pulled everything toward himself. Not only her eyes and all her senses but also inanimate things seemed to exist because of him, backdrops to his presence. Now that he had gone, these things, so long subdued by his presence, were glamorized in his wake.

Then one day, burrowing in a dresser drawer, she found what she had been looking for: proof that he had been there, his driver's license. It contained just what she needed for verification—his vital statistics: Born 1901, height 5′11″, weight 152 lbs., eyes brown, hair black, color black. Oh yes, skin black. Very black. So black that only a steady careful rubbing with steel wool would remove it, and as it was removed there was the glint of gold leaf and under the gold leaf the cold alabaster and deep, deep down under the cold alabaster more black only this time the black of warm loam.

But what was this? Albert Jacks? His name was Albert Jacks? A. Jacks. She had thought it was Ajax. All those years. Even from the time she walked by the pool hall and looked away from him sitting astride a wooden chair, looked away to keep from seeing the wide space of intolerable orderliness between his legs; the openness that held no sign, no sign at all, of the animal that lurked in his trousers; looked away from the insolent nostrils and the smile that kept slipping and falling, falling, falling so she wanted to reach out with her hand to catch it before it fell to the pavement and was sullied by the cigarette butts and bottle caps and spittle at his feet and the feet of other men who sat or stood around outside the pool hall, calling, singing out to her and Nel and grown women too with lyrics like *pig meat* and *brown sugar* and *jailbait* and *O Lord, what have I done to deserve the wrath*, and *Take me, Jesus, I have seen the promised land*, and *Do, Lord, remember me* in voices mellowed by hopeless passion into gentleness. Even then, when she and Nel were trying hard not to dream of him and not to think of him when they touched the softness in their underwear or undid their braids as soon as they left home to let the hair bump and wave around their ears, or wrapped the cotton binding around their chests so the nipples would not break through their blouses and give him cause to smile his slipping, falling smile, which brought the blood rushing to their skin. And even later, when for the first time in her life she had lain in bed with a man and said his name involuntarily or said it truly meaning *him*, the name she was screaming and saying was not his at all.

Sula stood with a worn slip of paper in her fingers and said aloud to no one, "I didn't even know his name. And if I didn't know his name, then there is nothing I did know and I have known nothing ever at all since the one thing I wanted was to know his name so how could he help but leave me since he was making love to a woman who didn't even know his name.

"When I was a little girl the heads of my paper dolls came off, and it was a long time before I discovered that my own head would not fall off if I bent my neck. I used to walk around holding it very stiff because I thought a strong wind or a heavy push would snap my neck. Nel was the one who told me the truth. But she was wrong. I did not hold my head stiff enough when I met him and so I lost it just like the dolls.

"It's just as well he left. Soon I would have torn the flesh from his face just to see if I was right about the gold and nobody would have understood that kind of curiosity. They would have believed that I wanted to hurt him just like the little boy who fell down the steps and broke his leg and the people think I pushed him just because I looked at it."

Holding the driver's license she crawled into bed and fell into a sleep full of dreams of cobalt blue.

When she awoke, there was a melody in her head she could not identify or recall ever hearing before. "Perhaps I made it up," she thought. Then it came to her—the name of the song and all its lyrics just as she had heard it many times before. She sat on the edge of the bed thinking, "There aren't any more new songs and I have sung all the ones there are. I have sung them all. I have sung all the songs there are." She lay down again on the bed and sang a little wandering tune made up of the words *I have sung all the songs all the songs I have sung all the songs there are* until, touched by her own lullaby, she grew drowsy, and in the hollow of near-sleep she tasted the acridness of gold, left the chill of alabaster and smelled the dark, sweet stench of loam.

1940

"I heard you was sick. Anything I can do for you?"

She had practiced not just the words but the tone, the pitch of her voice. It should be calm, matter-of-fact, but strong in sympathy—for the illness though, not for the patient.

The sound of her voice as she heard it in her head betrayed no curiosity, no pride, just the inflection of any good woman come to see about a sick person who, incidentally, had such visits from nobody else.

For the first time in three years she would be looking at the stemmed rose that hung over the eye of her enemy. Moreover, she would be doing it with the taste of Jude's exit in her mouth, with the resentment and shame that even yet pressed for release in her stomach. She would be facing the black rose that Jude had kissed and looking at the nostrils of the woman who had twisted her love for her own children into something so thick and monstrous she was afraid to show it lest it break loose and smother them with its heavy paw. A cumbersome bear-love that, given any rein, would suck their breath away in its crying need for honey.

Because Jude's leaving was so complete, the full responsibility of the household was Nel's. There were no more fifty dollars in brown envelopes to count on, so she took to cleaning rather than fret away the tiny seaman's pension her parents lived on. And just this past year she got a better job working as a chambermaid in the same hotel Jude had worked in. The tips were only fair, but the hours were good—she was home when the children got out of school.

At thirty her hot brown eyes had turned to agate, and her skin had taken on the sheen of maple struck down, split and sanded at the height of its green. Virtue, bleak and drawn, was her only mooring. It brought her to Number 7 Carpenter's Road and the door with the blue glass; it helped her to resist scratching the screen as in days gone by; it hid from her the true motives for her charity, and, finally, it gave her voice the timbre she wanted it to have: free of delight or a lip-smacking "I told you so" with which the news of Sula's illness had been received up in the Bottom—free of the least hint of retribution.

Now she stood in Eva's old bedroom, looking down at that dark rose, aware of the knife-thin arms sliding back and forth over the quilt and the boarded-up window Eva had jumped out of.

Sula looked up and without a second's pause followed Nel's example of leaving out the greeting when she spoke.

"As a matter of fact, there is. I got a prescription. Nathan usually goes for me but he . . . school don't let out till three. Could you run it over to the drugstore?"

"Where is it?" Nel was glad to have a concrete errand. Conversation would be difficult. (Trust Sula to pick up a relationship exactly where it lay.)

"Look in my bag. No. Over there."

Nel walked to the dresser and opened the purse with the beaded clasp. She saw only a watch and the folded prescription down inside. No wallet, no change purse. She turned to Sula: "Where's your . . ."

But Sula was looking at the boarded-up window. Something in her eye right there in the corner stopped Nel from completing her question. That and the slight flare of the nostrils—a shadow of a snarl. Nel took the piece of paper and picked up her own purse, saying, "OK. I'll be right back."

As soon as the door was shut, Sula breathed through her mouth. While Nel was in the room the pain had increased. Now that this new pain killer, the one she had been holding in reserve, was on the way her misery was manageable. She let a piece of her mind lay on Nel. It was funny, sending Nel off to that drugstore right away like that, after she had not seen her to speak to for years. The drugstore was where Edna Finch's Mellow House used to be years back when they were girls. Where they used to go, the two of them, hand in hand, for the 18-cent ice-cream sundaes, past the Time and a Half Pool Hall, where the sprawling men said "pig meat," and they sat in that cool room with the marble-top tables and ate the first ice-cream sundaes of their lives. Now Nel was going back there alone and Sula was waiting for the medicine the doctor said not to take until the pain got really bad. And she supposed "really bad" was now. Although you could never tell. She wondered for an instant what Nellie wanted; why she had come. Did she want to gloat? Make up? Following this line of thought required more concentration than she could muster. Pain was greedy; it demanded all of her attention. But it was good that this new medicine, the reserve, would be brought to her by her old friend. Nel, she remembered, always thrived on a crisis. The closed place in the water; Hannah's funeral. Nel was the best. When Sula imitated her, or tried to, those long years ago, it always ended up in some action noteworthy not for its coolness but mostly for its being bizarre. The one time she tried to protect Nel, she had cut off her own finger tip and earned not Nel's gratitude but her disgust. From then on she had let her emotions dictate her behavior.

She could hear Nel's footsteps long before she opened the door and put the medicine on the table near the bed.

As Sula poured the liquid into a sticky spoon, Nel began the sickroom conversation.

"You look fine, Sula."

"You lying, Nellie. I look bad." She gulped the medicine.

"No. I haven't seen you for a long time, but you look ..."

"You don't have to do that, Nellie. It's going to be all right."

"What ails you? Have they said?"

Sula licked the corners of her lips. "You want to talk about that?"

Nel smiled, slightly, at the bluntness she had forgotten. "No. No, I don't, but you sure you should be staying up here alone?"

"Nathan comes by. The deweys sometimes, and Tar Baby..."

"That ain't help, Sula. You need to be with somebody grown. Somebody who can . . ."

"I'd rather be here, Nellie."

"You know you don't have to be proud with me."

"Proud?" Sula's laughter broke through the phlegm. "What you talking about? I like my own dirt, Nellie. I'm not proud. You sure have forgotten me."

"Maybe. Maybe not. But you a woman and you alone."

"And you? Ain't you alone?"

"I'm not sick. I work."

"Yes. Of course you do. Work's good for you, Nellie. It don't do nothing for me."

"You never *had* to."

"I never would."

"There's something to say for it, Sula. 'Specially if you don't want people to have to do for you."

"Neither one, Nellie. Neither one."

"You can't have it all, Sula." Nel was getting exasperated with her arrogance, with her lying at death's door still smart-talking.

"Why? I can do it all, why can't I have it all?"

"You *can't* do it all. You a woman and a colored woman at that. You can't act like a man. You can't be walking around all independent-like, doing whatever you like, taking what you want, leaving what you don't."

"You repeating yourself."

"How repeating myself?"

"You say I'm a woman and colored. Ain't that the same as being a man?"

"I don't think so and you wouldn't either if you had children."

"Then I really would act like what you call a man. Every man I ever knew left his children."

"Some were taken."

"Wrong, Nellie. The word is 'left.' "

"You still going to know everything, ain't you?"

"I don't know everything, I just do everything."

"Well, you don't do what I do."

"You think I don't know what your life is like just because I ain't living it? I know what every colored woman in this country is doing."

"What's that?"

"Dying. Just like me. But the difference is they dying like a stump. Me, I'm going down like one of those red-woods. I sure did live in this world."

"Really? What have you got to show for it?"

"Show? To who? Girl, I got my mind. And what goes on in it. Which is to say, I got me."

"Lonely, ain't it?"

"Yes. But my lonely is *mine*. Now your lonely is some-body else's. Made by somebody else and handed to you. Ain't that something? A secondhand lonely."

Nel sat back on the little wooden chair. Anger skipped but she realized that Sula was probably just showing off. No telling what shape she was really in, but there was no point in saying anything other than what was the truth. "I always understood how you could take a man. Now I understand why you can't keep none."

"Is that what I'm supposed to do? Spend my life keep-ing a man?"

"They worth keeping, Sula."

"They ain't worth more than me. And besides, I never

loved no man because he was worth it. Worth didn't have nothing to do with it."

"What did?"

"My mind did. That's all."

"Well I guess that's it. You own the world and the rest of us is renting. You ride the pony and we shovel the shit. I didn't come up here for this kind of talk, Sula . . ."

"No?"

"No. I come to see about you. But now that you opened it up, I may as well close it." Nel's fingers closed around the brass rail of the bed. Now she would ask her. "How come you did it, Sula?"

There was a silence but Nel felt no obligation to fill it. Sula stirred a little under the covers. She looked bored as she sucked her teeth. "Well, there was this space in front of me, behind me, in my head. Some space. And Jude filled it up. That's all. He just filled up the space."

"You mean you didn't even love him?" The feel of the brass was in Nel's mouth. "It wasn't even loving him?"

Sula looked toward the boarded-up window again. Her eyes fluttered as if she were about to fall off into sleep.

"But . . ." Nel held her stomach in. "But what about me? What about me? Why didn't you think about me? Didn't I count? I never hurt you. What did you take him for if you didn't love him and why didn't you think about me?" And then, "I was good to you, Sula, why don't that matter?"

Sula turned her head away from the boarded window. Her voice was quiet and the stemmed rose over her eye was very dark. "It matters, Nel, but only to you. Not to anybody else. Being good to somebody is just like being mean to somebody. Risky. You don't get nothing for it."

Nel took her hands from the brass railing. She was annoyed with herself. Finally when she had gotten the nerve to ask the question, the right question, it made no difference. Sula couldn't give her a sensible answer because she didn't know. Would be, in fact, the last to know. Talking to her about right and wrong was like talking to the deweys. She picked at the fringe on Sula's bedspread and said softly, "We were friends."

"Oh, yes. Good friends," Sula said.

"And you didn't love me enough to leave him alone. To let him love me. You had to take him away."

"What you mean take him away? I didn't kill him, I just fucked him. If we were such good friends, how come you couldn't get over it?"

"You laying there in that bed without a dime or a friend to your name having done all the dirt you did in this town and you still expect folks to love you?"

Sula raised herself up on her elbows. Her face glistened with the dew of fever. She opened her mouth as though to say something, then fell back on the pillows and sighed. "Oh, they'll love me all right. It will take time, but they'll love me." The sound of her voice was as soft and distant as the look in her eyes. "After all the old women have lain with the teen-agers; when all the young girls have slept with their old drunken uncles; after all the black men fuck all the white ones; when all the white women kiss all the black ones; when the guards have raped all the jailbirds and after all the whores make love to their grannies; after all the faggots get their mothers' trim; when Lindbergh sleeps with Bessie Smith and Norma Shearer makes it with Stepin Fetchit; after all the dogs have fucked all the cats and every weathervane on every barn flies off the roof to mount the hogs . . . then there'll be a little love left over for me. And I know just what it will feel like."

She closed her eyes then and thought of the wind pressing her dress between her legs as she ran up the bank of the river to four leaf-locked trees and the digging of holes in the earth.

Embarrassed, irritable and a little bit ashamed, Nel rose to go. "Goodbye, Sula. I don't reckon I'll be back."

She opened the door and heard Sula's low whisper. "Hey, girl." Nel paused and turned her head but not enough to see her.

"How you know?" Sula asked.

"Know what?" Nel still wouldn't look at her.

"About who was good. How you know it was you?"

"What you mean?"

"I mean maybe it wasn't you. Maybe it was me."

Nel took two steps out the door and closed it behind her. She walked down the hall and down the four flights of steps. The house billowed around her light then dark, full of presences without sounds. The deweys, Tar Baby, the newly married couples, Mr. Buckland Reed, Patsy, Valentine, and the beautiful Hannah Peace. Where were they? Eva out at the old folks' home, the deweys living anywhere, Tar Baby steeped in wine, and Sula upstairs in Eva's bed with a boarded-up window and an empty pocketbook on the dresser.

. . .

When Nel closed the door, Sula reached for more medicine. Then she turned the pillow over to its cool side and thought about her old friend. "So she will walk on down that road, her back so straight in that old green coat, the strap of her handbag pushed back all the way to the elbow, thinking how much I have cost her and never remember the days when we were two throats and one eye and we had no price."

Pictures drifted through her head as lightly as dandelion spores: the blue eagle that swallowed the E of the Sherman's Mellowe wine that Tar Baby drank; the pink underlid of Hannah's eye as she probed for a fleck of coal dust or a lash. She thought of looking out of the windows of all those trains and buses, looking at the feet and backs of all those people. Nothing was ever different. They were all the same. All of the words and all of the smiles, every tear and every gag just something to do.

"That's the same sun I looked at when I was twelve, the same pear trees. If I live a hundred years my urine will flow the same way, my armpits and breath will smell the same. My hair will grow from the same holes. I didn't mean anything. I never meant anything. I stood there watching her burn and was thrilled. I wanted her to keep on jerking like that, to keep on dancing."

Then she had the dream again. The Clabber Girl Baking Powder lady was smiling and beckoning to her, one hand under her apron. When Sula came near she disintegrated into white dust, which Sula was hurriedly trying to stuff into the pockets of her blue-flannel housecoat. The disintegration was awful to see, but worse was the feel of the powder—its starchy slipperiness as she tried to collect it by handfuls. The more she scooped, the more it billowed. At last it covered her, filled her eyes, her nose, her throat, and she woke gagging and overwhelmed with the smell of smoke.

Pain took hold. First a fluttering as of doves in her stomach, then a kind of burning, followed by a spread of thin wires to other parts of her body. Once the wires of liquid pain were in place, they jelled and began to throb. She tried concentrating on the throbs, identifying them as waves, hammer strokes, razor edges or small explosions. Soon even the variety of the pain bored her and there was nothing to do, for it was joined by fatigue so great she could not make a fist or fight the taste of oil at the back of her tongue.

Several times she tried to cry out, but the fatigue barely let her open her lips, let alone take the deep breath necessary to scream. So she lay there wondering how soon she would gather enough strength to lift her arm and push the rough quilt away from her chin and whether she should turn her cheek to the cooler side of the pillow now or wait till her face was thoroughly soaked and the move would be more refreshing. But she was reluctant to move her face for another reason. If she turned her head, she would not be able to see the boarded-up window Eva jumped out of. And looking at those four wooden planks with the steel rod slanting across them was the only peace she had. The sealed window soothed her with its sturdy termination, its unassailable finality. It was as though for the first time she was completely alone—where she had always wanted to be—free of the possibility of distraction. It would be here, only here, held by this blind window high above the elm tree, that she might draw her legs up to her chest, close her eyes, put her thumb in her mouth and float over and down the tunnels, just missing the dark walls, down, down until she met a rain scent and would know the water was near, and she would curl into its heavy softness and it would envelop her, carry her, and wash her tired flesh always. Always. Who said that? She tried hard to think. Who was it that had promised her a sleep of water always? The effort to recall was too great; it loosened a knot in her chest that turned her thoughts again to the pain.

While in this state of weary anticipation, she noticed that she was not breathing, that her heart had stopped completely. A crease of fear touched her breast, for any second there was sure to be a violent explosion in her brain, a gasping for breath. Then she realized, or rather she sensed, that there was not going to be any pain. She was not breathing because she didn't have to. Her body did not need oxygen. She was dead.

Sula felt her face smiling. "Well, I'll be damned," she thought, "it didn't even hurt. Wait'll I tell Nel."

1941

The death of Sula Peace was the best news folks up in the Bottom had had since the promise of work at the tunnel. Of the few who were not afraid to witness the burial of a witch and who had gone to the cemetery, some had come just to verify her being put away but stayed to sing "Shall We Gather at the River" for politeness' sake, quite unaware of the bleak promise of their song. Others came to see that nothing went awry, that the shallow-minded and small-hearted kept their meanness at bay, and that the entire event be characterized by that abiding gentleness of spirit to which they themselves had arrived by the simple determination not to let anything—anything at all: not failed crops, not rednecks, lost jobs, sick children, rotten potatoes, broken pipes, bug-ridden flour, third-class coal, educated social workers, thieving insurance men, garlic-ridden hunkies, corrupt Catholics, racist Protestants, cowardly Jews, slaveholding Moslems, jack-leg nigger preachers, squeamish Chinamen, cholera, dropsy or the Black Plague, let alone a strange woman—keep them from their God.

In any case, both the raw-spirited and the gentle who came—not to the white funeral parlor but to the colored part of the Beechnut Cemetery—felt that either *because*

Sula was dead or just *after* she was dead a brighter day was dawning. There were signs. The rumor that the tunnel spanning the river would use Negro workers became an announcement. Planned, abandoned and replanned for years, this project had finally begun in 1937. For three years there were rumors that blacks would work it, and hope was high in spite of the fact that the River Road leading to the tunnel had encouraged similar hopes in 1927 but had ended up being built entirely by white labor—hillbillies and immigrants taking even the lowest jobs. But the tunnel itself was another matter. The craft work—no, they would not get that. But it was a major job, and the government seemed to favor opening up employment to black workers. It meant black men would not have to sweep Medallion to eat, or leave the town altogether for the steel mills in Akron and along Lake Erie.

The second sign was the construction begun on an old people's home. True, it was more renovation than construction, but the blacks were free, or so it was said, to occupy it. Some said that the very transfer of Eva from the ramshackle house that passed for a colored women's nursing home to the bright new one was a clear sign of the mystery of God's ways, His mighty thumb having been seen at Sula's throat.

So it was with a strong sense of hope that the people in the Bottom watched October close.

Then Medallion turned silver. It seemed sudden, but actually there had been days and days of no snow—just frost—when, late one afternoon, a rain fell and froze.

Way down Carpenter's Road, where the concrete side-walks started, children hurried to the sliding places before shopkeepers and old women sprinkled stove ashes, like ancient onyx, onto the new-minted silver. They hugged trees simply to hold for a moment all that life and large-ness stilled in glass, and gazed at the sun pressed against the gray sky like a worn doubloon, wondering all the while if the world were coming to an end. Grass stood blade by blade, shocked into separateness by an ice that held for days.

Late-harvesting things were ruined, of course, and fowl died of both chill and rage. Cider turned to ice and split the jugs, forcing the men to drink their cane liquor too soon. It was better down in the valley, since, as always, the hills protected it, but up in the Bottom black folks suf-fered heavily in their thin houses and thinner clothes. The ice-cold wind bled what little heat they had through windowpanes and ill-fitting doors. For days on end they were virtually housebound, venturing out only to coal-bins or right next door for the trading of vital foodstuffs. Never to the stores. No deliveries were being made any-way, and when they were, the items were saved for better-paying white customers. Women could not make it down the icy slopes and therefore missed days of wages they sorely needed.

The consequence of all that ice was a wretched Thanks-giving of tiny tough birds, heavy pork cakes, and pithy sweet potatoes. By the time the ice began to melt and the first barge was seen shuddering through the ice skim on the river, everybody under fifteen had croup, or scarlet fever, and those over had chilblains, rheumatism, pleurisy, earaches and a world of other ailments.

Still it was not those illnesses or even the ice that marked the beginning of the trouble, that self-fulfilled prophecy that Shadrack carried on his tongue. As soon as the silvering began, long before the cider cracked the jugs, there was something wrong. A falling away, a dislocation was taking place. Hard on the heels of the general relief that Sula's death brought a restless irritability took hold. Teapot, for example, went into the kitchen and asked his mother for some sugar-butter-bread. She got up to fix it and found that she had no butter, only oleomargarine. Too tired to mix the saffron-colored powder into the hard cake of oleo, she simply smeared the white stuff on the bread and sprinkled the sugar over it. Teapot tasted the difference and refused to eat it. This keenest of insults that a mother can feel, the rejection by a child of her food, bent her into fury and she beat him as she had not done since Sula knocked him down the steps. She was not alone. Other mothers who had defended their children from Sula's malevolence (or who had defended their positions as mothers from Sula's scorn for the role) now had nothing to rub up against. The tension was gone and so was the reason for the effort they had made. Without her mockery, affection for others sank into flaccid disrepair. Daughters who had complained bitterly about the responsibilities of taking care of their aged mothers-in-law had altered when Sula locked Eva away, and they began cleaning those old women's spittoons without a murmur. Now that Sula was dead and done with, they returned to a steeping resentment of the burdens of old people. Wives uncoddled their husbands; there seemed no further need to reinforce their vanity. And even those Negroes who had moved down from Canada to Medallion, who remarked every chance they got that they had never been slaves, felt a loosening of the reactionary compassion for Southern-born blacks Sula had inspired in them. They returned to their original claims of superiority.

The normal meanness that the winter brought was compounded by the small-spiritedness that hunger and scarlet fever produced. Even a definite and witnessed interview of four colored men (and the promise of more in the spring) at the tunnel site could not break the cold vise of that lean and bitter year's end.

Christmas came one morning and haggled everybody's nerves like a dull ax—too shabby to cut clean but too heavy to ignore. The children lay wall-eyed on creaking beds or pallets near the stove, sucking peppermint and oranges in between coughs while their mothers stomped the floors in rage at the cakes that did not rise because the stove fire had been so stingy; at the curled bodies of men who chose to sleep the day away rather than face the silence made by the absence of Lionel trains, drums, crybaby dolls and rocking horses. Teen-agers sneaked into the Elmira Theater in the afternoon and let Tex Ritter free them from the recollection of their fathers' shoes, yawning in impotence under the bed. Some of them had a bottle of wine, which they drank at the feet of the glittering Mr. Ritter, making such a ruckus the manager had to put them out. The white people who came with Christmas bags of rock candy and old clothes were hard put to get a *Yes'm, thank you,* out of those sullen mouths.

Just as the ice lingered in October, so did the phlegm of December—which explained the enormous relief brought on by the first three days of 1941. It was as though the season had exhausted itself, for on January first the temperature shot up to sixty-one degrees and slushed the whiteness overnight. On January second drab patches of grass could be seen in the fields. On January third the sun came out—and so did Shadrack with his rope, his bell and his childish dirge.

He had spent the night before watching a tiny moon. The people, the voices that kept him company, were with him less and less. Now there were long periods when he heard nothing except the wind in the trees and the plop of buckeyes on the earth. In the winter, when the fish were too hard to get to, he did picking-up jobs for small businessmen (nobody would have him in or even near their homes), and thereby continued to have enough money for liquor. Yet the drunk times were becoming deeper but more seldom. It was as though he no longer needed to drink to forget whatever it was he could not remember. Now he could not remember that he had ever forgotten anything. Perhaps that was why for the first time after that cold day in France he was beginning to miss the presence of other people. Shadrack had improved enough to feel lonely. If he was lonely before, he didn't know it because the noise he kept up, the roaring, the busyness,

protected him from knowing it. Now the compulsion to
activity, to filling up the time when he was not happily
fishing on the riverbank, had dwindled. He sometimes
fell asleep before he got drunk; sometimes spent whole
days looking at the river and the sky; and more and more
he relinquished the military habits of cleanliness in his
shack. Once a bird flew into his door—one of the robins
during the time there was a plague of them. It stayed,
looking for an exit, for the better part of an hour. When
the bird found the window and flew away, Shadrack was
grieved and actually waited and watched for its return.
During those days of waiting, he did not make his bed, or
sweep, or shake out the little rag-braid rug, and almost
forgot to slash with his fish knife the passing day on his
calendar. When he did return to housekeeping, it was not
with the precision he had always insisted upon. The messier
his house got, the lonelier he felt, and it was harder and
harder to conjure up sergeants, and orderlies, and invading
armies; harder and harder to hear the gunfire and keep the
platoon marching in time. More frequently now he looked
at and fondled the one piece of evidence that he once
had a visitor in his house: a child's purple-and-white belt.
The one the little girl left behind when she came to see
him. Shadrack remembered the scene clearly. He had
stepped into the door and there was a tear-stained face
turning, turning toward him; eyes hurt and wondering;
mouth parted in an effort to ask a question. She had
wanted something—from him. Not fish, not work, but
something only he could give. She had a tadpole over her
eye (that was how he knew she was a friend—she had the
mark of the fish he loved), and one of her braids had

come undone. But when he looked at her face he had seen also the skull beneath, and thinking she saw it too—knew it was there and was afraid—he tried to think of something to say to comfort her, something to stop the hurt from spilling out of her eyes. So he had said "always," so she would not have to be afraid of the change—the falling away of skin, the drip and slide of blood, and the exposure of bone underneath. He had said "always" to convince her, assure her, of permanency.

It worked, for when he said it her face lit up and the hurt did leave. She ran then, carrying his knowledge, but her belt fell off and he kept it as a memento. It hung on a nail near his bed—unfrayed, unsullied after all those years, with only the permanent bend in the fabric made by its long life on a nail. It was pleasant living with that sign of a visitor, his only one. And after a while he was able to connect the belt with the face, the tadpole-over-the-eye-face that he sometimes saw up in the Bottom. His visitor, his company, his guest, his social life, his woman, his daughter, his friend—they all hung there on a nail near his bed.

Now he stared at the tiny moon floating high over the ice-choked river. His loneliness had dropped down somewhere around his ankles. Some other feeling possessed him. A feeling that touched his eyes and made him blink. He had seen her again months? weeks? ago. Raking leaves for Mr. Hodges, he had gone into the cellar for two bushel baskets to put them in. In the hallway he passed an open door leading to a small room. She lay on a table there. It was surely the same one. The same little-girl face, same tadpole over the eye. So he had been wrong. Terribly

wrong. No "always" at all. Another dying away of someone whose face he knew.

It was then he began to suspect that all those years of
rope hauling and bell ringing were never going to do any
good. He might as well sit forever on his riverbank and
stare out of the window at the moon.

By his day-slashed calendar he knew that tomorrow
was the day. And for the first time he did not want to
go. He wanted to stay with the purple-and-white belt.
Not go. Not go.

Still, when the day broke in an incredible splash of sun,
he gathered his things. In the early part of the afternoon,
drenched in sunlight and certain that this would be the last
time he would invite them to end their lives neatly and
sweetly, he walked over the rickety bridge and on into
the Bottom. But it was not heartfelt this time, not loving
this time, for he no longer cared whether he helped them
or not. His rope was improperly tied; his bell had a tinny
unimpassioned sound. His visitor was dead and would
come no more.

Years later people would quarrel about who had been
the first to go. Most folks said it was the deweys, but one
or two knew better, knew that Dessie and Ivy had been
first. Said that Dessie had opened her door first and stood
there shielding her eyes from the sun while watching
Shadrack coming down the road. She laughed.

Maybe the sun; maybe the clots of green showing in the
hills promising so much; maybe the contrast between
Shadrack's doomy, gloomy bell glinting in all that sweet

sunshine. Maybe just a brief moment, for once, of not feeling fear, of looking at death in the sunshine and being unafraid. She laughed.

Upstairs, Ivy heard her and looked to see what caused the thick music that rocked her neighbor's breasts. Then Ivy laughed too. Like the scarlet fever that had touched everybody and worn them down to gristle, their laughter infected Carpenter's Road. Soon children were jumping about giggling and men came to the porches to chuckle. By the time Shadrack reached the first house, he was facing a line of delighted faces.

Never before had they laughed. Always they had shut their doors, pulled down the shades and called their children out of the road. It frightened him, this glee, but he stuck to his habit—singing his song, ringing his bell and holding fast to his rope. The deweys with their magnificent teeth ran out from Number 7 and danced a little jig around the befuddled Shadrack, then cut into a wild aping of his walk, his song and his bell-ringing. By now women were holding their stomachs, and the men were slapping their knees. It was Mrs. Jackson, who ate ice, who tripped down off her porch and marched—actually marched—along behind him. The scene was so comic the people walked into the road to make sure they saw it all. In that way the parade started.

Everybody, Dessie, Tar Baby, Patsy, Mr. Buckland Reed, Teapot's Mamma, Valentine, the deweys, Mrs. Jackson, Irene, the proprietor of the Palace of Cosmetology, Reba, the Herrod brothers and flocks of teen-agers got into the mood and, laughing, dancing, calling to one another, formed a pied piper's band behind Shadrack. As the initial group of about twenty people passed more houses, they called to the people standing in doors and leaning out of windows to join them; to help them open further this slit in the veil, this respite from anxiety, from dignity, from gravity, from the weight of that very adult pain that had undergirded them all those years before. Called to them to come out and play in the sunshine—as though the sunshine would last, as though there really was hope. The same hope that kept them picking beans for other farmers; kept them from finally leaving as they talked of doing; kept them knee-deep in other people's dirt; kept them excited about other people's wars; kept them solicitous of white people's children; kept them convinced that some magic "government" was going to lift them up, out and away from that dirt, those beans, those wars.

Some, of course, like Helene Wright, would not go. She watched the ruckus with characteristic scorn. Others, who understood the Spirit's touch which made them dance, who understood whole families bending their backs in a field while singing as from one throat, who understood the ecstasy of river baptisms under suns just like this one, did not understand this curious disorder, this headless display and so refused also to go.

Nevertheless, the sun splashed on a larger and larger crowd that strutted, skipped, marched, and shuffled down the road. When they got down to where the sidewalk started, some of them stopped and decided to turn back, too embarrassed to enter the white part of town whooping like banshees. But except for three or four, the fainthearted were put to shame by the more aggressive and abandoned,

and the parade danced down Main Street past Wool-
worth's and the old poultry house, turned right and moved
on down the New River Road.

At the mouth of the tunnel excavation, in a fever pitch
of excitement and joy, they saw the timber, the bricks, the
steel ribs and the tacky wire gate that glittered under ice
struck to diamond in the sun. It dazzled them, at first, and
they were suddenly quiet. Their hooded eyes swept over
the place where their hope had lain since 1927. There was
the promise: leaf-dead. The teeth unrepaired, the coal
credit cut off, the chest pains unattended, the school shoes
unbought, the rush-stuffed mattresses, the broken toilets,
the leaning porches, the slurred remarks and the staggering
childish malevolence of their employers. All there in blazing sunlit ice rapidly becoming water.

Like antelopes they leaped over the little gate—a wire
barricade that was never intended to bar anything but
dogs, rabbits and stray children—and led by the tough,
the enraged and the young they picked up the lengths of
timber and thin steel ribs and smashed the bricks they
would never fire in yawning kilns, split the sacks of lime-
stone they had not mixed or even been allowed to haul;
tore the wire mesh, tipped over wheelbarrows and rolled
forepoles down the bank, where they sailed far out on the
icebound river.

Old and young, women and children, lame and hearty,
they killed, as best they could, the tunnel they were forbidden to build.

They didn't mean to go in, to actually go down into
the lip of the tunnel, but in their need to kill it all, all of it,
to wipe from the face of the earth the work of the thin-

armed Virginia boys, the bull-necked Greeks and the knife-faced men who waved the leaf-dead promise, they went too deep, too far . . .

A lot of them died there. The earth, now warm, shifted; the first forepole slipped; loose rock fell from the face of the tunnel and caused a shield to give way. They found themselves in a chamber of water, deprived of the sun that had brought them there. With the first crack and whoosh of water, the clamber to get out was so fierce that others who were trying to help were pulled to their deaths. Pressed up against steel ribs and timber blocks young boys strangled when the oxygen left them to join the water. Outside, others watched in terror as ice split and earth shook beneath their feet. Mrs. Jackson, weighing less than 100 pounds, slid down the bank and met with an open mouth the ice she had craved all her life. Tar Baby, Dessie, Ivy, Valentine, the Herrod boys, some of Ajax's younger brothers and the deweys (at least it was supposed; their bodies were never found)—all died there. Mr. Buckland Reed escaped, so did Patsy and her two boys, as well as some fifteen or twenty who had not gotten close enough to fall, or whose timidity would not let them enter an unfinished tunnel.

And all the while Shadrack stood there. Having forgotten his song and his rope, he just stood there high up on the bank ringing, ringing his bell.

1965

Things were so much better in 1965. Or so it seemed. You could go downtown and see colored people working in the dime store behind the counters, even handling money with cash-register keys around their necks. And a colored man taught mathematics at the junior high school. The young people had a look about them that everybody said was new but which reminded Nel of the deweys, whom nobody had ever found. Maybe, she thought, they had gone off and seeded the land and growed up in these young people in the dime store with the cash-register keys around their necks.

They were so different, these young people. So different from the way she remembered them forty years ago.

Jesus, there were some beautiful boys in 1921! Look like the whole world was bursting at the seams with them. Thirteen, fourteen, fifteen years old. Jesus, they were fine. L. P., Paul Freeman and his brother Jake, Mrs. Scott's twins—and Ajax had a whole flock of younger brothers. They hung out of attic windows, rode on car fenders, delivered the coal, moved into Medallion and moved out, visited cousins, plowed, hoisted, lounged on the church steps, careened on the school playground. The sun heated them and the moon slid down their backs. God, the world was *full* of beautiful boys in 1921.

Nothing like these kids. Everything had changed. Even the whores were better then: tough, fat, laughing women with burns on their cheeks and wit married to their mean- ness: or widows couched in small houses in the woods with eight children to feed and no man. These modern-day whores were pale and dull before those women. These little clothes-crazy things were always embarrassed. Nasty but shamed. They didn't know what shameless was. They should have known those silvery widows in the woods who would get up from the dinner table and walk into the trees with a customer with as much embarrassment as a calving mare.

Lord, how time flies. She hardly recognized anybody in the town any more. Now there was another old people's home. Look like this town just kept on building homes for old people. Every time they built a road they built a old folks' home. You'd think folks was living longer, but the fact of it was, they was just being put out faster.

Nel hadn't seen the insides of this most recent one yet, but it was her turn in Circle Number 5 to visit some of the old women there. The pastor visited them regularly, but the circle thought private visits were nice too. There were just nine colored women out there, the same nine that had been in the other one. But a lot of white ones. White people didn't fret about putting their old ones away. It took a lot for black people to let them go, and even if somebody was old and alone, others did the dropping by, the floor washing, the cooking. Only when they got crazy

and unmanageable were they let go. Unless it was somebody like Sula, who put Eva away out of meanness. It was
true that Eva was foolish in the head, but not so bad as to
need locking up.

Nel was more than a little curious to see her. She had
been really active in church only a year or less, and that
was because the children were grown now and took up less
time and less space in her mind. For over twenty-five
years since Jude walked out she had pinned herself into a
tiny life. She spent a little time trying to marry again, but
nobody wanted to take her on with three children, and she
simply couldn't manage the business of keeping boyfriends.
During the war she had had a rather long relationship with
a sergeant stationed at the camp twenty miles down river
from Medallion, but then he got called away and everything was reduced to a few letters—then nothing. Then
there was a bartender at the hotel. But now she was fifty-
five and hard put to remember what all that had been
about.

It didn't take long, after Jude left, for her to see what
the future would be. She had looked at her children and
knew in her heart that that would be all. That they were
all she would ever know of love. But it was a love that, like
a pan of syrup kept too long on the stove, had cooked out,
leaving only its odor and a hard, sweet sludge, impossible
to scrape off. For the mouths of her children quickly forgot the taste of her nipples, and years ago they had begun
to look past her face into the nearest stretch of sky.

In the meantime the Bottom had collapsed. Everybody
who had made money during the war moved as close as
they could to the valley, and the white people were buying

down river, cross river, stretching Medallion like two strings on the banks. Nobody colored lived much up in the Bottom any more. White people were building towers for television stations up there and there was a rumor about a golf course or something. Anyway, hill land was more valuable now, and those black people who had moved down right after the war and in the fifties couldn't afford to come back even if they wanted to. Except for the few blacks still huddled by the river bend, and some undemolished houses on Carpenter's Road, only rich white folks were building homes in the hills. Just like that, they had changed their minds and instead of keeping the valley floor to themselves, now they wanted a hilltop house with a river view and a ring of elms. The black people, for all their new look, seemed awfully anxious to get to the valley, or leave town, and abandon the hills to whoever was interested. It was sad, because the Bottom had been a real place. These young ones kept talking about the community, but they left the hills to the poor, the old, the stubborn—and the rich white folks. Maybe it hadn't been a community, but it had been a place. Now there weren't any places left, just separate houses with separate televisions and separate telephones and less and less dropping by.

These were the same thoughts she always had when she walked down into the town. One of the last true pedestrians, Nel walked the shoulder road while cars slipped by. Laughed at by her children, she still walked wherever she wanted to go, allowing herself to accept rides only when the weather required it.

Now she went straight through the town and turned left at its farthest end, along a tree-lined walk that turned into a country road farther on and passed the cemetery, Beechnut Park.

When she got to Sunnydale, the home for the aged, it was already four o'clock and turning chill. She would be glad to sit down with those old birds and rest her feet.

A red-haired lady at the desk gave her a pass card and pointed to a door that opened onto a corridor of smaller doors. It looked like what she imagined a college dormitory to be. The lobby was luxurious—modern—but the rooms she peeped into were sterile green cages. There was too much light everywhere; it needed some shadows. The third door, down the hall, had a little name tag over it that read EVA PEACE. Nel twisted the knob and rapped a little on the door at the same time, then listened a moment before she opened it.

At first she couldn't believe it. She seemed so small, sitting at that table in a black-vinyl chair. All the heaviness had gone and the height. Her once beautiful leg had no stocking and the foot was in a slipper. Nel wanted to cry —not for Eva's milk-dull eyes or her floppy lips, but for the once proud foot accustomed for over a half century to a fine well-laced shoe, now stuffed gracelessly into a pink terrycloth slipper.

"Good evening, Miss Peace. I'm Nel Greene come to pay a call on you. You remember me, don't you?"

Eva was ironing and dreaming of stairwells. She had neither iron nor clothes but did not stop her fastidious lining up of pleats or pressing out of wrinkles even when she acknowledged Nel's greeting.

"Howdy. Sit down."

"Thank you." Nel sat on the edge of the little bed.

"You've got a pretty room, a real pretty room, Miss Peace."

"You eat something funny today?"

"Ma'am?"

"Some chop suey? Think back."

"No, ma'am."

"No? Well, you gone be sick later on."

"But I didn't have no chop suey."

"You think I come all the way over here for you to tell me that? I can't make visits too often. You should have some respect for old people."

"But Miss Peace, I'm visiting *you*. This is *your* room." Nel smiled.

"What you say your name was?"

"Nel Greene."

"Wiley Wright's girl?"

"Uh huh. You do remember. That makes me feel good, Miss Peace. You remember me and my father."

"Tell me how you killed that little boy."

"What? What little boy?"

"The one you threw in the water. I got oranges. How did you get him to go in the water?"

"I didn't throw no little boy in the river. That was Sula."

"You. Sula. What's the difference? You was there. You watched, didn't you? Me, I never would've watched."

"You're confused, Miss Peace. I'm Nel. Sula's dead."

"It's awful cold in the water. Fire is warm. How did you get him in?" Eva wet her forefinger and tested the iron's heat.

"Who told you all these lies? Miss Peace? Who told you? Why are you telling lies on me?"

"I got oranges. I don't drink they old orange juice. They puts something in it."

"Why are you trying to make out like I did it?"

Eva stopped ironing and looked at Nel. For the first time her eyes looked sane.

"You think I'm guilty?" Nel was whispering.

Eva whispered back, "Who would know that better than you?"

"I want to know who you been talking to." Nel forced herself to speak normally.

"Plum. Sweet Plum. He tells me things." Eva laughed a light, tinkly giggle—girlish.

"I'll be going now, Miss Peace." Nel stood.

"You ain't answered me yet."

"I don't know what you're talking about."

"Just alike. Both of you. Never was no difference between you. Want some oranges? It's better for you than chop suey. Sula? I got oranges."

Nel walked hurriedly down the hall, Eva calling after her, "Sula?" Nel couldn't see the other women today. That woman had upset her. She handed her pass back to the lady, avoiding her look of surprise.

Outside she fastened her coat against the rising wind. The top button was missing so she covered her throat with her hand. A bright space opened in her head and memory seeped into it.

Standing on the riverbank in a purple-and-white dress, Sula swinging Chicken Little around and around. His laughter before the hand-slip and the water closing quickly over the place. What had she felt then, watching Sula going around and around and then the little boy swinging out over the water? Sula had cried and cried when she came back from Shadrack's house. But Nel had remained calm.

"*Shouldn't we tell?*"

"*Did he see?*"

"*I don't know. No.*"

"*Let's go. We can't bring him back.*"

What did old Eva mean by *you watched?* How could she help seeing it? She was right there. But Eva didn't say *see,* she said *watched.* "I did not watch it. I just saw it." But it was there anyway, as it had always been, the old feeling and the old question. The good feeling she had had when Chicken's hands slipped. She hadn't wondered about that in years. "Why didn't I feel bad when it happened? How come it felt so good to see him fall?"

All these years she had been secretly proud of her calm, controlled behavior when Sula was uncontrollable, her compassion for Sula's frightened and shamed eyes. Now it seemed that what she had thought was maturity, serenity and compassion was only the tranquillity that follows a joyful stimulation. Just as the water closed peacefully over the turbulence of Chicken Little's body, so had contentment washed over her enjoyment.

She was walking too fast. Not watching where she placed her feet, she got into the weeds by the side of the road. Running almost, she approached Beechnut Park. Just over there was the colored part of the cemetery. She went in. Sula was buried there along with Plum, Hannah

and now Pearl. With the same disregard for name changes
by marriage that the black people of Medallion always
showed, each flat slab had one word carved on it. Together
they read like a chant: PEACE 1895–1921, PEACE 1890–
1923, PEACE 1910–1940, PEACE 1892–1959.

They were not dead people. They were words. Not
even words. Wishes, longings.

All these years she had been harboring good feelings
about Eva; sharing, she believed, her loneliness and unloved state as no one else could or did. She, after all, was
the only one who really understood why Eva refused to
attend Sula's funeral. The others thought they knew;
thought the grandmother's reasons were the same as their
own—that to pay respect to someone who had caused them
so much pain was beneath them. Nel, who did go, believed
Eva's refusal was not due to pride or vengeance but to a
plain unwillingness to see the swallowing of her own flesh
into the dirt, a determination not to let the eyes see what
the heart could not hold.

Now, however, after the way Eva had just treated her,
accused her, she wondered if the townspeople hadn't been
right the first time. Eva *was* mean. Sula had even said so.
There was no good reason for her to speak so. Feeble-
minded or not. Old. Whatever. Eva knew what she was
doing. Always had. She had stayed away from Sula's
funeral and accused Nel of drowning Chicken Little for
spite. The same spite that galloped all over the Bottom.
That made every gesture an offense, every off-center smile
a threat, so that even the bubbles of relief that broke in the
chest of practically everybody when Sula died did not
soften their spite and allow them to go to Mr. Hodges'

funeral parlor or send flowers from the church or bake a yellow cake.

She thought about Nathan opening the bedroom door the day she had visited her, and finding the body. He said he knew she was dead right away not because her eyes were open but because her mouth was. It looked to him like a giant yawn that she never got to finish. He had run across the street to Teapot's Mamma, who, when she heard the news, said, "Ho!" like the conductor on the train when it was about to take off except louder, and then did a little dance. None of the women left their quilt patches in disarray to run to the house. Nobody left the clothes halfway through the wringer to run to the house. Even the men just said "uhn," when they heard. The day passed and no one came. The night slipped into another day and the body was still lying in Eva's bed gazing at the ceiling trying to complete a yawn. It was very strange, this stubbornness about Sula. For even when China, the most rambunctious whore in the town, died (whose black son and white son said, when they heard she was dying, "She ain't dead yet?"), even then everybody stopped what they were doing and turned out in numbers to put the fallen sister away.

It was Nel who finally called the hospital, then the mortuary, then the police, who were the ones to come. So the white people took over. They came in a police van and carried the body down the steps past the four pear trees and into the van for all the world as with Hannah. When the police asked questions nobody gave them any information. It took them hours to find out the dead woman's first name. The call was for a Miss Peace at 7 Carpenter's

Road. So they left with that: a body, a name and an address. The white people had to wash her, dress her, prepare her and finally lower her. It was all done elegantly, for it was discovered that she had a substantial death policy. Nel went to the funeral parlor, but was so shocked by the closed coffin she stayed only a few minutes.

The following day Nel walked to the burying and found herself the only black person there, steeling her mind to the roses and pulleys. It was only when she turned to leave that she saw the cluster of black folk at the lip of the cemetery. Not coming in, not dressed for mourning, but there waiting. Not until the white folks left—the gravediggers, Mr. and Mrs. Hodges, and their young son who assisted them—did those black people from up in the Bottom enter with hooded hearts and filed eyes to sing "Shall We Gather at the River" over the curved earth that cut them off from the most magnificent hatred they had ever known. Their question clotted the October air, Shall We Gather at the River? The beautiful, the beautiful river? Perhaps Sula answered them even then, for it began to rain, and the women ran in tiny leaps through the grass for fear their straightened hair would beat them home.

Sadly, heavily, Nel left the colored part of the cemetery. Further along the road Shadrack passed her by. A little shaggier, a little older, still energetically mad, he looked at the woman hurrying along the road with the sunset in her face.

He stopped. Trying to remember where he had seen her before. The effort of recollection was too much for him and he moved on. He had to haul some trash out at Sunnydale and it would be good and dark before he got home.

He hadn't sold fish in a long time now. The river had killed them all. No more silver-gray flashes, no more flat, wide, unhurried look. No more slowing down of gills. No more tremor on the line.

Shadrack and Nel moved in opposite directions, each thinking separate thoughts about the past. The distance between them increased as they both remembered gone things.

Suddenly Nel stopped. Her eye twitched and burned a little.

"Sula?" she whispered, gazing at the tops of trees. "Sula?"

Leaves stirred; mud shifted; there was the smell of overripe green things. A soft ball of fur broke and scattered like dandelion spores in the breeze.

"All that time, all that time, I thought I was missing Jude." And the loss pressed down on her chest and came up into her throat. "We was girls together," she said as though explaining something. "O Lord, Sula," she cried, "girl, girl, girlgirlgirl."

It was a fine cry—loud and long—but it had no bottom and it had no top, just circles and circles of sorrow.

Song of Solomon

Daddy

*The fathers may soar
And the children may know their names*

Part I

Part 1

Chapter 1

The North Carolina Mutual Life Insurance agent promised to
fly from Mercy to the other side of Lake Superior at three
o'clock. Two days before the event was to take place he tacked
a note on the door of his little yellow house:

> At 3:00 p.m. on Wednesday the 18th of February,
> 1931, I will take off from Mercy and fly away on
> my own wings. Please forgive me. I loved you all.
>
> (signed) Robert Smith,
> Ins. agent

Mr. Smith didn't draw as big a crowd as Lindbergh had four
years earlier—not more than forty or fifty people showed up—
because it was already eleven o'clock in the morning, on the
very Wednesday he had chosen for his flight, before anybody
read the note. At that time of day, during the middle of the
week, word-of-mouth news just lumbered along. Children were
in school; men were at work; and most of the women were
fastening their corsets and getting ready to go see what tails or

entrails the butcher might be giving away. Only the unem-
ployed, the self-employed, and the very young were available—
deliberately available because they'd heard about it, or accidentally available because they happened to be walking at that exact
moment in the shore end of Not Doctor Street, a name the post
office did not recognize. Town maps registered the street as
Mains Avenue, but the only colored doctor in the city had lived
and died on that street, and when he moved there in 1896 his
patients took to calling the street, which none of them lived in or
near, Doctor Street. Later, when other Negroes moved there,
and when the postal service became a popular means of transferring messages among them, envelopes from Louisiana, Virginia,
Alabama, and Georgia began to arrive addressed to people at
house numbers on Doctor Street. The post office workers returned these envelopes or passed them on to the Dead Letter
Office. Then in 1918, when colored men were being drafted, a
few gave their address at the recruitment office as Doctor Street.
In that way, the name acquired a quasi-official status. But not for
long. Some of the city legislators, whose concern for appropriate
names and the maintenance of the city's landmarks was the
principal part of their political life, saw to it that "Doctor
Street" was never used in any official capacity. And since they
knew that only Southside residents kept it up, they had notices
posted in the stores, barbershops, and restaurants in that part of
the city saying that the avenue running northerly and southerly
from Shore Road fronting the lake to the junction of routes 6
and 2 leading to Pennsylvania, and also running parallel to and
between Rutherford Avenue and Broadway, had always been
and would always be known as Mains Avenue and not Doctor
Street.

It was a genuinely clarifying public notice because it gave
Southside residents a way to keep their memories alive and please
the city legislators as well. They called it Not Doctor Street, and
were inclined to call the charity hospital at its northern end No
Mercy Hospital since it was 1931, on the day following Mr.
Smith's leap from its cupola, before the first colored expectant

mother was allowed to give birth inside its wards and not on its steps. The reason for the hospital's generosity to that particular woman was not the fact that she was the only child of this Negro doctor, for during his entire professional life he had never been granted hospital privileges and only two of his patients were ever admitted to Mercy, both white. Besides, the doctor had been dead a long time by 1931. It must have been Mr. Smith's leap from the roof over their heads that made them admit her. In any case, whether or not the little insurance agent's conviction that he could fly contributed to the place of her delivery, it certainly contributed to its time.

When the dead doctor's daughter saw Mr. Smith emerge as promptly as he had promised from behind the cupola, his wide blue silk wings curved forward around his chest, she dropped her covered peck basket, spilling red velvet rose petals. The wind blew them about, up, down, and into small mounds of snow. Her half-grown daughters scrambled about trying to catch them, while their mother moaned and held the underside of her stomach. The rose-petal scramble got a lot of attention, but the pregnant lady's moans did not. Everyone knew the girls had spent hour after hour tracing, cutting, and stitching the costly velvet, and that Gerhardt's Department Store would be quick to reject any that were soiled.

It was nice and gay there for a while. The men joined in trying to collect the scraps before the snow soaked through them—snatching them from a gust of wind or plucking them delicately from the snow. And the very young children couldn't make up their minds whether to watch the man circled in blue on the roof or the bits of red flashing around on the ground. Their dilemma was solved when a woman suddenly burst into song. The singer, standing at the back of the crowd, was as poorly dressed as the doctor's daughter was well dressed. The latter had on a neat gray coat with the traditional pregnant-woman bow at her navel, a black cloche, and a pair of four-button ladies' galoshes. The singing woman wore a knitted navy cap pulled far down over her forehead. She had wrapped herself up in an old quilt instead of a winter coat. Her head cocked to one side, her eyes fixed on Mr. Robert Smith, she sang in a powerful contralto:

> *O Sugarman done fly away*
> *Sugarman done gone*
> *Sugarman cut across the sky*
> *Sugarman gone home. . . .*

A few of the half a hundred or so people gathered there nudged each other and sniggered. Others listened as though it were the helpful and defining piano music in a silent movie. They stood this way for some time, none of them crying out to Mr. Smith, all of them preoccupied with one or the other of the minor events about them, until the hospital people came.

They had been watching from the windows—at first with mild curiosity, then, as the crowd seemed to swell to the very walls of the hospital, they watched with apprehension. They wondered if one of those things that racial-uplift groups were always organizing was taking place. But when they saw neither placards nor speakers, they ventured outside into the cold: white-coated surgeons, dark-jacketed business and personnel clerks, and three nurses in starched jumpers.

The sight of Mr. Smith and his wide blue wings transfixed them for a few seconds, as did the woman's singing and the roses strewn about. Some of them thought briefly that this was probably some form of worship. Philadelphia, where Father Divine reigned, wasn't all that far away. Perhaps the young girls holding baskets of flowers were two of his virgins. But the laughter of a gold-toothed man brought them back to their senses. They stopped daydreaming and swiftly got down to business, giving orders. Their shouts and bustling caused great confusion where before there had been only a few men and some girls playing with pieces of velvet and a woman singing.

One of the nurses, hoping to bring some efficiency into the disorder, searched the faces around her until she saw a stout woman who looked as though she might move the earth if she wanted to.

"You," she said, moving toward the stout woman. "Are these your children?"

The stout woman turned her head slowly, her eyebrows lifted at the carelessness of the address. Then, seeing where the voice came from, she lowered her brows and veiled her eyes.

"Ma'am?"

"Send one around back to the emergency office. Tell him to tell the guard to get over here quick. That boy there can go. That one." She pointed to a cat-eyed boy about five or six years old.

The stout woman slid her eyes down the nurse's finger and looked at the child she was pointing to.

"Guitar, ma'am."

"What?"

"Guitar."

The nurse gazed at the stout woman as though she had spoken Welsh. Then she closed her mouth, looked again at the cat-eyed boy, and lacing her fingers, spoke her next words very slowly to him.

"Listen. Go around to the back of the hospital to the guard's office. It will say 'Emergency Admissions' on the door. A-D-M-I-S-I-O-N-S. But the guard will be there. Tell him to get over here—on the double. Move now. Move!" She unlaced her fingers and made scooping motions with her hands, the palms pushing against the wintry air.

A man in a brown suit came toward her, puffing little white clouds of breath. "Fire truck's on its way. Get back inside. You'll freeze to death."

The nurse nodded.

"You left out a *s*, ma'am," the boy said. The North was new to him and he had just begun to learn he could speak up to white people. But she'd already gone, rubbing her arms against the cold.

"Granny, she left out a *s*."

"And a 'please.' "

"You reckon he'll jump?"

"A nutwagon do anything."

"Who is he?"

"Collects insurance. A nutwagon."

"Who is that lady singing?"

"That, baby, is the very last thing in pea-time." But she smiled when she looked at the singing woman, so the cat-eyed boy listened to the musical performance with at least as much interest as he devoted to the man flapping his wings on top of the hospital.

The crowd was beginning to be a little nervous now that the law was being called in. They each knew Mr. Smith. He came to their houses twice a month to collect one dollar and sixty-eight cents and write down on a little yellow card both the date and their eighty-four cents a week payment. They were always half a month or so behind, and talked endlessly to him about paying ahead—after they had a preliminary discussion about what he was doing back so soon anyway.

"You back in here already? Look like I just got rid of you."

"I'm tired of seeing your face. Really tired."

"I knew it. Soon's I get two dimes back to back, here you come. More regular than the reaper. Do Hoover know about you?"

They kidded him, abused him, told their children to tell him they were out or sick or gone to Pittsburgh. But they held on to those little yellow cards as though they meant something—laid them gently in the shoe box along with the rent receipts, marriage licenses, and expired factory identification badges. Mr. Smith smiled through it all, managing to keep his eyes focused almost the whole time on his customers' feet. He wore a business suit for his work, but his house was no better than theirs. He never had a woman that any of them knew about and said nothing in church but an occasional "Amen." He never beat anybody up and he wasn't seen after dark, so they thought he was probably a nice man. But he was heavily associated with illness and death, neither of which was distinguishable from the brown picture of the North Carolina Mutual Life Building on the back of their yellow cards. Jumping from the roof of Mercy was the most interesting thing he had done. None of them had suspected he had it in him. Just goes to show, they murmured to each other, you never really do know about people.

The singing woman quieted down and, humming the tune, walked through the crowd toward the rose-petal lady, who was still cradling her stomach.

"You should make yourself warm," she whispered to her, touching her lightly on the elbow. "A little bird'll be here with the morning."

"Oh?" said the rose-petal lady. "Tomorrow morning?"

"That's the only morning coming."

"It can't be," the rose-petal lady said. "It's too soon."

"No it ain't. Right on time."

The women were looking deep into each other's eyes when a loud roar went up from the crowd—a kind of wavy *oo* sound. Mr. Smith had lost his balance for a second, and was trying gallantly to hold on to a triangle of wood that jutted from the cupola. Immediately the singing woman began again:

> *O Sugarman done fly*
> *O Sugarman done gone . . .*

Downtown the firemen pulled on their greatcoats, but when they arrived at Mercy, Mr. Smith had seen the rose petals, heard the music, and leaped on into the air.

The next day a colored baby was born inside Mercy for the first time. Mr. Smith's blue silk wings must have left their mark, because when the little boy discovered, at four, the same thing Mr. Smith had learned earlier—that only birds and airplanes could fly—he lost all interest in himself. To have to live without that single gift saddened him and left his imagination so bereft that he appeared dull even to the women who did not hate his mother. The ones who did, who accepted her invitations to tea and envied the doctor's big dark house of twelve rooms and the green sedan, called him "peculiar." The others, who knew that the house was more prison than palace, and that the Dodge sedan was for Sunday drives only, felt sorry for Ruth Foster and her dry daughters, and called her son "deep." Even mysterious.

"Did he come with a caul?"

"You should have dried it and made him some tea from it to drink. If you don't he'll see ghosts."

"You believe that?"

"I don't, but that's what the old people say."

"Well, he's a deep one anyway. Look at his eyes."

And they pried pieces of baked-too-fast sunshine cake from the roofs of their mouths and looked once more into the boy's eyes. He met their gaze as best he could until, after a pleading glance toward his mother, he was allowed to leave the room.

It took some planning to walk out of the parlor, his back washed with the hum of their voices, open the heavy double doors leading to the dining room, slip up the stairs past all those bedrooms, and not arouse the attention of Lena and Corinthians sitting like big baby dolls before a table heaped with scraps of red velvet. His sisters made roses in the afternoon. Bright, lifeless roses that lay in peck baskets for months until the specialty buyer at Gerhardt's sent Freddie the janitor over to tell the girls that they could use another gross. If he did manage to slip by his sisters and avoid their casual malice, he knelt in his room at the window sill and wondered again and again why he had to stay level on the ground. The quiet that suffused the doctor's house then, broken only by the murmur of the women eating sunshine cake, was only that: quiet. It was not peaceful, for it was preceded by and would soon be terminated by the presence of Macon Dead.

Solid, rumbling, likely to erupt without prior notice, Macon kept each member of his family awkward with fear. His hatred of his wife glittered and sparked in every word he spoke to her. The disappointment he felt in his daughters sifted down on them like ash, dulling their buttery complexions and choking the lilt out of what should have been girlish voices. Under the frozen heat of his glance they tripped over doorsills and dropped the salt cellar into the yolks of their poached eggs. The way he mangled their grace, wit, and self-esteem was the single excitement of their days. Without the tension and drama he ignited, they might not have known what to do with themselves. In his absence his daughters bent their necks over blood-red squares of velvet and waited eagerly for any hint of him, and his wife, Ruth, began her days stunned into stillness by her husband's contempt and ended them wholly animated by it.

When she closed the door behind her afternoon guests, and let the quiet smile die from her lips, she began the preparation of food her husband found impossible to eat. She did not try to make her meals nauseating; she simply didn't know how not to. She would notice that the sunshine cake was too haggled to put before him and decide on a rennet dessert. But the grinding of the veal and beef for a meat loaf took so long she not only forgot the pork, settling for bacon drippings poured over the meat, she had no time to make a dessert at all. Hurriedly, then, she began to set the table. As she unfolded the white linen and let it billow over the fine mahogany table, she would look once more at the large water mark. She never set the table or passed through the dining room without looking at it. Like a lighthouse keeper drawn to his window to gaze once again at the sea, or a prisoner automatically searching out the sun as he steps into the yard for his hour of exercise, Ruth looked for the water mark several times during the day. She knew it was there, would always be there, but she needed to confirm its presence. Like the keeper of the lighthouse and the prisoner, she regarded it as a mooring, a checkpoint, some stable visual object that assured her that the world was still there; that this was life and not a dream. That she was alive somewhere, inside, which she acknowledged to be true only because a thing she knew intimately was out there, outside herself.

Even in the cave of sleep, without dreaming of it or thinking of it at all, she felt its presence. Oh, she talked endlessly to her daughters and her guests about how to get rid of it—what might hide this single flaw on the splendid wood: Vaseline, tobacco juice, iodine, a sanding followed by linseed oil. She had tried them all. But her glance was nutritious; the spot became, if anything, more pronounced as the years passed.

The cloudy gray circle identified the place where the bowl filled every day during the doctor's life with fresh flowers had stood. Every day. And when there were no flowers, it held a leaf arrangement, a gathering of twigs and berries, pussy willow, Scotch pine. . . . But always something to grace the dinner table in the evening.

It was for her father a touch that distinguished his own family from the people among whom they lived. For Ruth it was the summation of the affectionate elegance with which she believed her childhood had been surrounded. When Macon married her and moved into Doctor's house, she kept up the centerpiece-arranging. Then came the time she walked down to the shore through the roughest part of the city to get some driftwood. She had seen an arrangement of driftwood and dried seaweed in the homemakers section of the newspaper. It was a damp November day, and Doctor was paralyzed even then and taking liquid food in his bedroom. The wind had lifted her skirt from around her ankles and cut through her laced shoes. She'd had to rub her feet down with warm olive oil when she got back. At dinner, where just the two of them sat, she turned toward her husband and asked him how he liked the centerpiece. "Most people overlook things like that. They see it, but they don't see anything beautiful in it. They don't see that nature has already made it as perfect as it can be. Look at it from the side. It is pretty, isn't it?"

Her husband looked at the driftwood with its lacy beige seaweed, and without moving his head, said, "Your chicken is red at the bone. And there is probably a potato dish that is supposed to have lumps in it. Mashed ain't the dish."

Ruth let the seaweed disintegrate, and later, when its veins and stems dropped and curled into brown scabs on the table, she removed the bowl and brushed away the scabs. But the water mark, hidden by the bowl all these years, was exposed. And once exposed, it behaved as though it were itself a plant and flourished into a huge suede-gray flower that throbbed like fever, and sighed like the shift of sand dunes. But it could also be still. Patient, restful, and still.

But there was nothing you could do with a mooring except acknowledge it, use it for the verification of some idea you wanted to keep alive. Something else is needed to get from sunup to sundown: a balm, a gentle touch or nuzzling of some sort. So Ruth rose up and out of her guileless inefficiency to claim her bit of balm right after the preparation of dinner and just before the return of her husband from his office. It was one of her two secret indulgences—the one that involved her son— and part of the pleasure it gave her came from the room in which she did it. A damp greenness lived there, made by the evergreen that pressed against the window and filtered the light. It was just a little room that Doctor had called a study, and aside from a sewing machine that stood in the corner along with a dress form, there was only a rocker and tiny footstool. She sat in this room holding her son on her lap, staring at his closed eyelids and listening to the sound of his sucking. Staring not so much from maternal joy as from a wish to avoid seeing his legs dangling almost to the floor.

In late afternoon, before her husband closed his office and came home, she called her son to her. When he came into the little room she unbuttoned her blouse and smiled. He was too young to be dazzled by her nipples, but he was old enough to be bored by the flat taste of mother's milk, so he came reluctantly, as to a chore, and lay as he had at least once each day of his life in his mother's arms, and tried to pull the thin, faintly sweet milk from her flesh without hurting her with his teeth.

She felt him. His restraint, his courtesy, his indifference, all of which pushed her into fantasy. She had the distinct impression that his lips were pulling from her a thread of light. It was as though she were a cauldron issuing spinning gold. Like the miller's daughter—the one who sat at night in a straw-filled room, thrilled with the secret power Rumpelstiltskin had given her: to see golden thread stream from her very own shuttle. And that was the other part of her pleasure, a pleasure she hated to give up. So when Freddie the janitor, who liked to pretend he was a friend of the family and not just their flunky as well as their tenant, brought his rent to the doctor's house late one day and looked in the window past the evergreen, the terror that sprang to Ruth's eyes came from the quick realization that she was to lose fully half of what made her daily life bearable. Freddie, however, interpreted her look as simple shame, but that didn't stop him from grinning.

"Have mercy. I be damn."

He fought the evergreen for a better look, hampered more by his laughter than by the branches. Ruth jumped up as quickly as she could and covered her breast, dropping her son on the floor and confirming for him what he had begun to suspect—that these afternoons were strange and wrong.

Before either mother or son could speak, rearrange themselves properly, or even exchange looks, Freddie had run around the house, climbed the porch steps, and was calling them between gulps of laughter.

"Miss Rufie. Miss Rufie. Where you? Where you all at?" He opened the door to the green room as though it were his now.

"I be damn, Miss Rufie. When the last time I seen that? I don't even know the last time I seen that. I mean, ain't nothing wrong with it. I mean, old folks swear by it. It's just, you know, you don't see it up here much. . . ." But his eyes were on the boy. Appreciative eyes that communicated some complicity she was excluded from. Freddie looked the boy up and down, taking in the steady but secretive eyes and the startling contrast between Ruth's lemony skin and the boy's black skin. "Used to be a lot of womenfolk nurse they kids a long time down South. Lot of 'em. But you don't see it much no more. I knew a family—the mother wasn't too quick, though—nursed hers till the boy, I reckon, was near 'bout thirteen. But that's a bit much, ain't it?" All the time he chattered, he rubbed his chin and looked at the boy. Finally he stopped, and gave a long low chuckle. He'd found the phrase he'd been searching for. "A milkman. That's what you got here, Miss Rufie. A natural milkman if ever I seen one. Look out, womens. Here he come. Huh!"

Freddie carried his discovery not only into the homes in Ruth's neighborhood, but to Southside, where he lived and where Macon Dead owned rent houses. So Ruth kept close to home and had no afternoon guests for the better part of two months, to keep from hearing that her son had been rechristened with a name he was never able to shake and that did nothing to improve either one's relationship with his father.

Macon Dead never knew how it came about—how his only son acquired the nickname that stuck in spite of his own refusal to use it or acknowledge it. It was a matter that concerned him a good deal, for the giving of names in his family was always surrounded by what he believed to be monumental foolishness. No one mentioned to him the incident out of which the nickname grew because he was a difficult man to approach—a hard man, with a manner so cool it discouraged casual or spontaneous conversation. Only Freddie the janitor took liberties with Macon Dead, liberties he purchased with the services he rendered, and Freddie was the last person on earth to tell him. So Macon Dead neither heard of nor visualized Ruth's sudden terror, her awkward jump from the rocking chair, the boy's fall broken by the tiny footstool, or Freddie's amused, admiring summation of the situation.

Without knowing any of the details, however, he guessed, with the accuracy of a mind sharpened by hatred, that the name he heard schoolchildren call his son, the name he overheard the ragman use when he paid the boy three cents for a bundle of old clothes—he guessed that this name was not clean. Milkman. It certainly didn't sound like the honest job of a dairyman, or bring to his mind cold bright cans standing on the back porch, glittering like captains on guard. It sounded dirty, intimate, and hot. He knew that wherever the name came from, it had something to do with his wife and was, like the emotion he always felt when thinking of her, coated with disgust.

This disgust and the uneasiness with which he regarded his son affected everything he did in that city. If he could have felt sad, simply sad, it would have relieved him. Fifteen years of regret at not having a son had become the bitterness of finally having one in the most revolting circumstances.

There had been a time when he had a head full of hair and when Ruth wore lovely complicated underwear that he deliberately took a long time to undo. When all of his foreplay was untying, unclasping, unbuckling the snaps and strings of what must have been the most beautiful, the most delicate, the whitest and softest underwear on earth. Each eye of her corset he toyed with (and there were forty—twenty on each side); each grosgrain ribbon that threaded its pale-blue way through the snowy top of her bodice he unlaced. He not only undid the blue bow; he pulled it all the way out of the hem, so she had to rethread it afterward with a safety pin. The elastic bands that connected her perspiration shields to her slip he unsnapped and snapped again, teasing her and himself with the sound of the snaps and the thrill of his fingertips on her shoulders. They never spoke during these undressings. But they giggled occasionally, and as when children play "doctor," undressing of course was the best part.

When Ruth was naked and lying there as moist and crumbly as unbleached sugar, he bent to unlace her shoes. That was the final delight, for once he had undressed her feet, had peeled her stockings down over her ankles and toes, he entered her and ejaculated quickly. She liked it that way. So did he. And in almost twenty years during which he had not laid eyes on her naked feet, he missed only the underwear.

Once he believed that the sight of her mouth on the dead man's fingers would be the thing he would remember always. He was wrong. Little by little he remembered fewer and fewer of the details, until finally he had to imagine them, even fabricate them, guess what they must have been. The image left him, but the odiousness never did. For the nourishment of his outrage he depended on the memory of her underwear; those round, innocent corset eyes now lost to him forever.

So if the people were calling his son Milkman, and if she was lowering her eyelids and dabbing at the sweat on her top lip when she heard it, there was definitely some filthy connection and it did not matter at all to Macon Dead whether anyone gave him the details or not.

And they didn't. Nobody both dared enough and cared enough to tell him. The ones who cared enough, Lena and Corinthians, the living proof of those years of undressing his wife, did not dare. And the one person who dared to but didn't care to was the one person in the world he hated more than his wife in spite of the fact that she was his sister. He had not crossed the tracks to see her since his son was born and he had no intention of renewing their relationship now.

Macon Dead dug in his pocket for his keys, and curled his fingers around them, letting their bunchy solidity calm him. They were the keys to all the doors of his houses (only four true houses; the rest were really shacks), and he fondled them from time to time as he walked down Not Doctor Street to his office. At least he thought of it as his office, had even painted the word OFFICE on the door. But the plate-glass window contradicted him. In peeling gold letters arranged in a semicircle, his business establishment was declared to be Sonny's Shop. Scraping the previous owner's name off was hardly worth the trouble since he couldn't scrape it from anybody's mind. His storefront office was never called anything but Sonny's Shop, although nobody now could remember thirty years back, when, presumably, Sonny did something or other there.

He walked there now—strutted is the better word, for he had a high behind and an athlete's stride—thinking of names. Surely, he thought, he and his sister had some ancestor, some lithe young man with onyx skin and legs as straight as cane stalks, who had a name that was real. A name given to him at birth with love and seriousness. A name that was not a joke, nor a disguise, nor a brand name. But who this lithe young man was, and where his cane-stalk legs carried him from or to, could never be known. No. Nor his name. His own parents, in some mood of perverseness or resignation, had agreed to abide by a naming done to them by somebody who couldn't have cared less. Agreed to take and pass on to all their issue this heavy name scrawled in perfect thoughtlessness by a drunken Yankee in the Union Army. A literal slip of the pen handed to his father on a piece of paper and which he handed on to his only son, and his son likewise handed on to his; Macon Dead who begat a second Macon Dead who married Ruth Foster (Dead) and begat Magdalene called Lena Dead and First Corinthians Dead and (when he least expected it) another Macon Dead, now known to the part of the world that mattered as Milkman Dead. And as if that were not enough, a sister named Pilate Dead, who would never mention to her brother the circumstances or the details of this foolish misnaming of his son because the whole thing would have delighted her. She would savor it, maybe fold it too in a brass box and hang it from her other ear.

He had cooperated as a young father with the blind selection of names from the Bible for every child other than the first male. And abided by whatever the finger pointed to, for he knew every configuration of the naming of his sister. How his father, confused and melancholy over his wife's death in childbirth, had thumbed through the Bible, and since he could not read a word, chose a group of letters that seemed to him strong and handsome; saw in them a large figure that looked like a tree hanging in some princely but protective way over a row of smaller trees. How he had copied the group of letters out on a piece of brown paper; copied, as illiterate people do, every curlicue, arch, and bend in the letters, and presented it to the midwife.

"That's the baby's name."

"You want this for the baby's name?"

"I want that for the baby's name. Say it."

"You can't name the baby this."

"Say it."

"It's a man's name."

"Say it."

"Pilate."

"What?"

"Pilate. You wrote down Pilate."

"Like a riverboat pilot?"

"No. Not like no riverboat pilot. Like a Christ-killing Pilate. You can't get much worse than that for a name. And a baby girl at that."

"That's where my finger went down at."

"Well, your brain ain't got to follow it. You don't want to give this motherless child the name of the man that killed Jesus, do you?"

"I asked Jesus to save me my wife."

"Careful, Macon."

"I asked him all night long."

"He give you your baby."

"Yes. He did. Baby name Pilate."

"Jesus, have mercy."

"Where you going with that piece of paper?"

"It's going back where it came from. Right in the Devil's flames."

"Give it here. It come from the Bible. It stays in the Bible."

And it did stay there, until the baby girl turned twelve and took it out, folded it up into a tiny knot and put it in a little brass box, and strung the entire contraption through her left earlobe. Fluky about her own name at twelve, how much more fluky she'd become since then Macon could only guess. But he knew for certain that she would treat the naming of the third Macon Dead with the same respect and awe she had treated the boy's birth.

Macon Dead remembered when his son was born, how she seemed to be more interested in this first nephew of hers than she was in her own daughter, and even that daughter's daughter. Long after Ruth was up and about, as capable as she ever would be—and that wasn't much—of running the house again, Pilate continued to visit, her shoelaces undone, a knitted cap pulled down over her forehead, bringing her foolish earring and sickening smell into the kitchen. He had not seen her since he was sixteen years old, until a year before the birth of his son, when she appeared in his city. Now she was acting like an in-law, like an aunt, dabbling at helping Ruth and the girls, but having no interest in or knowledge of decent housekeeping, she got in the way. Finally she just sat in a chair near the crib, singing to the baby. That wasn't so bad, but what Macon Dead remembered most was the expression on her face. Surprise, it looked like, and eagerness. But so intense it made him uneasy. Or perhaps it was more than that. Perhaps it was seeing her all those years after they had separated outside that cave, and remembering his anger and her betrayal. How far down she had slid since then. She had cut the last thread of propriety. At one time she had been the dearest thing in the world to him. Now she was odd, murky, and worst of all, unkempt. A regular source of embarrassment, if he would allow it. But he would not allow it.

Finally he had told her not to come again until she could show some respect for herself. Could get a real job instead of running a wine house.

"Why can't you dress like a woman?" He was standing by the stove. "What's that sailor's cap doing on your head? Don't you have stockings? What are you trying to make me look like in this town?" He trembled with the thought of the white men in the bank—the men who helped him buy and mortgage houses—discovering that this raggedy bootlegger was his sister. That the propertied Negro who handled his business so well and who lived in the big house on Not Doctor Street had a sister who had a daughter but no husband, and that daughter had a daughter but no husband. A collection of lunatics who made wine and sang in the streets "like common street women! Just like common street women!"

Pilate had sat there listening to him, her wondering eyes resting on his face. Then she said, "I been worried sick about you too, Macon."

Exasperated, he had gone to the kitchen door. "Go 'head,

Pilate. Go on now. I'm on the thin side of evil and trying not to break through."

Pilate stood up, wrapped her quilt around her, and with a last fond look at the baby, left through the kitchen door. She never came back.

When Macon Dead got to the front door of his office he saw a stout woman and two young boys standing a few feet away. Macon unlocked his door, walked over to his desk, and settled himself behind it. As he was thumbing through his accounts book, the stout woman entered, alone.

"Afternoon Mr. Dead, sir. I'm Mrs. Bains. Live over at number three on Fifteenth Street."

Macon Dead remembered—not the woman, but the circumstances at number three. His tenant's grandmother or aunt or something had moved in there and the rent was long overdue.

"Yes, Mrs. Bains. You got something for me?"

"Well, that's what I come to talk to you about. You know Cency left all them babies with me. And my relief check ain't no more'n it take to keep a well-grown yard dog alive—half alive, I should say."

"Your rent is four dollars a month, Mrs. Bains. You two months behind already."

"I do know that, Mr. Dead, sir, but babies can't make it with nothing to put in they stomach."

Their voices were low, polite, without any hint of conflict.

"Can they make it in the street, Mrs. Bains? That's where they gonna be if you don't figure out some way to get me my money."

"No, sir. They can't make it in the street. We need both, I reckon. Same as yours does."

"Then you better rustle it up, Mrs. Bains. You got till"—he swiveled around to consult the calendar on the wall—"till Saturday coming. Saturday, Mrs. Bains. Not Sunday. Not Monday. Saturday."

If she had been younger and had more juice, the glitter in her eyes would have washed down onto her cheeks. Now, at her time of life, it simply gleamed. She pressed the flat of her hand on Macon Dead's desk and, holding the gleam steady in her eyes, pushed herself up from the chair. She turned her head a little to look out the plate-glass window, and then back at him.

"What's it gonna profit you, Mr. Dead, sir, to put me and them children out?"

"Saturday, Mrs. Bains."

Lowering her head, Mrs. Bains whispered something and walked slowly and heavily from the office. As she closed the door to Sonny's Shop, her grandchildren moved out of the sunlight into the shadow where she stood.

"What he say, Granny?"

Mrs. Bains put a hand on the taller boy's hair and fingered it lightly, absently searching with her nails for tetter spots.

"He must've told her no," said the other boy.

"Do we got to move?" The tall boy tossed his head free of her fingers and looked at her sideways. His cat eyes were gashes of gold.

Mrs. Bains let her hand fall to her side. "A nigger in business is a terrible thing to see. A terrible, terrible thing to see."

The boys looked at each other and back at their grandmother. Their lips were parted as though they had heard something important.

When Mrs. Bains closed the door, Macon Dead went back to the pages of his accounts book, running his fingertips over the figures and thinking with the unoccupied part of his mind about the first time he called on Ruth Foster's father. He had only two keys in his pocket then, and if he had let people like the woman who just left have their way, he wouldn't have had any keys at all. It was because of those keys that he could dare to walk over to that part of Not Doctor Street (it was still Doctor Street then) and approach the most important Negro in the city. To lift the lion's paw knocker, to entertain thoughts of marrying the doctor's daughter was possible because each key represented a house which he owned at the time. Without those keys he would have floated away at the doctor's first word: "Yes?" Or he would have melted like new wax under the heat of that pale eye. Instead he was able to say that he had been introduced to his daughter, Miss Ruth Foster, and would appreciate having the doctor's permission to keep her company now and then. That his intentions were honorable and that he himself was certainly worthy of the doctor's consideration as a gentleman friend for Miss Foster since, at twenty-five, he was already a colored man of property.

"I don't know anything about you," the doctor said, "other than your name, which I don't like, but I will abide by my daughter's preference."

In fact the doctor knew a good deal about him and was more grateful to this tall young man than he ever allowed himself to show. Fond as he was of his only child, useful as she was in his house since his wife had died, lately he had begun to chafe under her devotion. Her steady beam of love was unsettling, and she had never dropped those expressions of affection that had been so lovable in her childhood. The good-night kiss was itself a masterpiece of slow-wittedness on her part and discomfort on his. At sixteen, she still insisted on having him come to her at night, sit on her bed, exchange a few pleasantries, and plant a kiss on her lips. Perhaps it was the loud silence of his dead wife, perhaps it was Ruth's disturbing resemblance to her mother. More probably it was the ecstasy that always seemed to be shining in Ruth's face when he bent to kiss her—an ecstasy he felt inappropriate to the occasion.

None of that, of course, did he describe to the young man who came to call. Which is why Macon Dead still believed the magic had lain in the two keys.

In the middle of his reverie, Macon was interrupted by rapid tapping on the window. He looked up, saw Freddie peeping through the gold lettering, and nodded for him to enter. A gold-toothed bantamweight, Freddie was as much of a town crier as Southside had. It was this same rapid tapping on the window-pane, the same flash-of-gold smile that had preceded his now-famous scream to Macon: "Mr. Smith went splat!" It was obvious to Macon that Freddie now had news of another calamity.

"Porter gone crazy drunk again! Got his shotgun!"

"Who's he out for?" Macon began closing books and opening desk drawers. Porter was a tenant and tomorrow was collection day.

"Ain't out for nobody in particular. Just perched himself up in the attic window and commenced to waving a shotgun. Say he gotta kill him somebody before morning."

"He go to work today?"

"Yep. Caught the eagle too."

"Drunk it all up?"

"Not all of it. He only got one bottle, and he still got a fist fulla money."

"Who's crazy enough to sell him any liquor?"

Freddie showed a few gold teeth but said nothing, so Macon knew it was Pilate. He locked all his drawers save one—the one he unlocked and took a small .32 from.

"Police warn every bootlegger in the county, and he still gets it somehow." Macon went on with the charade, pretending he didn't know his sister was the one Porter and anybody else—adult, child, or beast—could buy wine from. He thought for the hundredth time that she needed to be in jail and that he would be willing to put her there if he could be sure she wouldn't loudmouth him and make him seem trashy in the eyes of the law—and the banks.

"You know how to use that thing, Mr. Dead, sir?"

"I know how."

"Porter's crazy when he drunk."

"I know what he is."

"How you aiming to get him down?"

"I ain't aiming to get him down. I'm aiming to get my money down. He can go on and die up there if he wants to. But if he don't toss me my rent, I'm going to blow him out of that window."

Freddie's giggle was soft, but his teeth strengthened its impact. A born flunky, he loved gossip and the telling of it. He was the ear that heard every murmur of complaint, every name-calling; and his was the eye that saw everything: the secret loving glances, the fights, the new dresses.

Macon knew Freddie as a fool and a liar, but a reliable liar. He was always right about his facts and always wrong about the motives that produced the facts. Just as now he was right about Porter having a shotgun, being in the attic window, and being drunk. But Porter was not waiting to kill somebody, meaning anybody, before morning. In fact he was very specific about whom he wanted to kill—himself. However, he did have a precondition which he shouted down, loud and clear, from the attic. "I want to fuck! Send me up somebody to fuck! Hear me? Send me up somebody, I tell ya, or I'ma blow my brains out!"

As Macon and Freddie approached the yard, the women from the rooming house were hollering answers to Porter's plea.

"What kinda bargain is that?"

"Kill yourself first and then we'll send you somebody."

"Do it have to be a woman?"

"Do it got to be human?"

"Do it got to be alive?"

"Can it be a piece of liver?"

"Put that thing down and throw me my goddam money!" Macon's voice cut through the women's fun. "Float those dollars down here, nigger, then blow yourself up!"

Porter turned and aimed his shotgun at Macon.

"If you pull that trigger," shouted Macon, "you better not miss. If you take a shot you better make sure I'm dead, cause if you don't I'm gonna shoot your balls up in your throat!" He pulled out his own weapon. "Now get the hell outta that window!"

Porter hesitated for only a second, before turning the barrel of the shotgun toward himself—or trying to. Its length made it difficult; his drunkenness made it impossible. Struggling to get the right angle, he was suddenly distracted. He leaned his shotgun on the window sill, pulled out his penis and in a high arc, peed over the heads of the women, making them scream and run in a panic that the shotgun had not been able to create. Macon rubbed the back of his head while Freddie bent double with laughter.

For more than an hour Porter held them at bay: cowering, screaming, threatening, urinating, and interspersing all of it with pleas for a woman.

He would cry great shoulder-heaving sobs, followed by more screams.

"I love ya! I love ya all. Don't act like that. You women. Stop it. Don't act like that. Don't you see I love ya? I'd die for ya, kill for ya. I'm saying I love ya. I'm telling ya. Oh, God have mercy. What I'm gonna do? What in this fuckin world am I gonna dooooo?"

Tears streamed down his face and he cradled the barrel of the shotgun in his arms as though it were the woman he had been begging for, searching for, all his life. "Gimme hate, Lord," he whimpered. "I'll take hate any day. But don't give me love. I can't take no more love, Lord. I can't carry it. Just like Mr. Smith. He couldn't carry it. It's too heavy. Jesus, *you* know. You know all about it. Ain't it heavy? Jesus? Ain't love heavy? Don't you see, Lord? You own son couldn't carry it. If it killed Him, what You think it's gonna do to me? Huh? Huh?" He was getting angry again.

"Come down outta there, nigger!" Macon's voice was still loud, but it was getting weary.

"And you, you baby-dicked baboon"—he tried to point at Macon—"you the worst. You need killin, you really *need* killin. You know why? Well, I'm gonna tell you why. I *know* why. Everybody . . ."

Porter slumped down in the window, muttering, "Everybody know why," and fell fast asleep. As he sank deeper into it, the shotgun slipped from his hand, rattled down the roof, and hit the ground with a loud explosion. The shot zipped past a bystander's shoe and blew a hole in the tire of a stripped Dodge parked in the road.

"Go get my money," Macon said.

"Me?" Freddie asked. "Suppose he . . ."

"Go get me my money."

Porter was snoring. Through the blast of the gun and the picking of his pocket he slept like a baby.

When Macon walked out of the yard, the sun had disappeared behind the bread company. Tired, irritable, he walked down Fifteenth Street, glancing up as he passed one of his other houses, its silhouette melting in the light that trembled between dusk and twilight. Scattered here and there, his houses stretched up beyond him like squat ghosts with hooded eyes. He didn't like to look at them in this light. During the day they were reassuring to see; now they did not seem to belong to him at all—in fact he felt as though the houses were in league with one another to make him feel like the outsider, the propertyless, landless wanderer. It was this feeling of loneliness that made him decide to take a shortcut back to Not Doctor Street, even though to do so would lead him past his sister's house. In the gathering darkness, he was sure his passing would be unnoticed by her. He crossed a yard and followed a fence that led into Darling Street where Pilate lived in a narrow single-story house whose basement seemed to be rising from rather than settling into the ground. She had no electricity because she would not pay for the service. Nor for gas. At night she and her daughter lit the house with candles and kerosene lamps; they warmed themselves and cooked with wood and coal, pumped kitchen water into a dry sink through a pipeline from a well and lived pretty much as though progress was a word that meant walking a little farther on down the road.

Her house sat eighty feet from the sidewalk and was backed by four huge pine trees, from which she got the needles she stuck into her mattress. Seeing the pine trees started him thinking about her mouth; how she loved, as a girl, to chew pine needles and as a result smelled even then like a forest. For a dozen years she had been like his own child. After their mother died, she had come struggling out of the womb without help from throbbing muscles or the pressure of swift womb water. As a result, for all the years he knew her, her stomach was as smooth and sturdy as her back, at no place interrupted by a navel. It was the absence of a navel that convinced people that she had not come into this world through normal channels; had never lain, floated, or grown in some warm and liquid place connected by a tissue-thin tube to a reliable source of human nourishment. Macon knew otherwise, because he was there and had seen the eyes of the midwife as his mother's legs collapsed. And heard as well her shouts when the baby, who they had believed was dead also, inched its way headfirst out of a still, silent, and indifferent cave of flesh, dragging her own cord and her own afterbirth behind her. But the rest was true. Once the new baby's lifeline was cut, the cord stump shriveled, fell off, and left no trace of having ever existed, which, as a young boy taking care of his baby sister, he thought no more strange than a bald head. He was seventeen years old, irreparably separated from her and already pressing forward in his drive for wealth, when he learned that there was probably not another stomach like hers on earth.

Now, nearing her yard, he trusted that the dark would keep anyone in her house from seeing him. He did not even look to his left as he walked by it. But then he heard the music. They were singing. All of them. Pilate, Reba, and Reba's daughter, Hagar. There was no one on the street that he could see; people were at supper, licking their fingers, blowing into saucers of coffee, and no doubt chattering about Porter's escapade and Macon's fear-less confrontation of the wild man in the attic. There were no street lights in this part of town; only the moon directed the way of a pedestrian. Macon walked on, resisting as best he could the sound of the voices that followed him. He was rapidly approaching a part of the road where the music could not follow, when he saw, like a scene on the back of a postcard, a picture of where he was headed—his own home; his wife's narrow unyielding back; his daughters, boiled dry from years of yearning; his son, to whom he could speak only if his words held some command or criticism. "Hello, Daddy." "Hello, son, tuck your shirt in." "I found a dead bird, Daddy." "Don't bring that mess in this house. . . ." There was no music there, and tonight he wanted just a bit of music—from the person who had been his first caring for.

He turned back and walked slowly toward Pilate's house. They were singing some melody that Pilate was leading. A phrase that the other two were taking up and building on. Her powerful contralto, Reba's piercing soprano in counterpoint, and the soft voice of the girl, Hagar, who must be about ten or eleven now, pulled him like a carpet tack under the influence of a magnet.

Surrendering to the sound, Macon moved closer. He wanted no conversation, no witness, only to listen and perhaps to see the three of them, the source of that music that made him think of fields and wild turkey and calico. Treading as lightly as he could, he crept up to the side window where the candlelight flickered lowest, and peeped in. Reba was cutting her toenails with a kitchen knife or a switchblade, her long neck bent almost to her knees. The girl, Hagar, was braiding her hair, while Pilate, whose face he could not see because her back was to the window, was stirring something in a pot. Wine pulp, perhaps. Macon knew it was not food she was stirring, for she and her daughters ate like children. Whatever they had a taste for. No meal was ever planned or balanced or served. Nor was there any gathering at the table. Pilate might bake hot bread and each one of them would eat it with butter whenever she felt like it. Or there might be grapes, left over from the winemaking, or peaches for days on end. If one of them bought a gallon of milk they drank it until it was gone. If another got a half bushel of tomatoes or a dozen ears of corn, they ate them until they were gone too. They ate what they had or came across or had a craving for. Profits from their wine-selling evaporated like sea water in a hot wind—going for junk jewelry for Hagar, Reba's gifts to men, and he didn't know what all.

Near the window, hidden by the dark, he felt the irritability of the day drain from him and relished the effortless beauty of the women singing in the candlelight. Reba's soft profile, Hagar's hands moving, moving in her heavy hair, and Pilate. He knew her face better than he knew his own. Singing now, her face would be a mask; all emotion and passion would have left her features and entered her voice. But he knew that when she was neither singing nor talking, her face was animated by her constantly moving lips. She chewed things. As a baby, as a very young girl, she kept things in her mouth—straw from brooms, gristle, buttons, seeds, leaves, string, and her favorite, when he could find some for her, rubber bands and India rubber erasers. Her lips were alive with small movements. If you were close to her, you wondered if she was about to smile or was she merely shifting a straw from the baseline of her gums to her tongue. Perhaps she was dislodging a curl of rubber band from inside her cheek, or was she really smiling? From a distance she appeared to be whispering to herself, when she was only nibbling or splitting tiny seeds with her front teeth. Her lips were darker than her skin, wine-stained, blueberry-dyed, so her face had a cosmetic look—as though she had applied a very dark lipstick neatly and blotted away its shine on a scrap of newspaper.

As Macon felt himself softening under the weight of memory and music, the song died down. The air was quiet and yet Macon Dead could not leave. He liked looking at them freely this way. They didn't move. They simply stopped singing and Reba went on paring her toenails, Hagar threaded and unthreaded her hair, and Pilate swayed like a willow over her stirring.

Chapter 2

Only Magdalene called Lena and First Corinthians were genuinely happy when the big Packard rolled evenly and silently out
of the driveway. They alone had a sense of adventure and were
flagrant in their enjoyment of the automobile's plushness. Each
had a window to herself and commanded an unobstructed view
of the summer day flying past them. And each was both old
enough and young enough to actually believe she was a princess
riding in a regal chariot driven by a powerful coachman. In the
back seat, away from the notice of Macon and Ruth, they
slipped off their patent leather pumps, rolled their stockings
down over their knees, and watched the men walking down the
streets.

These rides that the family took on Sunday afternoons had
become rituals and much too important for Macon to enjoy. For
him it was a way to satisfy himself that he was indeed a successful man. It was a less ambitious ritual for Ruth, but a way,
nevertheless, for her to display her family. For the little boy it
was simply a burden. Pressed in the front seat between his

parents, he could see only the winged woman careening off the nose of the car. He was not allowed to sit on his mother's lap during the drive—not because she wouldn't have it, but because his father objected to it. So it was only by kneeling on the dove gray seat and looking out the back window that he could see anything other than the laps, feet, and hands of his parents, the dashboard, or the silver winged woman poised at the tip of the Packard. But riding backward made him uneasy. It was like flying blind, and not knowing where he was going—just where he had been—troubled him. He did not want to see trees that he had passed, or houses and children slipping into the space the automobile had left behind.

Macon Dead's Packard rolled slowly down Not Doctor Street, through the rough part of town (later known as the Blood Bank because blood flowed so freely there), over the bypass downtown, and headed for the wealthy white neighborhoods. Some of the black people who saw the car passing by sighed with good-humored envy at the classiness, the dignity of it. In 1936 there were very few among them who lived as well as Macon Dead. Others watched the family gliding by with a tiny bit of jealousy and a whole lot of amusement, for Macon's wide green Packard belied what they thought a car was for. He never went over twenty miles an hour, never gunned his engine, never stayed in first gear for a block or two to give pedestrians a thrill. He never had a blown tire, never ran out of gas and needed twelve grinning raggle-tailed boys to help him push it up a hill or over to a curb. No rope ever held the door to its frame, and no teen-agers leaped on his running board for a lift down the street. He hailed no one and no one hailed him. There was never a sudden braking and backing up to shout or laugh with a friend. No beer bottles or ice cream cones poked from the open windows. Nor did a baby boy stand up to pee out of them. He never let rain fall on it if he could help it and he walked to Sonny's Shop—taking the car out only on these occasions. What's more, they doubted that he had ever taken a woman into the back seat, because rumor was that he went to "bad houses" or lay, sometimes, with a slack or lonely female tenant. Other than the bright and roving eyes of Magdalene called Lena and First Corinthians, the Packard had no real lived life at all. So they called it Macon Dead's hearse.

First Corinthians pulled her fingers through her hair. It was long, lightweight hair, the color of wet sand. "Are you going anyplace special, or are we just driving around?" She kept her eyes on the street, watching the men and women walking by.

"Careful, Macon. You always take the wrong turn here." Ruth spoke softly from the right side of the car.

"Do you want to drive?" Macon asked her.

"You know I don't drive," she answered.

"Then let me do it."

"All right, but don't blame me if . . ."

Macon pulled smoothly into the left fork of the road that led through downtown and into a residential area.

"Daddy? Are we going any special place?"

"Honoré," Macon said.

Magdalene called Lena pushed her stockings farther down on her legs. "On the lake? What's out there? There's nothing out there, nobody."

"There's a beach community out there, Lena. Your father wants to look at it." Ruth reasserted herself into the conversation.

"What for? Those are white people's houses," said Lena.

"All of it's not white people's houses. Some of it's nothing. Just land. Way over on the other side. It could be a nice summer place for colored people. Beach houses. You understand what I mean?" Macon glanced at his daughter through the rear-view mirror.

"Who's going to live in them? There's no colored people who can afford to have two houses," Lena said.

"Reverend Coles can, and Dr. Singleton," Corinthians corrected her.

"And that lawyer—what's his name?" Ruth looked around at Corinthians, who ignored her.

"And Mary, I suppose." Lena laughed.

Corinthians stared coldly at her sister. "Daddy wouldn't sell property to a barmaid. Daddy, would you let us live next to a barmaid?"

"She owns that place, Corinthians," Ruth said.

"I don't care what she owns. I care about what she is. Daddy?" Corinthians leaned toward her father for confirmation.

"You're going too fast, Macon." Ruth pressed the toe of her shoe against the floorboard.

"If you say one more thing to me about the way I drive, you're going to walk back home. I mean it."

Magdalene called Lena sat forward and put her hand on her mother's shoulder. Ruth was quiet. The little boy kicked his feet against the underside of the dashboard.

"Stop that!" Macon told him.

"I have to go to the bathroom," said his son.

Corinthians held her head. "Oh, Lord."

"But you went before we left," said Ruth.

"I have to *go!*" He was beginning to whine.

"Are you sure?" his mother asked him. He looked at her. "I guess we better stop," Ruth said to nobody in particular. Her eyes grazed the countryside they were entering.

Macon didn't alter his speed.

"Are *we* going to have a summer place, or are you just selling property?"

"I'm not selling anything. I'm thinking of buying and then renting," Macon answered her.

"But are *we*—"

"I have to go," said the little boy.

"—going to live there too?"

"Maybe."

"By ourselves? Who else?" Corinthians was very interested.

"I can't tell you that. But in a few years—five or ten—a whole lot of coloreds will have enough to afford it. A whole lot. Take my word for it."

Magdalene called Lena took a deep breath. "Up ahead you could pull over, Daddy. He might mess up the seat."

Macon glanced at her in the mirror and slowed down. "Who's going to take him?" Ruth fiddled with the door handle. "Not you," Macon said to her.

Ruth looked at her husband. She parted her lips but didn't say anything.

"Not me," said Corinthians. "I have on high heels."

"Come on," Lena sighed. They left the car, little boy and big sister, and disappeared into the trees that reared up off the shoulder of the road.

"You really think there'll be enough colored people—I mean nice colored people—in this city to live there?"

"They don't have to be from this city, Corinthians. People will drive to a summer house. White people do it all the time." Macon drummed his fingers on the steering wheel, which trembled a little as the car idled.

"Negroes don't like the water." Corinthians giggled.

"They'll like it if they own it," said Macon. He looked out the window and saw Magdalene called Lena coming out of the trees. A large colorful bouquet of flowers was in her hand, but her face was crumpled in anger. Over her pale-blue dress dark wet stains spread like fingers.

"He wet on me," she said. "He wet me, Mama." She was close to tears.

Ruth clucked her tongue.

Corinthians laughed. "I told you Negroes didn't like water."

He didn't mean it. It happened before he was through. She'd stepped away from him to pick flowers, returned, and at the sound of her footsteps behind him, he'd turned around before he was through. It was becoming a habit—this concentration on things behind him. Almost as though there were no future to be had.

But if the future did not arrive, the present did extend itself, and the uncomfortable little boy in the Packard went to school and at twelve met the boy who not only could liberate him, but could take him to the woman who had as much to do with his future as she had his past.

Guitar said he knew her. Had even been inside her house.

"What's it like in there?" Milkman asked him.

"Shiny," Guitar answered. "Shiny and brown. With a smell."

"A bad smell?"

"I don't know. Her smell. You'll see."

All those unbelievable but entirely possible stories about his father's sister—the woman his father had forbidden him to go near—had both of them spellbound. Neither wished to live one more day without finding out the truth, and they believed they were the legitimate and natural ones to do so. After all, Guitar already knew her, and Milkman was her nephew.

They found her on the front steps sitting wide-legged in a long-sleeved, long-skirted black dress. Her hair was wrapped in black too, and from a distance, all they could really see beneath her face was the bright orange she was peeling. She was all angles, he remembered later, knees, mostly, and elbows. One foot pointed east and one pointed west.

As they came closer and saw the brass box dangling from her ear, Milkman knew that what with the earring, the orange, and the angled black cloth, nothing—not the wisdom of his father nor the caution of the world—could keep him from her.

Guitar, being older and already in high school, had none of the reluctance that his young buddy still struggled with, and was the first one to speak.

"Hi."

The woman looked up. First at Guitar and then at Milkman.

"What kind of word is that?" Her voice was light but gravel-sprinkled. Milkman kept on staring at her fingers, manipulating the orange. Guitar grinned and shrugged. "It means hello."

"Then say what you mean."

"Okay. Hello."

"That's better. What you want?"

"Nothin. We just passin by."

"Look like you standin by."

"If you don't want us here, Miss Pilate, we'll go." Guitar spoke softly.

"I ain't the one with the wants. You the one want something."

"We wanna ask you something." Guitar stopped feigning in-difference. She was too direct, and to keep up with her he had to pay careful attention to his language.

"Ask it."

"Somebody said you ain't got no navel."

"That the question?"

"Yes."

"Don't sound like a question. Sound like an answer. Gimme the question."

"Do you?"

"Do I what?"

"Do you have a navel?"

"No."

"What happened to it?"

"Beats me." She dropped a bright peeling into her lap and separated an orange section slowly. "Now do I get to ask a question?"

"Sure."

"Who's your little friend?"

"This here's Milkman."

"Do he talk?" Pilate swallowed a piece of the fruit.

"Yeah. He talk. Say something." Guitar shoved an elbow at Milkman without taking his eyes off Pilate.

Milkman took a breath, held it, and said, "Hi."

Pilate laughed. "You all must be the dumbest unhung Negroes on earth. What they telling you in them schools? You say 'Hi' to pigs and sheep when you want 'em to move. When you tell a human being 'Hi,' he ought to get up and knock you down."

Shame had flooded him. He had expected to feel it, but not that kind; to be embarrassed, yes, but not that way. She was the one who was ugly, dirty, poor, and drunk. The queer aunt whom his sixth-grade schoolmates teased him about and whom he hated because he felt personally responsible for her ugliness, her poverty, her dirt, and her wine.

Instead she was making fun of his school, of his teachers, of him. And while she looked as poor as everyone said she was, something was missing from her eyes that should have confirmed it. Nor was she dirty; unkempt, yes, but not dirty. The whites of her fingernails were like ivory. And unless he knew absolutely nothing, this woman was definitely not drunk. Of course she was anything but pretty, yet he knew he could have watched her all day: the fingers pulling thread veins from the orange sections, the berry-black lips that made her look as though she wore make-up, the earring. . . . And when she stood up, he all but gasped. She was as tall as his father, head and shoulders taller than himself. Her dress wasn't as long as he had thought; it came to just below her calf and now he could see her unlaced men's shoes and the silvery-brown skin of her ankles.

She held the peelings precisely as they had fallen in her lap, and as she walked up the steps she looked as though she were holding her crotch.

"Your daddy wouldn't like that. He don't like dumb peoples." Then she looked right at Milkman, one hand holding the peelings, the other on the doorknob. "I know your daddy. I know you too."

Again Guitar spoke up. "You his daddy's sister?"

"The only one he got. Ain't but three Deads alive."

Milkman, who had been unable to get one word out of his mouth after the foolish "Hi," heard himself shouting: "I'm a Dead! My mother's a Dead! My sisters. You and him ain't the only ones!"

Even while he was screaming he wondered why he was suddenly so defensive—so possessive about his name. He had always hated that name, all of it, and until he and Guitar became friends, he had hated his nickname too. But in Guitar's mouth it sounded clever, grown up. Now he was behaving with this strange woman as though having the name was a matter of deep personal pride, as though she had tried to expel him from a very special group, in which he not only belonged, but had exclusive rights.

In the heartbeat of silence that followed his shouts, Pilate laughed.

"You all want a soft-boiled egg?" she asked.

The boys looked at each other. She'd changed rhythm on them. They didn't want an egg, but they did want to be with her, to go inside the wine house of this lady who had one earring, no navel, and looked like a tall black tree.

"No, thanks, but we'd like a drink of water." Guitar smiled back at her.

"Well. Step right in." She opened the door and they followed her into a large sunny room that looked both barren and cluttered. A moss-green sack hung from the ceiling. Candles were stuck in bottles everywhere; newspaper articles and magazine pictures were nailed to the walls. But other than a rocking chair, two straight-backed chairs, a large table, a sink and stove, there was no furniture. Pervading everything was the odor of pine and fermenting fruit.

"You ought to try one. I know how to do them just right. I don't like my whites to move, you know. The yolk I want soft, but not runny. Want it like wet velvet. How come you don't just try one?"

She had dumped the peelings in a large crock, which like most everything in the house had been made for some other purpose. Now she stood before the dry sink, pumping water into a blue-and-white wash basin which she used for a saucepan.

"Now, the water and the egg have to meet each other on a kind of equal standing. One can't get the upper hand over the other. So the temperature has to be the same for both. I knock the chill off the water first. Just the chill. I don't let it get warm because the egg is room temperature, you see. Now then, the real secret is right here in the boiling. When the tiny bubbles come to the surface, when they as big as peas and just before they get big as marbles. Well, right then you take the pot off the fire. You don't just put the fire out; you take the pot off. Then you put a folded newspaper over the pot and do one small obligation. Like answering the door or emptying the bucket and bringing it in off the front porch. I generally go to the toilet. Not for a long stay, mind you. Just a short one. If you do all that, you got yourself a perfect soft-boiled egg.

"I remember the messes I used to make for my father when I cooked. Your father"—she directed a thumb at Milkman—"he couldn't cook worth poot. Once I made a cherry pie for him, or tried to. Macon was a nice boy and awful good to me. Be nice if you could have known him then. He would have been a real good friend to you too, like he was to me."

Her voice made Milkman think of pebbles. Little round pebbles that bumped up against each other. Maybe she was hoarse, or maybe it was the way she said her words, with both a drawl and a clip. The piny-winy smell was narcotic, and so was the sun streaming in, strong and unfettered because there were no curtains or shades at the windows that were all around the room, two in each of three walls, one on each side of the door, one on either side of the sink and the stove, and two on the farther wall. The fourth wall must back on the bedrooms, Milkman thought. The pebbly voice, the sun, and the narcotic wine smell weakened both the boys, and they sat in a pleasant semi-stupor, listening to her go on and on. . . .

"Hadn't been for your daddy, I wouldn't be here today. I would have died in the womb. And died again in the woods. Those woods and the dark would have surely killed me. But he saved me and here I am boiling eggs. Our papa was dead, you see. They blew him five feet up into the air. He was sitting on his fence waiting for 'em, and they snuck up from behind and blew him five feet into the air. So when we left Circe's big house we didn't have no place to go, so we just walked around and lived in them woods. Farm country. But Papa came back one day. We didn't know it was him at first, cause we both saw him blowed five feet into the air. We were lost then. And talking about dark! You think dark is just one color, but it ain't. There're five or six kinds of black. Some silky, some woolly.

Some just empty. Some like fingers. And it don't stay still. It moves and changes from one kind of black to another. Saying something is pitch black is like saying something is green. What kind of green? Green like my bottles? Green like a grasshopper? Green like a cucumber, lettuce, or green like the sky is just before it breaks loose to storm? Well, night black is the same way. May as well be a rainbow.

"Now, we lost and there was this wind and in front of us was the back of our daddy. We were some scared children. Macon kept telling me that the things we was scared of wasn't real. What difference do it make if the thing you scared of is real or not? I remember doing laundry for a man and his wife once, down in Virginia. The husband came into the kitchen one afternoon shivering and saying did I have any coffee made. I asked him what was it that had grabbed hold of him, he looked so bad. He said he couldn't figure it out, but he felt like he was about to fall off a cliff. Standing right there on that yellow and white and red linoleum, as level as a flatiron. He was holding on to the door first, then the chair, trying his best not to fall down. I opened my mouth to tell him wasn't no cliff in that kitchen. Then I remembered how it was being in those woods. I felt it all over again. So I told the man did he want me to hold on to him so he couldn't fall. He looked at me with the most grateful look in the world. 'Would you?' he said. I walked around back of him and locked my fingers in front of his chest and held on to him. His heart was kicking under his vest like a mule in heat. But little by little it calmed down."

"You saved his life," said Guitar.

"No such thing. His wife come in before it was time to let go. She asked me what I was doing and I told her."

"Told her what? What'd you say?"

"The truth. That I was trying to keep him from falling off a cliff."

"I bet he wished he had jumped off then. She believe you? Don't tell me she believed you."

"Not right away she didn't. But soon's I let go he fell dead-weight to the floor. Smashed his glasses and everything. Fell right on his face. And you know what? He went down so slow. I swear it took three minutes, three whole minutes to go from a standing upright position to when he mashed his face on the floor. I don't know if the cliff was real or not, but it took him three minutes to fall down it."

"Was he dead?" asked Guitar.

"Stone dead."

"Who shot your daddy? Did you say somebody shot him?" Guitar was fascinated, his eyes glittering with lights.

"Five feet into the air . . ."

"Who?"

"I don't know who and I don't know why. I just know what I'm telling you: what, when, and where."

"You didn't say where." He was insistent.

"I did too. Off a fence."

"Where was the fence?"

"On our farm."

Guitar laughed, but his eyes were too shiny to convey much humor. "Where was the farm?"

"Montour County."

He gave up on "where." "Well, when then?"

"When he sat there—on the fence."

Guitar felt like a frustrated detective. "What year?"

"The year they shot them Irish people down in the streets. Was a good year for guns and gravediggers, I know that." Pilate put a barrel lid on the table. Then she lifted the eggs from the wash basin and began to peel them. Her lips moved as she played an orange seed around in her mouth. Only after the eggs were split open, revealing moist reddish-yellow centers, did she return to her story. "One morning we woke up when the sun was nearly a quarter way cross the sky. Bright as anything. And blue. Blue like the ribbons on my mother's bonnet. See that streak of sky?" She pointed out the window. "Right behind them hickories. See? Right over there."

They looked and saw the sky stretching back behind the houses and the trees. "That's the same color," she said, as if she had discovered something important. "Same color as my mama's ribbons. I'd know her ribbon color anywhere, but I don't know her name. After she died Papa wouldn't let anybody say it. Well, before we could get the sand rubbed out of our eyes and take a good look around, we saw him sitting there on a stump. Right in the sunlight. We started to call him but he looked on off, like he was lookin at us and not lookin at us at the same time. Something in his face scared us. It was like looking at a face under water. Papa got up after a while and moved out of the sun on back into the woods. We just stood there looking at the stump. Shaking like leaves."

Pilate scraped the eggshells together into a little heap, her fingers fanning out over and over again in a gentle sweeping. The boys watched, afraid to say anything lest they ruin the next part of her story, and afraid to remain silent lest she not go on with its telling.

"Shaking like leaves," she murmured, "just like leaves."

Suddenly she lifted her head and made a sound like a hoot owl. "Ooo! Here I come!"

Neither Milkman nor Guitar saw or heard anyone approaching, but Pilate jumped up and ran toward the door. Before she reached it, a foot kicked it open and Milkman saw the bent back of a girl. She was dragging a large five-bushel basket of what looked like brambles, and a woman was pushing the other side of it, saying, "Watch the doorsill, baby."

"I got it," the girl answered. "Push."

"About time," said Pilate. "The light be gone before you know it."

"Tommy's truck broke down," the girl said, panting. When the two had managed to get the basket into the room, the girl stretched her back and turned around, facing them. But Milkman had no need to see her face; he had already fallen in love with her behind.

"Hagar." Pilate looked around the room. "This here's your brother, Milkman. And this is his friend. What's your name again, pretty?"

"Guitar."

"Guitar? You play any?" she asked.

"That ain't her brother, Mama. They cousins." The older woman spoke.

"Same thing."

"No it ain't. Is it, baby?"

"No," said Hagar. "It's different."

"See there. It's different."

"Well, what is the difference, Reba? You know so much."

Reba looked at the ceiling. "A brother is a brother if you both got the same mother or if you both—"

Pilate interrupted her. "I mean what's the difference in the way you act toward 'em? Don't you have to act the same way to both?"

"That's not the point, Mama."

"Shut up, Reba. I'm talking to Hagar."

"Yes, Mama. You treat them both the same."

"Then why they got two words for it 'stead of one, if they ain't no difference?" Reba put her hands on her hips and opened her eyes wide.

"Pull that rocker over here," said Pilate. "You boys have to give up your seats unless you gonna help."

The women circled the basket, which was full of blackberries still on their short, thorny branches.

"What we have to do?" Guitar asked.

"Get them little berries off them hateful branches without popping 'em. Reba, get that other crock."

Hagar looked around, all eyes and hair. "Why don't we pull a bed out the back room? Then we can all sit down."

"Floor's good enough for me," said Pilate, and she squatted down on her haunches and lifted a branch gently from the basket. "This all you got?"

"No." Reba was side-rolling a huge crock. "Two more outside."

"Better bring them in. Draw too many flies out there."

Hagar started for the door and motioned to Milkman. "Come on, brother. You can help."

Milkman jumped up, knocking his chair backward, and trotted after Hagar. She was, it seemed to him, as pretty a girl as he'd ever seen. She was much much older than he was. She must be as old as Guitar, maybe even seventeen. He seemed to be floating. More alive than he'd ever been, and floating. Together he and Hagar dragged two baskets up the porch stairs and into the house. She was as strong and muscular as he was.

"Careful, Guitar. Go slow. You keep on busting 'em."

"Leave him alone, Reba. He got to get the feel first. I asked you did you play any. That why they call you Guitar?"

"Not cause I do play. Because I wanted to. When I was real little. So they tell me."

"Where'd you ever see a guitar?"

"It was a contest, in a store down home in Florida. I saw it when my mother took me downtown with her. I was just a baby. It was one of those things where you guess how many beans in the big glass jar and you win a guitar. I cried for it, they said. And always asked about it."

"You should of called Reba. She'd get it for you."

"No, you couldn't buy it. You had to give the number of jellybeans."

"I heard you. Reba would of known how many. Reba wins things. She ain't never lost nothing."

"Really?" Guitar smiled, but he was doubtful. "She lucky?"

"Sure I'm lucky." Reba grinned. "People come from everywhere to get me to stand in for 'em at drawings and give them numbers to play. It works pretty well for them, and it always works for me. I win everything I try to win and lots of things I don't even try to win."

"Got to where won't nobody sell her a raffle ticket. They just want her to hold theirs."

"See this?" Reba put her hand down in the top of her dress and pulled out a diamond ring attached to a string. "I won this last year. I was the . . . what was it, Mama?"

"Five hundred thousandth."

"Five hundred . . . no it wasn't. That ain't what they said."

"Half a million is what they said."

"That's right. The half a millionth person to walk into Sears and Roebuck." Her laughter was gay and proud.

"They didn't want to give it to her," said Hagar, "cause she looked so bad."

Guitar was astonished. "I remember that contest, but I don't remember hearing nothing 'bout no colored person winning it." Guitar, a habitual street roamer, believed he knew every public thing going on in the city.

"Nobody did. They had picture-taking people and everything waiting for the next person to walk in the door. But they never did put my picture in the paper. Me and Mama looked, too, didn't we?" She glanced at Pilate for confirmation and went on. "But they put the picture of the man who won second prize in. He won a war bond. He was white."

"Second prize?" Guitar asked. "What kind of 'second prize'? Either you the half-millionth person or you ain't. Can't be no next-to-the-half-millionth."

"Can if the winner is Reba," Hagar said. "The only reason they got a second was cause she was the first. And the only reason they gave it to her was because of them cameras."

"Tell 'em why you was in Sears, Reba."

"Looking for a toilet." Reba threw her head back to let the laughter escape. Her hands were stained with blackberry juice, and when she wiped the tears from her eyes she streaked the purple from her nose to her cheekbone. Much lighter than Pilate or Hagar, Reba had the simple eyes of an infant. All of them had a guileless look about them, but complication and something more lurked behind Pilate's and Hagar's faces. Only Reba, with her light pimply skin and deferential manner, looked as though her simplicity might also be vacuousness.

"Ain't but two toilets downtown they let colored in: Mayflower Restaurant and Sears. Sears was closer. Good thing nature wasn't in a hurry. They kept me there fifteen minutes gettin my name and address to send the diamond over to me. But I wouldn't let 'em send it to me. I kept asking them, Is this a real contest? I don't believe you."

"It was worth a diamond ring to get you out of there. Drawing a crowd and getting ready to draw flies," said Hagar.

"What're you going to do with the ring?" Milkman asked her.

"Wear it. Seldom I win something I like."

"Everything she win, she give away," Hagar said.

"To a man," said Pilate.

"She don't never keep none of it. . . ."

"That's what she want to win—a man. . . ."

"Worse'n Santa Claus. . . ."

"Funny kind of luck ain't no luck at all. . . ."

"*He* comes just once a year. . . ."

Hagar and Pilate pulled the conversation apart, each yanking out some thread of comment more to herself than to Milkman or Guitar—or even Reba, who had dropped her ring back inside her dress and was smiling sweetly, and deftly separating the royal-purple berries from their twigs.

Milkman was five feet seven then but it was the first time in his life that he remembered being completely happy. He was with his friend, an older boy—wise and kind and fearless. He was sitting comfortably in the notorious wine house; he was surrounded by women who seemed to enjoy him and who laughed out loud. And he was in love. No wonder his father was afraid of them.

"When will this wine be ready?" he asked.

"This batch? Few weeks," Pilate said.

"You gonna let us have some?" Guitar smiled.

"Sure. You want some now? Plenty wine in the cellar."

"I don't want that. I want some of this. Some of the wine I made."

"You think you made this?" Pilate laughed at him. "You think this all there is to it? Picking a few berries?"

"Oh." Guitar scratched his head. "I forgot. We got to mash them in our bare feet."

"Feet? Feet?" Pilate was outraged. "Who makes wine with they feet?"

"Might taste good, Mama," said Hagar.

"Couldn't taste no worse," Reba said.

"Your wine any good, Pilate?" asked Guitar.

"Couldn't tell you."

"Why not?"

"Never tasted it."

Milkman laughed. "You sell wine you don't even taste?"

"Folks don't buy it for the taste. Buy it to get drunk."

Reba nodded. "Used to anyway. Ain't buying nothing now."

"Don't nobody want no cheap home brew. The Depression's over," Hagar said. "Everybody got work now. They can afford to buy Four Roses."

"Plenty still buy," Pilate told her.

"Where you get the sugar for it?" Guitar asked.

"Black market," said Reba.

"What 'plenty'? Tell the truth, Mama. If Reba hadn't won that hundred pounds of groceries, we'd have starved last winter."

"Would not." Pilate put a fresh piece of twig in her mouth.

"We *would* have."

"Hagar, don't contradict your mama," Reba whispered.

"Who was gonna feed us?" Hagar was insistent. "Mama can go for months without food. Like a lizard."

"Lizard live that long without food?" asked Reba.

"Girl, ain't nobody gonna let you starve. You ever had a hungry day?" Pilate asked her granddaughter.

"Course she ain't," said her mother.

Hagar tossed a branch to the heap on the floor and rubbed her fingers. The tips were colored a deep red. "Some of my days were hungry ones."

With the quickness of birds, the heads of Pilate and Reba shot up. They peered at Hagar, then exchanged looks.

"Baby?" Reba's voice was soft. "You been hungry, baby? Why didn't you say so?" Reba looked hurt. "We get you anything you want, baby. Anything. You *been* knowing that."

Pilate spit her twig into the palm of her hand. Her face went still. Without those moving lips her face was like a mask. It seemed to Milkman that somebody had just clicked off a light.

He looked at the faces of the women. Reba's had crumpled. Tears were streaming down her cheeks. Pilate's face was still as death, but alert as though waiting for some signal. Hagar's profile was hidden by her hair. She leaned forward, her elbows on her thighs, rubbing fingers that looked bloodstained in the lessening light. Her nails were very very long.

The quiet held. Even Guitar didn't dare break it.

Then Pilate spoke. "Reba. She don't mean food."

Realization swept slowly across Reba's face, but she didn't answer. Pilate began to hum as she returned to plucking the berries. After a moment, Reba joined her, and they hummed together in perfect harmony until Pilate took the lead:

> *O Sugarman don't leave me here*
> *Cotton balls to choke me*
> *O Sugarman don't leave me here*
> *Buckra's arms to yoke me. . . .*

When the two women got to the chorus, Hagar raised her head and sang too.

> *Sugarman done fly away*
> *Sugarman done gone*
> *Sugarman cut across the sky*
> *Sugarman gone home.*

Milkman could hardly breathe. Hagar's voice scooped up what little pieces of heart he had left to call his own. When he thought he was going to faint from the weight of what he was feeling, he risked a glance at his friend and saw the setting sun gilding Guitar's eyes, putting into shadow a slow smile of recognition.

Delicious as the day turned out to be for Milkman, it was even more so because it included secrecy and defiance, both of which dissipated within an hour of his father's return. Freddie had let Macon Dead know that his son had spent the afternoon "drinking in the wine house."

"He's lying! We didn't drink nothing. Nothing. Guitar didn't even get the glass of water he asked for."

"Freddie never lies. He misrepresents, but he never lies."

"He lied to you."

"About the wine-drinking? Maybe. But not about you being there, huh?"

"No, sir. Not about that." Milkman softened his tone a bit, but succeeded in keeping the edge of defiance in his voice.

"Now, what were your instructions from me?"

"You told me to stay away from there. To stay away from Pilate."

"Right."

"But you never told me why. They're our cousins. She's your own sister."

"And you're my own son. And you will do what I tell you to do. With or without explanations. As long as your feet are under my table, you'll do in this house what you are told."

At fifty-two, Macon Dead was as imposing a man as he had been at forty-two, when Milkman thought he was the biggest thing in the world. Bigger even than the house they lived in. But today he had seen a woman who was just as tall and who had made him feel tall too.

"I know I'm the youngest one in this family, but I ain't no baby. You treat me like I was a baby. You keep saying you don't have to explain nothing to me. How do you think that makes me feel? Like a baby, that's what. Like a twelve-year-old baby!"

"Don't you raise your voice to me."

"Is that the way your father treated you when you were twelve?"

"Watch your mouth!" Macon roared. He took his hands out of his pockets but didn't know what to do with them. He was momentarily confused. His son's question had shifted the scenery. He was seeing himself at twelve, standing in Milkman's shoes and feeling what he himself had felt for his own father. The numbness that had settled on him when he saw the man he loved and admired fall off the fence; something wild ran through him when he watched the body twitching in the dirt. His father had sat for five nights on a split-rail fence cradling a shotgun and in the end died protecting his property. Was that what this boy felt for him? Maybe it was time to tell him things.

"Well, did he?"

"I worked right alongside my father. Right alongside him. From the time I was four or five we worked together. Just the two of us. Our mother was dead. Died when Pilate was born. Pilate was just a baby. She stayed over at another farm in the daytime. I carried her over there myself in my arms every morning. Then I'd go back across the fields and meet my father. We'd hitch President Lincoln to the plow and . . . That's what we called her: President Lincoln. Papa said Lincoln was a good plow hand before he was President and you shouldn't take a good plow hand away from his work. He called our farm Lincoln's Heaven. It was a little bit a place. But it looked big to me then. I know now it must a been a little bit a place, maybe a hundred and fifty acres. We tilled fifty. About eighty of it was woods. Must of been a fortune in oak and pine; maybe that's what they wanted—the lumber, the oak and the pine. We had a pond that was four acres. And a stream, full of fish. Right down in the heart of a valley. Prettiest mountain you ever saw, Montour Ridge. We lived in Montour County. Just north of the Susquehanna. We had a four-stall hog pen. The big barn was forty feet by a hundred and forty—hip-roofed too. And all around in the mountains was deer and wild turkey. You ain't tasted nothing till you taste wild turkey the way Papa cooked it. He'd burn it real fast in the fire. Burn it black all over. That sealed it. Sealed the juices in. Then he'd let it roast on a spit for twenty-four hours. When you cut the black burnt part off, the meat underneath was tender, sweet, juicy. And we had fruit trees. Apple, cherry. Pilate tried to make me a cherry pie once."

Macon paused and let the smile come on. He had not said any of this for years. Had not even reminisced much about it recently. When he was first married he used to talk about Lincoln's Heaven to Ruth. Sitting on the porch swing in the dark, he would re-create the land that was to have been his. Or when he was just starting out in the business of buying houses, he would lounge around the barbershop and swap stories with the men there. But for years he hadn't had that kind of time, or interest. But now he was doing it again, with his son, and every detail of that land was clear in his mind: the well, the apple orchard, President Lincoln; her foal, Mary Todd; Ulysses S. Grant, their cow; General Lee, their hog. That was the way he knew what history he remembered. His father couldn't read, couldn't write; knew only what he saw and heard tell of. But he had etched in Macon's mind certain historical figures, and as a boy in school, Macon thought of the personalities of his horse, his hog, when he read about these people. His father may have called their plow horse President Lincoln as a joke, but Macon always thought of Lincoln with fondness since he had loved him first as a strong, steady, gentle, and obedient horse. He even liked General Lee, for one spring they slaughtered him and ate the best pork outside Virginia, "from the butt to the smoked ham to the ribs to the sausage to the jowl to the feet to the tail to the head cheese"—for eight months. And there was cracklin in November.

"General Lee was all right by me," he told Milkman, smiling. "Finest general I ever knew. Even his balls was tasty. Circe made up the best pot of maws she ever cooked. Huh! I'd forgotten that woman's name. That was it, Circe. Worked at a big farm some white people owned in Danville, Pennsylvania. Funny how things get away from you. For years you can't remember nothing. Then just like that, it all comes back to you. Had a dog run, they did. That was the big sport back then. Dog races. White people did love their dogs. Kill a nigger and comb their hair at the same time. But I've seen grown white men cry about their dogs."

His voice sounded different to Milkman. Less hard, and his speech was different. More southern and comfortable and soft. Milkman spoke softly too. "Pilate said somebody shot your father. Five feet into the air."

"Took him sixteen years to get that farm to where it was paying. It's all dairy country up there now. Then it wasn't. Then it was . . . nice."

"Who shot him, Daddy?"

Macon focused his eyes on his son. "Papa couldn't read, couldn't even sign his name. Had a mark he used. They tricked him. He signed something, I don't know what, and they told him they owned his property. He never read nothing. I tried to teach him, but he said he couldn't remember those little marks from one day to the next. Wrote one word in his life—Pilate's name; copied it out of the Bible. That's what she got folded up in that earring. He should have let me teach him. Everything bad that ever happened to him happened because he couldn't read. Got his name messed up cause he couldn't read."

"His name? How?"

"When freedom came. All the colored people in the state had to register with the Freedmen's Bureau."

"Your father was a slave?"

"What kind of foolish question is that? Course he was. Who hadn't been in 1869? They all had to register. Free and not free. Free and used-to-be-slaves. Papa was in his teens and went to sign up, but the man behind the desk was drunk. He asked Papa where he was born. Papa said Macon. Then he asked him who his father was. Papa said, 'He's dead.' Asked him who owned him, Papa said, 'I'm free.' Well, the Yankee wrote it all down, but in the wrong spaces. Had him born in Dunfrie, wherever the hell that is, and in the space for his name the fool wrote, 'Dead' comma 'Macon.' But Papa couldn't read so he never found out what he was registered as till Mama told him. They met on a wagon going North. Started talking about one thing and another, told her about being a freedman and showed off his papers to her. When she looked at his paper she read him out what it said."

"He didn't have to keep the name, did he? He could have used his real name, couldn't he?"

"Mama liked it. Liked the name. Said it was new and would wipe out the past. Wipe it all out."

"What was his real name?"

"I don't remember my mother too well. She died when I was four. Light-skinned, pretty. Looked like a white woman to me. Me and Pilate don't take nothing after her. If you ever have a doubt we from Africa, look at Pilate. She look just like Papa and he looked like all them pictures you ever see of Africans. A Pennsylvania African. Acted like one too. Close his face up like a door."

"I saw Pilate's face like that." Milkman felt close and confidential now that his father had talked to him in a relaxed and intimate way.

"I haven't changed my mind, Macon. I don't want you over there."

"Why? You still haven't said why."

"Just listen to what I say. That woman's no good. She's a snake, and can charm you like a snake, but still a snake."

"You talking about your own sister, the one you carried in your arms to the fields every morning."

"That was a long time ago. You seen her. What she look like to you? Somebody nice? Somebody normal?"

"Well, she . . ."

"Or somebody cut your throat?"

"She didn't look like that, Daddy."

"Well she *is* like that."

"What'd she do?"

"It ain't what she did; it's what she is."

"What is she?"

"A snake, I told you. Ever hear the story about the snake? The man who saw a little baby snake on the ground? Well, the man saw this baby snake bleeding and hurt. Lying there in the dirt. And the man felt sorry for it and picked it up and put it in his basket and took it home. And he fed it and took care of it till it was big and strong. Fed it the same thing he ate. Then one day, the snake turned on him and bit him. Stuck his poison tongue right in the man's heart. And while he was laying there dying, he turned to the snake and asked him, 'What'd you do that for?' He said, 'Didn't I take good care of you? Didn't I save your life?' The snake said, 'Yes.' 'Then what'd you do it for? What'd you kill me for?' Know what the snake said? Said, 'But you knew I was a snake, didn't you?' Now, I mean for you to stay out of that wine house and as far away from Pilate as you can."

Milkman lowered his head. His father had explained nothing to him.

"Boy, you got better things to do with your time. Besides, it's time you started learning how to work. You start Monday. After school come to my office; work a couple of hours there and learn what's real. Pilate can't teach you a thing you can use in this world. Maybe the next, but not this one. Let me tell you right now the one important thing you'll ever need to know: Own things. And let the things you own own other things. Then you'll own yourself and other people too. Starting Monday, I'm going to teach you how."

Chapter 3

Life improved for Milkman enormously after he began working
for Macon. Contrary to what his father hoped, there was more
time to visit the wine house. Running errands for Macon's rent
houses gave him leave to be in Southside and get to know the
people Guitar knew so well. Milkman was young and he was
friendly—just the opposite of his father—and the tenants felt at
ease enough with him to tease him, feed him, confide in him. But
it was hard to see much of Guitar. Saturdays were the only days
he was certain to find him. If Milkman got up early enough on
Saturday morning, he could catch his friend before Guitar went
roaming the streets and before he himself had to help Macon
collect rents. But there were days in the week when they agreed
to skip school and hang out, and on one of those days Guitar
took him to Feather's pool hall on Tenth Street, right in the
middle of the Blood Bank area.

It was eleven o'clock in the morning when Guitar pushed
open the door and shouted, "Hey, Feather! Give us a couple of
Red Caps."

Feather, a short squat man with sparse but curly hair, looked up at Guitar, then at Milkman, and frowned.

"Get him out of here."

Guitar stopped short and followed the little man's gaze to Milkman's face and back again. The half-dozen men there playing pool turned around at the sound of Feather's voice. Three of them were air force pilots, part of the 332nd Fighter Group. Their beautiful hats and gorgeous leather jackets were carefully arranged on chairs. Their hair was cut close to the skull; their shirt cuffs were turned neatly back on their forearms; their white scarves hung in snowy rectangles from their hip pockets. Silver chains glistened at their necks and they looked faintly amused as they worked chalk into the tips of their cues.

Guitar's face shone with embarrassment. "He's with me," he said.

"I said get him outta here."

"Come on, Feather, he's my friend."

"He's Macon Dead's boy, ain't he?"

"So what?"

"So get him outta here."

"He can't help who his daddy is." Guitar had his voice under control.

"Neither can I. Out."

"What his daddy do to you?"

"Nothing yet. That's why I want him outta here."

"He ain't like his daddy."

"He ain't got to be like him—*from* him is enough."

"I'll be responsible for—"

"Stop messing with me, Guitar. Get him out. He ain't old enough to have wet dreams."

The pilots laughed and a man in a gray straw hat with a white band said, "Aw, let the boy stay, Feather."

"You shut your mouth. I'm running this."

"What harm can he do? A twelve-year-old kid." He smiled at Milkman, who stopped himself from saying, No, thirteen.

"But it ain't your problem, is it?" asked Feather. "His daddy ain't your landlord, is he, and you ain't got no operating license to hang on to either. You ain't got nothing. . . ."

Feather turned on the man with the white hatband the same acid manner he'd used with the boys. Guitar took the opportunity offered by Feather's new target to shoot his hand out like a double-edged hatchet slamming into a tree, and shout, "Later for you, man. Come on. Let's shake this place." His voice now was loud and deep—loud enough and deep enough for two. Milkman slid his hands into his back pockets and followed his friend to the door. He stretched his neck a little to match the chilly height he hoped the soldiers had seen in his eyes.

Silently they ambled down Tenth Street until they reached a stone bench that jutted from the sidewalk near the curb. They stopped there and sat down, their backs to the eyes of two men in white smocks who were watching them. One of the men leaned in the doorway of a barbershop. The other sat in a chair tilted back to the plate-glass window of the shop. They were the owners of the barbershop, Railroad Tommy and Hospital Tommy. Neither boy spoke, not to the men nor to each other. They sat and watched the traffic go by.

"Have all the halls of academe crumbled, Guitar?" Hospital Tommy spoke from his chair. His eyes were milky, like those of very old people, but the rest of him was firm, lithe, and young-looking. His tone was casual but suggested authority nonetheless.

"No, sir." Guitar answered him over his shoulder.

"Then what, pray, are you doing out here in the streets at this time of day?"

Guitar shrugged. "We just took a day off, Mr. Tommy."

"And your companion? Is he on sabbatical too?"

Guitar nodded. Hospital Tommy talked like an encyclopedia and Guitar had to guess at most of his words. Milkman kept looking at the cars going by.

"Neither one of you appears to be having much fun on your holiday. You could have stayed in the halls of academe and looked evil."

Guitar fished for a cigarette and offered one to Milkman. "Feather made me mad is all."

"Feather?"

"Yeah. He wouldn't let us in. I go in there all the time. All the time and he don't say nothing. But today he throws us out. Said my friend here is too young. Can you beat that? Feather? Worrying about somebody's age?"

"I didn't know Feather had so much as a brain cell to worry with."

"He don't. Just showing off is all. He wouldn't even let me have a bottle of beer."

Railroad Tommy laughed softly from the doorway. "Is that all? He wouldn't let you have a beer?" He rubbed the back of his neck and then crooked a finger at Guitar. "Come over here, boy, and let me tell you about some other stuff you are not going to have. Come on over here."

Reluctantly they stood up and sidled closer to the laughing man.

"You think that's something? Not having a beer? Well, let me ask you something. You ever stood stock still in the galley of the Baltimore and Ohio dining car in the middle of the night when the kitchen closed down and everything's neat and ready for the next day? And the engine's highballing down the track and three of your buddies is waiting for you with a brand-new deck of cards?"

Guitar shook his head. "No, I never . . ."

"That's right, you never. And you never going to. That's one more thrill you not going to have, let alone a bottle of beer."

Guitar smiled. "Mr. Tommy," he began, but Tommy cut him off.

"You ever pull fourteen days straight and come home to a sweet woman, clean sheets, and a fifth of Wild Turkey? Eh?" He looked at Milkman. "Did you?"

Milkman smiled and said, "No, sir."

"No? Well, don't look forward to it, cause you not going to have that either."

Hospital Tommy drew a pinfeather toothpick from under his smock. "Don't tease the boy, Tommy."

"Who's teasing? I'm telling him the truth. He ain't going to have it. Neither one of 'em going to have it. And I'll tell you something else you not going to have. You not going to have no private coach with four red velvet chairs that swivel around in one place whenever you want 'em to. No. And you not going to have your own special toilet and your own special-made eight-foot bed either. And a valet and a cook and a secretary to travel with you and do everything you say. Everything: get the right temperature in your hot-water bottle and make sure the smoking tobacco in the silver humidor is fresh each and *every* day. That's something else you not going to have. You ever have five thousand dollars of cold cash money in your pocket and walk into a bank and tell the bank man you want such and such a house on such and such a street and he sell it to you right then? Well, you won't ever have it. And you not going to have a governor's mansion, or eight thousand acres of timber to sell. And you not going to have no ship under your command to sail on, no train to run, and you can join the 332nd if you want to and shoot down a thousand German planes all by yourself and land in Hitler's backyard and whip him with your own hands, but you never going to have four stars on your shirt front, or even three. And you not going to have no breakfast tray brought in to you early in the morning with a red rose on it and two warm croissants and a cup of hot chocolate. Nope. Never. And no pheasant buried in coconut leaves for twenty days and stuffed with wild rice and cooked over a wood fire so tender and delicate it make you cry. And no Rothschild '29 or even Beaujolais to go with it."

A few men passing by stopped to listen to Tommy's lecture. "What's going on?" they asked Hospital Tommy.

"Feather refused them a beer," he said. The men laughed.

"And *no* baked Alaska!" Railroad Tommy went on. "None! You never going to have that."

"No baked Alaska?" Guitar opened his eyes wide with horror and grabbed his throat. "You breaking my heart!"

"Well, now. That's something you will have—a broken heart." Railroad Tommy's eyes softened, but the merriment in them died suddenly. "And folly. A whole lot of folly. You can count on it."

"Mr. Tommy, suh," Guitar sang in mock humility, "we just wanted a bottle of beer is all."

"Yeah," said Tommy. "Yeah, well, welcome aboard."

"What's a baked Alaska?" They left the Tommys just as they had found them and continued down Tenth Street.

"Something sweet," answered Guitar. "A dessert."

"Taste good?"

"I don't know. I can't eat sweets."

"You can't?" Milkman was amazed. "Why not?"

"Makes me sick."

"You don't like nothing sweet?"

"Fruit, but nothing with sugar. Candy, cake, stuff like that. I don't even like to smell it. Makes me want to throw up."

Milkman searched for a physical cause. He wasn't sure he trusted anybody who didn't like sweets. "You must have sugar diabetes."

"You don't get sugar diabetes from not eating sugar. You get it from eating too much sugar."

"Then what is it, then?"

"I don't know. It makes me think of dead people. And white people. And I start to puke."

"Dead people?"

"Yeah. And white people."

"I don't get it."

Guitar said nothing, so Milkman continued, "How long you been like that?"

"Since I was little. Since my father got sliced up in a sawmill and his boss came by and gave us kids some candy. Divinity. A big sack of divinity. His wife made it special for us. It's sweet, divinity is. Sweeter than syrup. Real sweet. Sweeter than . . ." He stopped walking and wiped from his forehead the beads of sweat that were collecting there. His eyes paled and wavered. He spit on the sidewalk. "Ho—hold it," he whispered, and stepped into a space between a fried-fish restaurant and Lilly's Beauty Parlor.

Milkman waited on the sidewalk, staring at the curtained window of the beauty shop. Beauty shops always had curtains or shades up. Barbershops didn't. The women didn't want anybody on the street to be able to see them getting their hair done. They were ashamed.

When Guitar emerged, his eyes were teary from the effort of dry heaving. "Come on," he said. "Let's get us some weed. That's one thing I can have."

By the time Milkman was fourteen he had noticed that one of his legs was shorter than the other. When he stood barefoot and straight as a pole, his left foot was about half an inch off the floor. So he never stood straight; he slouched or leaned or stood with a hip thrown out, and he never told anybody about it— ever. When Lena said, "Mama, what is he walking like *that* for?" he said, "I'll walk any way I want to, including over your ugly face." Ruth said, "Be quiet, you two. It's just growing pains, Lena." Milkman knew better. It wasn't a limp—not at all—just the suggestion of one, but it looked like an affected walk, the strut of a very young man trying to appear more sophisticated than he was. It bothered him and he acquired movements and habits to disguise what to him was a burning defect. He sat with his left ankle on his right knee, never the other way around. And he danced each new dance with a curious stiff-legged step that the girls loved and other boys eventually copied. The deformity was mostly in his mind. Mostly, but not completely, for he did have shooting pains in that leg after several hours on a basketball court. He favored it, believed it was polio, and felt secretly connected to the late President Roosevelt for that reason. Even when everybody was raving about Truman because he had set up a Committee on Civil Rights,

Milkman secretly preferred FDR and felt very very close to him. Closer, in fact, to him than to his own father, for Macon had no imperfection and age seemed to strengthen him. Milkman feared his father, respected him, but knew, because of the leg, that he could never emulate him. So he differed from him as much as he dared. Macon was clean-shaven; Milkman was desperate for a mustache. Macon wore bow ties; Milkman wore four-in-hands. Macon didn't part his hair; Milkman had a part shaved into his. Macon hated tobacco; Milkman tried to put a cigarette in his mouth every fifteen minutes. Macon hoarded his money; Milkman gave his away. But he couldn't help sharing with Macon his love of good shoes and fine thin socks. And he did try, as his father's employee, to do the work the way Macon wanted it done.

Macon was delighted. His son belonged to him now and not to Ruth, and he was relieved at not having to walk all over town like a peddler collecting rents. It made his business more dignified, and he had time to think, to plan, to visit the bank men, to read the public notices, auctions, to find out what plots were going for taxes, unclaimed heirs' property, where roads were being built, what supermarkets, schools; and who was trying to sell what to the government for the housing projects that were going to be built. The quickie townlets that were springing up around war plants. He knew as a Negro he wasn't going to get a big slice of the pie. But there were properties nobody wanted yet, or little edges of property somebody didn't want Jews to have, or Catholics to have, or properties nobody knew were of any value yet. There was quite a bit of pie filling oozing around the edge of the crust in 1945. Filling that could be his. Everything had improved for Macon Dead during the war. Except Ruth. And years later when the war was over and that pie filling had spilled over into his very lap, had stickied his hands and weighed his stomach down into a sagging paunch, he still wished he had strangled her back in 1921. She hadn't stopped spending occasional nights out of the house, but she was fifty years old now and what lover could she have kept so long? What lover could there be that even Freddie didn't know about? Macon decided it was of no importance, and less and less often did he get angry enough to slap her. Particularly after the final time, which became final because his son jumped up and knocked him back into the radiator.

Milkman was twenty-two then and since he had been fucking for six years, some of them with the same woman, he'd begun to see his mother in a new light. She was no longer the person who worried him about galoshes and colds and food, who stood in the way of most of the little pleasures he could take at home because they all involved some form of dirt, noise, or disarray. Now he saw her as a frail woman content to do tiny things; to grow and cultivate small life that would not hurt her if it died: rhododendron, goldfish, dahlias, geraniums, imperial tulips. Because these little lives did die. The goldfish floated to the top of the water and when she tapped the side of the bowl with her fingernail they did not flash away in a lightning arc of terror. The rhododendron leaves grew wide and green and when their color was at its deepest and waxiest, they suddenly surrendered it and lapsed into limp yellow hearts. In a way she was jealous of death. Inside all that grief she felt when the doctor died, there had been a bit of pique too, as though he had chosen a more interesting subject than life—a more provocative companion than she was—and had deliberately followed death when it beckoned. She was fierce in the presence of death, heroic even, as she was at no other time. Its threat gave her direction, clarity, audacity. Regardless of what Macon had done, she'd always suspected that the doctor didn't have to die if he hadn't wanted to. And it may have been that suspicion of personal failure and rejection (plus a smidgen of revenge against Macon) that made her lead her husband down paths from which there was no exit save violence. Lena thought Macon's rages unaccountable. But Corinthians began to see a plan. To see how her mother had learned to bring her husband to a point, not of power (a nine-year-old girl could slap Ruth and get away with it), but of helplessness. She would begin by describing some incident in which she was a sort of honest buffoon. It began as a piece of pleasant dinner conversation, harmless on the surface because no one at the table was required to share her embarrassment; but all were able to admire her honesty and to laugh at her ignorance.

She had gone to the wedding of Mrs. Djvorak's granddaughter. Anna Djvorak was an old Hungarian woman who had been one of her father's patients. He'd had many working-class white patients and some middle-class white women who thought he was handsome. Anna Djvorak was convinced that the doctor had miraculously saved her son's life by not sending him to the tuberculosis sanatorium back in 1903. Almost everybody who did go to the "san," as they called it, died in it. Anna didn't know that the doctor had no practicing privileges there, just as he had none at Mercy. Nor did she know that the cure for tuberculosis in 1903 was precisely the one most detrimental to the patients. All she knew was that the doctor had prescribed a certain diet, hours of rest to be rigidly adhered to, and cod-liver oil twice a day. The boy survived. It was natural that she would want the miracle doctor's daughter at the wedding of this son's youngest daughter. Ruth went and when the congregation went to the altar to receive the host, she went also. Kneeling there with her head bowed, she was not aware that the priest was left with the choice of placing the wafer on her hat or skipping her. He knew immediately that she was not Catholic since she did not raise her head at his words and push out her tongue for the wafer to be carefully placed there.

"Corpus Domini Nostri Jesu Christi," said the priest, and then, to her, a sharp whisper: "Ssss. Raise your head!" She looked up, saw the wafer and the acolyte holding a little silver tray under it. "Corpus Domini Nostri Jesu Christi custodiat animam tuam . . ." The priest held the host toward her and she opened her mouth.

Later, at the reception, the priest asked her point-blank whether she was Catholic.

"No. I'm Methodist," she said.

"I see," he said. "Well, the sacraments of the Church are reserved for—" Just then old Mrs. Djvorak interrupted him.

"Father," she said, "I want you to meet one of my dearest

friends. Dr. Foster's daughter. Her father saved Ricky's life. Ricky wouldn't be here today if . . ."

Father Padrew smiled and shook Ruth's hand. "Very pleased to meet you, Miss Foster."

It was a simple occurrence, elaborately told. Lena listened and experienced each phrase of her mother's emotion from religious ecstasy to innocent confidence to embarrassment. Corinthians listened analytically, expectantly—wondering how her mother would develop this anecdote into a situation in which Macon would either lash out at her verbally or hit her. Milkman was only half listening.

" 'Are you Catholic?' he asked me. Well, I was embarrassed for a minute, but then I said, 'No. I'm Methodist.' And he started to tell me that only Catholics could take communion in a Catholic church. Well, I never heard of that. Anybody can take communion, I thought. At our church anybody can come up on the first Sunday. Well, before he could get it out, Anna came up and said, 'Father, I want you to meet one of my dearest friends. Dr. Foster's daughter.' Well, the priest was all smiles then. And shook my hand and said he was *very* pleased and honored to make my acquaintance. So it all turned out all right. But honestly, I didn't know. I went up there as innocent as a lamb."

"You didn't know that only Catholics take communion in a Catholic church?" Macon Dead asked her, his tone making it clear that he didn't believe her.

"No, Macon. How would I know?"

"You see them put up their own school, keep their kids out of public schools, and you still think their religious stuff is open to anybody who wants to drop in?"

"Communion is communion."

"You're a silly woman."

"Father Padrew didn't think so."

"You made a fool of yourself."

"Mrs. Djvorak didn't think so."

"She was just trying to keep the wedding going, keep you from fucking it up."

"Macon, please don't use that language in front of the children."

"What goddam children? Everybody in here is old enough to vote."

"There is no call for an argument."

"You make a fool of yourself in a Catholic church, embarrass everybody at the reception, and come to the table to gloat about how wonderful you were?"

"Macon . . ."

"And sit there lying, saying you didn't know any better?"

"Anna Djvorak wasn't the least bit—"

"Anna Djvorak don't even know your name! She called you *Dr. Foster's daughter!* I bet you one hundred dollars she still don't know your name! You by yourself ain't nobody. You your daddy's daughter!"

"That's so," said Ruth in a thin but steady voice. "I certainly am my daddy's daughter." She smiled.

Macon didn't wait to put his fork down. He dropped it on the table while his hand was on its way across the bread plate becoming the fist he smashed into her jaw.

Milkman hadn't planned any of it, but he had to know that one day, after Macon hit her, he'd see his mother's hand cover her lips as she searched with her tongue for any broken teeth, and discovering none, tried to adjust the partial plate in her mouth without anyone noticing—and that on that day he would not be able to stand it. Before his father could draw his hand back, Milkman had yanked him by the back of his coat collar, up out of his chair, and knocked him into the radiator. The window shade flapped and rolled itself up.

"You touch her again, one more time, and I'll kill you."

Macon was so shocked at being assaulted he could not speak. He had come to believe, after years of creating respect and fear wherever he put his foot down, after years of being the tallest man in every gathering, that he was impregnable. Now he crept along the wall looking at a man who was as tall as he was—and forty years younger.

Just as the father brimmed with contradictory feelings as he crept along the wall—humiliation, anger, and a grudging feeling of pride in his son—so the son felt his own contradictions. There was the pain and shame of seeing his father crumple before any man—even himself. Sorrow in discovering that the pyramid was not a five-thousand-year wonder of the civilized world, mysteriously and permanently constructed by generation after generation of hardy men who had died in order to perfect it, but that it had been made in the back room at Sears, by a clever window dresser, of papier-mâché, guaranteed to last for a mere lifetime.

He also felt glee. A snorting, horse-galloping glee as old as desire. He had won something and lost something in the same instant. Infinite possibilities and enormous responsibilities stretched out before him, but he was not prepared to take advantage of the former, or accept the burden of the latter. So he cock-walked around the table and asked his mother, "Are you all right?"

She was looking at her fingernails. "Yes, I'm fine."

Milkman looked at his sisters. He had never been able to really distinguish them (or their roles) from his mother. They were in their early teens when he was born; they were thirty-five and thirty-six now. But since Ruth was only sixteen years older than Lena, all three had always looked the same age to him. Now when he met his sisters' eyes over the table, they returned him a look of hatred so fresh, so new, it startled him. Their pale eyes no longer appeared to blur into their even paler skin. It seemed to him as though charcoal lines had been drawn around their eyes; that two drag lines had been smudged down their cheeks, and their rosy lips were swollen in hatred so full it was about to burst through. Milkman had to blink twice before their faces returned to the vaguely alarmed blandness he was accustomed to. Quickly he left the room, realizing there was no one to thank him—or abuse him. His action was his alone. It would change nothing between his parents. It would change nothing inside them. He had knocked his father down and perhaps there were some new positions on the chessboard, but the game would go on.

Sleeping with Hagar had made him generous. Or so he thought. Wide-spirited. Or so he imagined. Wide-spirited and generous enough to defend his mother, whom he almost never thought about, and to deck his father, whom he both feared and loved.

Back in his bedroom, Milkman fiddled with things on his dresser. There was a pair of silver-backed brushes his mother had given him when he was sixteen, engraved with his initials, the abbreviated degree designation of a doctor. He and his mother had joked about it and she hinted strongly that he ought to consider going to medical school. He'd foisted her off with "How would that look? M.D., M.D. If you were sick, would you go see a man called Dr. Dead?"

She laughed but reminded him that his middle name was Foster. Couldn't he use Foster as a last name? Dr. Macon Foster. Didn't that sound fine? He had to admit that it did. The silver-backed brushes were a constant reminder of what her wishes for him were—that he not stop his education at high school, but go on to college and medical school. She had as little respect for her husband's work as Macon had for college graduates. To Milkman's father, college was time spent in idleness, far away from the business of life, which was learning to own things. He was eager for his daughters to go to college—where they could have found suitable husbands—and one, Corinthians, did go. But it was pointless for Milkman, particularly since his son's presence was a real help to him in the office. So much so that he had been able to get his bank friends to speak to some of their friends and get his son moved out of 1-A draft classification and into a "necessary to support family" status.

Milkman stood before his mirror and glanced, in the low light of the wall lamp, at his reflection. He was, as usual, unimpressed with what he saw. He had a fine enough face. Eyes women complimented him on, a firm jaw line, splendid teeth. Taken apart, it looked all right. Even better than all right. But it lacked coherence, a coming together of the features into a total self. It was all very tentative, the way he looked, like a man peeping around a corner of someplace he is not supposed to be, trying to make up his mind whether to go forward or to turn back. The decision he made would be extremely important, but the way in which he made the decision would be careless, haphazard, and uninformed.

Standing there in the lamplight, trying not to think of how his father had looked creeping along the wall, he heard a knock at his door. He didn't want to see the face of Lena or Corinthians, nor to have any secret talk with his mother. But he was not any happier to see his father looming there in the hall. A line of blood was still visible in the thin cut at the corner of Macon's mouth. But he stood straight, and his eyes were steady.

"Look, Daddy," Milkman began, "I—"

"Don't say anything," Macon said, pushing past him. "Sit down."

Milkman moved toward the bed. "Look here, let's try to forget this. If you promise—"

"I told you to sit down. And down is what I mean." Macon's voice was low, but his face looked like Pilate's. He closed the door. "You a big man now, but big ain't nearly enough. You have to be a whole man. And if you want to be a whole man, you have to deal with the whole truth."

"You don't have to do any of this, you know. I don't need to know everything between you and Mama."

"I do have to do it and you do need to know it. If you're in the business of raising your fist at your father, you better have some intelligence behind that fist the next time you throw it. Nothing I'm about to say is by way of apology or excuse. It's just information.

"I married your mother in 1917. She was sixteen, living alone with her father. I can't tell you I was in love with her. People didn't require that as much as they do now. Folks were expected to be civilized to one another, honest, and—and clear. You relied on people being what they said they were, because there was no other way to survive. The important thing, when you took a wife, was that the two of you agreed on what was important.

"Your mother's father never liked me and I have to say I was very disappointed in him. He was just about the biggest Negro in this city. Not the richest, but the most respected. But a bigger hypocrite never lived. Kept all his money in four different banks. Always calm and dignified. I thought he was naturally that way until I found out he sniffed ether. Negroes in this town worshipped him. He didn't give a damn about them, though. Called them cannibals. He delivered both your sisters himself and each time all he was interested in was the color of their skin. He would have disowned you. I didn't like the notion of his being his own daughter's doctor, especially since she was also my wife. Mercy wouldn't take colored then. Anyway, Ruth wouldn't go to any other doctor. I tried to get a midwife for her, but the doctor said midwives were dirty. I told him a midwife delivered me, and if a midwife was good enough for my mother, a midwife was good enough for his daughter. Well, we had some words between us about it, and I ended up telling him that nothing could be nastier than a father delivering his own daughter's baby. That stamped it. We had very little to say after that, but they did it anyway. Both Lena and Corinthians. They let me do the naming by picking a word blind, but that was all. Your sisters are just a little over a year apart, you know. And both times he was there. She had her legs wide open and he was there. I know he was a doctor and doctors not supposed to be bothered by things like that, but he was a man before he was a doctor. I knew then they'd ganged up on me forever—the both of them—and no matter what I did, they managed to have things their way. They made sure I remembered whose house I was in, where the china came from, how he sent to England for the Waterford bowl, and again for the table they put it on. That table was so big they had to take it apart to get it in the door. He was always bragging about how he was the second man in the city to have a two-horse carriage.

"Where I'd come from, the farm we had, that was nothing to them. And what I was trying to do—they didn't have any interest in that. Buying shacks in shacktown, they called it.

'How's shacktown?' That's the way he'd greet me in the evenings.

"But it wasn't that. I could put up with that, because I knew what I wanted, and pretty much how to get it. So I could put up with that. Did put up with it. It was something else, something I couldn't put my finger on. I tried to get him to spend some of that money out of those four banks once. Some track land was going for a lot of money—railroad money. Erie Lackawanna was buying. I had a good hunch where the track would be laid. I walked all around over there, the Shore Road, the docks, the fork in routes 6 and 2. I figured out just where the tracks would have to go. And found land I could have got cheap and sold back to the railroad agents. He wouldn't lend me a dime. If he had, he would have died a rich man, instead of a fair-to-middling one. And I would have been way ahead. I asked your mother to talk him into it. I told her exactly where the Erie was headed. She said it had to be *his* decision; she couldn't influence him. She told me, her husband, that. Then I began to wonder who she was married to—me or him.

"Well, he took sick." Macon stopped, as though the mention of illness reminded him of his own frailty, and pulled a large white handkerchief out of his pocket. Gingerly he pressed it against the thin cut on his lip. He looked at the faint stain it made on his handkerchief. "All that ether," he said, "must have got in his blood. They had another name for it, but I know it was that ether. He just lay down and started swelling up. His body did; his legs and arms just wasted away. He couldn't see patients anymore, and for the first time in his life the pompous donkey found out what it was like to have to be sick and pay another donkey to make you well. One of them doctors, the one that was taking care of him—one of the same ones wouldn't let him set foot in their hospital, and who, if he had delivered *their* daughter's or wife's baby, had even thought of it, would have run him out of here on a rail—one of them, the ones he thought worth his attention, well, he came in here with some magic potion, Radiathor, and told him it would cure him. Ruth was all excited. And for a few days he was better. Then he got sicker. Couldn't move, holes were forming in his scalp. And he just lay there in that bed where your mother still sleeps and then he died there. Helpless, fat stomach, skinny arms and legs, looking like a white rat. He couldn't digest his food, you know. Had to drink all his meals and swallow something after every meal. I believe to this day that was ether too.

"The night he died, I'd been over on the other side of town, fixing a porch that fell down. Mr. Bradlee's house. Porch had been leaning for twenty years, and then just fell down, split clean away from the foundation. I got some men to help me and went over there to get it back up so the people wouldn't have to jump to get out the house and climb up three feet to get in it. Somebody tiptoed up to me and said, 'Doctor died.' Ruth, they said, was upstairs with him. I figured she was upset and went up right away to comfort her. I didn't have time to change clothes from working on the porch, but I went up anyway. She was sitting in a chair next to his bed, and the minute she saw me she jumped up and screamed at me, 'You dare come in here like that? Clean yourself! Clean up before you come in here!' It vexed me some, but I do respect the dead. I went and washed up. Took a bath, put on a clean shirt and collar, and went back in." Macon paused again and touched his cut lip as though that were where the pain that showed in his eyes was coming from.

"In the bed," he said, and stopped for so long Milkman was not sure he was going to continue. "In the bed. That's where she was when I opened the door. Laying next to him. Naked as a yard dog, kissing him. Him dead and white and puffy and skinny, and she had his fingers in her mouth.

"Now, I want you to know I had a terrible time after that. I started thinking all sorts of things. If Lena and Corinthians were my children. I come to know pretty quick they were, cause it was clear that bastard couldn't fuck nothing. Ether took care of whatever he had in that area long before I got there. And he wouldn't have been so worried about what color skin they had unless they were coming from me. Then I thought about his delivering Ruth's babies. I'm not saying that they had contact. But there's lots of things a man can do to please a woman, even if he can't fuck. Whether or not, the fact is she was in that bed sucking his fingers, and if she do that when he was dead, what'd she do when he was alive? Nothing to do but kill a woman like that. I swear, many's the day I regret she talked me out of killing her. But I wasn't looking forward to spending the rest of my days on some rock pile. But you see, Macon, sometimes I can't catch hold of myself quick enough. It just gets out. Tonight, when she said, 'Yes, I am my daddy's daughter,' and gave that little smirk . . ." Macon looked up at his son. The door of his face had opened; his skin looked iridescent. With only a minor break in his voice, he told him, "I am not a bad man. I want you to know that. Or believe it. No man ever took his responsibilities more seriously than I have. I'm not making claims to sainthood, but you have to know it all. I'm forty years older than you and I don't have another forty in me. Next time you take it into your head to jump me, I want you to think about the man you think you whipping. And think about the fact that next time I might not let you. Old as I am, I might not let you."

He stood up and pushed his handkerchief into his back pocket.

"Don't say anything now. But think about everything I've said."

Macon turned the doorknob, and without a backward glance, left the room.

Milkman sat on the edge of his bed; everything was still except for the light buzzing in his head. He felt curiously disassociated from all that he had heard. As though a stranger that he'd sat down next to on a park bench had turned to him and begun to relate some intimacy. He was entirely sympathetic to the stranger's problems—understood perfectly his view of what had happened to him—but part of his sympathy came from the fact that he himself was not involved or in any way threatened by the stranger's story. It was quite the opposite from the feeling he'd had an hour or less ago. The alien who had just walked out of his room was also the man he felt passionately enough about to strike with all the fervor he could summon up. Even now he could feel the tingle in his shoulder that had signaled the uncontrollable urge to smash his father's face. On the way upstairs to his room he had felt isolated, but righteous. He was a man who saw another man hit a helpless person. And he had interfered. Wasn't that the history of the world? Isn't that what men did? Protected the frail and confronted the King of the Mountain? And the fact that the frail was his mother and the King of the Mountain his father made it more poignant, but did not change the essential facts. No. He would not pretend that it was love for his mother. She was too insubstantial, too shadowy for love. But it was her vaporishness that made her more needful of defense. She was not a maternal drudge, her mind pressed flat, her shoulders hunched under the burden of housework and care of others, brutalized by a bear of a man. Nor was she the acid-tongued shrew who defended herself with a vicious vocabulary and a fast lip. Ruth was a pale but complicated woman given to deviousness and ultra-fine manners. She seemed to know a lot and understand very little. It was an interesting train of thought, and new for him. Never had he thought of his mother as a person, a separate individual, with a life apart from allowing or interfering with his own.

Milkman put on his jacket and left the house. It was seven-thirty in the evening and not yet dark. He wanted to walk and breathe some other air. He wouldn't know what to feel until he knew what to think. And it was difficult thinking in that room where the silver-backed brushes with the M.D. initials shone in the light and where the chair his father had just sat in still held the imprint of his buttocks in the cushion. As the stars made themselves visible, Milkman tried to figure what was true and what part of what was true had anything to do with him. What was he supposed to do with this new information his father had dumped on him? Was it an effort to cop a plea? How was he supposed to feel about the two of them now? Was it *true*, first of all? Did his mother . . . had his mother made it with her own father? Macon had said no. That the doctor was impotent. How did he know? Well, he must have known what he was talking about, because he was much too eager for it to be true to let it go if there were any possibility it could have taken place. Still, he had admitted there were "other things" a man could do to please a woman. "Goddam," Milkman said aloud. "What the fuck did he tell me all that shit for?" He didn't want to know any of it. There was nothing he could do about it. The doctor was dead. You can't do the past over.

Milkman's confusion was rapidly turning to anger. "Strange motherfuckers," he whispered. "Strange." If he wanted me to lay off, he thought, why didn't he just say that? Just come to me like a man and say, Cool it. You cool it and I'll cool it. We'll both cool it. And I'd say, Okay, you got it. But no. He comes to me with some way-out tale about how come and why.

Milkman was heading toward Southside. Maybe he could find Guitar. A drink with Guitar would be just the thing. Or if he couldn't find Guitar, he'd go see Hagar. No. He didn't want to talk to Hagar, to any woman, just yet. Talk about strange. Now, that was a really strange bunch. His whole family was a bunch of crazies. Pilate singing all day and talking off the wall. Reba turning on for everything in pants. And Hagar . . . well, she was just fine, but still, she wasn't regular. She had some queer ways. But at least they were fun and not full of secrets.

Where would Guitar be? Never anywhere when you really needed him. A real pop-up. Popped up anywhere, anytime, but never on time. Milkman realized he was whispering every now and then and that people on the street were looking at him. Suddenly it seemed to him that there were a lot of people out for that time of day. Where the hell was everybody going? He made an effort not to vocalize his thoughts.

"You want to be a whole man, you have to deal with the whole truth," his father had said. Couldn't I be a whole man without knowing all that? "You better have some intelligence behind that fist." Okay. What intelligence? That my mama screwed her daddy. That my grandfather was a high-yellow

nigger who loved ether and hated black skin. So what did he let
you marry his daughter for? So he could screw her without the
neighbors knowing it? Did you ever catch them doing it? No.
You just felt something you couldn't put your finger on. His
money, probably. He wouldn't let you put your finger on that,
would he? And his daughter wouldn't help you, would she? So
you figured they must be gettin it on the operating table. If he'd
given you those four bankbooks to do what you liked, to buy
up the Erie Lackawanna Railroad, he could have had her all he
liked, right? He could have come right in your bed, and the
three of you could have had a ball. He'd get one tit and you'd
get . . . the . . . other. . . .

Milkman stopped dead in his tracks. Cold sweat broke out on
his neck. People jostled him trying to get past the solitary man
standing in their way. He had remembered something. Or believed he remembered something. Maybe he'd dreamed it and it
was the dream he remembered. The picture was developing, of
the two men in the bed with his mother, each nibbling on a
breast, but the picture cracked and in the crack another picture
emerged. There was this green room, a very small green room,
and his mother was sitting in the green room and her breasts
were uncovered and somebody was sucking them and the somebody was himself. So? So what? My mother nursed me. Mothers
nurse babies. Why the sweat? He walked on, hardly noticing
the people pushing past him, their annoyed, tight faces. He tried
to see more of the picture, but couldn't. Then he heard something that he knew was related to the picture. Laughter. Somebody he couldn't see, in the room laughing . . . at him and at
his mother, and his mother is ashamed. She lowers her eyes and
won't look at him. "Look at me, Mama. Look at me." But she
doesn't and the laughter is loud now. Everybody is laughing.
Did he wet his pants? Is his mother ashamed because while he
was nursing he wet his pants? What pants? He didn't wear pants
then. He wore diapers. Babies always wet their diapers. Why
does he think he has pants on? Blue pants with elastic around the
calf. Little blue corduroy knickers. Why is he dressed that way?

Is that what the man is laughing at? Because he is a tiny baby dressed in blue knickers? He sees himself standing there. "Look at me, Mama," is all he can think of to say. "Please look at me." Standing? He is a tiny baby. Nursing in his mother's arms. He can't stand up.

"I couldn't stand up," he said aloud, and turned toward a shop window. There was his face leaning out of the upturned collar of his jacket, and he knew. "My mother nursed me when I was old enough to talk, stand up, and wear knickers, and somebody saw it and laughed and—and that is why they call me Milkman and that is why my father never does and that is why my mother never does, but everybody else does. And how did I forget that? And why? And if she did that to me when there was no reason for it, when I also drank milk and Ovaltine and everything else from a glass, then maybe she did other things with her father?"

Milkman closed his eyes and then opened them. The street was even more crowded with people, all going in the direction he was coming from. All walking hurriedly and bumping against him. After a while he realized that nobody was walking on the other side of the street. There were no cars and the street lights were on, now that darkness had come, but the sidewalk on the other side of the street was completely empty. He turned around to see where everybody was going, but there was nothing to see except their backs and hats pressing forward into the night. He looked again at the other side of Not Doctor Street. Not a soul.

He touched the arm of a man in a cap who was trying to get past him. "Why is everybody on this side of the street?" he asked him.

"Watch it, buddy," the man snapped, and moved on with the crowd.

Milkman walked on, still headed toward Southside, never once wondering why he himself did not cross over to the other side of the street, where no one was walking at all.

He believed he was thinking coldly, clearly. He had never

loved his mother, but had always known that she had loved him. And that had always seemed right to him, the way it should be. Her confirmed, eternal love of him, love that he didn't even have to earn or deserve, seemed to him natural. And now it was decomposing. He wondered if there was anyone in the world who liked him. Liked him for himself alone. His visits to the wine house seemed (before his talk with his father) an extension of the love he had come to expect from his mother. Not that Pilate or Reba felt the possessive love for him that his mother did, but they had accepted him without question and with all the ease in the world. They took him seriously too. Asked him questions and thought all his responses to things were important enough to laugh at or quarrel with him about. Everything he did at home was met with quiet understanding from his mother and his sisters (or indifference and criticism from his father). The women in the wine house were indifferent to nothing and understood nothing. Every sentence, every word, was new to them and they listened to what he said like bright-eyed ravens, trembling in their eagerness to catch and interpret every sound in the universe. Now he questioned them. Questioned everybody. His father had crept along the wall and then come upstairs with a terrible piece of news. His mother had been portrayed not as a mother who simply adored her only son, but as an obscene child playing dirty games with whatever male was near—be it her father or her son. Even his sisters, the most tolerant and accommodating of all the women he knew, had changed their faces and rimmed their eyes with red and charcoal dust.

Where was Guitar? He needed to find the one person left whose clarity never failed him, and unless he was out of the state, Milkman was determined to find him.

His first stop, Tommy's Barbershop, was fruitful. Guitar was there with several other men, leaning in various attitudes, but all listening to something.

As Milkman entered and spotted Guitar's back, he was so relieved he shouted, "Hey, Guitar!"

"Sh!" said Railroad Tommy. Guitar turned around and mo-

tioned him to come in but to be quiet. They were listening to
the radio and muttering and shaking their heads. It was some
time before Milkman discovered what they were so tense about.
A young Negro boy had been found stomped to death in Sun-
flower County, Mississippi. There were no questions about who
stomped him—his murderers had boasted freely—and there
were no questions about the motive. The boy had whistled at
some white woman, refused to deny he had slept with others,
and was a Northerner visiting the South. His name was Till.

Railroad Tommy was trying to keep the noise down so he
could hear the last syllable of the newscaster's words. In a few
seconds it was over, since the announcer had only a few speculations and even fewer facts. The minute he went on to another
topic of news, the barbershop broke into loud conversation.
Railroad Tommy, the one who had tried to maintain silence, was
himself completely silent now. He moved to his razor strop
while Hospital Tommy tried to keep his customer in the chair.
Porter, Guitar, Freddie the janitor, and three or four other men
were exploding, shouting angry epithets all over the room.
Apart from Milkman, only Railroad Tommy and Empire State
were quiet—Railroad Tommy because he was preoccupied with
his razor and Empire State because he was simple, and probably
mute, although nobody seemed sure about that. There was no
question whatever about his being simple.

Milkman tried to focus on the crisscrossed conversations.

"It'll be in the morning paper."

"Maybe it will, and maybe it won't," said Porter.

"It was on the radio! Got to be in the paper!" said Freddie.

"They don't put that kind of news in no white paper. Not
unless he raped somebody."

"What you bet? What you bet it'll be in there?" said Freddie.

"Bet anything you can lose," Porter answered.

"You on for five."

"Wait a minute," Porter shouted. "Say where."

"What you mean, 'where'? I got five says it'll be in the morning paper."

"On the sports page?" asked Hospital Tommy.

"Or the funny papers?" said Nero Brown.

"No, man. Front page. I bet five dollars on front page."

"What the fuck is the difference?" shouted Guitar. "A kid is stomped and you standin round fussin about whether some cracker put it in the paper. He stomped, ain't he? Dead, ain't he? Cause he whistled at some Scarlett O'Hara cunt."

"What'd he do it for?" asked Freddie. "He knew he was in Mississippi. What he think that was? Tom Sawyer Land?"

"So he whistled! So what!" Guitar was steaming. "He supposed to die for that?"

"He from the North," said Freddie. "Acting big down in Bilbo country. Who the hell he think he is?"

"Thought he was a man, that's what," said Railroad Tommy.

"Well, he thought wrong," Freddie said. "Ain't no black men in Bilbo country."

"The hell they ain't," said Guitar.

"Who?" asked Freddie.

"Till. That's who."

"He dead. A dead man ain't no man. A dead man is a corpse. That's all. A corpse."

"A living coward ain't a man either," said Porter.

"Who you talking to?" Freddie was quick to get the personal insult.

"Calm down, you two," said Hospital Tommy.

"You!" shouted Porter.

"You calling me a coward?" Freddie wanted to get the facts first.

"If the shoe fits, put your rusty foot in it."

"You all gonna keep that up, you have to get out of my shop."

"Tell that nigger somethin," said Porter.

"I'm serious now," Hospital Tommy went on. "There is no cause for all this. The boy's dead. His mama's screaming. Won't let them bury him. That ought to be enough colored blood on the streets. You want to spill blood, spill the crackers' blood that bashed his face in."

"Oh, they'll catch them," said Walters.

"Catch 'em? Catch 'em?" Porter was astounded. "You out of your fuckin mind? They'll catch 'em, all right, and give 'em a big party and a medal."

"Yeah. The whole town planning a parade," said Nero.

"They got to catch 'em."

"So they catch 'em. You think they'll get any time? Not on your life!"

"How can they *not* give 'em time?" Walters' voice was high and tight.

"How? Just *don't*, that's how." Porter fidgeted with his watch chain.

"But everybody knows about it now. It's all over. Everywhere. The law is the law."

"You wanna bet? This is sure money!"

"You stupid, man. Real stupid. Ain't no law for no colored man except the one sends him to the chair," said Guitar.

"They say Till had a knife," Freddie said.

"They always say that. He could of had a wad of bubble gum, they'd swear it was a hand grenade."

"I still say he shoulda kept his mouth shut," said Freddie.

"You should keep yours shut," Guitar told him.

"Hey, man!" Again Freddie felt the threat.

"South's bad," Porter said. "Bad. Don't nothing change in the good old U.S. of A. Bet his daddy got his balls busted off in the Pacific somewhere."

"If they ain't busted already, them crackers will see to it. Remember them soldiers in 1918?"

"Ooooo. Don't bring all that up. . . ."

The men began to trade tales of atrocities, first stories they had heard, then those they'd witnessed, and finally the things that had happened to themselves. A litany of personal humiliation, outrage, and anger turned sicklelike back to themselves as humor. They laughed then, uproariously, about the speed with which they had run, the pose they had assumed, the ruse they had invented to escape or decrease some threat to their manliness, their humanness. All but Empire State, who stood, broom in hand and drop-lipped, with the expression of a very intelligent ten-year-old. •

And Guitar. His animation had died down, leaving its traces in his eyes.

Milkman waited until he could get his attention. Then they both left, walking silently down the street.

"What is it? You looked pissed when you came in."

"Nothing," said Milkman. "Where can we get a drink?"

"Mary's?"

"Naw. Too many broads hasslin you."

"It's just eight-thirty. Cedar Lounge don't open till nine."

"Shit. *You* think. I'm tired."

"I got a taste at the pad," Guitar offered.

"Solid. Your box working?"

"Uh uh. Still broke."

"I need some music. Music and a taste."

"Then it'll have to be Miss Mary. I'll keep the ladies working elsewhere."

"Yeah? I want to see you tell those ladies what to do."

"Come on, Milk. This ain't New York; choices are limited."

"Okay. Mary's."

They walked a few blocks to the corner of Rye and Tenth streets. When they passed a tiny bakery, Guitar swallowed hard and quickened his steps. Mary's was the bar/lounge that did the best business in the Blood Bank—although each of the three other corners had a similar place—because of Mary herself, a pretty but overpainted barmaid/part-owner, who was sassy, funny, and good company for the customers. Whores worked her bar in safety; lonely drunks could drink there in peace; cruisers found chickens or hawks—whichever they preferred, even jailbait; restless housewives were flattered there and danced their heels off; teen-agers learned "life rules" there; and everybody found excitement there. For in Mary's the lights made everybody beautiful, or if not beautiful, then fascinating. The music gave tone and texture to conversations that would put you to sleep anywhere else. And the food and drink provoked people into behavior that resembled nothing less than high drama.

But all that began around eleven o'clock. It was practically empty at eight-thirty in the evening, when Guitar and Milkman arrived. They slid into a booth and ordered Scotch and water. Milkman drank his up quickly and ordered another before asking Guitar, "How come they call me Milkman?"

"How the fuck would I know? That's your name, ain't it?"

"My name is Macon Dead."

"You drag me all the way over here to tell me your name?"

"I need to know it."

"Aw, drink up, man."

"You know your name, don't you?"

"Cut the shit. What's on your mind?"

"I decked my old man."

"Decked?"

"Yeah. Hit him. Knocked him into the fuckin radiator."

"What'd he do to you?"

"Nothin."

"Nothin? You just up and popped him?"

"Yeah."

"For no reason?"

"He hit my mother."

"Oh."

"He hit her. I hit him."

"That's tough."

"Yeah."

"I mean it."

"I know." Milkman sighed heavily. "I know."

"Listen. I can understand how you feel."

"Uh uh. You can't understand. Unless it happens to you, you can't understand."

"Yes I can. You know I used to hunt a lot. When I was a kid down home—"

"Oh, shit, do we have to hear about Alabama again?"

"Not Alabama. Florida."

"Whatever."

"Just listen, Milkman. Listen to me. I used to hunt a lot. From the time I could walk almost and I was good at it. Everybody said I was a natural. I could hear anything, smell anything, and see like a cat. You know what I mean? A natural. And I was never scared—not of the dark or shadows or funny sounds, and I was never afraid to kill. Anything. Rabbit, bird, snakes, squirrels, deer. And I was little. It never bothered me. I'd take a shot at anything. The grown men used to laugh about it. Said I was a natural-born hunter. After we moved up here with my grandmother, that was the only thing about the South I missed. So when my grandmother used to send us kids back home in the summer, all I thought about was hunting again. They'd pile us on the bus and we'd spend the summer with my grandmother's sister, Aunt Florence. Soon's I got there I looked for my uncles, to go out in the woods. And one summer—I was about ten or eleven, I guess—we all went out and I went off on my own. I thought I saw deer tracks. It wasn't the season for deer, but that didn't bother me any. If I saw one I killed one. I was right about the tracks; it was a deer, but spaced funny—not wide apart like I thought they should be, but still a deer. You know they step in their own prints. If you never saw them before you'd think a two-legged creature was jumping. Anyway, I stayed on the trail until I saw some bushes. The light was good and all of a sudden I saw a rump between the branches. I dropped it with the first shot and finished it with the next. Now, I want to tell you I was feeling good. I saw myself showing my uncles what I'd caught. But when I got up to it—and I was going real slow because I thought I might have to shoot it again—I saw it was a doe. Not a young one; she was old, but she was still a doe. I felt . . . bad. You know what I mean? I killed a doe. A doe, man."

Milkman was gazing at Guitar with the wide steady eyes of a man trying to look sober.

"So I know how you felt when you saw your father hit your mother. It's like that doe. A man shouldn't do that. You couldn't help what you felt."

Milkman nodded his head, but it was clear to Guitar that nothing he had said had made any difference. Chances were Milkman didn't even know what a doe was, and whatever it was, it wasn't his mother. Guitar ran his finger around the rim of his glass.

"What'd she do, Milk?"

"Nothin. Smiled. He didn't like her smile."

"You're not making sense. Talk sense. And slow down. You know you can't hold liquor."

"What you mean, I can't hold liquor?"

" 'Scuse me. Help yourself."

"I'm trying to have a serious conversation and you talking shit, Guitar."

"I'm listening."

"And I'm talking."

"Yes, you talking, but what are you saying? Your papa clips your mama cause she smiles at him. You clip him cause he clipped her. Now, is that the way you all spend the evening in your house or is there something else you're trying to say?"

"Came up to talk to me afterwards."

"Who?"

"My old man."

"What'd he say?"

"Said I had to be a whole man and know the whole thing."

"Go on."

"He was gonna buy the Erie Lackawanna, but my mother wouldn't let him."

"Oh, yeah? Maybe she needs beatin."

"That's very funny, man."

"Why ain't you laughing, then?"

"I am laughing. Inside."

"Milk?"

"Yeah?"

"Your daddy slapped your mama, right?"

"Right. Right."

"You hit him, right?"

"Right."

"Nobody appreciates what you did. Right?"

"Hey, Guitar. You right again."

"Not your mother, not your sisters, and your daddy appreciates it least of all."

"Least of all. Right."

"So he bawls you out."

"Yep. No. No. He . . ."

"He talks quiet to you?"

"Right!"

"Explains things to you."

"Yeah."

"About why he hit her."

"Uh huh."

"And it's all about something that happened a long time ago? Before you were born?"

"You got it! You are a very smart little colored boy. And I am going to tell Oxford University about you."

"And you wish he'd kept it to himself because it don't concern you and you can't do nothin about it anyway."

"You have just passed the course. Guitar Bains, Ph.D."

"But it bothers you just the same?"

"Let me think." Milkman closed his eyes and tried to prop his chin on his hand, but it was too difficult. He was trying to get as drunk as possible as rapidly as possible. "Yes. Well, it did bother me. Before I came in here it did. I don't know, Guitar." He became serious and his face had the still and steady look of a grown man trying not to vomit . . . or cry.

"Forget it, Milk. Whatever it is, forget it. It ain't nothin. Whatever he told you, forget it."

"I hope I can. I sure hope I can."

"Listen, baby, people do funny things. Specially us. The cards are stacked against us and just trying to stay in the game, stay alive and in the game, makes us do funny things. Things we can't help. Things that make us hurt one another. We don't even know why. But look here, don't carry it inside and don't give it to nobody else. Try to understand it, but if you can't, just forget it and keep yourself strong, man."

"I don't know, Guitar. Things seem to be getting to me, you know?"

"Don't let 'em. Unless you got a plan. Look at Till. They got to him too. Now he's just an item on WJR's evening news."

"He was crazy."

"No. Not crazy. Young, but not crazy."

"Who cares if he fucks a white girl? Anybody can do that. What's he bragging for? Who cares?"

"Crackers care."

"Then they're crazier'n he is."

"Of course. But they're alive and crazy."

"Yeah, well, fuck Till. I'm the one in trouble."

"Did I hear you right, brother?"

"All right. I didn't mean that. I . . ."

"What's your trouble? You don't like your name?"

"No." Milkman let his head fall to the back of the booth. "No, I don't like my name."

"Let me tell you somethin, baby. Niggers get their names the way they get everything else—the best way they can. The best way they can."

Milkman's eyes were blurred now and so were his words. "Why can't we get our stuff the right way?"

"The best way is the right way. Come on. I'll take you home."

"No, I can't go back there."

"No? Where then?"

"Let me stay in your pad."

"Oh, man, you know my situation. One of us'll have to sleep on the floor. Besides . . ."

"I'll sleep on the floor."

"Besides, I may have company."

"No shit?"

"No shit. Come on, let's go."

"I ain't going home, Guitar. Hear me?"

"Want me to take you over to Hagar's?" Guitar motioned to the waitress for the check.

"Hagar's. Yeah. Sweet Hagar. Wonder what her name is."

"You just said it."

"I mean her last name. Her daddy's name."

"Ask Reba." Guitar paid their bar bill and helped Milkman negotiate to the door. The wind had risen and cooled. Guitar flapped his elbows against the cold.

"Ask anybody *but* Reba," said Milkman. "Reba don't know her own last name."

"Ask Pilate."

"Yeah. I'll ask Pilate. Pilate knows. It's in that dumb-ass box hanging from her ear. Her own name and everybody else's. Bet mine's in there too. I'm gonna ask her what my name is. Say, you know how my old man's daddy got his name?"

"Uh uh. How?"

"Cracker gave it to him."

"Sho 'nough?"

"Yep. And he took it. Like a fuckin sheep. Somebody should have shot him."

"What for? He was already Dead."

Chapter 4

Once again he did his Christmas shopping in a Rexall drugstore. It was late, the day before Christmas Eve, and he hadn't had the spirit or energy or presence of mind to do it earlier or thoughtfully. Boredom, which had begun as a mild infection, now took him over completely. No activity seemed worth the doing, no conversation worth having. The fluttery preparations at home seemed fake and dingy. His mother was going on as she did every year about the incredible price of trees and butter. As though their tree would be anything other than it had always been: the huge shadowy thing in a corner burdened with decorations she had had since she was a girl. As if her fruitcakes were edible, or her turkey done all the way to the bone. His father gave them all envelopes of varying amounts of money, never thinking that just once they might like something he actually went into a department store and selected.

The gifts Milkman had to buy were few and easily chosen in a drugstore. Cologne and dusting powder for Magdalene called Lena; a compact for Corinthians; a five-pound box of chocolates for his mother. And some shaving equipment for his father. In fifteen minutes he was done. The only problem gift was Hagar's. It was hard to select something hurriedly for her since she liked everything but preferred nothing. More important, he wasn't sure he wanted to keep it up. Keep up the whole business of "going with" Hagar. He seldom took her anywhere except to the movies and he never took her to parties where people of his own set danced and laughed and developed intrigues among themselves. Everybody who knew him knew about Hagar, but she was considered his private honey pot, not a real or legitimate girl friend—not someone he might marry. And only one or two of the various women he dated "seriously" ever put up a fight about her since they believed she was less than a rival.

Now, after more than a dozen years, he was getting tired of her. Her eccentricities were no longer provocative and the stupefying ease with which he had gotten and stayed between her legs had changed from the great good fortune he'd considered it, to annoyance at her refusal to make him hustle for it, work for it, do something difficult for it. He didn't even have to pay for it. It was so free, so abundant, it had lost its fervor. There was no excitement, no galloping of blood in his neck or his heart at the thought of her.

She was the third beer. Not the first one, which the throat receives with almost tearful gratitude; nor the second, that confirms and extends the pleasure of the first. But the third, the one you drink because it's there, because it can't hurt, and because what difference does it make?

Perhaps the end of the year was a good time to call it off. It wasn't going anywhere and it was keeping him lazy, like a pampered honey bear who had only to stick out his paw for another scoop, and so had lost the agility of the tree-climbers, the bee-fighters, but not the recollection of how thrilling the search had been.

He would buy her something for Christmas, of course, something nice to remember him by, but nothing that would give her any ideas about marriage. There was some costume jewelry on

display. She might like that, but it would pale before the diamond ring Reba had stuck down in her dress. A Timex? She
would never look at it. Staring at the glass tube that housed the
watches, he found himself getting angry. All this indecision
about what to get for Hagar was new. At Christmases past he
simply chose (or had his sisters choose) from a long list of things
that Hagar had mentioned specifically. Things quite out of place
in her household: a navy-blue satin bathrobe (this for a woman
who lived in a house that had no bathroom); a chubby; a snood
with a velvet bow; a rhinestone bracelet with earrings to match;
patent leather pumps; White Shoulders cologne. Milkman used
to wonder at her specificity and her acquisitiveness until he reminded himself that Pilate and Reba celebrated no holidays. Yet
their generosity was so wholehearted it looked like carelessness,
and they did their best to satisfy every whim Hagar had. When
he first took her in his arms, Hagar was a vain and somewhat
distant creature. He liked to remember it that way—that he
took her in his arms—but in truth it was she who called him
back into the bedroom and stood there smiling while she unbuttoned her blouse.

From the time he first saw her, when he was twelve and she
was seventeen, he was deeply in love with her, alternately awkward and witty in her presence. She babied him, ignored him,
teased him—did anything she felt like, and he was grateful just
to see her do anything or be any way. A good part of the
enthusiasm with which he collected his father's rents was because of the time it gave him to visit the wine house and, hope-
fully, find Hagar there. He was free to drop in anytime and
after school he tried to make sure he saw her.

Years passed and his puppy breath came as fast as ever in
Hagar's presence. It slowed finally, after Guitar took him to his
first Southside party, and after he found himself effortlessly
popular with girls of his own age and in his own neighborhood.
But while his breath was no longer that of a puppy, Hagar could
still whip it into a pant when he was seventeen and she was
twenty-two. Which she did on the dullest flattest day he could

remember, a throw-away day in March when he drove his father's two-tone Ford over to her house for two bottles of wine. Milkman was much sought after and depended upon to secure the liquor he and his under-twenty-one friends believed vital to a party. When he got to Pilate's he walked in on a domestic crisis.

Reba's new man friend had asked her for a small loan and she had told him that she didn't have any money at all. The man, who had received two or three nice presents from her unasked, thought she was lying and was trying to tell him to shove off. They were quarreling in the backyard—that is, the man was quarreling. Reba was crying and trying to convince him that what she'd said was true. Just after Milkman opened the door, Hagar came running from the bedroom, where she'd been looking out the back window. She screamed to Pilate, "Mama! He's hitting her! I saw him! With his fist, Mama!"

Pilate looked up from a fourth-grade geography book she was reading and closed it. Slowly, it seemed to Milkman, she walked over to a shelf that hung over the dry sink, put the geography book on it, and removed a knife. Slowly still, she walked out the front door—there was no back door—and as soon as she did, Milkman could hear Reba's screams and the man's curses.

It didn't occur to him to stop Pilate—her mouth was not moving and her earring flashed fire—but he did follow her, as did Hagar, around to the back of the house, where, approaching the man from the back, she whipped her right arm around his neck and positioned the knife at the edge of his heart. She waited until the man felt the knife point before she jabbed it skillfully, about a quarter of an inch through his shirt into the skin. Still holding his neck, so he couldn't see but could feel the blood making his shirt sticky, she talked to him.

"Now, I'm not going to kill you, honey. Don't you worry none. Just be still a minute, the heart's right here, but I'm not going to stick it in any deeper. Cause if I stick it in any deeper, it'll go straight through your heart. So you have to be real still, you hear? You can't move a inch cause I might lose control. It's just a little hole now, honey, no more'n a pin scratch. You might lose about two tablespoons of blood, but no more. And if you're real still, honey, I can get it back out without no mistake. But before I do that, I thought we'd have a little talk."

The man closed his eyes. Sweat ran from his temples down the sides of his face. A few neighbors who had heard Reba's screams had gathered in Pilate's backyard. They knew right away that the man was a newcomer to the city. Otherwise he would have known a few things about Reba, one of which was that she gave away everything she had and if there was a case quarter in that house she'd have given it to him; and more important, he would have known not to fool with anything that belonged to Pilate, who never bothered anybody, was helpful to everybody, but who also was believed to have the power to step out of her skin, set a bush afire from fifty yards, and turn a man into a ripe rutabaga—all on account of the fact that she had no navel. So they didn't have much sympathy for him. They just craned their necks to hear better what Pilate was telling him.

"You see, darlin, that there is the only child I got. The first baby I ever had, and if you could turn around and see my face, which of course you can't cause my hand might slip, you'd know she's also the last. Women are foolish, you know, and mamas are the most foolish of all. And you know how mamas are, don't you? You got a mama, ain't you? Sure you have, so you know what I'm talking about. Mamas get hurt and nervous when somebody don't like they children. First real misery I ever had in my life was when I found out somebody—a little teeny tiny boy it was—didn't like my little girl. Made me so mad, I didn't know what to do. We do the best we can, but we ain't got the strength you men got. That's why it makes us so sad if a grown man start beating up on one of us. You know what I mean? I'd hate to pull this knife out and have you try some other time to act mean to my little girl. Cause one thing I know for sure: whatever she done, she's been good to *you*. Still, I'd hate to push it in more and have your mama feel like I do now. I confess, I don't know what to do. Maybe you can help me. Tell me, what should I do?"

The man struggled for breath and Pilate eased up on his throat but not his heart.

"Lemme go," he whispered.

"Hmmmmm?"

"Lemme go. I . . . won't never . . . put a hand on her. I promise."

"A real promise, sugar?"

"Yeah. I promise. You won't never see me no more."

Reba sat on the ground, her arms around her knees, staring through her unswollen eye at the scene as though she were at a picture show. Her lip was split and her cheek was badly bruised, and though her skirt and hands were stained with her effort to stop the blood pouring from her nose, a little still trickled down.

Pilate plucked the knife out of the man's shirt and took her arm away. He lurched a little, looked down at the blood on his clothes and up at Pilate, and licking his lips, backed all the way to the side of the house under Pilate's gaze. Her lips didn't start moving again until he was out of sight and running down the road.

All attention turned to Reba, who was having difficulty trying to stand up. She said she thought something was broken inside in the place where he'd kicked her. Pilate felt her ribs and said nothing was broken. But Reba said she wanted to go to the hospital. (It was her dream to be a patient in a hospital; she was forever trying to get admitted, since in her picture-show imagination, it was a nice hotel. She gave blood there as often as they would let her, and stopped only when the blood bank was moved to an office-type clinic some distance away from Mercy.) She was insistent now, and Pilate surrendered her judgment to Reba's. A neighbor offered to drive them and off they went, leaving Milkman to buy his wine from Hagar.

He was delighted with the performance and followed Hagar into the house to laugh and talk excitedly about it. She was as tranquil as he was agitated, as monosyllabic as he was garrulous.

"Was that something? Wow! She's two inches taller than he is, and she's talking about weak."

"We are weak."

"Compared to what? A B-52?"

"Every woman's not as strong as she is."

"I hope not. Half as strong is too much."

"Well, muscle strength is one thing. I meant women are weak in other ways."

"Name some. I want you to name some for me. Where are you weak?"

"I don't mean me. I mean other women."

"You don't have any weakness?"

"I haven't found any."

"I suppose you think you can whip me." It was the seventeen-year-old's constant preoccupation—who could whip him.

"Probably," said Hagar.

"Ha! Well, I guess I better not try to prove you wrong. Pilate might be back with her knife."

"Pilate scare you?"

"Yeah. Don't she scare you?"

"No. Nobody scares me."

"Yeah. You tough. I know you tough."

"Not tough. I just don't let people tell me what to do. I do what I want."

"Pilate tells you what to do."

"But I don't have to do it, if I don't want to."

"Wish I could say the same for my mother."

"Your mother boss you?"

"Well . . . not boss exactly." Milkman floundered for a word to describe the nagging he thought he was a victim of.

"How old are you now?" asked Hagar. She lifted her eyebrows like a woman mildly interested in the age of a small child.

"Seventeen."

"You old enough to be married." Hagar said it with the strong implication that he should not allow his mother to have any say about what he did.

"I'm waiting for you," he said, trying to regain (or acquire) some masculine flippancy.

"Be a long wait."

"Why?"

Hagar sighed as if her patience was being tried. "I'd like to be in love with the man I marry."

"Try me. You could learn if you'd try."

"You're too young for me."

"State of mind," he said.

"Uh huh. My mind."

"You're like all women. Waiting for Prince Charming to come trotting down the street and pull up in front of your door. Then you'll sweep down the steps and powie! Your eyes meet and he'll yank you up on his horse and the two of you ride off into the wind. Violins playing and 'courtesy of MGM' stamped on the horse's butt. Right?"

"Right," she said.

"What you going to do in the meantime?"

"Watch the lump grow in a little boy's pants."

Milkman smiled, but he was not amused. Hagar laughed. He jumped up to grab her, but she ran into the bedroom and shut the door. He rubbed his chin with the back of his hand and looked at the door. Then he shrugged and picked up the two bottles of wine.

"Milkman?" Hagar stuck her head out the door. "Come in here."

He turned around and put the bottles down on the table. The door was open, but he couldn't see her, could only hear her laughing, a low private laugh as though she had won a bet. He moved so quickly he forgot to duck the green sack hanging from the ceiling. A hickey was forming on his forehead by the time he got to her. "What you all got in there?" he asked her.

"That's Pilate's stuff. She calls it her inheritance." Hagar was unbuttoning her blouse.

"What'd she inherit? Bricks?" Then he saw her breasts.

"This is what I do in the meantime," she said.

Their tossing and giggling had been free and open then and they began to spend as much time in Guitar's room when he was at work as Guitar himself did when he was home. She became a quasi-secret but permanent fixture in his life. Very much a tease, sometimes accommodating his appetites, sometimes refusing. He never knew when or why she would do either. He assumed Reba and Pilate knew, but they never made any reference to the change in his relationship to Hagar. While he had lost some of his twelve-year-old's adoration of her, he was delighted to be sleeping with her and she was odd, funny, quirky company, spoiled, but artlessly so and therefore more refreshing than most of the girls his own age. There were months when Hagar would not see him, and then he'd appear one day and she was all smiles and welcome.

After about three years or so of Hagar's on-again-off-again passion, her refusals dwindled until finally, by the time he'd hit his father, they were nonexistent. Furthermore, she began to wait for him, and the more involved he got with the other part of his social life, the more reliable she became. She began to pout, sulk, and accuse him of not loving her or wanting to see her anymore. And though he seldom thought about his age, she was very aware of hers. Milkman had stretched his carefree boyhood out for thirty-one years. Hagar was thirty-six—and nervous. She placed duty squarely in the middle of their relationship; he tried to think of a way out.

He paid the clerk for the presents he had chosen and left the drugstore, having made up his mind to call it off.

I'll remind her that we are cousins, he thought. He would not buy her a present at all; instead he would give her a nice piece of money. Explain that he wanted her to get something really nice for herself, but that his gift-giving was compromising her. That he was not what she needed. She needed a steady man who could marry her. He was standing in her way. And since they were related and all, she should start looking for someone else. It hurt him, he would say, deeply hurt him, after all these years, but if you loved somebody as he did her, you had to think of them first. You couldn't be selfish with somebody you loved.

Having thought so carefully of what he would say to her, he felt as though he had already had the conversation and had settled everything. He went back to his father's office, got some cash out of the safe, and wrote Hagar a nice letter which ended: "Also, I want to thank you. Thank you for all you have meant to me. For making me happy all these years. I am signing this letter with love, of course, but more than that, with gratitude."

And he did sign it with love, but it was the word "gratitude" and the flat-out coldness of "thank you" that sent Hagar spinning into a bright blue place where the air was thin and it was silent all the time, and where people spoke in whispers or did not make sounds at all, and where everything was frozen except for an occasional burst of fire inside her chest that crackled away until she ran out into the streets to find Milkman Dead.

Long after he'd folded the money and the letter into an envelope, Milkman sat on at his father's desk. He added and re-added columns of figures, always eighty cents too little or eighty cents too much. He was still distracted and edgy, and all of it was not because of the problem of Hagar. He'd had a conversation with Guitar some time ago about the dragnet. A young boy, about sixteen years old, on his way home from school, had been strangled with what was believed to be a rope, and his head was bashed in. The state troopers cooperating with the local police said the way in which the boy had been killed was similar to the way another boy had been killed on New Year's Eve in 1953, and the way four grown men had been killed in 1955—the strangulation, the smashing of the face. In the poolrooms and in Tommy's Barbershop, the word was that Winnie Ruth Judd had struck again. The men laughed about it and repeated for the benefit of newcomers the story of how, in 1932, Winnie Ruth, a convicted murderer, who axed and dismembered her victims and stuffed them in trunks, was committed to a state asylum for the criminally insane, and escaped two or three times each year.

Once she had walked two hundred miles through two states before they caught her. Because there was a brutal killing in the city in December of that year, during the time Winnie Ruth was at large, Southside people were convinced that she had done it. From then on when some particularly nasty murder was reported, the Negroes said it was Winnie Ruth. They said that because Winnie Ruth was white and so were the victims. It was their way of explaining what they believed was white madness—crimes planned and executed in a truly lunatic manner against total strangers. Such murders could only be committed by a fellow lunatic of the race and Winnie Ruth Judd fit the description. They believed firmly that members of their own race killed one another for good reasons: violation of another's turf (a man is found with somebody else's wife); refusal to observe the laws of hospitality (a man reaches into his friend's pot of mustards and snatches out the meat); or verbal insults impugning their virility, honesty, humanity, and mental health. More important, they believed the crimes they committed were legitimate because they were committed in the heat of passion: anger, jealousy, loss of face, and so on. Bizarre killings amused them, unless of course the victim was one of their own.

They speculated about Winnie Ruth's motives for this recent murder. Somebody said she was raunchy from being cooped up and went looking for a lay. But she knew better than to expect a grown man to want her, so she went for a schoolboy. Another said she probably didn't like saddle shoes and when she got out of the loony bin and walked four hundred miles to safety, the first thing she saw was a kid wearing saddle shoes and she couldn't take it—ran amok.

Amid the jokes, however, was a streak of unspoken terror. The police said there had been a witness who thought he saw a "bushy-haired Negro" running from the schoolyard where the body was found.

"The same bushy-haired Negro they saw when Sam Sheppard axed his wife," said Porter.

"Hammered, man," said Guitar. "Twenty-seven hammer blows."

"Great Jesus. Why he do twenty-seven? That's a hard killin."

"Every killing is a hard killing," said Hospital Tommy. "Killing anybody is hard. You see those movies where the hero puts his hands around somebody's neck and the victim coughs a little bit and expires? Don't believe it, my friends. The human body is robust. It can gather strength when it's in mortal danger."

"You kill anybody in the war, Tommy?"

"I put my hand to a few."

"With your hands?"

"Bayonet, friend. The men of the Ninety-second used bayonets. Belleau Wood glittered with them. Fairly glittered."

"How'd it feel?"

"Unpleasant. Extremely unpleasant. Even when you know he'll do the same to you, it's still a very indelicate thing to do."

They laughed as usual at Tommy's proper way of speaking.

"That's because you didn't want to be in the army no way," said a fat man. "What about if you was roaming the streets and met up with Orval Faubus?"

"Boy, I'd love to kill that sucker," a heavy-set man said.

"Keep saying that. They'll soon have your ass downtown."

"My hair ain't bushy."

"They'll make it bushy."

"They'll take some brass knuckles and make your *head* bushy and call it hair."

Aside from Empire State's giggle, which was wholehearted, it had seemed to Milkman then that the laughter was wan and nervous. Each man in that room knew he was subject to being picked up as he walked the street and whatever his proof of who he was and where he was at the time of the murder, he'd have a very uncomfortable time being questioned.

And there was one more thing. For some time Milkman had been picking up hints that one or more of these murders had in fact been either witnessed or committed by a Negro. Some slip, someone knowing some detail about the victim. Like whether or not Winnie Ruth couldn't stand saddle shoes. Did the boy have on saddle shoes? Did the newspaper say so? Or was that just one of the fanciful details a good jokester would think of.

The two Tommys were cleaning up. "Closed," they said to a

man who poked his face in the door. "Shop's closing." The conversation died down and the men who were just hanging around seemed reluctant to go. Guitar too, but finally he slipped on his jacket, shadow-boxed with Empire State, and joined Milkman at the door. Southside shops were featuring feeble wreaths and lights, made more feeble by the tacky Yuletide streamers and bells the city had strung up on the lampposts. Only downtown were the lights large, bright, festive, and full of hope.

The two men walked down Tenth Street, headed for Guitar's room.

"Freaky," said Milkman. "Some freaky shit."

"Freaky world," said Guitar. "A freaky, fucked-up world."

Milkman nodded. "Railroad Tommy said the boy had on saddle shoes."

"Did he?" Guitar asked.

"Did he? You know he did. You were laughing right along with the rest of us."

Guitar glanced at him. "What you opening your nose for?"

"I know when I'm being put off."

"Then that's what it is, man. Nothing else. Maybe I don't feel like discussing it."

"You mean you don't feel like discussing it with me. You were full of discussion in Tommy's."

"Look, Milk, we've been tight a long time, right? But that don't mean we're not different people. We can't always think the same way about things. Can't we leave it like that? There are all kinds of people in this world. Some are curious, some ain't; some talk, some scream; some are kickers and other people are kicked. Take your daddy, now. He's a kicker. First time I laid eyes on him, he was kicking us out of our house. That was a difference right there between you and me, but we got to be friends anyway. . . ."

Milkman stopped and forced Guitar to stop too and turn around. "I know you're not going to give me a bullshit lecture."

"No lecture, man. I'm trying to tell you something."

"Well, tell me. Don't give me no fuckin bullshit lecture."

"What do you call a lecture?" asked Guitar. "When *you* don't talk for two seconds? When you have to listen to somebody else instead of talk? Is that a lecture?"

"A lecture is when somebody talks to a thirty-one-year-old man like he's a ten-year-old kid."

"You want me to talk or not?"

"Go ahead. Talk. Just don't talk to me in that funny tone. Like you a teacher and I'm some snot-nosed kid."

"That's the problem, Milkman. You're more interested in my tone than in what I'm saying. I'm trying to say that we don't have to agree on everything; that you and me are different; that—"

"You mean you got some secret shit you don't want me to know about."

"I mean there are things that interest me that don't interest you."

"How you know they don't interest me?"

"I know you. Been knowing you. You got your high-tone friends and your picnics on Honoré Island and you can afford to spend fifty percent of your brainpower thinking about a piece of ass. You got that red-headed bitch and you got a Southside bitch and no telling what in between."

"I don't believe it. After all these years you putting me down because of where I live?"

"Not where you live—where you hang out. You don't live nowhere. Not Not Doctor Street *or* Southside."

"You begrudge me—"

"I don't begrudge you a thing."

"You're welcome everywhere I go. I've tried to get you to come to Honoré—"

"Fuck Honoré! You hear me? The only way I'll go to that nigger heaven is with a case of dynamite and a book of matches."

"You used to like it."

"I never liked it! I went with you, but I never liked it. Never."

"What's wrong with Negroes owning beach houses? What

do you want, Guitar? You mad at every Negro who ain't scrubbing floors and picking cotton. This ain't Montgomery, Alabama."

Guitar looked at him, first in rage, and then he began to laugh. "You're right, Milkman. You have never in your life said a truer word. This definitely is not Montgomery, Alabama. Tell me. What would you do if it was? If this turned out to be another Montgomery?"

"Buy a plane ticket."

"Exactly. Now you know something about yourself you didn't know before: who you are and what you are."

"Yeah. A man that refuses to live in Montgomery, Alabama."

"No. A man that can't live there. If things ever got tough, you'd melt. You're not a serious person, Milkman."

"Serious is just another word for miserable. I know all about serious. My old man is serious. My sisters are serious. And nobody is more serious than my mother. She's so serious, she wasting away. I was looking at her in the backyard the other day. It was as cold as a witch's tit out there, but she had to get some bulbs in the ground before the fifteenth of December, she said. So there she was on her knees, digging holes in the ground."

"So? I miss the point."

"The point is that she wanted to put those bulbs in. She didn't have to. She likes to plant flowers. She really likes it. But you should have seen her face. She looked like the unhappiest woman in the world. The most miserable. So where's the fun? I've never in my whole life heard my mother laugh. She smiles sometimes, even makes a little sound. But I don't believe she has ever laughed out loud."

Without the least transition and without knowing he was going to, he began to describe to Guitar a dream he had had about his mother. He called it a dream because he didn't want to tell him it had really happened, that he had really seen it.

He was standing at the kitchen sink pouring the rest of his coffee down the drain when he looked through the window and saw Ruth digging in the garden. She made little holes and tucked something that looked like a small onion in them. As he stood there, mindlessly watching her, tulips began to grow out of the holes she had dug. First a solitary thin tube of green, then two leaves opened up from the stem—one on each side. He rubbed his eyes and looked again. Now several stalks were coming out of the ground behind her. Either they were bulbs she had already planted or they had been in the sack so long they had germinated. The tubes were getting taller and taller and soon there were so many of them they were pressing up against each other and up against his mother's dress. And still she didn't notice them or turn around. She just kept digging. Some of the stems began to sprout heads, bloody red heads that bobbed over and touched her back. Finally she noticed them, growing and nodding and touching her. Milkman thought she would jump up in fear—at least surprise. But she didn't. She leaned back from them, even hit out at them, but playfully, mischievously. The flowers grew and grew, until he could see only her shoulders above them and her flailing arms high above those bobbing, snapping heads. They were smothering her, taking away her breath with their soft jagged lips. And she merely smiled and fought them off as though they were harmless butterflies.

He knew they were dangerous, that they would soon suck up all the air around her and leave her limp on the ground. But she didn't seem to guess this at all. Eventually they covered her and all he could see was a mound of tangled tulips bent low over her body, which was kicking to the last.

He described all of that to Guitar as though the dream emphasized his point about the dangers of seriousness. He tried to be as light-hearted as possible in the telling, but at the end, Guitar looked him in the eyes and said, "Why didn't you go help her?"

"What?"

"Help her. Pull her out from underneath."

"But she liked it. She was having fun. She liked it."

"Are you sure?" Guitar was smiling.

"Sure I'm sure. It was my dream."

"It was *your* mother too."

"Aw, man, why you making something out of it that ain't there? You're making the whole thing into something superserious, just to prove your point. First I'm wrong for not living in Alabama. Then I'm wrong for not behaving right in my own dream. Now I'm wrong for dreaming it. You see what I mean? The least little thing is a matter of life and death to you. You're getting to be just like my old man. He thinks if a paper clip is in the wrong drawer, I should apologize. What's happening to everybody?"

"Looks like everybody's going in the wrong direction but you, don't it?"

Milkman swallowed. He remembered that long-ago evening after he hit his father how everybody was crammed on one side of the street, going in the direction he was coming from. Nobody was going his way. It was as though Guitar had been in that dream too.

"Maybe," he said. "But I know where I'm going."

"Where?"

"Wherever the party is."

Guitar smiled. His teeth were as white as the snowflakes that were settling on his jacket. "Merry Christmas," he said, "and Happy New Year." He waved his hand and cut around the corner to his street. He was lost in the snowy shadows of Southside before Milkman could ask him where he was going or tell him to wait.

Now he closed the accounts book in Sonny's Shop and gave up on the column of numbers. Something was happening to Guitar, had already happened to him. He was constantly chafing Milkman about how he lived, and that conversation was just one more example of how he'd changed. No more could Milkman run up the stairs to his room to drag him off to a party or a bar. And he didn't want to talk about girls or getting high. Sports were about the only things he was still enthusiastic about, and music. Other than that, he was all gloom and golden eyes. And politics.

It was that atmosphere of earnestness he provoked that led
Milkman to talking about his family more than he would normally do and that also led him to defend with flippant remarks
the kind of life he led. Pussy and Honoré parties. Guitar knew
that wasn't all he was interested in, didn't he? He knew Milkman had other interests. Such as? he asked himself. Well, he was
very good in his father's business, for one thing. Excellent, in
fact. But he had to admit right away that real estate was of no
real interest to him. If he had to spend the rest of his life thinking about rents and property, he'd lose his mind. But he was
going to spend the rest of his life doing just that, wasn't he?
That's what his father assumed and he supposed that was what
he had assumed as well.

Maybe Guitar was right—partly. His life was pointless, aimless, and it was true that he didn't concern himself an awful lot
about other people. There was nothing he wanted bad enough
to risk anything for, inconvenience himself for. Still, what right
had Guitar to talk? He didn't live in Montgomery either; all he
did was work at that automobile factory and sneak off places—
nobody knew where—and hang around Tommy's Barbershop.
He never kept a woman more than a few months—the time span
that he said was average before she began to make "permanent-
arrangement-type noises."

He ought to get married, Milkman thought. Maybe I should
too. Who? There were lots of women around and he was very
much the eligible bachelor to the Honoré crowd. Maybe he'd
pick one—the redhead. Get a nice house. His father would help
him find one. Go into a real partnership with his father and . . .
And what? There had to be something better to look forward
to. He couldn't get interested in money. No one had ever denied
him any, so it had no exotic attraction. Politics—at least barbershop politics and Guitar's brand—put him to sleep. He was
bored. Everybody bored him. The city was boring. The racial
problems that consumed Guitar were the most boring of all. He
wondered what they would do if they didn't have black and
white problems to talk about. Who would they be if they
couldn't describe the insults, violence, and oppression that their

lives (and the television news) were made up of? If they didn't have Kennedy or Elijah to quarrel about? They excused themselves for everything. Every job of work undone, every bill unpaid, every illness, every death was The Man's fault. And Guitar was becoming just like them—except he made no excuses for himself—just agreed, it seemed to Milkman, with every grievance he heard.

Milkman went into the bathroom, which served also as a pantry, and plugged in the hot plate to make himself some instant coffee. While he was there, he heard a rapid tapping on the windowpane. He stepped back into the office and saw Freddie's eyes through the lettering. Milkman unlocked the door.

"Hey, Freddie. What's up?"

"Looking for a warm spot. They got me runnin tonight. Christmas comin and all, all I do is run up and down the street." Freddie's janitor duties at the department store were supplemented by his function as a messenger and package deliverer.

"They give you a new truck yet?" Milkman asked him.

"You crazy? The engine have to fall out on the ground before they give me a decent one."

"I put some coffee water on. Have a cup?"

"Just what I'm lookin for. Saw your lights and thought there's got to be a hot cup a coffee in there. You wouldn't happen to have a little taste to go in it, would ya?"

"Just so happens I do."

"Atta boy."

Milkman went into the bathroom, lifted the lid from the toilet tank, and took out the half-pint bottle he kept hidden from Macon, who wouldn't have alcohol on the premises. He brought the bottle into the office, put it on the desk, and went back to make up two cups of coffee. When he reentered, Freddie was trying to look as though he hadn't already turned the pint up to his mouth. They laced their coffee and Milkman looked around for his cigarettes.

"Hard times, boy," Freddie said absently, after his first sip. "Hard times." Then, as though he noticed something missing, he asked, "Where's your buddy?"

"You mean Guitar?"

"Yeah. Guitar. Where's he?"

"Haven't seen him in a few days. You know Guitar. He'll disappear on you in a minute." Milkman noticed how white Freddie's hair was.

"How old are you, Freddie?"

"Who knows? They made dirt in the morning and me that afternoon." He giggled. "But I been around a long long time."

"You born here?"

"Naw. Down south. Jacksonville, Florida. Bad country, boy. Bad, bad country. You know they ain't even got an orphanage in Jacksonville where colored babies can go? They have to put 'em in jail. I tell people that talk about them sit-ins I was *raised* in jail, and it don't scare me none."

"I didn't know you were an orphan."

"Well, not a regular orphan. I had people and all, but my mama died and nobody would take me in. It was on account of the way she died that nobody would take me."

"How'd she die?"

"Ghosts."

"Ghosts?"

"You don't believe in ghosts?"

"Well"—Milkman smiled—"I'm willing to, I guess."

"You better believe, boy. They're here."

"Here?" Milkman didn't glance around the office, but he wanted to. The wind howled outside in the blackness and Freddie, looking like a gnome, flashed his gold teeth. "I don't mean in this room necessarily. Although they could be." He cocked his head and listened. "No. I mean they in the world."

"You've seen some?"

"Plenty. Plenty. Ghosts killed my mother. I didn't see that, of course, but I seen 'em since."

"Tell me about them."

"No I ain't. I don't do no talkin 'bout the ghosts I seen. They don't like that."

"Well, tell me about the one you didn't see. The one killed your mother."

"Oh. Well. That one. She was walking cross the yard with this neighbor friend of hers and they both looked up and saw a woman comin down the road. They stopped and waited to see who she was. When the woman got near, the neighbor called out howdy and soon's she said the word, the woman turned into a white bull. Right before their eyes. My mama fell down on the ground in labor pain right then and there. When I was born and they showed me to her, she screamed and passed out. Never *did* come to. My father died two months before I was born, and they couldn't get none of my people and nobody else to take a baby brought here by a white bull."

Milkman started laughing. He didn't mean to hurt Freddie's feelings, but he couldn't stop the laughter, and the more he tried, the more it came.

Freddie looked more surprised than hurt. "You don't believe me, do you?"

Milkman couldn't answer, he was laughing so hard.

"Okay," Freddie said, and threw up his hands. "Okay, laugh on. But they's a lot of strange things you don't know nothin about, boy. You'll learn. Lot of strange things. Strange stuff goin on right in this here town."

Milkman's laughter was under control now. "What? What strange stuff is happening in this town? I haven't seen any white bulls lately."

"Open your eyes. Ask your buddy. He knows."

"What buddy?"

"Your buddy Guitar. Ask him what strange stuff been happenin. Ask him how come he runnin round with Empire State all of a sudden."

"Empire State?"

"That's right. Empire State."

"Nobody runs around with Empire State. He's a nut. He just stands around with a broom, dribbling spit. He can't even talk."

"He *don't* talk. That don't mean he can't. Only reason he don't is cause he found his wife in bed with another man long time ago, and ain't found nothing to say since then."

"Well, what's Guitar doing with him?"

"Good question. Police would like to know the answer to that too."

"How'd you get from Empire State to the police?"

"You ain't heard? People say the police is lookin for a colored man what killed that white boy in the schoolyard."

"I know that. Everybody knows that."

"Well, the description fits State. And Guitar been takin him places. Hidin him, I believe."

"What's so strange about that? You know Guitar is like that. He'll hide anybody the law is looking for. He hates white people, especially cops, and anybody they're after can count on him for help."

"You don't understand. Him and State ain't actin like they just hidin him. They actin like he did it."

"You a little drunk, Freddie?"

"Yeah, I'm a little drunk, but that don't change nothin. Look here. Remember when Emmet Till was killed? Back in fifty-three? Well, right after that, a white boy was killed in the schoolyard, wasn't he?"

"I don't know. I can't remember the dates of murders I haven't committed."

"You don't know?" Freddie was incredulous.

"No. Are you saying State did it?"

"I'm sayin he acts like it and I'm sayin Guitar knows, and I'm sayin somethin strange is goin on. That's what I'm sayin."

He's mad at me, thought Milkman, because I laughed at his mother and that white bull story. So he's trying to get back at me.

"Keep your eyes open," Freddie went on. "Just keep them open." He looked in the pint bottle, saw it was empty, and got up to leave. "Yep. Some strange goings on round here. But don't put my name in it if you hear anything. Was just like this when that insurance man jumped off the roof. Ever hear tell of him?"

"Seems like I did."

"That must a been when you was a little bitty baby, 1931.

Well, it was some strange stuff then too." Freddie buttoned his coat and pulled his flap-eared cap down as far as it would go. "Well, thanks for the coffee, boy. Did me a lot of good. A lot of good." He took his gloves out of his pocket and moved to the door.

"You're welcome, Freddie. Merry Christmas if I don't see you before that."

"Same to you. And your folks. Tell Mr. Dead and your mother I said Merry Christmas." He was smiling again. When he reached the door he put on his gloves. Then he turned his head slowly and faced Milkman. "Tell you somebody else might know about what's goin on. Corinthians. Ask Corinthians."

He flashed his gold merrily and was gone.

Chapter 5

Nothing happened to the fear. He lay in Guitar's bed face-up in the sunlight, trying to imagine how it would feel when the ice pick entered his neck. But picturing a spurt of wine-red blood and wondering if the ice pick would make him cough didn't help. Fear lay like a pair of crossed paws on his chest.

He closed his eyes and threw his arm over his face to keep the light from overexposing his thoughts. In the darkness that his arm made he could see ice picks coming down faster than raindrops had when he tried as a little boy to catch them with his tongue.

Five hours ago, before he knocked on Guitar's door, he had stood on the top step, dripping in the summer rain that still patted the window, imagining that the drops were tiny steely picks. Then he knocked on the door.

"Yeah?" The voice was lightly aggressive; Guitar never opened his door to a knock anymore before finding out who it was.

"Me—Milkman," he answered, and waited for the clicking sounds of three locks being released.

Milkman walked in, hunching his shoulders under his wet suit jacket. "Anything to drink?"

"Now, you know better'n that." Guitar was smiling, his golden eyes dimmed for the moment. They had not seen much of each other since that argument about Honoré versus Alabama, but the quarrel had been cleansing for both of them. They were easy with each other now that they didn't have to pretend. When in conversation they came to the battleground of difference, their verbal sparring was full of good humor. Furthermore, their friendship had been tested in more immediate ways. The last six months had been dangerous for Milkman, and Guitar had come to his aid over and over again.

"Coffee, then," said Milkman. He sat on the bed with the heaviness of a very old man. "How long you gonna keep that up?"

"Forever. It's over, man. No booze. How about some tea?"

"Jesus."

"Loose too. Bet you thought tea grew in little bags."

"Oh, Christ."

"Like Louisiana cotton. Except the black men picking it wear diapers and turbans. All over India that's all you see. Bushes with little bitsy white tea bags blossoming. Right?"

"Gimme the tea, Guitar. Just the tea. No geography."

"No geography? Okay, no geography. What about some history in your tea? Or some sociopolitico— No. That's still geography. Goddam, Milk, I do believe my whole life's geography."

"Don't you wash pots out for people before you cook water in them?"

"For example, I live in the North now. So the first question come to mind is North of what? Why, north of the South. So North exists because South does. But does that mean North is different from South? No way! South is just south of North. . . ."

"You don't put the fuckin leaves in the boiling water. You pour the water *over* the leaves. In a pot, man. In a teapot!"

"But there is some slight difference worth noticing. Northerners, for example—born and bred ones, that is—are picky about their food. Well, not about the food. They actually don't give a shit about the food. What they're picky about is the trappings. You know what I mean? The pots and shit. Now, they're real funny about pots. But tea? They don't know Earl Grey from old man Lipton's instant."

"I want tea, man. Not won-ton shredded wheat."

"Old man Lipton dye him up some shredded *New York Times* and put it in a cute little white bag and northern Negroes run amok. Can't contain themselves. Ever notice that? How they love them little white bags?"

"Oh, Jesus."

"He's a Northerner too. Lived in Israel, but a Northerner in His heart. His bleeding heart. His cute little old bleeding red heart. Southerners think they own Him, but that's just because the first time they laid eyes on Him, He was strung up on a tree. They can relate to that, see. Both the stringer and the strung. But Northerners know better. . . ."

"Who you talking about? Black people or white people?"

"Black? White? Don't tell me you're one of those racial Negroes? Who said anything about black people? This is just a geography lesson." Guitar handed Milkman a steaming cup of tea.

"Yeah, well, if this is tea, I'm a soft-fried egg."

"See what I mean? Picky. Why you got to be a *soft*-fried egg? Why can't you be just a fried egg? Or just a plain old egg? And why a egg anyway? Negro's been a lotta things, but he ain't never been no egg."

Milkman began to laugh. Guitar had done it again. He'd come to the door sopping wet, ready to roll over and die, and now he was laughing, spilling tea, and choking out his reply: "How come? How come a nigger can't be a egg? He can be a egg if he wants to."

"Nope. Can't be no egg. It ain't in him. Something about his genes. His genes won't let him be no egg no matter how hard he tries. Nature says no. 'No, you can't be no egg, nigger. Now, you can be a crow if you wanna. Or a big baboon. But not no egg. Eggs is difficult, complicated. Fragile too. And white.' "

"They got brown eggs."

"Miscegenation. Besides, don't nobody want 'em."

"French people do."

"In France, yeah. But not in the Congo. Frenchman in the Congo won't touch a brown egg."

"Why won't he?"

"Scared of 'em. Might do something to his skin. Like the sun."

"French people love the sun. They're always trying to get in the sun. On the Riviera—"

"They try to get in the French sun, but not the Congo sun. In the Congo they hate the sun."

"Well, I got a right to be what I want to be, and I want to be a egg."

"Fried?"

"Fried."

"Then somebody got to bust your shell."

Quicker than a pulse beat, Guitar had changed the air. Milkman wiped his mouth, avoiding Guitar's eyes because he knew the phosphorus was back in them. The little room stood at attention in the quiet. It was a second-story porch walled in to make a room-for-rent so the landlady could get an income from it and have a watchman too. Its outside stairway made it perfect for a bachelor. Especially a secretive one like Guitar Bains.

"Can I have the pad tonight?" Milkman asked him. He examined his fingernails.

"To cop?"

Milkman shook his head.

Guitar didn't believe him. Didn't believe his friend really wanted to be alone the night before the day of his own murder. "That's scary, man. Very scary."

Milkman didn't answer.

"You're not obliged to go through no number, you know. Not for me. Everybody knows you're brave when you want to be."

Milkman looked up but still did not answer.

"Still and all," Guitar went on carefully, "you might get your heart cut out. Then you'll be just another brave nigger what got wasted."

Milkman reached for the Pall Mall package. It was empty, so he pulled a longish butt from the Planter's peanut butter jar top that was Guitar's ashtray for the day. He stretched out on the bed, letting his long fingers rub the pocket places in his clothes where matches might be. "Everything's cool," he said.

"Shit," said Guitar. "Ain't nothing cool. Nothing, nowhere. Even the North Pole ain't cool. You think so, go on up there and watch them fuckin glaciers ice your ass. And what the glaciers don't get the polar bears will." Guitar stood up, his head almost touching the ceiling. Annoyed by Milkman's indifference, he relieved his agitation by straightening up the room. He pulled an empty crate from underneath the straight-backed chair leaning in the corner, and started dumping trash into the box: dead matches from the window sill, pork bones from the barbecue he had eaten the day before. He crumpled the pleated paper cups that had been overflowing with cole slaw and fired them into the crate. "Every nigger I know wants to be cool. There's nothing wrong with controlling yourself, but can't nobody control other people." He looked sideways at Milkman's face, alert for any sign, any opening. This kind of silence was new. Something must have happened. Guitar was genuinely worried about his friend, but he also didn't want anything to happen in his room that would bring the police there. He picked up the peanut-butter-top ashtray.

"Wait. There's still some good butts in there." Milkman spoke softly.

Guitar dumped the whole ashtray into the box.

"What'd you do that for? You know we don't have no cigarettes."

"Then move your ass and go get some."

"Come on, Guitar. Cut the shit." Milkman rose from the bed and reached for the crate. He would have gotten it except Guitar stepped back and flung it all the way across the room, letting the mess settle right back where it came from. Graceful and economical as a cat, he arced his arm out of the swing and slammed his fist up against the wall, forming a barrier to any move Milkman might make.

"Pay attention." Guitar's voice was low. "Pay attention when I'm trying to tell you something."

Head to head, toe to toe they stood. Milkman's left foot hovered above the floor, and Guitar's eyes with their phosphorous lights singed his heart a little, but he took the stare. "And if I don't? What then, man? You gonna do me in? My name is Macon, remember? I'm already Dead."

Guitar didn't smile at the familiar joke, but there was enough recognition of it in his face to soften the glare in his eyes.

"Somebody ought to tell your murderer that," said Guitar.

Milkman gave a short laugh and moved back toward the bed. "You worry too much, Guitar."

"I worry just enough. But right now I need to know how come you ain't worried at all. You come up here knowing it's the thirtieth day. Knowing if anybody wants to find you they come here if not first then last. And you ask me to leave you by yourself. Just tell me what you doing."

"Look," Milkman said. "Out of all those times, I was scared just twice: the first time and the third. I've been handling it ever since, right?"

"Yeah, but something's funny this time."

"Ain't nothing funny."

"Yeah, it is. You. You funny."

"No I'm not. Just tired. Tired of dodging crazy people, tired of this jive town, of running up and down these streets getting nowhere. . . ."

"Well, you're home free if tired is all you are. Soon you'll have all the rest you ever need. Can't promise you the bed's comfortable, but morticians don't make mattresses."

"Maybe she won't come this time."

"She ain't missed in six months. You countin on her taking a holiday or something?"

"I can't hide from that bitch no more. I got to stop it. I don't want to go through this again a month from now."

"Why don't you get her people to do something?"

"I am her people."

"Listen, Milk, I'll split if you say so. But just listen to me a minute. That broad had a Carlson skinning knife last time. You know how sharp a Carlson skinning knife is? Cut you like a laser, man."

"I know."

"No, you don't know. You was up under the bar when me and Moon grabbed her."

"I know what she had."

"Won't be no Moon in this room tomorrow. And no Guitar either, if I listen to you. This time she might have a pistol."

"What fool is gonna give a colored woman a pistol?"

"Same fool that gave Porter a shotgun."

"That was years ago."

"It ain't even that that bothers me. It's the way you acting. Like you want it. Like you looking forward to it."

"Where'd you think that up?"

"Look at you. You all dressed up."

"I had to work in Sonny's Shop. You know my old man makes me dress up like this when I'm behind the desk."

"You had time to change. It's past midnight."

"Okay. So I'm clean. So I'm looking forward to it. I just got through telling you I don't want to hide no more. . . ."

"It's a secret, ain't it? You got yourself a secret."

"That makes two of us."

"Two? You and her?"

"No. You and me. You've been making some funny smoke screens lately." Milkman looked up at Guitar and smiled. "Just so you don't think I ain't noticed."

Guitar grinned back. Now that he knew there was a secret, he settled down into the groove of their relationship.

"Okay, Mr. Dead, sir. You on your own. Would you ask your visitor to kind of neaten things up a little before she goes? I don't want to come back and have to look through a pile of cigarette butts for your head. Be nice if it was laying somewhere I could spot it right off. And if it's her head that's left behind, well, there's some towels in the closet on the shelf in the back."

"Rest your mind, boy. Ain't nobody giving up no head."

They laughed then at the suitableness of the unintended pun, and it was in the sound of this laughter that Guitar picked up his brown leather jacket and started out the door.

"Cigarettes!" Milkman called after him. "Bring me some cigarettes before you disappear."

"Gotcha!" Guitar was halfway down the stairs. Already his thoughts had left Milkman and had flown ahead to the house where six old men waited for him.

He didn't come back that night.

Milkman lay quietly in the sunlight, his mind a blank, his lungs craving smoke. Gradually his fear of and eagerness for death returned. Above all he wanted to escape what he knew, escape the implications of what he had been told. And all he knew in the world about the world was what other people had told him. He felt like a garbage pail for the actions and hatreds of other people. He himself did nothing. Except for the one time he had hit his father, he had never acted independently, and that act, his only one, had brought unwanted knowledge too, as well as some responsibility for that knowledge. When his father told him about Ruth, he joined him in despising her, but he felt put upon; felt as though some burden had been given to him and that he didn't deserve it. None of that was his fault, and he didn't want to have to think or be or do something about any of it.

In that mood of lazy righteousness he wallowed in Guitar's bed, the same righteousness that had made him tail his mother like a secret agent when she left the house a week or so ago.

Returning home from a party, he had hardly pulled Macon's Buick up to the curb and turned off the car lights when he saw his mother walking a little ahead of him down Not Doctor Street. It was one-thirty in the morning, but in spite of the hour and her turned-up coat collar, there was no air of furtiveness about her at all. She was walking in what seemed to him a determined manner. Neither hurried nor aimless. Just the even-paced walk of a woman on her way to some modest but respectable work.

When Ruth turned the corner, Milkman waited a minute and started up the car. Creeping, not letting the engine slide into high gear, he drove around the corner. She was standing at the bus stop, so Milkman waited in the shadows until the bus came and she boarded it.

Surely this was no meeting of lovers. The man would have picked her up nearby somewhere. No man would allow a woman he had any affection for to come to him on public transportation in the middle of the night, especially a woman as old as Ruth. And what man wanted a woman over sixty anyway?

Following the bus was a nightmare; it stopped too often, too long, and it was difficult to tail it, hide, and watch to see if she got off. Milkman turned on the car radio, but the music, which he hoped would coat his nerve ends, only splayed them. He was very nervous and thought seriously about turning back.

Finally the bus pulled up at the intracounty train station. Its last stop. There, among the few remaining passengers, he saw her go into the lobby of the station. He believed he'd lost her. He'd never find out what train she was taking. He thought again of going back home. It was late, he was exhausted, and he wasn't sure he wanted to know any more about his mother. But having come this far, he realized it was foolish to turn back now and leave things forever up in the air. He parked in the lot and walked slowly toward the station. Maybe she's not taking a train, he thought. Maybe he meets her in the station.

He looked around carefully before pushing open the doors. There was no sign of her inside. It was a small, plain building. Old but well lit. Looming over the modest waiting room was the Great Seal of Michigan, in vivid Technicolor, painted, probably, by some high school art class. Two pink deer reared up on their hind legs, facing each other, and an eagle perched at eye level between them. The eagle's wings were open and looked like raised shoulders. Its head was turned to the left; one fierce eye bored into that of a deer. Purple Latin words stretched in a long ribbon beneath the seal: *Si Quaeris Peninsulam Amoenam Circumspice.* Milkman didn't understand the Latin and he didn't understand why the wolverine state had a buck painted on the seal. Or were they does? He remembered Guitar's story about killing one. "A man shouldn't do that." Milkman felt a quick beat of something like remorse, but he shook it off and resumed his search for his mother. He walked to the back of the station. Still no sight of her. Then he noticed that there was an upper platform, stairs leading to it, and an arrow with the words FAIR-FIELD AND NORTHEASTERN SUBURBS painted on it. Perhaps she was up there. He moved cautiously toward the stairs, glancing up and all around lest he see her or miss her. A loudspeaker broke the silence, announcing the arrival of the two-fifteen train to Fairfield Heights, leaving from the upper platform. He dashed up the stairs then just in time to see Ruth step into a car, and to jump into another car himself.

The train made ten stops at about ten-minute intervals. He leaned out between the cars at each stop to see if she was getting off. After the sixth stop, he asked the conductor when the next train returned to the city. "Five forty-five a.m.," he said.

Milkman looked at his watch. It was already three o'clock. When the conductor called out, "Fairfield Heights. Last stop," a half hour later, Milkman looked out again and this time he saw her disembark. He darted behind the three-sided wooden structure that sheltered waiting passengers from the wind until he heard her wide rubber heels padding down the steps.

Beyond the shelter along the street below were stores—all closed now: newsstands, coffee shops, stationery shops, but no houses. The wealthy people of Fairfield did not live near a train station and very few of their houses could even be seen from the road. Nevertheless, Ruth walked in her even-paced way down the street and in just a few minutes was at the wide winding lane that led into Fairfield Cemetery.

As Milkman stared at the ironwork arched over the entrance, he remembered snatches of his mother's chatter about having looked so very carefully for a cemetery for the doctor's body—someplace other than the one where Negroes were all laid together in one area. And forty years ago Fairfield was farm country with a county cemetery too tiny for anybody to care whether its dead were white or black.

Milkman leaned against a tree and waited at the entrance. Now he knew, if he'd had any doubts, that all his father had told him was true. She was a silly, selfish, queer, faintly obscene woman. Again he felt abused. Why couldn't anybody in his whole family just be normal?

He waited for an hour before she came out.

"Hello, Mama," he said. He tried to make his voice sound as coolly cruel as he felt; just as he tried to frighten her by stepping out suddenly from behind the tree.

He succeeded. She stumbled in alarm and took a great gulp of air into her mouth.

"Macon! Is that you? You're here? Oh, my goodness. I . . ." She tried desperately to normalize the situation, smiling wanly and blinking her eyes, searching for words and manners and civilization.

Milkman stopped her. "You come to lay down on your father's grave? Is that what you've been doing all these years? Spending a night every now and then with your father?"

Ruth's shoulders seemed to slump, but she said in a surprisingly steady voice, "Let's walk toward the train stop."

Neither said a word during the forty-five minutes they waited in the little shelter for the train back to the city. The sun came up and pointed out the names of young lovers painted on the wall. A few men were walking up the stairs to the platform.

When the train backed in from its siding they still had not spoken. Only when the wheels were actually turning and the engine had cleared its throat did Ruth begin, and she began in the middle of a sentence as though she had been thinking it all through since she and her son left the entrance to Fairfield Cemetery.

". . . because the fact is that I am a small woman. I don't mean little; I mean small, and I'm small because I was pressed small. I lived in a great big house that pressed me into a small package. I had no friends, only schoolmates who wanted to touch my dresses and my white silk stockings. But I didn't think I'd ever need a friend because I had him. I was small, but he was big. The only person who ever really cared whether I lived or died. Lots of people were *interested* in whether I lived or died, but he cared. He was not a good man, Macon. Certainly he was an arrogant man, and often a foolish and destructive one. But he cared whether and he cared how I lived, and there was, and is, no one else in the world who ever did. And for that I would do anything. It was important for me to be in his presence, among his things, the things he used, had touched. Later it was just important for me to know that he was in the world. When he left it, I kept on reigniting that cared-for feeling that I got from him.

"I am not a strange woman. I am a small one.

"I don't know what all your father has told you about me down in that shop you all stay in. But I know, as well as I know my own name, that he told you only what was flattering to him. I know he never told you that he killed my father and that he tried to kill you. Because both of you took my attention away from him. I know he never told you that. And I know he never told you that he threw my father's medicine away, but it's true. And I couldn't save my father. Macon took away his medicine and I just didn't know it, and I wouldn't have been able to save you except for Pilate. Pilate was the one brought you here in the first place."

"Pilate?" Milkman was coming awake. He had begun listening to his mother with the dulled ear of someone who was about to be conned and knew it.

"Pilate. Old, crazy, sweet Pilate. Your father and I hadn't had physical relations since my father died, when Lena and Corinthians were just toddlers. We had a terrible quarrel. He threatened to kill me. I threatened to go to the police about what he had done to my father. We did neither. I guess my father's money was more important to him than the satisfaction of killing me. And I would have happily died except for my babies. But he did move into another room and that's the way things stayed until I couldn't stand it anymore. Until I thought I'd really die if I had to live that way. With nobody touching me, or even looking as though they'd like to touch me. That's when I started coming to Fairfield. To talk. To talk to somebody who wanted to listen and not laugh at me. Somebody I could trust. Somebody who trusted me. Somebody who was . . . interested in me. For my own self. I didn't care if that somebody was under the ground. You know, I was twenty years old when your father stopped sleeping in the bed with me. That's hard, Macon. Very hard. By the time I was thirty . . . I think I was just afraid I'd die that way.

"Then Pilate came to town. She came into this city like she owned it. Pilate, Reba, and Reba's little baby. Hagar. Pilate came to see Macon right away and soon as she saw me she knew what my trouble was. And she asked me one day, 'Do you want him?' 'I want somebody,' I told her. 'He's as good as anybody,' she said. 'Besides, you'll get pregnant and your baby ought to be his. He ought to have a son. Otherwise this be the end of us.'

"She gave me funny things to do. And some greenish-gray grassy-looking stuff to put in his food." Ruth laughed. "I felt like a doctor, like a chemist doing some big important scientific experiment. It worked too. Macon came to me for four days. He even came home from his office in the middle of the day to be with me. He looked puzzled, but he came. Then it was over. And two months later I was pregnant. When he found out about it, he immediately suspected Pilate and he told me to get rid of the baby. But I wouldn't and Pilate helped me stand him off. I wouldn't have been strong enough without her. She saved my life. And yours, Macon. She saved yours too. She watched you like you were her own. Until your father threw her out."

Milkman leaned his head against the cold handbar that was attached to the seat in front of him. He held it there, letting its chill circle his head. Then he turned to his mother. "Were you in the bed with your father when he was dead? Naked?"

"No. But I did kneel there in my slip at his bedside and kiss his beautiful fingers. They were the only part of him that wasn't . . ."

"You nursed me."

"Yes."

"Until I was . . . old. Too old."

Ruth turned toward her son. She lifted her head and looked deep into his eyes. "And I also prayed for you. Every single night and every single day. On my knees. Now you tell me. What harm did I do you on my knees?"

That was the beginning. Now it was all going to end. In a little while she would walk in the door and this time he would let her do it. Afterward there would be no remembrance of who he was or where. Of Magdalene called Lena and First Corinthians, of his father trying to stop him dead before he was born. Of the brilliant bitterness between his father and his mother, a bitterness as smooth and fixed as steel. And he wouldn't have those waking dreams or hear those awful words his mother had spoken to him: What harm? What harm did I do you on my knees?

He could hear her footsteps, and then the sound of the door-knob turning, sticking, and turning again. He knew, without uncovering his eyes, that she was right there, looking at him through the window.

Hagar. Killing, ice-pick-wielding Hagar, who, shortly after a Christmas thank-you note, found herself each month searching the barrels and cupboards and basement shelves for some comfortably portable weapon with which to murder her true love.

The "thank you" cut her to the quick, but it was not the

reason she ran scurrying into cupboards looking for weapons. That had been accomplished by the sight of Milkman's arms around the shoulders of a girl whose silky copper-colored hair cascaded over the sleeve of his coat. They were sitting in Mary's, smiling into glasses of Jack Daniel's on the rocks. The girl looked a little like Corinthians or Lena from the back, and when she turned, laughing, toward Milkman, and Hagar saw her gray eyes, the fist that had been just sitting in her chest since Christmas released its forefinger like the blade of a skinning knife. As regularly as the new moon searched for the tide, Hagar looked for a weapon and then slipped out of her house and went to find the man for whom she believed she had been born into the world. Being five years older than he was and his cousin as well did nothing to dim her passion. In fact her maturity and blood kinship converted her passion to fever, so it was more affliction than affection. It literally knocked her down at night, and raised her up in the morning, for when she dragged herself off to bed, having spent another day without his presence, her heart beat like a gloved fist against her ribs. And in the morning, long before she was fully awake, she felt a longing so bitter and tight it yanked her out of a sleep swept clean of dreams.

She moved around the house, onto the porch, down the streets, to the fruit stalls and the butchershop, like a restless ghost, finding peace nowhere and in nothing. Not in the first tomato off the vine, split open and salted lightly, which her grandmother put before her. Not the six-piece set of pink glass dishes Reba won at the Tivoli Theater. And not the carved wax candle that the two of them made for her, Pilate dipping the wick and Reba scratching out tiny flowers with a nail file, and put in a genuine store-bought candleholder next to her bed. Not even the high fierce sun at noon, nor the ocean-dark evenings. Nothing could pull her mind away from the mouth Milkman was not kissing, the feet that were not running toward him, the eye that no longer beheld him, the hands that were not touching him.

She toyed, sometimes, with her unsucked breasts, but at some point her lethargy dissipated of its own accord and in its place was wilderness, the focused meanness of a flood or an avalanche of snow which only observers, flying in a rescue helicopter, believed to be an indifferent natural phenomenon, but which the victims, in their last gulp of breath, knew was both directed and personal. The calculated violence of a shark grew in her, and like every witch that ever rode a broom straight through the night to a ceremonial infanticide as thrilled by the black wind as by the rod between her legs; like every fed-up-to-the-teeth bride who worried about the consistency of the grits she threw at her husband as well as the potency of the lye she had stirred into them; and like every queen and every courtesan who was struck by the beauty of her emerald ring as she tipped its poison into the old red wine, Hagar was energized by the details of her mission. She stalked him. Whenever the fist that beat in her chest became that pointing finger, when any contact with him at all was better than none, she stalked him. She could not get his love (and the possibility that he did not think of her at all was intolerable), so she settled for his fear.

On those days, her hair standing out from her head like a thundercloud, she haunted Southside and Not Doctor Street until she found him. Sometimes it took two days, or three, and the people who saw her passed the word along that Hagar "done took off after Milkman again." Women watched her out of their windows. Men looked up from their checker games and wondered if she'd make it this time. The lengths to which lost love drove men and women never surprised them. They had seen women pull their dresses over their heads and howl like dogs for lost love. And men who sat in doorways with pennies in their mouths for lost love. "Thank God," they whispered to themselves, "thank God I ain't never had one of them graveyard loves." Empire State himself was a good example of one. He'd married a white girl in France and brought her home. Happy as a fly and just as industrious, he lived with her for six years until he came home to find her with another man. Another black man. And when he discovered that his white wife loved not only him, not only this other black man, but the whole race, he sat down, closed his mouth, and never said another word. Railroad Tommy had given him a janitor's job to save him from the poorhouse, workhouse, or nuthouse, one.

So Hagar's forays were part and parcel of the mystery of having been "lifed" by love, and while the manifestation it took was a source of great interest to them, the consequences were not. After all, it served him right, messing with his own cousin.

Luckily for Milkman, she had proved, so far, to be the world's most inept killer. Awed (even in the midst of her anger) by the very presence of her victim, she trembled violently and her knife thrusts and hammer swings and ice-pick jabs were clumsy. As soon as the attempt had been thwarted by a wrist grab from behind or a body tackle from the front or a neat clip on the jaw, she folded up into herself and wept cleansing tears right there and later under Pilate's strap—to which she submitted with relief. Pilate beat her, Reba cried, and Hagar crouched. Until the next time. Like this time when she turned the doorknob of Guitar's little bachelor room.

It was locked. So she swung one leg over the porch railing and fiddled with the window. Milkman heard the noises, heard the window shake, but refused to move or take his arm away from his eyes. Even when he heard the tinkle and clatter of glass he did not move.

Hagar put her shoe back on before reaching into the window hole she had made and turning the catch. It took her the longest time to raise the window. She was hanging lopsided over the railing, one leg supporting her weight. The window slid in a crooked path up its jamb.

Milkman refused to look. Perspiration collected in the small of his back and ran out of his armpit down his side. But the fear was gone. He lay there as still as the morning light, and sucked the world's energy up into his own will. And willed her dead. Either she will kill me or she will drop dead. Either I am to live in this world on my terms or I will die out of it. If I am to live in it, then I want her dead. One or the other. Me or her. Choose.

Die, Hagar. Die. Die. Die.

But she didn't. She crawled into the room and walked over to the little iron bed. In her hand was a butcher knife, which she raised high over her head and brought down heavily toward the smooth neck flesh that showed above his shirt collar. The knife struck his collarbone and angled off to his shoulder. A small break in the skin began to bleed. Milkman jerked, but did not move his arm nor open his eyes. Hagar raised the knife again, this time with both hands, but found she could not get her arms down. Try as she might, the ball joint in her shoulders would not move. Ten seconds passed. Fifteen. The paralyzed woman and the frozen man.

At the thirtieth second Milkman knew he had won. He moved his arm and opened his eyes. His gaze traveled to her strung-up, held-up arms.

Oh, she thought, when she saw his face, I had forgotten how beautiful he is.

Milkman sat up, swung his legs over the side of the bed, and stood.

"If you keep your hands just that way," he said, "and then bring them down straight, straight and fast, you can drive that knife right smack in your cunt. Why don't you do that? Then all your problems will be over." He patted her cheek and turned away from her wide, dark, pleading, hollow eyes.

She stood that way for a long time, and it was an even longer time before anybody found her. They could have guessed where she was, though. If anybody missed her for a while they could guess. Even Ruth knew now. A week earlier she had learned from Freddie that Hagar had tried to kill Milkman six times in as many months. She stared at his golden teeth and said, "Hagar?" She hadn't laid eyes on her in years; had been to Pilate's house only once in her life—a very long time ago.

"Hagar?"

"Hagar. Shore Hagar."

"Does Pilate know?"

"Course she do. Whip her every time, but it don't do no good."

Ruth was relieved. For a moment she imagined that Pilate, who had brought her son to life in the first place, was now bound to see him dead. But right after that moment of relief, she felt hurt because Milkman had not told her himself. Then she realized that he really didn't tell her anything, and hadn't for years. Her son had never been a person to her, a separate real person. He had always been a passion. Because she had been so desperate to lie with her husband and have another baby by him, the son she bore was first off a wished-for bond between herself and Macon, something to hold them together and reinstate their sex lives. Even before his birth he was a strong feeling—a feeling about the nasty greenish-gray powder Pilate had given her to be stirred into rain water and put into food. But Macon came out of his few days of sexual hypnosis in a rage and later when he discovered her pregnancy, tried to get her to abort. Then the baby became the nausea caused by the half ounce of castor oil Macon made her drink, then a hot pot recently emptied of scalding water on which she sat, then a soapy enema, a knitting needle (she inserted only the tip, squatting in the bathroom, crying, afraid of the man who paced outside the door), and finally, when he punched her stomach (she had been about to pick up his breakfast plate, when he looked at her stomach and punched it), she ran to Southside looking for Pilate. She had never walked through that part of town, but she knew the street Pilate lived on, though not the house. Pilate had no telephone and no number on her house. Ruth had asked some passer-by where Pilate lived and was directed to a lean brown house set back from the unpaved road. Pilate was sitting on a chair; Reba was cutting Pilate's hair with a barber's clippers. That was the first time she saw Hagar, who was four or five years old then. Chubby, with four long braids, two like horns over each ear, two like tails at the back of her neck. Pilate comforted Ruth, gave her a peach, which Ruth could not eat because the fuzz made her sick. She listened to what Ruth said and sent Reba to the store for a box of Argo cornstarch. She sprinkled a little of it into her hand and offered it to Ruth, who obediently took a lump and put it in her mouth. As soon as she tasted it, felt its crunchiness, she asked for more, and ate half a box before she left. (From then on she ate cornstarch, cracked ice, nuts, and once in a fit she put a few tiny pebbles of gravel in her mouth. "When you expectin, you have to eat what the baby craves," Pilate said, " 'less it come in the world hongry for what you denied it." Ruth could not bite enough. Her teeth were on edge with the yearning. Like the impulse of a cat to claw, she searched for crunchy things, and when there was nothing, she would grind her teeth.)

Gnashing the cornstarch, Ruth let Pilate lead her into the bedroom, where the woman wrapped her in a homemade-on-the-spot girdle—tight in the crotch—and told her to keep it on until the fourth month and "don't take no more mess off Macon and don't ram another thing up in your womb." She also told her not to worry. Macon wouldn't bother her no more; she, Pilate, would see to it. (Years later Ruth learned that Pilate put a small doll on Macon's chair in his office. A male doll with a small painted chicken bone stuck between its legs and a round red circle painted on its belly. Macon knocked it out of the chair and with a yardstick pushed it into the bathroom, where he doused it with alcohol and burned it. It took nine separate burnings before the fire got down to the straw and cotton ticking of its insides. But he must have remembered the round fire-red stomach, for he left Ruth alone after that.)

When the baby was born the day after she stood in the snow, with cloth roses at her feet and a man with blue wings above her head, she regarded him as a beautiful toy, a respite, a distraction, a physical pleasure as she nursed him—until Freddie (again Freddie) caught her at it; then he was no longer her velveteened toy. He became a plain on which, like the cowboys and Indians in the movies, she and her husband fought. Each one befuddled by the values of the other. Each one convinced of his own purity and outraged by the idiocy he saw in the other. She was the Indian, of course, and lost her land, her customs, her integrity to the cowboy and became a spread-eagled footstool resigned to her fate and holding fast to tiny irrelevant defiances.

But who was this son of hers? This tall man who had flesh on the outside and feelings on the inside that she knew nothing of, but somebody did, knew enough about him to want to kill him. Suddenly, the world opened up for her like one of her imperial tulips and revealed its evil yellow pistil. She had been husbanding her own misery, shaping it, making of it an art and a Way. Now she saw a larger, more malevolent world outside her own. Outside the fourposter bed where Doctor had bubbled and rotted (all but his beautiful hands, which were the only things his grandson had inherited). Outside her garden and the fishbowl where her goldfish died. She had thought it was all done. That she had won out over the castor oil, and the pot of steam that had puckered and burned her skin so she could not bear to urinate or sit with her daughters at the table where they cut and sewed. She had had the baby anyway, and although it did nothing to close the break between herself and Macon, there he was, her single triumph.

Now Freddie was telling her that it wasn't done and over yet. Somebody was still trying to kill him. To deprive her of the one aggressive act brought to royal completion. And the person who was threatening his life was someone who shared Macon's blood.

"That hurts," she said aloud to Freddie as she folded into her pocket the rent money he handed her. "That hurts, you know."

She climbed the porch steps and went into the kitchen. Without knowing what her foot was planning to do, she kicked the cabinet door with the worn lock under the sink. It answered her kick with a tiny whine before it sneaked open again. Ruth looked at it and kicked it closed once more. Again it whined and opened right back up.

"I want you closed," she whispered. "Closed."

The door stayed open.

"Closed. You hear me? Closed. Closed. Closed." She was screaming by now.

Magdalene called Lena, hearing her shouts, ran down the stairs and into the kitchen. She found her mother staring at the sink and commanding it.

"Mother?" Lena was frightened.

Ruth looked up at her. "What is it?"

"I don't know. . . . I thought I heard you saying something."

"Get somebody to fix that door. I want it shut. Tight."

Lena stared as Ruth hurried past and when she heard her mother running up the stairs, she put her fingers to her lips in disbelief. Ruth was sixty-two years old. Lena had no idea she could move that fast.

Her passions were narrow but deep. Long deprived of sex, long dependent on self-manipulation, she saw her son's imminent death as the annihilation of the last occasion she had been made love to.

With the same determined tread that took her to the graveyard six or seven times a year, Ruth left the house and caught the number 26 bus and sat down right in back of the driver. She took her glasses off and wiped them on the hem of her skirt. She was serene and purposeful as always when death turned his attention to someone who belonged to her, as she was when death breathed in her father's wispy hair and blew the strands about. She had the same calmness and efficiency with which she cared for the doctor, putting her hand on death's chest and holding him back, denying him, keeping her father alive even past the point where he wanted to be alive, past pain on into disgust and horror at having to smell himself in his next breath. Past that until he was too sick to fight her efforts to keep him alive, lingering in absolute hatred of this woman who would not grant him peace, but kept her shining lightish eyes fixed on him like magnets holding him from the narrow earth he longed for.

Ruth wiped her glasses clean so she could see the street signs as they passed ("Eat cherries," Pilate had told her, "and you won't have to wear them little windows over your eyes"), her mind empty except for getting there—to Darling Street, where Pilate lived and where, she supposed, Hagar lived too. How had that chubby little girl weighed down with hair become a knife-

wielding would-be killer out to get her son? Maybe Freddie lied.
Maybe. She'd see.

When the banks disappeared and small shops in between
rickety houses came into view, Ruth pulled the cord. She
stepped down and walked toward the underpass that cut across
Darling Street. It was a long walk and she was sweating by the
time she got to Pilate's house. The door was open, but nobody
was inside. The house smelled fruity and she remembered how
the peach had nauseated her the last time she was there. Here
was the chair she had collapsed in. There the candlemaker's
rack, the pan where Pilate's homemade soap hardened into a
yellowish-brown slab. This house had been a haven then, and in
spite of the cold anger she felt now, it still looked like an inn, a
safe harbor. A flypaper roll entirely free of flies curled down
from the ceiling not far from a sack that hung there too. Ruth
looked into the bedroom and saw three little beds, and like
Goldilocks, she walked over to the nearest one and sat down.
There was no back door to this two-room house, just a big room
where they lived and this bedroom. It had a cellar that one could
enter only from the outside under a metal door that slanted away
from the house and opened onto stone stairs.

Ruth sat still, letting the anger and determination jell. She
wondered whose bed it was and lifted up the blanket and saw
only mattress ticking. The same was true of the next bed, but
not of the third. It had sheets, a pillow, and a pillow slip. That
would be Hagar's, she thought. The anger unjelled and flooded
through her. She left the room, pressing her fury back so she
would be able to wait and wait until somebody returned. Pacing
the floor of the outer room, her elbows in the palms of her
hands, she suddenly heard humming that seemed to be coming
from the back of the house. Pilate, she thought. Pilate hummed
and chewed things all the time. Ruth would ask her first if what
Freddie said was true. She needed Pilate's calm view, her
honesty and equilibrium. Then she would know what to do.
Whether to unfold her arms and let the rage out to do whatever
it might, or . . . She tasted again the Argo cornstarch and felt

the marvelous biting and crunching it allowed her. Now she merely ground her teeth as she stepped out to the porch and made her way around the side of the house through the nicotiana growing all wild and out of control.

A woman sat on a bench, her hands clasped between her knees. It was not Pilate. Ruth stood still and looked at the woman's back. It didn't look like death's back at all. It looked vulnerable, soft, like an easily wounded shin, full of bone but susceptible to the slightest pain.

"Reba?" she said.

The woman turned around and fastened on her the most sorrowful eyes Ruth had ever seen.

"Reba's gone," she said, the second word sounding as if the going were permanent. "Can I do something for you?"

"I'm Ruth Foster."

Hagar stiffened. A lightning shot of excitement ran through her. Milkman's mother: the silhouette she had seen through the curtains in an upstairs window on evenings when she stood across the street hoping at first to catch him, then hoping just to see him, finally just to be near the things he was familiar with. Private vigils held at night, made more private because they were expressions of public lunacy. The outline she'd seen once or twice when the side door opened and a woman shook crumbs from a tablecloth or dust from a small rug onto the ground. Whatever Milkman had told her about his mother, whatever she had heard from Pilate and Reba, she could not remember, so overwhelmed was she in the presence of *his* mother. Hagar let her morbid pleasure spread across her face in a smile.

Ruth was not impressed. Death always smiled. And breathed. And looked helpless like a shinbone, or a tiny speck of black on the Queen Elizabeth roses, or film on the eye of a dead goldfish.

"You are trying to kill him." Ruth's voice was matter-of-fact. "If you so much as bend a hair on his head, so help me Jesus, I will tear your throat out."

Hagar looked surprised. She loved nothing in the world except this woman's son, wanted him alive more than anybody, but hadn't the least bit of control over the predator that lived inside her. Totally taken over by her anaconda love, she had no self left, no fears, no wants, no intelligence that was her own. So it was with a great deal of earnestness that she replied to Ruth. "I'll try not to. But I can't make you a for-certain promise."

Ruth heard the supplication in her words and it seemed to her that she was not looking at a person but at an impulse, a cell, a red corpuscle that neither knows nor understands why it is driven to spend its whole life in one pursuit: swimming up a dark tunnel toward the muscle of a heart or an eye's nerve end that it both nourished and fed from.

Hagar lowered her eyelids and gazed hungrily down the figure of the woman who had been only a silhouette to her. The woman who slept in the same house with him, and who could call him home and he would come, who knew the mystery of his flesh, had memory of him as long as his life. The woman who knew him, had watched his teeth appear, stuck her finger in his mouth to soothe his gums. Cleaned his behind, Vaselined his penis, and caught his vomit in a fresh white diaper. Had fed him from her own nipples, carried him close and warm and safe under her heart, and who had opened her legs far far wider than she herself ever had for him. Who even now could walk freely into his room if she wanted to and smell his clothes, stroke his shoes, and lay her head on the very spot where he had lain his. But what was more, so much more, this thin lemon-yellow woman knew with absolute certainty what Hagar would willingly have her throat torn out to know: that she would see him this very day. Jealousy loomed so large in her it made her tremble. Maybe you, she thought. Maybe it's you I should be killing. Maybe then he will come to me and let me come to him. He is my home in this world. And then, aloud, "He is my home in this world."

"And I am his," said Ruth.

"And he wouldn't give a pile of swan shit for either one of you."

They turned then and saw Pilate leaning on the window sill. Neither knew how long she'd been there.

"Can't say as I blame him neither. Two growed-up women

talkin 'bout a man like he was a house or needed one. He ain't a house, he's a man, and whatever he need, don't none of you got it."

"Leave me alone, Mama. Just leave me alone."

"You already alone. If you want more alone, I can knock you into the middle of next week, and leave you there."

"You're botherin me!" Hagar was shouting and digging her fingers in her hair. It was an ordinary gesture of frustration, but its awkwardness made Ruth know that there was something truly askew in this girl. That here was the wilderness of Southside. Not the poverty or dirt or noise, not just extreme unregulated passion where even love found its way with an ice pick, but the absence of control. Here one lived knowing that at any time, anybody might do anything. Not wilderness where there was system, or the logic of lions, trees, toads, and birds, but wild wilderness where there was none.

She had not recognized it in Pilate, whose equilibrium overshadowed all her eccentricities and who was, in any case, the only person she knew of strong enough to counter Macon. Although Ruth had been frightened of her the first time she saw her—when she knocked on the kitchen door way back then, looking, as she said, for her brother Macon. (Ruth was still frightened of her a little. Not just her short hair cut regularly like a man's, or her large sleepy eyes and busy lips, or the smooth smooth skin, hairless, scarless, and wrinkleless. For Ruth had actually seen it. The place on her stomach where a navel should have been and was not. Even if you weren't frightened of a woman who had no navel, you certainly had to take her very seriously.)

Now she held up her hand, imperiously, and silenced Hagar's whines.

"Sit down there. Sit down and don't leave this yard."

Hagar slumped and moved slowly back to her bench.

Pilate turned her eyes to Ruth. "Come on in. Rest yourself before you hop on that bus again."

They sat down at the table facing each other.

"Peaches kind of dried up on me in this heat," said Pilate, and she reached for a peck basket which held about a half dozen. "But there should be some good ones left in here. Can I slice you up some?"

"No, thank you," said Ruth. She was trembling a little now. After the tension, the anger, the bravado of her earlier state of mind, followed by the violence of Pilate's words to her granddaughter, this quiet social-tea tone disarmed her, threw her too soon and too suddenly back into the mannered dignity that was habitual for her. Ruth pressed her hands together in her lap to stop the shaking.

They were so different, these two women. One black, the other lemony. One corseted, the other buck naked under her dress. One well read but ill traveled. The other had read only a geography book, but had been from one end of the country to another. One wholly dependent on money for life, the other indifferent to it. But those were the meaningless things. Their similarities were profound. Both were vitally interested in Macon Dead's son, and both had close and supportive posthumous communication with their fathers.

"The last time I was here you offered me a peach. My visit was about my son then too."

Pilate nodded her head and with her right thumbnail slit the peach open.

"You won't never be able to forgive her. For just tryin to do it you won't never be able to forgive her. But it looks to me like you ought to be able to understand her. Think on it a minute. You ready now to kill her—well, maim her anyway—because she's tryin to take him away from you. She's the enemy to you because she wants to take him out of your life. Well, in her eyes there's somebody who wants to take him out of her life too—him. So he's her enemy. He's the one who's tryin to take himself out of her life. And she'll kill him before she lets him do that. What I'm sayin is that you both got the same idea.

"I do my best to keep her from it. She's my baby too, you know, but I tear her up every time she try. Just for the tryin, mind you, because I know one thing sure: she'll never pull it off. He come in the world tryin to keep from gettin killed. Layin in your stomach, his own papa was tryin to do it. And you helped some too. He had to fight off castor oil and knittin needles and being blasted with hot steam and I don't know what all you and Macon did. But he made it. When he was at his most helpless, he made it. Ain't nothin goin to kill him but his own ignorance, and won't no woman ever kill him. What's likelier is that it'll be a woman save his life."

"Nobody lives forever, Pilate."

"Don't?"

"Of course not."

"Nobody?"

"Of course, nobody."

"I don't see why not."

"Death is as natural as life."

"Ain't nothin natural about death. It's the most unnatural thing they is."

"You think people should live forever?"

"Some people. Yeah."

"Who's to decide? Which ones should live and which ones shouldn't?"

"The people themselves. Some folks want to live forever. Some don't. I believe they decide on it anyway. People die when they want to and if they want to. Don't nobody have to die if they don't want to."

Ruth felt a chill. She'd always believed that her father wanted to die. "I wish I could count on your faith as far as my son was concerned. But I think I'd be a really foolish woman if I did that. You saw your own father die, just like I did; you saw him killed. Do you think he wanted to die?"

"I saw Papa shot. Blown off a fence five feet into the air. I saw him wigglin on the ground, but not only did I not see him die, I seen him since he was shot."

"Pilate. You all buried him yourselves." Ruth spoke as if she were talking to a child.

"Macon did."

"It's the same thing."

"Macon seen him too. After he buried him, after he was blown off that fence. We both seen him. I see him still. He's helpful to me, real helpful. Tells me things I need to know."

"What things?"

"All kinds of things. It's a good feelin to know he's around. I tell you he's a person I can always rely on. I tell you somethin else. He's the *only* one. I was cut off from people early. You can't know what that was like. After my papa was blown off that fence, me and Macon wandered around for a few days until we had a fallin out and I went off on my own. I was about twelve, I think. When I cut out by myself, I headed for Virginia. I thought I remembered that was where my papa had people. Or my mother did. Seemed to me like I remembered somebody sayin that. I don't remember my mother because she died before I was born."

"*Before* you were born? How could she . . . ?"

"She died and the next minute I was born. But she was dead by the time I drew air. I never saw her face. I don't even know what her name was. But I do remember thinkin she come from Virginia. Anyways, that's where I struck out for. I looked around for somebody to take me in, give me a little work for a while so I could earn some money to get on down there. I walked for seven days before I found a place with a preacher's family. A nice place except they made me wear shoes. They sent me to school, though. A one-room place, where everybody sat. I was twelve, but since this was my first school I had to sit over there with the little bitty children. I didn't mind it too much; matter of fact, I liked a lot of it. I loved the geography part. Learning about that made me want to read. And the teacher was tickled at how much I liked geography. She let me have the book and I took it home with me to look at. But then the preacher started pattin on me. I was so dumb I didn't know enough to stop him. But his wife caught him at it, thumbin my breasts, and put me out. I took my geography book off with me.

I could of stayed in that town cause they was plenty of colored people to take me in. In them days, anybody too old to work kept the children. Grown folks worked and left their kids in other people's houses. But him being the preacher and all like that, I figured I ought to make tracks. I was broke as a haint cause the place didn't carry no wages. Just room and board. So I just took my geography book and a rock I picked up for a souvenir and lit out.

"It was a Sunday when I met up with some pickers. Folks call 'em migrants nowadays; then they was just called pickers. They took me in and treated me fine. I worked up in New York State pickin beans, then we'd move to another place and pick a different crop. Everyplace I went I got me a rock. They was about four or five families all together in the crew. All of them related one way or another. But they was good people and treated me fine. I stayed with them for three years, I believe, and the main reason I stayed on was a woman there I took to. A root worker. She taught me a lot and kept me from missin my own family, Macon and Papa. I didn't have a thought in my head of ever leavin them, but I did. I had to. After a while they didn't want me around no more." Pilate sucked a peach stone and her face was dark and still with the memory of how she was "cut off" so early from other people.

The boy. The nephew, or was it the cousin, of the woman who worked roots. When she was fifteen, and the rain was so heavy they had to stay in the shacks (those who had them—the others had tents) because nothing could be harvested in that pouring rain, the boy and Pilate lay down together. He was no older than she was and while everything about her delighted him, nothing about her surprised him. So it was with no malice whatsoever that one evening after supper he mentioned to some of the men (but within listening distance of the women) that he didn't know that some folks had navels and some didn't. The men and the women raised their eyes at his remark, and asked him to explain what he meant. He got it out, finally, after many false starts—he thought they were alarmed because he had taken the pretty girl with the single earring to bed—but he soon discovered that the navel thing was what bothered them.

The root woman was assigned the job of finding out if what he said was true or not. She called Pilate into her shack one day later. "Lay down," she said. "I want to check on something." Pilate lay down on the straw pallet. "Now lift up your dress," the woman said. "More. All the way up. Higher." And then her eyes flew open wide and she put her hand over her mouth. Pilate leaped up. "What? What is it?" She looked down at herself, thinking a snake or a poisonous spider had crawled over her legs.

"Nothin," the woman said. Then, "Child, where's your navel?"

Pilate had never heard the word "navel" and didn't know what the woman was talking about. She looked down at her legs, parted on the rough ticking. "Navel?" she asked.

"You know. This." And the woman pulled up her own dress and slipped the elastic of her bloomers down over her fat stomach. Pilate saw the little corkscrew thing right in the middle, the little piece of skin that looked like it was made for water to drain down into, like the little whirlpools along the edges of a creek. It was just like the thing her brother had on his stomach. He had one. She did not. He peed standing up. She squatting down. He had a penis like a horse did. She had a vagina like the mare. He had a flat chest with two nipples. She had teats like the cow. He had a corkscrew in his stomach. She did not. She thought it was one more way in which males and females were different. The boy she went to bed with had one too. But until now she had never seen another woman's stomach. And from the horror on the older woman's face she knew there was something wrong with not having it.

"What's it for?" she asked.

The woman swallowed. "It's for . . . it's for people who were born natural."

Pilate didn't understand that, but she did understand the conversation she had later with the root worker and some other women in the camp. She was to leave. They were very sorry, they liked her and all, and she was such a good worker and a big help to everybody. But she had to leave just the same.

"On account of my stomach?" But the women would not answer her. They looked at the ground.

Pilate left with more than her share of earnings, because the women did not want her to go away angry. They thought she might hurt them in some way if she got angry, and they also felt pity along with their terror of having been in the company of something God never made.

Pilate went away. Again she headed for Virginia. But now she knew how to harvest in a team and looked for another migrant crew, or a group of women who had followed their men to some seasonal work as brickmakers, iron workers, shipyard workers. In her three years picking, she had seen a number of these women, their belongings stuffed into wagons heading for the towns and cities that sought out and transported black men to various crafts that could be practiced only when the weather permitted. The companies did not encourage the women to come—they did not want an influx of poor colored settlers in those towns—but the women came anyway and took jobs as domestics and farm helpers in the towns, and lived wherever housing was free or dirt cheap. But Pilate did not want a steady job in a town where a lot of colored people lived. All her encounters with Negroes who had established themselves in businesses or trades in those small midwestern towns had been unpleasant. Their wives did not like the trembling unhampered breasts under her dress, and told her so. And though the men saw many raggedy black children, Pilate was old enough to disgrace them. Besides, she wanted to keep moving.

Finally she was taken on by some pickers heading home, stopping for a week's work here and there, wherever they could find it. Again she took a man to bed, and again she was expelled. Only this time there was no polite but firm pronouncement, nor any generous share of profits. They simply left her one day, moved out while she was in the town buying thread. She got back to campground to find nothing but a dying fire, a bag of rocks, and her geography book propped up on a tree. They even took her tin cup.

She had six copper pennies, five rocks, the geography book, and two spools of black thread—heavyweight No. 30. Right there she knew she must decide on whether to get to Virginia or settle in a town where she would probably have to wear shoes. So she did both—the latter to make the former possible. With the six pennies, the book, the rocks, and the thread, she walked back to town. Black women worked in numbers at two places in that town: the laundry and, across the street from it, the hotel/ whorehouse. Pilate chose the laundry and walked in, saying to the three young girls elbow deep in water there, "Can I stay here tonight?"

"Nobody in here at night."

"I know. Can I stay?"

They shrugged. The next day Pilate was hired as a washer-woman at ten cents a day. She worked there, ate there, slept there, and saved her dimes. Her hands, well calloused from years of harvesting, were stripped of their toughness and became soft in the wash water. Before her hands could get the different but equally tough skin of a laundress, her knuckles split with the rubbing and wringing, and ran blood into the rinse tubs. She almost ruined an entire batch of sheets, but the other girls covered for her, giving the sheets a second rinse.

One day she noticed a train steaming away from the town. "Where does it go to?" she asked.

"South," they said.

"How much does it cost?"

They laughed. "They freight trains," they told her. Only two passenger cars, and no colored allowed.

"Well, how do colored people get where they want to go?"

"Ain't supposed to go nowhere," they said, "but if they do, have to go by wagon. Ask at the livery stable when the next wagon is going down. The livery people always know when somebody is getting ready to take off."

She did, and by the end of October, just before cold weather set in, she was on her way to West Virginia, which was close anyway, according to her geography book. When she got to Virginia itself, she realized that she didn't know in what part of the state to look for her people. There were more Negroes there than she'd ever seen, and the comfort she felt in their midst she kept all her life.

Pilate had learned, whenever she was asked her name, to give only her first name. The last name had a bad effect on people. Now she was forced to ask if anybody knew of a family called Dead. People frowned and said, "No, never heard of any such."

She was in Culpeper, Virginia, washing clothes in a hotel, when she learned that there was a colony of Negro farmers on an island off the coast of Virginia. They grew vegetables, had cattle, made whiskey, and sold a little tobacco. They did not mix much with other Negroes, but were respected by them and self-sustaining. And you could get to them only by boat. On a Sunday, she convinced the ferryman to take her there, when his work was done, in his skiff.

"What you want over there?" he asked.

"Work."

"You don't want to work over there," he said.

"Why not?"

"Them folks keep to theyselves too much."

"Take me. I'll pay."

"How much?"

"A nickel."

"Great Jesus! You on. Be here at nine-thirty."

There were twenty-five or thirty families on that island and when Pilate made it clear that she wasn't afraid of work, but didn't like the mainland and the confinement of town, she was taken in. She worked there for three months, hoeing, fishing, plowing, planting, and helping out at the stills. All she had to do, she thought, was keep her belly covered. And it was true. At sixteen now, she took a lover from one of the island families and managed to keep direct light from ever hitting her stomach. She also managed to get pregnant, and to the great consternation of the island women, who were convinced their menfolk were the most desirable on earth—which accounted for so much intermarrying among them—Pilate refused to marry the man, who was eager to take her for his wife. Pilate was afraid that she wouldn't be able to hide her stomach from a husband forever. And once he saw that uninterrupted flesh, he would respond the same way everybody else had. Yet, incredible as they found her decision, nobody asked her to leave. They watched over her and gave her fewer and lighter chores as her time drew near. When her baby was born, a girl, the two midwives in attendance were so preoccupied with what was going on between her legs they never even noticed her smooth balloon of a stomach.

The first thing the new mother looked for in her baby girl was the navel, which she was relieved to see. Remembering how she got the name that was folded in her ear, when the nine days' waiting was done she asked one of the women for a Bible. There was a hymnal, they said, but not a Bible on the island. Everybody who wanted to go to services had to go to the mainland.

"Can you tell me a nice name for a girl that's in the Bible?" Pilate asked.

"Oh, plenty," they said, and reeled off a score, from which she chose Rebecca and shortened it to Reba.

It was right after Reba was born that her father came to her again. Pilate had become extremely depressed and lonely after the birth. The baby's father was forbidden to see her, since she had not "healed" yet, and she spent some dark lonely hours along with the joyous ones with the baby. Clear as day, her father said, "Sing. Sing," and later he leaned in at the window and said, "You just can't fly on off and leave a body."

Pilate understood all of what he told her. To sing, which she did beautifully, relieved her gloom immediately. And she knew he was telling her to go back to Pennsylvania and collect what was left of the man she and Macon had murdered. (The fact that she had struck no blow was irrelevant. She was part of her brother's act, because, then, she and he were one.) When the child was six months old, she asked the mother of the baby's father to keep it, and left the island for Pennsylvania. They tried to discourage her because it was getting to be winter, but she paid them no attention.

A month later she returned with a sack, the contents of which she never discussed, which she added to her geography book and the rocks and the two spools of thread.

When Reba was two years old, Pilate was seized with restlessness. It was as if her geography book had marked her to roam the country, planting her feet in each pink, yellow, blue or green state. She left the island and began the wandering life that she kept up for the next twenty-some-odd years, and stopped only after Reba had a baby. No place was like the island ever again. Having had one long relationship with a man, she sought another, but no man was like that island man ever again either.

After a while, she stopped worrying about her stomach, and stopped trying to hide it. It occurred to her that although men fucked armless women, one-legged women, hunchbacks and blind women, drunken women, razor-toting women, midgets, small children, convicts, boys, sheep, dogs, goats, liver, each other, and even certain species of plants, they were terrified of fucking her—a woman with no navel. They froze at the sight of that belly that looked like a back; became limp even, or cold, if she happened to undress completely and walked straight toward them, showing them, deliberately, a stomach as blind as a knee.

"What are you? Some kinda *mer*maid?" one man had shouted, and reached hurriedly for his socks.

It isolated her. Already without family, she was further isolated from her people, for, except for the relative bliss on the island, every other resource was denied her: partnership in marriage, confessional friendship, and communal religion. Men frowned, women whispered and shoved their children behind them. Even a traveling side show would have rejected her, since her freak quality lacked that important ingredient—the grotesque. There was really nothing to see. Her defect, frightening and exotic as it was, was also a theatrical failure. It needed intimacy, gossip, and the time it took for curiosity to become drama.

Finally Pilate began to take offense. Although she was hampered by huge ignorances, but not in any way unintelligent, when she realized what her situation in the world was and would probably always be she threw away every assumption she had learned and began at zero. First off, she cut her hair. That was one thing she didn't want to have to think about anymore. Then she tackled the problem of trying to decide how she wanted to live and what was valuable to her. When am I happy and when am I sad and what is the difference? What do I need to know to stay alive? What is true in the world? Her mind traveled crooked streets and aimless goat paths, arriving sometimes at profundity, other times at the revelations of a three-year-old. Throughout this fresh, if common, pursuit of knowledge, one conviction crowned her efforts: since death held no terrors for her (she spoke often to the dead), she knew there was nothing to fear. That plus her alien's compassion for troubled people ripened her and—the consequence of the knowledge she had made up or acquired—kept her just barely within the boundaries of the elaborately socialized world of black people. Her dress might be outrageous to them, but her respect for other people's privacy—which they were all very intense about—was balancing. She stared at people, and in those days looking straight into another person's eyes was considered among black people the height of rudeness, an act acceptable only with and among children and certain kinds of outlaws—but she never made an impolite observation. And true to the palm oil that flowed in her veins, she never had a visitor to whom she did not offer food before one word of conversation—business or social—began. She laughed but never smiled and in 1963, when she was sixty-eight years old, she had not shed a tear since Circe had brought her cherry jam for breakfast.

She gave up, apparently, all interest in table manners or hygiene, but acquired a deep concern for and about human relationships. Those twelve years in Montour County, where she had been treated gently by a father and a brother, and where she herself was in a position to help farm animals under her care, had taught her a preferable kind of behavior. Preferable to that of the men who called her mermaid and the women who swept up her footprints or put mirrors on her door.

She was a natural healer, and among quarreling drunks and fighting women she could hold her own, and sometimes mediated a peace that lasted a good bit longer than it should have because it was administered by someone not like them. But most important, she paid close attention to her mentor—the father who appeared before her sometimes and told her things. After Reba was born, he no longer came to Pilate dressed as he had been on the woods' edge and in the cave, when she and Macon had left Circe's house. Then he had worn the coveralls and heavy shoes he was shot in. Now he came in a white shirt, a blue collar, and a brown peaked cap. He wore no shoes (they were tied together and slung over his shoulder), probably because his feet hurt, since he rubbed his toes a lot as he sat near her bed or on the porch, or rested against the side of the still. Along with winemaking, cooking whiskey became the way Pilate began to make her steady living. That skill allowed her more freedom hour by hour and day by day than any other work a woman of no means whatsoever and no inclination to make love for money could choose. Once settled in as a small-time bootlegger in the colored section of a town, she had only occasional police or sheriff problems, for she allowed none of the activities that often accompanied wine houses—women, gambling—and she more often than not refused to let her customers drink what they bought from her on the premises. She made and sold liquor. Period.

After Reba grew up and began to live from one orgasm to another, taking time out to produce one child, Hagar, Pilate thought it might be time for a change. Not because of Reba, who was quite content with the life her mother and she lived, but because of her granddaughter. Hagar was prissy. She hated, even as a two-year-old, dirt and disorganization. At three she was already vain and beginning to be proud. She liked pretty clothes. Astonished as Pilate and Reba were by her wishes, they enjoyed trying to fulfill them. They spoiled her, and she, as a favor to their indulgence, hid as best she could the fact that they embarrassed her.

Pilate decided to find her brother, if he was still alive, for the child, Hagar, needed family, people, a life very different from what she and Reba could offer, and if she remembered anything about Macon, he would be different. Prosperous, conventional, more like the things and people Hagar seemed to admire. In addition, Pilate wanted to make peace between them. She asked her father where he was, but he just rubbed his feet and shook his head. So for the first time, Pilate went voluntarily to the police, who sent her to the Red Cross, who sent her to the Salvation Army, who sent her to the Society of Friends, who sent her back to the Salvation Army, who wrote to their command posts in large cities from New York to St. Louis and from Detroit to Louisiana and asked them to look in the telephone directory, where in fact one captain's secretary found him listed. Pilate was surprised that they were successful, but the captain was not, because there could hardly be many people with such a name.

They made the trip in style (one train and two buses), for Pilate had a lot of money; the crash of 1929 had produced so many buyers of cheap home brew she didn't even need the collection the Salvation Army took up for her. She arrived with suitcases, a green sack, a full-grown daughter, and a granddaughter, and found her brother truculent, inhospitable, embarrassed, and unforgiving. Pilate would have moved on immediately except for her brother's wife, who was dying of lovelessness then, and seemed to be dying of it now as she sat at the table across from her sister-in-law listening to her life story, which Pilate was making deliberately long to keep Ruth's mind off Hagar.

Chapter 6

"I took her home. She was standing in the middle of the room when I got there. So I just took her home. Pitiful. Really pitiful."

Milkman shrugged. He didn't want to talk about Hagar, but it was a way to sit Guitar down and get around to asking him something else.

"What'd you do to her?" asked Guitar.

"What'd I do to *her*? You saw her with a butcher knife and you ask me that?"

"I mean before. That's a messed-up lady."

"I did what you do to some woman every six months—called the whole thing off."

"I don't believe you."

"It's the truth."

"No. It had to be something more."

"You calling me a liar?"

"Take it any way you want. But that girl's hurt—and the hurt came from you."

"What's the matter with you? You've been watching her try

to kill me for months and I never laid a hand on her. Now you sit there worried about her. All of a sudden you're police. You've been wearing a halo a lot lately. You got a white robe too?"

"What's that supposed to mean?"

"It means I'm tired of being criticized by you. I know we don't see eye to eye on a lot of things. I know you think I'm lazy—not serious, you say—but if we're friends . . . I don't meddle you, do I?"

"No. Not at all."

Several minutes passed while Milkman played with his beer and Guitar sipped tea. They were sitting in Mary's Place on a Sunday afternoon a few days after Hagar's latest attempt on his life.

"You're not smoking?" asked Milkman.

"No. I quit. Feel a hell of a lot better too." There was another pause before Guitar continued. "You ought to stop yourself."

Milkman nodded. "Yeah. If I stay around you I will. I'll stop smoking, fucking, drinking—everything. I'll take up a secret life and hanging out with Empire State."

Guitar frowned. "Now who's meddling?"

Milkman sighed and looked straight at his friend. "I am. I want to know why you were running around with Empire State last Christmas."

"He was in trouble. I helped him."

"That's all?"

"What else?"

"I don't know what else. But I know there is something else. Now, if it's something I can't know, okay, say so. But something's going on with you. And I'd like to know what it is."

Guitar didn't answer.

"We've been friends a long time, Guitar. There's nothing you don't know about me. I can tell you anything—whatever our differences, I know I can trust you. But for some time now it's been a one-way street. You know what I mean? I talk to you, but you don't talk to me. You don't think I can be trusted?"

"I don't know if you can or not."

"Try me."

"I can't. Other people are involved."

"Then don't tell me about other people; tell me about you."

Guitar looked at him for a long time. Maybe, he thought. Maybe I can trust you. Maybe not, but I'll risk it anyway because one day . . .

"Okay," he said aloud, "but you have to know that what I tell you can't go any further. And if it does, you'll be dropping a rope around my neck. Now do you still want to know it?"

"Yeah."

"You sure?"

"I'm sure."

Guitar poured some more hot water over his tea. He looked into his cup for a minute while the leaves settled slowly to the bottom. "I suppose you know that white people kill black people from time to time, and most folks shake their heads and say, 'Eh, eh, eh, ain't that a shame?' "

Milkman raised his eyebrows. He thought Guitar was going to let him in on some deal he had going. But he was slipping into his race bag. He was speaking slowly, as though each word had to count, and as though he were listening carefully to his own words. "I can't suck my teeth or say 'Eh, eh, eh.' I had to do something. And the only thing left to do is balance it; keep things on an even keel. Any man, any woman, or any child is good for five to seven generations of heirs before they're bred out. So every death is the death of five to seven generations. You can't stop them from killing us, from trying to get rid of us. And each time they succeed, they get rid of five to seven generations. I help keep the numbers the same.

"There is a society. It's made up of a few men who are willing to take some risks. They don't initiate anything; they don't even choose. They are as indifferent as rain. But when a Negro child, Negro woman, or Negro man is killed by whites and nothing is done about it by *their* law and *their* courts, this society selects a similar victim at random, and they execute him or her in a similar manner if they can. If the Negro was hanged, they hang; if a Negro was burnt, they burn; raped and murdered, they rape and murder. If they can. If they can't do it precisely in the same manner, they do it any way they can, but they do it. They call themselves the Seven Days. They are made up of seven men. Always seven and only seven. If one of them dies or leaves or is no longer effective, another is chosen. Not right away, because that kind of choosing takes time. But they don't seem to be in a hurry. Their secret is time. To take the time, to last. Not to grow; that's dangerous because you might become known. They don't write their names in toilet stalls or brag to women. Time and silence. Those are their weapons, and they go on forever.

"It got started in 1920, when that private from Georgia was killed after his balls were cut off and after that veteran was blinded when he came home from France in World War I. And it's been operating ever since. I am one of them now."

Milkman had held himself very still all the time Guitar spoke. Now he felt tight, shriveled, and cold.

"You? You're going to kill people?"

"Not people. White people."

"But why?"

"I just told you. It's necessary; it's got to be done. To keep the ratio the same."

"And if it isn't done? If it just goes on the way it has?"

"Then the world is a zoo, and I can't live in it."

"Why don't you just hunt down the ones who did the killing? Why kill innocent people? Why not just those who did it?"

"It doesn't matter who did it. Each and every one of them could do it. So you just get any one of them. There are no innocent white people, because every one of them is a potential nigger-killer, if not an actual one. You think Hitler surprised them? You think just because they went to war they thought he was a freak? Hitler's the most natural white man in the world. He killed Jews and Gypsies because he didn't have us. Can you see those Klansmen shocked by him? No, you can't."

"But people who lynch and slice off people's balls—they're crazy, Guitar, crazy."

"Every time somebody does a thing like that to one of us,

they say the people who did it were crazy or ignorant. That's like saying they were drunk. Or constipated. Why isn't cutting a man's eyes out, cutting his nuts off, the kind of thing you never get too drunk or ignorant to do? Too crazy to do? Too constipated to do? And more to the point, how come Negroes, the craziest, most ignorant people in America, don't get that crazy and that ignorant? No. White people are unnatural. As a race they are unnatural. And it takes a strong effort of the will to overcome an unnatural enemy."

"What about the nice ones? Some whites made sacrifices for Negroes. Real sacrifices."

"That just means there are one or two natural ones. But they haven't been able to stop the killing either. They are outraged, but that doesn't stop it. They might even speak out, but that doesn't stop it either. They might even inconvenience themselves, but the killing goes on and on. So will we."

"You're missing the point. There're not just one or two. There're a lot."

"Are there? Milkman, if Kennedy got drunk and bored and was sitting around a potbellied stove in Mississippi, he might join a lynching party just for the hell of it. Under those circumstances his unnaturalness would surface. But I know I wouldn't join one no matter how drunk I was or how bored, and I know you wouldn't either, nor any black man I know or ever heard tell of. Ever. In any world, at any time, just get up and go find somebody white to slice up. But they *can* do it. And they don't even do it for profit, which is why they do most things. They do it for fun. Unnatural."

"What about . . ." Milkman searched his memory for some white person who had shown himself unequivocally supportive of Negroes. "Schweitzer. Albert Schweitzer. Would he do it?"

"In a minute. He didn't care anything about those Africans. They could have been rats. He was in a laboratory testing *himself*—proving he could work on human dogs."

"What about Eleanor Roosevelt?"

"I don't know about the women. I can't say what their women would do, but I do remember that picture of those white mothers holding up their babies so they could get a good look at some black men burning on a tree. So I have my suspicions about Eleanor Roosevelt. But *none* about Mr. Roosevelt. You could've taken him and his wheelchair and put him in a small dusty town in Alabama and given him some tobacco, a checkerboard, some whiskey, and a rope and he'd have done it too. What I'm saying is, under certain conditions they would *all* do it. And under the same circumstances we would not. So it doesn't matter that some of them *haven't* done it. I listen. I read. And now I know that they know it too. They know they are unnatural. Their writers and artists have been saying it for years. Telling them they are unnatural, telling them they are depraved. They call it tragedy. In the movies they call it adventure. It's just depravity that they try to make glorious, natural. But it ain't. The disease they have is in their blood, in the structure of their chromosomes."

"You can prove this, I guess. Scientifically?"

"No."

"Shouldn't you be able to prove it before you act on something like that?"

"Did they prove anything scientifically about us before they killed us? No. They killed us first and then tried to get some scientific proof about why we should die."

"Wait a minute, Guitar. If they are as bad, as unnatural, as you say, why do you want to be like them? Don't you want to be better than they are?"

"I am better."

"But now you're doing what the worst of them do."

"Yes, but I am reasonable."

"Reasonable? How?"

"I am not, one, having fun; two, trying to gain power or public attention or money or land; three, angry at anybody."

"You're not angry? You must be!"

"Not at all. I hate doing it. I'm afraid to do it. It's hard to do it when you aren't angry or drunk or doped up or don't have a personal grudge against the person."

"I can't see how it helps. I can't see how it helps anybody."

"I told you. Numbers. Balance. Ratio. And the earth, the land."

"I'm not understanding you."

"The earth is soggy with black people's blood. And before us Indian blood. Nothing can cure them, and if it keeps on there won't be any of us left and there won't be any land for those who are left. So the numbers have to remain static."

"But there are more of them than us."

"Only in the West. But still the ratio can't widen in their favor."

"But you should want everybody to know that the society exists. Then maybe that would help stop it. What's the secrecy for?"

"To keep from getting caught."

"Can't you even let other Negroes know about it? I mean to give us hope?"

"No."

"Why not?"

"Betrayal. The possibility of betrayal."

"Well, let *them* know. Let white people know. Like the Mafia or the Klan; frighten them into behaving."

"You're talking foolishness. How can you let one group know and not the other? Besides, we are not like them. The Mafia is unnatural. So is the Klan. One kills for money, the other kills for fun. And they have huge profits and protection at their disposal. We don't. But it's not about other people knowing. We don't even tell the victims. We just whisper to him, 'Your Day has come.' The beauty of what we do is its secrecy, its smallness. The fact that nobody needs the unnatural satisfaction of talking about it. Telling about it. We don't discuss it among ourselves, the details. We just get an assignment. If the Negro was killed on a Wednesday, the Wednesday man takes it; if he was killed on Monday, the Monday man takes that one. And we just notify one another when it's completed, not how or who. And if it ever gets to be too much, like it was for Robert Smith, we do *that* rather than crack and tell somebody. Like Porter. It was getting him down. They thought somebody would have to take over his day. He just needed a rest and he's okay now."

Milkman stared at his friend and then let the spasm he had been holding back run through him. "I can't buy it, Guitar."

"I know that."

"There's too much wrong with it."

"Tell me."

"Well, for one thing, you'll get caught eventually."

"Maybe. But if I'm caught I'll just die earlier than I'm supposed to—not better than I'm supposed to. And how I die or when doesn't interest me. What I die *for* does. It's the same as what I live for. Besides, if I'm caught they'll accuse me and kill me for one crime, maybe two, never for all. And there are still six other days in the week. We've been around for a long long time. And believe me, we'll be around for a long long time to come."

"You can't marry."

"No."

"Have children."

"No."

"What kind of life is that?"

"Very satisfying."

"There's no love in it."

"No love? No love? Didn't you hear me? What I'm doing ain't about hating white people. It's about loving us. About loving you. My whole life is love."

"Man, you're confused."

"Am I? When those concentration camp Jews hunt down Nazis, are they hating Nazis or loving dead Jews?"

"It's not the same thing."

"Only because they have money and publicity."

"No; because they turn them over to the courts. You kill and you don't kill the killers. You kill innocent people."

"I told you there are no—"

"And you don't correct a thing by—"

"We poor people, Milkman. I work at an auto plant. The rest

of us barely eke out a living. Where's the money, the state, the country to finance our justice? You say Jews try their catches in a court. Do we have a court? Is there one courthouse in one city in the country where a jury would convict them? There are places right now where a Negro still can't testify against a white man. Where the judge, the jury, the court, are legally bound to ignore anything a Negro has to say. What that means is that a black man is a victim of a crime only when a white man says he is. Only then. If there was anything like or near justice or courts when a cracker kills a Negro, there wouldn't have to be no Seven Days. But there ain't; so we are. And we do it without money, without support, without costumes, without newspapers, without senators, without lobbyists, and without illusions!"

"You sound like that red-headed Negro named X. Why don't you join him and call yourself Guitar X?"

"X, Bains—what difference does it make? I don't give a damn about names."

"You miss his point. His point is to let white people know you don't accept your slave name."

"I don't give a shit what white people know or even think. Besides, I do accept it. It's part of who I am. Guitar is *my* name. Bains is the slave master's name. And I'm all of that. Slave names don't bother me; but slave status does."

"And knocking off white folks changes your slave status?"

"Believe it."

"Does it do anything for my slave status?"

Guitar smiled. "Well, doesn't it?"

"Hell, no." Milkman frowned. "Am I going to live any longer because you all read the newspaper and then ambush some poor old white man?"

"It's not about you living longer. It's about how you live and why. It's about whether your children can make other children. It's about trying to make a world where one day white people will think before they lynch."

"Guitar, none of that shit is going to change how I live or how any other Negro lives. What you're doing is crazy. And something else: it's a habit. If you do it enough, you can do it to anybody. You know what I mean? A torpedo is a torpedo, I don't care what his reasons. You can off anybody you don't like. You can off me."

"We don't off Negroes."

"You hear what you said? *Negroes*. Not Milkman. Not 'No, I can't touch *you*, Milkman,' but 'We don't off Negroes.' Shit, man, suppose you all change your parliamentary rules?"

"The Days are the Days. It's been that way a long time."

Milkman thought about that. "Any other young dudes in it? Are all the others older? You the only young one?"

"Why?"

"Cause young dudes are subject to change the rules."

"You worried about yourself, Milkman?" Guitar looked amused.

"No. Not really." Milkman put his cigarette out and reached for another one. "Tell me, what's your day?"

"Sunday. I'm the Sunday man."

Milkman rubbed the ankle of his short leg. "I'm scared for you, man."

"That's funny. I'm scared for you too."

Chapter 7

Truly landlocked people know they are. Know the occasional Bitter Creek or Powder River that runs through Wyoming; that the large tidy Salt Lake of Utah is all they have of the sea and that they must content themselves with *bank*, *shore*, and *beach* because they cannot claim a coast. And having none, seldom dream of flight. But the people living in the Great Lakes region are confused by their place on the country's edge—an edge that is border but not coast. They seem to be able to live a long time believing, as coastal people do, that they are at the frontier where final exit and total escape are the only journeys left. But those five Great Lakes which the St. Lawrence feeds with memories of the sea are themselves landlocked, in spite of the wandering river that connects them to the Atlantic. Once the people of the lake region discover this, the longing to leave becomes acute, and a break from the area, therefore, is necessarily dream-bitten, but necessary nonetheless. It might be an appetite for other streets, other slants of light. Or a yearning to be surrounded by strangers. It may even be a wish to hear the solid click of a door closing behind their backs.

For Milkman it was the door click. He wanted to feel the heavy white door on Not Doctor Street close behind him and know that he might be hearing the catch settle into its groove for the last time.

"You'll own it all. All of it. You'll be free. Money is freedom, Macon. The only real freedom there is."

"I know, Daddy, I know. But I have to get away just the same. I'm not leaving the country; I just want to be on my own. Get a job on my own, live on my own. You did it at sixteen. Guitar at seventeen. Everybody. I'm still living at home, working for you—not because I sweated for the job, but because I'm your son. I'm over thirty years old."

"I need you here, Macon. If you were going to go, you should have gone five years ago. Now I've come to depend on you." It was difficult for him to beg, but he came as close to it as he could.

"Just a year. One year. Stake me for a year and let me go. When I come back, I'll work a year for nothing and pay you back."

"It's not the money. It's you being here, taking care of this. Taking care of all I'm going to leave you. Getting to know it, know how to handle it."

"Let me use some of it now, when I need it. Don't do like Pilate, put it in a green sack and hang it from the wall so nobody can get it. Don't make me wait until—"

"What did you say?" As suddenly as an old dog drops a shoe when he smells raw meat, Macon Dead dropped his pleading look and flared his nostrils with some new interest.

"I said give me a little bit—"

"No. Not that. About Pilate and a sack."

"Yeah. Her sack. You've seen it, haven't you? That green sack she got hanging from the ceiling? She calls it her inheritance. You can't get from one side of the room to the other without cracking your head on it. Don't you remember it?"

Macon was blinking rapidly, but he managed to calm himself and say, "I've never set foot in Pilate's house in my life. I looked in there once, but it was dark and I didn't see anything hanging down from the ceiling. When's the last time you saw it?"

"Maybe nine or ten months ago. What about it?"

"You think it's still there?"

"Why wouldn't it be?"

"You say it's green. You know for sure it's green?"

"Yeah, green. Grass green. What is it? What's bothering you?"

"She told you it was her inheritance, huh?" Macon was smiling, but so craftily that Milkman could hardly recognize it as a smile.

"No. She didn't; Hagar did. I was walking across the room toward the . . . uh . . . toward the other side and I'm tall enough for it to be in my way. I bumped my head on it. Made a hickey too. When I asked Hagar what it was she said, 'Pilate's inheritance.' "

"And it made a hickey on your head?"

"Yeah. Felt like bricks. What're you going to do, sue her?"

"You had any lunch?"

"It's ten-thirty, Daddy."

"Go to Mary's. Get us a couple of orders of barbecue. Meet me in the park across from Mercy. We'll eat lunch there."

"Daddy . . ."

"Go on now. Do what I say. Go on, Macon."

They met in the little public park across the street from Mercy Hospital. It was full of pigeons, students, drunks, dogs, squirrels, children, trees, and secretaries. The two colored men sat down on an iron bench a little away from the most crowded part, but not the edge. They were very well dressed, too well dressed to be eating pork out of a box, but on that warm September day it seemed natural, a perfect addition to the mellowness that pervaded the park.

Milkman was curious about his father's agitation, but not alarmed. So much had been going on, so many changes. Besides, he knew whatever was making his father fidget and look around to see if anyone was too near had to do with something his father wanted, not something he wanted himself. He could look at his father coolly now that he had sat on that train and listened to his mother's sad sad song. Her words still danced around in his head. "What harm did I do you on my knees?"

Deep down in that pocket where his heart hid, he felt used. Somehow everybody was using him for something or as something. Working out some scheme of their own on him, making him the subject of their dreams of wealth, or love, or martyrdom. Everything they did seemed to be about him, yet nothing he wanted was part of it. Once before he had had a long talk with his father, and it ended up with his being driven further from his mother. Now he had had a confidential talk with his mother, only to discover that before he was born, before the first nerve end had formed in his mother's womb, he was the subject of great controversy and strife. And now the one woman who claimed to love him more than life, more than her life, actually loved him more than *his* life, for she had spent half a year trying to relieve him of it. And Guitar. The one sane and constant person he knew had flipped, had ripped open and was spilling blood and foolishness instead of conversation. He was a fit companion for Empire State. So now he waited with curiosity, but without excitement or hope, for this latest claim.

"Listen to me. Just eat your meat and listen to me. Don't interrupt, because I might lose my train of thought.

"A long time ago, I told you about when I was a boy on the farm. About Pilate and me. About my father getting killed. I never finished the story; I never told you all of it. The part I left out was about me and Pilate. I tried to keep you away from her and said she was a snake. Now I'm going to tell you why."

A red ball rolled to his feet, and Macon picked it up and threw it back to a little girl. He made sure she was safely back in her mother's view before he began his story.

Six days after the first Macon Dead died, his children, a twelve-year-old Pilate and a sixteen-year-old Macon Dead, found themselves homeless. Bewildered and grieving, they went to the house of the closest colored person they knew: Circe, the midwife who had delivered them both and who was there when their mother died and when Pilate was named. She worked in a large house—a mansion—outside Danville, for a family of what was then called gentlemen farmers. The orphans called to Circe from the vegetable garden early in the morning as soon as they saw the smoke from the cook stove rising. Circe let them in, pressing her hands together with relief, and saying how glad she was to see them alive. She hadn't known what had happened to them after the killing. Macon explained that he had buried his father himself, down by that part of the stream on Lincoln's Heaven where they used to fish together, the place where he had caught that nine-pound trout. The grave was shallower than it ought to be, but he'd piled rocks there.

Circe told them to stay with her until they could all figure out what to do, someplace for them to go. She hid them in that house easily. There were rooms the family seldom went into, but if they weren't safe, she was prepared to share her own room (which was off limits to everybody in the house). It was small, though, so they agreed to stay in a pair of rooms on the third floor that were used only for storage. Circe would bring them food, water to wash in, and she would empty their slop jar.

Macon asked if they couldn't work there; would her mistress take them on as kitchen help, yard help, anything?

Circe bit her tongue trying to get the words out. "You crazy? You say you saw the men what killed him. You think they don't know you saw them? If they kill a growed man, what you think they do to you? Be sensible. We got to plan and figure this thing out."

Macon and Pilate stayed there two weeks, not a day longer. He had been working hard on a farm since he was five or six years old and she was born wild. They couldn't bear the stillness, the walls, the boredom of having nothing to do but wait for the day's excitement of eating and going to the toilet. Anything was better than walking all day on carpeting, than eating the soft bland food white people ate, than having to sneak a look at the sky from behind ivory curtains.

Pilate began to cry the day Circe brought her white toast and cherry jam for breakfast. She wanted her own cherries, from her own cherry tree, with stems and seeds; not some too-sweet mashed mush. She thought she would die if she couldn't hold her mouth under Ulysses S. Grant's teat and squirt the warm milk into her mouth, or pull a tomato off its vine and eat it where she stood. Craving certain specific foods had almost devastated her. That, plus the fact that her earlobe was sore from the operation she had performed on herself, had her near hysteria. Before they left the farm, she'd taken the scrap of brown paper with her name on it from the Bible, and after a long time trying to make up her mind between a snuffbox and a sunbonnet with blue ribbons on it, she took the little brass box that had belonged to her mother. Her miserable days in the mansion were spent planning how to make an earring out of the box which would house her name. She found a piece of wire, but couldn't get it through. Finally, after much begging and whining, Circe got a Negro blacksmith to solder a bit of gold wire to the box. Pilate rubbed her ear until it was numb, burned the end of the wire, and punched it through her earlobe. Macon fastened the wire ends into a knot, but the lobe was swollen and running pus. At Circe's instruction she put cobwebs on it to draw the pus out and stop the bleeding.

On the night of the day she cried so about the cherries, the two of them decided that when her ear got better, they would leave. It was too much of a hardship on Circe anyway for them to stay there, and if her white folks found out about them, they might let her go.

One morning Circe climbed all the way to the third floor with a covered plate of scrapple and found two empty rooms. They didn't even take a blanket. Just a knife and a tin cup.

The first day out was joyous for them. They ate raspberries and apples; they took off their shoes and let the dewy grass and sun-warmed dirt soothe their feet. At night they slept in a hay-stack, so grateful for open air even the field mice and the ticks were welcome bedmates.

The next day was pleasant but less exciting. They bathed in a curve of the Susquehanna and then wandered in a southerly direction, keeping to fields, woods, stream beds, and little-used paths, headed, they thought, for Virginia, where Macon believed they had people.

On the third day they woke to find a man that looked just like their father sitting on a stump not fifty yards away. He was not looking at them; he was just sitting there. They would have called out to him or run toward him except he was staring right past them with such distance in his eyes, he frightened them. So they ran away. All day long at various intervals they saw him: staring down into duck ponds; framed by the Y of a sycamore tree; shading his eyes from the sun as he peered over a rock at the wide valley floor beneath them. Each time they saw him they backed off and went in the opposite direction. Now the land itself, the only one they knew and knew intimately, began to terrify them. The sun was blazing down, the air was sweet, but every leaf that the wind lifted, every rustle of a pheasant hen in a clump of ryegrass, sent needles of fear through their veins. The cardinals, the gray squirrels, the garden snakes, the butter-flies, the ground hogs and rabbits—all the affectionate things that had peopled their lives ever since they were born became ominous signs of a presence that was searching for them, follow-ing them. Even the river's babbling sounded like the call of a liquid throat waiting, just waiting for them. That was in the daylight. How much more terrible was the night.

Just before dark, when the sun had left them alone, when they were coming out of some woods looking around for the crest of the hill where they could see, perhaps, a farm, an aban-doned shed—anyplace where they could spend the night—they saw a cave, and at its mouth stood their father. This time he motioned for them to follow him. Faced with the choice of the limitless nighttime woods and a man who looked like their father, they chose the latter. After all, if it was their father, he wouldn't hurt them, would he?

Slowly they approached the mouth of the cave, following their father's beckoning hand and his occasional backward glance.

They looked into the cave and saw nothing but a great maw of darkness. Their father had disappeared. If they stayed near the lip, they thought, it was as good a place as any to spend the night; perhaps he was simply looking out for them, showing them what to do and where to go. They made themselves as comfortable as they could on a rock formation that jutted out like a shelf from a hip-high mass of stone. There was nothing behind them that they could see and only the certainty of bats to disturb them. Yet it was nothing to that other darkness—outside.

Toward morning, Macon woke from a light and fitful sleep, with a terrific urge to relieve his bowels, the consequence of three days' diet of wild fruit. Without waking his sister, he climbed off the shelf, and shy of squatting on the crown of a hill in a new sun, he walked a little farther back into the cave. When he was finished, the darkness had disintegrated somewhat, and he saw, some fifteen feet in front of him, a man stirring in his sleep. Macon tried to button his pants and get away without waking him, but the leaves and twigs crunching under his feet pulled the man all the way out of his sleep. He raised his head, turned over, and smiled. Macon saw that he was very old, very white, and his smile was awful.

Macon stepped back, one hand outstretched behind him, thinking all the while of how his father's body had twitched and danced for whole minutes in the dirt. He touched the cave's wall and a piece of it gave way in his hand. Closing his fingers around it, he threw it at the grinning man's head, hitting him just above the eye. Blood spurted out and knocked the smile off the pale face, but did not stop the man from coming and coming, all the time wiping blood from his face and smearing it on his shirt.

Macon got hold of another rock, but missed that time. The man kept coming.

The scream that boomed down the cave tunnel and woke the bats came just when Macon thought he had taken his last living breath. The bleeding man turned toward the direction of the scream and looked at the colored girl long enough for Macon to pull out his knife and bring it down on the old man's back. He crashed forward, then turned his head to look up at them. His mouth moved and he mumbled something that sounded like "What for?" Macon stabbed him again and again until he stopped moving his mouth, stopped trying to talk, and stopped jumping and twitching on the ground.

Panting with the exertion of slashing through an old man's rib cage, Macon ran back to get the blanket the man had been sleeping on. He wanted the dead man to disappear, to be covered, hidden, to be gone. When he snatched the blanket, a large tarpaulin came with it and he saw three boards positioned across what looked like a shallow pit. He paused and then kicked the boards aside. Underneath were little gray bags, their necks tied with wire, arranged like nest eggs. Macon picked one of them up and was amazed at its weight.

"Pilate," he called. "Pilate."

But she was growing roots where she stood, and staring open-mouthed at the dead man. Macon had to pull her by the arm over to the hole where the bags lay. After some difficulty with the wire (he ended up having to use his teeth), he got one open and shook the gold nuggets it held out into the leaves and twigs that lay on the floor of the cave.

"Gold," he whispered, and immediately, like a burglar out on his first job, stood up to pee.

Life, safety, and luxury fanned out before him like the tail-spread of a peacock, and as he stood there trying to distinguish each delicious color, he saw the dusty boots of his father standing just on the other side of the shallow pit.

"It *is* Papa!" said Pilate. And as if in answer to her recognition, he took a deep breath, rolled his eyes back, and whispered, "Sing. Sing," in a hollow voice before he melted away again.

Pilate darted around the cave calling him, looking for him, while Macon piled the sacks of gold into the tarpaulin.

"Let's go, Pilate. Let's get out of here."

"We can't take that." She pointed a finger at his bundle.

"What? Not take it? You lost your mind?"

"That's stealing. We killed a man. They'll be after us, all over. If we take his money, then they'll think that's why we did it. We got to leave it, Macon. We can't get caught with no bags of money."

"This ain't money; it's gold. It'll keep us for life, Pilate. We can get us another farm. We can—"

"Leave it, Macon! Leave it! Let them find it just where it was!" Then she began to shout, "Papa! Papa!"

Macon slapped her and the little brass box dangled on her ear. She cupped it in her hands for a moment and then leaped on her brother like an antelope. They fought right there in front of the dead man's staring eyes. Pilate was almost as strong as Macon, but no real match for him, and he probably would have beaten her unconscious had she not got his knife, not yet dry from the old man's blood, and held it ready for his heart.

Macon stood very still and watched her eyes. He began calling her ugly names, but she didn't answer. He backed out of the cave and walked a little distance away.

All day he waited for her to come out. All day she stayed there. When night came he just sat, at the foot of a tree, unafraid of all the night things that had terrified him before, eyes wide open, waiting for her to stick her woolly head out of the cave. There was no sound from her direction and he waited the whole night. At dawn he crept forward a foot at a time, hoping he would catch her asleep. Just then he heard some dogs and knew hunters were walking nearby. He ran as fast as he could through the woods until he couldn't hear the dogs anymore.

Another day and a night he spent trying to work his way back to the cave and avoid the hunters if they were still about. Finally he got there, three days and two nights later. Inside the cave the dead man was still looking placidly up at him, but the tarpaulin and the gold were gone.

The secretaries went away. So did the children and the dogs. Only the pigeons, the drunks, and the trees were left in the little park.

Milkman had eaten almost none of his barbecue. He was watching his father's face, shining with perspiration and the emotions of memory.

"She took it, Macon. After all that, she took the gold."

"How do you know? You didn't see her take it," said Milkman.

"The tarpaulin was green." Macon Dead rubbed his hands together. "Pilate came to this city in 1930. Two years later they call back all the gold. I figured she spent it all in the twenty or so years since I'd seen her, since she was living like poor trash when she got here. It was natural for me to believe she'd got rid of it all. Now you tell me she got a green sack full of something hard enough to give you a hickey on your head when you bumped into it. That's the gold, boy. That's it!"

He turned to his son full face and licked his lips. "Macon, get it and you can have half of it; go wherever you want. Get it. For both of us. Please get it, son. Get the gold."

Chapter 8

Every night now Guitar was seeing little scraps of Sunday dresses—white and purple, powder blue, pink and white, lace and voile, velvet and silk, cotton and satin, eyelet and grosgrain. The scraps stayed with him all night and he remembered Magdalene called Lena and Corinthians bending in the wind to catch the heart-red pieces of velvet that had floated under the gaze of Mr. Robert Smith. Only Guitar's scraps were different. The bits of Sunday dresses that he saw did not fly; they hung in the air quietly, like the whole notes in the last measure of an Easter hymn.

Four little colored girls had been blown out of a church, and his mission was to approximate as best he could a similar death of four little white girls some Sunday, since he was the Sunday man. He couldn't do it with a piece of wire, or a switchblade. For this he needed explosives, or guns, or hand grenades. And that would take money. He knew that the assignments of the Days would more and more be the killing of white people in groups, since more and more Negroes were being killed in groups. The single, solitary death was going rapidly out of fashion, and the Days might as well prepare themselves for it.

So when Milkman came to him with a proposal to steal and share a cache of gold, Guitar smiled. "Gold?" He could hardly believe it.

"Gold."

"Nobody got gold, Milkman."

"Pilate does."

"It's against the law to have gold."

"That's why she got it. She can't use it, and she can't report its being stolen since she wasn't supposed to have it in the first place."

"How do we get rid of it—get greenbacks for it?"

"Leave that to my father. He knows bank people who know other bank people. They'll give him legal tender for it."

"Legal tender." Guitar laughed softly. "How much legal tender will it bring?"

"That's what we have to find out."

"What's the split?"

"Three ways."

"Your papa know that?"

"Not yet. He thinks it's two ways."

"When you gonna tell him?"

"Afterwards."

"Will he go for it?"

"How can he *not* go for it?"

"When do we get it?"

"Whenever we want to."

Guitar spread his palm. "My man." Milkman slapped his hand. "Legal tender. Legal tender. I love it. Sounds like a virgin bride." Guitar rubbed the back of his neck and lifted his face to the sun in a gesture of expansiveness and luxury.

"Now we have to come up with something. A way to get it," said Milkman.

"Be a breeze. A cool cool breeze," Guitar continued, smiling at the sun, his eyes closed as though to ready himself for the gold by trying out a little bit of the sun's.

"A breeze?" Now that Guitar was completely enthusiastic, Milkman's own excitement was blunted. Something perverse made him not want to hand the whole score to his friend on a platter. There should be some difficulty, some complication in this adventure. "We just walk over there and snatch it off the wall, right? And if Pilate or Reba say anything, we just knock them out the way. That what you have in mind?" He summoned as much irony as he could into his voice.

"Defeatism. That's what you got. Defeatism."

"Common sense is what I got."

"Come on, old dude. Your pappy give you a good thing and you want to fight it."

"I'm not fighting. I just want to get out alive and breathing so what I snatch does me some good. I don't want to have to give it to a brain surgeon to pull an ice pick out the back of my head."

"Can't no ice pick get through the back of your head, nigger."

"Can get through my heart."

"What you doin with a heart anyway?"

"Pumping blood. And I'd like to keep on pumping it."

"Okay. We got us a problem. A little bitty problem: how can two big men get a fifty-pound sack out of a house with three women in it—women who all together don't weigh three hundred pounds."

"What you have to weigh to pull a trigger?"

"What trigger? Nobody in that house got a gun."

"You don't know what Hagar's got."

"Look, Milk. She's been trying to kill you for almost a year. Used everything she could get her hands on and never once did she use a gun."

"So? Maybe she's thinking. Wait till next month."

"Next month she'll be too late, won't she?" Guitar leaned his head over to the side and smiled at Milkman, an engaging boyish smile. Milkman hadn't seen him this relaxed and cordial in a long

long time. He wondered if that's why he had let him in on it. Obviously he could pull it off alone, but maybe he wanted to see Guitar warm and joking again, his face open and smiling instead of with that grim reaper look.

They met again on Sunday on route 6 away from the colored part of town. A road consisting of used-car lots, Dairy Queens, and White Castle hamburger places. It was empty of shoppers that morning—nothing but the occasional sound of automobiles breaking the graveyard silence of the cars in the lots, lined up like tombstones.

Since that last conversation—the important one in which Guitar explained his work, not the brief chancy talks they'd had afterward—Milkman wished he had the nerve to ask Guitar the question that was bothering him. "Has he?" He could hardly phrase the question in his own mind, and certainly could never say it aloud. Guitar had impressed him with the seriousness and the dread of the work of the Days, and the danger. He had said that the Days never even talked about the details among themselves, so Milkman was sure any inquiry from him would only make Guitar sullen again. And cold. But the question was there. "Has he done it? Has he really killed somebody?" Like the old men on Tenth Street, now he bought the morning and evening papers, and once every two weeks the black newspaper, and read nervously, looking for reports of murders that appeared suspicious, pointless. When he found one, he followed the news stories until a suspect was found. Then he had to see if there were any black people murdered by someone other than their own.

"Did you do it yet?" He was like a teen-age girl wondering about the virginity of her friend, the friend who has a look, a manner newly minted—different, separate, focused somehow. "Did you do it yet? Do you know something both exotic and ordinary that I have not felt? Do you now know what it's like to risk your one and only self? How did it feel? Were you afraid? Did it change you? And if I do it, will it change me too?"

Maybe he could ask him one day, but not this day when it was so much like old times. Taking risks together the way they did when Milkman was twelve and Guitar was a teen-ager and they swaggered, haunched, leaned, straddled, ran all over town trying to pick fights or at least scare somebody: other boys, girls, dogs, pigeons, old women, school principals, drunks, ice cream vendors, and the horses of junkyard men. When they succeeded they rode the wind and covered their mouths to aggravate their laughter. And when they didn't, when somebody out-insulted them, or ignored them, or sent them running, they wisecracked and name-called until the sweat of embarrassment evaporated from the palms of their hands. Now they were men, and the terror they needed to provoke in others, if for no other reason than to feel it themselves, was rarer but not lighter. Dominion won by fear and secured by fear was still sweeter than any that could be got another way. (Except for women, whom they liked to win with charm but keep with indifference.)

It was like that again now, and Milkman didn't want to lose it.

There was something else too. Guitar had placed himself willingly and eagerly in a life cause that would always provide him with a proximity to knife-cold terror. Milkman knew his own needs were milder, for he could thrive in the presence of someone who inspired fear. His father, Pilate, Guitar. He gravitated toward each one, envious of their fearlessness now, even Hagar's, in spite of the fact that she was no longer a threat, but a fool who wanted not his death so much as his attention. Guitar could still create the sense of danger and life lived on the cutting edge. So Milkman had brought him into this scheme only partially for his help. Mostly because this escapade cried out for a cutting edge to go with its larklike quality. With Guitar as his co-conspirator, Milkman could look forward to both fun and fear.

They sauntered on down route 6, stopping frequently to examine the cars, gesticulating, bantering each other about the best way to burglarize a shack that, as Guitar said, "didn't have a door or window with a lock."

"But it's got people," Milkman insisted. "Three. All crazy."

"Women."

"Crazy women."

"Women."

"You're forgetting, Guitar, how Pilate got the gold in the first place. She waited in a cave with a dead man for three days to haul it out, and that was when she was twelve. If she did that at twelve to get it, what you think she'll do now when she's almost seventy to keep it?"

"We don't have to be rough. Cunning is all we need to be."

"Okay. Tell me how you gonna cunning them out of the house."

"Well, let's see now." Guitar stopped to scratch his back on a telephone pole. He closed his eyes, in either the ecstasy of relief or the rigors of concentration. Milkman stared off into the sky for inspiration, and while glancing toward the rooftops of the used-car places, he saw a white peacock poised on the roof of a long low building that served as headquarters for Nelson Buick. He was about to accept the presence of the bird as one of those waking dreams he was subject to whenever indecisiveness was confronted with reality, when Guitar opened his eyes and said, "Goddam! Where'd that come from?"

Milkman was relieved. "Must of come from the zoo."

"That raggedy-ass zoo? Ain't nothing in there but two tired monkeys and some snakes."

"Well, where then?"

"Beats me."

"Look—she's flying down." Milkman felt again his unrestrained joy at anything that could fly. "Some jive flying, but look at her strut."

"He."

"Huh?"

"He. That's a he. The male is the only one got that tail full of jewelry. Son of a bitch. Look at that." The peacock opened its tail wide. "Let's catch it. Come on, Milk," and Guitar started to run toward the fence.

"What for?" asked Milkman, running behind him. "What we gonna do if we catch him?"

"Eat him!" Guitar shouted. He swung easily over the double pipes that bordered the lot and began to circle the bird at a distance, holding his head a little to the side to fool the peacock, which was strutting around a powder-blue Buick. It closed its tail and let the tips trail in the gravel. The two men stood still, watching.

"How come it can't fly no better than a chicken?" Milkman asked.

"Too much tail. All that jewelry weighs it down. Like vanity. Can't nobody fly with all that shit. Wanna fly, you got to give up the shit that weighs you down."

The peacock jumped onto the hood of the Buick and once more spread its tail, sending the flashy Buick into oblivion.

"Faggot." Guitar laughed softly. "White faggot."

Milkman laughed too, and they watched a while more before leaving the used cars and the pure white peacock.

But the bird had set them up. Instead of continuing the argument about how they would cop, they began to fantasize about what the gold could buy when it became legal tender. Guitar, eschewing his recent asceticism, allowed himself the pleasure of waking up old dreams: what he would buy for his grandmother and her brother, Uncle Billy, the one who had come up from Florida to help raise them all after his father died; the marker he would buy for his father's grave, "pink with lilies carved on it"; then stuff for his brother and sisters, and his sisters' children. Milkman fantasized too, but not for the stationary things Guitar described. Milkman wanted boats, cars, airplanes, and the command of a large crew. He would be whimsical, generous, mysterious with his money. But all the time he was laughing and going on about what he would do and how he planned to live, he was aware of a falseness in his voice. He wanted the money—desperately, he believed—but other than making tracks out of the city, far away from Not Doctor Street, and Sonny's Shop, and Mary's Place, and Hagar, he could not visualize a life that much different from the one he had. New people. New places. Command. That was what he wanted in his life. And he couldn't get deep into Guitar's talk of elegant clothes for himself and his brother, sumptuous meals for Uncle Billy, and week-long card games in which the stakes would be a yard and a half and then a deuce and a quarter. He screamed and shouted "Wooeeeee!" at Guitar's list, but because his life was not unpleasant and even had a certain amount of luxury in addition to its comfort, he felt off center. He just wanted to beat a path away from his parents' past, which was also their present and which was threatening to become his present as well. He hated the acridness in his mother's and father's relationship, the conviction of righteousness they each held on to with both hands. And his efforts to ignore it, transcend it, seemed to work only when he spent his days looking for whatever was light-hearted and without grave consequences. He avoided commitment and strong feelings, and shied away from decisions. He wanted to know as little as possible, to feel only enough to get through the day amiably and to be interesting enough to warrant the curiosity of other people—but not their all-consuming devotion. Hagar had given him this last and more drama than he could ever want again. He'd always believed his childhood was sterile, but the knowledge Macon and Ruth had given him wrapped his memory of it in septic sheets, heavy with the odor of illness, misery, and unforgiving hearts. His rebellions, minor as they were, had all been in the company of, or shared with, Guitar. And this latest Jack and the Beanstalk bid for freedom, even though it had been handed to him by his father—assigned almost—stood some chance of success.

He had half expected his friend to laugh at him, to refuse with some biting comment that would remind Milkman that Guitar was a mystery man now, a man with blood-deep responsibilities. But when he watched Guitar's face as he described what could be had almost for the asking, he knew right away he hadn't guessed wrong. Maybe the professional assassin had had enough, or had changed his mind. Had he . . .? "Did you . . .?" As

he listened to him go over each detail of meals, clothes, tombstones, he wondered if Guitar simply could not resist the lure of
something he had never had—money.

Guitar smiled at the sun, and talked lovingly of televisions,
and brass beds, and week-long card games, but his mind was on
the wonders of TNT.

By the time they'd exhausted their imaginative spending, it
was almost noon and they were back on the edge of Southside.
They picked up where they'd left off in the discussion of the
scheme. Guitar was ready now; Milkman was still cautious. Too
cautious for Guitar.

"I don't understand you. You come running after me with a
dynamite proposition, and for three days we talk about it, the
best news I've had since pussy, but when we get down to business, you come up with some shit about how it can't be done.
You shucking me or what?"

"What would I be shucking for? I didn't have to tell you
about it."

"I don't know. I don't even know why you doing it. You
know about me—you can guess why I'm in it. But money ain't
never been what you needed or couldn't get."

Milkman ignored the reference to why Guitar was "in it," and
said as calmly as he could, "I need it to get away. I told you,
man. I got to get out of here. Be on my own."

"On *your* own? With a million-dollar wallet, you call that on
your own?"

"Fuck you. What difference does it make why I want it?"

"Cause I'm not sure you do want it. At least not bad enough
to go ahead and cop."

"I just want it right. No hassles. No . . . You know, burglary is a serious crime. I don't want to end up in—"

"What burglary? This ain't no burglary. This is Pilate."

"So?"

"So! They're your people."

"They're still people, and people scream."

"What's the worst? What's the worst thing can happen? We

bust in, right? Suppose all three of them are there. They're women. What can they do? Whip us?"

"Maybe."

"Come on! Who? Hagar? Right up in your face she blows it. Pilate? She loves you, boy. She wouldn't touch you."

"You believe that?"

"Yeah, I believe it! Look. You got qualms, tell me about them. Because you related? Your daddy's more related than you are, and it's his idea."

"It's not that."

"Then what?"

"They're crazy, Guitar. Nobody knows what they'll do; *they* don't even know."

"I know they're crazy. Anybody live like they do, selling fifty-cent wine and peeing in a bucket, with one million dollars hanging over their nappy heads, has to be. You scared of craziness? If you are, *you're* crazy."

"I don't want to be caught, that's all. I don't want to do time. I want to plan it so neither one happens. How come that's too much to ask? To plan."

"It don't look like planning. Looks like stalling."

"It is planning. Planning how to get them out the house. How to get us in the house. How to cut that sack off the ceiling and then get back out the house and on down the street. And it's hard to plan with them. They're not regular. They don't have regular habits. And then there's the wineheads. One of them liable to drop in any old time. They're not clock people, Guitar. I don't believe Pilate knows how to tell time except by the sun."

"They sleep at night."

"Anybody sleep can wake up."

"Anybody woke up can be knocked down."

"I don't want to knock nobody down. I want them gone when we hit."

"And what's gonna make them leave?"

Milkman shook his head. "An earthquake, maybe."

"Then let's make an earthquake."

"How?"

"Set the house on fire. Put a skunk in there. A bear. Something. Anything."

"Be serious, man."

"I'm trying, baby. I'm trying. Don't they go nowhere?"

"All together?"

"All together."

Milkman shrugged. "Funerals. They go to funerals. And circuses."

"Oh, man! We have to wait for somebody to die? Or for Ringling Brothers to come to town?"

"I'm trying to figure it out is all. At the moment we don't have a chance."

"Well, if a man don't *have* a chance, then he has to *take* a chance!"

"Be reasonable."

"Reasonable? You can't get no pot of gold being reasonable. Can't nobody get no gold being reasonable. You have to be unreasonable. How come you don't know that?"

"Listen to me. . . ."

"I just quit listening. You listen! You got a life? Live it! Live the motherfuckin life! Live it!"

Milkman's eyes opened wide. He tried hard not to swallow, but the clarion call in Guitar's voice filled his mouth with salt. The same salt that lay in the bottom of the sea and in the sweat of a horse's neck. A taste so powerful and necessary that stallions galloped miles and days for it. It was new, it was delicious, and it was his own. All the tentativeness, doubt, and inauthenticity that plagued him slithered away without a trace, a sound.

Now he knew what his hesitation had been all about. It was not to give an unnatural complexity to a simple job; nor was it to keep Guitar on hold. He had simply not believed in it before. When his father told him that long story, it really seemed like Jack and the Beanstalk . . . some fairy tale mess. He hadn't believed it was really there, or really gold, or that he could really have it just for the taking. It was too simple. But Guitar believed it, gave it a crisp concreteness, and what's more, made it into an act, an important, real, and daring thing to do. He felt a self inside himself emerge, a clean-lined definite self. A self that could join the chorus at Railroad Tommy's with more than laughter. He could tell this. The only other real confrontation he'd had was hitting his father, but that wasn't the kind of story that stirred the glitter up in the eyes of the old men in Tommy's.

Milkman didn't think through any of this clearly. He only tasted the salt and heard the hunter's horn in Guitar's voice.

"Tomorrow," he said. "Tomorrow night."

"What time?"

"One-thirty. I'll pick you up."

"Beautiful."

Far down the road, a long way from Milkman and Guitar, the peacock spread its tail.

On autumn nights, in some parts of the city, the wind from the lake brings a sweetish smell to shore. An odor like crystallized ginger, or sweet iced tea with a dark clove floating in it. There is no explanation for the smell either, since the lake, on September 19, 1963, was so full of mill refuse and the chemical wastes of a plastics manufacturer that the hair of the willows that stood near the shore was thin and pale. Carp floated belly up onto the beach, and the doctors at Mercy knew, but did not announce, that ear infections were a certainty for those who swam in those waters.

Yet there was this heavy spice-sweet smell that made you think of the East and striped tents and the *sha-sha-sha* of leg bracelets. The people who lived near the lake hadn't noticed the smell for a long time now because when air conditioners came, they shut their windows and slept a light surface sleep under the motor's drone.

So the ginger sugar blew unnoticed through the streets, around the trees, over roofs, until, thinned out and weakened a little, it reached Southside. There, where some houses didn't even have screens, let alone air conditioners, the windows were thrown wide open to whatever the night had to offer. And there the ginger smell was sharp, sharp enough to distort dreams and make the sleeper believe the things he hungered for were right at hand. To the Southside residents who were awake on such nights, it gave all their thoughts and activity a quality of being both intimate and far away. The two men standing near the pines on Darling Street—right near the brown house where wine drinkers went—could smell the air, but they didn't think of ginger. Each thought it was the way freedom smelled, or justice, or luxury, or vengeance.

Breathing the air that could have come straight from a marketplace in Accra, they stood for what seemed to them a very long time. One leaned against a tree, his foot hovering off the ground. Finally one touched the elbow of the other and they both moved toward an open window. With no trouble at all, they entered. Although they had stood deliberately in the dark of the pine trees, they were unprepared for the deeper darkness that met them there in that room. Neither had seen that kind of blackness, not even behind their own eyelids. More unsettling than the darkness, however, was the fact that in contrast to the heat outside (the slumbering ginger-laden heat that had people wiping sweat from their neck folds), it was as cold as ice in Pilate's house.

Suddenly the moon came out and shone like a flashlight right into the room. They both saw it at the same time. It hung heavy, hung green like the green of Easter eggs left too long in the dye. And like Easter, it promised everything: the Risen Son and the heart's lone desire. Complete power, total freedom, and perfect justice. Guitar knelt down before it and wove his fingers together into a footstep. Milkman hoisted himself up, one hand on Guitar's head, and shifted himself until he sat on Guitar's shoulders. Slowly Guitar stood up. Milkman felt upward along the sack until he found its neck. He thought the rope would have to be cut, and was annoyed to find the sack hung by wire instead.

He hoped the knife would be enough, because they hadn't figured on wire and had brought neither pincers nor a wire cutter.
The sound of the grating knife filled the room. No one, he
thought, could sleep through that. At last some few strands
broke and it was only a moment before the entire blackness was
severed. They'd figured on the weight of the sack being enough
to tumble them the minute it was cut free, and planned that at a
whispered signal, Guitar would bend his knees and sink down so
Milkman's feet would hit the floor almost immediately. But
there was no need for this graceful footwork; the bag was much
lighter than they had anticipated, and Milkman made it down
quite easily. As soon as they both regained balance, there was a
huge airy sigh that each one believed was made by the other.
Milkman handed his knife to Guitar, who closed it and tucked it
in his back pocket. There was the deep sigh again and an even
more piercing chill. Holding the sack by its neck and its bottom,
Milkman followed Guitar to the window. Once Guitar had
cleared the sill, he reached back to help Milkman over. The
moonlight was playing tricks on him, for he thought he saw the
figure of a man standing right behind his friend. Enveloped by
the heat they'd left a few minutes earlier, they walked swiftly
away from the house and out onto the road.

At another open window on the same side of the house, the
one next to the sink where Hagar washed her hair and where
Reba put pintos to soak, a woman's face appeared. "What the
devil they want that for?" she wondered. Then she picked at the
window sill until she had a splinter of wood and put it in her
mouth.

Chapter 9

Amanuensis. That was the word she chose, and since it was straight out of the nineteenth century, her mother approved, relishing the blank stares she received when she told her lady guests what position her daughter had acquired with the State Poet Laureate. "She's Michael-Mary Graham's amanuensis." The rickety Latin word made the work her daughter did (she, after all, wasn't required to work) sound intricate, demanding, and totally in keeping with her education. And the women didn't dare ask for further details (they tried to remember its sound, but still couldn't find it in the dictionary), for they were suitably impressed by the name of Michael-Mary Graham. It was a lie, of course, even as the simpler word "secretary" was a lie, but Ruth repeated it with confidence because she believed it was true. She did not know then, and never found out, that Corinthians was Miss Graham's maid.

Unfit for any work other than the making of red velvet roses, she had a hard time finding employment befitting her degree. The three years she had spent in college, a junior year in France, and being the granddaughter of the eminent Dr. Foster should have culminated in something more elegant than the two uniforms that hung on Miss Graham's basement door. That all these advantages didn't was still incredible to her. It had been assumed that she and Magdalene called Lena would marry well—but hopes for Corinthians were especially high since she'd gone to college. Her education had taught her how to be an enlightened mother and wife, able to contribute to the civilization—or in her case, the civilizing—of her community. And if marriage was not achieved, there were alternative roles: teacher, librarian, or . . . well, something intelligent and public-spirited. When neither of these fates tapped her on the forehead right away, she simply waited. High toned and high yellow, she believed what her mother was also convinced of: that she was a prize for a professional man of color. So there were vacations and weekends in other cities as well as visits and teas in her own, where and when such men appeared. The first of the black doctors to move there, in the forties when she graduated, had a son five years her junior. The second, a dentist, had two infant girls; the third was a very old physician (rumored to be an alcoholic), whose two sons were already raising families. Then there were teachers, two lawyers, a mortician—but on the few occasions when eligible bachelors were among them, Corinthians was not their choice. She was pretty enough, pleasant enough, and her father had the money they could rely on if needed, but she lacked drive. These men wanted wives who could manage, who were not so well accustomed to middle-class life that they had no ambition, no hunger, no hustle in them. They wanted their wives to like the climbing, the acquiring, and the work it took to maintain status once it was achieved. They wanted wives who would sacrifice themselves and appreciate the hard work and sacrifice of their husbands. Corinthians was a little too elegant. Bryn Mawr in 1940. France in 1939. That was a bit much. Fisk, Howard, Talledega, Tougaloo—that was their hunting territory. A woman who spoke French and who had traveled on the *Queen Mary* might not have the proper attitude toward future patients or clients, and if the man was a teacher, he steered clear of a woman who had a better education than he did. At one point post office workers were even being considered suitable for Lena and Corinthians, but that was long after they had reached thirty-five, and after Ruth came to terms with the savage fact that her daughters were not going to marry doctors. It was a shock to them all, which they managed to withstand by not accepting a more complete truth: that they probably were not going to marry anybody.

Magdalene called Lena seemed resigned to her life, but when Corinthians woke up one day to find herself a forty-two-year-old maker of rose petals, she suffered a severe depression which lasted until she made up her mind to get out of the house. So her search for work—which was shock number two—was intense. The twenty-one years that she had been out of college worked against her for a teaching job. She had none of the "new" courses now required by the board of education. She considered going to the state teachers' school to take the required courses, even went to the administration building to register. But the sight of those torpedo breasts under fuzzy blue sweaters, the absolute nakedness of those young faces, drove her out of the building and off the campus like a leaf before a hailstorm. Which was too bad, because she had no real skills. Bryn Mawr had done what a four-year dose of liberal education was designed to do: unfit her for eighty percent of the useful work of the world. First, by training her for leisure time, enrichments, and domestic mindlessness. Second, by a clear implication that she was too good for such work. After graduation she returned to a work world in which colored girls, regardless of their background, were in demand for one and only one kind of work. And by 1963, Corinthians' main concern was simply that her family not know that she had been doing it for two years.

She avoided the other maids on the street, and those whom she saw regularly on the bus assumed that she had some higher household position than theirs since she came to work in high-heeled shoes and only a woman who didn't have to be on her feet all day could stand the pressure of heels on the long ride home. Corinthians was careful; she carried no shopping bag of shoes, aprons, or uniforms. Instead she had a book. A small gray book on which *Contes de Daudet* was printed in gold lettering on its cover. Once she was inside Miss Graham's house she changed into her uniform (which was a discreet blue anyway, not white) and put on a pair of loafers before she dropped to her knees with the pail of soapy water.

Miss Graham was delighted with Corinthians' dress and slightly uppity manners. It gave her house the foreign air she liked to affect, for she was the core, the very heartbeat, of the city's literary world. Michael-Mary Graham was very considerate of Corinthians. When she had large dinner parties, a Swedish cook was hired and the heavy work was done by the old white rummy she shared with the Goodwill Industries. Nor was she impatient with Corinthians' undistinguished everyday cooking, for Michael-Mary ate several small plain meals. It was also a pleasure and a relief to have a maid who read and who seemed to be acquainted with some of the great masters of literature. So nice to give a maid a copy of *Walden* for Christmas rather than that dreary envelope, and to be able to say so to her friends. In the world Michael-Mary Graham inhabited, her mild liberalism, a residue of her Bohemian youth, and her posture of sensitive lady poet passed for anarchy.

Corinthians was naïve, but she was not a complete fool. She never let her mistress know she had ever been to college or Europe or could recognize one word of French that Miss Graham had not taught her (*entrez*, for example). Actually, the work Corinthians did was good for her. In that house she had what she never had in her own: responsibility. She flourished in a way, and exchanged arrogance occasionally for confidence. The humiliation of wearing a uniform, even if it was blue, and deceiving people was tempered by the genuine lift which came of having her own money rather than receiving an allowance like a child. And she was surprised to discover that the amount of neatly folded bills Michael-Mary handed her each Saturday at noon was within two dollars of the amount real secretaries took home each week.

Other than scrubbing the kitchen tile and keeping a hard shine on the wooden floors, the work was not hard. The poetess lived alone and shaped her time and activities carefully in order to meet the heavy demands of artistic responsibility. Being a poet she could, of course, do little else. Marriage, children—all had been sacrificed to the Great Agony and her home was a tribute to the fastidiousness of her dedication (and the generosity of her father's will). Colors, furnishings, and appointments had been selected for their inspirational value. And she was fond of saying, in deprecating some item, "I couldn't write a line with *that* in the house." *That* might be a vase, the new toilet bowl the plumbers hauled in, a plant, or even the Christmas wreath St. John's third-grade class presented to her in gratitude for the moving reading she'd given at their holiday assembly. Every morning between ten and noon she wrote, and every afternoon between three and four-fifteen. Evenings were often given over to discussions and meetings with local poets, painters, musicians, and writers of fiction, at which they praised or condemned other artists, scorned the marketplace and courted it. Of this group Michael-Mary Graham was the queen, for her poetry had been published—first in 1938, in a volume called *Seasons of My Soul;* there was a second collection in 1941, called *Farther Shores.* What was more, her poems had appeared in at least twenty small literary magazines, two "slicks," six college journals, and the Sunday supplements of countless newspapers. She was also the winner, between 1938 and 1958, of nine Poet of the Year awards, culminating finally in the much-coveted State Poet Laureateship. At the ceremony, her most famous poem, "Watchword," was performed by the Choral Speech Society of St. John's High School. None of that, however, had mitigated the reluctance of her publishers to bring out her complete collected works (tentatively called *The Farthest Shore*). But there was no question in her mind that they would come around.

When Miss Graham first saw Corinthians, she was not at all

impressed with her. First, because the prospective employee came ten minutes early for the interview and Michael-Mary, who adhered to her schedule to the minute, was forced to answer the door in a print peignoir. Already irritated by this lapse, she was further disenchanted by the woman's delicate frame. Obviously she could not put up the screens, take down the storm windows, or endure any sustained heavy cleaning. But when she learned the woman's name, Michael-Mary was so charmed by the sound of "Corinthians Dead," she hired her on the spot. As she told friends later, her poetic sensibility overwhelmed her good judgment.

They got on well together, mistress and maid, and by the sixth month of her stay, Michael-Mary suggested that she learn how to type. So Corinthians was almost on her way to becoming an amanuensis after all.

Shortly after Miss Graham encouraged her to take typing so she might be helpful with some of her mistress's work, a black man sat down next to Corinthians on the bus. She took little notice of him—only that he was ill-dressed and appeared elderly. But soon she became aware that he was staring at her. A quick corner-of-the-eye peek to verify this was met by his radiant smile. Corinthians turned her head and kept it so until he got off.

The next day he was there again. Once more she made her disdain clear. The rest of the week passed without his watchful eyes. But on the following Monday he was back, looking at her with an expression that stopped just short of a leer. These occasional meetings went on for a month or so. Corinthians thought she should be afraid of him, for something in his manner suggested waiting—a confident, assured waiting. Then one morning he dropped a white envelope on the seat beside her just before he got off the bus. She let it lie there all the way to her stop, but couldn't resist scooping it up as surreptitiously as possible when she stood to pull the cord.

Standing at the stove, waiting for Michael-Mary's milk to skim, she opened the envelope and withdrew a greeting card.

Raised letters of the word "Friendship" hung above a blue and yellow bouquet of flowers and were repeated inside above a verse.

> *Friendship is an outstretched hand,*
> *A smile of warm devotion.*
> *I offer both to you this day,*
> *With all the heart's emotion.*

A white hand of no particular sex held another, smaller, blue and yellow bouquet. There was no signature.

Corinthians threw it in the brown paper bag opened for the day's garbage. It stayed there all day, but it also stayed on her mind. When evening came, she reached down through the grapefruit rind, the tea leaves, and the salami casing to find it, brush it clean, and transfer it to her purse. She couldn't explain to herself why. The man was a complete nuisance and his flirtation an insult. But no one, not anyone at all, had made any attempt (any serious attempt) to flirt with her in a long time. At the very least the card was good for conversation. She wished he had signed it, not because she wanted to know his name, but so it would look more authentic—otherwise somebody might think she bought it herself.

For two weeks afterward the man was not on the bus. When he did appear, it was hard for Corinthians not to speak or acknowledge his presence. As they neared the place where he usually got off, he leaned over to her and said, "I truly hope you didn't mind." She looked up, gave him a small smile, and shook her head. He said nothing more.

But on subsequent days they did exchange greetings and finally they began to talk. In a while they were chatting (carefully, guardedly) and she, at least, was looking forward to his being there. By the time she knew that his name was Henry Porter and that he had occasional yard work in that part of town, she was glad she had never shown or mentioned either the card or the man to anyone.

Pleasant as their conversations were, they were also curious.

Each took care not to ask the other certain questions—for fear he or she would have to volunteer the same information. What part of town do you live in? Do you know Mr. So-and-so?

Eventually Mr. Porter offered to pick Corinthians up after work. He didn't own a car, he said, but borrowed a friend's sometimes. Corinthians agreed, and the result was a pair of middle-aged lovers who behaved like teen-agers—afraid to be caught by their parents in a love relationship they were too young for. He took her for rides in an old gray Oldsmobile—to the country, to drive-in movies—and they sat over bad coffee in certain dime stores where they were not likely to be recognized.

Corinthians knew she was ashamed of him, that she would have to add him to the other secret, the nature of her work, that he could never set foot in her house. And she hated him a lot for the shame she felt. Hated him sometimes right in the middle of his obvious adoration of her, his frequent compliments about her looks, her manners, her voice. But those swift feelings of contempt never lasted long enough for her to refuse those drive-in movie sessions where she was the sole object of someone's hunger and satisfaction.

At some point Corinthians began to suspect that Porter's discretion was not only in deference to who she was (her position and all), but also because he too didn't want to be discovered. Her first thought was that he was married. His denials, accompanied by a wistful smile which she interpreted as a sly one, only aggravated her suspicions. Finally, to prove his bachelorhood as well as to indulge himself in a real bed, he invited her to his room. She declined immediately and repeatedly for several days until he accused her of the very thing that was absolutely true: that she was ashamed of him.

"Ashamed of you?" Her eyes and mouth went wide with surprise (genuine surprise, because she never thought he would guess it). "If I were ashamed I wouldn't see you at all, let alone *this* way." Her hand pointed toward the world outside the car they sat in: the row upon row of automobiles in the hot drive-in movie lot.

Porter traced her cheek line with his knuckle. "Well, then? The things you tell me can't be true and not true at the same time."

"I've never told you anything except what was true. I thought we both knew . . . understood . . . the problem."

"Maybe," he said. "Let's hear it, Corrie." His knuckles stroked her jaw line. "Let's hear the problem."

"My father. It's only my father . . . the way he is."

"How is he?"

Corinthians shrugged. "You know as well as I do. He never wanted us to mix with . . . people. He's very strict."

"And that's the reason you won't come home with me?"

"I'm sorry. I have to live there. I can't let him know about us. Not yet." But when? she thought. If not at forty-four, then when? If not now, when even my pubic hair is turning gray and when my breasts have dropped of their own accord—then when?

Porter spoke her own question aloud. "When, then?" And she could not answer him right away. She put her fingers to her forehead and said, "I don't know. I honestly don't know."

It was such a fake gesture to go along with her fake feelings of moral and filial commitment that she knew right away how foolish she seemed. The things they did in that old car, the things she'd let her tongue say, as recently as five minutes ago . . . and now to caress her temples and say in Michael-Mary's reading voice, "I don't know," embarrassed her and must have disgusted Porter, for he took his hand from her face and put it on the steering wheel. Right at the beginning of the second feature, he started the car and moved it slowly down the gravel aisle.

Neither spoke until the car entered downtown traffic. It was ten-thirty. She'd told her mother she would be typing manuscript for Miss Graham until very late. "In this heat?" was all her mother said. Corinthians sat quietly, feeling shame but not thinking the word, until she realized that he was driving her to the bus stop where he always let her out to walk home the way she normally would. In a sudden flash she knew he was never going to see her again, and the days rolled out before her like a dingy gray carpet in an unfurnished, unpeopled hall-for-rent.

"Are you taking me home?" She succeeded in keeping the anxiety out of her voice—succeeded too well, for her words sounded arrogant and careless.

He nodded and said, "I don't want a doll baby. I want a woman. A grown-up woman that's not scared of her daddy. I guess you don't want to be a grown-up woman, Corrie."

She stared through the windshield. A grown-up woman? She tried to think of some. Her mother? Lena? The dean of women at Bryn Mawr? Michael-Mary? The ladies who visited her mother and ate cake? Somehow none of them fit. She didn't know any grown-up women. Every woman she knew was a doll baby. Did he mean like the women who rode on the bus? The other maids, who were not hiding what they were? Or the black women who walked the streets at night?

"You mean like those women on the bus? You can have one of *them*, you know. Why don't you drop a greeting card in one of *their* laps?" His words had hit home; she had been compared —unfavorably, she believed—with the only people she knew for certain she was superior to. "They'd love to have a greeting card dropped in their lap. Just love it. But oh, I forgot. You couldn't do that, could you, because they wouldn't be able to read it. They'd have to take it home and wait till Sunday and give it to the preacher to read it to them. Of course when they heard it they might not know what it meant. But it wouldn't matter— they'd see the flowers and the curlicues all over the words and they'd be happy. It wouldn't matter a bit that it was the most ridiculous, most clichéd, most commercial piece of tripe the drugstore world has to offer. They wouldn't know mediocrity if it punched them right in their fat faces. They'd laugh and slap their fat thighs and take you right on into their kitchens. Right up on the breakfast table. But you wouldn't give them a fifteen-cent greeting card, would you?—no matter how silly and stupid it was—because they're grown-up women and you don't have to court *them*. You can just come right out and say, 'Hello there, come on to my room tonight.' Right? Isn't that so? Isn't that so?" She was close to screaming. "But no. You wanted a lady. Somebody who knows how to sit down, how to dress, how to eat the food on her plate. Well, there is a difference between a woman and a lady, and I know you know which one I am."

Porter pulled the car over to the curb, and without shutting off the motor, leaned across her and opened the door. Corinthians got out and did her best to slam it, but the rusty hinges of the borrowed Oldsmobile did not accommodate her. She had to settle for the gesture.

By the time she reached number 12 Not Doctor Street, her trembling had become uncontrollable. Suddenly the shaking stopped and she froze at the steps. Two seconds later she turned on her heel and ran back down the street to where Porter had stopped the car. The moment she had put her foot on the step leading up to the porch, she saw her ripeness mellowing and rotting before a heap of red velvet scraps on a round oak table. The car was still there, its motor purring. Corinthians ran toward it faster than she had ever run in her life, faster than she'd cut across the grass on Honoré Island when she was five and the whole family went there for a holiday. Faster even than the time she flew down the stairs having seen for the first time what the disease had done to her grandfather. She put her hand on the door handle and found it locked. Porter was sitting pretty much the way he was when she'd tried to slam the door. Bending down, she rapped on the window. Porter's profile did not move. She rapped again, louder, mindless of who might see her under the gray beech tree just around the corner from home. So close and yet so far, she felt as though she were in a dream; there, but not there, within a hair's breadth but not reaching it.

She was First Corinthians Dead, daughter of a wealthy property owner and the elegant Ruth Foster, granddaughter of the magnificent and worshipped Dr. Foster, who had been the second man in the city to have a two-horse carriage, and a woman who had turned heads on every deck of the *Queen Mary* and had Frenchmen salivating all over Paris. Corinthians Dead, who had held herself pure all these years (well, almost all, and almost pure), was now banging on the car-door window of a yardman. But she would bang forever to escape the velvet. The red velvet that had flown all over the snow that day when she and Lena and her mother had walked past the hospital on their way to the department store. Her mother was pregnant—a fact that had embarrassed Corinthians when first she learned of it. All she could think of was how her friends would laugh when they found out she had a pregnant mother. Her relief was sweet when she discovered that it was too soon to show. But by February her mother was heavy and needed to get out of the house, to exercise a little. They'd walked slowly through the snow, watching carefully for icy places. Then as they passed Mercy, there was a crowd watching a man on the roof. Corinthians had seen him before her mother did, but when Ruth looked up she was so startled she dropped the basket, scattering the roses everywhere. Corinthians and Lena busied themselves picking them up, wiping the snow from the cloth on their coats, all the while peeping at the man in blue wings on the hospital roof. They were laughing, Lena and she; collecting the roses, looking up at the man, and laughing from fear, embarrassment, and giddiness. It was all mixed together—the red velvet, the screams, and the man crashing down on the pavement. She had seen his body quite clearly, and to her astonishment, there was no blood. The only red in view was in their own hands and in the basket. Her mother's moans were getting louder and she seemed to be sinking into the ground. A stretcher came at last for the doll-broken body (all the more doll-like because there was no blood), and finally a wheelchair for her mother, who was moving straight into labor.

Corinthians continued to make roses, but she hated that stupid hobby and gave Lena any excuse to avoid it. They spoke to her of death. First the death of the man in the blue wings. Now her own. For if Porter did not turn his head and lean toward the door to open it for her, Corinthians believed she would surely die. She banged her knuckles until they ached to get the attention of the living flesh behind the glass, and would have smashed her fist through the window just to touch him, feel his heat, the only thing that could protect her from a smothering death of dry roses.

He did not move. In a panic, lest he shift gears and drive away, leaving her alone in the street, Corinthians climbed up on the fender and lay full out across the hood of the car. She didn't look through the windshield at him. She just lay there, stretched across the car, her fingers struggling for a grip on steel. She thought of nothing. Nothing except what her body needed to do to hang on, to never let go. Even if he drove off at one hundred miles an hour, she would hang on. Her eyes were shut tight with the effort of clinging to the hood, and she didn't hear the door open and shut, nor Porter's footsteps as he moved around to the front of the car. She screamed at first when he put his hand on her shoulders and began pulling her gently into his arms. He carried her to the passenger's side of the car, stood her on her feet while he opened the door and helped her ease into the seat. In the car, he pressed her head onto his shoulder and waited for her soft crying to wane before he left the driver's seat to pick up the purse she had let fall on the sidewalk. He drove away then to number 3 Fifteenth Street, a house owned by Macon Dead, where sixteen tenants lived, and where there was an attic window, from which this same Henry Porter had screamed, wept, waved a shotgun, and urinated over the heads of the women in the yard.

It was not yet midnight and hot—hot enough to make people angry, had it not been for a pleasant smell in the air, like sweet ginger. Corinthians and Porter entered the hall that opened off the front door. Except for a hem of light under the kitchen door, where a card game was in progress, there was no sign of any other tenant.

Corinthians saw only the bed, an iron bed painted hospital white. She sank down on it as soon as she got into the room and stretched out, feeling bathed, scoured, vacuumed, and for the first time simple. Porter undressed after she did and lay down beside her. They were quiet for a minute, then he turned over and parted her legs with his.

Corinthians looked down at him. "Is this for me?" she asked.

"Yes," he said. "Yes, this is for you."

"Porter."

"This is . . . for you. Instead of roses. And silk underwear and bottles of perfume."

"Porter."

"Instead of chocolate creams in a heart-shaped box. Instead of a big house and a great big car. Instead of long trips . . ."

"Porter."

". . . in a clean white boat."

"No."

"Instead of picnics . . ."

"No."

". . . and fishing . . ."

"No."

". . . and being old together on a porch."

"No."

"This is for you, girl. Oh, yes. This is for you."

They woke at four o'clock in the morning, or rather she did. When she opened her eyes she saw him staring at her and those were either tears in his eyes or sweat. It was very hot in that room in spite of the open window.

"The bathroom," she murmured. "Where is the bathroom?"

"Down the hall," he said. Then, apologetically, "Can I get you something?"

"Oh." She pushed a few strands of matted damp hair from her forehead. "Something to drink, please. Something cold."

He dressed quickly, leaving off his shirt and his socks, and left the room. Corinthians got up too and began to put her clothes on. Since there seemed to be no mirror in the room, she stood in front of the open window and used the upper part of the pane, dark enough to show her reflection, to smooth her hair. Then she noticed the walls. What she had assumed to be wallpaper as she entered and fell on the bed was in fact calendars. Row after row of calendars: S. &. J. Automobile Parts, featuring a 1939 Hudson; the Cuyahoga River Construction Company ("We build to please—We're pleased to build"); Lucky Hart Beauty Products (a wavy-haired lady smiling out of a heavily powdered face); the *Call and Post* newspaper. But most of them were from the North Carolina Mutual Life Insurance Company. They literally covered the walls, each one turned to December. It was as though he'd kept every calendar since 1939. Some of them were large cards displaying all twelve months and on those she noticed circles drawn around dates.

Porter came in while she was gazing at them. He held a glass of iced water, the cubes jammed to the rim.

"Why do you keep calendars?" she asked.

He smiled. "Passes the time. Here. Drink your drink. It'll cool you."

She took the glass and sipped a little from it, trying to keep the ice from touching her teeth as she looked at him over the rim. Standing there, barefoot, her hair damp with sweat and sticking to her cheeks like paint, she felt easy. In place of vanity she now felt a self-esteem that was quite new. She was grateful to him, this man who rented a tiny room from her father, who ate with a knife and did not even own a pair of dress shoes. A perfect example of the men her parents had kept her from (and whom she had also kept herself from) all her life because such a man was known to beat his woman, betray her, shame her, and leave her. Corinthians moved close to him, tilted his chin up with her fingers, and planted a feathery kiss on his throat. He held her head in his hands until she closed her eyes and tried to set the glass down on a tiny table.

"Uh uh. It'll be light soon. Gotta get you home."

She obeyed and finished dressing herself. They walked as softly as possible down the stairs and past the wide triangle of light that lay on the floor in front of the kitchen door. The men were still at their card game, but the door was partially open now. Porter and Corinthians moved quickly past, just out of the light.

Still a voice called, "Who that? Mary?"

"No. Just me. Porter."

"Porter?" The voice was incredulous. "What shift you on?"

"Catch you later," said Porter and opened the front door before the speaker's curiosity could propel him into the hall.

Corinthians slid as close to Porter as the floor gear of the car allowed, her head resting on the seat back. She closed her eyes once more and took deep breaths of the sweet air her brother had been inhaling three hours ago.

"Hadn't you better fix your hair?" Porter asked. He thought she was beautiful like that, girlish, but he didn't want her excuse to her parents, if they were still awake, to sound ridiculous.

She shook her head. She wouldn't have collected her hair into a ball at her nape now for anything in the world.

Porter parked under the same tree where Corinthians had thrown herself across the hood of the car. Now, after a whispered confession, she walked the four blocks, no longer afraid to mount the porch steps.

As soon as she closed the door she heard voices and instinctively touched her loose hair. The voices came from beyond the dining room, from behind the closed kitchen door. Men's voices. Corinthians blinked. She had just come from a house in which men sat in a lit kitchen talking in loud excited voices, only to meet an identical scene at home. She wondered if this part of the night, a part she was unfamiliar with, belonged, had always belonged, to men. If perhaps it was a secret hour in which men rose like giants from dragon's teeth and, while the women slept, clustered in their kitchens. On tiptoe she approached the door. Her father was speaking.

"You still haven't explained to me why you brought him along."

"What difference does it make now?" That was her brother's voice.

"He knows about it," said her father. "That's what difference."

"About what? There's nothing to know. It was a bust." Milkman's voice swelled like a blister.

"It was a mistake, not a bust. It just means it's somewhere else. That's all."

"Yeah. The mint. You want me to go to the mint?"

"No!" Macon struck the table. "It's got to be there. It's got to."

Corinthians couldn't make sense out of what they were talking about with so much passion, and she didn't want to stay there and learn, lest it distract her from the contentment she was feeling. She left them and climbed the stairs to her own bed.

Downstairs in the kitchen, Milkman folded his arms on the table and put his head down. "I don't care. I don't care where it is."

"It was just a mistake," said his father. "One little mess-up. That don't mean we have to pull out."

"You call being thrown in jail a little mess-up?"

"You out, ain't you? You was only there twenty minutes."

"Two hours."

"Wouldn't have been two minutes if you had called me soon's you got there. Sooner. Should have called me soon's they picked you up."

"Police cars don't have telephones in them." Milkman was weary. He lifted his head and let it rest in his hand, directing his words into his shirt sleeve.

"They would have let you, if it had just been you. Soon as you told them your name they would have let you go. But you was with that Southside nigger. That's what did it."

"That is *not* what did it. It was riding around with a sack of rocks and human bones that did it. Human bones. Which is, if you're a halfway intelligent cop, a hint that there must have been a human being connected to them bones at one time."

"Of course at one time. But not tonight. There couldn't have been a human attached to the bones yesterday. It takes time for a body to be a skeleton. They know that. And don't tell me it wasn't Guitar they was suspicious of. That yellow-eyed nigger looks like he might do anything."

"They didn't see his eyes when they told us to pull over. They didn't see nothing. They just sideswiped us, and told us to get out. Now, what was that for? What'd they stop us for? We wasn't speeding. Just driving along." Milkman searched for cigarettes. He got angry again when he thought about bending over the car, his legs spread, his hands on the hood, while the policeman fingered his legs, his back, his ass, his arms. "What business they got stopping cars that ain't speeding?"

"They stop anybody they want to. They saw you was colored, that's all. And they're looking for the Negro that killed that boy."

"Who said it was a Negro?"

"Paper said it."

"They always say that. Every time . . ."

"What difference does it make? If you'd been alone and told them your name they never would have hauled you in, never would have searched the car, and never would have opened that sack. They know me. You saw how they acted when I got there."

"They didn't act any different when you got there. . . ."

"What?"

"They acted different when you took that sucker off in the corner and opened your wallet."

"You better be thankful I got a wallet."

"I am. God knows I am."

"And that would have been the end of it, except for that Southside nigger. Hadn't been for him, they wouldn't of had to get Pilate down there." Macon rubbed his knees. The idea of having to depend on Pilate to get his son out of jail humiliated him. "Raggedy bootlegging bitch."

"She's still a bitch?" Milkman began to chuckle. Exhaustion and the slow release of tension made him giddy. "You thought she stole it. All these years . . . all these years you've been holding that against her." He was laughing out right now. "How she sneaked out of some cave with a big bag of gold that must have weighed a hundred pounds over her shoulder, all over the country for fifty years and didn't spend none of it, just hung it from the ceiling like a fuckin sack of onions." Milkman put his head back and let the laughter fill the kitchen. Macon was silent. "Fifty years . . . You been thinking about that gold for fifty years! Oh, shit. This is some crazy shit. . . ." Tears of laughter were running from his eyes. "Crazy. All of you. Just straight-out, laid-back crazy. I should of known. The whole thing was crazy; everything about it was crazy—the whole idea."

"What's crazier? Her hauling a sack of gold around all this time, or hauling a dead man's bones around? Huh? Which one?" Macon asked.

"I don't know. I really don't know."

"If she do one, she could do the other. She's the one they should have kept. When you all told them the bones belonged to her, they should have locked her up soon's she walked in the door."

Milkman wiped the tears on his sleeve. "Lock her up for what? After that story she told?" He started laughing again. "She came in there like Louise Beaver and Butterfly McQueen all rolled up in one. 'Yassuh, boss. Yassuh, boss. . . .'"

"She didn't say that."

"Almost. She even changed her voice."

"I told you she was a snake. Drop her skin in a split second."

"She didn't even look the same. She looked short. Short and pitiful."

"That's cause she wanted it back. She wanted them to let her have the bones back."

"Her poor husband's bones, that she didn't have no money to bury. Pilate got a husband somewhere?"

"Does the Pope?"

"Well, she got 'em back. They gave 'em to her."

"She knew what she was doing, all right."

"Yeah, she knew. But how did she know so fast? I mean she came in there . . . you know . . . prepared. She had it all together when she got there. Cop must have told her everything when he picked her up and brought her to the station."

"Uh uh. They don't do that."

"Then how did she know?"

"Who knows what Pilate knows?"

Milkman shook his head. "Only The Shadow knows." He was still amused, but earlier, when he and Guitar had sat hand-cuffed on a wooden bench, his neck skin had crawled with fear.

"White man's bones," Macon said. He stood up and yawned. The dark of the sky was softened now. "Nigger bitch roaming around with a white man's bones." He yawned again. "I'll never understand that woman. I'm seventy-two years old and I'm going to die not understanding one thing about her." Macon walked toward the kitchen door and opened it. Then he turned around and said to Milkman, "But you know what that means, don't you? If she took the white man's bones and left the gold, then the gold must still be there." He shut the door before his son could protest.

Well, it would rot there, thought Milkman. If anybody even mentions the word "gold," I'm going to have to take his teeth out. He sat on there in the kitchen, wishing for more coffee, but too tired to get up and fix it. In a minute his mother would be downstairs; she had got up when he and Macon had come in, but Macon sent her back upstairs. Milkman fished for another ciga-rette and watched dawn eclipse the electric light over the sink. It was a cheery sun, which suggested another hot day. But the stronger it got, the more desolate he became. Alone, without Macon, he let the events of the night come back to him—he remembered little things, details, and yet he wasn't sure these details had really happened. Perhaps he made them up. Pilate *had* been shorter. As she stood there in the receiving room of the jail, she didn't even come up to the sergeant's shoulder—and the sergeant's head barely reached Milkman's own chin. But Pilate was as tall as he was. When she whined to the policeman, verify-ing Milkman's and Guitar's lie that they had ripped off the sack as a joke on an old lady, she had to look up at him. And her hands were shaking as she described how she didn't know the sack was gone until the officer woke her up; that she couldn't imagine why anybody would want to run off with her husband's bones; that her husband had been lynched in Mississippi fifteen years ago, and that they wouldn't let her cut him down, and that she left town then and that when she went back the body had dropped off the rope of its own accord, so she collected it and tried to bury it, but the "funeral peoples" wanted fifty dollars for a coffin, and the carpenter wanted twelve-fifty for a pine box and she just didn't have no twelve dollars and fifty cents so she just carried what was left of Mr. Solomon (she always called him Mr. Solomon cause he was such a dignified colored man) and put it in a sack and kept it with her. "Bible say what so e'er the Lord hath brought together, let no man put asunder—Matthew Twenty-one: Two. We was bony fide and legal wed, suh," she pleaded. Even her eyes, those big sleepy old eyes, were small as she went on: "So I thought I just as well keep him near me and when I die they can put him in the same hole as me. We'll raise up to Judgment Day together. Hand in hand."

Milkman was astonished. He thought Pilate's only acquaintance with the Bible was the getting of names out of it, but she quoted it, apparently, verse and chapter. Furthermore, she had looked at Milkman and Guitar and Macon like she didn't know who exactly they were. In fact, when asked if she knew them, she pointedly said, "Not this man, here," looking at her brother, "but I do believe I've noticed this fella around the neighborhood." Here she motioned toward Guitar, who sat there like marble with the eyes of a dead man. Later, as Macon drove them all home—Pilate sitting in front, Guitar and himself in the back—Guitar never said a word. His anger was like heat shimmering out of his skin, making the hot air blowing in through the open window seem refreshing by comparison.

And again there was a change. Pilate was tall again. The top of her head, wrapped in a silk rag, almost touched the roof of the car, as did theirs. And her own voice was back. She spoke, but to Macon only, and nobody else spoke at all. In a conversational tone, like somebody picking up a story that had been interrupted in the telling, she told her brother something quite different from what she told the policemen.

"I spent that whole day and night in there, and when I looked out the next morning you was gone. I was scared I would run into you, but I didn't see hide nor hair of you. It was three years or more 'fore I went back. The winter it was. Snow was everywhere and I couldn't hardly find my way. I looked up Circe first, then went looking for the cave. It was a hard trek, I can tell you, and I was in frail condition. Snow piled up every which way. But you should of known better than to think I'd go back there for them little old bags. I wasn't stuttin 'em when I first laid eyes on 'em, I sure wasn't thinking about them three years later. I went cause Papa told me to. He kept coming to see me, off and on. Tell me things to do. First he just told me to sing, to keep on singing. 'Sing,' he'd whisper. 'Sing, sing.' Then right after Reba was born he came and told me outright: 'You just can't fly on off and leave a body,' he tole me. A human life is precious. You shouldn't fly off and leave it. So I knew right away what he meant cause he was right there when we did it. He meant that if you take a life, then you own it. You responsible for it. You can't get rid of nobody by killing them. They still there, and they yours now. So I had to go back for it. And I did find the cave. And there he was. Some wolves or something must have drug it cause it was right in the mouth of the cave, laying up, sitting up almost, on that very rock we slept on. I put him in my sack, piece by piece. Some cloth was still on him, but his bones was clean and dry. I've had it every since. Papa told me to, and he was right, you know. You can't take a life and walk off and leave it. Life is life. Precious. And the dead you kill is yours. They stay with you anyway, in your mind. So it's a better thing, a more better thing to have the bones right there with you wherever you go. That way, it frees up your mind."

Fucks up your mind, thought Milkman, fucks it up for good. He pulled himself up from the table. He had to get some sleep before he went looking for Guitar.

Staggering up the stairs, he remembered Pilate's back as she got out of the Buick—not bent at all under the weight of the sack. And he remembered how Guitar glared at her as she walked away from the car. When Macon dropped him off, he neither answered nor turned his head at Milkman's "See y' later."

Milkman woke at noon. Somebody had come into his room and placed a small fan on the floor near the foot of his bed. He listened to the whirring for a long time before he got up and went into the bathroom to fill the tub. He lay there in lukewarm water, still sweating, too hot and tired to soap himself. Every now and then he flicked water on his face, letting it wet his two-day-old beard. He wondered if he could shave without slicing his chin open. The tub was uncomfortable, too short for him to stretch out, though he remembered when he could almost swim in it. Now he looked down at his legs. The left one looked just as long as the other. His eyes traveled up his body. The touch of the policeman's hand was still there—a touch that made his flesh jump like the tremor of a horse's flank when flies light on it. And something more. Something like shame stuck to his skin. Shame at being spread-eagled, fingered, and handcuffed. Shame at having stolen a skeleton, like a kid on a Halloween trick-or-treat prank rather than a grown man making a hit. Shame at needing both his father and his aunt to get him off. Then more shame at seeing his father—with an accommodating "we all understand how it is" smile—buckle before the policemen. But nothing was like the shame he felt as he watched and listened to Pilate. Not just her Aunt Jemima act, but the fact that she was both adept at it and willing to do it—for him. For the one who had just left her house carrying what he believed was her inheritance. It didn't matter that he also believed she had "stolen" it. . . . From whom? From a dead man? From his father, who was also stealing it? Then and now? He had stolen it too, and what's more, he had been prepared—at least he told himself he had been prepared—to knock her down if she had come into the room while he was in the act of stealing it. To knock down an old black lady who had cooked him his first perfect egg, who had shown him the sky, the blue of it, which was like her mother's ribbons, so that from then on when he looked at it, it had no distance, no remoteness, but was intimate, familiar, like a room that he lived in, a place where he belonged. She had told him stories, sung him songs, fed him bananas and corn bread and, on the first cold day of the year, hot nut soup. And if his mother was right, this old black lady—in her late sixties, but with the skin and agility of a teen-aged girl—had brought him into the world when only a miracle could have. It was this woman, whom he would have knocked senseless, who shuffled into the police station and did a little number for the cops—opening herself up wide for their amusement, their pity, their scorn, their mockery, their disbelief, their meanness, their whimsy, their annoyance, their power, their anger, their boredom—whatever would be useful to her and to himself.

Milkman sloshed his legs in the water. He thought again of how Guitar had looked at Pilate—the jeweled hatred in his eyes. He had no right to that look. Suddenly, Milkman knew the answer to the question he had never been able to ask Guitar. Guitar could kill, would kill, and probably had killed. The Seven Days was the consequence of this ability, but not its origin. No. He had no cause to look at her like that, Milkman thought, and heaving himself upright in the tub, he soaped himself hurriedly.

The September heat blasted him as soon as he got outside, and wiped out the pleasant effects of his bath. Macon had taken the Buick—age forced him to walk less—so Milkman went on foot to Guitar's house. As he rounded the corner, he noticed a familiar-looking gray Oldsmobile, a jagged crack in the rear window, parked in front of the house. Several men were inside and two were standing outside: Guitar and Railroad Tommy. Milkman slowed his steps. Tommy was talking, while Guitar nodded his head. Then the two men shook hands—a handshake Milkman had never seen before: first Tommy held Guitar's hand in both his own, then Guitar held Tommy's hand in his two. Tommy got in the car and Guitar dashed around the house to the side stairs that led to his room. The Oldsmobile—Milkman figured it was a 1953 or 1954 model—made a tight U-turn and headed toward him. When it passed by, all the occupants looked straight ahead. Porter was driving, with Empire State in the middle and Railroad Tommy on the far side, and in the back seat was Hospital Tommy and a man named Nero. Milkman didn't know the other man.

That must be *them*, he thought. His heart beat wildly. Six men, one of them Porter, and Guitar. Those are the Days. And that car. That was the car that let Corinthians off near the house sometimes. Milkman had first assumed his sister had an occasional lift home from her job. Later, since she never mentioned it, and also because she seemed quieter and rounder lately, he decided she was seeing some man on the sly. He thought it funny, sweet and a little sad. But now he knew that whoever she was seeing belonged to that car and belonged to the Seven Days. Foolish woman, he thought. Of all the people to pick. She was so silly. So silly. Jesus!

He wasn't up to Guitar now. He would see him later.

People behaved much better, were more polite, more understanding when Milkman was drunk. The alcohol didn't change him at all, but it had a tremendous impact on whomever he saw while he was under its influence. They looked better, never spoke above a whisper, and when they touched him, even to throw him out of the house party because he had peed in the kitchen sink, or when they picked his pockets as he dozed on a bench at the bus station, they were gentle, loving.

He stayed that way, swaying from light buzz to stoned, for two days and a night, and would have extended it to at least another day but for a sobering conversation with Magdalene called Lena, to whom he had not said more than four consecutive sentences since he was in the ninth grade.

She was waiting for him at the top of the stairs when he came home early one morning. Wrapped in a rayon robe and without her glasses, she looked unreal yet kind, like the man who had picked his pocket a short while ago.

"Come here. I want to show you something. Can you come in here for a minute?" She was whispering.

"Can't it wait?" He was kind too; and he was proud of the civility in his voice, considering how tired he was.

"No," she said. "No. You have to see it now. Today. Just look at it."

"Lena, I'm really beat out . . ." he began in sweet reason-ableness.

"It won't take more'n a minute. It's important."

He sighed and followed her down the hall into her bedroom. She walked to the window and pointed. "Look down there."

In what seemed to him like elegant if slow motion, Milkman went to the window, parted the curtain, and followed her point-ing finger with his eyes. All he saw was the lawn at the side of the house. Not a thing was moving there, but in the light of early day he thought he might have missed it.

"What?"

"That little maple. Right there." She pointed to a tiny maple tree about four feet high. "The leaves should be turning red now. September is almost over. But they're not; they're just shriveling and falling down green."

He turned to her and smiled. "You said it was important." He was not angry, not even irritated, and he enjoyed his equa-nimity.

"It is important. Very important." Her voice was soft; she kept on staring at the tree.

"Then tell me. I've got to go to work in a few minutes."

"I know. But you can spare me a minute, can't you?"

"Not to stare at a dead bush, I can't."

"It's not dead yet. But it will be soon. The leaves aren't turn-ing this year."

"Lena, you been in the sherry?"

"Don't make fun of me," she said, and there was a hint of steel in her voice.

"But you have, haven't you?"

"You're not paying any attention to me."

"I am. I'm standing here listening to you tell me the news of the day—that a bush is dying."

"You don't remember it, do you?"

"Remember it?"

"You peed on it."

"I what?"

"You peed on it."

"Lena, maybe we can discuss this later. . . ."

"And on me."

"Uh . . . Lena, I have done some things in my life. Some things I don't feel too good about. But I swear to God I never peed on you."

"It was summer. The year Daddy had that Packard. We went for a ride and you had to go to the bathroom. Remember?"

Milkman shook his head. "No. I don't remember that."

"I took you. We were in the country and there was no place else to go. So they made me take you. Mama wanted to, but Daddy wouldn't let her. And he wouldn't go himself. Corinthians turned up her nose and refused outright, so they made me go. I had on heels too. I was a girl too, but they made me go. You and I had to slide down a little slope off the shoulder of the road. It was pretty back in there. I unbuttoned your pants and turned away so you could be private. Some purple violets were growing all over the grass, and wild jonquil. I picked them and took some twigs from a tree. When I got home I stuck them in the ground right down there." She nodded toward the window. "Just made a hole and stuck them in. I always liked flowers, you know. I was the one who started making artificial roses. Not Mama. Not Corinthians. Me. I loved to do it. It kept me . . . quiet. That's why they make those people in the asylum weave baskets and make rag rugs. It keeps them quiet. If they didn't have the baskets they might find out what's really wrong and . . . do something. Something terrible. After you peed on me, I wanted to kill you. I even tried to once or twice. In little ways:

leaving soap in your tub, things like that. But you never slipped and broke your neck, or fell down the stairs or anything." She laughed a little. "But then I saw something. The flowers I'd stuck in the ground, the ones you peed on—well, they died, of course, but not the twig. It lived. It's that maple. So I wasn't mad about it anymore—the pee, I mean—because the tree was growing. But it's dying now, Macon."

Milkman rubbed the corner of his eye with his ring finger. He was so sleepy. "Yeah, well, that was a helluva piss, wouldn't you say? You want me to give it another shot?"

Magdalene called Lena drew one hand out of the pocket of her robe and smashed it across his mouth. Milkman stiffened and made an incomplete gesture toward her. She ignored it and said, "As surely as my name is Magdalene, you are the line I will step across. I thought because that tree was alive that it was all right. But I forgot that there are all kinds of ways to pee on people."

"You listen here." Milkman was sober now and he spoke as steadily as he could. "I'm going to make some allowance for your sherry—up to a point. But you keep your hands off me. What is all this about peeing on people?"

"You've been doing it to us all your life."

"You're crazy. When have I ever messed over anybody in this house? When did you ever see me telling anybody what to do or giving orders? I don't carry no stick; I live and let live, you know that."

"I know you told Daddy about Corinthians, that she was seeing a man. Secretly. And—"

"I *had* to. I'd love for her to find somebody, but I *know* that man. I—I've been around him. And I don't think he . . ." Milkman stopped, unable to explain. About the Days, about what he suspected.

"Oh?" Her voice was thick with sarcasm. "You have somebody else in mind for her?"

"No."

"No? But he's Southside, and not good enough for her? It's good enough for you, but not for her, right?"

"Lena . . ."

"What do you know about somebody not being good enough
for somebody else? And since when did you care whether
Corinthians stood up or fell down? You've been laughing at us
all your life. Corinthians. Mama. Me. Using us, ordering us, and
judging us: how we cook your food; how we keep your house.
But now, all of a sudden, you have Corinthians' welfare at heart
and break her up from a man you don't approve of. Who are
you to approve or disapprove anybody or anything? I was
breathing air in the world thirteen years before your lungs were
even formed. Corinthians, twelve. You don't know a single
thing about either one of us—we made roses; that's all you knew
—but now you know what's best for the very woman who
wiped the dribble from your chin because you were too young
to know how to spit. Our girlhood was spent like a found nickel
on you. When you slept, we were quiet; when you were
hungry, we cooked; when you wanted to play, we entertained
you; and when you got grown enough to know the difference
between a woman and a two-toned Ford, everything in this
house stopped for you. You have yet to wash your own underwear, spread a bed, wipe the ring from your tub, or move a fleck
of your dirt from one place to another. And to this day, you
have never asked one of us if we were tired, or sad, or wanted a
cup of coffee. You've never picked up anything heavier than
your own feet, or solved a problem harder than fourth-grade
arithmetic. Where do you get the *right* to decide our lives?"

"Lena, cool it. I don't want to hear it."

"I'll tell you where. From that hog's gut that hangs down
between .your legs. Well, let me tell you something, baby
brother: you will need more than that. I don't know where you
will get it or who will give it to you, but mark my words, you
will need more than that. He has forbidden her to leave the
house, made her quit her job, evicted the man, garnisheed his
wages, and it is all because of you. You are exactly like him.
Exactly. I didn't go to college because of him. Because I was
afraid of what he might do to Mama. You think because you hit

him once that we all believe you were protecting her. Taking her side. It's a lie. You were taking over, letting us know you had the right to tell her and all of us what to do."

She stopped suddenly and Milkman could hear her breathing. When she started up again, her voice had changed; the steel was gone and in its place was a drifting, breezy music. "When we were little girls, before you were born, he took us to the ice-house once. Drove us there in his Hudson. We were all dressed up, and we stood there in front of those sweating black men, sucking ice out of our handkerchiefs, leaning forward a little so as not to drip water on our dresses. There were other children there. Barefoot, naked to the waist, dirty. But we stood apart, near the car, in white stockings, ribbons, and gloves. And when he talked to the men, he kept glancing at us, us and the car. The car and us. You see, he took us there so they could see us, envy us, envy him. Then one of the little boys came over to us and put his hand on Corinthians' hair. She offered him her piece of ice and before we knew it, *he* was running toward us. He knocked the ice out of her hand into the dirt and shoved us both into the car. First he displayed us, then he splayed us. All our lives were like that: he would parade us like virgins through Babylon, then humiliate us like whores in Babylon. Now he has knocked the ice out of Corinthians' hand again. And you are to blame." Magdalene called Lena was crying. "You are to blame. You are a sad, pitiful, stupid, selfish, hateful man. I hope your little hog's gut stands you in good stead, and that you take good care of it, because you don't have anything else. But I want to give you notice." She pulled her glasses out of her pocket and put them on. Her eyes doubled in size behind the lenses and were very pale and cold. "I don't make roses anymore, and you have pissed your last in this house."

Milkman said nothing.

"Now," she whispered, "get out of my room."

Milkman turned and walked across the room. It was good advice, he thought. Why not take it? He closed the door.

Part II

Chapter 10

When Hansel and Gretel stood in the forest and saw the house
in the clearing before them, the little hairs at the nape of their
necks must have shivered. Their knees must have felt so weak
that blinding hunger alone could have propelled them forward.
No one was there to warn or hold them; their parents, chastened
and grieving, were far away. So they ran as fast as they could to
the house where a woman older than death lived, and they ignored the shivering nape hair and the softness in their knees. A
grown man can also be energized by hunger, and any weakness
in his knees or irregularity in his heartbeat will disappear if he
thinks his hunger is about to be assuaged. Especially if the object
of his craving is not gingerbread or chewy gumdrops, but gold.

   Milkman ducked under the boughs of black walnut trees and
walked straight toward the big crumbling house. He knew that
an old woman had lived in it once, but he saw no signs of life
there now. He was oblivious to the universe of wood life that
did live there in layers of ivy grown so thick he could have sunk
his arm in it up to the elbow. Life that crawled, life that slunk

and crept and never closed its eyes. Life that burrowed and scurried, and life so still it was indistinguishable from the ivy stems on which it lay. Birth, life, and death—each took place on the hidden side of a leaf. From where he stood, the house looked as if it had been eaten by a galloping disease, the sores of which were dark and fluid.

One mile behind him were macadam and the reassuring sounds of an automobile or two—one of which was Reverend Cooper's car, driven by his thirteen-year-old nephew.

Noon, Milkman had told him. Come back at noon. He could just as easily have said twenty minutes, and now that he was alone, assaulted by what city people regard as raucous silence, he wished he had said five minutes. But even if the boy hadn't had chores to do, it would be foolish to be driven fifteen miles outside Danville on "business" and stay a hot minute.

He should never have made up that elaborate story to disguise his search for the cave; somebody might ask him about it. Besides, lies should be very simple, like the truth. Excessive detail was simply excess. But he was so tired after the long bus ride from Pittsburgh, coming right after the luxury of the flight, he was afraid he wouldn't be convincing.

The airplane ride exhilarated him, encouraged illusion and a feeling of invulnerability. High above the clouds, heavy yet light, caught in the stillness of speed ("Cruise," the pilot said), sitting in intricate metal become glistening bird, it was not possible to believe he had ever made a mistake, or could. Only one small thought troubled him—that Guitar was not there too. He would have loved it—the view, the food, the stewardesses. But Milkman wanted to do this by himself, with no input from anybody. This one time he wanted to go solo. In the air, away from real life, he felt free, but on the ground, when he talked to Guitar just before he left, the wings of all those other people's nightmares flapped in his face and constrained him. Lena's anger, Corinthians' loose and uncombed hair, matching her slack lips, Ruth's stepped-up surveillance, his father's bottomless greed, Hagar's hollow eyes—he did not know whether he deserved any of that, but he knew he was fed up and he knew he had to leave quickly. He told Guitar of his decision before he told his father.

"Daddy thinks the stuff is still in the cave."

"Could be." Guitar sipped his tea.

"Anyway, it's worth checking out. At least we'll know once and for all."

"I couldn't agree more."

"So I'm going after it."

"By yourself?"

Milkman sighed. "Yeah. Yeah. By myself. I need to get out of here. I mean I really have to go away somewhere."

Guitar put his cup down and folded his hands in front of his mouth. "Wouldn't it be easier with the two of us? Suppose you have trouble?"

"It might be easier, but it might look more suspicious with two men instead of one roaming around the woods. If I find it, I'll haul it back and we'll split it up just like we agreed. If I don't, well, I'll be back anyway."

"When you leaving?"

"Tomorrow morning."

"What's your father say about you going alone?"

"I haven't told him yet. You're the only one knows so far." Milkman stood up and went to the window that looked out on Guitar's little porch. "Shit."

Guitar was watching him carefully. "What's the matter?" he asked. "Why you so low? You don't act like a man on his way to the end of the rainbow."

Milkman turned around and sat on the sill. "I hope it *is* a rainbow, and nobody has run off with the pot, cause I need it."

"Everybody needs it."

"Not as bad as me."

Guitar smiled. "Look like you really got the itch now. More than before."

"Yeah, well, everything's worse than before, or maybe it's the same as before. I don't know. I just know that I want to live my own life. I don't want to be my old man's office boy no more. And as long as I'm in this place I will be. Unless I have my own money. I have to get out of that house and I don't want to owe anybody when I go. My family's driving me crazy. Daddy wants me to be like him and hate my mother. My mother wants me to think like her and hate my father. Corinthians won't speak to me; Lena wants me out. And Hagar wants me chained to her bed or dead. Everybody wants something from me, you know what I mean? Something they think they can't get anywhere else. Something they think I got. I don't know what it is—I mean what it is they really want."

Guitar stretched his legs. "They want your life, man."

"My life?"

"What else?"

"No. Hagar wants my life. My family . . . they want—"

"I don't mean that way. I don't mean they want your dead life; they want your living life."

"You're losing me," said Milkman.

"Look. It's the condition our condition is in. Everybody wants the life of a black man. Everybody. White men want us dead or quiet—which is the same thing as dead. White women, same thing. They want us, you know, 'universal,' human, no 'race consciousness.' Tame, except in bed. They like a little racial loincloth in the bed. But outside the bed they want us to be individuals. You tell them, 'But they lynched my papa,' and they say, 'Yeah, but you're better than the lynchers are, so forget it.' And black women, they want your whole self. Love, they call it, and understanding. 'Why don't you *understand* me?' What they mean is, Don't love anything on earth except me. They say, 'Be responsible,' but what they mean is, Don't go anywhere where I ain't. You try to climb Mount Everest, they'll tie up your ropes. Tell them you want to go to the bottom of the sea—just for a look—they'll hide your oxygen tank. Or you don't even have to go that far. Buy a horn and say you want to play. Oh, they love the music, but only after you pull eight at the post office. Even if you make it, even if you stubborn and mean and you get to the top of Mount Everest, or you do play and you good, real good—that still ain't enough. You blow your lungs out on the horn and they want what breath you got left to hear about how you love them. They want your full attention. Take a risk and they say you not for real. That you don't love them. They won't even let you risk your own life, man, your *own* life—unless it's over them. You can't even die unless it's about them. What good is a man's life if he can't even choose what to die for?"

"Nobody can choose what to die for."

"Yes you can, and if you can't, you can damn well try to."

"You sound bitter. If that's what you feel, why are you playing your numbers game? Keeping the racial ratio the same and all? Every time I ask you what you doing it for, you talk about love. Loving Negroes. Now you say—"

"It *is* about love. What else but love? Can't I love what I criticize?"

"Yeah, but except for skin color, I can't tell the difference between what the white women want from us and what the colored women want. You say they all want our life, our living life. So if a colored woman is raped and killed, why do the Days rape and kill a white woman? Why worry about the colored woman at all?"

Guitar cocked his head and looked sideways at Milkman. His nostrils flared a little. "Because she's *mine*."

"Yeah. Sure." Milkman didn't try to keep disbelief out of his voice. "So everybody wants to kill us, except black men, right?"

"Right."

"Then why did my father—who is a very black man—try to kill me before I was even born?"

"Maybe he thought you were a little girl; I don't know. But I don't have to tell you that your father is a very strange Negro. He'll reap the benefits of what we sow, and there's nothing we can do about that. He behaves like a white man, thinks like a white man. As a matter of fact, I'm glad you brought him up. Maybe you can tell me how, after losing everything his own father worked for to some crackers, after *seeing* his father shot down by them, how can he keep his knees bent? Why does he love them so? And Pilate. She's worse. She saw it too and, first, goes back to get a cracker's bones for some kind of crazy self-punishment, and second, leaves the cracker's gold right where it was! Now, is that voluntary slavery or not? She slipped into those Jemima shoes cause they fit."

"Look, Guitar. First of all, my father doesn't care whether a white man lives or swallows lye. He just wants what they have. And Pilate is a little nuts, but she wanted us out of there. If she hadn't been smart, both our asses would be cooling in the joint right now."

"My ass. Not yours. She wanted you out, not me."

"Come on. That ain't even fair."

"No. Fair is one more thing I've given up."

"But to Pilate? What for? She knew what we did and still she bailed us out. Went down for us, clowned and crawled for us. You saw her face. You ever see anything like it in your life?"

"Once. Just once," said Guitar. And he remembered anew how his mother smiled when the white man handed her the four ten-dollar bills. More than gratitude was showing in her eyes. More than that. Not love, but a willingness to love. Her husband was sliced in half and boxed backward. He'd heard the mill men tell how the two halves, not even fitted together, were placed cut side down, skin side up, in the coffin. Facing each other. Each eye looking deep into its mate. Each nostril inhaling the breath the other nostril had expelled. The right cheek facing the left. The right elbow crossed over the left elbow. And he had worried then, as a child, that when his father was wakened on Judgment Day his first sight would not be glory or the magnificent head of God—or even the rainbow. It would be his own other eye.

Even so, his mother had smiled and shown that willingness to love the man who was responsible for dividing his father up throughout eternity. It wasn't the divinity from the foreman's wife that made him sick. That came later. It was the fact that instead of life insurance, the sawmill owner gave his mother forty dollars "to tide you and them kids over," and she took it happily and bought each of them a big peppermint stick on the very day of the funeral. Guitar's two sisters and baby brother sucked away at the bone-white and blood-red stick, but Guitar couldn't. He held it in his hand until it stuck there. All day he held it. At the graveside, at the funeral supper, all the sleepless night. The others made fun of what they believed was his miserliness, but he could not eat it or throw it away, until finally, in the outhouse, he let it fall into the earth's stinking hole.

"Once," he said. "Just once." And felt the nausea all over again. "The crunch is here," he said. "The big crunch. Don't let them Kennedys fool you. And I'll tell you the truth: I hope your daddy's right about what's in that cave. And I sure hope you don't have no second thoughts about getting it back here."

"What's that supposed to mean?"

"It means I'm nervous. Real nervous. I need the bread."

"If you're in a hurt, I can let you have—"

"Not *me*. *Us*. We have work to do, man. And just recently"—Guitar squinted his eyes at Milkman—"just recently one of us was put out in the streets, by somebody I don't have to name. And his wages were garnisheed cause this somebody said two months rent was owing. This somebody needs two months rent on a twelve-by-twelve hole in the wall like a fish needs side pockets. Now we have to take care of this man, get him a place to stay, pay the so-called back rent, and—"

"That was my fault. Let me tell you what happened. . . ."

"No. Don't tell me nothing. You ain't the landlord and you didn't put him out. You may have handed him the gun, but you didn't pull the trigger. I'm not blaming you."

"Why not? You talk about my father, my father's sister, and you'll talk about my sister too if I let you. Why you trust me?"

"Baby, I hope I never have to ask myself that question."

It ended all right, that gloomy conversation. There was no real anger and nothing irrevocable was said. When Milkman left, Guitar opened his palm as usual and Milkman slapped it. Maybe it was fatigue, but the touching of palms seemed a little weak.

At the Pittsburgh airport he discovered that Danville was 240 miles northeast, and not accessible by any public transportation other than a Greyhound bus. Reluctantly, unwilling to give up the elegance he had felt on the flight, he taxied from the airport to the bus station and settled himself for two idle hours before the Greyhound left. By the time he boarded, the inactivity, the picture magazines he'd read, the strolls in the streets near the station, had exhausted him. He fell asleep fifteen minutes outside Pittsburgh. When he woke it was late in the afternoon, with an hour more to go before he reached Danville. His father had raved about the beauty of this part of the country, but Milkman saw it as merely green, deep into its Indian summer but cooler than his own city, although it was farther south. The mountains, he thought, must make for the difference in temperature. For a few minutes he tried to enjoy the scenery running past his window, then the city man's boredom with nature's repetition overtook him. Some places had lots of trees, some did not; some fields were green, some were not, and the hills in the distance were like the hills in every distance. Then he watched signs—the names of towns that lay twenty-two miles ahead, seventeen miles to the east, five miles to the northeast. And the names of junctions, counties, crossings, bridges, stations, tunnels, mountains, rivers, creeks, landings, parks, and lookout points. Everybody had to do his act, he thought, for surely anybody who was interested in Dudberry Point already knew where it was.

He had two bottles of Cutty Sark in his suitcase, along with two shirts and some underwear. The large suitcase, he thought, would have its real load on the return trip. Now he wished he had not checked it under the bus, for he wanted a drink right then. According to his watch, the gold Longines his mother had given him, it would be another twenty minutes before a stop. He lay back on the headrest and tried to fall asleep. His eyes

were creasing from the sustained viewing of uneventful countryside.

In Danville he was astonished to learn that the bus depot was a
diner on route 11 where the counterman sold bus tickets, hamburgers, coffee, cheese and peanut butter crackers, cigarettes,
candy and a cold-cut plate. No lockers, no baggage room, no
taxi, and now he realized no men's room either.

Suddenly he felt ridiculous. What was he supposed to do? Put
his suitcase down and ask the man: Where is the cave near the
farm where my father lived fifty-eight years ago? He knew
nobody, had no names except the first name of an old lady who
was now dead. And rather than call any more attention to himself in this tiny farming town than his beige three-piece suit, his
button-down light-blue shirt and black string tie, and his beautiful Florsheim shoes had already brought, he asked the counterman if he could check his bag there. The man gazed at the
suitcase and seemed to be turning the request over in his mind.

"I'll pay," said Milkman.

"Leave 'er here. Back a the pop crates," the man said. "When
you wanna pick 'er up?"

"This evening," he said.

"Fine. She'll be right here."

Milkman left the diner/bus station with a small satchel of
shaving things and walked out into the streets of Danville, Pennsylvania. He'd seen places like this in Michigan, of course, but he
never had to do anything in them other than buy gas. The three
stores on the street were closing up for the night. It was five-
fifteen and about a dozen people, all told, were walking on the
sidewalks. One of them was a Negro. A tall man, elderly, with a
brown peaked cap and an old-fashioned collar. Milkman followed him for a while, then caught up to him and said, "Say, I
wonder if you could help me." He smiled as he spoke.

The man turned around but did not answer. Milkman wondered if he had offended him in some way. Finally the man
nodded and said, "Do what I can." He had a slight country lilt,
like that of the white man at the counter.

"I'm looking for . . . Circe, a lady named Circe. Well, not

her, but her house. Do you know where she used to live? I'm from out of town. I just got off the bus. I have some business to take care of here, an insurance policy, and I need to check on some property out there."

The man was listening and apparently not going to interrupt him, so Milkman ended his sentence lamely with: "Can you help me?"

"Reverend Cooper would know," said the man.

"Where can I find him?" Milkman felt something missing from the conversation.

"Stone Lane. Follow this here street till you come to the post office. Go on around the post office and that'll be Windsor. The next street is Stone Lane. He lives in there."

"Will there be a church there?" Milkman assumed a preacher lived next door to his church.

"No. No. Church ain't got no parsonage. Reverend Cooper lives in Stone Lane. Yella house, I believe."

"Thanks," said Milkman. "Thanks a lot."

"Mighty welcome," said the man. "Good evenin'." And he walked away.

Milkman considered whether to go back for his suitcase, abandoned the idea, and followed the directions given him. An American flag identified the post office, a frame structure next to a drugstore that served also as the Western Union office. He turned left at the corner, but noticed there were no street signs anywhere. How could he find Windsor or Stone Lane if there were no signs? He walked through a residential street, another and another, and he was just about to go back to the drugstore and look under "A.M.E." or "A.M.E. Zion" in the telephone directory when he saw a yellow-and-white house. Maybe this is it, he thought. He climbed the steps, determined to mind his manners. A thief should be polite and win goodwill.

"Good evening. Is Reverend Cooper here?"

A woman was standing in the doorway. "Yes, he's here. Would you like to come in? I'll call him."

"Thank you." Milkman entered a tiny hall and waited.

A short chubby man appeared, fingering his glasses. "Yes, sir? You wanted to see me?" His eyes ran rapidly over Milkman's clothes, but his voice betrayed no excessive curiosity.

"Yes. Uh . . . how are you?"

"Fine. Fine. And you?"

"Pretty good." Milkman felt as awkward as he sounded. He had never had to try to make a pleasant impression on a stranger before, never needed anything from a stranger before, and did not remember ever asking anybody in the world how they were. I might as well say it all, he thought. "I could use your help, sir. My name is Macon Dead. My father is from around—"

"Dead? Macon Dead, you say?"

"Yes." Milkman smiled apologetically for the name. "My father—"

"Well, I'll be." Reverend Cooper took off his glasses. "Well, I'll be! Esther!" He threw his voice over his shoulder without taking his eyes off his guest. "Esther, come here!" Then to Milkman: "I know your people!"

Milkman smiled and let his shoulders slump a little. It was a good feeling to come into a strange town and find a stranger who knew your people. All his life he'd heard the tremor in the word: "I live here, but my *people* . . ." or: "She acts like she ain't got no *people*," or: "Do any of your *people* live there?" But he hadn't known what it meant: links. He remembered Freddie sitting in Sonny's Shop just before Christmas, saying, "None of my people would take me in." Milkman beamed at Reverend Cooper and his wife. "You do?"

"Sit on down here, boy. You the son of the Macon Dead I knew. Oh, well, now, I don't mean to say I knew him all that well. Your daddy was four or five years older than me, and they didn't get to town much, but everybody round here remembers the old man. Old Macon Dead, your granddad. My daddy and him was good friends. A blacksmith, my daddy was. I'm the only one got the call. Well well well." Reverend Cooper grinned and massaged his knees. "Oh, Lord, I'm forgetting myself. You must be hungry. Esther, get him something to fill himself up on."

"Oh, no. No, thank you, sir. Maybe a little something to drink. I mean if you do drink, that is."

"Sure. Sure. Nothing citified, I'm sorry to say, but— Esther!" She was on her way to the kitchen. "Bring some glasses and get that whiskey out the cupboard. This here's Macon Dead's boy and he's tired and needs a drink. Tell me, how'd you find me? Don't tell me your daddy remembered me?"

"He probably does, but I met a man in the street and he told me how to find you."

"You asked him for me?" Reverend Cooper wanted to get all the facts straight. Already he was framing the story for his friends: how the man came to his house first, how he asked for him. . . .

Esther returned with a Coca-Cola tray, two glasses, and a large mayonnaise jar of what looked like water. Reverend Cooper poured it warm and neat into the two glasses. No ice, no water—just pure rye whiskey that almost tore Milkman's throat when he swallowed it.

"No. I didn't ask for you by name. I asked him if he knew where a woman named Circe used to live."

"Circe? Yes. Lord, old Circe!"

"He told me to talk to you."

Reverend Cooper smiled and poured more whiskey. "Everybody round here knows me and I know everybody."

"Well, I know my father stayed with her awhile, after they . . . when they . . . after his father died."

"They had a fine place. Mighty fine. Some white folks own it now. Course that's what they wanted. That's why they shot him. Upset a lot of people here, a whole lot of people. Scared 'em too. But didn't your daddy have a sister name of Pilate?"

"Yes, sir. Pilate."

"Still living, is she?"

"Oh, yes. Very much living."

"Issat so? Pretty girl, real pretty. My daddy was the one made the earring for her. That's how we knew they was alive. After Old Macon Dead was killed, nobody knew whether the children was dead too or what. Then a few weeks passed and Circe came to my daddy's shop. Right across from where the post office is now—that's where my daddy's blacksmith shop was. She came in there with this little metal box with a piece of paper bag folded up in it. Pilate's name was written on it. Circe didn't tell Daddy anything, but that he was to make a earring out of it. She stole a brooch from the folks she worked for. My daddy took the gold pin off it and soldered it to the box. So we knew they was alive and Circe was taking care of 'em. They'd be all right with Circe. She worked for the Butlers—rich white folks, you know—but she was a good midwife in those days. Delivered everybody. Me included."

Maybe it was the whiskey, which always made other people gracious when he drank it, but Milkman felt a glow listening to a story come from this man that he'd heard many times before but only half listened to. Or maybe it was being there in the place where it happened that made it seem so real. Hearing Pilate talk about caves and woods and earrings on Darling Street, or his father talk about cooking wild turkey over the automobile noise of Not Doctor Street, seemed exotic, something from another world and age, and maybe not even true. Here in the parsonage, sitting in a cane-bottomed chair near an upright piano and drinking homemade whiskey poured from a mayonnaise jar, it was real. Without knowing it, he had walked right by the place where Pilate's earring had been fashioned, the earring that had fascinated him when he was little, the fixing of which informed the colored people here that the children of the murdered man were alive. And this was the living room of the son of the man who made the earring.

"Did anybody ever catch the men who did it—who killed him?"

Reverend Cooper raised his eyebrows. "Catch?" he asked, his face full of wonder. Then he smiled again. "Didn't have to catch 'em. They never went nowhere."

"I mean did they have a trial; were they arrested?"

"Arrested for what? Killing a nigger? Where did you say you was from?"

"You mean nobody did anything? Didn't even try to find out who did it?"

"Everybody knew who did it. Same people Circe worked for—the Butlers."

"And nobody did anything?" Milkman wondered at his own anger. He hadn't felt angry when he first heard about it. Why now?

"Wasn't nothing to do. White folks didn't care, colored folks didn't dare. Wasn't no police like now. Now we got a county sheriff handles things. Not then. Then the circuit judge came through just once or twice a year. Besides, the people what did it owned half the county. Macon's land was in their way. Folks just was thankful the children escaped."

"You said Circe worked for the people who killed him. Did she know that?"

"Course she did."

"And she let them stay there?"

"Not out in the open. She hid them."

"Still, they were in the same house, right?"

"Yep. Best place, I'd say. If they came to town somebody'd see 'em. Nobody would think of looking there."

"Did Daddy—did my father know that?"

"I don't know what he knew, if Circe ever told him. I never saw him after the murder. None of us did."

"Where are they? The Butlers. They still live here?"

"Dead now. Every one of 'em. The last one, the girl Elizabeth, died a couple years back. Barren as a rock and just as old. Things work out, son. The ways of God are mysterious, but if you live it out, just live it out, you see that it always works out. Nothing they stole or killed for did 'em a bit a good. Not one bit."

"I don't care whether it did them good. The fact is they did somebody else harm."

Reverend Cooper shrugged. "White folks different up your way?"

"No, I guess not. . . . Sometimes, though, you can do something."

"What?" The preacher looked genuinely interested.

Milkman couldn't answer except in Guitar's words, so he said nothing.

"See this here?" The reverend turned around and showed Milkman a knot the size of a walnut that grew behind his ear. "Some of us went to Philly to try and march in an Armistice Day parade. This was after the First World War. We were invited and had a permit, but the people, the white people, didn't like us being there. They started a fracas. You know, throwing rocks and calling us names. They didn't care nothing 'bout the uniform. Anyway, some police on horseback came—to quiet them down, we thought. They ran *us* down. Right under their horses. This here's what a hoof can do. Ain't that something?"

"Jesus God."

"You wouldn't be here to even things up, would you?" The preacher leaned over his stomach.

"No. I'm passing through, that's all. Just thought I'd look around. I wanted to see the farm. . . ."

"Cause any evening up left to do, Circe took care of."

"What'd she do?"

"Hah! What didn't she do?"

"Sorry I didn't come out here long time ago. I would have liked to meet her. She must have been a hundred years old when she died."

"Older. Was a hundred when I was a boy."

"Is the farm nearby?" Milkman appeared mildly interested.

"Not too far."

"I sort of wanted to see where it was since I'm out this way. Daddy talked so much about it."

"It's right back of the Butler place, about fifteen miles out. I can take you there. My old piece of car's in the shop, but it was supposed to be ready yesterday. I'll check on it."

Milkman waited four days for the car to be ready. Four days at Reverend Cooper's house as his guest, and the purpose of long visits from every old man in the town who remembered his father or his grandfather, and some who'd only heard. They all repeated various aspects of the story, all talked about how beautiful Lincoln's Heaven was. Sitting in the kitchen, they looked at Milkman with such rheumy eyes, and spoke about his grandfather with such awe and affection, Milkman began to miss him too. His own father's words came back to him: "I worked right alongside my father. Right alongside him." Milkman thought then that his father was boasting of his manliness as a child. Now he knew he had been saying something else. That he loved his father; had an intimate relationship with him; that his father loved him, trusted him, and found him worthy of working "right alongside" him. "Something went wild in me," he'd said, "when I saw him on the ground."

His was the genuine feeling that Milkman had faked when Reverend Cooper described the hopelessness of "doing anything." These men remembered both Macon Deads as extraordinary men. Pilate they remembered as a pretty woods-wild girl "that couldn't nobody put shoes on." Only one of them remembered his grandmother. "Good-lookin, but looked like a white woman. Indian, maybe. Black hair and slanted-up eyes. Died in childbirth, you know." The more the old men talked—the more he heard about the only farm in the county that grew peaches, real peaches like they had in Georgia, the feasts they had when hunting was over, the pork kills in the winter and the work, the backbreaking work of a going farm—the more he missed something in his life. They talked about digging a well, fashioning traps, felling trees, warming orchards with fire when spring weather was bad, breaking young horses, training dogs. And in it all was his own father, the second Macon Dead, their contemporary, who was strong as an ox, could ride bareback and barefoot, who, they agreed, outran, outplowed, outshot, outpicked, outrode them all. He could not recognize that stern, greedy, unloving man in the boy they talked about, but he loved the boy they described and loved that boy's father, with his hip-roofed barn, his peach trees, and Sunday break-of-dawn fishing parties in a fish pond that was two acres wide.

They talked on and on, using Milkman as the ignition that gunned their memories. The good times, the hard times, things that changed, things that stayed the same—and head and shoulders above all of it was the tall, magnificent Macon Dead, whose death, it seemed to him, was the beginning of their own dying even though they were young boys at the time. Macon Dead was the farmer they wanted to be, the clever irrigator, the peach-tree grower, the hog slaughterer, the wild-turkey roaster, the man who could plow forty in no time flat and sang like an angel while he did it. He had come out of nowhere, as ignorant as a hammer and broke as a convict, with nothing but free papers, a Bible, and a pretty black-haired wife, and in one year he'd leased ten acres, the next ten more. Sixteen years later he had one of the best farms in Montour County. A farm that colored their lives like a paintbrush and spoke to them like a sermon. "You see?" the farm said to them. "See? See what you can do? Never mind you can't tell one letter from another, never mind you born a slave, never mind you lose your name, never mind your daddy dead, never mind nothing. Here, this here, is what a man can do if he puts his mind to it and his back in it. Stop sniveling," it said. "Stop picking around the edges of the world. Take advantage, and if you can't take advantage, take disadvantage. We live here. On this planet, in this nation, in this county right here. Nowhere else! We got a home in this rock, don't you see! Nobody starving in my home; nobody crying in my home, and if I got a home you got one too! Grab it. Grab this land! Take it, hold it, my brothers, make it, my brothers, shake it, squeeze it, turn it, twist it, beat it, kick it, kiss it, whip it, stomp it, dig it, plow it, seed it, reap it, rent it, buy it, sell it, own it, build it, multiply it, and pass it on—can you hear me? Pass it on!"

But they shot the top of his head off and ate his fine Georgia peaches. And even as boys these men began to die and were dying still. Looking at Milkman in those nighttime talks, they

yearned for something. Some word from him that would re-
kindle the dream and stop the death they were dying. That's
why Milkman began to talk about his father, the boy they
knew, the son of the fabulous Macon Dead. He bragged a little
and they came alive. How many houses his father owned (they
grinned); the new car every two years (they laughed); and
when he told them how his father tried to buy the Erie Lackawanna (it sounded better that way), they hooted with joy.
That's him! That's Old Macon Dead's boy, all right! They
wanted to know everything and Milkman found himself rattling
off assets like an accountant, describing deals, total rents income,
bank loans, and this new thing his father was looking into—the
stock market.

Suddenly, in the midst of his telling, Milkman wanted the
gold. He wanted to get up right then and there and go get it.
Run to where it was and snatch every grain of it from under the
noses of the Butlers, who were dumb enough to believe that if
they killed one man his whole line died. He glittered in the light
of their adoration and grew fierce with pride.

"Who'd your daddy marry?"

"The daughter of the richest Negro doctor in town."

"That's him! That's Macon Dead!"

"Send you all to college?"

"Sent my sisters. I work right alongside him in our office."

"Hah! Keep you home to get that money! Macon Dead
gonna always make him some money!"

"What kinda car he drive?"

"Buick. Two-twenty-five."

"Great God, a deuce and a quarter! What year?"

"This year!"

"That's him! That's Macon Dead! He gonna buy the Erie
Lackawanna! If he want it, he'll get it! Bless my soul. Bet he
worry them white folks to death. Can't nobody keep him down!
Not no Macon Dead! Not in this world! And not in the next!
Haw! Goddam! The Erie Lacka*wan*na!"

After all the waiting, Reverend Cooper couldn't go. His preaching income was supplemented by freightyard work and he was called for an early shift. His nephew, called Nephew since he was their only one, was assigned to drive Milkman out to the farm—as close as they could get. Nephew was thirteen and barely able to see over the steering wheel.

"Does he have a license?" Milkman asked Mrs. Cooper.

"Not yet," she said, and when she saw his consternation she explained that farm kids drove early—they had to.

Milkman and Nephew started out right after breakfast. It took them the better part of an hour because the roads were curving two-lanes and they spent twenty minutes behind a light truck they couldn't pull around. Nephew spoke very little. He seemed interested only in Milkman's clothes, which he took every opportunity to examine. Milkman decided to give him one of his shirts, and asked him to stop by the bus station to pick up the suitcase he'd left there.

Finally Nephew slowed down on a stretch of road that showed no houses at all. He stopped.

"What's the matter? You want me to drive?"

"No, sir. This is it."

"What's it? Where?"

"Back in there." He pointed to some bushes. "The road to the Butler place is in there and the farm's back behind it. You got to walk it. Car won't make it."

Nothing was truer; as it turned out, Milkman's feet could hardly make it over the stony road covered with second growth. He had asked Nephew to wait, thinking he would survey the area quickly and come back later on his own. But the boy had chores, he said, and would be back whenever Milkman wanted him to be there.

"An hour," said Milkman.

"Take me an hour just to get back to town," said Nephew.

"Reverend Cooper said you were to take me. Not leave me stranded."

"My mama whip me, I don't do my chores."

Milkman was annoyed, but because he didn't want the boy to think he was nervous about being left out there alone, he agreed to having him come back at—he glanced at his heavy, overdesigned watch—at noon. It was nine o'clock then.

His hat had been knocked off by the first branches of the old walnut trees, so he held it in his hand. His cuffless pants were darkened by the mile-long walk over moist leaves. The quiet fairly roared in his ears. He was uncomfortable and a little anxious, but the gold loomed large in his mind, as did the faces of the men he'd drunk with last night, and he stepped firmly onto the gravel and leaves of the driveway which circled the biggest house he'd ever seen.

This is where they stayed, he thought, where Pilate cried when given cherry jam. He stood still a moment. It must have been beautiful, must have seemed like a palace to them, but neither had ever spoken of it in any terms but how imprisoned they felt, how difficult it was to see the sky from their room, how repelled they were by the carpets, the draperies. Without knowing who killed their father, they instinctively hated the murderers' house. And it did look like a murderer's house. Dark, ruined, evil. Never, not since he knelt by his window sill wishing he could fly, had he felt so lonely. He saw the eyes of a child peer at him over the sill of the one second-story window the ivy had not covered. He smiled. Must be myself I'm seeing—thinking about how I used to watch the sky out the window. Or maybe it's the light trying to get through the trees. Four graceful columns supported the portico, and the huge double door featured a heavy, brass knocker. He lifted it and let it fall; the sound was soaked up like a single raindrop in cotton. Nothing stirred. He looked back down the path and saw the green maw out of which he had come, a greenish-black tunnel, the end of which was nowhere in sight.

The farm, they said, was right in back of the Butler place, but knowing how different their concept of distance was, he thought he'd better get moving. If he found what he was looking for he would have to come back at night—with equipment, of course, but also with some familiarity with the area. On impulse he reached out his hand and tried to turn the doorknob. It didn't budge. Half turning to leave—literally as an afterthought —he pushed the door and it swung open with a sigh. He leaned in. The smell prevented him from seeing anything more than the absence of light did. A hairy animal smell, ripe, rife, suffocating. He coughed and looked for somewhere to spit, for the odor was in his mouth, coating his teeth and tongue. He pulled a handkerchief from his back pocket, held it over his nose, backed away from the open door, and had just begun to spill the little breakfast he'd eaten when the odor disappeared and, quite suddenly, in its place was a sweet spicy perfume. Like ginger root—pleasant, clean, seductive. Surprised and charmed by it, he retraced his steps and went inside. After a second or two he was able to see the hand-laid and hand-finished wooden floor in a huge hall, and at its farther end a wide staircase spiraling up into the dark. His eyes traveled up the stairs.

He had had dreams as a child, dreams every child had, of the witch who chased him down dark alleys, between lawn trees, and finally into rooms from which he could not escape. Witches in black dresses and red underskirts; witches with pink eyes and green lips, tiny witches, long rangy witches, frowning witches, smiling witches, screaming witches and laughing witches, witches that flew, witches that ran, and some that merely glided on the ground. So when he saw the woman at the top of the stairs there was no way for him to resist climbing up toward her outstretched hands, her fingers spread wide for him, her mouth gaping open for him, her eyes devouring him. In a dream you climb the stairs. She grabbed him, grabbed his shoulders and pulled him right up against her and tightened her arms around him. Her head came to his chest and the feel of that hair under his chin, the dry bony hands like steel springs rubbing his back, her floppy mouth babbling into his vest, made him dizzy, but he knew that always, always at the very instant of the pounce or the gummy embrace he would wake with a scream and an erection. Now he had only the erection.

Milkman closed his eyes, helpless to pull away before the completion of the dream. What made him surface from it was a humming sound around his knees. He looked down and there, surrounding him, was a pack of golden-eyed dogs, each of which had the intelligent child's eyes he had seen from the window. Abruptly the woman let him go and he looked down at her too. Beside the calm, sane, appraising eyes of the dogs, her eyes looked crazy. Beside their combed, brushed gun-metal hair, hers was wild and filthy.

She spoke to the dogs. "Go on away. Helmut, go on. Horst, move." She waved her hands and the dogs obeyed.

"Come, come," she said to Milkman. "In here." She took his hand in both of hers, and he followed her—his arm outstretched, his hand in hers—like a small boy being dragged reluctantly to bed. Together they weaved among the bodies of the dogs that floated around his legs. She led him into a room, made him sit on a gray velvet sofa, and dismissed all the dogs but two that lay at her feet.

"Remember the Weimaraners?" she asked, settling herself, pulling her chair close to him.

She was old. So old she was colorless. So old only her mouth and eyes were distinguishable features in her face. Nose, chin, cheekbones, forehead, neck all had surrendered their identity to the pleats and crochetwork of skin committed to constant change.

Milkman struggled for a clear thought, so hard to come by in a dream: Perhaps this woman is Circe. But Circe is dead. This woman is alive. That was as far as he got, because although the woman was talking to him, she might in any case still be dead— as a matter of fact, she *had* to be dead. Not because of the wrinkles, and the face so old it could not be alive, but because out of the toothless mouth came the strong, mellifluent voice of a twenty-year-old girl.

"I knew one day you would come back. Well, that's not entirely true. Some days I doubted it and some days I didn't think about it at all. But you see, I was right. You did come."

It was awful listening to that voice come from that face. Maybe something was happening to his ears. He wanted to hear the sound of his own voice, so he decided to take a chance on logic.

"Excuse me. I'm his son. I'm Macon Dead's son. Not the one you knew."

She stopped smiling.

"My name is Macon Dead too, but I'm thirty-two years old. You knew my father and his father too." So far, so good. His voice was the same. Now he needed only to know if he had assessed the situation correctly. She did not answer him. "You're Circe, aren't you?"

"Yes; Circe," she said, but she seemed to have lost all interest in him. "My name is Circe."

"I'm just visiting," he said. "I spent a couple of days with Reverend Cooper and his wife. They're the ones brought me out here."

"I thought you were him. I thought you came back to see me. Where is he? *My* Macon?"

"Back home. He's alive. He told me about you. . . ."

"And Pilate. Where is she?"

"There too. She's fine."

"Well, you look like him. You really do." But she didn't sound convinced.

"He's seventy-two years old now," said Milkman. He thought that would clear things up, make her know he couldn't be the Macon she knew, who was sixteen when she last saw him. But all she said was "Uhn," as though seventy-two, thirty-two, any age at all, meant nothing whatsoever to her. Milkman wondered how old she really was.

"Are you hungry?" she asked.

"No. Thank you. I ate breakfast."

"So you've been staying with that little Cooper boy?"

"Yes, ma'am."

"A runt. I told him not to smoke, but children don't listen."

"Do you mind if I do?" Milkman was relaxing a little and he hoped the cigarette would relax him more.

She shrugged. "Do what you like. Everybody does what he likes nowadays anyway."

Milkman lit the cigarette and the dogs hummed at the sound of the match, their eyes glittering toward the flame.

"Ssh!" whispered Circe.

"Beautiful," said Milkman.

"What's beautiful?"

"The dogs."

"They're not beautiful, they're strange, but they keep things away. I'm completely worn out taking care of 'em. They belonged to Miss Butler. She bred them, crossbred them. Tried for years to get them in the AKC. They wouldn't permit it."

"What did you call them?"

"Weimaraners. German."

"What do you do with them?"

"Oh, I keep some. Sell some. Till we all die in here together." She smiled.

She had dainty habits which matched her torn and filthy clothes in precisely the way her strong young cultivated voice matched her wizened face. Her white hair—braided, perhaps; perhaps not—she touched as though replacing a wayward strand from an elegant coiffure. And her smile—an opening of flesh like celluloid dissolving under a drop of acid—was accompanied by a press of fingers on her chin. It was this combination of daintiness and cultivated speech that misled Macon and invited him to regard her as merely foolish.

"You should get out once in a while."

She looked at him.

"Is this your house now? Did they will you this? Is that why you have to stay here?"

She pressed her lips over her gums. "The only reason I'm here alone is because she died. She killed herself. All the money was gone, so she killed herself. Stood right there on the landing where you were a minute ago and threw herself off the banister. She didn't die right away, though; she lay in the bed a week or two and there was nobody here but us. The dogs were in the kennel then. I brought her in the world, just like I did her mother and her grandmother before that. Birthed just about everybody in the county, I did. Never lost one either. Never lost nobody but your mother. Well, grandmother, I guess she was. Now I birth dogs."

"Some friend of Reverend Cooper said she looked white. My grandmother. Was she?"

"No. Mixed. Indian mostly. A good-looking woman, but fierce, for the young woman I knew her as. Crazy about her husband too, overcrazy. You know what I mean? Some women love too hard. She watched over him like a pheasant hen. Nervous. Nervous love."

Milkman thought about this mixed woman's great-granddaughter, Hagar, and said, "Yes. I know what you mean."

"But a good woman. I cried like a baby when I lost her. Like a baby. Poor Sing."

"What?" He wondered if she lisped.

"I cried like a baby when I—"

"No. I mean what did you call her?"

"Sing. Her name was Sing."

"Sing? Sing Dead. Where'd she get a name like that?"

"Where'd you get a name like yours? White people name Negroes like race horses."

"I suppose so. Daddy told me how they got their name."

"What'd he tell you?"

Milkman told her the story about the drunken Yankee.

"Well, he didn't have to keep the name. She made him. She made him keep that name," Circe said when he was through.

"She?"

"Sing. His wife. They met on a wagon going North. Ate pecans all the way, she told me. It was a wagonful of ex-slaves going to the promised land."

"Was she a slave too?"

"No. No indeed. She always bragged how she was never a slave. Her people neither."

"Then what was she doing on that wagon?"

"I can't answer you because I don't know. Never crossed my mind to ask her."

"Where were they coming from? Georgia?"

"No. Virginia. Both of them lived in Virginia, her people and his. Down around Culpeper somewhere. Charlemagne or something like that."

"I think that's where Pilate was for a while. She lived all over the country before she came to us."

"Did she ever marry that boy?"

"What boy?"

"The boy she had the baby by."

"No. She didn't marry him."

"Didn't think she would. She was too ashamed."

"Ashamed of what?"

"Her stomach."

"Oh, that."

"Borned herself. I had very little to do with it. I thought they were both dead, the mother and the child. When she popped out you could have knocked me over. I hadn't heard a heartbeat anywhere. She just came on out. Your daddy loved her. Hurt me to hear they broke away from one another. So it does me good to hear they're back together again." She had warmed up talking about the past and Milkman decided not to tell her that Macon and Pilate just lived in the same city. He wondered how she knew about their split, and if she knew what they broke apart about.

"You knew about their quarrel?" he asked quietly, nonchalantly.

"Not the substance. Just the fact. Pilate came back here just after her baby was born. One winter. She told me they split up when they left here and she hadn't seen him since."

"Pilate told me they lived in a cave for a few days after they left this house."

"Is that right? Must have been Hunters Cave. Hunters used it to rest up in there sometimes. Eat. Smoke. Sleep. That's where they dumped Old Macon's body."

"They who? I thought . . . My father said he buried him. Down by a creek or a river someplace where they used to fish."

"He did. But it was too shallow and too close to the water. The body floated up at the first heavy rain. Those children hadn't been gone a month when it floated up. Some men were fishing down there and saw this body, a Negro. So they knew who it was. Dumped it in the cave, and it was summer too. You'd think they would have buried a body in the summer. I told Mrs. Butler I thought it was a disgrace."

"Daddy doesn't know that."

"Well, don't tell him. Let him have his peace. It's hard enough with a murdered father; he don't need to know what happened to the body."

"Did Pilate tell you why she came back here?"

"Yes. She said her father told her to. She had visits from him, she said."

"I'd like to see that cave. Where he's . . . where they put him."

"Won't be anything left to see now. That's been a long time ago."

"I know, but maybe there's something I can bury properly."

"Now, that's a thought worth having. The dead don't like it if they're not buried. They don't like it at all. You won't have trouble finding it. You go back out the road you came in on. Go north until you come to a stile. It's falling down, but you'll see it's a stile. Right in there the woods are open. Walk a little way in and you'll come to a creek. Cross it. There'll be some more woods, but ahead you'll see a short range of hills. The cave is right on the face of those hills. You can't miss it. It's the only one there. Tell your daddy you buried him properly, in a graveyard. Maybe with a headstone. A nice headstone. I hope they find me soon enough and somebody'll take pity on me." She looked at the dogs. "Hope they find me soon and don't let me lay in here too long."

Milkman swallowed as her thought touched his mind. "People come to see you, don't they?"

"Dog buyers. They come every now and then. They'll find me, I guess."

"Reverend Cooper . . . They think you're dead."

"Splendid. I don't like those Negroes in town. Dog people come and the man that delivers the dog food once a week. They come. They'll find me. I just hope it's soon."

He loosened his collar and lit another cigarette. Here in this dim room he sat with the woman who had helped deliver his father and Pilate; who had risked her job, her life, maybe, to hide them both after their father was killed, emptied their slop jars, brought them food at night and pans of water to wash. Had even sneaked off to the village to have the girl Pilate's name and snuffbox made into an earring. Then healed the ear when it got infected. And after all these years was thrilled to see what she believed was one of them. Healer, deliverer, in another world she would have been the head nurse at Mercy. Instead she tended Weimaraners and had just one selfish wish: that when she died somebody would find her before the dogs ate her.

"You should leave this place. Sell the damn dogs. I'll help you. You need money? How much?" Milkman felt a flood of pity and thought gratitude made her smile at him. But her voice was cold.

"You think I don't know how to walk when I want to walk? Put your money back in your pocket."

Rebuffed from his fine feelings, Milkman matched her cold tone: "You loved those white folks that much?"

"Love?" she asked. "Love?"

"Well, what are you taking care of their dogs for?"

"Do you know why she killed herself? She couldn't stand to see the place go to ruin. She couldn't live without servants and money and what it could buy. Every cent was gone and the taxes took whatever came in. She had to let the upstairs maids go, then the cook, then the dog trainer, then the yardman, then the chauffeur, then the car, then the woman who washed once a week. Then she started selling bits and pieces—land, jewels, furniture. The last few years we ate out of the garden. Finally she couldn't take it anymore. The thought of having no help, no money—well, she couldn't take that. She had to let everything go."

"But she didn't let you go." Milkman had no trouble letting his words snarl.

"No, she didn't let me go. She killed herself."

";And you still loyal."

"You don't listen to people. Your ear is on your head, but it's not connected to your brain. I said she killed herself rather than do the work I'd been doing all my life!" Circe stood up, and the dogs too. "Do you hear me? She saw the work I did all her days and *died*, you hear me, *died* rather than live like me. Now, what do you suppose she thought I was! If the way I lived and the work I did was so hateful to her she killed herself to keep from having to do it, and you think I stay on here because I loved her, then you have about as much sense as a fart!"

The dogs were humming and she touched their heads. One stood on either side of her. "They loved this place. Loved it. Brought pink veined marble from across the sea for it and hired men in Italy to do the chandelier that I had to climb a ladder and clean with white muslin once every two months. They loved it. Stole for it, lied for it, killed for it. But I'm the one left. Me and the dogs. And I will never clean it again. Never. Nothing. Not a speck of dust, not a grain of dirt, will I move. Everything in this world they lived for will crumble and rot. The chandelier already fell down and smashed itself to pieces. It's down there in the ballroom now. All in pieces. Something gnawed through the cords. Ha! And I want to see it all go, make sure it does go, and that nobody fixes it up. I brought the dogs in to make sure. They keep strangers out too. Folks tried to get in here to steal things after she died. I set the dogs on them. Then I just brought them all right in here with me. You ought to see what they did to her bedroom. Her walls didn't have wallpaper. No. Silk brocade that took some Belgian women six years to make. She loved it—oh, how much she loved it. Took thirty Weimaraners one day to rip it off the walls. If I thought the stink wouldn't strangle you, I'd show it to you." She looked at the walls around her. "This is the last room."

"I wish you'd let me help you," he said after a while.

"You have. You came in here and pretended it didn't stink and told me about Macon and my sweet little Pilate."

"Are you sure?"

"Never surer."

They both stood and walked down the hall. "Mind how you step. There's no light." Dogs came from everywhere, humming. "Time for their feeding," she said. Milkman started down the stairs. Halfway down, he turned and looked up at her.

"You said his wife made him keep the name. Did you ever know his real name?"

"Jake, I believe."

"Jake what?"

She shrugged, a Shirley Temple, little-girl-helpless shrug. "Jake was all she told me."

"Thanks," he called back, louder than he needed to, but he wanted his gratitude to cut through the stink that was flooding back over the humming of the dogs.

But the humming and the smell followed him all the way back down the tunnel to the macadam road. When he got there it was ten-thirty. Another hour and a half before Nephew would be back. Milkman paced the shoulder of the road, making plans. When should he return? Should he try to rent a car or borrow the preacher's? Had Nephew got his suitcase? What equipment would he need? Flashlight and what else? What story should be in his mind in case he was discovered? Of course: looking for his grandfather's remains—to collect them and take them for a proper burial. He paced further, and then began to stroll in the direction Nephew would be coming from. After a few minutes, he wondered if he was going the right way. He started back, but just then saw the ends of two or three wooden planks sticking out of the brush. Maybe this was the stile Circe had described to him. Not exactly a stile, but the remains of one. Circe had not left that house in years, he thought. Any stile she knew of would have to be in disrepair now. And if her directions were accurate, he might make it there and back before twelve. At least he would be able to check it out in the daylight.

Gingerly, he parted the brush and walked a little way into the woods. He didn't see even a trace of a track. But as he kept on a bit, he heard water and followed the sound, which seemed to be just ahead of the next line of trees. He was deceived. He walked for fifteen minutes before he came to it. "Cross it," she'd said, and he thought there would be a bridge of some sort. There was none. He looked across and saw hills. It must be there. Right there. He calculated that he could just make it in the hour or so left before he should be back on the road. He sat down, took off his shoes and socks, stuffed the socks in his pocket, and rolled up his pants. Holding his shoes in his hand, he waded in. Unprepared for the coldness of the water and the slimy stones at the bottom, he slipped to one knee and soaked his shoes trying to break his fall. He righted himself with difficulty and poured the water out of his shoes. Since he was already wet, there was no point in turning back; he waded on out. After half a minute, the creek bed dropped six inches and he fell again, only now he went completely under and got a glimpse of small silvery translucent fish as his head went down. Snorting water, he cursed the creek, which was too shallow to swim and too rocky to walk. He should have pulled a stick to check depth before he put his foot down, but his excitement had been too great. He went on, feeling with his toes for firm footing before he put his weight down. It was slow moving—the water was about two or three feet deep and some twelve yards wide. If he hadn't been so eager, maybe he could have found a narrower part to cross. Thoughts of what he should have done instead of just plunging in, fruitless as they were, irritated him so that they kept him moving until he made it to the other side. He threw his shoes on the dry ground and hoisted himself up and out on the bank. Breathless, he reached for his cigarettes and found them soaked. He lay back on the grass and let the high sunshine warm him. He opened his mouth so the clear air could bathe his tongue.

After a while he sat up and put on the wet socks and shoes. He looked at his watch to check the time. It ticked, but the face was splintered and the minute hand was bent. Better move, he thought, and struck out for the hills, which, deceptive as the sound of the creek, were much farther away than they seemed. He had no idea that simply walking through trees, bushes, on untrammeled ground could be so hard. Woods always brought to his mind City Park, the tended woods on Honoré Island where he went for outings as a child and where tiny convenient paths led you through. "He leased ten acres of virgin woods and cleared it all," said the men describing the beginning of Old Macon Dead's farm. Cleared this? Chopped down this? This stuff he could barely walk through?

He was sweating into his wet shirt and just beginning to feel the result of sharp stones on his feet. Occasionally he came to a clear space and he'd alter his direction as soon as the low hills came back into view.

Finally flat ground gave way to a gentle upward slope of bushes, saplings, and rock. He walked along its edge, looking for an opening. As he moved southward, the skirts of the hills were rockier and the saplings fewer. Then he saw, some fifteen to twenty feet above him, a black hole in the rock which he could get to by a difficult, but not dangerous, climb, made more difficult by the thin smooth soles of his shoes. He wiped sweat from his forehead on his coat sleeve, slipped off the narrow black tie that hung open around his collar and put it in his pocket.

The salt taste was back in his mouth and he was so agitated by what he believed, hoped, he would find there, he had to put his hands on warm stone to dry them. He thought of the pitiful hungry eyes of the old men, their eagerness for some word of defiant success accomplished by the son of Macon Dead; and of the white men who strutted through the orchards and ate the Georgia peaches after they shot his grandfather's head off. Milkman took a deep breath and began to negotiate the rocks.

As soon as he put his foot on the first stone, he smelled money, although it was not a smell at all. It was like candy and sex and soft twinkling lights. Like piano music with a few strings in the background. He'd noticed it before when he waited under the pines near Pilate's house; more when the moon lit up the green sack that hung like a kept promise from her ceiling; and most when he tumbled lightly to the floor, sack in hand. Las Vegas and buried treasure; numbers dealers and Wells Fargo wagons; race track pay windows and spewing oil wells; craps, flushes, and sweepstakes tickets. Auctions, bank vaults, and heroin deals. It caused paralysis, trembling, dry throats, and sweaty palms. Urgency, and the feeling that "they" had been mastered or were on your side. Quiet men stood up and threw a queen down on the table hard enough to break her neck. Women sucked their bottom lips and put little red disks down in numbered squares. Lifeguards, A-students, eyed cash registers and speculated on how far away the door was. To win. There was nothing like it in the world.

Milkman became agile, pulling himself up the rock face, digging his knees into crevices, searching with his fingers for solid earth patches or ledges of stone. He left off thinking and let his body do the work. He stood up, finally, on level ground twenty feet to the right of the mouth of the cave. There he saw a crude footpath he might have found earlier if he had not been so hasty. That was the path the hunters used and that Pilate and his father had also used. None of them tore their clothes as he had, climbing twenty feet of steep rock.

He entered the cave and was blinded by the absence of light. He stepped back out and reentered, cupping his eyes. After a while, he could distinguish the ground from the wall of the cave. There was the ledge of rock where they'd slept, much larger than he had pictured. And worn places on the floor where fires had once burned, and several boulders standing around the entrance—one with a kind of V-shaped crown. But where were the bones? Circe said they dumped him in here. Farther back, probably, back where the shallow pit was. Milkman had no flashlight and his matches were certainly wet, but he tried to find a dry one anyway. Only one or two even sputtered. The rest were dead. Still, his eyes were getting used to the dark. He pulled a branch from a bush that grew near the entrance and bending forward, let it graze the ground before him as he walked. He had gone thirty or forty feet when he noticed the cave's walls were closer together. He could not see the roof at all. He stopped and began to move slowly sideways, the branch tip scratching a yard or so ahead. The side of his hand grazed rock and he flung the dry bat shit off it and moved to the left. The branch struck air. He stopped again, and lowered the tip until it touched ground again. Raising it up and down, and pressing it back and around, he could tell that he had found the pit. It was about two feet deep and maybe eight feet wide. Frantically he scraped the branch around the bottom. It hit something hard, again something else hard. Milkman swallowed and dropped to his knees. He squinted his eyes as hard as he could, but he couldn't see a thing. Suddenly he remembered a lighter in his vest pocket. He dropped the branch and fumbled for it, almost faint from the money smell—the twinkling lights, the piano music. He pulled it out, praying it would light. On the second try, it burst into flame and he peered down. The lighter went out. He snapped it back and held his hand over its fragile flame. At the bottom of the hole he saw rocks, boards, leaves, even a tin cup, but no gold. Stretched out on his stomach, holding the lighter in one hand, he swept the bottom with the other, clawing, pulling, fingering, poking. There were no fat little pigeon-breasted bags of gold. There was nothing. Nothing at all. And before he knew it, he was hollering a long, *awwww* sound into the pit. It triggered the bats, which swooped suddenly and dived in the darkness over his head. They startled him and he leaped to his feet, whereupon the sole of his right shoe split away from the soft cordovan leather. The bats drove him out in a lopsided run, lifting his foot high to accommodate the flopping sole.

In the sunlight once more, he stopped for breath. Dust, tears, and too bright light were in his eyes, but he was too angry and disgusted to rub them. He merely threw the lighter in a wide

high arc into the trees at the foot of the hills and limped down
the footpath, paying no attention to the direction he was going.
He put his feet down wherever was most convenient. Quite
suddenly, it seemed to him, he was at the creek again, but up-
stream where the crossing—about twelve feet here and so shallow he could see the stony bottom—was laid across with boards.
He sat down and lashed the sole of his shoe to its top with his
black string tie, then walked across the homemade bridge. The
woods on the other side had a pathway.

Milkman began to shake with hunger. Real hunger, not the
less than top-full feeling he was accustomed to, the nervous desire to taste something good. Real hunger. He believed if he
didn't get something to eat that instant he would pass out. He
examined the bushes, the branches, the ground for a berry, a
nut, anything. But he didn't know what to look for, nor how
they grew. Trembling, his stomach in a spasm, he tore off a few
leaves and put them in his mouth. They were as bitter as gall,
but he chewed them anyway, spit them out, and got others. He
thought of the breakfast food Mrs. Cooper had put before him,
which had disgusted him then. Fried eggs covered with grease,
fresh-squeezed orange juice with seed and pulp floating in it,
thick hand-cut bacon, a white-hot mound of grits and biscuits. It
was her best effort, he knew, but perhaps because of the whiskey he'd drunk the night before, he could only bring himself to
drink two cups of black coffee and eat two biscuits. The rest
had nauseated him, and what he did eat he had left at Circe's
door.

Some brush closed in on him and when he swept it angrily
aside, he saw a stile and the road in front of him. Macadam,
automobiles, fence posts, civilization. He looked at the sky to
gauge the hour. The sun was a quarter of the way down from
what even he knew was high noon. About one o'clock, he
guessed. Nephew would have come and gone. He felt in his
back pocket for his wallet. It was discolored at the edges from
the water, but the contents were dry. Five hundred dollars, his
driver's license, phone numbers on slips of paper, social security

card, airline ticket stub, cleaners receipts. He looked up and down the road. He had to get food, and started walking south, where he believed Danville lay, hoping to hitch as soon as a car came by. He was not only ravenous; his feet hurt. The third car to pass stopped—a 1954 Chevrolet—and the driver, a black man, showed the same interest in Milkman's clothes that Nephew had shown. He seemed not to notice or care about the rip at the knee or under the arm, the tie-tied shoe, the leaves in Milkman's hair, or the dirt all over the suit.

"Where you headed, partner?"

"Danville. As close as I can get."

"Hop on in, then. Little out my way. I cut over to Buford, but I'll get you closer than you was."

" 'Preciate it," answered Milkman. He loved the car seat, loved it. And sank his weary back into its nylon and sighed.

"Good cut of suit," the man said. "I guess you ain't from here'bouts."

"No. Michigan."

"Sure 'nough? Had a aunt move out there. Flint. You know Flint?"

"Yeah. I know Flint." Milkman's feet were singing, the tender skin of the ball louder than the heels. He dared not spread his toes, lest the singing never stop.

"What kinda place is it, Flint?"

"Jive. No place you'd want to go to."

"Thought so. Name sounds good, but I thought it'd be like that."

Milkman had noticed a six-bottle carton of Coca-Cola on the back seat when he got in the car. It was on his mind.

"Could I buy one of those Coca-Colas from you? I'm kinda thirsty."

"It's warm," said the man.

"Long as it's wet."

"Help yourself."

Milkman reached around and pulled a bottle out of its case.

"Got a bottle opener?"

The man took the bottle from him and put its head in his mouth and slowly pried the top off. Foam shot all over his chin and his lap before Milkman could take it from him.

"Hot." The man laughed and wiped himself with a navy-and-white handkerchief.

Milkman gulped the Coke, foam and all, in three or four seconds.

"Like another?"

He did but he said no. Just a cigarette.

"Don't smoke," said the man.

"Oh," said Milkman, and struggled against and lost to a long belch.

"Bus station's right around the bend there." They were just outside Danville. "You can make it easy."

"I really do thank you." Milkman opened the door. "What do I owe you? For the Coke and all?"

The man was smiling, but his face changed now. "My name's Garnett, Fred Garnett. I ain't got much, but I can afford a Coke and a lift now and then."

"I didn't mean . . . I . . ."

But Mr. Garnett had reached over and closed the door. Milkman could see him shaking his head as he drove off.

Milkman's feet hurt him so, he could have cried, but he made it to the diner/bus station and looked for the man behind the counter. He wasn't there, but a woman offered to help. There followed a long discussion in which he discovered that the bag was not there, the man was not there, she didn't know if a colored boy had picked it up or not, they didn't have a checkroom and she was mighty sorry but he could look at the stationmaster's if the boy didn't have it, and was there anything else she could do?

"Hamburgers," he said. "Give me some hamburgers and a cup of coffee."

"Yes, sir. How many?"

"Six," he said, but his stomach cramped on the fourth and bent him double with a pain that lasted off and on all the way to Roanoke. But before he left, he telephoned Reverend Cooper. His wife answered and told him that her husband was still at the freightyard and he could catch him there if he hurried. Milkman thanked her and hung up. Walking like a pimp in delicate shoes, he managed to get to the yard, which was fairly close to the bus station. He entered the gate and asked the first man he saw if Reverend Cooper was still there.

"Coop?" the man said. "I think he went on over to the station house. See it? Right over there."

Milkman followed his finger, and hobbled over the gravel and ties to the station house.

It was empty save for an old man dragging a crate.

"Excuse me," Milkman said. "Is Rev—is Coop still here?"

"Just left. If you run you can catch him," the man said. He wiped the sweat of exertion from his forehead.

Milkman thought about running anywhere on his tender feet and said, "Oh, well. I'll try to catch him another time." He turned to go.

"Say," said the man. "If you ain't gonna try to catch him, could you give me a hand with this?" He pointed down to the huge crate at his feet. Too tired to say no or explain, Milkman nodded. The two of them grunted and groaned over the box, and finally got it up on a dolly, where they could push it to the weighing platform. Milkman slumped over the crate and caught his breath, barely able to nod to the old man's thank yous. Then he went out of the station into the street.

He was tired now. Really tired. He didn't want to see Reverend Cooper and his success-starved friends again. And he certainly didn't want to explain anything to his father or Guitar just yet. So he hobbled back to the bus station and asked for the next bus leaving that was going south. It had to be south. And it had to be Virginia. Because now he thought he knew how to find out what had happened to the gold.

.   .

Full of hamburgers, sore of foot, sick to his stomach, but at least sitting down, he couldn't even feel the disappointment that lay in the pit in the cave. He slept heavily for several hours on the bus, woke and daydreamed, napped a little more, woke again at a rest stop and ate a bowl of pea soup. He went into a drugstore and replaced the shaving equipment and toilet articles he'd left at Reverend Cooper's, and decided to wait and get his shoe fixed (it was sealed with chewing gum now), his suit mended, and a new shirt in Virginia.

The Greyhound bus made a sound like the hum of the Weimaraners as it sped down the road, and Milkman shivered a little, the way he had when Circe glanced at them, sitting in the "last room," wondering if she would outlive them. But there were over thirty of them and reproducing all the time.

The low hills in the distance were no longer scenery to him. They were real places that could split your thirty-dollar shoes. More than anything in the world he'd wanted it to be there, for row upon row of those little bags to turn their fat pigeon chests up to his hands. He thought he wanted it in the name of Macon Dead's Georgia peaches, in the name of Circe and her golden-eyed dogs, and especially in the name of Reverend Cooper and his old-timey friends who began to die before their facial hair was out when they saw what happened to a black man like them—"ignorant as a hammer and broke as a convict"—who had made it anyway. He also thought he wanted it in the name of Guitar, to erase what looked like doubt in his face when Milkman left, the "I-know-you-gonna-fuck-up" look. There wasn't any gold, but now he knew that all the fine reasons for wanting it didn't mean a thing. The fact was he wanted the gold because it was gold and he wanted to own it. Free. As he had sat chomping the hamburgers in the bus station, imagining what going home would be like now—not only to have to say there was no gold, but also to know he was trapped there—his mind had begun to function clearly.

Circe said that Macon and Sing had boarded that wagon in Virginia, where they both came from. She also said Macon's body rose up from the ground at the first heavy rain, and that the Butlers, or somebody, dumped it in the hunters' cave one summer night. One summer night. And it was a body, a corpse, when they hauled it away, because they recognized him as a Negro. Yet Pilate said it was winter when she was there, and there were only bones. She said she went to see Circe and visited the cave four years later, in the snow, and took the white man's bones. Why didn't she see her father's bones? There should have been two skeletons. Did she step over one and collect the other? Surely Circe had told her the same thing she told him—that her father's body was in the cave. Did Pilate tell Circe that they had killed a man in there? Probably not, since Circe didn't mention it. Pilate said she took the white man's bones and didn't even look for the gold. But she lied. She had not mentioned the second skeleton because it wasn't there when she got to the cave. She didn't come back four years later—or if she did, it was her *second* trip. She came back *before* they dumped the Negro they found in the cave. She took the bones, all right; Milkman had seen them on the table in the jailhouse. But that's not all she took. She took the gold. To Virginia. And maybe somebody in Virginia would know.

Milkman followed in her tracks.

Chapter 11

The women's hands were empty. No pocketbook, no change purse, no wallet, no keys, no small paper bag, no comb, no handkerchief. They carried nothing. Milkman had never in his life seen a woman on the street without a purse slung over her shoulder, pressed under her arm, or dangling from her clenched fingers. These women walked as if they were going somewhere, but they carried nothing in their hands. It was enough to let him know he was really in the backwoods of Virginia, an area the signs kept telling him was the Blue Ridge Mountains. Danville, with its diner/bus station and its post office on the main street was a thriving metropolis compared to this no-name hamlet, a place so small nothing financed by state funds or private enterprise reared a brick there. In Roanoke, Petersburg, Culpeper he'd asked for a town named Charlemagne. Nobody knew. The coast, some said. Tidewater. A valley town, said others. He ended up at an AAA office, and after a while they discovered it and its correct name: Shalimar. How do I get there? Well, you can't walk it, that's for sure. Buses go there? Trains? No. Well, not very near. There is one bus, but it just goes to . . . He ended up buying a fifty-dollar car for seventy-five dollars out of a young man's yard. It broke down before he could get to the gas station and fill the tank. And when he got pushed to the station, he spent $132 on a fan belt, brake lining, oil filter, gas line filter, two retreads, and a brand-new oil pan, which he didn't need but bought before the mechanic told him the gasket was broken. It was a hard and bitter price to pay. Not because it wasn't worth it, and not because it had to be in cash since the garage owner looked at his Standard Oil credit card like it was a three-dollar bill, but because he had got used to prices in the South: socks two pairs for a quarter, resoled shoes thirty cents, shirt $1.98, and the two Tommys needed to know that he got a shave *and* a haircut for fifty cents.

By the time he bought the car, his morale had soared and he was beginning to enjoy the trip: his ability to get information and help from strangers, their attraction to him, their generosity (Need a place to stay? Want a good place to eat?). All that business about southern hospitality was for real. He wondered why black people ever left the South. Where he went, there wasn't a white face around, and the Negroes were as pleasant, wide-spirited, and self-contained as could be. He earned the rewards he got here. None of the pleasantness was directed at him because of his father, as it was back home, or his grandfather's memory, as it was in Danville. And now, sitting behind a steering wheel, he felt even better. He was his own director—relieving himself when he wanted to, stopping for cold beer when he was thirsty, and even in a seventy-five-dollar car the sense of power was strong.

He'd had to pay close attention to signs and landmarks, because Shalimar was not on the Texaco map he had, and the AAA office couldn't give a nonmember a charted course—just the map and some general information. Even at that, watching as carefully as he could, he wouldn't have known he had arrived if the fan belt hadn't broken again right in front of Solomon's General Store, which turned out to be the heart and soul of Shalimar, Virginia.

He headed for the store, nodding at the four men sitting outside on the porch, and side-stepping the white hens that were
strolling about. Three more men were inside, in addition to the
man behind the counter, who he assumed was Mr. Solomon
himself. Milkman asked him for a cold bottle of Red Cap, please.

"No beer for sale on Sunday," the man said. He was a light-
skinned Negro with red hair turning white.

"Oh. I forgot what day it was." Milkman smiled. "Pop, then.
I mean soda. Got any on ice?"

"Cherry smash. That suit you?"

"Fine. Suit me fine."

The man walked over to the side of the store and slid open the
door of an ancient cooler. The floor was worn and wavy with
years of footsteps. Cans of goods on the shelf were sparse, but
the sacks, trays, and cartons of perishables and semiperishables
were plentiful. The man pulled a bottle of red liquid from the
cooler and wiped it dry on his apron before handing it to
Milkman.

"A nickel if you drink it here. Seven cents if you don't."

"I'll drink it here."

"Just get in?"

"Yeah. Car broke down. Is there a garage nearby?"

"Naw. Five miles yonder is one, though."

"Five miles?"

"Yep. What's the trouble? Mebbe one a us can fix it. Where
you headed?"

"Shalimar."

"You standin in it."

"Right here? This is Shalimar?"

"Yes, suh. Shalimar." The man pronounced it *Shalleemone*.

"Good thing I broke down. I would have missed it for sure."
Milkman laughed.

"Your friend almost missed it too."

"My friend? What friend?"

"The one lookin for you. Drove in here early this mornin and
axed for ya."

"Asked for me by name?"

"No. He never mentioned your name."

"Then how do you know he was looking for me?"

"Said he was lookin for his friend in a three-piece beige suit. Like that." He pointed to Milkman's chest.

"What'd he look like?"

"Dark-skinned man. 'Bout your complexion. Tall. Thin. What's a matter? Y'all get your wires crossed?"

"Yeah. No. I mean . . . what was his name?"

"Didn't say. Just asked for you. He come a long way to meet you, though. I know that. Drove a Ford with Michigan tags."

"Michigan? You sure Michigan?"

"Sure I'm sure. Was he supposed to meet you in Roanoke?" When Milkman looked wild-eyed, the man said, "I seen your tags."

Milkman sighed with relief. And then said, "I wasn't sure where we were going to meet up. And he didn't say his name?"

"Naw. Just said to give you some good-luck message if I was to see you. Lemme see . . ."

"Good luck?"

"Yeah. Said to tell you your day was sure coming or your day . . . something like that . . . your day is here. But I know it had a day in it. But I ain't sure if he said it was comin or was already here." He chuckled. "Wish mine was here. Been waitin fifty-seven years and it ain't come yet."

The other men in the store laughed congenially, while Milkman stood frozen, everything in him quiet but his heart. There was no mistaking the message. Or the messenger. Guitar was looking for him, was following him, and for professional reasons. Unless . . . Would Guitar joke about that phrase? That special secret word the Seven Days whispered to their victims?

"The drink abuse you?" Mr. Solomon was looking at him. "Sweet soda water don't agree with me."

Milkman shook his head and swallowed the rest hurriedly. "No," he said. "I'm just . . . car weary. I think I'll sit outside awhile." He started toward the door.

"You want me to see 'bout your car for you?" Mr. Solomon sounded slightly offended.

"In a minute. I'll be right back."

Milkman pushed the screen door and stepped outside on the porch. The sun was blazing. He took off his jacket and held it on his forefinger over his shoulder. He gazed up and down the dusty road. Shotgun houses with wide spaces between them, a few dogs, chickens, children, and the women with nothing in their hands. They sat on porches, and walked in the road swaying their hips under cotton dresses, bare-legged, their unstraightened hair braided or pulled straight back into a ball. He wanted one of them bad. To curl up in a cot in that one's arms, or that one, or that. That's the way Pilate must have looked as a girl, looked even now, but out of place in the big northern city she had come to. Wide sleepy eyes that tilted up at the corners, high cheekbones, full lips blacker than their skin, berry-stained, and long long necks. There must be a lot of intermarriage in this place, he thought. All the women looked alike, and except for some light-skinned red-headed men (like Mr. Solomon), the men looked very much like the women. Visitors to Shalimar must be rare, and new blood that settled here nonexistent.

Milkman stepped off the porch, scattering the hens, and walked down the road toward a clump of trees near a building that looked like a church or clubhouse of some sort. Children were playing behind the trees. Spreading his jacket on the burnt grass, he sat down and lit a cigarette.

Guitar was here. Had asked for him. But why was he afraid? They were friends, close friends. So close he had told him all about the Seven Days. There was no trust heavier than that. Milkman was a confidant, almost an accomplice. So why was he afraid? It was senseless. Guitar must have left that particular message so Milkman could know who was looking for him without his giving his name. Something must have happened back home. Guitar must be running, from the police, maybe, and decided to run toward his friend—the only one other than the Days who would know what it was all about and whom he could trust. Guitar needed to find Milkman and he needed help. That was it. But if Guitar knew Milkman was headed for Shalimar, he must have found that out in Roanoke, or Culpeper—or maybe even in Danville. And if he knew that, why didn't he wait? Where was he now? Trouble. Guitar was in trouble.

Behind him the children were singing a kind of ring-around-the-rosy or Little Sally Walker game. Milkman turned to watch. About eight or nine boys and girls were standing in a circle. A boy in the middle, his arms outstretched, turned around like an airplane, while the others sang some meaningless rhyme:

> *Jay the only son of Solomon*
> *Come booba yalle, come booba tambee*
> *Whirl about and touch the sun*
> *Come booba yalle, come booba tambee . . .*

They went on with several verses, the boy in the middle doing his imitation of an airplane. The climax of the game was a rapid shouting of nonsense words accompanied by more rapid twirling: "Solomon rye balaly *shoo*; yaraba medina hamlet *too*"—until the last line. "Twenty-one children the last one *Jay!*" At which point the boy crashed to earth and the others screamed.

Milkman watched the children. He'd never played like that as a child. As soon as he got up off his knees at the window sill, grieving because he could not fly, and went off to school, his velvet suit separated him from the other children. White and black thought he was a riot and went out of their way to laugh at him and see to it that he had no lunch to eat, nor any crayons, nor ever got through the line to the toilet or the water fountain. His mother finally surrendered to his begging for corduroy knickers or straights, which helped a little, but he was never asked to play those circle games, those singing games, to join in anything, until Guitar pulled those four boys off him. Milkman smiled, remembering how Guitar grinned and whooped as the four boys turned on him. It was the first time Milkman saw anybody really enjoy a fight. Afterward Guitar had taken off his baseball cap and handed it to Milkman, telling him to wipe the blood from his nose. Milkman bloodied the cap, returned it, and Guitar slapped it back on his head.

Remembering those days now, Milkman was ashamed of having been frightened or suspicious of Guitar's message. When he turned up, he would explain everything and Milkman would do what he could to help. He stood up and brushed his jacket. A black rooster strutted by, its blood-red comb draped forward like a wicked brow.

Milkman walked back toward Solomon's store. He needed a place to stay, some information, and a woman, not necessarily in that order. He would begin wherever the beginning was. In a way it was good Guitar had asked for him. Along with waiting for him and waiting for some way to get a new fan belt, he had a legitimate reason to dawdle. Hens and cats gave up their places on the steps as he approached them.

"Feelin better, are ya?" asked Mr. Solomon.

"Much better. Just needed a stretch, I guess." He jutted his chin toward the window. "Nice around here. Peaceful. Pretty women too."

A young man sitting on a chair tilted to the wall pushed his hat back from his forehead and let the front legs of the chair hit the floor. His lips were open, exposing the absence of four front teeth. The other men moved their feet. Mr. Solomon smiled but didn't say anything. Milkman sensed that he'd struck a wrong note. About the women, he guessed. What kind of place was this where a man couldn't even ask for a woman?

He changed the subject. "If my friend, the one who stopped by this morning, was going to wait for me here, where would he be likely to find a place to stay? Any rooming houses around here?"

"Rooming houses?"

"Yeah. Where a man can spend the night."

Mr. Solomon shook his head. "Nothin like that here."

Milkman was getting annoyed. What was all the hostility for? He looked at the men sitting around the store. "You think maybe one of them could help with the car?" he asked Mr. Solomon. "Maybe get another belt somewhere?"

Mr. Solomon kept his eyes on the counter. "Guess I could ask them." His voice was soft; he spoke as if he was embarrassed about something. There was none of the earlier chattiness he'd been full of when Milkman arrived.

"If they can't find one, let me know right away. I may have to buy another car to get back home."

Every one of the faces of the men turned to look at him, and Milkman knew he had said something else wrong, although he didn't know what. He only knew that they behaved as if they'd been insulted.

In fact they had been. They looked with hatred at the city Negro who could buy a car as if it were a bottle of whiskey because the one he had was broken. And what's more, who had said so in front of them. He hadn't bothered to say his name, nor ask theirs, had called them "them," and would certainly despise their days, which should have been spent harvesting their own crops, instead of waiting around the general store hoping a truck would come looking for mill hands or tobacco pickers in the flatlands that belonged to somebody else. His manner, his clothes were reminders that they had no crops of their own and no land to speak of either. Just vegetable gardens, which the women took care of, and chickens and pigs that the children took care of. He was telling them that they weren't men, that they relied on women and children for their food. And that the lint and tobacco in their pants pockets where dollar bills should have been was the measure. That thin shoes and suits with vests and smooth smooth hands were the measure. That eyes that had seen big cities and the inside of airplanes were the measure. They had seen him watching their women and rubbing his fly as he stood on the steps. They had also seen him lock his car as soon as he got out of it in a place where there couldn't be more than two keys twenty-five miles around. He hadn't found them fit enough or good enough to want to know their names, and believed himself too good to tell them his. They looked at his skin and saw it was as black as theirs, but they knew he had the heart of the white men who came to pick them up in the trucks when they needed anonymous, faceless laborers.

Now one of them spoke to the Negro with the Virginia license and the northern accent.

"Big money up North, eh?"

"Some," Milkman answered.

"Some? I hear tell everybody up North got big money."

"Lotta people up North got nothing." Milkman made his voice pleasant, but he knew something was developing.

"That's hard to believe. Why would anybody want to stay there if they ain't no big money?"

"The sights, I guess." Another man answered the first. "The sights and the women."

"You kiddin," said the first man in mock dismay. "You mean to tell me pussy different up North?"

"Naw," said the second. "Pussy the same everywhere. Smell like the ocean; taste like the sea."

"Can't be," said a third. "Got to be different."

"Maybe the pricks is different." The first man spoke again.

"Reckon?" asked the second man.

"So I hear tell," said the first man.

"How different?" asked the second man.

"Wee little," said the first man. "Wee, wee little."

"Naw!" said the second man.

"So they tell me. That's why they pants so tight. That true?" The first man looked at Milkman for an answer.

"I wouldn't know," said Milkman. "I never spent much time smacking my lips over another man's dick." Everybody smiled, including Milkman. It was about to begin.

"What about his ass hole? Ever smack your lips over that?"

"Once," said Milkman. "When a little young nigger made me mad and I had to jam a Coke bottle up his ass."

"What'd you use a bottle for? Your cock wouldn't fill it?"

"It did. After I took the Coke bottle out. Filled his mouth too."

"Prefer mouth, do you?"

"If it's big enough, and ugly enough, and belongs to a ignorant motherfucker who is about to get the livin shit whipped out of him."

The knife glittered.

Milkman laughed. "I ain't seen one of those since I was fourteen. Where I come from *boys* play with knives—if they scared they gonna lose, that is."

The first man smiled. "That's me, motherfucker. Scared to death I'm gonna lose."

Milkman did the best he could with a broken bottle, but his face got slit, so did his left hand, and so did his pretty beige suit, and he probably would have had his throat cut if two women hadn't come running in screaming, "Saul! Saul!"

The store was full of people by then and the women couldn't get through. The men tried to shush them, but they kept on screaming and provided enough lull for Mr. Solomon to interrupt the fight.

"All right. All right. That's enough of that."

"Shut your mouth, Solomon."

"Get them women outta here."

"Stick him, Saul, stick that cocksucker."

But Saul had a jagged cut over his eye and the blood pouring from it made it hard to see. It was difficult but not impossible for Mr. Solomon to pull him away. He left cursing Milkman, but his fervor was gone.

Milkman backed up against the counter, waiting to see if anybody else was going to jump him. When it looked as if no one was, and when the people were drifting outside to watch Saul scuffling and cursing at the men pulling him away, he slumped a little and wiped his face. When the entire store save for the owner was empty, Milkman hurled the broken bottle into a corner. It careened by the cooler and bounced off the wall before splintering on the floor. He walked outside, still panting, and looked around. Four older men still sat on the porch, as though nothing had happened. Blood was streaming down Milkman's face, but it had dried on his hand. He kicked at a white hen and sat down on the top step, wiping the blood with his handkerchief. Three young women with nothing in their hands stood in the road looking at him. Their eyes were wide but noncommittal. Children joined them, circling the women like birds. Nobody said anything. Even the four men on the porch

were quiet. Nobody came toward him, offered him a cigarette
or a glass of water. Only the children and the hens walked
around. Under the hot sun, Milkman was frozen with anger. If
he'd had a weapon, he would have slaughtered everybody in
sight.

"You pretty good with a bottle. How you with a shotgun?"
One of the older men had sidled up to him. The smile on his face
was faint. It was as though now that the young men had had
their chance, with unsatisfactory results, the older men would
take over. Their style, of course, would be different. No name-
calling toilet contest for them. No knives either, or hot breath
and knotted neck muscles. They would test him, match and beat
him, probably, on some other ground.

"Best shot there is," Milkman lied.

"That so?"

"Yeah, it's so."

"Some of us is going huntin later on. Care to join us?"

"That toothless motherfucker going too?"

"Saul? No."

"Cause I might have to knock the rest of them out."

The man laughed. "Sheriff took the others—with the butt of
a gun."

"Yeah? Good."

"Well, you comin?"

"Sure I'm coming. Just get me the gun."

He laughed again. "Name's Omar."

"Macon Dead."

Omar blinked at the name, but didn't comment on it. He
merely told him to come by King Walker's, a gas station about
two miles up the road, right around sundown. "It's straight up
yonder. Ain't no way in the world you can miss it."

"I won't miss it." Milkman stood up and walked to his car. He
fumbled for the car keys, opened the door, and slid into the seat.
He rolled down all four windows, found a towel in the back

seat, and stretched out, using his jacket for a pillow and the towel as a bandage for his face. His feet stuck out the open door. Fuck 'em. Who were all these people roaming the world trying to kill him? His own father had tried while he was still in his mother's stomach. But he'd lived. And he had lived the last year dodging a woman who came every month to kill him, and he had lain just like this, with his arm over his eyes, wide open to whatever she had in her hand. He'd lived through that too. Then a witch had stepped out of his childhood nightmares to grab him, and he'd lived through that. Some bats had driven him out of a cave—and he'd lived through that. And at no time did he have a weapon. Now he walked into a store and asked if somebody could fix his car and a nigger pulled a knife on him. And he still wasn't dead. Now what did these black Neanderthals think they were going to do? Fuck 'em. My name's Macon; I'm already dead. He had thought this place, this Shalimar, was going to be home. His original home. His people came from here, his grandfather and his grandmother. All the way down South people had been nice to him, generous, helpful. In Danville they had made him the object of hero worship. In his own home town his name spelled dread and grudging respect. But here, in his "home," he was unknown, unloved, and damn near killed. These were some of the meanest unhung niggers in the world.

He slept, unmolested by everything and everybody except a dream in which he thought he saw Guitar looking down on him. When he woke he bought two cans of pineapple and a box of crackers from Mr. Solomon. He ate on the porch with the hens. The men were gone, and the sun was leaving. Only the children stayed to watch him eat. When he poured the last of the pineapple juice down his throat, one of the children stepped forward to ask, "Can we have your can, mister?" He held it out and they snatched the can and ran off to fashion some game out of it.

He started out for King Walker's. Even if he could have come up with a way to get out of the hunt, he wouldn't have taken it, in spite of the fact that he had never handled a firearm in his life. He had stopped evading things, sliding through, over, and around difficulties. Before he had taken risks only with Guitar. Now he took them alone. Not only had he let Hagar stab him; he had let the nightmare witch catch him and kiss him. To a man surviving that, anything else was a joke.

King Walker was nothing like his name suggested. He was a small man, bald, with a left cheek bulging with tobacco. Years ago he'd been a star pitcher in one of the black baseball leagues and the history of his career was nailed and pasted all over his shop. They had not lied when they said no garage or mechanic on duty was nearer than five miles. King Walker's station had obviously gone broke a long time ago. The pumps were dry; there wasn't even a can of oil in the place. Now it seemed to be used as a kind of clubhouse for the men and Walker lived in the back of the station. In addition to King Walker, who wasn't going, there was Omar and another man who had also been on the porch and who introduced himself as Luther Solomon—no relation to the grocery store Solomon. They were waiting for some others, who came soon after Milkman got there, driving an old Chevy. Omar introduced them as Calvin Breakstone and Small Boy.

Calvin seemed to be the most congenial of them, and followed the introductions with a command to King Walker to "get this city boy some shoes for his feet." King rummaged around, spitting tobacco, and came up with some mud-caked brogans. They outfitted Milkman completely, laughing all the while at his underwear, fingering his vest—Small Boy tried to get his wrestler's arms into Milkman's jacket—and wondering what had happened to his feet. Bits of skin still peeled from his toes because of the two days he had spent in wet shoes and socks. King Walker made him sprinkle Arm & Hammer soda on them before he put on the thick socks they gave him. When Milkman was dressed in World War II army fatigues with a knit cap on his head, they opened some Falstaff beer and began to talk about guns. At which point the revelry mixed with meanness abated and King Walker handed Milkman his Winchester .22.

"Ever use a twenty-two?"

"Not in a good while," Milkman said.

The five men piled into the Chevy and drove off into the lessening light. From what Milkman could tell, after fifteen minutes or so they were going up to high ground. As the car swerved through narrow roads, the conversation picked up again and they talked about other trips, game, kills, misses. Soon the only light came from the moon and it was getting cool enough for Milkman to be grateful for his knit cap. The car pulled ahead and around some sharp bends. In the rear-view mirror Milkman thought he glimpsed the headlights of another car and wondered briefly if they were being met by others. The sky was dark enough now for stars.

"Better make time, Calvin. Coon be done ate and gone on home."

Calvin pulled over and stopped the car.

"Let 'em rip," he said, and handed the car keys to Small Boy, who walked around to the back and unlocked the trunk. Three hounds leaped out, sniffing and wagging their tails. But they didn't make a sound.

"You brought Becky?" asked Luther. "Oh, man! We gonna get some coon tonight!"

The dogs' nervousness, their eagerness to hear the signal that would allow them to race off into the trees, made Milkman jittery. What was he supposed to do? Two feet in any direction from the headlights was black night.

Omar and Small Boy hauled equipment from the trunk: four lamps, one flashlight, rope, shells, and a pint bottle of liquor. When all four lamps were ablaze, they asked Milkman if he wanted to use a lamp or a flashlight. He hesitated, and Calvin said, "He can run with me. Give him the torch."

Milkman put it in his back pocket.

"Take that change out your pocket," said Calvin. "Makes too much noise."

Milkman did as he was told and took King's shotgun, a piece of rope, and a deep swig from the bottle they were passing around.

The dogs padded about, silent, panting, almost faint with excitement. But still they made no sound. Calvin and Omar both loaded their double-gauge shotguns with .22 shells in one barrel and buckshot in the other. Small Boy clapped his hands once, and the three hounds sped screaming into the night. The men didn't take off after them at once, as Milkman had supposed they would. Instead they stood quietly and listened for a while. Small Boy laughed lightly, shaking his head. "Becky's leadin. Let's go. Calvin, you and Macon go off to the right. We'll head this a way, and circle over by the gulch. Don't shoot no bears, now."

"Shoot him if I see him," said Calvin as he and Milkman moved away.

As they left the Chevy, the car that Milkman had noticed sped past them. Obviously, there were no others in the hunting party. Calvin was ahead, the burning lamp swinging low from his hand. Milkman flicked on his flashlight.

"Better save it," said Calvin. "You don't need it now."

They plodded on in a direction that may have been toward the screaming dogs, but Milkman couldn't tell.

"Any bears out here?" he asked in what he hoped was an interested but not anxious voice.

"Just us, and we got the guns." Calvin laughed and was suddenly swallowed up by the dark, only the low swinging lamp marking his path. Milkman watched the lamp until he realized that focusing on it kept him from seeing anything else. If he was to grow accustomed to the dark, he would have to look at what it was possible to see. A long moan sailed up through the trees somewhere to the left of where they were. It sounded like a woman's voice, sobbing, and mingling with the dogs' yelps and the men's shouts. A few minutes later, the distant screaming of the dogs and the calls of the three men stopped. There was only the soughing wind and his and Calvin's footsteps. It took Milkman a while to figure out how to pick up his feet and miss the roots and stones; to distinguish a tree from a shadow; to keep his head down and away from the branches that swept back from Calvin's hand into his face. They were walking upland. Every now and then Calvin stopped, threw his lamplight on a tree, and examined it closely from about three feet off the ground to up as far as his arm could go. Other times he lowered the lamp over the ground, and squatting down on his haunches, peered into the dirt. Each time he seemed to be whispering. Whatever he discovered he kept to himself and Milkman didn't ask him. All he wanted to do was keep up, be ready to shoot whatever the game was when it appeared, and look out for an attempt any of them might make on his life. Within an hour after arriving in Shalimar, a young man had tried to kill him in public. What these older men, under cover of night, were capable of he could only guess.

He heard the sound of the sobbing woman again and asked Calvin, "What the hell is that?"

"Echo," he said. "Ryna's Gulch is up ahead. It makes that sound when the wind hits a certain way."

"Sounds like a woman crying," said Milkman.

"Ryna. Folks say a woman name Ryna is cryin in there. That's how it got the name."

Calvin stopped, but so suddenly that Milkman, deep in thought about Ryna, bumped into him. "Hush!" Calvin closed his eyes and tilted his head into the wind. All Milkman could hear was the dogs again, yelping, but more rapidly, he thought, than before. Calvin whistled. A faint whistle came back to them.

"Son of a fuckin bitch!" Calvin's voice broke with agitation. "Bobcat! Come on, man!" He literally sprang away and Milkman did the same. Now they moved at double time, still on land that sloped upward. It was the longest trek Milkman had ever made in his life. Miles, he thought; we must be covering miles. And hours; it must be two hours now since he whistled. On they walked, and Calvin never broke his stride for anything except an occasional shout and an occasional pause to listen to the sound that came back.

The light was changing and Milkman was getting very tired. The distance between himself and Calvin's lamp was getting wider and wider. He was twenty years younger than Calvin, but found himself unable to keep up the pace. And he was getting clumsy—stepping over big stones rather than around them, dragging his feet and catching them in humped roots, and now that Calvin was not directly in front, he had to push the branches away from his face himself. The doubling down and under branches and pushing things out of his way were as exhausting as the walk. His breath was coming in shorter and shorter gasps and he wanted to sit down more than anything in the world. He believed they were circling now, for it seemed to him that this was the third time he had seen that double-humped rock in the distance. Should they be circling? he wondered. Then he thought he remembered hearing that certain prey circled when it was being stalked. Did bobcat? He didn't even know what a bobcat looked like.

At last he surrendered to his fatigue and made the mistake of sitting down instead of slowing down, for when he got up again, the rest had given his feet an opportunity to hurt him and the pain in his short leg was so great he began to limp and hobble. Soon it wasn't possible for him to walk longer than five minutes at a time without pausing to lean against a sweet gum tree. Calvin was a pinpoint of light bobbing ahead in and out of the trees. Finally Milkman could take no more; he had to rest. At the next tree he sank down to the ground and put his head back on its bark. Let them laugh if they wanted to; he would not move until his heart left from under his chin and went back down into his chest where it belonged. He spread his legs, pulled the flashlight out of his hip pocket, and put his Winchester down near his right leg. At rest now, he could feel the blood pulsing in his temple and the cut on his face stinging in the night wind from the leaf juice and tree sap the branches had smeared on it.

When he was breathing almost normally, he began to wonder what he was doing sitting in the middle of a woods in Blue Ridge country. He had come here to find traces of Pilate's journey, to find relatives she might have visited, to find anything he could that would either lead him to the gold or convince him that it no longer existed. How had he got himself involved in a hunt, involved in a knife-and-broken-bottle fight in the first place? Ignorance, he thought, and vanity. He hadn't been alert early enough, hadn't seen the signs jutting out everywhere around him. Maybe this was a mean bunch of black folk, but he should have guessed it, sensed it, and part of the reason he hadn't was the easy, good treatment he had received elsewhere. Or had he? Maybe the glow of hero worship (twice removed) that had bathed him in Danville had also blinded him. Perhaps the eyes of the men in Roanoke, Petersburg, Newport News, had not been bright with welcome and admiration. Maybe they were just curious or amused. He hadn't stayed in any place long enough to find out. A meal here, gas there—the one real contact was the buying of the car, and the seller needing a buyer would naturally be friendly under those circumstances. The same thing held when he'd had to have those elaborate repairs. What kind of savages were these people? Suspicious. Hot-tempered. Eager to find fault and despise any outsider. Touchy. Devious, jealous, traitorous, and evil. He had done nothing to deserve their contempt. Nothing to deserve the explosive hostility that engulfed him when he said he might have to buy a car. Why didn't they respond the way the man in Roanoke did when he bought the car? Because in Roanoke he did not have a car. Here he had one and wanted another, and perhaps it was that that upset them. Furthermore, he hadn't even suggested that he would trade the old one in. He had hinted that he would abandon the "broken" one and just get another. But so what? What business was it of theirs what he did with his money? He didn't deserve . . .

It sounded old. *Deserve.* Old and tired and beaten to death. Deserve. Now it seemed to him that he was always saying or thinking that he didn't deserve some bad luck, or some bad treatment from others. He'd told Guitar that he didn't "deserve" his family's dependence, hatred, or whatever. That he didn't even "deserve" to hear all the misery and mutual accusations his parents unloaded on him. Nor did he "deserve" Hagar's vengeance. But why shouldn't his parents tell him their personal problems? If not him, then who? And if a stranger could try to kill him, surely Hagar, who knew him and whom he'd thrown away like

a wad of chewing gum after the flavor was gone—she had a
right to try to kill him too.

Apparently he thought he deserved only to be loved—from a
distance, though—and given what he wanted. And in return he
would be . . . what? Pleasant? Generous? Maybe all he was
really saying was: I am not responsible for your pain; share your
happiness with me but not your unhappiness.

They were troublesome thoughts, but they wouldn't go
away. Under the moon, on the ground, alone, with not even the
sound of baying dogs to remind him that he was with other
people, his self—the cocoon that was "personality"—gave way.
He could barely see his own hand, and couldn't see his feet. He
was only his breath, coming slower now, and his thoughts. The
rest of him had disappeared. So the thoughts came, unobstructed
by other people, by things, even by the sight of himself. There
was nothing here to help him—not his money, his car, his
father's reputation, his suit, or his shoes. In fact they hampered
him. Except for his broken watch, and his wallet with about two
hundred dollars, all he had started out with on his journey was
gone: his suitcase with the Scotch, the shirts, and the space for
bags of gold; his snap-brim hat, his tie, his shirt, his three-piece
suit, his socks, and his shoes. His watch and his two hundred
dollars would be of no help out here, where all a man had was
what he was born with, or had learned to use. And endurance.
Eyes, ears, nose, taste, touch—and some other sense that he
knew he did not have: an ability to separate out, of all the things
there were to sense, the one that life itself might depend on.
What did Calvin see on the bark? On the ground? What was he
saying? What did he hear that made him know something unex-
pected had happened some two miles—perhaps more—away,
and that that something was a different kind of prey, a bobcat?
He could still hear them—the way they had sounded the last
few hours. Signaling one another. What were they saying?
"Wait up?" "Over here?" Little by little it fell into place. The
dogs, the men—none was just hollering, just signaling location
or pace. The men and the dogs were talking to each other. In

distinctive voices they were saying distinctive, complicated things. That long *yah* sound was followed by a specific kind of howl from one of the dogs. The low *howm howm* that sounded like a string bass imitating a bassoon meant something the dogs understood and executed. And the dogs spoke to the men: single-shot barks—evenly spaced and widely spaced—one every three or four minutes, that might go on for twenty minutes. A sort of radar that indicated to the men where they were and what they saw and what they wanted to do about it. And the men agreed or told them to change direction or to come back. All those shrieks, those rapid tumbling barks, the long sustained yells, the tuba sounds, the drumbeat sounds, the low liquid *howm howm*, the reedy whistles, the thin *eeeee*'s of a cornet, the *unh unh unh* bass chords. It was all language. An extension of the click people made in their cheeks back home when they wanted a dog to follow them. No, it was not language; it was what there was before language. Before things were written down. Language in the time when men and animals did talk to one another, when a man could sit down with an ape and the two converse; when a tiger and a man could share the same tree, and each understood the other; when men ran *with* wolves, not from or after them. And he was hearing it in the Blue Ridge Mountains under a sweet gum tree. And if they could talk to animals, and the animals could talk to them, what didn't they know about human beings? Or the earth itself, for that matter. It was more than tracks Calvin was looking for—he whispered to the trees, whispered to the ground, touched them, as a blind man caresses a page of Braille, pulling meaning through his fingers.

Milkman rubbed the back of his head against the bark. This was what Guitar had missed about the South—the woods, hunters, killing. But something had maimed him, scarred him like Reverend Cooper's knot, like Saul's missing teeth, and like his own father. He felt a sudden rush of affection for them all, and out there under the sweet gum tree, within the sound of men tracking a bobcat, he thought he understood Guitar now. Really understood him.

Down either side of his thighs he felt the sweet gum's surface roots cradling him like the rough but maternal hands of a grand-father. Feeling both tense and relaxed, he sank his fingers into the grass. He tried to listen with his fingertips, to hear what, if anything, the earth had to say, and it told him quickly that someone was standing behind him and he had just enough time to raise one hand to his neck and catch the wire that fastened around his throat. It cut like a razor into his fingers, tore into the skin so deeply he had to let go. The wire pressed into his neck then and took his breath. He thought he heard himself gurgling and saw a burst of many-colored lights dancing before his eyes. When the music followed the colored lights, he knew he had just drawn the last sweet air left for him in the world. Exactly the way he'd heard it would be, his life flashed before him, but it consisted of only one image: Hagar bending over him in perfect love, in the most intimate sexual gesture imaginable. In the midst of that picture he heard the voice of the someone holding the wire say, "Your Day has come," and it filled him with such sadness to be dying, leaving this world at the fingertips of his friend, that he relaxed and in the instant it took to surrender to the overwhelming melancholy he felt the cords of his struggling neck muscles relax too and there was a piece of a second in which the wire left him room enough to gasp, to take another breath. But it was a living breath this time, not a dying one. Hagar, the lights, the music, disappeared, and Milkman grabbed the Winchester at his side, cocked it, and pulled the trigger, shooting into the trees in front of him. The blast startled Guitar, and the wire slipped again. Guitar pulled it back, but Milkman knew his friend would need both hands to keep it that way. He turned the shotgun backward as far as he could and managed awkwardly, to pull the trigger again, hitting only branches and dirt. He was wondering if there was another blast in the gun when he heard right up close the wild, wonderful sound of three baying dogs who he knew had treed a bobcat. The wire dropped and he heard Guitar breaking into a fast run through the trees. Milkman stood up and grabbed his flashlight, pointing it in the direction of the sound of running feet. He saw nothing but branches resettling themselves. Rubbing his neck, he moved toward the sound of the dogs. Guitar did not have a gun, otherwise he would have used it, so Milkman felt secure heading for the dogs with the gun in his hand even though it had no more shot. He didn't miss; his sense of direction was accurate and he came upon Calvin, Small Boy, Luther, and Omar crouching on the ground a few feet away from the dogs and the glistening night eyes of a bobcat in a tree.

The dogs were trying their best to get up into the tree, and the men were considering whether to shoot the bobcat down, shoot a limb and make him jump down and fight the dogs, or what. They decided to try and kill the cat where he lay. Omar stood up and took his lamp over to the left. The cat crept a little ways out, following the light. Then Small Boy took aim and put a bullet just under the left foreleg and the bobcat dropped through the branches into the jaws of Becky and her companions.

There was a lot of life in the cat; he fought well until Calvin hollered the dogs away and shot it again, and once more, and then it was still.

They held the lamps over the carcass and groaned with pleasure at the size, the ferocity, the stillness of it. All four got down on their knees, pulling rope and knives, cutting a branch the width of a wrist, tying it and binding it for the long walk back.

They were so pleased with themselves it was some time before anybody remembered to ask Milkman what he was shooting at back there. Milkman hoisted the stake he was carrying a little higher and said, "I dropped the gun. I tripped and it went off. Then when I picked it up it went off again."

They burst into laughter. "Tripped? What'd you have the safety off for? Was you scared?"

"Scared to death," said Milkman. "Scared to death."

They hooted and laughed all the way back to the car, teasing Milkman, egging him on to tell more about how scared he was. And he told them. Laughing too, hard, loud, and long. Really laughing, and he found himself exhilarated by simply walking the earth. Walking it like he belonged on it; like his legs were stalks, tree trunks, a part of his body that extended down down down into the rock and soil, and were comfortable there—on the earth and on the place where he walked. And he did not limp.

They met dawn in King Walker's gas station for a rehash of the night they had spent. Milkman was the butt of their humor, but it was good-humored humor, quite unlike the laughter the trip had begun with. "Lucky to be alive. Cat wasn't the problem; this here nigger was the problem. Blastin away at us while we got a mean cat gettin ready to chew us and the dogs up both. Shootin all through the woods. Could have blown his own head off. Don't you city boys know how to handle yourself?"

"You country niggers got it all over us," Milkman answered.

Omar and Small Boy slapped him on the shoulders. Calvin hollered to Luther, "Go get Vernell. Tell her to get breakfast ready. Soon's we skin this cat, we comin in there with a appetite and she better be ready to meet it!"

Milkman went with them to the back of the station, where, on a small cemented area covered by a corrugated tin roof, the dead bobcat lay. Milkman's neck had swollen so it was difficult for him to lower his chin without pain.

Omar sliced through the rope that bound the bobcat's feet. He and Calvin turned it over on its back. The legs fell open. Such thin delicate ankles.

"Everybody wants a black man's life."

Calvin held the forefeet open and up while Omar pierced the curling hair at the point where the sternum lay. Then he sliced all the way down to the genitals. His knife pointed upward for a cleaner, neater incision.

"Not his dead life; I mean his living life."

When he reached the genitals he cut them off, but left the scrotum intact.

"It's the condition our condition is in."

Omar cut around the legs and the neck. Then he pulled the hide off.

"What good is a man's life if he can't even choose what to die for?"

The transparent underskin tore like gossamer under his fingers.

"Everybody wants the life of a black man."

Now Small Boy knelt down and slit the flesh from the scrotum to the jaw.

"Fair is one more thing I've given up."

Luther came back and, while the others rested, carved out the rectal tube with the deft motions of a man coring an apple.

"I hope I never have to ask myself that question."

Luther reached into the paunch and lifted the entrails. He dug under the rib cage to the diaphragm and carefully cut around it until it was free.

"It is about love. What else but love? Can't I love what I criticize?"

Then he grabbed the windpipe and the gullet, eased them back, and severed them with one stroke of his little knife.

"It is about love. What else?"

They turned to Milkman. "You want the heart?" they asked him. Quickly, before any thought could paralyze him, Milkman plunged both hands into the rib cage. "Don't get the lungs, now. Get the heart."

"What else?"

He found it and pulled. The heart fell away from the chest as easily as yolk slips out of its shell.

"What else? What else? What else?"

Now Luther went back into the stomach cavity and yanked the entrails out altogether. They sucked up like a vacuum through the hole that was made at the rectum. He slipped the entrails into a paper bag while the others began cleaning up, hosing down, salting, packing, straightening, and then they turned the cat over to let the blood drain down on its own hide.

"What are you going to do with it?" asked Milkman.

"Eat him!"

A peacock soared away and lit on the hood of a blue Buick.

Milkman looked at the bobcat's head. The tongue lay in its mouth as harmless as a sandwich. Only the eyes held the menace of the night.

Hungry as he was, he couldn't eat much of Vernell's breakfast, so he pushed the scrambled eggs, hominy, fried apples around in the plate, gulped coffee and talked a lot. And, somehow, he had to get around to the purpose of his visit to Shalimar.

"You know, my grandfather came from somewhere near here. My grandmother too."

"Did? From around here? What's their name?"

"I don't know her maiden name, but her first name was Sing. Any of you ever know anybody with a name like that?"

They shook their heads. "Sing? No. Never heard of nobody name that."

"I had an aunt live down this way too. Name of Pilate. Pilate Dead. Ever hear of her?"

"Ha! Sound like a newspaper headline: Pilot Dead. She do any flying?"

"No. *P-i-l-a-t-e*, Pilate."

"*P-i-l-a-t-e*. That spell *Pie-late*," Small Boy said.

"Naw, nigger. Not no *Pie-late*. Pilate like in the Bible, dummy."

"He don't read the Bible."

"He don't read nothin."

"He can't read nothin."

They teased Small Boy until Vernell interrupted them. "You all hush. You say Sing?" she asked Milkman.

"Yeah. Sing."

"I believe that was the name of a girl my gran used to play with. I remember the name cause it sounded so pretty. Gran used to talk about her all the time. Seem like her folks didn't like her to play with the colored children from over this way, so her and my gran used to sneak off and go fishin and berry-pickin. You know what I mean? She'd have to meet her in secret." Vernell eyed Milkman carefully. "This Sing girl was light-skinned, with straight black hair."

"That's her!" Milkman said. "She was mixed or Indian, one."

Vernell nodded. "Indian. One of old Heddy's children. Heddy was all right, but she didn't like her girl playin with coloreds. She was a Byrd."

"A what?"

"A Byrd. Belonged to the Byrd family over by the ridge. Near Solomon's Leap."

"Oh, yeah?" said one of the men. "One of Susan Byrd's people?"

"That's right. One of them. They never was too crazy 'bout colored folks. Susan either."

"Do they still live there?" asked Milkman.

"Susan do. Right behind the ridge. Only house back in there with a brick front. She by herself now. All the others moved out so they could pass."

"Can I walk it?" he asked.

"Most folks could, I reckon," said Omar. "But after last night I don't recommend it for you." He laughed.

"Can you drive a car through?"

"Part of the way you can. But the road is narrow and messy back up in there," said Vernell. "Horse, maybe, but not no car."

"I'll make it. Might take me a week, but I'll make it," said Milkman.

"Just don't carry no guns"—Calvin cooled his coffee in his saucer—"and you'll be all right." They all laughed again.

Milkman thought about that. Guitar was out there someplace, and since he seemed to know everything Milkman was doing or getting ready to do, he'd also know he was going out to some ridge. He touched his swollen neck. He didn't want to go anywhere alone without a gun.

"You ought to have a rest before you go trottin off any-

where," Omar said, looking at him. "There's a nice lady up the
road a ways. She'd be proud to take you in." The look in his
eyes was unmistakable. "Pretty woman too. Real pretty." Vernell grunted and Milkman smiled. Hope she's got a gun, he
thought.

She didn't, but she had indoor plumbing and her smile was
just like her name, Sweet, as she nodded her head to Milkman's
query about whether he could take a bath. The tub was the
newest feature in the tiny shotgun house and Milkman sank
gratefully into the steaming water. Sweet brought him soap and
a boar's-bristle brush and knelt to bathe him. What she did for
his sore feet, his cut face, his back, his neck, his thighs, and the
palms of his hands was so delicious he couldn't imagine that the
lovemaking to follow would be anything but anticlimactic. If
this bath and this woman, he thought, are all that come out of
this trip, I will rest easy and do my duty to God, country, and
the Brotherhood of Elks for the rest of my life. I will walk hot
coals with a quart of kerosene in my hand for this. I will walk
every railroad tie from here to Cheyenne and back for this. But
when the lovemaking came, he decided he would crawl.

Afterward he offered to bathe her. She said he couldn't because the tank was small and there wasn't enough water for
another hot bath.

"Then let me give you a cool one," he said. He soaped and
rubbed her until her skin squeaked and glistened like onyx. She
put salve on his face. He washed her hair. She sprinkled talcum
on his feet. He straddled her behind and massaged her back. She
put witch hazel on his swollen neck. He made up the bed. She
gave him gumbo to eat. He washed the dishes. She washed his
clothes and hung them out to dry. He scoured her tub. She
ironed his shirt and pants. He gave her fifty dollars. She kissed
his mouth. He touched her face. She said please come back. He
said I'll see you tonight.

Chapter 12

At four o'clock he knocked on the door of the only house back of the ridge with a brick front. Fresh and shining in the army fatigues Sweet had washed and pressed, he had tramped along feeling ready for anything. But he didn't think Guitar would jump him in the daytime on a winding path (which they called a road) that cut through hilly land that was nevertheless tilled and had a smattering of houses and people. If he did confront him (with anything other than a gun) Milkman was sure he could take him, but it would be best to get back before nightfall. He didn't know what was on Guitar's mind, but he knew it had something to do with the gold. If he knows I'm here and where I have been and what I did in each place, then he must know that I'm trying to get it, doing just what I said I would do. Why would he try to kill me before I got it or even found out what happened to it? Most of it was a total mystery to him, but the part that was clear was enough to keep him alert and jittery all the way.

The Byrd house sat on a neat lawn separated by a white picket fence from the field grass on either side of the property. A child's swing dangled from a cedar tree; four little steps painted blue led up to the porch, and from the window, between fluttering curtains, came the smell of gingerbread baking.

A woman who looked to be about his mother's age answered the door.

"Miss Byrd?" Milkman asked her.

"Yes?"

"How are you? My name is, uh, Macon, and I'm visiting here for a few days. I'm from Michigan and I think some of my people lived here a long time ago. I was hoping you'd be able to help me."

"Help you what?" She sounded arch and Milkman had the distinct impression that this lady did not like the color of his skin.

"Find them. I mean find out about them. We're all split up, my family, and some folks in town thought you might know some of them."

"Who's that, Susan?" Another woman's voice came from behind her.

"Somebody to see *me*, Grace."

"Well, why don't you ask him in? Don't make him state his business on the steps."

Miss Byrd sighed. "Please come in, Mr. Macon."

Milkman followed her into a pleasant living room full up with sunshine. "Excuse me," she said. "I didn't mean to be rude. Please have a seat." She motioned to a gray velvet wing-back chair. A woman in a two-piece print dress came into the room, clutching a paper napkin in her hand and chewing on something.

"Who'd you say?" She addressed her question to Miss Byrd, but ran inquisitive eyes over Milkman.

Miss Byrd held out a hand. "This is a friend of mine—Miss Long. Grace Long—Mr. . . ."

"How do you do?" Grace held out her hand to him.

"Fine, thank you."

"Mr. Macon, is it?"

"Yes."

"Susan, perhaps Mr. Macon would like some refreshment." Miss Long smiled and sat on the sofa facing the gray chair.

"Well, he just stepped foot in the door, Grace. Give me time." Miss Byrd turned to Milkman. "Would you like a cup of coffee or some tea?"

"Sure. Thanks."

"Which one?"

"Coffee's all right."

"You've got butter cookies, Susan. Give him some of those butter cookies."

Miss Byrd gave her friend a tired frown. "I'll just be a minute," she said to Milkman, and left the room.

"Yes, well. Did I hear you say you were visiting in these parts? We don't see too many visitors." Grace crossed her ankles. Like Susan Byrd, she wore black laced shoes and cotton stockings. As she made herself comfortable, she inched her dress up a little.

"Yes, visiting."

"You in the service?"

"Ma'am? Oh, no. I was hunting last night. Some friends lent me these." He smoothed the seam Sweet had made in the fatigues.

"Hunting? Oh, Lord, don't tell me you're one of them. I can't stand those hunting people. They make me sick, always prowling round other people's property. Day and night they're shooting up the world. I tell my students—I'm a schoolteacher, you know, I teach over at the normal school. Have you seen it yet?"

"No, not yet."

"Well, there's nothing to see, really. Just a school, like any other. But you're welcome to stop by. We'd be pleased to have you. Where you from again?"

"Michigan."

"I thought so. Susan!" She turned around. "He's from up North." Then back to Milkman: "Where are you staying?"

"Well, nowhere yet. I just met a few people in town and . . ."

Susan Byrd came in with a tray of coffee cups and a plate of wide pale cookies.

"He's from Michigan," said Grace.

"I heard him. How do you take your coffee?"

"Black."

"Black? No cream or sugar at all?" asked Grace. "Wish I could do that; maybe I could get back into a twelve. But it's never going to happen now." She pressed one hand on her hip and smiled at Milkman.

"What did you want to see me about?" Susan Byrd placed a mild but clear stress on the word "me."

"I'm trying to locate anybody who might have known my grandmother. Her name was Sing."

Grace clapped her hands to her mouth and gave a little squeal. "Relatives! You all are relatives!" Milkman put his cup down. "Well, I'll be!" Grace's eyes were lit and dancing.

"You've come to the right place," said Susan, "but I doubt if I can help you any."

"What are you talking about, Susan? Your mother was named Sing, wasn't she?"

"No, she wasn't, Grace, and if you let me finish a sentence you might learn something you don't know too."

"I thought you said—"

"My mother's name was Mary. *M-a-r-y*, Mary."

"Well, excuse *me*."

Susan turned to Milkman. "My father, Crowell Byrd, had a sister named Sing."

"That must be her! My grandmother! Sing. Did she marry a man named—"

"I knew there was somebody in your family named Sing!"

"She didn't marry anybody that I know of." Susan interrupted them both.

"Oh, this is really something. A stranger walks right into your house and he's your own . . . what? Cousin? I hate to say it, but this is a small world. Isn't it? You have got to visit my class, Mr. Macon."

Milkman joined Susan Byrd in ignoring Grace Long. "Where did she live?" he asked her.

"The last time my father saw her, she was on a wagon headed for Massachusetts to a private school up there. A Quaker school."

"Your people Quakers? You never told me that. See, Mr. Macon, what your friends hide from you? I bet she'd hide you too."

"And she never married?" Milkman couldn't take the time to acknowledge Grace's attentions.

"Not anybody we heard of. After she went to that Quaker school they lost track of her. I believe they tried to locate her, mostly because my grandmother—her name was Heddy—she was so torn up about it. I always believed the same thing my father believed: that she didn't want to be found after she left that school."

"You know darn well she didn't," said Grace. "She probably started passing like the rest of 'em, that's what." She leaned toward Milkman. "There used to be a lot of that. A lot of it. Not so much nowadays, but there used to be a lot of 'em did it—if they could." She shot a glance at Susan. "Like your cousins, Susan. They're passing now. Lilah, John. I know John is, and he knows I know he is."

"Everybody knows that, Grace."

"Mr. Macon doesn't know it. I saw John on the street in Mayville—"

"Mr. Macon doesn't need to know it. He's not even interested."

"How do you know he's not?"

"Because he said the woman he's looking for was his grandmother, and if she's his grandmother she'd be too dark to . . ." Susan Byrd hesitated. "Well, too dark to pass. Wouldn't she?" She flushed a little.

Milkman ignored the question. "And you say she lived in Massachusetts, right?"

"Yes. Boston."

"I see." It looked like a dead end, so he decided to follow another line. "Did you ever know or hear of a woman around here named Pilate?"

"Pilate. No. Never. Have you, Grace?"

Grace shook her head. "No, and I've been here most of my life."

"I've been here *all* of mine," said Susan. "Both my parents were born here and so was I. Never been farther away than St. Phillips County. I have people in South Carolina, but I've never even been to visit them."

"That's because they're passing too. Just like John. You couldn't visit them if you wanted to." Grace leaned over the plate of cookies and selected one.

"They're not the only family I have left." Susan was indignant.

"I hope not. It's a sad thing, Mr. Macon, when you're left without any people to claim you. I keep up with my family. I'm not married, you know, not yet anyway, but my family is *very* close." She gave him a meaningful look. Milkman turned his wrist and looked down to see what time it was.

"Oh, look at that." Grace pointed to his hand. "What a good-looking watch. May I see it?" Milkman stood up to hand it to her and remained standing. "Look, Susan, it doesn't have a single number on it. Just dots. Now, how can anybody figure out what time it is from those dots?"

Susan rose too. "You ever been down here before, Mr. Macon?"

"No. This is my first visit."

"Well, I hope it won't be your last. How long will you be here?"

"Oh, I think I'll get on back tonight or tomorrow at the latest." He looked out the window. The sun was dropping.

"That soon?" asked Grace. "Why don't you give him something to take with him, Susan? Would you like to take some butter cookies with you, Mr. Macon?"

"No, thank you."

"You'll be happy to have them later." The woman was wearing him down. He smiled, though, and said, "If you like."

"I'll fix a little package for you. Okay, Susan?" She fled from the room.

Susan managed a small smile. "Wish you could stay and visit with us awhile." Her words were as mechanical as her smile.

"So do I," he said, "but, well, maybe I'll be back."

"That'd be nice. Sorry I couldn't be of any help to you."

"You have been."

"Have I?"

"Oh, sure. You have to know what's wrong before you can find what's right."

She smiled a genuine smile then. "It's important to you, is it, to find your people?"

Milkman thought about it. "No. Not really. I was just passing through, and it was just—just an idea. It's not important."

Grace returned with a little parcel wrapped in white paper napkins. "Here you are," she said. "You'll appreciate this later on."

"Thank you. Thank you both."

"Nice meeting you."

"And you."

He left the house feeling tired and off center. I'll spend one more night here and then leave, he thought. The car should be fixed by now. There's nothing here to know, no gold or any traces of it. Pilate lived in Virginia, but not in this part of the state. Nobody at all has heard of her. And the Sing that lived here went to Boston, not Danville, Pennsylvania, and passed for white. His grandmother would have been "too dark to pass." She had actually blushed. As though she'd discovered something shameful about him. He was both angry and amused and wondered what Omar and Sweet and Vernell thought of Miss Susan Byrd.

He was curious about these people. He didn't feel close to

them, but he did feel connected, as though there was some cord or pulse or information they shared. Back home he had never felt that way, as though he belonged to anyplace or anybody. He'd always considered himself the outsider in his family, only vaguely involved with his friends, and except for Guitar, there was no one whose opinion of himself he cared about. Once, long ago, he had cared what Pilate and Hagar thought of him, but having conquered Hagar and having disregarded Pilate enough to steal from her, all that was gone. But there was something he felt now—here in Shalimar, and earlier in Danville—that reminded him of how he used to feel in Pilate's house. Sitting in Susan Byrd's living room, lying with Sweet, eating with those men at Vernell's table, he didn't have to get over, to turn on, or up, or even out.

And there was something more. It wasn't true what he'd said to Susan Byrd: that it wasn't important to find his people. Ever since Danville, his interest in his own people, not just the ones he met, had been growing. Macon Dead, also known as Jake somebody. Sing. Who were they, and what were they like? The man who sat for five nights on a fence with a gun, waiting. Who named his baby girl Pilate, who tore a farm out of a wilderness. The man who ate pecans on a wagon going North. Did he have brothers or sisters whom he left behind? Who was his mother, his father? And his wife. Was she the Boston Sing? If so, what was she doing on a wagon? Why would she go off to a northern private school on a wagon? Not a carriage or a train, but a wagon—full of ex-slaves. Maybe she never got to Boston. Maybe she didn't pass. She could have changed her mind about school and run off with the boy she ate pecans with. And whoever she was, why did she want her husband to keep that awful name? To wipe out the past? What past? Slavery? She was never a slave. *His* slave past? And why didn't his own father, and Pilate, know any of their own relatives? Wasn't there any family to notify when the father died? Macon didn't ever try to get to Virginia. Pilate headed straight for it.

Milkman opened the parcel Grace had fixed for him and took

out a cookie. A little piece of paper fluttered to the ground. He picked it up and read: "Grace Long 40 Route 2 three houses down from the Normal School." He smiled. That's why it took her so long to wrap up four cookies. He bit into one of them and sauntered along, crumpling the napkins and Grace's invitation into a wad. The questions about his family still knocked around in his head like billiard balls. If his grandfather, this Jake, was born in the same place his wife was, in Shalimar, why did he tell the Yankee he was born in Macon, thereby providing him with the raw material for the misnaming? And if he and his wife were born in the same place, why did Pilate and his father and Circe all say they "met" on that wagon? And why did the ghost tell Pilate to sing? Milkman chuckled to himself. That wasn't what he was telling her at all; maybe the ghost was just repeating his wife's name, Sing, and Pilate didn't know it because she never knew her mother's name. After she died Macon Dead wouldn't let anybody say it aloud. That was funny. He wouldn't speak it after she died, and after he died that's all he ever said—her name.

Jesus! Here he was walking around in the middle of the twentieth century trying to explain what a ghost had done. But why not? he thought. One fact was certain: Pilate did not have a navel. Since that was true, anything could be, and why not ghosts as well?

He was near the road leading to the town now, and it was getting dark. He lifted his wrist to look at his watch and remembered that Grace had not given it back to him. "Damn," he murmured aloud. "I'm losing everything." He stood still, trying to make up his mind whether to go back for it now or later. If he went now, he'd be forced to return in deep darkness. Totally defenseless before a hit from Guitar. But it would be a real bother to have to come all the way back here—where no car could make it—tomorrow when he was going to leave. But Guitar might be—

"I can't let him direct and determine what I do, where I go or when. If I do that now I'll do it all my life and he'll run me off the earth."

He didn't know what to do, but decided finally that a watch was not worth worrying about. All it could do was tell him the time of day and he really wasn't interested. Wiping cookie crumbs from his mustache, he turned into the main road, and there, outlined in cobalt blue, stood Guitar. Leaned, rather, against a persimmon tree. Milkman stopped, surprised at the calm, steady beat of his heart—the complete absence of fear. But then, Guitar was cleaning his fingernails with a harmless match stick. Any weapon he had would have to be hidden in his denim jacket or pants.

They looked at each other for a minute. No, less. Just long enough for the heart of each man to adjust its throb to the downbeat of the other. Guitar spoke first.

"My man."

Milkman ignored the greeting. "Why, Guitar? Just tell me why."

"You took the gold."

"What gold? There wasn't any gold."

"You took the gold."

"The cave was empty, man. I got down on my stomach and looked in that pit. I put my hands—"

"You took the gold."

"You're crazy, Guitar."

"Angry. Never crazy."

"There wasn't any gold!" Milkman tried hard not to shout.

"I saw you, motherfucker."

"Saw me what?"

"Take the gold."

"Where?"

"In Danville."

"You saw me with gold in Danville?"

"I saw you with gold in Danville."

"You've got to be kidding. What was I doing with it?"

"Shipping it."

"Shipping it?"

"Yeah. Why the game, man? You just greedy, like your old

man? Or what?" Guitar's eyes rested on the last butter cookie in Milkman's hand. He frowned and began to breathe through his lips.

"Guitar, I didn't ship no gold. There wasn't any gold to ship. You couldn't have seen me."

"I saw you, baby. I was in the station."

"What fuckin station?"

"The freight station in Danville."

Milkman remembered then, going to look for Reverend Cooper, looking all over for him. Then going into the station house to see if he'd gone, and there helping a man lift a huge crate onto the weighing platform. He started to laugh. "Oh, shit. Guitar, that wasn't no gold. I was just helping that man lift a crate. He asked me to help him. Help him lift a big old crate. I did and then I split."

Guitar looked at the cookie again, then back into Milkman's eyes. Nothing changed in his face. Milkman knew it sounded lame. It was the truth, but it sounded like a lie. A weak lie too. He also knew that in all his life, Guitar had never seen Milkman give anybody a hand, especially a stranger; he also knew that they'd even discussed it, starting with Milkman's not coming to his mother's rescue in a dream he had. Guitar had accused him of selfishness and indifference; told him he wasn't serious, and didn't have any fellow feeling—none whatsoever. Now he was standing there saying that he willingly, spontaneously, had helped an old white man lift a huge, heavy crate. But it was true. It was true. And he'd prove it.

"Guitar, why am I here? If I was shipping gold back home, why am I here dressed like this? Would I be roaming around in the country like a fool with a crate of gold off somewhere? Would I? What the fuck would I do that for and then come here?"

"Maybe you shipped the gold *here*, you jive-ass."

"What the fuck are you talking about?"

"I looked! I saw it! You hear me? I drove down there, followed you there, because I had a funny feeling that you were pulling a fast one. I wasn't sure, but I felt it. If I was wrong, I'd help you get it. But I wasn't wrong. I got into Danville that afternoon. I drove right past the freight depot and there you were in your little beige suit. I parked and followed you into the station. When I got there I saw you shipping it. Giving it to the man. I waited until you left, and I went back in and asked the cracker if my friend"—he slurred the word—"had shipped a crate to Michigan. The man said no. Just one crate on the load, he said. Just one crate. And when I asked him where it was going, all he could remember was Virginia." Guitar smiled. "The bus you caught wasn't headed for Michigan. It was headed for Virginia. And here you are."

Milkman felt whipped. There was nothing to do but let it play.

"Was my name on the crate?"

"I didn't look."

"Would I send a crate of gold to Virginia—*gold*, man."

"You might. You did."

"Is that why you tried to kill me?"

"Yes."

"Because I ripped you off?"

"Because you ripped *us* off! You are fuckin with our work!"

"You're wrong. Dead wrong."

"The 'dead' part is you."

Milkman looked down at the cookie in his hand. It looked foolish and he started to throw it away, but changed his mind. "So my Day has come?"

"Your Day has come, but on *my* schedule. And believe it: I will run you as long as there is ground. Your name is Macon, but you ain't dead yet."

"Tell me something. When you saw me in the station, with the crate, why did you back off and hide? Why didn't you just walk up to me? It could have been settled there."

"I told you. I had this funny funny feeling."

"That I was going to cut you out?"

"Cut *us* out. Yes."

"And you believe I did?"
"Yes."
"Back there in the woods you were angry."
"Yes."
"Now you're going to wait till the gold comes."
"Yes."
"And I pick it up."
"You won't be able to pick it up."
"Do me a favor. When it gets here. Check it first to see if there's gold in it."
"First?"
"Or last. But before you haul it all the way back home."
"Don't worry yourself about it."
"One more thing. Why the message? Why'd you warn me with a message at the store?"
"You're my friend. It's the least I could do for a friend."
"My man. I want to thank you."
"You're welcome, baby."

Milkman slipped into Sweet's bed and slept the night in her perfect arms. It was a warm dreamy sleep all about flying, about sailing high over the earth. But not with arms stretched out like airplane wings, nor shot forward like Superman in a horizontal dive, but floating, cruising, in the relaxed position of a man lying on a couch reading a newspaper. Part of his flight was over the dark sea, but it didn't frighten him because he knew he could not fall. He was alone in the sky, but somebody was applauding him, watching him and applauding. He couldn't see who it was.

When he awoke the next morning and set about seeing to the repair of his car, he couldn't shake the dream, and didn't really want to. In Solomon's store he found Omar and Solomon shaking sacks of okra into peck baskets and he still felt the sense of lightness and power that flying had given him.

"Got a belt for your car," said Omar. "Ain't new, but it ought to fit."

"Hey, that's good. Thanks, Omar."

"You leavin us right away?"

"Yeah, I have to get on back."

"You see that Byrd woman all right?"

"Yeah, I saw her."

"She help you any?" Omar wiped the okra fuzz from his hands onto his trousers.

"No. Not much."

"Well, King Walker say he be down this morning and put the belt on. You probably ought to get a good checkup on that car once you get on the road."

"I plan to."

"Sweet give you any breakfast?" asked Solomon.

"She tried, but I wanted to get over here early to see about the car."

"What about a cup a coffee; there's a full pot in back."

"No, thanks. I think I'll walk around a little till he comes."

It was six-thirty in the morning and the town was bustling as though it were high noon. Life and business began early in the South so the coolest part of the day could be taken advantage of. People had already eaten, women had already washed clothes and were spreading them on bushes, and in a few days, when the school in the next town opened, children at this hour would already be walking, running over the roads and fields to class. Now they were sauntering about, doing chores, teasing cats, throwing bread to stray chickens, and some of them were playing their endless round games. Milkman could hear them singing and wandered off toward them and the huge cedar that reared up over their heads. Again their sweet voices reminded him of the gap in his own childhood, as he leaned against the cedar to watch them. The boy in the middle of the circle (it seemed always to be a boy) spun around with his eyes closed and his arm stretched out, pointing. Round and round he went until the song ended with a shout and he stopped, his finger pointing at a child Milkman could not see. Then they all dropped to their knees and he was surprised to hear them begin another song at this point, one he had heard off and on all his life. That old blues song Pilate sang all the time: "O Sugarman don't leave me here," except the children sang, "Solomon don't leave me here."

Milkman smiled, remembering Pilate. Hundreds of miles away, he was homesick for her, for her house, for the very people he had been hell-bent to leave. His mother's quiet, crooked, apologetic smile. Her hopeless helplessness in the kitchen. The best years of her life, from age twenty to forty, had been celibate, and aside from the consummation that began his own life, the rest of her life had been the same. He hadn't thought much of it when she'd told him, but now it seemed to him that such sexual deprivation would affect her, hurt her in precisely the way it would affect and hurt him. If it were possible for somebody to force him to live that way, to tell him, "You may walk and live among women, you may even lust after them, but you will not make love for the next twenty years," how would he feel? What would he do? Would he continue as he was? And suppose he were married and his wife refused him for fifteen years. His mother had been able to live through that by a long nursing of her son, some occasional visits to a grave-yard. What might she have been like had her husband loved her?

And his father. An old man now, who acquired things and used people to acquire more things. As the son of Macon Dead the first, he paid homage to his own father's life and death by loving what that father had loved: property, good solid property, the bountifulness of life. He loved these things to excess because he loved his father to excess. Owning, building, acquiring—that was his life, his future, his present, and all the history he knew. That he distorted life, bent it, for the sake of gain, was a measure of his loss at his father's death.

As Milkman watched the children, he began to feel uncomfortable. Hating his parents, his sisters, seemed silly now. And the skim of shame that he had rinsed away in the bathwater after having stolen from Pilate returned. But now it was as thick and as tight as a caul. How could he have broken into that house—

the only one he knew that achieved comfort without one article of comfort in it. No soft worn-down chair, not a cushion or a pillow. No light switch, no water running free and clear after a turn of a tap handle. No napkins, no tablecloth. No fluted plates or flowered cups, no circle of blue flame burning in a stove eye. But peace was there, energy, singing, and now his own remembrances.

His mind turned to Hagar and how he had treated her at the end. Why did he never sit her down and talk to her? Honestly. And what ugly thing was it he said to her the last time she tried to kill him? And God, how hollow her eyes had looked. He was never frightened of her; he never actually believed that she would succeed in killing him, or that she really wanted to. Her weapons, the complete lack of cunning or intelligence even of conviction, in her attacks were enough to drain away any fear. Oh, she could have accidentally hurt him, but he could have stopped her in any number of ways. But he hadn't wanted to. He had used her—her love, her craziness—and most of all he had used her skulking, bitter vengeance. It made him a star, a celebrity in the Blood Bank; it told men and other women that he was one bad dude, that he had the power to drive a woman out of her mind, to destroy her, and not because she hated him, or because he had done some unforgivable thing to her, but because he had fucked her and she was driven wild by the absence of his magnificent joint. His hog's gut, Lena had called it. Even the last time, he used her. Used her imminent arrival and feeble attempt at murder as an exercise of his will against hers— an ultimatum to the universe. "Die, Hagar, die." Either this bitch dies or I do. And she stood there like a puppet strung up by a puppet master who had gone off to some other hobby.

O Solomon don't leave me here.

The children were starting the round again. Milkman rubbed the back of his neck. Suddenly he was tired, although the morning was still new. He pushed himself away from the cedar and sank to his haunches.

Song of Solomon

> *Jay the only son of Solomon*
> *Come booba yalle, come . . .*

Everybody in this town is named Solomon, he thought wearily. Solomon's General Store, Luther Solomon (no relation), Solomon's Leap, and now the children were singing "*Solomon* don't leave me" instead of "*Sugarman.*" Even the name of the town sounded like Solomon: Shalimar, which Mr. Solomon and everybody else pronounced *Shalleemone.*

Milkman's scalp began to tingle. Jay the only son of Solomon? Was that *Jake* the only son of Solomon? Jake. He strained to hear the children. That was one of the people he was looking for. A man named Jake who lived in Shalimar, as did his wife, Sing.

He sat up and waited for the children to begin the verse again. "Come booba yalle, come booba tambee," it sounded like, and didn't make sense. But another line—"Black lady fell down on the ground"—was clear enough. There was another string of nonsense words, then "Threw her body all around." Now the child in the center began whirling, spinning to lyrics sung in a different, faster tempo: "Solomon 'n' Reiner Belali Shalut . . ."

Solomon again, and Reiner? Ryna? Why did the second name sound so familiar? Solomon and Ryna. The woods. The hunt. Solomon's Leap and Ryna's Gulch, places they went to or passed by that night they shot the bobcat. The gulch was where he heard that noise that sounded like a woman crying, which Calvin said came from Ryna's Gulch, that there was an echo there that folks said was "a woman name Ryna" crying. You could hear her when the wind was right.

But what was the rest: Belali . . . Shalut . . . Yaruba? If Solomon and Ryna were names of people, the others might be also. The verse ended in another clear line. "Twenty-one children, the last one *Jake!*" And it was at the shout of *Jake* (who was also, apparently, "the only son of Solomon") that the twirling boy stopped. Now Milkman understood that if the child's finger pointed at nobody, missed, they started up again. But if it pointed directly to another child, that was when they fell to their knees and sang Pilate's song.

Milkman took out his wallet and pulled from it his airplane ticket stub, but he had no pencil to write with, and his pen was in his suit. He would just have to listen and memorize it. He closed his eyes and concentrated while the children, inexhaustible in their willingness to repeat a rhythmic, rhyming action game, performed the round over and over again. And Milkman memorized all of what they sang.

> *Jake the only son of Solomon*
> *Come booba yalle, come booba tambee*
> *Whirled about and touched the sun*
> *Come konka yalle, come konka tambee*
>
> *Left that baby in a white man's house*
> *Come booba yalle, come booba tambee*
> *Heddy took him to a red man's house*
> *Come konka yalle, come konka tambee*
>
> *Black lady fell down on the ground*
> *Come booba yalle, come booba tambee*
> *Threw her body all around*
> *Come konka yalle, come konka tambee*
>
> *Solomon and Ryna Belali Shalut*
> *Yaruba Medina Muhammet too.*
> *Nestor Kalina Saraka cake.*
> *Twenty-one children, the last one Jake!*
>
> *O Solomon don't leave me here*
> *Cotton balls to choke me*
> *O Solomon don't leave me here*
> *Buckra's arms to yoke me*
>
> *Solomon done fly, Solomon done gone*
> *Solomon cut across the sky, Solomon gone home.*

He almost shouted when he heard "Heddy took him to a red man's house." Heddy was Susan Byrd's grandmother on her father's side, and therefore Sing's mother too. And "red man's house" must be a reference to the Byrds as Indians. Of course! Sing was an Indian or part Indian and her name was Sing Byrd or, more likely, Sing Bird. No—Singing Bird! That must have been her name originally—Singing Bird. And her brother, Crowell Byrd, was probably Crow Bird, or just Crow. They had mixed their Indian names with American-sounding names. Milkman had four people now that he could recognize in the song: Solomon, Jake, Ryna and Heddy, and a veiled reference to Heddy's Indianness. All of which seemed to put Jake and Sing together in Shalimar, just as Circe had said they were. He couldn't be mistaken. These children were singing a story about his own people! He hummed and chuckled as he did his best to put it all together.

Jake's father was Solomon. Did Jake whirl about and touch the sun? Did Jake leave a baby in a white man's house? No. If the "Solomon don't leave me" line was right, Solomon was the one who left, who "flew away"—meaning died or ran off—not Jake. Maybe it was the baby, or Jake himself, who was begging him to stay. But who was the "black lady" who fell down on the ground? Why did she throw her body all around? It sounded like she was having a fit. Was it because somebody took her baby first to a white man's house, then to an Indian's house? Ryna? Was Ryna the black lady still crying in the gulch? Was Ryna Solomon's daughter? Maybe she had an illegitimate child, and her father— No. It's Solomon she is crying for, not a baby. "Solomon don't leave me." He must have been her lover.

Milkman was getting confused, but he was as excited as a child confronted with boxes and boxes of presents under the skirt of a Christmas tree. Somewhere in the pile was a gift for him.

Yet there were many many missing pieces. Susan Byrd, he thought—she would have to know more than she had told him. Besides, he had to get his watch back.

He ran back to Solomon's store and caught a glimpse of himself in the plate-glass window. He was grinning. His eyes were shining. He was as eager and happy as he had ever been in his life.

Chapter 13

It was a long time after he left, that warm September morning, that she was able to relax enough to drop the knife. When it clattered to the linoleum, she brought her arms down, oh, so slowly, and cradled her breasts as though they were two mangoes thumbed over in the marketplace and pushed aside. She stood that way in the little rented room with the sunshine pouring in until Guitar came home. He could not get her to speak or move, so he picked her up in his arms and carried her downstairs. He sat her on the bottom step while he went to borrow a car to drive her home.

Terrible as he thought the whole business was, and repelled as he was by mindlessness in love, he could not keep the deep wave of sorrow from engulfing him as he looked at this really rather pretty woman sitting straight as a pole, holding her breasts, and staring in front of her out of hollow eyes.

The engine of the old car he'd borrowed roared, but Guitar spoke softly to her. "You think because he doesn't love you that you are worthless. You think because he doesn't want you anymore that he is right—that his judgment and opinion of you are correct. If he throws you out, then you are garbage. You think he belongs to you because you want to belong to him. Hagar, don't. It's a bad word, 'belong.' Especially when you put it with somebody you love. Love shouldn't be like that. Did you ever see the way the clouds love a mountain? They circle all around it; sometimes you can't even see the mountain for the clouds. But you know what? You go up top and what do you see? His head. The clouds never cover the head. His head pokes through, because the clouds let him; they don't wrap him up. They let him keep his head up high, free, with nothing to hide him or bind him. Hear me, Hagar?" He spoke to her as he would to a very young child. "You can't own a human being. You can't lose what you don't own. Suppose you did own him. Could you really love somebody who was absolutely nobody without you? You really want somebody like that? Somebody who falls apart when you walk out the door? You don't, do you? And neither does he. You're turning over your whole life to him. Your whole life, girl. And if it means so little to you that you can just give it away, hand it to him, then why should it mean any more to him? He can't value you more than you value yourself." He stopped. She did not move or give any sign that she had heard him.

Pretty woman, he thought. Pretty little black-skinned woman. Who wanted to kill for love, die for love. The pride, the conceit of these doormat women amazed him. They were always women who had been spoiled children. Whose whims had been taken seriously by adults and who grew up to be the stingiest, greediest people on earth and out of their stinginess grew their stingy little love that ate everything in sight. They could not believe or accept the fact that they were unloved; they believed that the world itself was off balance when it appeared as though they were not loved. Why did they think they were so lovable? Why did they think their brand of love was better than, or even as good as, anybody else's? But they did. And they loved their love so much they would kill anybody who got in its way.

He looked at her again. Pretty. Pretty little black girl. Pretty little black-skinned girl. What had Pilate done to her? Hadn't anybody told her the things she ought to know? He thought of his two sisters, grown women now who could deal, and the litany of their growing up. Where's your daddy? Your mama know you out here in the street? Put something on your head. You gonna catch your death a cold. Ain't you hot? Ain't you cold? Ain't you scared you gonna get wet? Uncross your legs. Pull up your socks. I thought you was goin to the Junior Choir. Your slip is showin. Your hem is out. Come back in here and iron that collar. Hush your mouth. Comb your head. Get up from there and make that bed. Put on the meat. Take out the trash. Vaseline get rid of that ash.

Neither Pilate nor Reba knew that Hagar was not like them. Not strong enough, like Pilate, nor simple enough, like Reba, to make up her life as they had. She needed what most colored girls needed: a chorus of mamas, grandmamas, aunts, cousins, sisters, neighbors, Sunday school teachers, best girl friends, and what all to give her the strength life demanded of her—and the humor with which to live it.

Still, he thought, to have the object of your love, worthy or not, despise you, or leave you . . .

"You know what, Hagar? Everything I ever loved in my life left me. My father died when I was four. That was the first leaving I knew and the hardest. Then my mother. There were four of us and she just couldn't cut it when my father died. She ran away. Just ran away. My aunt took care of us until my grandmother could get there. Then my grandmother took care of us. Then Uncle Billy came. They're both close to dead now. So it was hard for me to latch on to a woman. Because I thought if I loved anything it would die. But I did latch on. Once. But I guess once is all you can manage." Guitar thought about it and said, "But I never wanted to kill her. *Him*, yeah. But not her." He smiled, but Hagar wasn't looking, wasn't even listening, and when he led her out of the car into Reba's arms her eyes were still empty.

All they knew to do was love her and since she would not speak, they brought things to please her. For the first time in life Reba *tried* to win things. And, also for the first time, couldn't. Except for a portable television set, which they couldn't connect because they had no electricity, Reba won nothing. No raffle ticket, no Bingo, no policy slip, no clearing-house number, no magazine sweepstakes, no, nor any unpierced carnival balloon succumbed to her magic. It wore her down. Puzzled and luck-less, she dragged herself home clutching stalks of anything that blossomed along the edges of lots and other people's gardens. These she presented to her daughter, who sat in a chair by the window or lay in bed fingering, fingering her hair.

They cooked special things for her; searched for gifts that they hoped would break the spell. Nothing helped. Pilate's lips were still and Reba's eyes full of panic. They brought her lip-stick and chocolate milk, a pink nylon sweater and a fuchsia bed jacket. Reba even investigated the mysteries of making jello, both red and green. Hagar didn't even look at it.

One day Pilate sat down on Hagar's bed and held a compact before her granddaughter's face. It was trimmed in a goldlike metal and had a pink plastic lid.

"Look, baby. See here?" Pilate turned it all around to show it off and pressed in the catch. The lid sprang open and Hagar saw a tiny part of her face reflected in the mirror. She took the compact then and stared into the mirror for a long while.

"No wonder," she said at last. "Look at that. No wonder. No wonder."

Pilate was thrilled at the sound of Hagar's voice. "It's yours, baby," she said. "Ain't it pretty?"

"No wonder," said Hagar. "No wonder."

"No wonder what?" asked Pilate.

"Look at how I look. I look awful. No wonder he didn't want me. I look terrible." Her voice was calm and reasonable, as though the last few days hadn't been lived through at all. "I need to get up from here and fix myself up. No *wonder!*" Hagar threw back the bedcover and stood up. "Ohhh. I smell too. Mama, heat me some water. I need a bath. A long one. We got any bath salts left? Oh, Lord, my head. Look at that." She peered into the compact mirror again. "I look like a ground hog. Where's the comb?"

Pilate called Reba and together they flew through the house to find the comb, but when they found it Hagar couldn't get the teeth through her roped and matted hair.

"Wash it," said Reba. "Wash it and we'll comb it while it's wet."

"I need shampoo, then. Real shampoo. I can't use Mama's soap."

"I'll go get some." Reba was trembling a little. "What kind?"

"Oh, any kind. And get some hair oil, Reba. Posner's, and some . . . Oh, never mind. Just that. Mama? Have you seen my . . . Oh, my God. No wonder. No wonder."

Pilate pulled a piece of string from Hagar's bedspread and put it in her mouth. "I'll heat up the water," she said.

When Reba got back she washed Hagar's hair, brushed it, and combed it gently.

"Just make me two braids, Reba. I'm going to have to go to the beauty shop. Today. Oh, and I need something to wear." Hagar stood at the door of the little cardboard closet, running her hands over the shoulders of dresses. "Everything's a mess in here. A mess. All wrinkled . . ."

"Water's hot. Where you want the tub?"

"Bring it in here."

"You think you should be taking a bath so soon?" Reba asked. "You just got up."

"Hush, Reba," said Pilate. "Let the child take care of herself."

"But she's been in the bed three days."

"All the more reason."

"I can't put these things on. Everything's a mess." Hagar was almost in tears.

Reba looked at Pilate. "I hope you right. I don't approve of getting up too fast and jumping right in some water."

"Help me with this tub and stop grumbling."

"All wrinkled. What am I going to wear?"

"That ain't enough water to cover her feet."

"It'll grow when she sits down."

"Where's my yellow dress? The one that buttons all the way down?"

"Somewhere in there, I reckon."

"Find it for me and press it, would you? I know it's a mess. Everything's a mess."

Reba found and pressed the yellow dress. Pilate helped Hagar bathe. Finally a clean and clothed Hagar stood before the two women and said, "I have to buy some clothes. New clothes. Everything I have is a mess."

They looked at each other. "What you need?" asked Pilate.

"I need everything," she said, and everything is what she got. She shopped for everything a woman could wear from the skin out, with the money from Reba's diamond. They had seventy-five cents between them when Hagar declared her needs, and six dollars owed to them from customers. So the two-thousand-dollar two-carat diamond went to a pawnshop, where Reba traded it for thirty dollars at first and then, accompanied by storming Pilate, she went back and got one hundred and seventy more for it. Hagar stuffed two hundred dollars and seventy-five cents into her purse and headed downtown, still whispering to herself every now and then, "No wonder."

She bought a Playtex garter belt, I. Miller No Color hose, Fruit of the Loom panties, and two nylon slips—one white, one pink—one pair of Joyce Fancy Free and one of Con Brio ("Thank heaven for little Joyce heels"). She carried an armful of skirts and an Evan-Picone two-piece number into the fitting room. Her little yellow dress that buttoned all the way down lay on the floor as she slipped a skirt over her head and shoulders, down to her waist. But the placket would not close. She sucked in her stomach and pulled the fabric as far as possible, but the teeth of the zipper would not join. A light sheen broke out on her forehead as she huffed and puffed. She was convinced that her whole life depended on whether or not those aluminum teeth would meet. The nail of her forefinger split and the balls of her thumbs ached as she struggled with the placket. Dampness became sweat and her breath came in gasps. She was about to weep when the saleswoman poked her head through the curtain and said brightly, "How are you doing?" But when she saw Hagar's gnarled and frightened face, the smile froze.

"Oh, my," she said, and reached for the tag hanging from the skirt's waist. "This is a five. Don't force it. You need, oh, a nine or eleven, I should think. Please. Don't force it. Let me see if I have that size."

She waited until Hagar let the plaid skirt fall down to her ankles before disappearing. Hagar easily drew on the skirt the woman brought back, and without further search, said she would take it and the little two-piece Evan-Picone.

She bought a white blouse next and a nightgown—fawn trimmed in sea foam. Now all she needed was make-up.

The cosmetics department enfolded her in perfume, and she read hungrily the labels and the promise. Myrurgia for primeval woman who creates for him a world of tender privacy where the only occupant is you, mixed with Nina Ricci's L'Air du Temps. Yardley's Flair with Tuvaché's Nectaroma and D'Orsay's Intoxication. Robert Piguet's Fracas, and Calypso and Visa and Bandit. Houbigant's Chantilly. Caron's Fleurs de Rocaille and Bellodgia. Hagar breathed deeply the sweet air that hung over the glass counters. Like a smiling sleepwalker she circled. Round and round the diamond-clear counters covered with bottles, wafer-thin disks, round boxes, tubes, and phials. Lipsticks in soft white hands darted out of their sheaths like the shiny red penises of puppies. Peachy powders and milky lotions were grouped in front of poster after cardboard poster of gorgeous grinning faces. Faces in ecstasy. Faces somber with achieved seduction. Hagar believed she could spend her life there among the cut glass, shimmering in peaches and cream, in satin. In opulence. In luxe. In love.

It was five-thirty when Hagar left the store with two shopping bags full of smaller bags gripped in her hands. And she didn't put them down until she reached Lilly's Beauty Parlor.

"No more heads, honey." Lilly looked up from the sink as Hagar came in.

Hagar stared. "I have to get my hair done. I have to hurry," she said.

Lilly looked over at Marcelline. It was Marcelline who kept the shop prosperous. She was younger, more recently trained, and could do a light press that lasted. Lilly was still using red-hot irons and an ounce of oil on every head. Her customers were loyal but dissatisfied. Now she spoke to Marcelline. "Can you take her? I can't, I know."

Marcelline peered deeply into her customer's scalp. "Hadn't planned on any late work. I got two more coming. This is my eighth today."

No one spoke. Hagar stared.

"Well," said Marcelline. "Since it's you, come on back at eight-thirty. Is it washed already?"

Hagar nodded.

"Okay," said Marcelline. "Eight-thirty. But don't expect nothing fancy."

"I'm surprised at you," Lilly chuckled when Hagar left. "You just sent two people away."

"Yeah, well, I don't feel like it, but I don't want no trouble with that girl Hagar. No telling what she might do. She jump that cousin of hers, no telling what she might do to me."

"That the one going with Macon Dead's boy?" Lilly's customer lifted her head away from the sink.

"That's her. Ought to be shamed, the two of them. *Cousins.*"

"Must not be working out if she's trying to kill him."

"I thought he left town."

"Wouldn't you?"

"Well, I know I don't want to truck with her. Not me."

"She don't bother nobody but him."

"Well, Pilate, then. Pilate know I turned her down, she wouldn't like it. They spoil that child something awful."

"Didn't you order fish from next door?"
"All that hair. I hope she don't expect nothing fancy."
"Call him up again. I'm getting hungry."
"Be just like her. No appointment. No nothing. Come in here all late and wrong and want something fancy."

She probably meant to wait somewhere. Or go home and return to Lilly's at eight-thirty. Yet the momentum of the thing held her—it was all of a piece. From the moment she looked into the mirror in the little pink compact she could not stop. It was as though she held her breath and could not let it go until the energy and busyness culminated in a beauty that would dazzle him. That was why, when she left Lilly's, she looked neither right nor left but walked on and on, oblivious of other people, street lights, automobiles, and a thunderous sky. She was thoroughly soaked before she realized it was raining and then only because one of the shopping bags split. When she looked down, her Evan-Picone white-with-a-band-of-color skirt was lying in a neat half fold on the shoulder of the road, and she was far far from home. She put down both bags, picked the skirt up and brushed away the crumbs of gravel that stuck to it. Quickly she refolded it, but when she tried to tuck it back into the shopping bag, the bag collapsed altogether. Rain soaked her hair and poured down her neck as she stooped to repair the damage. She pulled out the box of Con Brios, a smaller package of Van Raalte gloves, and another containing her fawn-trimmed-in-seafoam shortie nightgown. These she stuffed into the other bag. Retracing her steps, she found herself unable to carry the heavier bag in one hand, so she hoisted it up to her stomach and hugged it with both arms. She had gone hardly ten yards when the bottom fell out of it. Hagar tripped on Jungle Red (Sculptura) and Youth Blend, and to her great dismay, saw her box of Sunny Glow toppling into a puddle. She collected Jungle Red and Youth Blend safely, but Sunny Glow, which had tipped completely over and lost its protective disk, exploded in light peach puffs under the weight of the raindrops. Hagar scraped up as much of it as she could and pressed the wilted cellophane disk back into the box.

Twice before she got to Darling Street she had to stop to retrieve her purchases from the ground. Finally she stood in Pilate's doorway, limp, wet, and confused, clutching her bundles in whatever way she could. Reba was so relieved to see her that she grabbed her, knocking Chantilly and Bandit to the floor. Hagar stiffened and pulled away from her mother.

"I have to hurry," she whispered. "I have to hurry."

Loafers sluicing, hair dripping, holding her purchases in her arms, she made it into the bedroom and shut the door. Pilate and Reba made no move to follow her.

Hagar stripped herself naked there, and without taking time to dry her face or hair or feet, she dressed herself up in the white-with-a-band-of-color skirt and matching bolero, the Maidenform brassiere, the Fruit of the Loom panties, the no color hose, the Playtex garter belt and the Joyce con brios. Then she sat down to attend to her face. She drew charcoal gray for the young round eye through her brows, after which she rubbed mango tango on her cheeks. Then she patted sunny glow all over her face. Mango tango disappeared under it and she had to put it on again. She pushed out her lips and spread jungle red over them. She put baby clear sky light to outwit the day light on her eyelids and touched bandit to her throat, earlobes, and wrists. Finally she poured a little youth blend into her palm and smoothed it over her face.

At last she opened the door and presented herself to Pilate and Reba. And it was in their eyes that she saw what she had not seen before in the mirror: the wet ripped hose, the soiled white dress, the sticky, lumpy face powder, the streaked rouge, and the wild wet shoals of hair. All this she saw in their eyes, and the sight filled her own with water warmer and much older than the rain. Water that lasted for hours, until the fever came, and then it stopped. The fever dried her eyes up as well as her mouth.

She lay in her little Goldilocks'-choice bed, her eyes sand dry and as quiet as glass. Pilate and Reba, seated beside the bed, bent over her like two divi-divi trees beaten forward by a wind always blowing from the same direction. Like the trees, they offered her all they had: love murmurs and a protective shade.

"Mama." Hagar floated up into an even higher fever.

"Hmmm?"

"Why don't he like my hair?"

"Who, baby? Who don't like your hair?"

"Milkman."

"Milkman does too like your hair," said Reba.

"No. He don't. But I can't figure out why. Why he never liked my hair."

"Of course he likes it. How can he not like it?" asked Pilate.

"He likes silky hair." Hagar was murmuring so low they had to bend down to hear her.

"Silky hair? Milkman?"

"He don't like hair like mine."

"Hush, Hagar."

"Silky hair the color of a penny."

"Don't talk, baby."

"Curly, wavy, silky hair. He don't like mine."

Pilate put her hand on Hagar's head and trailed her fingers through her granddaughter's soft damp wool. "How can he not love your hair? It's the same hair that grows out of his own armpits. The same hair that crawls up out his crotch on up his stomach. All over his chest. The very same. It grows out of his nose, over his lips, and if he ever lost his razor it would grow all over his face. It's all over his head, Hagar. It's his hair too. He got to love it."

"He don't love it at all. He hates it."

"No he don't. He don't know what he loves, but he'll come around, honey, one of these days. How can he love himself and hate your hair?"

"He loves silky hair."

"Hush, Hagar."

"Penny-colored hair."

"Please, honey."
"And lemon-colored skin."
"Shhh."
"And gray-blue eyes."
"Hush now, hush."
"And thin nose."
"Hush, girl, hush."
"He's never going to like my hair."
"Hush. Hush. Hush, girl, hush."

The neighbors took up a collection because Pilate and Reba had spent everything getting Hagar the things needed to fix herself up. It didn't amount to much, though, and it was touch and go whether she'd have a decent funeral until Ruth walked down to Sonny's Shop and stared at Macon without blinking. He reached into his cash drawer and pulled out two twenty-dollar bills and put them down on the desk. Ruth didn't stretch out her hand to pick them up, or even shift her feet. Macon hesitated, then wheeled around in his chair and began fiddling with the combination to his safe. Ruth waited. Macon dipped into the safe three separate times before Ruth unclasped her hands and reached for the money. "Thank you," she said, and marched off to Linden Chapel Funeral Home to make the fastest arrangements possible.

Two days later, halfway through the service, it seemed as though Ruth was going to be the lone member of the bereaved family there. A female quartet from Linden Baptist Church had already sung "Abide with Me"; the wife of the mortician had read the condolence cards and the minister had launched into his "Naked came ye into this life and naked shall ye depart" sermon, which he had always believed suitable for the death of a young woman; and the winos in the vestibule who came to pay their respects to "Pilate's girl," but who dared not enter, had begun to sob, when the door swung open and Pilate burst in, shouting, "Mercy!" as though it were a command. A young man stood up and moved toward her. She flung out her right arm and almost knocked him down. "I want mercy!" she shouted, and began walking toward the coffin, shaking her head from side to side as though somebody had asked her a question and her answer was no.

Halfway up the aisle she stopped, lifted a finger, and pointed. Then slowly, although her breathing was fast and shallow, she lowered her hand to her side. It was strange, the languorous, limp hand coming to rest at her side while her breathing was coming so quick and fast. "Mercy," she said again, but she whispered it now. The mortician scurried toward her and touched her elbow. She moved away from him and went right up to the bier. She tilted her head and looked down. Her earring grazed her shoulder. Out of the total blackness of her clothes it blazed like a star. The mortician tried to approach her again, and moved closer, but when he saw her inky, berry-black lips, her cloudy, rainy eyes, the wonderful brass box hanging from her ear, he stepped back and looked at the floor.

"Mercy?" Now she was asking a question. "Mercy?"

It was not enough. The word needed a bottom, a frame. She straightened up, held her head high, and transformed the plea into a note. In a clear bluebell voice she sang it out—the one word held so long it became a sentence—and before the last syllable had died in the corners of the room, she was answered in a sweet soprano: "I hear you."

The people turned around. Reba had entered and was singing too. Pilate neither acknowledged her entrance nor missed a beat. She simply repeated the word "Mercy," and Reba replied. The daughter standing at the back of the chapel, the mother up front, they sang.

> *In the nighttime.*
> *Mercy.*
> *In the darkness.*
> *Mercy.*
> *In the morning.*
> *Mercy.*

At my bedside.
Mercy.
On my knees now.
Mercy. Mercy. Mercy. Mercy.

They stopped at the same time in a high silence. Pilate reached out her hand and placed three fingers on the edge of the coffin. Now she addressed her words to the woman bordered in gray satin who lay before her. Softly, privately, she sang to Hagar the very same reassurance she had promised her when she was a little girl.

Who's been botherin my sweet sugar lumpkin?
Who's been botherin my baby?
Who's been botherin my sweet sugar lumpkin?
Who's been botherin my baby girl?

Somebody's been botherin my sweet sugar lumpkin.
Somebody's been botherin my baby.
Somebody's been botherin my sweet sugar lumpkin.
Somebody's been botherin my baby girl.

I'll find who's botherin my sweet sugar lumpkin.
I'll find who's botherin my baby.
I'll find who's botherin my sweet sugar lumpkin.
I'll find who's botherin my baby girl.

"My baby girl." The three words were still pumping in her throat as she turned away from the coffin. Looking about at the faces of the people seated in the pews, she fastened on the first pair of eyes that were directed toward her. She nodded at the face and said, "My baby girl." She looked for another pair of eyes and told him also, "My baby girl." Moving back down the aisle, she told each face turned toward her the same piece of news. "My baby girl. That's my baby girl. My baby girl. My baby girl. My baby girl."

Conversationally she spoke, identifying Hagar, selecting her away from everybody else in the world who had died. First she spoke to the ones who had the courage to look at her, shake their heads, and say, "Amen." Then she spoke to those whose nerve failed them, whose glance would climb no higher than the long black fingers at her side. Toward them especially she leaned a little, telling in three words the full story of the stumped life in the coffin behind her. "My baby girl." Words tossed like stones into a silent canyon.

Suddenly, like an elephant who has just found his anger and lifts his trunk over the heads of the little men who want his teeth or his hide or his flesh or his amazing strength, Pilate trumpeted for the sky itself to hear, "And she was *loved!*"

It startled one of the sympathetic winos in the vestibule and he dropped his bottle, spurting emerald glass and jungle-red wine everywhere.

Chapter 14

Perhaps it was because the sun had hit the rim of the horizon, but Susan Byrd's house looked different. The cedar tree was a silvery gray and its bark crinkled all the way up. It looked to Milkman like the leg of an ancient elephant. And now he noticed that the ropes that held the swing were frayed and the picket fence that had looked so bright and perky before was really flaked, peeling, even leaning to the left. The blue steps leading to the porch were faded into a watery gray. In fact the whole house looked seedy.

He lifted his hand to knock on the door and noticed the doorbell. He rang it and Susan Byrd opened the door.

"Hello again," he said.

"Well," she said, "you're as good as your word."

"I'd like to talk to you some more, if you don't mind. About Sing. May I come in?"

"Of course." She stood back from the door and the odor of another batch of gingerbread wafted out. Again they sat in the living room—he in the gray wing-back chair, she on the sofa this time. Miss Long was nowhere in sight.

"I know you don't know who Sing married or if she married, but I was wondering—"

"Of course I know who she married. That is if they *did* marry. She married Jake, that black boy her mother took care of."

Milkman felt dizzy. Everybody kept changing right in front of him. "But yesterday you said nobody heard from her after she left."

"Nobody did. But they knew who she left with!"

"Jake?"

"Jake. Black Jake. Black as coal."

"Where—where did they live? Boston?"

"I don't know where they ended up. North, I guess. We never heard."

"I thought you said she went to a private school in Boston."

She dismissed the whole notion with a wave of her hand. "I just said that in front of *her*, Grace. She talks so much, you know. Carries tales all over the county. It's true she was supposed to go to some school, but she didn't. She left on that double-team wagon with that black boy, Jake. A whole lot of slaves got together. Jake was driving. Can you imagine it? Riding off with a wagonload of slaves?"

"What was Jake's last name? Can you tell me?"

She shrugged. "I don't think he had one. He was one of those flying African children. They must all be dead a long time now."

"Flying African children?"

"Um hm, one of Solomon's children. Or Shalimar. Papa said Heddy always called him Shalimar."

"And Heddy was . . ."

"My grandmother. Sing's mother and Papa's too. An Indian woman. She was the one who took care of Jake when his father left them all. She found him and took him home and raised him. She didn't have any boy children then. My father, Crowell, came later." She leaned forward and whispered, "She didn't have a husband, Heddy. I didn't want to go into all of that with Grace. You can imagine what she'd do with that information.

You're a stranger, so it doesn't matter. But Grace . . ." Susan Byrd looked pleadingly at the ceiling. "This Jake was a baby she found, and he and Sing grew up together, and I guess rather than be packed off to some Quaker school, she ran away with him. You know colored people and Indians mixed a lot, but sometimes, well, some Indians didn't like it—the marrying, I mean. But neither one of them knew their own father, Jake nor Sing. And my own father didn't know his. Heddy never said. I don't know to this day if he was white, red, or—well—*what*. Sing's name was Singing Bird. And my father's name was Crow at first. Later he changed it to Crowell Byrd. After he took off his buckskin." She smiled.

"Why did you call Solomon a flying African?"

"Oh, that's just some old folks' lie they tell around here. Some of those Africans they brought over here as slaves could fly. A lot of them flew back to Africa. The one around here who did was this same Solomon, or Shalimar—I never knew which was right. He had a slew of children, all over the place. You may have noticed that everybody around here claims kin to him. Must be over forty families spread in these hills calling themselves Solomon something or other. I guess he must have been hot stuff." She laughed. "But anyway, hot stuff or not, he disappeared and left everybody. Wife, everybody, including some twenty-one children. And they say they all saw him go. The wife saw him and the children saw him. They were all working in the fields. They used to try to grow cotton here. Can you imagine? In these hills? But cotton was king then. Everybody grew it until the land went bad. It was cotton even when I was a girl. Well, back to this Jake boy. He was supposed to be one of Solomon's original twenty-one—all boys and all of them with the same mother. Jake was the baby. The baby and the wife were right next to him when he flew off."

"When you say 'flew off' you mean he ran away, don't you? Escaped?"

"No, I mean flew. Oh, it's just foolishness, you know, but according to the story he wasn't running away. He was flying.

He flew. You know, like a bird. Just stood up in the fields one day, ran up some hill, spun around a couple of times, and was lifted up in the air. Went right on back to wherever it was he came from. There's a big double-headed rock over the valley named for him. It like to killed the woman, the wife. I guess you could say 'wife.' Anyway she's supposed to have screamed out loud for days. And there's a ravine near here they call Ryna's Gulch, and sometimes you can hear this funny sound by it that the wind makes. People say it's the wife, Solomon's wife, crying. Her name was Ryna. They say she screamed and screamed, lost her mind completely. You don't hear about women like that anymore, but there used to be more—the kind of woman who couldn't live without a particular man. And when the man left, they lost their minds, or died or something. Love, I guess. But I always thought it was trying to take care of children by themselves, you know what I mean?"

She talked on and on while Milkman sat back and listened to gossip, stories, legends, speculations. His mind was ahead of hers, behind hers, with hers, and bit by bit, with what she said, what he knew, and what he guessed, he put it all together.

Sing had said she was going to a Quaker school, but she joined Jake on his wagonful of ex-slaves heading for Boston or somewhere. They must have dropped their passengers all along the way. And then Jake, at the reins, took a wrong turn, because he couldn't read, and they ended up in Pennsylvania.

"But there's a children's game they play around here. And in the game they sing, 'Jake the *only* son of Solomon.' *Only*." He looked at her, hoping she wouldn't mind the interruption.

"Well, they're wrong. He wasn't the only son. There were twenty others. But he was the only one Solomon tried to take with him. Maybe that's what it means. He lifted him up, but dropped him near the porch of the big house. That's where Heddy found him. She used to come over there and help with the soapmaking and the candlemaking. She wasn't a slave, but she worked over at the big house certain times of year. She was melting tallow when she looked up and saw this man holding a baby and flying toward the ridge. He brushed too close to a tree and the baby slipped out of his arms and fell through the branches to the ground. He was unconscious, but the trees saved him from dying. Heddy ran over and picked him up. She didn't have any male children, like I said, just a little bitty girl, and this one just dropped out of the sky almost in her lap. She never named him anything different; she was afraid to do that. She found out the baby was Ryna's, but Ryna was out of her mind. Heddy lived a good ways off from the place Solomon and them others worked on. She tried to keep the girl away from that place too. And you can imagine how she felt when both of them ran off. Just my father was left."

"Did Jake have to register at the Freedmen's Bureau before he left the state?"

"Everybody did. Everybody who had been slaves, that is. Whether they left the state or not. But we were never slaves, so—"

"You told me that. Weren't any of Jake's brothers registering too?"

"I couldn't say. Those must have been some times, back then. Some bad times. It's a wonder anybody knows who anybody is."

"You've helped me a lot, Miss Byrd. I'm grateful." He thought then about asking her if she had a photo album. He wanted to see Sing, Crowell, even Heddy. But he decided against it. She might start asking him questions, and he didn't want to trouble her with a new-found relative who was as black as Jake.

"Now, that's not the woman you're looking for, is it? Pilate?"

"No," he said. "Couldn't be." He made motions of departure and then remembered his watch.

"By the way, did I leave my watch here? I'd like it back."

"Watch?"

"Yes. Your friend wanted to see it. Miss Long. I handed it to her but I forgot—" Milkman stopped. Susan Byrd was laughing out loud.

"Well, you can say goodbye to it, Mr. Macon. Grace will go to dinner all over the county telling people about the watch you gave her."

"What?"

"Well, you know. She doesn't mean any real harm, but it's a quiet place. We don't have many visitors, especially young men who wear gold watches and have northern accents. I'll get it back for you."

"Never mind. Never mind."

"You'll just have to forgive her otherwise. This is a dull place, Mr. Macon. There's absolutely nothing in the world going on here. Not a thing."

Chapter 15

The fan belt didn't last long enough for him to get to the next gasoline station. It broke on the edge of a little town called Jistann, the needle trembling at H. Milkman sold it to the tow-truck man for twenty dollars and caught the first bus out. It was probably best that way, for over the humming wheels, his legs folded in the little space in front of his seat, he had time to come down from the incredible high that had begun as soon as he slammed the Byrd woman's door.

He couldn't get back to Shalimar fast enough, and when he did get there, dusty and dirty from the run, he leaped into the car and drove to Sweet's house. He almost broke her door down. "I want to swim!" he shouted. "Come on, let's go swimming. I'm dirty and I want waaaaater!"

Sweet smiled and said she'd give him a bath.

"Bath! You think I'd put myself in that tight little porcelain box? I need the sea! The whole goddam sea!" Laughing, hollering, he ran over to her and picked her up at the knees and ran around the room with her over his shoulder. "The sea! I have to swim in the sea. Don't give me no itty bitty teeny tiny tub, girl. I need the whole entire complete deep blue sea!"

He stood her on her feet. "Don't you all swim around here?"

"Over at the quarry is where the kids go sometimes."

"Quarry? You all don't have no sea? No ocean?"

"Naw; this hill country."

"Hill country. Mountain country. Flying country."

"A man was here to see you."

"Oh, yeah? That would be Mr. Guitar Bains."

"He didn't give his name."

"He don't have to! He's Guitar Bains. *Gi*tar, *Gi*tar, *Gi*tar Bains!" Milkman did a little dance and Sweet covered her mouth, laughing.

"Come on, Sweet, tell me where the sea is."

"They some water comin down below the ridge on the other side. Real deep; wide too."

"Then let's go! Come on!" He grabbed her arm and pulled her out to the car. He sang all the way: " 'Solomon 'n Ryna Belali Shalut . . .' "

"Where you learn that?" she asked him. "That's a game we used to play when we was little."

"Of course you did. Everybody did. Everybody but me. But I can play it now. It's my game now."

The river in the valley was wide and green. Milkman took off his clothes, climbed a tree and dived into the water. He surfaced like a bullet, iridescent, grinning, splashing water. "Come on. Take them clothes off and come on in here."

"Naw. I don't wanna swim."

"Come in here, girl!"

"Water moccasins in there."

"Fuck 'em. Get in here. Hurry up!"

She stepped out of her shoes, pulled her dress over her head and was ready. Milkman reached up for her as she came timidly down the bank, slipping, stumbling, laughing at her own awkwardness, then squealing as the cold river water danced up her legs, her hips, her waist. Milkman pulled her close and kissed her mouth, ending the kiss with a determined effort to pull her under the water. She fought him. "Oh, my hair! My hair's gonna get wet."

"No it ain't," he said, and poured a handful right in the middle of her scalp. Wiping her eyes, spluttering water, she turned to wade out, shrieking all the way. "Okay, okay," he bellowed. "Leave me. Leave me in here by myself. I don't care. I'll play with the water moccasins." And he began to whoop and dive and splash and turn. "He could fly! You hear me? My great-granddaddy could fly! Goddam!" He whipped the water with his fists, then jumped straight up as though he too could take off, and landed on his back and sank down, his mouth and eyes full of water. Up again. Still pounding, leaping, diving. "The son of a bitch could fly! You hear me, Sweet? That motherfucker could fly! Could fly! He didn't need no airplane. Didn't need no fuckin tee double you ay. He could fly his own self!"

"Who you talkin 'bout?" Sweet was lying on her side, her cheek cupped in her hand.

"Solomon, that's who."

"Oh, him." She laughed. "You belong to that tribe of niggers?" She thought he was drunk.

"Yeah. That tribe. That flyin motherfuckin tribe. Oh, man! He didn't need no airplane. He just took off; got fed up. *All the way up!* No more cotton! No more bales! No more orders! No more shit! He flew, baby. Lifted his beautiful black ass up in the sky and flew on home. Can you dig it? Jesus God, that must have been something to see. And you know what else? He tried to take his baby boy with him. My grandfather. Wow! Woooee! Guitar! You hear that? Guitar, my great-granddaddy could flyyyyyy and the whole damn town is named after him. Tell him, Sweet. Tell him my great-granddaddy could fly."

"Where'd he go, Macon?"

"Back to Africa. Tell Guitar he went back to Africa."

"Who'd he leave behind?"

"Everybody! He left everybody down on the ground and he sailed on off like a black eagle. 'O-o-o-o-o-o Solomon done fly,

Solomon done gone /Solomon cut across the sky, Solomon gone
home!' "

He could hardly wait to get home. To tell his father, Pilate;
and he would love to see Reverend Cooper and his friends. "You
think Macon Dead was something? Huh. Let me tell you about
his daddy. You ain't heard nothin yet."

Milkman turned in his seat and tried to stretch his legs. It was
morning. He'd changed buses three times and was now speeding
home on the last leg of his trip. He looked out the window. Far
away from Virginia, fall had already come. Ohio, Indiana,
Michigan were dressed up like the Indian warriors from whom
their names came. Blood red and yellow, ocher and ice blue.

He read the road signs with interest now, wondering what lay
beneath the names. The Algonquins had named the territory he
lived in Great Water, *michi gami*. How many dead lives and
fading memories were buried in and beneath the names of the
places in this country. Under the recorded names were other
names, just as "Macon Dead," recorded for all time in some
dusty file, hid from view the real names of people, places, and
things. Names that had meaning. No wonder Pilate put hers in
her ear. When you know your name, you should hang on to it,
for unless it is noted down and remembered, it will die when
you do. Like the street he lived on, recorded as Mains Avenue,
but called Not Doctor Street by the Negroes in memory of his
grandfather, who was the first colored man of consequence in
that city. Never mind that he probably didn't deserve their
honor—they knew what kind of man he was: arrogant, color-
struck, snobbish. They didn't care about that. They were paying their respect to whatever it was that made him *be* a doctor in
the first place, when the odds were that he'd be a yardman all of
his life. So they named a street after him. Pilate had taken a rock
from every state she had lived in—because she *had* lived there.
And having lived there, it was hers—and his, and his father's, his

grandfather's, his grandmother's. Not Doctor Street, Solomon's Leap, Ryna's Gulch, Shalimar, Virginia.

He closed his eyes and thought of the black men in Shalimar, Roanoke, Petersburg, Newport News, Danville, in the Blood Bank, on Darling Street, in the pool halls, the barbershops. Their names. Names they got from yearnings, gestures, flaws, events, mistakes, weaknesses. Names that bore witness. Macon Dead, Sing Byrd, Crowell Byrd, Pilate, Reba, Hagar, Magdalene, First Corinthians, Milkman, Guitar, Railroad Tommy, Hospital Tommy, Empire State (he just stood around and swayed), Small Boy, Sweet, Circe, Moon, Nero, Humpty-Dumpty, Blue Boy, Scandinavia, Quack-Quack, Jericho, Spoonbread, Ice Man, Dough Belly, Rocky River, Gray Eye, Cock-a-Doodle-Doo, Cool Breeze, Muddy Waters, Pinetop, Jelly Roll, Fats, Leadbelly, Bo Diddley, Cat-Iron, Peg-Leg, Son, Shortstuff, Smoky Babe, Funny Papa, Bukka, Pink, Bull Moose, B.B., T-Bone, Black Ace, Lemon, Washboard, Gatemouth, Cleanhead, Tampa Red, Juke Boy, Shine, Staggerlee, Jim the Devil, Fuck-Up, and *Dat* Nigger.

Angling out from these thoughts of names was one more—the one that whispered in the spinning wheels of the bus: "Guitar is biding his time. Guitar is biding his time. Your day has come. Your day has come. Guitar is biding his time. Guitar is a very good Day. Guitar is a very good Day. A very good Day, a very good Day, and biding, biding his time."

In the seventy-five-dollar car, and here on the big Greyhound, Milkman felt safe. But there were days and days ahead. Maybe if Guitar was back in the city now, among familiar surroundings, Milkman could defuse him. And certainly, in time, he would discover his foolishness. There was no gold. And although things would never be the same between them, at least the man-hunt would be over.

Even as he phrased the thought in his mind, Milkman knew it was not so. Either Guitar's disappointment with the gold that was not there was so deep it had deranged him, or his "work" had done it. Or maybe he simply allowed himself to feel about

Milkman what he had always felt about Macon Dead and the Honoré crowd. In any case, he had snatched the first straw, limp and wet as it was, to prove to himself the need to kill Milkman. The Sunday-school girls deserved better than to be avenged by that hawk-headed raven-skinned Sunday man who included in his blood sweep four innocent white girls and one innocent black man.

Perhaps that's what all human relationships boiled down to: Would you save my life? or would you take it?

"Everybody wants a black man's life."

Yeah. And black men were not excluded. With two exceptions, everybody he was close to seemed to prefer him out of this life. And the two exceptions were both women, both black, both old. From the beginning, his mother and Pilate had fought for his life, and he had never so much as made either of them a cup of tea.

Would you save my life or would you take it? Guitar was exceptional. To both questions he could answer yes.

"Should I go home first, or go to Pilate's first?" Out in the street, late at night with autumn air blowing cold off the lake, he tried to make up his mind. He was so eager for the sight of Pilate's face when he told her what he knew, he decided to see her first. He'd have a long time at his own house. He took a taxi to Darling Street, paid the driver, and bounded up the stairs. He pushed the door open and saw her standing over a tub of water, rinsing out the green bottles she used for her wine.

"Pilate!" he shouted. "Have I got stuff to tell you!"

She turned around. Milkman opened his arms wide so he could hold all of her in a warm embrace. "Come here, sweetheart," he said, grinning. She came and broke a wet green bottle over his head.

When he came to, he was lying on his side in the cellar. He opened one eye and considered the option of not coming to for a little while more. For a long time now he knew that anything could appear to be something else, and probably was. Nothing could be taken for granted. Women who loved you tried to cut your throat, while women who didn't even know your name scrubbed your back. Witches could sound like Katharine Hepburn and your best friend could try to strangle you. Smack in the middle of an orchid there might be a blob of jello and inside a Mickey Mouse doll, a fixed and radiant star.

So he lay on the cool damp floor of the cellar and tried to figure out what he was doing there. What did Pilate knock him out for? About the theft of her sack of bones? No. She'd come to his rescue immediately. What could it be, what else could he have done that would turn her against him? Then he knew. Hagar. Something had happened to Hagar. Where was she? Had she run off? Was she sick or . . . Hagar was dead. The cords of his neck tightened. How? In Guitar's room, did she . . . ?

What difference did it make? He had hurt her, left her, and now she was dead—he was certain of it. He had left her. While he dreamt of flying, Hagar was dying. Sweet's silvery voice came back to him: "Who'd he leave behind?" He left Ryna behind and twenty children. Twenty-one, since he dropped the one he tried to take with him. And Ryna had thrown herself all over the ground, lost her mind, and was still crying in a ditch. Who looked after those twenty children? Jesus Christ, he left twenty-one children! Guitar and the Days chose never to have children. Shalimar left his, but it was the children who sang about it and kept the story of his leaving alive.

Milkman rolled his head back and forth on the cellar floor. It was his fault, and Pilate knew it. She had thrown him in the cellar. What, he wondered, did she plan to do with him? Then he knew that too. Knew what Pilate's version of punishment was when somebody took another person's life. Hagar. Something of Hagar's must be nearby. Pilate would put him someplace near something that remained of the life he had taken, so he could *have* it. She would abide by this commandment from her father herself, and make him do it too. "You just can't fly on off and leave a body."

Suddenly Milkman began to laugh. Curled up like a Polish sausage, a rope cutting his wrists, he laughed.

"Pilate!" he called. "Pilate! That's not what he meant. Pilate! He didn't mean that. He wasn't talking about the man in the cave. Pilate! He was talking about himself. His own father flew away. He was the 'body.' The body you shouldn't fly off and leave. Pilate! Pilate! Come here. Let me tell you what your father said. Pilate, he didn't even tell you to sing, Pilate. He was calling for his wife—your mother. Pilate! Get me out of here!"

Light exploded in his face. The cellar door opened over his head. Pilate's feet appeared on the stone steps, and paused.

"Pilate," said Milkman, softly now, "that's not what he meant. I know what he meant. Come, let me tell you. And Pilate, those bones. They're not that white man's bones. He probably didn't even die. I went there. I saw. He wasn't there and the gold wasn't there either. Somebody found it and found him too. They must have, Pilate. Long before you got there. But, Pilate . . ."

She descended a few steps.

"Pilate?"

She came all the way down and he looked in her eyes and at her still mouth. "Pilate, your father's body floated up out of the grave you all dug for him. One month later it floated up. The Butlers, somebody, put his body in the cave. Wolves didn't drag the white man to the front of the cave and prop him on a rock. That was your father you found. You've been carrying your father's bones—all this time."

"Papa?" she whispered.

"Yes. And, Pilate, you have to bury him. He wants you to bury him. Back where he belongs. On Solomon's Leap."

"Papa?" she asked again.

Milkman did not speak; he watched her long fingers travel up her dress, to rest like the wing of a starling on her face. "I've been carryin Papa?" Pilate moved toward Milkman, stopped and looked at him for a while. Then her eyes turned to a rickety wooden table that stood against the stone wall of the cellar. It was in a part of the room so dark he had not even seen it. She walked over to the table and lifted from it a green-and-white shoe box, its cover held down with a rubber band. "Joyce," it said on the box. "Thank heaven for little Joyce heels."

"If I bury Papa, I guess I ought to bury this too—somewhere." She looked back at Milkman.

"No," he said. "No. Give it here."

When he went home that evening, he walked into the house on Not Doctor Street with almost none of the things he'd taken with him. But he returned with a box of Hagar's hair.

She wouldn't set foot on an airplane, so he drove. She seemed happy now. Her lips mobile again, she sat next to him in Macon's Buick, a mink stole Reba had won wrapped around her shoulders over her old black dress. The knit cap was pulled down on her forehead and her shoes still had no laces. Every now and then she glanced at the back seat to check on the sack. Peace circled her.

Milkman felt it too. His return to Not Doctor Street was not the triumph he'd hoped it would be, but there was relief in his mother's crooked smile. And Lena, though unforgiving as ever, was civil to him, since Corinthians had moved to a small house in Southside, which she shared with Porter. The Seven Days, Milkman guessed, would be looking for a new recruit, as they had to when Robert Smith jumped off the roof of Mercy. But there were long rambling talks with his father, who could not hear it enough—the "boys" who remembered him in Danville; his mother's running off with his father; the story about his father and his grandfather. He wasn't a bit interested in the flying part, but he liked the story and the fact that places were named for his people. Milkman softened his description of Circe, saying simply that she was alive, and taking care of the dogs.

"I ought maybe to take me a trip down there," said Macon.

"Virginia?" Milkman asked him.

"Danville. I ought to go by and see some of those boys before these legs stop moving. Let Freddie pick up the rents, maybe."

It was nice. No reconciliation took place between Pilate and Macon (although he seemed pleased to know that they were going to bury their father in Virginia), and relations between Ruth and Macon were the same and would always be. Just as the consequences of Milkman's own stupidity would remain, and regret would always outweigh the things he was proud of having done. Hagar was dead and he had not loved her one bit. And Guitar was . . . somewhere.

In Shalimar there was general merriment at his quick return, and Pilate blended into the population like a stick of butter in a churn. They stayed with Omar's family, and on the second and last evening, Milkman and Pilate walked up the road to the path that led to Solomon's Leap. It was the higher of two outcroppings of rock. Both flat-headed, both looking over a deep valley. Pilate carried the sack, Milkman a small shovel. It was a long way to the top, but neither stopped for breath. At the very top, on the plateau, the trees that could stand the wind at that height were few. They looked a long time for an area of earth among the rock faces large enough for the interment. When they found one, Pilate squatted down and opened the sack while Milkman dug. A deep sigh escaped from the sack and the wind turned chill. Ginger, a spicy sugared ginger smell, enveloped them. Pilate laid the bones carefully into the small grave. Milkman heaped dirt over them and packed it down with the back of his shovel.

"Should we put a rock or a cross on it?" Milkman asked.

Pilate shook her head. She reached up and yanked her earring from her ear, splitting the lobe. Then she made a little hole with her fingers and placed in it Sing's snuffbox with the single word Jake ever wrote. She stood up then, and it seemed to Milkman that he heard the shot after she fell. He dropped to his knees and cradled her lolling head in the crook of his arm, barking at her, "You hurt? You hurt, Pilate?"

She laughed softly and he knew right away that she was reminded of the day he first met her and said the most stupid thing there was to say.

The twilight had thickened and all around them it was getting dark. Milkman moved his hand over her chest and stomach, trying to find the place where she might be hit. "Pilate? You okay?" He couldn't make out her eyes. His hand under her head was sweating like a fountain. "Pilate?"

She sighed. "Watch Reba for me." And then, "I wish I'd a knowed more people. I would of loved 'em all. If I'd a knowed more, I would a loved more."

Milkman bent low to see her face and saw darkness staining his hand. Not sweat, but blood oozing from her neck down into his cupped hand. He pressed his fingers against the skin as if to force the life back in her, back into the place it was escaping from. But that only made it flow faster. Frantically he thought of tourniquets and could even hear the rip of cloth he should have been tearing. He shifted his weight and was about to lay her down, the better to wrap her wound, when she spoke again.

"Sing," she said. "Sing a little somethin for me."

Milkman knew no songs, and had no singing voice that anybody would want to hear, but he couldn't ignore the urgency in her voice. Speaking the words without the least bit of a tune, he sang for the lady. "Sugargirl don't leave me here/ Cotton balls to choke me/Sugargirl don't leave me here/ Buckra's arms to yoke me." The blood was not pulsing out any longer and there was something black and bubbly in her mouth. Yet when she moved her head a little to gaze at something behind his shoulder, it took a while for him to realize that she was dead. And when he did, he could not stop the worn old words from coming, louder and louder as though sheer volume would wake her. He woke only the birds, who shuddered off into the air. Milkman laid her head down on the rock. Two of the birds circled round them. One dived into the new grave and scooped something shiny in its beak before it flew away.

Now he knew why he loved her so. Without ever leaving the ground, she could fly. "There must be another one like you," he whispered to her. "There's got to be at least one more woman like you."

Even as he knelt over her, he knew there wouldn't be another mistake; that the minute he stood up Guitar would try to blow his head off. He stood up.

"Guitar!" he shouted.

Tar tar tar, said the hills.

"Over here, brother man! Can you see me?" Milkman cupped his mouth with one hand and waved the other over his head. "Here I am!"

Am am am am, said the rocks.

"You want me? Huh? You want my life?"

Life life life life.

Squatting on the edge of the other flat-headed rock with only the night to cover him, Guitar smiled over the barrel of his rifle. "My man," he murmured to himself. "My main man." He put the rifle on the ground and stood up.

Milkman stopped waving and narrowed his eyes. He could just make out Guitar's head and shoulders in the dark. "You want my life?" Milkman was not shouting now. "You need it? Here." Without wiping away the tears, taking a deep breath, or even bending his knees—he leaped. As fleet and bright as a lodestar he wheeled toward Guitar and it did not matter which one of them would give up his ghost in the killing arms of his brother. For now he knew what Shalimar knew: If you surrendered to the air, you could *ride* it.